A TASTE OF GOLD AND IRON

ALSO BY
ALEXANDRA ROWLAND

A Conspiracy of Truths
A Choir of Lies
Some by Virtue Fall
Over All the Earth

Finding Faeries

A TASTE OF GOLD AND IRON

ALEXANDRA
ROWLAND

A Tom Doherty Associates Book / New York

A TASTE OF GOLD AND IRON

Copyright © 2022 by Alexandra Rowland

A Tordotcom Book
Published by Tom Doherty Associates
120 Broadway
New York, NY 10271

www.tor.com

Tor® is a registered trademark of Macmillan Publishing Group, LLC.

Library of Congress Cataloging-in-Publication Data

Names: Rowland, Alexandra, author.
Title: A taste of gold and iron / Alexandra Rowland.
Description: First Edition. | New York : Tordotcom, a Tom Doherty
    Associates Book, 2022.
Identifiers: LCCN 2022007994 (print) | LCCN 2022007995 (ebook) |
    ISBN 9781250800381 (hardcover) | ISBN 9781250800404 (ebook)
Classification: LCC PS3618.O8767 T37 2022 (print) | LCC PS3618.O8767
    (ebook) | DDC 813/.6—dc23
LC record available at https://lccn.loc.gov/2022007994
LC ebook record available at https://lccn.loc.gov/2022007995

Our books may be purchased in bulk for promotional, educational,
or business use. Please contact your local bookseller or the Macmillan
Corporate and Premium Sales Department at 1-800-221-7945,
extension 5442, or by email at MacmillanSpecialMarkets@macmillan.com.

First Edition: 2022

Printed in the United States of America

0 9 8 7 6 5 4 3 2 1

For the fanfiction writers,
who taught me everything I know—
including, most especially, the pursuit of joy

A TASTE OF GOLD AND IRON

CHAPTER ONE

Halfway through his twenty-fifth year, and to his acute relief, Prince Kadou became an uncle.

Despite Kadou spending the entirety of his sister's pregnancy in terror and worry, the whole affair ended up being quite as routine as such things could be, but for the fact that the niece in question pushed him one joyous rung further down the line of succession. The night of Zeliha's labors, Kadou prayed fervently in the temple for hours until, finally, the good news arrived with the sudden crack of fireworks above, the shower of colored splendor—and Kadou felt like he could breathe easy for the first time in months. Years, maybe. It was the lamp of the lighthouse above him, at last, after a long, stormy night at sea.

Of course, peace and relief were a luxury that not even princes could easily afford for more than a moment or two: Princess Eyne's birth was followed by days of celebration—for the court, for the people of the capital and the rest of the kingdom, for the hundreds of kahyalar who served throughout the palace and the government with loyalty and devotion. With his sister the sultan indisposed (and gleefully taking advantage of her own opportunity for some peace), the duties of representing House Mahisti to the populace naturally fell to Kadou, as did a greater than usual proportion of the daily concerns of the realm—a very alarming break-in at the Shipbuilder's Guild on the night of the birth itself; a wealthy merchant from Oissos caught committing one of the most blasphemous crimes Kadou could conceive of, several days later; a number of perplexing tantrums thrown by Siranos, the body-father of the new princess (which Kadou's already shaky nerves found as upsetting and alarming on a personal level as the former two catastrophes were on a larger scale) . . . All these added up to a solid whirlwind week during which time Kadou barely had a chance to breathe, let alone hold his new niece for more than a minute or two the morning after she was born.

But waters rising to the peak of a hectic king-tide meant only that they would inevitably fall back to a time of dull lax-tides. It seemed Her Majesty decidedly agreed, and moreover felt that it was up to her to hurry things along.

"You look thin," Zeliha had told him, not two days before, in a very bossy, big-sister sort of voice when they'd finally found a moment to speak beyond Kadou's hectic official reports. Zeliha had waved off any further need for rest and recovery from childbirth when she'd heard what the Oissic merchant had been arrested for, declaring that she would attend to that matter herself so that Kadou could give his full attention to the Shipbuilder's Guild. They had heard that a satyota from Inacha was visiting the city—a truthwitch, as they were called in the slangy street-dialect—and had hired him to question Azuta Melachrinos tou Thorikou about where, precisely, she had received the *huge* amount of counterfeits with which she'd attempted to pay a gambling debt. The interrogation hadn't gone well. Azuta was too clever to answer a question straight when she could reply with a rhetorical question or a half-truth instead. But when Azuta had been dragged off back to her cell, Zeliha and Kadou had had a brief moment alone, free of anyone who they had to playact formality for. "You look like a wrung-out dishcloth. Are you eating? Are you sleeping?"

He hadn't been, particularly, on either count. He'd been too worried about the progress that wasn't being made on the investigation at the Shipbuilder's Guild, about Siranos arrogantly inserting himself into conversations he didn't belong in and passionately declaring that Azuta Melachrinos, his fellow countrywoman, deserved a fair trial and representation in court . . .

Too worried about having confided some of these worries to the wrong people.

No, of course he hadn't been sleeping, nor eating more than scratches here and there.

But before he'd been able to answer her, Zeliha had declared that it was high time they all got out of the palace for a day and thought about literally anything besides kingdom-running. A hunt, she said, would be just the thing.

✻

It was said that in ancient times when the great conqueror Asanbughaa had come to this coast and declared that here was where she would build the capital of her new kingdom, it had been one of her sorcerers who had raised the great plateau where the palace now stood. The rest of the land around was mostly flat forest or open farmland, rising to gentle hills further inland, and thence to mountains deep in the backcountry to the east and north.

The inland side of the plateau had a path downward, to match the winding switchbacks of the kingsroad along the face overlooking the city. The back path was even steeper and more carefully concealed—it was deliberately left in a state of slight neglect: bare dirt, rather than cobblestones, with trees and shrubs allowed to grow wild along its edges and turns, the better to disguise it from casual observers. It was barely wide enough for two horses to pass each other, and in some places their riders would have had to dismount to do it.

In the forest below, there was a particular clearing, the usual staging area for the beginning of royal hunts. Servants had come ahead hours before—or perhaps even the day before—to assemble airy, colorful tents and pavilions, floored with carpets and cushions. The grandest of these was the sultan's, of course, and Kadou was surprised to see Zeliha already waiting when he arrived with the few other courtiers who had not returned to the countryside after the week's festivities wound down.

She was lounging on a low couch, surrounded by ministers, with Princess Eyne cuddled in her arms. Her pavilion, heavy blue silk embroidered with silver and topped by a fountain of white feathers at its peak, cast cool, watery light over her. She looked up at the sound of hooves. "Kadou!" she called. "Little brother, do come here."

"Majesty," he replied, scrambling off his horse and bowing. "I wasn't expecting you to come."

"I arranged it, didn't I?" she replied dryly, shifting Eyne a bit so she could free a hand to wave Kadou over. "Come here, I said. The rest of you are dismissed, thank you."

"I hadn't thought you would have recovered enough to hunt." Kadou handed Wing's reins off to one of his kahyalar and ducked his head to clear the hanging drape of the pavilion's walls, which had been pulled back and tied off to the corner posts to let the breeze flow through. The ministers, withdrawing as ordered, bowed to him as they passed.

"Oh, I definitely haven't," she said, and gestured to a seat near her. Kadou took it. "The kahyalar hauled me here in fine style in a sedan chair like I'm already a dowager. It'll be a few more weeks yet before I can bear to sit on a horse. By the way, please help yourself," she said, nodding to a tray of sliced fruits that had been laid within reach, and plucked a piece of melon for herself. "I don't recommend childbirth, Kadou," she said seriously. "You ought to endeavor to avoid it."

He rolled his eyes at her, and let her see it too, and she grinned. It was better out here, away from the palace and the court—easier to pretend they were both still children or adolescents, just the prince and the crown princess, with very few concerns beyond tutors and scholars harrying them at every moment, kahyalar fluttering nervously around them while Zeliha announced some new adventure and dragged Kadou along after her.

"Truly, though," she said, "I can't imagine having a baby without six kahyalar to help. And even then, they always disappear just at the wrong moment. Can you take her? My arms are about to fall off. She's deceptively heavy."

Kadou dragged his chair closer to oblige and, between the two of them, they managed to get Eyne transferred into his arms with no more than a few ominous grumbles from the child. She was, somehow, already notably bigger and plumper than she'd been the week before. Kadou had had no idea that babies grew that fast. "If you can't enjoy the hunt yourself, why drag all of us out here?"

She sighed heavily, stretching and flexing the stiffness out of her arms. "I'm sick to death of hearing about Azuta Melachrinos. I've stared at so many counterfeits that my eyes ache."

"Are they at least . . . *bad* counterfeits?" Kadou asked, without much hope.

"See for yourself." Zeliha took a pair of coins from her pocket and held them out. A gold altın. A silver yira. He freed a hand from holding Eyne and, feeling like he might be jinxing himself, gingerly touched the altın.

The instant the metal brushed his skin, he flinched. His gift for touch-tasting—the Araşti sense for metal—was only faint, manifesting as a few wisps of sense-memory. The sensation that met his fingertips as he touched the counterfeit was a flat *clank*, a dull and hollow sound like an empty bucket dropped on flagstones. It was so *wrong* feeling and so startling that he snatched his hand away and flexed his fingers before he tried again.

In one of his two very earliest memories, he was knee-high to all the adults, clutching at the skirts of his mother's silk kaftan and burying his face in them from shyness whenever strangers looked at him—and there were so many strangers looking at him, smiling at him, bowing to him and Mama. There was a lot of activity around them, a loud jumble of noises and talking, and the air smelled sooty and dirty, and it was very warm, and Mama was talking to one of the strangers and only absently petting his hair as he pushed his face against her leg, and the kahya assigned as his nurse had disappeared somewhere, and—

Mama had bent down and picked him up, settling him on her hip, and he'd put his face into her hair and neck to hide, but she'd said, "Look, sweetheart, it's your grandfather." When he'd looked, she'd held up a coin—perfect, round and shining as the sun, with a little picture of Grandfather on it in profile, wearing his crown. And then, "Look, watch how the nice lady makes them," and the smiling stranger sitting at the anvil in front of Mama picked up a flat, blank circle of gold with tongs from a plate near the fire beside her, placed it between two mysterious pieces of iron on the anvil, and *struck* it with a hammer, a loud, clear clang that made him jump. She set down the hammer, took off the top part of the thing she'd hit, and—there was Grandfather's picture again, as if by magic.

The stranger had plucked it out and handed it to Mama, and Mama had tucked it into his palm. It had still been a little warm from the fire, as if it had been lying in the sunshine. "Do you know how much gold is in an altın, love?" Mama had asked.

He'd replied in a little whisper so the strangers couldn't hear him, "Nine, eight, six." She had smiled as bright as new-minted coin and kissed his cheek and told him to keep his altın safe and not to put it in his mouth.

Nine eight six. Nine hundred and eighty-six parts pure gold out of every thousand, he knew now, a fineness that had been set hundreds of years before and had never once changed, not for generations, not for *dynasties*. He still had that altın somewhere, and even now, part of the signature for coin gold as he experienced it— proper coins, that is, genuine ones—was the clear, bell-like chime of a hammer striking a die.

The counterfeit had to be mostly gold, because the rest of the signature had seemed mostly the same as usual—the smooth flow of warm, thick cream poured from a pitcher, the flash of sunshine on nearly still water. But when he plucked it off Zeliha's palm and rubbed it between his fingertips, savoring the metal as closely as he could, he could just barely distinguish other differences. The water-sparkle tasted faintly reddish, as if it were the light of sunset, or colored by the smoke of a wildfire.

Looking at it with his eyes rather than just the senses in his fingertips, he could see that the counterfeit was extremely well made. If he had only glanced at it lying on the table, perhaps amongst genuine altınlar, he wouldn't have taken any notice of it.

He drew his hand back, feeling a little sick. Zeliha snorted and tucked the coins away again, murmuring, "Yes, that's the face that all the other touch-tasters have made, too." Kadou wasn't surprised. The consistency of the value of their coinage was the foundation their nation was built on. The Araşti mercantile empire was vast and robust enough that their currency could be used nearly anywhere around the Sea of Serpents and in many places further beyond, because everyone, everywhere, knew that an Araşti coin was a coin you could trust. If a merchant in Imakami, Map Sut, Oissos, Aswijan, Mangar-Khagra, Kaskinen, or N'gaka was offered an altın, they would know *exactly* what its relative value was.

The country's power did not come from the edge of a sword, nor from enormous tracts of conquered territory, nor from even the navy, though Araşt had the fastest ships in the world. Their power came instead from the clink of coin, an open palm, a smile. Theirs was an empire built on the bedrock of reputation before all else.

"The ambassador of Oissos is behaving with no sense of decorum whatsoever," Zeliha went on. "She keeps following me around and *declaiming* as if she's in the middle of her Senate. I don't know who thought a Senate was a good idea. All it seems to do is turn out a load of annoying power-hungry bureaucrats."

Kadou snuggled Eyne a little closer, flexing his hand again to rid himself of the sense-memory of the befouled coin. "I don't know," he said quietly. "It must have made sense to someone, once." It might be nicer to *choose* power than to be stuck with it, he sometimes thought. Being prince often felt like he was seated on the back of a ferocious wild horse that could bite or trample anyone around him who didn't have a horse of their own. He had to be careful of it and aware of it all the time, lest it yank the reins out of his hands and buck him out of a solid seat. And who was to say that he was the best rider to tame it, simply because he had been born to it?

But then, Zeliha was right too—the Oissic Senate did seem to draw power-hungry bureaucrats, primarily.

"Anyway," she said. "It's a nice day, and investigating Azuta Melachrinos won't go any faster whether I'm there to hover over it or not. I needed a break and some fresh air and entertainment, and there's really nothing more entertaining than watching a bunch of fussy people traipse around on their ponies and try to kill things without getting their hands or their hems dirty." She picked over the tray of fruit without looking at him. "And I missed you," she added. "You usually call me *Majesty* these days, and it makes me feel far away from you." She shrugged, looked away.

"I miss you too," he said softly. He bit his lip and occupied himself with fussing over the wrinkles and folds of Eyne's swaddling cloths. She stared up at him solemnly as he did it—her eyes were huge and already quite dark grey, promising to darken to the classic blue-black of the Mahisti family, the same as his and Zeliha's.

"And," Zeliha said, her tone shifting, "I haven't gotten to talk to you about what happened at the kahyalar's party when you went for the Visit. You were *very* naughty, I heard."

He nearly choked, and it was only because he was terrified of dropping Eyne that he forced the wave of panic back.

Someone must have seen him talking to Tadek at the Visit.

(Gods, he realized immediately, of course they had seen it. He and Tadek had been right out in the open, they hadn't been subtle in the *least*—)

There were times when Kadou acted and only later realized, in a flash of crushing humiliation just like this one, how his actions might look from the outside. It had rather been at the top of his mind lately due to the troubles with Eyne's body-father, the way he stalked around Kadou, scrutinizing him so closely, glaring at him, making it clear with every glance that he believed that Kadou was up to something.

But who could blame him? Siranos's family had been devastated two generations ago by the machinations of a jealous second son, and he had no reason to believe that Kadou would behave any differently. Most people in his position, Kadou supposed, *wouldn't* have been joyfully happy to find themselves a step further away from the throne. But it made him nervous to be the target of such suspicion. He'd been second-guessing himself constantly, worrying and half-confused over his own motivations, lying awake at night wondering whether it was an inevitable matter of *when* he brought harm to his sister and niece, rather than an impossible, unthinkable *if*.

Someone had seen him talking to Tadek at the Visit. How could he explain? Was there any explanation that would be sufficient?

The night of Eyne's birth, Commander Eozena had come to the temple where Kadou was praying to give him news about the Shipbuilder's Guild break-in, had asked him to take charge of the matter since Her Majesty was indisposed in childbed, and had escorted him to the royal administrative offices so they could hurriedly scrawl out orders to secure the guild and limit passage out of the city, buying them time until they could ensure that the crucial secret held within the guild was secure and had not been . . . taken. It had been past midnight when she had left to see those orders executed. Kadou and Melek, one of the kahyalar assigned to his personal service, had remained behind to search through the files and find out whether any other incidents or concerns had been recently reported by the guild.

They'd been up to their elbows in documents when Siranos had come in, demanded to know what Kadou thought he was doing, and had not-quite-accused him of making his move against Her Majesty and his new daughter. Kadou had denied it—of course he had, the thought was horrifying to him—but Siranos had escalated, had seized Kadou's arm hard enough to bruise . . . It was only Melek, so firm and calm that çe hadn't even needed to raise çir voice, who had finally convinced Siranos to back down and leave.

No matter that Zeliha had brushed all these incidents off the very next morning when Kadou reported to her—all except the finer details of what Siranos had said and done, of course, because *that* felt like retaliation, like making a fuss about nothing, like escalating the conflict again after Melek had gone to all the trouble of deflecting it. It was no crime for Siranos to be a little out of sorts on the night of his body-child's birth, after all. But resolving to keep the peace made no difference in the privacy of his own mind, and neither did the fact that Zeliha had cheerfully agreed with Eozena's executive decision to delegate responsibility. Kadou did what he always did with incidents like these—he held tight to it, interrogated it from every angle, worried over it, ate himself up with anxiety until he was a shaking, nervous wreck. He hadn't been able to stop circling his mind around it all week—why was Siranos so suspicious of him? Was he seeing something in Kadou that Kadou hadn't yet noticed in himself?

All that would have been fine, but then . . .

He'd confided his fears to Tadek—another of the kahyalar, who he had known for some time, and who he had once been . . . close to. Tadek, who was so easy to talk to, even about matters Kadou barely dared to whisper aloud to anyone else.

Tadek had comforted and reassured him, had kissed his hands and smiled at him, had offered to ask around as to whether anyone else had heard mention of what Kadou had done (or was doing) to make Siranos so angry and suspicious. That was the point where things had started to go . . . awkward. Awkward, even before this moment, when his perspective wrenched and he was able to look at it from an outsider's perspective: Sending a kahya after Siranos was tantamount to having him *tailed*. Anyone else would conclude that easily.

Zeliha had a *whole ministry* of professional spies whose job it was to know everything that went on in every corner of the palace, in every alley of the capital, and in every village in the country. Of course she knew. Someone would have reported to her that Tadek, who had been assigned to Kadou's personal service last year, had suddenly been asking around about Siranos, about his motives, about any gossip surrounding him. That too would have been forgivable. But Tadek was a kahya of the core-guard, and that meant loyalty, and devotion, and a certain inclination to go above and beyond the call of duty.

Tadek—clever Tadek, too cunning for his own good, that expression of sly hazel mischief always sparkling in his eyes—had done just that. He'd asked other questions of his fellow kahyalar as well—questions that Kadou certainly had *not* asked him to investigate and *would not have* asked. When Kadou had paid his formal visit to the kahyalar's enormous celebration of the birth of the princess, Tadek had come to Kadou in the crowd, bearing news and secrets and whispers like guest-gifts. They had briefly left the courtyard of the garrison for a discreet walk. *I know a dozen kahyalar who would happily die for you,* Tadek had murmured to him, as if that were at all what Kadou wanted. Fireworks had been cracking and hissing overhead, reflecting bright off the surface of the garrison's laundry pond as they strolled around it and Tadek whispered all he'd found. *I myself, Highness, would of course lay down my life to protect you without hesitation, particularly from a—well, we can't yet call him a villain, can we?*

Gods, what had he been doing? He'd been gathering spies of his own.

"I'm—I don't—I can't—" He was trembling a little, and Eyne made a soft warning noise. "It's complicated, I swear it's not what it looked like, and I didn't mean anything by it, and—"

"Goodness, take a breath, Kadou!" Zeliha stared at him. "What in the world is the matter?"

"I'm really sorry," he said. His eyes prickled with tears.

Zeliha sat up. "Kadou, goodness, calm yourself. I was only going to—ohhh." She smiled and shook a finger at him. "Clever boy. *You're* teasing *me,* aren't you?" She sat back again, satisfied. "You're wasted as Duke of Harbors, you know. Maybe General Mirize's lessons on war tactics didn't fall on entirely uninterested ears after all."

He breathed, as his sovereign commanded. "I'm not teasing. I'm serious. I—you're right, I made some errors of judgment and I didn't mean anything by it, I should have thought more about how it would seem to other people . . ." He found himself clutching Eyne close. She was oddly comforting to hold.

"Kadou, gods! You're not teasing, are you? Gods, calm down. It was just flirting, right?"

Wait—"What?"

"All right, and drinking. And a very amusing speech, apparently, so well done there. By all accounts it was one of the better speeches we've given at one of the kahyalar's parties, they're all telling me so. But no one minded the rest of it. Why are you so upset?"

She wasn't even talking about Siranos. He breathed again, and it came easier this time. "I—I thought you might have, um, felt like I was behaving disgracefully."

She shrugged again. "There are times for perfect decorum and there are times to, ah, loosen one's sashes. As it were." She shot him a wry sidelong glance, and he felt his face go scarlet and wished his hands were free so he could hide his face. He suspected now that Zeliha had given him an infant to hold for exactly this reason. "Nothing wrong with a moonlit walk around such romantic environs as a laundry pond. It was a laundry pond, wasn't it?" The discreet walk *had* taken them around some kind of pond, but Kadou hadn't noted much about it. "But I'd better stop teasing, or you'll blush so hard you'll have an aneurysm." She dropped her voice. "In all seriousness, though . . . Tadek Hasira? Really?"

He looked back down and found a loose thread to fiddle with on the lace-trimmed hem of Eyne'e swaddling. "What about him?"

"You're seeing a lot of him lately. Again. Not *just* moonlit walks, I hear."

"It's not like that."

"*He* seems to think it is. Look, I have no problem with you taking a lover in *theory*, and if your heart is called—or whatever bit; maybe it's not about hearts—"

"*Zeliha.*"

"Sorry, fine, sorry—if your *heart* is called by one of our ka-hyalar then I trust you're doing your due diligence in having sensible, honest conversations with him about the complex issues that might come up, expectations and so on. My concerns have nothing to do with that. I merely . . . question your taste about this *particular* one."

The low thrum of anxiety he felt every time he thought of Tadek these days—too much initiative, too cunning for his own good, asking questions Kadou didn't want to know the answers to—was enough to quench his blush, at least. "It's not like that

anymore. It used to be, and then we . . . stopped. He was reassigned. Now we just . . ." He waved vaguely. "Talk. Sometimes."

Zeliha looked even more dubious. "You're *not* sleeping with
him?" Their attachment, such as it was, had been brief. When
Zeliha had announced her pregnancy, Kadou had been *wretched*
with terror about losing her. Tadek, stationed right at the door of
his very chambers, had witnessed him have a few of his episodes
of nerves. He had been so *kind* about it, and so warm, and had
worked hard to make light of it, to make Kadou smile, to hold
his hand and comfort him, and . . . things had happened. They
both knew nothing could come of it—they'd even talked about it
afterward, still naked and sticky in Kadou's bed—and Tadek had
only laughed off all Kadou's worries and ethical concerns, and had
kissed his eyes and told him that he was at His Highness's service
for as long as His Highness required and in *whatever* capacity he
desired—this last, of course, murmured directly against Kadou's
neck with a slow smile. It had not made Kadou's sense of ethics
feel any better to know that Tadek thought of this as part of his
service or his duty, but he had been so afraid, and he'd felt so alone,
and he had known in his *bones* that he couldn't breathe a word to a
single soul of his episodes of being overcome with cowardice over
imaginary terrors. Tadek had been all he'd had, his only confidant,
and Kadou had been too desperate for comfort to turn down his
offers as he should have. But the months had passed, and eventually it was time for the core-guard assignments to be shuffled
again, and since Kadou had not requested Tadek's attendance to
continue, their intimacy had come to a natural end—until Tadek
had come across him in one of his episodes again, and Kadou had
given in to yet another moment of weakness and confided in him
about Siranos.

"I'm not sleeping with him anymore," Kadou said firmly. "I'm
not. I just . . . He's nice." Sometimes. Sort of. He was also catty,
a fiend for gossip, and didn't take anything seriously, which was
sometimes . . . exasperating, though Kadou felt hideously guilty
even thinking such a thing in the privacy of his own mind.

"Nice," she mused. "*He's nice.* The boys must simply swoon

for poetry like that. Do they?" She took one look at his face and snorted. "The thunderstorm look is better on you than blushing. Seriously, though—nice? That's the best you can say about him?"

"Well . . ." He fidgeted, shifted Eyne to a better position. What hope did he have of explaining it to her? It was difficult to give Tadek's words any weight. Words were cheap, and Tadek had so many of them, and he flung them hither and yon like he was feeding chickens. Still, he was essentially a good person, and Kadou liked him. Liked being around him. Liked it when Tadek made him laugh, or took his mind off of whatever was troubling him.

But it was difficult to navigate any kind of intimate connection with him, not only because of their relative positions, but because it was frustrating to try to figure out what Tadek wanted from him other than sex. Perhaps he didn't want anything else besides Kadou's good regard, which he would have had anyway.

Perhaps it was similar to whatever Zeliha saw in Siranos. In both her position and Kadou's, having a friend or having a lover were both equally complicated, so you took what you could get and you didn't ask for anything more than what the person was willing to give you—and when you found someone who saw you and treated you like a *person*, you grabbed hold of that and cherished it.

Zeliha sighed heavily. "You need better standards. Surely there's *someone* in the palace of whom you have a higher opinion than *he's nice*."

"Not really. Not like that."

Zeliha sat up, looking off behind Kadou. "Speaking of lovers. We'll continue this conversation later," she said firmly, and then: "Siranos, welcome. Do join us, won't you?"

Kadou's muscles locked in place.

※

Zeliha, perhaps sensing a little of the tension between him and Siranos (which had increased exponentially the moment Siranos spotted Eyne cuddled in Kadou's arms), shoved them out of the pavilion toward their horses as soon as the mistress of the hunt sounded her horn, and said, "Now, look after each other and come back soon."

That rather spoiled Kadou's plans to stay quietly at the back of the hunt and enjoy the scenery and relative solitude. Instead, he'd be obliged to ride beside Siranos, his guards and Kadou's own kahyalar arrayed around them—including, gods help him, Tadek, who gave Kadou a respectful bow and a cheeky wink when their eyes first met, and who ambled right up to Kadou to hold Wing's reins as he mounted.

"Highness," he murmured. "Are you well?"

"Managing," Kadou said back, softly.

Tadek's bright eyes met his again. Kadou was expecting a wry smirk, a flirtatious comment, but Tadek's glance flicked over to Siranos. "Shall I ride beside you?" Tadek asked lightly. "I have all manner of silly gossip and chatter to fill the air with."

Ah, and there it was—a prime example of why Kadou kicked himself whenever he fell to the temptation of being exasperated with Tadek. The same things that he found so tiresome in some circumstances could be painfully useful in others.

But he couldn't rely entirely on Tadek, and with the earlier conversation with Zeliha . . . He suppressed a wince. "Not today," he whispered. "I ought to make an effort, at least."

Tadek cast another sharp, assessing glance at Siranos. It made Kadou more nervous than even the most egregious flirting would have. "As you wish, Highness. Just give me a sign if you change your mind. It's me, Gülpaşa, Balaban, Yulad, and Selçuk at your back today. We asked to be assigned to you specially."

Just wonderful. The person who he had to be most conscientious of and the four staunchest of Kadou's "supporters," according to Tadek. Oh, what a bad idea it had been to ask for his help with anything covert. Several times now Kadou had attempted to explain to Tadek that he'd gotten the wrong idea, he'd misunderstood what Kadou was asking of him, but time and again, Tadek's only response was to clasp Kadou's hands, kiss his palms, and assure him that Tadek had it all under control.

Siranos rode a glossy black gelding, a little heavier than Kadou preferred for his hunting horses—Wing was a mare of a delicately built breed from south Qeteren, bred for endurance riding through the foothills of the mountains on the edge of the desert. She was desert-colored too, a shade that Vintish horsemasters called isabelline, a honey-cream that shone like pale gold.

Siranos had said little to him when he had strode up to Zeliha's pavilion, and he said absolutely nothing to him now. Kadou longed to turn and catch Tadek's eye, let him fill the air as he'd volunteered to do—undoubtedly he'd have harmless gossip about the results of the recent exams, and which of the kahyalar had merited promotion from the fringe-guard to the core-guard, and who would be assigned to more direct government service, and so on. He resisted the urge, and so the frosty silence continued, broken only by the jingling of the tack and the crunching of old leaves under the horses' hooves, the panting of the dogs loping alongside them, and the sounds of other people talking or laughing or singing in the distance.

By their very nature, hunts were often long periods of peace (or even boredom) followed by a sudden frantic burst of activity. This one was no different—after an hour or more of riding, Kadou caught a flash in the corner of his eye and hauled Wing's head around in the next heartbeat. He shouted to her, to the others, and kicked her sides. She flung herself forward through the underbrush and Kadou caught a glimpse of the quarry—it was a grey doe, a little on the small side. Wing was already gaining on her.

One-handed, he unclipped his shortbow from the saddle, loosened an arrow from the quiver at his hip. He had a clear shot—the underbrush was thinner here, and there was a long stretch of flat ground. The dogs bayed around him, gathering one by one out of the woods to run with them. He hooked Wing's reins over the pommel and stayed seated low in the saddle, nocking the arrow, hooking the string with his draw-ring, and pulling to his ear—

Something slammed into him from the side. The arrow slipped and went wide, and the world tipped. Kadou scrambled for the pommel, for the reins, for Wing's mane, and fell heavily to the forest floor. It was only by the grace of the gods that his feet didn't get tangled in the stirrups. He lay dazed and winded, shaken to his bones, his bow fallen a few feet away. The dogs, still in pursuit, swarmed around him and leapt over him.

There was a buzzing in his ears, and he heard someone bellow, as if off in the distance. Everything hurt; he couldn't make himself move—he watched Wing slow and stop within four strides, just as she'd been trained . . .

Hooves thudded around him. He heard the twang of bow-strings, the slick shimmering sound of blades drawn from their sheaths, shouting—

"Treason! Treachery!"

He blinked his eyes hard and rolled onto his back. His right arm and side throbbed with pain.

"Stand down!" he heard Tadek shout.

Oh, Kadou thought. *Shit.* He pushed himself up just in time to see his kahyalar, all mounted, wheeling around and charging at Siranos and his guards, weapons drawn. In the next heartbeat, before he could call out, there was the shattering scream of injured horses and soldiers. "Treachery!" someone shouted. "Get him away!" The words were in Oissika—it was one of Siranos's guards.

Kadou scrambled to his feet. "Hold!" he cried. "Hold!"

Two of the horses were already struggling and falling to their knees, dying on the ground, great saber slashes in their necks pouring blood onto the leaves. Three people fell before his eyes too—he couldn't see which, just the colors of their uniforms: two Mahisti blue-and-white, one without uniform—Siranos's personal retinue. All three bore saber slashes, and one of them had been shot by four arrows—eye, shoulder, chest, side.

Kadou felt sick. Time seemed to be going very slowly. "Hold!" he screamed again. "As you love me, drop your weapons!"

It was pure chance that Tadek turned his horse and saw Kadou. "Highness!" The expression on his face couldn't have been faked—true relief, true shock, true fear.

Kadou dove forward and seized Tadek's reins, dragging his horse out of the fray, and shouted again, "*Hold!*" and Tadek joined him then, doubling their volume.

The fighting faltered, and Siranos's remaining guard fled back in the direction of camp—Siranos himself had already disappeared.

Kadou felt the pain again with every heaving gasp of breath he drew and clamped his hand to his aching side.

Tadek flung himself off his horse and caught Kadou up in his arms. Kadou groaned, sore but not, he thought, badly hurt. Tadek stepped back, his hands fluttering over Kadou's face, his shoulder and side. His eyes were filling with tears, Kadou noticed distantly. "He drew an arrow, and then—something happened with his horse and he crashed into you. I thought it was intentional—I saw you fall—I thought you were—I swear he had a knife in his hand, I swear it—"

Just a glint of sun on the arrowhead, more likely. "I'm fine," Kadou said through gritted teeth. "Attend to the others. There's dead."

"We have to get you away from them!" Tadek said, shaking his head. "Take your horse, ride for camp, ride for your life—"

"Tadek!" he shouted, and Tadek cringed and subsided. "No one tried to kill me!"

"I know what I saw!"

But even Kadou's paranoia couldn't color it—an accident, he was sure of it. Tadek had spent so much time gossiping that he was seeing ghosts where there were none.

He pushed Tadek aside without another glance and limped toward the two fallen kahyalar. His stomach turned again. He pressed his hand to his mouth and knelt slowly. He touched Gülpaşa's face, then Balaban's.

Dead. Certainly dead—she bore a long slash across her neck. He was the one pincushioned with arrows. He looked across to Siranos's guard: a young man, younger even than Kadou himself. He didn't know his name.

He swallowed hard and looked up. The other kahyalar were bloodied. "I'm sorry," he said, his voice breaking. "It wasn't—I lost my seat, that's all. I didn't . . ."

He couldn't even blame Tadek for putting the kahyalar on edge.

He'd only been doing what Kadou had told him to do. Kadou had put the idea into his head that Siranos might try to hurt him, and so at the first trivial accident, Tadek had seen something much worse. Stupid Tadek, but stupider *him*.

He pushed himself to his feet, wiping the leaves and dirt off his face with the cuffs of his kaftan. His hands were shaking.

They all stood silent until Zeliha's kahyalar arrived, a tempest of horse and armor, and they were bundled together and hauled back to the palace. Passing through the hunting camp, Kadou saw only pale, distraught faces of the cadets and servants. They were already striking the tents and packing things back into wagons.

Zeliha's kahyalar led him to the throne room. It was a wide chamber floored in black marble; one of the long sides was open, framed by a series of archways leading out to a covered balcony that overlooked the city far below and the ocean beyond. The throne, an imposing couch wide enough for three to sit comfortably side by side, stood at the far end of the chamber, blazing gold and white on a raised platform, covered with an awning of thickly embroidered blue velvet, like a more decorated version of the tent at the hunting camp.

Zeliha paced before the platform and turned sharply toward him when her kahya pushed him—pushed him!—in front of her. One look from her and he cringed, drawing in small.

"What. Happened."

"They thought," he began, but his voice broke and he had to clear his throat. "They thought I was hurt. Dead."

"Who?"

"My kahyalar." He bit his lip. "It was just . . . sudden. It happened in—in seconds." She said nothing, just looked hard at him, like granite, like fire. "It wasn't Siranos's fault, you mustn't blame him. I saw a deer and gave chase, and Siranos was close to me, and his horse—something happened; I don't know, maybe he lost his balance—I fell off Wing." He gestured to his clothes, the dirt ground into the fabric, the leaves and grass stains. "My kahyalar were a little farther back. All they saw was the collision, and my fall, and they assumed the worst. But it was just an accident."

"It seems awfully convenient," she said quietly, her voice no less sharp. "No—it seems implausible. *Both* sides of the story do."

"I don't know what else to tell you. Tadek—"

"Ah," she said, "Yes. Tadek. Tadek, who you're so close to. Let's talk about Tadek, shall we?" She stepped up to the platform and sat slowly on the throne, drawing one foot up, resting her bent arm on her knee. "You said that you and he had stopped being lovers. When *did* the two of you start getting close again?"

"We . . . we just walked by the pond at the kahyalar's party, you know that part already," he said. How much did she know? He should confess the rest. His tongue was like wood in his mouth.

"And what happened there?"

"We talked. He offered to come back to my rooms with me. I said no."

"You're leaving something out," she snarled. "There's a gap as wide as the sea between declining Tadek's company for the evening and Tadek flinging himself at my lover and the body-father of my child and screaming about traitors." She narrowed her eyes. "And I happen to know he had visited your rooms several days earlier, with no message from you. At least, not by any formal channels. It was his day off, and he chose to spend part of it in your chambers. So apparently you weren't just getting close at the kahyalar's party. You know, when you said you weren't sleeping with him, I thought you might be . . . let's not use the word *lying*. Being discreet."

"It—it was the night of Eyne's birth. He saw the fireworks. He came to offer his congratulations, that's all." And instead of finding Kadou exultant, he'd found him having an episode, one of the worse kind, when fear came upon him so powerfully that there was nothing he could do but curl into a ball and *shake* until his bones rattled. Maybe Tadek took things more seriously than Kadou thought. Tadek had reassured him, had dismissed all Kadou's worries . . . Kadou had babbled everything just to try to make him *understand*—everything about Siranos's own accusations of treachery earlier that night, about how Siranos had gotten physical—

"Tell me," Zeliha said. "Does Tadek hate Siranos, or do you?"

"Neither," Kadou choked out. "Neither! Tadek is not at fault—"

"If he isn't, then you are. He was part of your guard. He was acting under your command, and now three people are dead, two more injured. Two horses killed in the fray, two more put out of their misery afterward. Now, what *happened*?"

"Siranos," he said. His voice was thick, his throat tight. His hands shook harder than ever. "It was when—when Eozena came to me at the temple, as I told you—the night there was the break-in at the Shipbuilder's Guild, the night Eyne was born. I didn't know what to do, so Eozena and I went to your offices—I told you that part too, and about how Siranos saw me there and confronted me."

"Yes, I recall." Her voice was cold. "What did you leave out?"

"He was saying all sorts of things. He thought I was interfering with something. He accused me of—of underhanded behavior for disloyal motives. He was frightened," Kadou added quickly. "That's all. He didn't know why the kahyalar were following my orders—he's *Oissika*, he doesn't understand about—"

"He's not an idiot," Zeliha snapped. "Why didn't you tell anyone about Siranos's accusations? Why didn't you tell me? Why did you make Melek swear not to speak of it?"

After a long moment, he said, "I told Tadek. I was afraid. Just afraid, that's all. I went back to my chambers, and Tadek arrived unexpectedly to say congratulations, and he made me feel better, and—and I asked him to . . . He was just trying to protect me."

"So Tadek does hate Siranos."

"No!"

"Whatever you said to him," she said, slow and quiet. "Whatever you said about Siranos, it made Tadek ready to kill him for you. Not just willing, but *ready*. *Prepared*. He was on edge, and it was because of something you said."

"It's my fault," Kadou managed, finally. His mouth was dry. "Is that what you want me to say? It is. I know it is, I knew it was from the moment I saw what happened. But it was an accident, I swear it. Sister. Sister, I swear to you, I never wanted anyone to be hurt. By the heavens and the seas, I swear it."

"And yet you kept secrets from me. You didn't trust me."

"I'm sorry." He wiped the tears from his face. "I should have told you, it's not that I didn't trust you, but—"

"But what?"

"I thought it would be a burden," he whispered. "You're very busy, and with Eyne, and I didn't want to cause trouble . . . And I was worried he was right, that I was too far out of line, that I might have done something that would hurt you. But I wouldn't. I wouldn't, not ever. You're my *sister*."

She sighed and stood again, walking to the balcony, her hands clasped behind her back. "I have told Siranos in the past that I do not share his opinion of you. He has spoken to me several times about his concerns regarding you and your position. I thought it enough to brush him off. Now I see that it was *not*. It was never going to be enough." She paced along the length of the balcony and back. Kadou wasn't sure if he should follow her or stay. He stayed. "He found your behavior objectionable and suspicious. He thought you were skulking—that was the word he used—and I said you were simply doing as duty commanded.

"The two of you have put me into an uncomfortable and unfortunate position. If I do not address these problems, they will grow—you and I both know they will. Our tutors made *sure* we knew. You have power by your birth; he has some by Eyne's, for better or worse, regardless of whether I grant him claim on her." She sighed, her mouth thinning. "If I could go back nine months, I would tell myself not to get so . . . fixated on one person. I would tell myself to visit another lover, or two, to confuse the issue. It would have been better. Cleaner. But I blithely owned to the fact that Siranos was the body-father, and now he has a few threads of natural claim on Eyne, even if none of them are recognized in the eyes of the law." She turned on her heel, the skirts of her short kaftan swinging wide around her knees, the leather soles of her embroidered slippers hushing against the floor. "So. Something must be done while the problem is small and manageable, before it gets even more gruesome than it already is." She shot him a glance. "Before it gets any more like what happened to Siranos's own family in his grandfather's youth."

Kadou dropped his eyes to the floor. A jealous younger brother had happened. It was no wonder Siranos hated him.

"I won't stand to have childish squabbles in my court turning into a matter of blood and live steel. I won't stand to see factions this potentially severe breaking out in front of my eyes. But how do I solve it without breaking my relationships with my brother or with the body-father of my heir?" She didn't seem to be looking for an answer; she didn't even seem to be speaking directly to him anymore. "The answer lies, I think, in showing restraint where neither you nor Siranos have done so. Perhaps it is understandable that such unpleasantness, to use poetic understatement, might break out. Tensions have been running high. Things are new and different for all of us—I've only been sultan for, what, not even two years? And now Eyne. So perhaps the thing to do, before I take any drastic measures, is to deal with the root of the problem: The tension. The chaos." She turned again and looked right at Kadou. "You need some time. You've never been comfortable in court, and I can't imagine that all this reshuffling of positions and responsibilities has been easy on you. So! I would strongly, strongly suggest that you take a vacation. Maybe spend the summer at the hunting lodge in the mountains. Get away from it all, get some peace and quiet and fresh air. I'll see that there are people to attend to any of your business in the city."

"You're sending me away," Kadou said. He felt . . . blank. Blank, but for an ache where his heart was supposed to be. "You're . . . exiling me?"

"Exile is a very strong word," Zeliha said, raising one finger. "And that's definitely not what I'm doing. But you're responsible for three deaths, Kadou," she said. "This decision is born of my own selfishness. If I were a better monarch, I would punish you more harshly." She scowled at him.

"I didn't mean for anyone to be hurt. I was only afraid."

"If you're so afraid of Siranos that you are jumping at shadows and not trusting me to keep you safe, then you need something else to occupy your attention."

"I'm still responsible for the investigation—the Shipbuilder's Guild—"

"Lieutenant Armagan has it well under control. And I'm sure we could manage it without your oversight. So why, pray tell, do you need to be in the palace?"

There was one benefit to chronic cowardice, and that was that he had an intimate relationship with fear. For as many times as his nerves had screamed in panic at him that there was some imminent disaster happening around him, it meant that now, in a *real* moment of catastrophe, when he looked for an inward place of calm, he found it. The very fact that the terrible thing *wasn't* just in his own imagination was a comfort and a relief.

"It won't look good," he said. "If anyone finds out I've gone—they won't know what you said in here." His voice shook just a little, but not nearly as much as he expected it to. Thank goodness this was real. It was something he could put his hands on and fight, not just a pressing sense of aimless dread he was helpless against. "If it looks like you've sent your little brother into exile, and it sounds like it, and the effect is the same . . ."

Her glare sharpened. "That's *not* what I'm doing."

"How many kahyalar know about what happened today? All of them will, if they don't already—you *know* how they gossip. One thousand three hundred and seven in the palace, and that's not counting the cadets. Their families will know about this by dinnertime, their neighbors by lunch tomorrow, the city by breakfast the day after. It's a very bad situation. I'm responsible. But if you send me away, it will be so much worse. It will look like—"

"Like we're weak? Like my brother and the body-father of the heir were conspiring against each other right under my nose?"

"Zeliha," he whispered. He wanted so badly for her to be his *sister* now, instead of his sultan. "The first lesson."

Three words to stop her in her tracks.

She let out a long slow breath.

"Do you remember how old we were?" he asked. "I don't remember much of it."

"I was nine. You were five," she said through gritted teeth. "You were too young for that lesson, but you begged and begged to come and I couldn't shake you off my sleeve. And you regretted it after, didn't you? You cried for days."

"The first lesson: Don't use power impulsively or in anger," Kadou said. "Like sticking your hand into a fire, but the people smaller and weaker than you are the ones who get burned."

"You're not so much smaller or weaker than I am," she said flatly.

"The kahyalar are. Their families are." Her eye twitched. "Send me away and you'll have punished me and satisfied your anger, and I'll be miserable. But you know as well as I do that if there are consequences, *we* won't be the ones suffering for them. What if—what if N'gaka thinks we're weak and distracted, and decides to break our alliance and invade? In a war, thousands die before we do."

She scoffed. "An unlikely scenario."

"Yes, but not impossible. We have no idea how this will affect anything. We have no way of predicting it, and there are far too many pieces on the chessboard for us to estimate the cost. We are the descendants of merchants—are you willing to buy something without knowing the price of it?" Had he convinced her? Was this line of argument working at all? Would it have been better to cling to her sleeve and weep and beg, like he was five again? That had worked all through their childhood. It might well work again. "Please," he said, because he couldn't resist trying. "Please. You may give me whatever punishment you want. But keep it a family matter, as much as we can."

"A family matter," she said, incredulous. "Involving two dead kahyalar, a dead Oissika and several more injured ones—you know the Oissic ambassador is already furious with me over Azuta Melachrinos and her counterfeits."

"All the more reason to not make this a national incident," he said quickly. "Between the counterfeits and the Shipbuilder's Guild, there are already too many fires to put out. Tell the ambassador it was a hunting accident, and that we mourn their dead countryman and—and we'll send money to his family and honor him equally alongside our fallen kahyalar."

"And Siranos?" she said. "What's your great plan for him?"

Oh, by all means send him *away,* his mind suggested with a manic kind of brightness. "Restrict him to the Gold Court." The innermost area of the palace, residence of only the royal family and the highest-ranking courtiers when they visited from the country. "It's—it's house arrest, but it'll look like an honor."

"They'll think I intend to give him claim on Eyne," she said coldly. "He will think he's being rewarded."

"If you send him away but not me, he'll go home to Oissos, and he'll probably be as upset and angry to be sent away as I would be. His family is wealthy—they might be offended to be snubbed, and if they have connections . . . it could damage our relationship with Oissos. You . . ." He winced. "You have to keep both of us near you."

"I don't want to see either of your faces right now," she spat. "Men! Fools and idiots!"

"I'm sorry."

"And what's *your* punishment?"

"I'll pay for all the funerals. I'll send the consolement purses, both to the fallen guard and to the injured ones. I'll . . . apologize to Siranos."

"And that's supposed to convince me that you've learned anything?" she said. "What about your punishment for mistrusting me, for keeping things from me, for your *own* part in weakening the family?"

He cringed. "Is there *any* punishment that could fit those crimes without injuring us further?"

They were both silent for a long time. He dropped his eyes

to the floor; he could almost feel her anger, barely banked, still burning at the edges of him. At length, she stalked over to the gold-inlaid divan and sat. "Come here." She gestured to the floor at her feet. "There is another matter."

He obeyed, sitting near her. Another time, she would have given him one of the cushions, and he might have lounged comfortably against the side of the throne. Another time, she might have invited him to sit beside her. A knot of dread twisted through his already soured stomach. "What other matter?"

"Tadek."

His blood went cold. "You were right. Anything he did was under my orders," he blurted. "I take responsibility for that too."

"Did you tell him to meddle with the kahyalar? Did you tell him to raise support for you?"

"No. No, of course not, he—he was just overenthusiastic. I wasn't clear about what I was asking of him, and . . . It's my fault. It is." When someone pledged you their service, when they showed that they really were quite serious about their willingness to lay their life down for yours, that required a certain amount of care in return. Tadek had tried, genuinely, to protect him. Kadou was bound by oath and by honor to do the same. "What's going to happen to him?"

"Court-martial," Zeliha said. All the fiery anger had run out of her voice—now she just sounded tired. "There will have to be an inquest."

Kadou's breath caught.

"There's not much of a choice," she continued. "Depending on the outcome . . . The best he can hope for, the absolute, *absolute* best, is a dismissal without dishonor. More likely, *with* dishonor. Even more likely is imprisonment—he's been a kahya of the core-guard. He has certainly been privy to secrets we wouldn't want wandering out in the general population. And at worst? If things go poorly and he speaks unwisely, or if we uncover anything uglier . . . execution."

Kadou closed his eyes. "Majesty. Sister. Please, I'll take any punishment you give me, and I'll do it gracefully and honorably, but . . ." He swallowed, and shifted onto his knees facing Zeliha and into more formal speech. He bent to press his forehead to the floor in abject supplication, as he had to the goddess in her temple the night Eyne was born. "Please, Majesty, please allow me to beg mercy on his behalf. He was acting under my command, with only the information I gave him, and I believe with all my heart that he thought he was acting in accordance with the oaths he swore as a kahya."

"Kadou," Zeliha said, pained and regretful as if she were about to explain to him that his request was impossible.

"Majesty," he choked. Now he had to frame it thus: as a boon he begged of his *sovereign* rather than his sister. "*Please.*"

"Sit up, Your Highness," she said softly, and with a pang in his heart, he knew she understood. He obeyed, keeping his eyes downcast. His hands trembled and he clenched them on his knees.

"Majesty, there is precedent," he said, speaking quickly. "In the hundred and seventeenth year of the Ahak dynasty, one of the provincial governors—" His voice cracked and he almost expected her to interrupt, to be dry at him for citing their tutors' lessons at her, but she said nothing, only let him collect himself and speak again: "One of the provincial governors heard that several of his subordinates had plotted to steal grain from the sultan's tax caravan, but that they had been apprehended. He begged the sultan to lay their lives in his hands. Sultan Tamas granted his request, and the criminals were moved to reform themselves and served faithfully for many years after . . ." He trailed off.

She didn't say anything for a long time. "You would have me lay Tadek's life in your hands?"

"He doesn't deserve to die for this, Your Majesty. The responsibility is mine," he whispered. "*Please.*"

"If I grant your request, he will be dismissed from the kahyalar corps. He will be yours entirely, your sworn armsman. He will be paid, clothed, boarded, and fed from your household's coffers, and he will enjoy none of the benefits of his former station."

"Understood," Kadou said quietly. He'd asked for Tadek's life laid in his hands—he hadn't expected it to be weightless.

"Kadou," Zeliha said again, in an entirely different tone. "Are you sure?"

"Yes."

"He was a fool. He will continue being a fool."

"I can't abandon him," he said more firmly. "I won't. If things had been different, then we'd be calling him a hero now."

He glanced up just in time to see Zeliha roll her eyes. "Oh, of course, there's no difference between a fool and a hero besides everything else in the world around them. What wisdom." She was silent again for a time. "Fine. His life is yours. Make of him what you will. Or what you can."

He slumped with relief. "Thank you."

"You'd both do well to look for better influences," she said, and then paused. "Ah."

"What?"

She tapped her fingertips on her knee. "I'm thinking of punishments. Your personal guard needs to be reassigned, I think. I wonder if Commander Eozena would have time to supervise. You've already been working with her for the Shipbuilder's Guild investigation. Keep doing that and she can easily keep an eye on you for me."

If it had been anyone else, he might have resented it more. All the kahyalar were considered family, in theory, but with Eozena it was real. She was warm and familiar, solid. She was a lifeline: real and incontrovertible proof that Zeliha saw a constructive way forward and wouldn't change her mind later, sending him away or cutting him out of the family for good. Both of them loved Eozena like an aunt, and her loyalty and love in return was beyond question. His very earliest memory was of her saving his life: He'd been little more than an infant, and he'd toddled into a fountain. He could remember struggling in the water, the rippling light of the surface that he couldn't reach, and then Eozena's strong hands plunging down, and her warm skin as she held him very close against her neck and cuddled him until he breathed again and then as he cried.

"She has nearly thirty years of irreproachable service," Zeliha said, clearly warming to her idea. "You'll do well with someone really steady and prudent to talk to, someone who won't let your foolishness hold your common sense hostage. You know her, I know her, we both trust her. Don't we?"

Kadou could only nod. Eozena wouldn't lead him wrong. Sooner that the sun would rise in the west. Sooner that the sea-wall would crumble into the waves before Eozena let him misstep again.

"But she doesn't have time to hang around you every moment of the day, and she's not a common kahya anyway. She has important things to do besides watch over you. You need a new primary. Not Tadek, of course."

"Melek's my primary right now," he said.

"Melek is sweet and gullible," Zeliha said. "Çe won't do at all. You need an anchor. Someone . . . rule-oriented. Disciplined. Someone who will be a good example to Tadek of what he should have been as a kahya." She tapped her fingers once again. "Do you know Evemer Hoşkadem?"

CHAPTER TWO

Late on Tegridem afternoon, the day before the promotion exams began, Evemer went to accompany his mother to the temple near her house, where she lit candles to Usmim and prayed that Evemer's trials would be easy ones. Kneeling beside his mother as she prayed, his hands flat on his thighs, he made calm and steady eye contact with Usmim's statue. He was ready. His training and practice and studies were sufficient. He had done his best. That was all that Usmim ever asked. After this trial, there would be another, because Usmim always sent another trial—such was the nature of life. Evemer would be ready for that one too, and he would do his best again. He could not imagine any situation he could not handle. He had always done his best, and it had always been sufficient.

He went home to his mother's house that night instead of the kahyalar dormitories in the palace, and she made him his favorite meal, and when he'd finished eating, she took his face between her cool hands and looked hard into his eyes. Evemer looked back, open and honest and wordless, thinking *I'm ready* as firmly as he could, and then she nodded to mean *You're ready,* and he'd gone upstairs to bed.

On İkinç, two days later, he finished the exams and knew he had done well. They had not been difficult for him; he had been ready. Usmim had never sent a trial that was truly beyond Evemer's ability, only some that required greater determination, preparation, and care. After all, what would be the point of a trial that you were *supposed* to fail?

On the evening of Törtinç, two days after that, he returned

to the palace, taking the winding road up the cliff by foot, passed through the immense double doors of the Copper Gate, and went to the dormitories, where he found the entire garrison in chaos and heard the terrible news of what had happened on the hunt that day.

The next morning, he reported to his commanding officer, who handed him a chit of passage and ordered him immediately to present himself before Commander Eozena, who could be found past the Gold Gate. By this, Evemer understood that he had done well enough to earn promotion to the core-guard, and felt a quiet bloom of satisfaction in his chest, which he carefully kept from reaching his face.

Sergeant Benefşe did not deign to provide him with any further indication of what his new assignment would be, and so Evemer did not ask her for any clarification. He bowed himself out, went through the Silver Gate, where the daily business of the government happened, and then through the Gold Gate. The area beyond was as splendid as he had been told—quieter and cozier than the Silver Court, with jewel-like mosaics framing every window, all of which seemed to look out over cool shady gardens. He could hear birdsong and the bubbling sound of fountains whenever he stopped and listened, broken only by the murmur of distant voices.

He had never been past the Gold Gate, even as a cadet—he'd given his service years in the city watch instead. Balaban had mentored him there for a year or so, before he himself had been promoted to the core-guard.

Balaban was dead now. He kept forgetting. It was strange to think that someone he respected was just . . . gone, and uselessly. That was the part that stung most—not that Balaban had died, but that he had sworn to give his life to protect the royal family and then his death had been *pointless*.

Evemer set the thought aside firmly. It was not the time.

Commander Eozena was waiting for him in one of the courtyards leading into the residential wing of the Gold Court. During the winter, the provincial governors would swarm in from their holdings in the countryside and set up households in the palace's apartments. As it was the end of spring, they had all left again, so the Court was serene and quiet.

"Morning, Hoşkadem," Eozena said as he approached. She was an inch taller than him, dark-skinned and dark-eyed, her hair styled in hundreds of long, thin locs and decorated with a scatter of bright silver bands and charms. Besides knowing her by reputation and at a distance, he'd also had the great honor of meeting her on the sparring fields on several occasions. He'd been utterly trounced, of course—she was the *commander*.

If it had been anyone else, it might have been embarrassing to lose so definitively, but in Evemer's estimation, being beaten by the commander was better than winning against anyone else. She had always smiled and helped him up out of the dust, offered him brisk words of advice and encouragement as he brushed himself off, like she was pleased to see his progress and more pleased at the thought that he could progress further still. She was his direct commanding officer now, and that thought made the glow of satisfaction burn in his chest again.

"Commander," he said, saluting.

"Congratulations on your exams, and welcome to the coreguard. Did they show you the results?"

"No, Commander."

She smiled at him in a way that made her look terribly like his mother, though Eozena was more than a foot taller than her. "Best marks out of everyone. You should be very proud of yourself."

"Thank you, Commander."

"Now, I expect you have questions—they didn't tell you anything before they sent you over, did they?"

"No, Commander."

"Good. You're being given a great honor, you know. A very important assignment."

"Yes, Commander." Promotion to the core-guard was indeed an important assignment, although . . . it was odd that he was receiving orientation all on his own. He'd expected that he would be inducted in a small group. There *had* been years when only one person had marks high enough to merit the core-guard, but only rarely.

"Her Majesty picked you for this one herself," Eozena said. That was . . . alarming. That Her Majesty knew his *name* was something he wouldn't have ever dared to hope for. "Are you a nervous sort, Hoşkadem? Do you need a moment?"

"No, Commander," he said. Perhaps if anyone had given him a hint about what the assignment was, he might have.

She clapped him on the shoulder. "Good man. Well. Let's go introduce you, then. I don't think you've had a chance to meet him properly yet."

Him? Evemer had a sudden horrible suspicion of whose service, precisely, he was being assigned to.

Eozena led him inside, through doors guarded by pairs of ka-hyalar in full dress uniform, armed to the teeth and glittering in the sun—he himself had not yet been issued his core-guard uniform with its darker blues and bright silver braid. If it had been mandatory, he would have been sent to the requisitions offices first to be outfitted properly. He concluded, therefore, that he should not feel embarrassed to be underdressed.

The commander stopped at a pair of carved mahogany doors. "Listen," she said in a soft voice. "He's not a difficult charge. Very quiet, keeps to himself. I've known him since before he could walk—he's always been good. Do you understand?"

Oh, no. Evemer knew exactly who he was being assigned to. "Commander," he said, faintly strangled.

She nodded once and rapped on the door before cracking it open. "Pardon, Highness. Hoşkadem is here. May I introduce you?"

Highness. The prince.

Damn.

There was a long silence. "Yes" came a tired voice. "He can come in, if he likes." Eozena nodded briskly and opened the door the rest of the way, waving Evemer in before her.

He looked at her. He looked at the doorway. He looked at her.

She raised her eyebrow at him, the most fearsome expression he could possibly conceive of.

He entered the room.

It was just as splendid as the rest of the Gold Court. The vaulted ceilings were painted with a lace-like pattern of delicate vines and flowers, rich-colored carpets covered the floors, and the windows stood wide open, the curtains fluttering in the spring breeze.

In the center of the room there was a low table, set for a breakfast that had not been touched. On the opposite side of the table, not touching his breakfast, was the prince.

The prince—Kadou—was but two or three years younger than Evemer, smaller and slighter than him in every respect. His hands, wrapped around a brimming cup that was no longer steaming, were slender and well-manicured. His ink-black hair spilled long and shining in waves and soft curls down to his elbows, and his eyes were large, luminous, and the blue-black color of the ocean on a dark night.

Evemer had noticed all those things before. The first time he'd laid eyes on the prince up close had been at the Grand Temple on the night of Princess Eyne's birth when Commander Eozena had brought him and several other of the fringe-guards to run messages for her in the wake of the Shipbuilder's Guild break-in. That night, His Highness had looked tired, harried, distracted— and rather like he'd rolled out of bed in a hurry and only flung on a dressing gown over his nightshirt to run to the temple. A little disrespectful to the gods, Evemer had thought, but excusable in the circumstances.

The second time he'd seen the prince had been at the Shipbuilder's Guild itself the next morning. Evemer had been posted on guard at the door, and His Highness had arrived on horseback to hear the first reports from the investigation. Evemer had held the bridle while His Highness dismounted. He'd already looked exhausted, but he had paid enough attention to smile at Evemer and say thank you, and then he'd asked tentatively if Evemer could be spared to fetch him a cool drink—the morning had been unseasonably warm, and His Highness had been wearing heavy, high-formal court robes. Evemer had run off to do just that, thinking that mere well water wasn't nearly good enough for the prince of Araşt, that he would have to seek a street merchant willing to sell him something nicer.

Prince Kadou had gone inside to see to the hysterical guildmaster. When he'd come back out, he'd mounted up on his beautiful milk-gold horse again as if he'd forgotten the request. Evemer had offered him the flask he'd bought from a vendor down the street, and he watched His Highness's face as he took a deep draft from it and tasted the sharbat sekanjabin, cold and sweet and snapping with the refreshing edge of vinegar.

The exhaustion had cleared from His Highness's face, and a sparkle of light and pleasure had come into his eyes, and he'd looked down at Evemer, smiling gratefully, and he'd sighed, "Oh, you're a godsend."

All Evemer had done was bring him a cool drink, but it had felt like that one smile had shoved him six inches out of alignment. He'd been thunderstruck with that moment for days afterward, and still felt a little of it now when he remembered it. He'd thought perhaps he'd been embellishing it in his own memory.

But then His Highness was also the one who had gotten Balaban and Gülpaşa killed.

Evemer found that he was angry. The shock was beginning to settle in now. Balaban had been someone he admired. Gülpaşa was the closest thing he'd had to a friend—not a particularly intimate one, but he had respected her. They had both helped him prepare for the exams. They'd each, on separate occasions, heard him confess in a whisper that admittance to the core-guard was what he'd wanted most in all the world. It was the one thing he had been striving toward for as long as he could remember.

He felt as if His Highness had somehow deceived him with that shining moment at the Shipbuilder's Guild—as if he'd tricked Evemer into thinking well of him and only then revealed the truth in his heart.

Evemer thought again of that moment, of His Highness on his milk-gold horse, resplendent in blue and silver, glittering in the sun with the light on his hair and in his eyes, as radiant as a god-kissed prince out of legend as he asked graciously for Evemer's service. That kind of display should have *meant something*.

But it hadn't. Perhaps it was Evemer's own fault. Perhaps he was lying to himself if he thought any of that could have been real and true.

"Hello," said Prince Kadou.

"Hello," said Evemer. "Your Highness."

"Your Highness, this is Evemer Hoşkadem, newly promoted to first lieutenant in Her Majesty's service." She pronounced his first name with a little of the city accent, closer to *Afennür*, the standard form—not the worst mispronunciation he'd ever heard, but he was used to it and had learned to answer to it. "I will personally vouch for his loyalty and devotion to duty—I would quite readily trust him with any of my own secrets, were I required to confide them in someone, and I assure you on my honor that you can do the same. He is the best we have, and I know he will serve you well." Evemer heard the praise distantly, like it was someone talking in the next room. He was too busy schooling his face into blankness. Duty, yes.

He was not serving this . . . man. He was serving Her Majesty and Commander Eozena. He was obeying *their* commands. "I am honored to serve, Your Highness," he said, because that was nearly true.

"Hoşkadem, His Highness Prince Kadou. I trust he needs no other introduction."

"No, Commander," said Evemer.

"Good," said the commander. "You'll be His Highness's primary until further notice. If you have any questions, please consider me your first resource." This was said with enough of an edge that it wasn't, apparently, empty invitation. She sketched an alarmingly casual bow to the prince. "Unless you need anything else from me, I'll excuse myself," she said, and His Highness nodded morosely.

The door clicked behind her as she left.

Silence settled into the room like a cat curling up in a basket.

Evemer was completely at a loss for what to do or say. He stared

hard at His Highness, studying his face, his hands. He was wearing a loosely belted dressing gown over his snow-white underlayer,
and his hair was tousled. No one had bothered yet to groom and
arrange it. No one had even bothered to give him a shave.

Evemer clenched his jaw. He'd been under the impression that
there were certain standards in the Gold Court. Someone should
have attended His Highness this morning. Even if Evemer was the
new primary, there was no reason to wait for him to arrive and be
officially appointed and introduced—*someone* should have attended
Prince Kadou. It would be shameful, a dishonor on *Evemer*, if His
Highness were to appear like this in front of anyone else.

The prince looked . . . unhappy. Tense. Perhaps he knew
something of Evemer. Perhaps he was just as disappointed with
this situation as Evemer was.

Likely he would have preferred it to be one of his favorites.
Like that Tadek Hasira. His *lover*.

Everyone in the garrison knew about Tadek—when Evemer
had still been on fringe-duty, he'd known about Tadek. Even
before then, from their time as cadets in the kahyalar academy
together years and years ago, Evemer had been vaguely aware of
Tadek, and he had despised him almost instantly. They had never
spoken, so far as Evemer could remember, and Evemer had never
heard anything about the man that would recommend him: Tadek
was vain and had a reputation for being rather free with his affec-
tions. He wasn't serious; he was careless, flighty, and negligent—
qualities he shared with the prince, evidently.

And, of course, he too was also directly responsible for the
deaths of two good and loyal kahyalar.

Tadek should have been court-martialed for his part in what
he'd done, but the prince had saved his life, though none of last
night's gossip could quite agree on the exact truth of what had
happened. Evemer had collected at least eight different ludicrous
tales from twelve different kahyalar and cadets, and the only thing
that was the same across all of them was that the prince—*this*
prince, this careless, flighty, negligent man—had knelt at Her

Majesty's feet to ask her to show his lover mercy instead of allowing him take his punishment with honor.

No wonder they were lovers. They must get along splendidly.

His Highness seemed . . . shy? He kept glancing at Evemer
and away, worrying his lip with his teeth, his brow all twisted up.
The sign of a guilty conscience, maybe, or perhaps a simple weakness of character.

"I'm sorry about this," His Highness said suddenly.

He didn't sound sorry. He sounded like he was offering words
to Evemer like carefully arranged sweets on a tray at a banquet.

"I beg your pardon, Highness?"

His Highness looked away, then down at his hands, twisting
in his lap. Evemer took the opportunity to freely clench his jaw.
What sort of a prince was this, who couldn't even look at the person he spoke to? "I suppose you know that I'm not exactly held in
high favor at the moment."

"Your Highness," said Evemer.

"I don't want you to think that—that you're being punished,
or that this is going to be an obstacle to the advancement of your
career."

Of course he hadn't been thinking such a thing—Her Majesty
had appointed him to this post specifically. "Is there anything that
Your Highness requires?"

His Highness sighed and looked at the breakfast things,
looked down into his cup—coffee rather than tea. Rather luxuri-
ous for so early in the morning, Evemer thought. If His Highness
had regretted yesterday's events in the slightest, he might have
confined himself to more humble and modest fare to reflect his
repentance. Evemer eyed the myriad array of small plates and
bowls on the table as well, far more food than one person could
eat—several kinds of cheese, olives, eggs poached in red sauce, a
startling selection of jams, su borek, sliced and fried sausage, and
three types of bread. One of the breads was the same ring-shaped,
sesame-crusted simit that Evemer and his mother ate in their own
house—this, of all things, gave him pause. It was a ubiquitous

bread down in the city, one that everyone ate. But Evemer hadn't expected "everyone" to include the prince.

He didn't know how to feel about that.

Frustrated and angry, he decided after a moment's reflection. Princes were not *normal people*, so they oughtn't eat the same foods that normal people did.

"If you'll summon a cadet to clear breakfast away," His Highness said, and got to his feet. He still wore sleep trousers beneath his underlayer, and his feet were bare. "And then I suppose you can come dress me."

When the first order had been attended to, Evemer silently followed deeper into the prince's apartments—the other door in the room led into a bedchamber, as expansive and airy as the parlor had been, though since they were both north-facing, the light was a little dim. His Highness was standing at a massive wardrobe, rummaging shoulder-deep. At the front of the shelves, Evemer could see dozens of neatly folded robes and kaftans in colors as bright as flowers and butterfly wings, but deeper within there was the rustle of paper—the finer and more rarely worn items, he could guess.

His Highness pulled out a parcel and unwrapped it. He nodded, tossed it onto the bed, and turned to Evemer. To his credit (and Evemer begrudged him even this), he didn't ask if Evemer knew what he was doing—Evemer wouldn't have been allowed within a hundred yards of these apartments if he didn't meet the required standards of the position.

His Highness silently took a seat in the chair by the window and said, gesturing to a dresser nearby, "Everything's in that drawer." By *everything* he meant brushes, combs, nail files, pumice stones, several different types of scissors, straight razors, a leather strop for sharpening, shaving soaps, oils, lengths of clean white linen. Evemer took a careful inventory—it was neat enough, he supposed. It could be neater. He would have to inspect everything in one of his free moments.

He stropped the razor to a perfect edge and lathered the soap. His Highness tipped his head back, baring his throat. Evemer didn't allow himself to think of anything those next few minutes but the careful glide of the blade, the scrape of the edge against skin and hair.

His Highness kept his eyes closed, kept perfectly still and silent until Evemer had finished, and then he took the damp cloth and wiped the rest of the soap from his face. "Arrange my hair for mourning, please."

Mourning, was it? He cast an eye to the paper-wrapped parcel on the bed—was it going to be mourning clothes too? "Highness," he said, and even to his own ear his voice sounded cool.

Mourning, at least for the upper classes and royalty who wore their hair long like His Highness's, meant severe arrangements— Evemer brushed out the heavy, silken mass of black until it shone like wet ink, braided it as tightly as he could, and pinned it up into a knot at the nape of Kadou's neck. His Highness sprang out of the chair the moment the last pin was in place and went to the bed as if the parcel were a vicious animal that was going to spring up and bite him.

It was, indeed, mourning clothes. There was a velvet kaftan in funereal colors—a red so dark it was nearly black, lined with black silk, a deep purple underlayer embroidered with mountain laurel and acanthus, and black trousers. By the time Evemer had gotten all the soaps, brushes, razors, and cloths tidied away, His Highness had already changed into the trousers and was doing up the tiny black-pearl buttons of the underlayer with shaking hands.

Evemer silently took over. He could not resist the temptation to firmly brush His Highness's hands away—even in this, he wasn't the man Evemer had expected him to be. A prince ought to accept service graciously, rather than scrambling about trying to do trivial things for himself that should have been beneath his notice.

Evemer shook out the heavy velvet kaftan next—the cloth was so dark that it seemed to draw light into it, except where it flashed bright at the folds. Being more formal, it was fitted tighter through the shoulders than usual, with sleeves so restrictively narrow that they had to be buttoned from the elbow—His Highness, thankfully, did not attempt again to do these up, nor the silk-and-black-jadeite frog closures at the front. He stood as still and quiet for this as he had for the shave. There was just the terrible weight of this silence between them.

Surely he must know that Evemer knew.

Evemer unfolded the sash that went with the kaftan—a long length of black silk veiling, fine enough that even soft hands might snag the fabric if it was handled carelessly. His Highness raised his arms, and Evemer looped it around his waist twice and knotted it neatly in a sober style—one of the more fashionable knots wouldn't have been at all appropriate. The trailing ends of the sash reached nearly to the ground.

Evemer stood back and assessed him from head to toe.

"Do I pass inspection?" His Highness asked with a watery smile—an attempt at a joke.

"Highness," Evemer said in clipped tones, and His Highness's expression shuttered off again, into that closed and miserable wretchedness. "How long will Your Highness be in full mourning?"

"Five days," His Highness said. It was uncertain, almost a question. Was he looking for Evemer's approval?

Five days was excessive. Evemer risked another sharp glance at him—five days was how you mourned a parent, spouse, sibling, or child. Five days for a pair of kahyalar, even if they had been ones that Kadou knew well, smacked of performative grief. As if His Highness were publicly showing off how contrite and unhappy he was. "Highness," Evemer said, and his anger mounted higher to see His Highness wince.

※

The sentient, walking blank wall that had been assigned to him followed Kadou out of his chambers, out through the Gold Gate, and into the Silver Court, silent every step of the way.

At least, sort of a blank wall. He must think himself very accomplished at that stony facade, and Kadou was sure that it probably worked on most people. But Kadou could read him at a glance, just as he'd been able to at the Shipbuilder's Guild, when he had thanked the distractingly handsome kahya at the door for fetching him something to drink, and the kahya had straightened his shoulders and glowed at him without changing his expression a hair's breadth.

What he was reading now was cold, hidden fury that Evemer apparently thought he was concealing. He wasn't the only one who was upset—Melek had cried a bit, the night before, but pretended like çe hadn't. Istani had, unusually, refrained from grumbling about anything at all. Selime and Hafza, who had stood guard at the door, hadn't even made eye contact with him when he returned at last to his chambers, let alone smiled as they usually did. The cadets bringing in his meals had fled as quickly as possible.

This one, though, had worked himself up into a rage. Kadou had watched the storm brew darker over Lieutenant Hoşkadem's face as he'd entered the room and pinned Kadou in place with only the weight of his cold eyes and colder judgment. It made Kadou want to huddle down as small as possible.

Kadou led the way to the offices of the intelligence ministry— the kahyalar here were stiff and cool to him too, and he swept past them quickly with his eyes fixed on the ground and Evemer's steady step just behind him.

Lieutenant Armagan was waiting in one of the ministry's chambers, solemn faced. "Your Highness," çe said tonelessly. "I would have been more than happy to come to you instead. You needn't have made the walk."

It sounded almost like a rebuke—perhaps Armagan didn't want to be seen with him either. Kadou wouldn't blame çem for it. "It's no trouble. I'm happy to meet with you wherever you'd prefer," he said softly.

Armagan grunted. "That's the thing, Highness. I don't think we will have much reason to meet anymore."

Kadou's heart nearly stopped in his chest, and for a moment he thought Armagan might be about to declare that çe couldn't possibly work with Kadou's oversight. "What do you mean?" he managed.

"The investigation. It's a dead end, Highness."

"But you said just the other day that there was progress. You said slow, but . . . is that not the case?"

"I'm sorry that you came all this way for such bad news, Your Highness," Armagan said. "We're wasting our time on it, in my opinion. There's nothing that would give us clues about the identity of the thieves or how to track them, and nothing to suggest they actually got their hands on any sensitive information."

"But surely there's *something*—it's only been a few days, surely we can't just give up." It was too important. Araşti ships, shipbuilders, and sailors were the best in the world, and getting better every year—the guild had been responsible for recent developments in hull technology that several very clever people had attempted to explain to Kadou using lots of new terms like *fluid dynamics*. All that research had been stored in the guild's records room, but that wasn't what Kadou was most concerned about. The research being stolen would be a blow, but the nature of research was that anyone else would have been able to re-create it, if they had enough time.

No, the thing that kept Kadou up at night, the thing that had made this break-in an issue of national security was that besides all the research, the Shipbuilder's Guild held one-third of the most precious and lucrative secret in, arguably, the world: the trick of passing safely across the sea when the serpents of the deep rose for their breeding season and roved lust-maddened and hungry near the surface, or clustered in their writhing, frothing mating swarms, powerful and violent enough to tear holes in the bottoms of even the thickest-hulled vessels. For six weeks in the summer, the Sea of Serpents—the mercantile center of the world, it was said—was functionally impassable to all but Araşti ships sailed by Araşti captains. Six weeks when theirs were the only ships that would dare leave port for open waters. Six weeks when only they were safe. Six weeks of a total monopoly on trade, at least in this part of the world.

But that secret had been endangered, and so the investigation, in Kadou's opinion, remained quite literally a matter of national importance.

"Highness, we don't even know what they used to batter down

the doors," Armagan said. "All we know is that they used the noise of the fireworks on the night of Her Highness's birth to cover up the noise—that's *it*. There is *nothing* to go on. Highness, I've seen a dozen cases like this. There've been times I've worked my fingers to the bone only to turn up nothing. There are better ways to spend our energy—reinforcing security at the guilds, perhaps, so that it doesn't happen again; learning from what mistakes or infelicities happened here. That sort of thing. But with the search for answers or explanations . . ." Çe sighed. "Sometimes we just have to accept failure."

Those last words lodged in Kadou's chest like a crossbow quarrel. "I see," he said. "Well. I'll . . . I'll have to tell Her Majesty—"

"No need. I've already sent a report to Her Majesty and to Minister Selim."

Çe had gone over Kadou's head, in other words, likely because çe really *couldn't* stomach the idea of working with him and probably hadn't thought that he could be relied upon to accept good advice. "Oh. I see." There was an awkward beat of silence, and Armagan's eyes flicked to the door. Kadou got the hint immediately. "Well. Thank you for your service, then. I'm sure you did the best you could, and I'll be sure to commend you to Her Majesty."

Empty, rote words. Words that felt wrong in his mouth, that he *knew* were wrong. He should have insisted. He should have demanded answers. But he was no expert in such things, and he wasn't trained for this—the purpose of ministers like Armagan was to provide wisdom and counsel, but what good was that if their expertise was not heeded?

Kadou felt the familiar shivering beginning at the core of him, the cracks that would run through all his glass-fragile nerves until he shattered to pieces. He paused just long enough for Armagan to bow, and then he fled.

※

Evemer's duty was to the sultan, he reminded himself again and again that day. Not to the prince.

He followed His Highness from the embarrassingly short

meeting with Lieutenant Armagan to a series of equally short ones with other people, watching as the prince got quieter and more withdrawn with each person he spoke to. Evemer didn't know how to interpret it—was His Highness surprised that so many people were upset with him? Was he taken aback that no one was commenting on his performance of mourning? He was quite pale by noon, his face stark against the deep black-red of his kaftan, and he kept having little spells of shivering, as if he were cold.

He remembered, belatedly, that His Highness had not touched his breakfast, and promptly decided that it was not within the required standards of a kahya for Evemer to remind him to eat lunch. It would build character and discipline for him to go a little hungry.

By midafternoon, the prince's posture was terrible, like a meek child who thought they might be slapped at any moment. Evemer mentally shoved at him, willing him to straighten and stiffen his back, to raise his chin, to stop *fiddling* so with his cuffs. He knew His Highness was capable of it. He'd seen it in his effortless seat on that fine horse at the Shipbuilder's Guild.

Evemer straightened his own spine until it was as erect and rigid and unyielding as cold iron. His muscles ached in protest.

He could show enough discipline for both of them. He wouldn't allow himself a dram of ease as long as His Highness was slinking around like that as if no one were watching him, as if there were a single soul in the palace who wasn't paying attention to his every move. Evemer wondered how a person could be so oblivious, and then remembered—not oblivious. Just careless and negligent.

Evemer served the sultan. He obeyed Commander Eozena.

※

The very moment that Kadou felt he could reasonably return to his chambers, he did so, charging through the doors and striding across his parlor to his bedroom without waiting to see who, if anyone, followed. He staggered toward the bed and collapsed into it, rolling onto his back and clasping both hands to the center of his chest.

His clothes were far too tight—the collar around his neck, the sleeves, the waist. He couldn't move in them, couldn't breathe. The velvet was too heavy and too hot, even in the mild warmth of midspring.

"Highness," Evemer said from the door. "Do you require a doctor?"

"No. Don't. It's nothing." Kadou struggled suddenly back to his feet, stumbled across the room, and fumbled at the latches on the window. "I want this open. It's so stuffy in here."

Evemer came forward and brushed Kadou's hands aside, swinging the glass open to the inside and propping it open with the chair so the wind couldn't blow it closed. Kadou clawed at the black silk frog-closures of his kaftan with shaking hands and leaned against the windowsill—he managed a few of them, and even that was a sharp relief.

He'd failed. Zeliha had been right—he should have let her send him away somewhere to be useful. He shouldn't have talked her out of it, because now here he was, a failure and an embarrassment who couldn't even oversee the simplest investigation, let alone a crucially important one. What more could he have done? Surely there must have been something.

"I was not made aware of Your Highness having any medical conditions," Evemer said.

"I don't. It's nothing," Kadou said firmly. "It's not a medical condition. There's nothing wrong." He forced a laugh. "You might as well know. You'll find out eventually anyway. What's the point of hiding it? It's not a medical condition. I'm just a coward."

Evemer said nothing.

"You needn't worry," Kadou said. He closed his eyes and, though his hands were shaking, managed to undo two of the closures of his underlayer at his neck. The cotton stuck to his skin, sticky and overwarm, and Evemer had braided his hair so tightly that morning that his scalp was aching. "It comes upon me unexpectedly. Or . . . expectedly. Cowardice, after all. But that's all it is. Pay it no mind."

He stumbled back toward the bed, but Evemer caught him by the shoulder. "Your clothes, Highness."

The velvet was not so delicate that it would have been the worse for Kadou throwing himself into bed. A curse on all kahyalar and their universally inconvenient obsession with his presentation. Suppressing the impulse to scream, he propped himself up against one of the bedposts and shoved everything within him away while Evemer unknotted the sash, made quick work of the rest of the kaftan's buttons down Kadou's front and at his wrists, and peeled the mourning kaftan off of him. Then Evemer turned away, as if he didn't care at all now whether Kadou toppled into bed or not, now that he'd saved the velvet from being crushed.

It *was* desperately more comfortable without the weight of it dragging him down, at least. "Send a message to the kitchens," he said, falling into the sheets. "I'll be eating here in my rooms for dinner." He wondered when Evemer's relief shift would be sent. Perhaps he'd have to choke down a few bites of food under that cold gaze. He deserved it—it so clearly said that he had taken Kadou's measure and calculated precisely how much he'd fallen short.

"Yes, Highness," said Evemer. He folded the velvet kaftan neatly and laid it atop the dresser. Then, as if the words were being drawn from him with a team of oxen, "Is there anything else you require?"

"Send for Eozena," he said, barely keeping the quaver out of his voice. He was utterly appalled with himself. He'd be burdening her. She had better things to do than come to talk to him. "And— and can you please find out where my armsman is?" *And then bring me quite a lot of wine,* he did not add. Better to wait a little longer for that.

Evemer's moment of silence had a vaguely astonished quality. "Your armsman, Your Highness?"

"Tadek Hasira. He's—he's somewhere in the palace, unless they've sent him on leave—but they wouldn't have, because he's under *my* command now, and I didn't tell him—just send someone to find out where he is. Please."

"Yes, Highness."

He pulled all the pins out of his hair and unbraided it—his

scalp ached even more to be released from that tight binding—
and spent the next half hour staring into nothing and reviewing
every word that he had said to anyone that day, inspecting each
interaction from several angles to determine which ones he should
be crushingly embarrassed about, and to what degree.

Eozena saved him from himself. Coming in, she shut the
door and dragged the chair over to the edge of the bed, turning it
around so she could straddle it with her arms crossed on the back.
"Rough day?"

"Are *you* angry at me?"

"Nope," she said. "A tiny bit exasperated, perhaps. Is everyone
else angry?"

"I think so." He took a miserable breath. "Lieutenant Armagan
is shutting down the investigation."

She frowned. "Already?"

"That was my response too." He rolled onto his side to face her.
"Did I ruin it?"

"How could you have ruined it?"

"I must have, somehow."

She shook her head. "Nonsense. But what did Armagan say?"

"Just that there wasn't any progress, no clues, no leads. Çe said
it would be a waste of time, and that çe already informed Zeliha
and Minister Selim that çe was going to recommend shutting it
all down." Only that thing about the fireworks—which meant the
thieves had been prepared, which meant . . . probably nothing except that the gossip mill in the palace was in fine working condition. It had not been a secret that Her Majesty was pregnant, and
it definitely wouldn't have been a secret when her labors started.

"That's unusual," Eozena said, her frown deepening. "It's been—
what, just over a week?"

Kadou pushed himself up to a seat, crossing his legs tailor-style
and picking at a loose thread in the quilt. "I didn't know what else
to say—I barely know what I'm *doing* with this. Just . . . taking
reports and saying, 'Yes, good job,' right? If Armagan says there's
no point, then who am I to contradict that?"

"You could ask çem for the reports. You could review everything yourself. You could go back down to the Shipbuilder's Guild. I'd go with you."

Kadou squirmed with discomfort. "I don't know." His nerves were getting worse now—just the thought of indicating to Armagan that Kadou thought çir work was lacking in some way was too horrific to contemplate at the moment. It was all too much.

"Are you all right? Are you getting sick?"

"Maybe." That was easier than explaining—it was one thing to admit his cowardice to Evemer, who already was contemptuous of him. It was another to say it to Eozena, who might well be the only person in the palace who didn't hate him. "Do you . . ." He swallowed. "Do you know where Tadek is? He hasn't come."

"Of course he hasn't. He's not a kahya anymore. He isn't even allowed into the Gold Court except by royal decree, and . . . you haven't decreed it. They found him a room in the cadet dormitory for his lodging, I think."

Kadou swore and rolled out of bed. The cadet dormitory? For someone who, two days ago, was a kahya of the core-guard? Gods, how humiliating it must be—Tadek of all people didn't deserve to be humiliated.

Kadou went immediately to his writing desk, scrawled out a note, and marked it with his personal seal in sapphire-blue wax. "So," Eozena said, behind him. "You're going to continue things with him, then?"

He froze. "What do you mean?"

"You're summoning him to your side right away? What's he going to do here? Will you keep him in jewels and silks?"

Kadou flushed and dropped his eyes. "No. Just . . . he could serve as my valet, I suppose. Take some of the burden off the kahyalar." Then he wouldn't have to suffer through any more of those endless awkward silences with Evemer, or watch him glower from across the room, or have his hair braided so tightly that it hurt him all day. Strange how someone who had at first made Kadou look twice was now making him want to look anywhere *but* at him. "How long have you known about me and Tadek?" he asked. "It was the palace's gossip network, I suppose?"

"I'm commander of the guard, Kadou. I'm privy to ninety percent of the intelligence the crown receives. And . . . well, yes, you're partly right; kahyalar are *gossips*. If it was supposed to be a state secret, you could have done better."

"It wasn't. Not really."

"You were reasonably discreet, except for that little romantic walk at the party the other night. I certainly don't blame you for having something with him. From all I've witnessed and heard, it seems you treated each other well, before yesterday's . . . incident." Her expression turned sympathetic. "And I know it must be lonely. I imagine that it felt easier to turn to someone who had already sworn himself to you, someone you knew you could trust. Someone who made you feel safe."

Kadou nodded miserably. Not many courtiers his own age in the palace, and fewer that he was interested in, and fewer still who returned his interest. The boating accident that had killed his parents when he was ten years old had also taken a great many of the young people who should have grown to be Kadou's peers and friends. These days, the palace was only crowded around holidays and during the winter—the rest of the year, the families of the provincial governors resided at their country holdings. The kahyalar assigned to his service, rotating out every six or eight months, were and had always been the greatest part of his social life. As for them, there were many who, regardless of interest, wouldn't cross that line or be comfortable with him crossing it. Especially in the core-guard, the ones Kadou had the most interaction with—they had a tendency to be upright and tight-laced, as Evemer was.

He looked down at the letter in his hand. He was letting his weakness get the better of him again. One bad day and he was already backsliding, ready to dump everything on Tadek . . .

But what if Tadek was angry too? What if he would have preferred to be dismissed from the kahyalar corps entirely? Kadou hadn't asked what he wanted. He'd just . . . done what he thought he had to do to protect someone who was almost a friend. But if that had been some new violation of correct and caring behavior, then . . . then Tadek would be well within his rights to be furious at Kadou.

He was mortified that the thought hadn't even occurred to him before this moment. Eozena was right—Tadek was safe and comforting, and . . . And it wasn't fair for Kadou to use him like that, just for his own benefit. So, therefore, he shouldn't summon him. He *knew* what the right thing to do was—he ought to meet Tadek quietly in some neutral space, and let him be angry if he was angry, and then offer him whatever he wanted to make up for what Kadou had done to him. Maybe that would help.

Or maybe that too was another opportunity to fail spectacularly. Another opportunity to upset everyone, or give them material to gossip about. Another opportunity to disappoint Zeliha and Eozena.

He put the summons back on his desk. Tomorrow, maybe. He needed to agonize about it first. "I'm quite tired," he said. "I'm sorry. It's been a long day."

Eozena nodded and got up. "You going to be all right?"

"Yes," he lied. "Just fine."

"And the investigation? Do you want me to come with you to the guild tomorrow?"

"Perhaps not tomorrow." He was fully planning on staying in his chambers all day tomorrow, preferably with the sheets pulled over his head.

"I'll have all the reports brought here, then," she said.

"Oh—oh, no, you needn't go to the trouble."

"Kadou." He stopped, looked at her. She looked steadily, calmly back at him. "I'm going to commandeer the reports and say you wanted me to fetch them for you. Then I'm going to take them back to my own rooms and read them. Then I'm going to bring them here. But I can't do that middle bit without the first one. Do you mind terribly?"

The thought of even this little subterfuge being discovered sent another shockwave of nausea through him. But he trusted her better than he trusted himself, and so he said, "If you think it's best."

She looked askance, but nodded. "Send for me again if you need anything, all right? Day or night, you know that."

"Of course," he lied, again.

And then he was alone, with dinner and dusk still hours away, with a growing sense of unease pressing upon him—it felt very much like it had in the early months of Zeliha's pregnancy, when he'd worried himself into fits of shuddering terror on a near-daily basis. Tadek had been here then. Tadek had been his primary.

The letter to grant Tadek access to the Gold Court lay on his desk, taking up a disproportionate amount of space in his mind for such a small and unassuming object.

He shut his eyes and turned sharply away from it, pacing through the room, shoving his hands into his hair to rub his aching head and banish some of the shattered-glass feeling he was developing along all his edges.

He couldn't stay cooped up in his rooms. He'd worry himself to bits in here, or drive himself mad.

He whirled toward the wardrobe and yanked out the first kaftan his hands fell on—green linen, delicately embroidered along the bottom hem with an elegant, masculine profusion of flowers—and pulled it on, charging out the door a moment later, still doing up the buttons.

Evemer was sitting in a chair by the parlor door, cradling a half-full glass teacup in both hands. He looked up immediately and took in Kadou's mismatched clothing. "Highness," he said.

"I'm going for a walk in the garden."

"Highness." Evemer set aside his tea.

"You don't need to come with me."

Kadou turned away before he could see Evemer's expression, whatever it was—and Evemer followed him anyway. Kadou strode forward as if he could outpace the fear-creature lurking around the edges of his brain, growling a low and throbbing snarl and waiting for the moment to pounce and devour him. He went aimlessly, not always keeping to the paths, ducking his way under branches and clambering over low walls while Evemer followed behind without a single grumble. Damn him. Did he have that sharp stare of judgment fixed on Kadou now? The moment he had the thought, he could almost feel the weight of Evemer's eyes at his back.

He went until he was breathless, and then he found himself

in front of one of the palace's smaller shrines—it had twelve in total, including the Grand Temple, each dedicated to one of the two gods.

This one was for Usmim, the Lord of Trials. Of course his feet would lead him here, of all places. The building was no bigger than a large cottage or his own chambers, and inside it would be dim, cool, and quiet. Perhaps if he begged Usmim ardently enough, he would take pity and grant Kadou a moment's peace from his own mind.

✳

Her Majesty was a strong leader, someone Evemer was genuinely pleased and honored to be sworn to—the sort of liege he had thought of when he was a child: someone powerful, armed and armored and on a white horse, blazing in the sunlight, a banner snapping above, with eyes both stern and kind. Someone you could kneel to, swear your life to, and serve with honor, receiving equal honor in return. Someone you could die for, and not feel that your life or your death had been wasted.

His Highness, by comparison, was only affirming Evemer's assessment of careless-flighty-negligent.

At this moment, Evemer was profoundly embarrassed to be seen out in public with him, inasmuch as the extremely secure enclosure of the Gold Court could be considered public. His Highness had re-dressed himself, which was both annoying and offensive. If it had been anyone else, Evemer might have thought they were hinting that his service was somehow unsatisfactory.

He knew that it wasn't. His service was more than sufficient— the exams had proven so. Kadou was just . . . *like that*. Evemer hadn't tried to stop him at the doors of his chambers, hadn't tried to argue him into putting on something nicer than a linen kaftan that looked like it was more appropriate for a hunting excursion or a sweaty, dusty day at the training grounds than for hurling oneself aimlessly around the paths of the formal gardens. The skirts of the beautiful purple underlayer showed in vibrant flashes whenever the prince turned, garish and odd next to the subdued green outer layer.

His Highness swerved toward a little shrine to Usmim, paused, started forward again, paused again, repeated this five or seven times until Evemer allowed himself a brief moment of speculation about whether he'd be convicted for treason if he were to strangle him.

No, Evemer didn't actually want to do that. *Shaking* him, though, yes, very much. He'd grab this stupid little prince by his shoulders and shake him until his bones rattled and then maybe, just maybe, he'd come to his senses and stop being so much . . . *like this*.

His Highness charged forward to the shrine so suddenly that Evemer mentally cursed and had to scramble to keep up, and then stopped so abruptly on the threshold that Evemer nearly crashed into his back.

It took Evemer's eyes a moment to adjust to the gloom, and then he saw the person sitting there on the floor in front of Usmim's altar. Whoever it was hadn't lit any candles as they would have if they were properly praying, and something about it scraped across Evemer's instincts and set him on edge. He had the sudden impulse to step in front of Kadou, put his body between the prince and . . . whoever that was.

"Sorry," His Highness said. "I didn't know there was anyone in here."

The person turned, and in a wintry voice said, "Your Highness."

Evemer didn't notice how much restless, fidgeting energy Kadou had actually been carrying until it vanished. "Oh," His Highness said. "Siranos."

It took Evemer a moment to place the name—the princess's body-father? What was *he* doing in the Gold Court? He didn't belong here. The urge to put himself between them grew keener, but the doorway was too narrow to sidle around Kadou.

Siranos turned back to the altar. "Come in or don't. I don't care."

His Highness did five more verses of that stop-start hesitation before he slunk forward, keeping close to the wall as if . . . as if he were afraid of Siranos. Something really *was* wrong, then.

Kadou took a candle from the filigree box by the wall. When he'd lit it and stuck it into a sconce—the one furthest away from Siranos—he retreated to sit an awkward distance away from the altar. It took him a moment, evidently, to center himself: He flexed his hands open and closed for a minute before he moved into the first position of prayer.

Evemer kept an eye on Siranos and a hand on the hilt of the sword at his hip. He had only ever seen the man at a distance before, and would not have been able to put the name and face together before this. He was of a height with Her Majesty, lean and well-formed, with sharp narrow features, excellent cheekbones, and an immaculately trimmed beard. Oddly, he wore his hair very short, like a commoner, though it was styled with an expensive fragrant oil that Evemer could smell faintly even from ten feet away. The short hair showed that he didn't have his ears pierced— also like a commoner, though he wore a large gold ring with a yellow stone on his right hand. To Evemer's eye, the whole effect was of incompletion and inelegance: a man rich enough to afford fine clothing and jewels, but either too miserly to employ a competent body-servant who might advise him on how to better present himself, or else too obstinate to listen to that advice.

Evemer didn't like this. Why didn't he like this? Less than ten words from Siranos and he was wound tighter than the warp on his mother's loom.

His Highness had progressed to the third position of prayer when Siranos spoke again: "I'm told that it is thanks to you that I have been granted residence here," he said. His voice echoed oddly against the bare stone floors and walls, the high ceiling. Evemer was too appalled to do anything but stare at him. Who did he think he was to *interrupt* someone at prayer? That was only permissible for temple dedicates—even Tadek wouldn't be so rude.

"It was nothing," His Highness said. He kept his eyes squeezed closed, his hands raised in orans.

"So you don't expect me to show gratitude. Excellent."

A long silence. Evemer shifted closer to Kadou until he was nearly touching him—Kadou, sitting tailor-style, could have leaned back against Evemer's knees.

"Did you find what you were looking for?" Siranos asked suddenly. "That night you were in Her Majesty's offices, rummaging through her things?" Evemer calmly filed this into his inventory of everything objectionable about His Highness, then paused, took it out again, and mentally turned it over once or twice. *With a grain of salt*, said his mother's voice in his head. *Possibly a handful.* Evemer had accompanied His Highness and Commander Eozena to those very offices before he'd been sent off to run messages.

"I wasn't harming anything," His Highness said. "I was supposed to be there." True, as far as Evemer knew. The commander, whose years of service and heroism had proven her beyond reproach, had asked him to accompany her.

"It was about the matter at the Shipbuilder's Guild, wasn't it?" His Highness lowered his hands. "How did you . . . ?"

"You told me yourself," Siranos said.

"Did I?"

"Yes."

Exasperatingly, His Highness didn't seem to care about the interruptions to his prayer. Evemer wished with some annoyance that Siranos would at least address His Highness properly—whether or not the prince was careless-flighty-negligent, he was still the *prince*, and Siranos just some rich, good-looking nobody from Oissos. But then, the Oissika didn't understand about princes in the first place—they didn't have them. So Siranos could not be expected to behave with proper comportment.

"I don't remember what I said," His Highness murmured.

"You said," Siranos replied, a little too smoothly, "that there was something the matter at the Shipbuilder's Guild and that you had to write orders to someone about it. An investigation, I suppose."

His Highness shifted and said nothing, just . . . looked at Siranos. His head was turned just enough that Evemer, standing behind and above him, could see how knotted his brow was.

"How is the investigation going?" Siranos asked. "Well, I hope?"

"I'm sorry, but it—it wouldn't be right for me to—discuss state matters like that."

"What harm is there? I live in the Gold Court now, don't I? Now and for the foreseeable future, evidently. And I am the law-father of your niece."

"Body-father," His Highness said. "The word is *body-father*. I know it must be confusing if you're not familiar with the language. Easy to mix those words up—they must sound very similar to your ear." From another person's lips, this might have been a dig, but Evemer couldn't read a drop of sarcasm in His Highness's voice.

Siranos made an annoyed noise. "Body-father, law-father, love-father." He said these mockingly, mispronouncing each of the three words. "I can't see what the distinction is, but you fussy Araşti keep insisting there is one!" Evemer filed this away too—he had heard some rumors that Siranos didn't understand this either. As a cadet in the academy, Evemer's teachers had told them that in Oissos, children automatically belonged as much to their sire as they did to their mother, even if the two weren't married, which seemed a strange and backward way of doing things. Perhaps that was why the Oissika took such a funny angle on marriage. In Araşt, it all came down to *claim*: Someone who became pregnant retained full claim on their child unless they specifically shared that claim with the child's sire. That was the reason Her Majesty had very wisely not gotten married, and indeed *wouldn't* be getting married, because then another house (or, gods forbid, another *country*, if Her Majesty married some foreign noble) would have claim on any of the future heirs to the throne. Far more prudent for Her Majesty to get her children from lovers, as she had with Siranos—it was the main benefit of having a sovereign capable of bearing: House Mahisti would maintain full and exclusive claim on their heirs. His Majesty the former sultan, on the other hand—Kadou and Zeliha's grandfather—had *had* to get married, since he wouldn't have been guaranteed claim on his body-children otherwise.

And then there were His Highness's parents. That, Evemer

had heard, was a simple love story. An outlier. His Highness couldn't reasonably expect a love-match, though they were unremarkable and commonplace in the lower classes.

"In any case," Siranos was saying bitterly. "What's the harm of me knowing anything? Who am I going to tell?"

"Whether or not you have anyone to tell," His Highness said softly to Siranos, "it doesn't make it right for me to speak of it. I shouldn't have even told you about the Shipbuilder's Guild. It's a state matter."

Siranos snorted. "Fine. As you wish. I suppose I'll ask Zeliha instead."

Evemer would not stand to let *that* sort of ill manners slide. A prince was one thing, the sultan quite another. "*Her Majesty,*" Evemer said. His Highness and Siranos both started. "You will address Sultan Zeliha with the proper honorifics, whether or not you are in her presence."

In the light from the single candle and what light spilled through the doorway behind them, Siranos sneered. "Do you always let your guards speak out of turn?"

His Highness's spine stiffened until his posture was nearly one that Evemer could approve of. "He's not a guard, he's a *kahya.*"

"Even after a year, I fail to discern the difference there too."

"A guard is just someone you hire off the street," His Highness said, and now he even *sounded* a bit like a prince. There was a banked fire in his voice. "The kahyalar are the future ministers of the government and military. They're educated in law, history, literature, the skills of war, and a hundred practical matters. I imagine Evemer could shoe a horse if there were no farrier available, or measure and sew clothing, or play music, or navigate by the stars, or run through all twenty verses of Beydamur's progression for the sword upon command." All of this was true, and more besides, but Evemer didn't give His Highness any credit for it—might as well applaud him for knowing that the sky was blue. "And they take oaths," His Highness added. "So yes, we let our kahyalar speak. They're people, not automatons. If we are entrusting these people with our lives, if we trust them to know when to draw their swords, why not trust them to know when to hold their tongues?"

"And his hypocrisy? He rebukes me for rudeness but I don't even get a *sir*?" He looked at Evemer again as if daring him to reply. Evemer stared back at him. "If it were me, I'd have him whipped. I'd do it myself."

His Highness dropped his hands from orans and folded them on his knees. "If my kahya's words have offended you, then I shall take it upon myself to apologize." His voice was soft again. "I beg your forgiveness."

Evemer snapped his eyes to the altar and glared hard at it. Siranos wanted *him* whipped? He ought to be whipped himself for speaking like that in the presence of his betters.

And the apology! His Highness was a prince; he owed no apology to anyone, particularly not to Siranos, of all people. Evemer had done absolutely nothing that could be considered even mildly improper—how dare the prince apologize for him?

At least Siranos could find nothing to say in reply. He turned back to the altar, and after a moment His Highness raised his hands again and returned to prayer.

"Is it true your mother was an adulteress?" asked Siranos quite suddenly. Evemer very nearly drew steel on him.

"No," Kadou said. His voice had gone rather . . . vague. Distant, perhaps, or dazed.

"Are you sure—"

"Yes," Evemer snapped. "And Her Majesty will thank you not to slander her mother like that."

"I thought it a reasonable question," Siranos said, with the silky satisfaction of one whose fencing riposte had landed just right.

"It isn't."

"One hears such rumors."

"Hold your tongue." Except yes, one did hear such rumors—the kahyalar were all terrible gossips, and Evemer had often received a whispered piece of gossip framed as *Now, you must be aware of the things people say sometimes so that you won't be surprised . . .*

Kadou's mother, the princess Mihrişah, had married Lord

Arslan, a very minor landholder from the backcountry, barely more than a gentleman farmer. His holdings had been only a day's ride from the mountain village where Evemer had been born. The fact that the crown princess had married at all should have been the first big scandal, but . . . Well, even now, thirty years later, the kahyalar in the garrison were still sighing over the sweeping, splendid romance of it all.

The second scandal had been when Kadou's grandfather had sent Princess Mihrişah on a diplomatic mission to Vinte without her husband, yet she had returned, fourteen months later, with a five-month-old infant son. Perhaps it might have blown over with no more than a few grumbles from the worst busybodies, since most people could add nine months to five months and come up with fourteen, and therefore there was no reason to suspect that she had violated her oaths by having a child with someone besides her husband . . . Except for the fact that she'd named the child something funny and foreign. *Kadou*. Vintish, apparently.

It had been just enough to cast a shadow of a doubt as to whether the claim she and Arslan shared on the child was tainted, though everyone who had told Evemer this story was quick to assure him that Prince Kadou was the spitting image of the late prince-consort Arslan, only with better hair and the Mahisti eyes.

Siranos was looking over his shoulder now with a strange smile. "I beg your pardon? Hold my tongue?"

His Highness heaved himself to his feet. He hadn't finished the prayer—there were three more positions to move through. "Good day," he mumbled to Siranos, already scuttling toward the door. Evemer clenched his jaw and followed. Evidently the prince hadn't been lying about cowardice. Well, at least he knew that about himself.

Siranos laughed behind them as they left.

Kadou moved more slowly now. His face, when Evemer caught a glimpse of it, was wide-eyed and expressionless. He stumbled once, catching himself before Evemer could catch him, and sat down heavily on the first bench he came across. His hands clutched the edge of it, white-knuckled.

Evemer said nothing. He stood at parade rest nearby, angling himself to face the way they'd come, just in case Siranos decided to follow them.

"I'm sorry," His Highness said. "I'm sorry he spoke to you like that."

"His opinion is beneath me," Evemer said. *As it should be beneath you,* he added in the safety of his own thoughts.

"He shouldn't have threatened to have you whipped. He shouldn't have called you a *guard.*" Life and fire came into Kadou's voice.

"That was hardly the most upsetting thing he said, Highness," Evemer allowed himself to say.

"He can attack *me* all he likes. He doesn't get to turn on my kahya."

It was just *words.* What did words matter? Evemer lifted his chin. "Highness."

"Oh, for the gods' sake—would you speak? Don't just *Highness* me."

"As you wish, Your Highness." And then, for reasons he couldn't have quite identified, he said, "I would have killed him if he talked about my mother like that."

His Highness laughed hollowly. "You got assigned to me because Her Majesty thought there was a chance I might have him killed, Evemer."

Evemer barely suppressed a flinch. "Apologies, Highness."

"Shall we go tell her that I've already beguiled you into my faction?" He laughed again, now wild and nervous, almost manic. "You can tell her how I convinced you to hate Siranos, just like I convinced the others."

Grain of salt, his mother's voice whispered in his head again. "Did you convince them? Or did they witness something like this?"

"He laid hands on me, the night of Eyne's birth. Bruised my arm, threatened me. Melek saw it. Çe can tell you everything, if you won't believe me."

"Highness," Evemer said, because that was all that could be said.

Kadou dragged himself to his feet—he was wavering like he was tipsy, like he'd forgotten which way was up. Evemer did not offer his arm, and Kadou didn't ask for it, just wove his way down the gravel path. "Do you—" he began, and then stopped.

"Highness?"

"Do you have any questions? About . . . anything he said back there?"

About his mother, he meant. Evemer should say that everyone knew those rumors were nonsense, that His Highness should put it out of his mind. He wouldn't, of course. He didn't owe Kadou comfort or care beyond what was professionally demanded. "No, Highness."

"Nothing? Nothing at all?"

Why was he pushing? Did he *want* Evemer to demand answers of him? Evemer carefully kept all emotion from his face and stared steadily down the path, but the ill-mannered, undisciplined parts of himself bared their teeth with annoyance. Those parts had several impertinent questions and wouldn't have minded making demands at all.

He must have taken too long tamping down his irritation, because His Highness said dully, "If you don't ask, I'm going to feel like I'm waiting for a sword to fall on my neck the rest of the day."

There was a moment, just one, where Evemer could nearly feel the mass of the questions on his tongue, filling his mouth. "I have nothing to ask, Highness."

Kadou could be as upset as he pleased; Evemer wouldn't budge for him.

✳

Kadou's heart was racing, and had been since he had first laid eyes on Siranos—since before that, too, but that moment was when he had started to *feel* it against the back of his ribs. He had to stop and rest twice more on the walk back to his chambers—he longed to run for them, but he was barely able to stay upright.

It was nothing, he kept telling himself. It was nothing. It was *nothing*. Perhaps if he said it enough times, it would become true.

He felt Evemer's presence at his back like a looming dread, and several times he thought of whirling to face him, shouting at him, striking him, begging him—whatever it took to get him to just say something. *Please*, Kadou would cry. *Please, just look me in the eye and tell me you hate me, because it can't be as bad out in the open air as it is inside my head, and it's eating me alive. Please.*

But because Evemer hated him, because Evemer knew that Kadou would suffer more this way, he would hold his tongue. He wouldn't say a word besides "Highness," even if Kadou dropped to his knees in the dust and cried.

Kadou's mind whirled from Evemer to Siranos to Zeliha, round and round: Here is how you've failed, and also here, and *here*, and *here* and *here* and *hereandhereandhere*—

The kahya at the door to his chambers opened it, and Kadou hurled himself through. Dinner had been laid out—he ignored all the food and seized on the carafe of wine, pouring far too much of it into the glass. He could feel Evemer's cold gaze boring into the back of his head as he drank deep. It was a white, as sweet and fresh as snowmelt and honey. "Send for more of this," he said, refilling his glass and pouring that down his gullet too. He heard Evemer open the door again, speak quietly to the other kahya.

He forced himself to slow down when pouring the third glass emptied the carafe. He sat heavily at the table and surveyed the food. The wine had hit his stomach with a rush of warmth, and he was acutely aware that he had not eaten all day. It would help his nerves if he could manage a few bites, but . . . No. No, he couldn't do it. The idea of having to spend energy on chewing was unaccountably upsetting and pushed him right to the edge of tears.

What was wrong with him? Why was he like this? Why did he let his own mind terrorize him so?

Evemer was moving around the room, lighting lamps and tidying the arrangement of the cushions and furniture. Kadou wondered wildly if he meant it as a code of some sort, an unspoken criticism of Kadou himself.

He couldn't stand it. He couldn't endure this, no one could possibly endure this.

"My armsman," he choked out.

"Armsman Tadek Hasira," Evemer began, prompt and serene, "is quartered in cadet dormitory seven—"

"Send for him. Now, please. There's a letter on my desk." He waved his hand toward his bedroom door. Did he dare to order them to hurry? Did he dare to flex his power needlessly like that? Well, who could it possibly harm that he hadn't harmed already? He had already ruined everything that could be ruined. "Have the messenger run," he said, gripping the edge of the table. "Tell them to have Tadek run too." Best to find out whether Tadek was angry sooner rather than later. Best to throw himself at it and get it over with, so he would know whether or not he should completely surrender to despair.

"Highness," said Evemer tonelessly, and went to Kadou's room to fetch the letter.

Kadou lost himself for a moment, staring unfocused across the room. He felt unmoored, but only a little, just enough that it was a welcome relief from the screeching of his own mind. The Vintish ambassador had brought a troupe of musicians from his homeland several years ago—one of them had a violin, a funny stringed instrument played with a bow. It had been rather like an oddly shaped kemençe, but in tone it had been more similar to the yowling of a cat, and it had set Kadou's teeth on edge. It had hardly been music at all, but that's what Kadou's brain sounded like in moments like these.

When he came out of the moment with a sharp jolt, Evemer was moving around the room again and the second carafe of wine had appeared on the table. How deep had he been drifting that he hadn't noticed a cadet enter to deliver it? Had Evemer already sent off the letter? He must have, or he wouldn't have returned to his previous task.

He was touching nearly everything in the room, it seemed like. Nothing satisfied him as it was. It all had to be aligned with military precision to everything else, all crisp right angles and symmetry.

Kadou sloshed some of the new carafe of wine into his glass

and thence into his mouth, and promptly choked, the acridness of the dry wine turning bitter on his tongue against the remaining sweetness of the white. Evemer glanced over at him sharply. "It's nothing," he said, coughing.

"Highness," Evemer said, and returned to his tasks.

Amazing vocabulary on that man. He had such a way of using a single word for so many different meanings. That one, Kadou supposed, meant *You're a lush and an embarrassment; please stop.*

He was, though. He was a foolish, stupid thing.

He peered down into the glass—it was a black wine, heavy and thick, more suitable for the evening. He would have preferred a red, if he'd been given the choice, something faintly floral that wouldn't clash so wretchedly against the white.

He gulped the rest of his glass down, grimacing, and pushed aside the carafe. He ought to eat. He hadn't eaten all day. He ought to.

Evemer was fussing with the alignment of the cushions on one of the divans, and it was going to make Kadou cry. He forced himself to watch—could Zeliha have known how incisive a punishment this would be? How deep it would cut to have someone like Evemer looming behind him at every step, judging his every word and gesture, exerting his will on Kadou's environment to demonstrate how overwhelmingly insufficient he was in a thousand tiny ways?

How could anyone have thought that Kadou was competent enough to repair his relationship with his niece's body-father? Or oversee the investigation at the guild?

So Kadou kept watching, dully letting it all wash over him while the wine settled in his stomach and then crept into his blood, until everything was wonderfully soft and even the embarrassment and humiliations he was hoarding like a magpie's pile of baubles were blunted into irrelevance.

There was, at length, a tap on the door. Kadou's heart lurched in his chest and he got halfway to his feet—but Evemer swung the door open first and let Tadek in.

Kadou froze.

He'd never seen Tadek wearing anything but the deep, rich co-balt of the core-guard's uniform. He'd been stripped of that honor with all the rest, of course. To replace it, they'd given him the uniform of a cadet, trousers and an ill-fitting knee-length kaftan of the palest blue, two shades off white.

That particular shade came from a dye made of dogwood bark and hyacinths—cheap materials, in comparison with those used for the fringe-guard and core-guard's uniforms. There were nearly three times as many cadets as the two upper levels combined. As a person rose through the ranks, they were given uniforms made of more precious materials—finer cloth and buttons, better tailoring, more vibrant dyes ... An outward expression of the increasing value in which House Mahisti held them, the investment of time and training and education.

Someone had looked Tadek in the eye and told him that he wasn't valuable anymore. They'd taken his beautiful cobalt uni-form which had been made just for him, and they'd put him back in this.

Kadou swallowed a lump of anger. Tadek was his armsman, wasn't he? He was of Kadou's household now, and Kadou could see him dressed in whatever colors he wished. He could put Tadek back in—well, not actual kahya blues, not unless he wanted to step on the toes of the entire garrison, but ... Something else. Something that wouldn't be such a public humiliation as *cadet whites*.

"Hello," Kadou said.

"Highness," Tadek murmured in reply. He wasn't meeting Kadou's eyes, but he had his chin tipped up in that way he had, as if he weren't going to let anyone see that he was shamed.

Kadou sat back down, swallowed another lump of complicated emotion. He was too drunk for this. "Come in, please."

He'd made a mistake. He'd made an awful mistake. Tadek clearly didn't want to be here.

"How can I serve you?" Tadek asked, still in that low, uncharac-teristic voice. No brightness in his voice, none of that sly, sidelong laughter that seemed to leave every word laden with two or three layers of meaning and scandal.

"I . . . I don't actually need anything," Kadou began. "I just . . ." Mistake. Mistake.

"If His Highness does not require you, you can come help me change the sheets on the bed," Evemer said flatly.

Then Tadek met Kadou's eyes. The life flashed back into them, a moment of anger and then hilarity, as if he were inviting Kadou to share in a joke—*can you believe this?* "Of course," he said lightly, no hint of anything in his voice. "If you need an extra pair of hands, I'm happy to assist."

Kadou put his head in his hands as the two of them went out of the room—they left the door open and he could hear the murmur of Tadek's voice as they worked, but he was too drunk to make out any words. It didn't sound like Tadek was going to try to murder—

That wasn't a good joke. Even in the privacy of his own mind, that wasn't a good joke at all.

He staggered to his feet and contemplated the wine for a moment before drifting toward his bedroom.

"Well, you're so new," Tadek was saying, very kind and warm, "so no wonder you're still folding the corners like that. Scripture-perfect, aren't they? There's faster ways I can show you." Kadou leaned on the doorjamb and watched Evemer's shoulders go tense and his posture stiffen in that secretly offended way he had. "Speaking of that—listen, I had five years in the core-guard, so if you have any questions, just let me know, all right?"

"Yes, I expect after five years, you would know your way around bedsheets," Evemer said tonelessly, and Kadou's heart skipped a beat.

Gods. Of course he knew Kadou had been sleeping with Tadek. Everyone did, by this point, didn't they? Kadou met Tadek's eyes—he shrugged minutely, and Kadou mentally wrung his hands and shoved the thought aside.

Evemer smoothed the last wrinkles out of the sheets and stood at attention. "Your Highness, may I be excused for dinner?"

"Of course," Kadou said, waving vaguely. "You can eat mine, if you want. I'm not going to."

Evemer paused for half a heartbeat. "Highness," he said, and walked out.

Kadou stood aside to let him pass, and shuffled into the room to sit on the edge of the bed, ruining all the work they'd done to smooth the sheets.

Tadek stood before him, hands empty at his sides.

"Can we talk sometime?" Tadek said. The door was still open. Neither of them moved to close it.

"What have we to talk about?" Kadou said. "Everything is terrible. My fault. I ruined it."

"You saved my life," Tadek said. "I want to talk about that, if you'll allow me. I haven't had a chance to say thank you."

"It was nothing."

"You asked Her Majesty to lay my life in your hands."

Kadou flushed hot. "I couldn't just leave you to it. You ought to be angry—it's my fault that you—"

Tadek sank to his knees before him, took Kadou's hands in his own, pressed the backs of them to his forehead. "Highness," he said. The warmth and assurance of his manner finally broke on that word, like a cliff crumbling into the sea.

"Don't. Don't," he said. Gods, he was tired. And drunk. Tadek's forehead against his hand was very warm. "You serve me, I protect you. That's the—the oath, isn't it? I was only doing what I thought was my duty—I'm so sorry."

Tadek lifted his head. "Oh, bullshit, Kadou—what *duty*? You could have left me behind. You could have told Her Majesty anything you liked!"

"What happened," Kadou said slowly, "was my fault. I gave you orders that led us to this. It was only right that I take responsibility. Don't thank me for not being horrible. It's my *job* to look after you, and if I failed the first time by giving you bad orders, then I wasn't going to fail the second time. And—and I'm sorry. I'm sorry I've ruined your career." His voice cracked. "If I hadn't interfered, you could have—you would have been court-martialed, but at least you could have defended yourself. You could have . . . done better than this, maybe, if you were lucky. But this was the deal she offered me, and I couldn't leave it to chance, or to someone else's decision. I had to make sure you were safe."

Tadek flinched. "I won't try to convince you I'm not upset about—about being cut off. But there is no possibility I would have been able to remain with the kahyalar corps. There is nothing I could have said."

"I'm sorry I wasn't better. I really was afraid."

Tadek pressed his lips to the back of Kadou's hand, then turned it over and kissed his palm. "When you fell off Wing, you were lying so still I thought you were dead," he whispered. "In all my life, I don't think I've ever been truly afraid, not until that moment." He looked up at Kadou. "I haven't been able to stop thinking about it. About what it was like to see you get up and then start shouting—I went straight to Usmim's temple as soon as I was able and left bread and honey at his feet." He laughed bitterly. "I hardly recognized myself—I don't even believe in the gods, and there I was, groveling in gratitude to the Lord of Trials, just because I'd seen your face again after I'd thought you were dead."

Kadou's heart skipped another beat, this time rather more pleasantly. Tadek wasn't at all angry with him, and after the day he'd had, that felt almost too good to be true. He really was terribly drunk. His eyes flicked from Tadek's bright hazel eyes down to his mouth, lovely and clever and soft.

"Please don't shut me out," Tadek whispered. "I've been waiting for you to summon me. I thought you might be angry with me. But then I thought that wouldn't make sense. Just don't do that again, Highness, please. Don't shut me out. You're all I have now."

"I know," he rasped. "I'm going to try to do better." But what did better mean, in this new, strange world where Tadek's very life had been laid in his hands? Tadek was right, that was the thing. Kadou *was* all he had now.

A life was a terrifying burden to carry.

He squeezed Tadek's hands, and Tadek pressed his forehead

to them again. "May I sleep here? On the divan?" he whispered into Kadou's palm, looking up at him beseechingly. His cheek was a little rough under Kadou's fingertips. He hadn't shaved that morning. "I don't want to go back to the cadet dormitories. I could stay, and we could talk. We can sort this mess out."

Kadou closed his eyes. How good would that be? Oh, very. They were the only two who really understood what had happened—they could speak honestly and openly to each other about it. That was all that Kadou really wanted. They could talk, and then Tadek would flirt, because Tadek always flirted, and Kadou would let himself be convinced into bed—it wouldn't be very difficult, especially not after the day he'd had—and Kadou could lose the rest of himself in Tadek's arms, in his soft mouth. Just like before, months ago, when his terrors over Zeliha's pregnancy had torn him up and Tadek had been there to help him past it.

He'd be making a liar of himself, of course, if he did that. Everything he'd said to Eozena and Zeliha about how that part of things with Tadek had ended ages ago, how he wasn't going to do that again—well, all of it had been true when he'd *said* it. What did it matter, anyway? He'd wrecked everything else already, what was a little bit more? And wasn't he allowed to want anything for himself? Wasn't he allowed to ask for comfort? Wasn't Tadek allowed to offer it, or ask for the same for himself?

"Highness," Tadek breathed against his skin. "Please. I'm yours."

It couldn't make anything worse, and it might make both of them feel a little better. Tadek was really the only one here who knew how he felt, who understood the whole story in all its complexity.

He wondered vaguely if this was one of Usmim's trials, sent to test the mettle of Kadou's character. The only problem was what the trial concerned—was it about the struggle of resisting temptation? Or was it about the struggle of accepting warmth and comfort when he felt that he didn't deserve either? Perhaps it was both, and Usmim was only interested in seeing *which* path he would choose to face.

He opened his eyes. He'd been rubbing his thumb against Tadek's cheekbone. He'd only just noticed. "Yes, all right," he whispered. Maybe Tadek wouldn't even have to convince him.

No, he definitely wouldn't. Tadek's eyes were so bright and pretty, his mouth so soft, his presence and scent so familiar that it hurt a little in the center of Kadou's chest . . . He wouldn't have to be convincing in the slightest. Kadou was eighty percent of the way there himself already.

Maybe closer to ninety percent. Certainly no higher than ninety-eight and a half—

Kadou gave up on thinking that he wasn't going to do it. He licked his lips. "Can I—" He dipped forward just a little, hesitant, and Tadek surged up, meeting his mouth with an eager noise, burying his hands in Kadou's hair.

This was probably a very bad idea.

※

Evemer sat at the table and felt no shame at all in listening to what he could hear of the quiet conversation through the half-open door while he ate from the untouched platters of Kadou's dinner, right up until it got conspicuously silent for a time. Then, even more conspicuously, the bedroom door slammed closed.

He was still eating when Melek tapped on the door and let çemself in. "Here for the night watch," çe said with a smile. "Ah, good, I was so hoping to pass you at the shift change when I heard you were joining us! Congratulations on the promotion, the gods themselves willed it. I had a *feeling* it was going to be you, you know." Melek beamed at him, and Evemer inclined his head politely in thanks. "Everyone's pretending like they're not mad with jealousy about your exam scores—the whole garrison is talking about it," çe added impishly, then eyed the food. "Is that all *your* dinner, or . . . ?"

"His Highness didn't eat today," Evemer said. He wasn't about to go reminding the *prince* about it, but someone else should know. "Other than approximately five glasses of wine."

"Oh." Melek frowned. "Is he already in bed?"

"He is in his room. In private conversation."

"With whom? The commander?"

Evemer weighed his options—a kahya should be discreet about his lord's activities, but Melek had been serving His Highness for months now. In all likelihood, çe already knew about it. "He's with his armsman," Evemer said. If Melek knew, then çe would know what that meant. If çe didn't, then it revealed nothing.

"Oh." Melek gazed at the bedroom door for a long moment. "So it'll probably be a while before he needs anything, then."

"I don't presume to make assumptions about His Highness's plans for the evening."

"Right, of course, yes," çe said, nodding. "But it's not really an assumption, is it." There was some soft noise from behind the door, just loud enough for them to hear, and Melek gestured grandly at the door, as if to say, *You see!* "Look, I haven't had a chance to eat dinner properly yet either—I know I'm supposed to take over for you now, but you're not finished with your food . . . Will you be angry if I go to the kitchens for a bit?" Melek pressed çir palms together in supplication and adopted a pleading expression. "I won't take long, I promise."

"I won't be angry," Evemer said. "Go, if you want to go." Things were . . . surprisingly lax here in the core-guard, he was discovering. There was less attention paid to strict routine than in the cadets or the fringe-guard. Perhaps it was just Prince Kadou's tendency toward flightiness—his kahyalar had to be ready to adapt and be flexible. It wasn't like Evemer had anywhere to be. As Prince Kadou's primary, he had a small room down the hall. As soon as Melek returned, he'd go there, read for a little while, write a letter to his mother, and sleep.

"I'll owe you one," Melek said, grinning.

"I do not require you to do so."

"Just keep it in mind." Çe paused at the door. "Actually, do you like the day shift? Getting up at the crack of dawn to attend him until he falls asleep?"

"I am honored to serve however I am commanded."

"Well, sure, yes, me too. But if you wanted to sleep in . . . We could ask His Highness if he'd mind us adjusting the shifts. I'm not much of a night owl, honestly—I'd be happy to take the dawn shift if you didn't like it. We could divide it at noon and midnight instead of dawn and dusk."

"I would never presume to ask His Highness to accommodate my trivial preferences."

Melek opened çir mouth, closed it again. "All right. I'll be back in a bit, then."

Evemer finished eating, packed all the platters up for the cadets to clear away, and made a circuit of the chambers to check the fastenings on the windows, peer out into the darkness to observe the watch pairs circle past on the garden paths and, farther away, on the walls that bounded the Gold Court.

Every now and then, there was a barely audible noise from the bedchamber.

He hadn't really wanted to believe the rumors, but here he was, and there *they* were, not even doing him the courtesy of being loud enough that he could easily block it out. They were mostly terribly quiet about it, so that every time he settled into patient vigilance, he'd hear some rustle, or someone's voice, and all his instincts would lock up and scream, *Listen!! Danger?*

Tadek was irresponsible. What if someone managed to get past all the kahyalar on the walls and in the gardens, and climbed into His Highness's room through one of the windows? What if Tadek was distracted until it was too late?

Evemer hadn't any call to be finding fault with His Highness's personal affairs, but it was outright stupid to be carrying on with someone who had also proven themselves to be as useless and impulsive as Tadek. Surely His Highness couldn't think that Tadek was any good for him—but perhaps that was the root of the attraction. Careless-flighty-negligent, after all. And there'd been that outrageous situation with the corners of the bedsheets; Tadek clearly didn't give a damn about propriety or doing small things the way they should be done just because that was the way to do them. If he did, neither of them would have gotten into this situation, and Evemer would have gotten some other assignment.

They deserved each other.

Evemer was just starting to wonder fiercely where Melek had gone off to and whether çe was actually planning on returning when Tadek stuck his head out the door, wildly rumpled, his color high. "Oh, good," he said, seeing Evemer. "I was hoping you were still there. Is there any food left? *Now* he says he's hungry," he added with an eyeroll.

"Yes," Evemer said.

Tadek opened the door the rest of the way and Evemer stared stonily out the window. Tadek hadn't bothered to get properly dressed again but for his trousers. "He needs to eat regularly," he said, picking through the trays for whatever tasty bits Evemer had left. "Keep a closer eye on him in the future—sometimes you have to bully him a little, especially if he's in one of his moods." He picked up a platter in one hand and the wine in the other and looked around. "Hm. Also, could you pop out and get us a basin of water and some cloths?"

Evemer stared at him.

"What?" Tadek said, smirking. "Something wrong?"

"You ought to at least *attempt* discretion," Evemer hissed.

"But you already knew."

There were murmurs about the sort of relationships that might occasionally develop between a kahya and their liege—the consensus was that it was only to be expected from time to time, when two people who trusted each other became close and spent a great deal of time in proximity. There were stories, too, of more than one former kahya who, upon being promoted out of the ranks of the core-guard to illustrious political office, had then married one of the people to whom they had formerly been appointed in service.

But on the other side of the coin . . . All through the time he had been in the cadets and the fringe-guard, they had gotten lectures about procedures for addressing unwanted attentions from both superiors within their own ranks and those whom they were otherwise sworn to serve. Just because such things were not unheard of did not make them entirely proper, and it certainly didn't make them a matter that Evemer would have entrusted to two people who had already shown themselves to be careless, flighty, negligent.

But all Evemer said was "Do you think His Highness wants you to advertise it?"

"I think His Highness doesn't want to go to sleep sticky." Tadek swept back into the room and kicked the door closed.

CHAPTER THREE

Kadou opened his eyes and instantly regretted it.

Now *that* was a hangover.

He rolled over, instinctively reaching for a pillow to shove his head beneath. His arm landed on skin rather than fabric.

He cracked his eyes open again. Oh. Of course. Tadek.

Damn it.

"You awake?" Tadek mumbled. "Give me a minute, lovely."

Kadou rolled onto his back and forced his eyes open, enduring the stabbing agony of the morning light. At least the windows were north-facing. Small mercies.

Kadou took stock of himself, of Tadek, of the bed. Respectively: naked, mostly naked, mussed to hell. He'd had a momentary hope that all that had been merely a dream. What *had* he been thinking? Well, other than the screaming of his own mind, like shrieking violins, like the snarl of a beast made of fear that lurked around the edges of the shadows until, like last night, it could rush upon him and tear him to shreds as easily as a piece of delicate cloth. Other than how he was all Tadek had left. Other than how Tadek was the only one who knew what it was like.

Yes, that did cast a different light on it. He understood himself, at least, even if he wasn't proud of it. His brain was slow and aching.

Tadek yawned and stretched, flexing his joints until they popped. "I could sleep in another hour or so, honestly," he said, yawning again.

"I ought to get up," Kadou said, pushing halfheartedly at the mattress to heave himself queasily vertical. "Breakfast. A bath.

Have to talk with Eozena." He looked blearily around the room. "Find something to do so I don't go mad." Avoid going outside, for fear of running into Siranos . . .

He felt Tadek's fingertips trace down his spine and shivered. "We could take another twenty minutes or so."

Kadou groaned. "Thanks, but—hangover. Thinking of clawing my own eyes out."

"Ah," Tadek said, sounding more alert. "We can't be having that. Shall I fetch you something?"

"Please."

Tadek rolled out of bed and scooped his cadet whites off the floor, pulling them on and tying them closed haphazardly with his sash. "Be right back," he said, leaning over Kadou for a kiss.

Kadou turned his face away. "Morning breath," he said, which was . . . well, part of the truth.

Tadek only laughed. "Yours or mine?"

"Both."

Tadek went to the vanity and brought him a tooth-stick, softwood that had been infused with mint and orange-blossom water, and took one for himself as well. "Back in a minute."

As soon as Tadek opened the door across the room, Kadou heard Eozena. "Good, you're awake. Is His Highness?"

"Are you awake for the commander, Highness?" Tadek asked, looking back over his shoulder.

Kadou winced and nodded, flopping back into the pillows and gnawing on the end of tooth-stick until the end frayed enough to scrape his teeth clean. The sweetness of the flavors was already clearing the stale taste out of his mouth.

He heard the door shut. Eozena's footsteps.

He pulled the sheets over his head, tooth-stick and all.

She stopped at the foot of the bed. "Good morning, Your Highness," she said. "As we are alone, I am using my discretion to dispense with formalities, as per the privileges granted to me by my rank."

"Yep," he mumbled around the stick. "Go right ahead. I deserve it."

"You sure made a decision, eh? There was a decision to be made there, and you really just made the *shit* out of it. My gods."

"I know," he groaned, and pulled a pillow over his head too. "But he made some really good points."

"Oh, I bet he did." She snorted. "Unbury yourself a bit, wouldn't you?" Kadou flung the pillow off, but did not take the sheet down enough to look at her. "I'm not here to lecture you or tell you what sort of relationship you ought to have with your armsman. That is not the relationship that *I* wish to have with you. However, I do feel it is my duty, as a person who has known you and loved you since you were born, to sharply prod you from time to time to keep you on your toes. I have now completed that obligation. I feel it is also my duty as the commander of your guard to warn my liege of dangers when I see them, and so I say: Have a care, Kadou. You do not have the luxury of indulging in mere moments of weakness because you're lonely or upset."

"In my defense, that's explicitly what he was offering," Kadou took the tooth-stick out of his mouth and tugged the sheets down under his chin, peering at her. "I wouldn't have presumed to ask, otherwise."

"It might have been what he was offering when he was a kahya," she said. "But you may find things have changed now. Everything is different—I'm sure you'd be the first to admit that, no?"

"Yes," he whispered.

"You didn't see him when he was demoted. He was wrecked. He is as upset as you are. He is not handling it well, no matter how good he is at keeping up a front. So again I advise you: Have a care. Make no assumptions. What he wanted last week is not the same as what he wants now." That was chillingly true. A week ago, Tadek never would have claimed, even in jest, that Kadou was all he had. Now it was stony fact. "Now, would you like to get up? I've brought you Armagan's files about the investigation. I thought we could discuss them over breakfast."

Kadou shoved down the shivering flare of uncertainty in his chest. He hadn't done anything wrong. He *hadn't*. She was only warning him, not rebuking him. There was no reason to tear himself to pieces over it. He'd already admitted she was right; all she expected him to do was to go forward carefully, which he would have done anyway. He didn't need to apologize for anything. But gods, he wanted to. "Could you call in whoever's on duty to dress me?"

"What for? You think I'm so out of practice that I can't manage your buttons myself? Such insolence." Though this last was said with a smile, though he *knew* she was only teasing, it struck him in the place already made tender by her previous warning.

"I didn't mean that," he said. "Um. Hand me a dressing gown? They're hanging in the wardrobe."

She found one and tossed it to him. He wrapped it around himself, shoving his arms through the sleeves and knotting the ties down the front before flinging the sheets back. He sat in the chair by the window and allowed her to brush his hair while he finished cleaning his teeth. Without needing to be told, she bound his hair up in a knot at his nape, appropriate for mourning and much more comfortable than Evemer's version the day before—she really hadn't lost the knack for kahyalar duties.

"Your intelligence network is very good," he muttered to her. "To know about this," he gestured to his hair, "and about Tadek."

She patted him on the shoulder. "When you go wandering around the Silver Court in full formal mourning, it doesn't take long for me to hear about it. Nor when you have your armsman summoned to your chambers after dinner with the greatest urgency so that the messenger has to race past every set of eyes from here to the Copper Gate, and then your armsman has to take the same path at the same pace, but in cadet whites. At dusk. It was conspicuous."

Kadou put his head in his hands and cursed himself. Could he never once think things through?

"Kadou," she said. "Kadou, love, would it help if I were a bit closer, the next few weeks? There are my own duties to attend to, of course, and I won't step on Lieutenant Hoşkadem's toes by presuming to take over as your primary, but . . . Shall I be nearby? Something of an advisor?"

"I couldn't possibly trouble you like that," he said. He stood, smoothing out the fabric of his underlayer. She caught his elbow and turned him to face her.

She was taller than him, taller even than Evemer. "Kadou. Do you have anyone to tell you no?"

"Just Zeliha," he whispered. And Evemer, who would say *Highness* in that tone—that was nearly the same. "I'm sorry. I'll do better. You shouldn't bother yourself with my foolishness. You're not just any kahya, after all. Things like this are . . . beneath you. There are more important matters that you can be working on besides brushing my hair and telling me I'm being an idiot. I should be able to do that for myself."

He glanced up just in time to see the corner of her mouth quirk. She shrugged. "As you prefer, Highness. Though I would argue that there is nothing my liege could ask of me that I would consider beneath me."

She led him out to the parlor, where breakfast had been laid. Evemer was seated like a granite statue in a chair by the door, and Tadek stood awkwardly near the table with a cup of something gently steaming. Kadou smelled it as soon as Tadek handed it over—it was medicinal, an infusion of willowbark and bitter herbs, and he had to choke it down all in one go.

Tadek lingered until Kadou and Eozena had settled at the table and, evidently seeing that he was not going to be invited to partake, excused himself with a murmur and returned to the bedroom, shutting the door behind him.

Eozena poured coffee for herself. Kadou, still a little wary of the state of his stomach, had salep. It was hot and milky and as thick as gravy, sweetened with honey and brightened with cinnamon to balance the underlying earthy flavor of it, like the smell of an approaching thunderstorm in the heat of a dry summer.

"My excellent intelligence network also told me that you didn't eat much yesterday," Eozena said. "Please mind your health. If that nonsense continues today, I'm going to come back at dinnertime and we can have an argument about it, which I will win."

Of course she'd win. There was no doubt about that. *She* had no compunctions about fighting dirty in arguments like that. "I'll eat," he said. "Lunch and dinner, at least."

She gave him a dry, skeptical look. "See that you do." She hauled a satchel closer and pulled out a thick sheaf of papers, covered with neat, tiny script. "All the records from Lieutenant Armagan's investigation. I reviewed them last night."

Kadou's head really was aching too much to easily read anything right now. "It's useless, isn't it?"

"I don't know." She pushed the papers across the table to him. Armagan's handwriting made his head throb. "Look how neat and tidy they are. Look how methodical." She gestured to the pages— Armagan did indeed write with an exceptionally clear, fluid hand, the letters tiny with large spaces between each line of text, presumably so çe could go back later and easily add any necessary notes. "Not that handwriting has anything to do with personality, but . . ." She shrugged. "Armagan's a meticulous sort of person too. I've been aware of çem for years. Çe's done excellent work ever since çe was promoted, and I've heard nothing but good things from çir former supervisors."

Kadou looked up from the pages, frowning. "So çe's not likely to have missed anything."

"It would be uncharacteristic, at the very least. Armagan is thorough. So," she said, pulling the papers back toward her and spreading them out between the two of them. She propped her elbows on the table, steepling her fingers at her lips. "I can't help but wonder why çe concluded so quickly that there was nothing more to be done."

"You think that's . . . wrong?"

Eozena tilted her head side to side, uncertain; a few of her locs tumbled over her shoulder. "I almost always think that it's wise to get a second opinion. One's own perceptions can lie so easily."

Well . . . that was true. Kadou knew that intellectually, even if the obsessively terrified parts of his mind couldn't always remember it. "What should I do? You said you reviewed these—did you spot anything?"

"Nothing obvious, nothing in *here*." She paused. "But . . . I have this excellent intelligence network in the palace."

"So I've heard," he said slowly. "And?"

"And I'm told that the people reporting to Armagan discussed the case with çem that morning, and then çe left the palace. Armagan shut down the investigation when çe came back. Almost immediately. Started reassigning people right and left, talking about how it was pointless and nothing would come of it."

Kadou frowned. "That's . . . odd."

"*Yes*. Yes, it is."

"Where did Armagan go, when çe left?"

"That's the other thing. It doesn't seem that anyone can give me a definite answer. It's all just guesses or assumptions. Lots of people blinking at me and saying, 'Um, I think çe went out, maybe to talk to some witnesses or something?'"

Kadou didn't want to say it out loud, didn't want to have to ask. But . . . Oh, Mother of All, give him strength. "Do you think çe was . . . involved?"

"We have to suspect that *someone* in the palace was involved— the thieves timed the break-in so the fireworks would cover the noise, remember. Someone told them to be on standby. Could have been Armagan. Could have been someone else." Eozena tapped her steepled fingers against her chin. "It's worth keeping an eye on çem, I think. Worth paying close attention, and being thorough and meticulous ourselves."

This should have been a comfort—it wasn't his fault. He hadn't ruined it. There was some other, external force, something that they hadn't seen. And yet . . . The stakes were even higher now. If he fumbled this, he could ruin Armagan's career, just like he ruined Tadek's, just like how he'd gotten Balaban and Gülpaşa killed, just like—

He forced himself to breathe. Eozena was here. Eozena wouldn't let him muck it up. "What should we do? What should *I* do?"

She shuffled the papers back into a neat pile. "Read through these with me. Tell me if you see anything that sticks out. We'll go from there."

He nodded. "Yes, all right." His head ached. His stomach churned. Eozena distributed the notes between them, and he tried to focus enough to read.

Tadek eventually emerged from the bedchamber, all the laundry bundled in his arms. He put it in the antechamber to be collected by a cadet, then sat down at the table with a few of Kadou's informal underlayers and began to inspect them for loose buttons, stray threads, popped seams. "Mind if I help myself to coffee?"

Kadou practically *felt* a wave of disapproval from Evemer's side of the room, and ignored it. "Go ahead," he said, trying for an absent tone of voice. He kept his eyes fixed on the papers as if he were terribly focused on them, and that was enough to keep Tadek from talking to him.

He'd made an awful mistake. Eozena was right—she was always right. Tadek wanted something different now than what he'd wanted before, and the situation had changed . . . He was Kadou's responsibility, Kadou's to care for and look after.

He couldn't risk it. One wrong move and Tadek would be hurt, with nowhere to go unless he wanted to throw away his entire livelihood.

Tadek seemed like he was in a good mood, though—as he mended the clothes, he was humming under his breath, some song Kadou didn't recognize.

Kadou stared at Armagan's notes without processing a single word, and nearly jumped out of his skin when a soft tap sounded on the door. Evemer got up to answer it, and immediately stood aside to let in Melek. "Morning, all," çe said brightly. "Commander, Highness, are you terribly busy?"

"Sort of," Kadou said. "What is it?"

"I wanted to talk about the shift schedule."

Tadek looked up from the mending. "Oh, yes. Me too."

Kadou felt a brief throb of panic at Tadek's words. He glanced up, met Eozena's eyes, and she quirked an eyebrow at him. It said a thousand things, and he wished he could be as expressive back at her. "Could we discuss it later?"

Eozena sat back. "I don't mind a brief interruption, since we're all here," she said. "I'd have to sign off on any schedule changes anyway, so you might as well make use of me while you've got me."

Kadou gestured to one of the other cushions at the table. He shuffled the papers together and put them aside as Melek settled çemself.

Çe took a piece of paper from çir pocket and unfolded it. "Evemer's got the dawn-to-dusk shift, six days a week. Tomorrow, Tegridem, is his day off. I'm the dusk-to-dawn shift, and I'm off on İkinç." Melek rattled off the rest of the shift assignments—who was on the door duty, and who was Kadou's designated secondary for each shift, and who was tapped to be the substitute primary on the days Melek and Evemer were off, and the names of the cadets currently appointed to this area of the palace, and . . . well, it was really far more information than Kadou had been expecting, and his head reeled trying to follow it all. He poured himself another cup of salep. "So," Melek said triumphantly, "I've been thinking there might be a smarter way to arrange things."

"Oh?" Kadou said faintly.

Melek glanced at Tadek. "I'll have to design a new draft if . . . Is Tadek getting shifts to attend you?"

Tadek looked up hopefully; Kadou froze.

"Not at this time," Eozena said, firm but not unkind. "Attending to household matters is one thing. Armsman Hasira, I'm sure you can see that it would be improper to continue serving overtly as a kahya after you have been demoted. Perhaps in the future we can revisit the issue, but for now it is out of the question."

Tadek had dropped his eyes back to the mending, his jaw set in a particular way that pushed Kadou's already wobbly nerves even further off-balance.

Melek was nodding mildly. "Right. Well, here's the thing, Highness, Commander. I hope you don't mind me being forthright, but I'd rather get up early than stay up late."

"You . . . want to switch with Evemer? Have days instead of nights?" That was . . . It couldn't be done, no matter how much the idea appealed to him. Zeliha herself had appointed Evemer his primary. It would offend both her and him if Kadou were to shuffle him off into the night watch.

"Not quite like that," Melek said. Çe looked over çir shoulder. "Stop glowering, Evemer, I'm not going to put you out. Look, if the shift changes happened at midnight and at noon, instead of dawn and dusk, then we'd both have a bit of time during the daylight to get other things done. What time did you wake up for training this morning?"

"The fourth hour," Evemer said flatly. Kadou bit his tongue to stop a burst of surprised laughter, but no one else seemed to think it even faintly funny—he'd just sounded so offended, as if they should all *know* that of course he'd be up well before dawn.

"Look here," Melek said, turning çir attention back to Kadou and Eozena, "Evemer would still attend His Highness for most of the important things—those usually happen in the afternoons and evenings, right? And you know how awkward it is to hand off a shift during the middle of a banquet or a meeting. It'd be so much smoother to do it at noon and—"

Kadou held up a desperate hand to forestall any more campaigning. "It's up to you and Evemer," he said quickly. Eozena nodded silently. "If you two prefer to do it that way, I have no objections." This way, he'd have Melek at his back for half the day, and . . . "You'd want the morning shift? Midnight to noon?" Melek nodded.

Melek was always cheerful and pleasant in the mornings, and wouldn't braid Kadou's hair so tightly that it hurt him, and wouldn't glare him out of bed, and wouldn't make judgmental eyes about Kadou's sartorial choices . . .

"I see no harm in it," Eozena said with a shrug.

Kadou shoved aside all his selfishness. "It's not fair to make Evemer change his habits unless he wants to."

Evemer had gone stiff in that way he had that looked almost

offended from certain angles. "I am pleased to serve however I am required, Highness."

"That's not an answer," Kadou murmured.

Evemer's eyes fixed on him. He looked as if he thought Kadou was challenging him. "I would be honored to take the afternoon, if Melek wants the mornings," he said.

"What a noble sacrifice," Tadek said wryly. "May I ask a question?"

Another throb of terror. Kadou swallowed it. "Of course."

"What are my duties to be?" There was no rancor in his voice, just mild curiosity and an amused drawl. "Or shall I just putter around and make myself useful however I see fit?"

"That seems like a good place to start, doesn't it?" Eozena said, rolling her coffee cup between her palms. "I'd be happy to help find things for you to do, if you're feeling at loose ends."

His mouth quirked in a wry smile, but the edges of it were brittle. He gestured to the mending in his lap. "Useful things it is, then."

"I'll still pay your stipend, if you'd like it," Kadou blurted. The enrichment stipend was considered one of the great perks of the kahyalar corps, a generous and regular sum of money that a kahya was expected to spend on advancing their education in some way that wasn't already provided by the palace—some spent it on specialized weapons training from experts, or lessons in music or foreign languages, or lectures on academic subjects. Nowadays, too, some spent it on books: They'd become unbelievably cheap in the last five or so years, what with those new printing presses.

Without the stipend, Tadek had little hope of advancing his position or eventually turning elsewhere to use skills to which he was better suited. Kadou felt, again, the weight of the life laid in his hands.

But perhaps it had sounded like he was playing favorites? He panicked all over again. "And," he added quickly to Melek and Evemer, "if either of you want to spend your stipend on something unusual, I'll inform the bursar that you're to be allowed. I won't even check what you're spending it on. You can use it for whatever you like, or save it. No restrictions. Tadek too."

Eozena looked hard at all of them. "His Highness is very generous. I hope you use it wisely."

"Oh, don't worry about me, Commander," Tadek said with a sunny grin—Kadou couldn't tell if this one was genuine or not. It seemed to be. "Don't really need mine anymore anyway. I usually spent it on . . . *cultural enrichment,* as the clerks in the bursar's office call it."

Melek frowned. "Why?"

"Why not? I enjoyed it. Twice a week, I'd go to the theater and music halls. I could tell you about any major theatrical performance from the last ten years." He laughed. "That's not much use now, though, is it. What do you use yours for?"

"Usually I go find someone who knows how to do something interesting, and I pay them to teach me. I know about dyes and lockpicking and acrobatics . . . I went abseiling down the side of the plateau once."

Tadek laughed again. Kadou was watching him very, very carefully, trying to spot another crack in Tadek's mien, but there were none now. He seemed entirely relaxed, even merry. "You never spend it on anything fun? That's what it's *for.*"

"It's *for* expanding your skills and knowledge," Evemer said sternly, while Melek muttered, "Abseiling was fun."

Tadek rolled his eyes. "If you want to word it so prissily, Evemer, sure. It was established to promote general literacy amongst the kahyalar—do you know how that's defined? Have you read the guidelines about what you're allowed to use it for, or did you just listen to the boring examples they suggested when you were first promoted to the fringe? You know there's even more things you can use it for now that you're core-guard, don't you?" Kadou glanced back and forth between them. Evemer was glowering openly now; Tadek had leaned back on one hand, showily careless and unimpressed. "If you haven't read them—which would not surprise me, because almost no one bothers—then you'd know."

"I have read them, in fact," Evemer snapped.

"If you're going to fight, you can take it outside," Eozena said sharply. "Don't burden His Highness with your squabbling."

It's no trouble, Kadou wanted to say. *It's nothing. You don't have to hide yourselves from me.* But . . . perhaps they did. Perhaps it was that he didn't have the right to be shown. And after what Eozena had reminded him of that morning . . . It was better to be silent about some things.

※

Evemer fumed to himself as Melek wrapped up çir business and left for bed. He'd had a lifetime of practicing discipline and self-control, but he'd been barely twenty-four hours in the core-guard and he'd already lost his temper in front of His Highness and Commander Eozena.

And *Tadek,* of all people.

Most of Usmim's little tests could be weathered with sheer, stubborn force of will, but the Lord of Trials appeared to be sending him some subtler, more insidious ones now, and those were more difficult to guard against.

He would go to the temple at dusk, when he was released from the day's service. He would attend one of the lectures, where doubtless one of the temple aunts would be earnestly giving a crowd of people the usual platitudes about committing to the improvement of themselves, the virtues of patience, the way a trial turned sideways was just an opportunity. If he didn't feel better after that, it would be his own fault.

He would not allow them to get to him.

"Evemer, you're still fresh from the exams," Eozena said, looking up from the papers and ledgers that she and Kadou had returned to upon Melek's departure. "You must have studied up on arithmetic and accounting."

"Yes, Commander."

She looked terribly relieved. "Excellent, come check this over for me, then. I can balance my own accounts, but this"—she flicked her hand at the table—"is giving me a headache."

"I can handle it by myself," His Highness said quickly to her.

"I did say so." He had, although not very firmly—it had sounded like a politeness more than a strong assertion.

"And I've been saying that nobody audits a guild all by their lonesome, and that you'd have to be mad to want to," she replied sharply. "Take the help you have available. Evemer's already been on the investigation." Evemer would have blinked in surprise at her tone, but—well, it was not his place to criticize his superior officer.

His Highness gestured at Evemer. "Maybe he has his own things to attend to!"

"Oh, come now," Tadek said, glancing up from his mending with a smile. "He's just waiting by the door, all the way across the room. Anyone would prefer to spend time close to *you*, Highness."

This again. Evemer tightened his jaw. It was one thing to carry on with His Highness behind closed doors, in private. Doing so— flirting!—right in the open, in front of all of them, was an entirely different matter. Whatever made Tadek think he had the right?

Evemer was unsurprised to see Eozena's eyes narrow, but it was with some curiosity that he noticed Kadou's expression too: He didn't look pleased, which was . . . odd. Quite odd. There was an element of embarrassment, yes, and rightly so, but . . . What was the rest? Guilt? Discomfort? It had lasted only a fraction of a second, and then His Highness had dropped his attention back to the papers, and the curtain of his hair swung forward to shield his face, and Tadek had already turned back to his task . . .

Odd.

Evemer said, "I am at His Highness's disposal."

"See?" said Tadek cheerfully. "Even the walking stone wall wants to be near you."

"Tadek," Eozena said, as Evemer clenched his fists and steeled his spine.

Tadek looked up again, feigning surprise excellently. "What? Did I say something?"

Kadou's expression had gotten stormy, and his hands, resting on the table, were clenched. His knuckles were white, just like when he'd clamped his hands on the windowsill during that strange episode of nerves the day before. "You'd better apologize."

"Oh." Tadek sat there for moments too long, glancing between Kadou and the commander, who had sat back and crossed her arms. "Sorry, Highness. Commander. I was only trying to lighten the mood. You've been working on that for ages now and I can see how bored you are." He grinned brilliantly. "But I suppose I've often been told I should talk a bit less. I'll hold my tongue."

"No," Kadou said. "I meant apologize to Evemer."

"Wait, what for?" Tadek asked, so wondering and bewildered that Evemer had to assume it was sincere.

"For taunting him like you're a little boy trying to start a street scuffle," Eozena said.

"Say sorry, and that you won't do it again," Kadou added.

"It was just a—"

"If you disobey a direct order from His Highness, I'll drag you out of here by the scruff of your neck for a *very* serious conversation in the courtyard," Eozena said, calm and quiet.

Tadek turned to Evemer. "I'm sorry. I won't do it again."

"Thank you," he replied automatically. "Already forgotten." He was too astonished to do anything else, and probably just as bewildered as Tadek was. Tadek could have said anything he liked—Evemer wasn't going to take offense at some few careless words. They weren't the worst he'd ever heard, even of that particular genre, directed at that specific aspect of his demeanor.

Tadek turned back and sketched a short bow to Kadou and Eozena. "If you'll both excuse me," he murmured. "I think I'll take my work out into the garden. Where the light's better."

"You're excused," Eozena said.

Evemer glanced again at His Highness. Odd. Just . . . very odd. Still careless and negligent—he did have blood on his hands, after all. But flighty . . . Hm.

Evemer compromised with himself: He mentally appended a question mark. Careless-flighty(?)-negligent. That would do.

He made himself comfortable at the table as Tadek gathered

up his tasks. He waited for someone to explain to him what he was supposed to be doing, but His Highness and Eozena silently watched Tadek leave the room, and as soon as the door shut, the tension . . . failed to release.

Kadou dropped his face into his hands, his elbows on the desk. Eozena patted his shoulder. "I could have handled that, if you'd asked. But you did well."

"Did I?" Kadou asked, strangled.

"Mm," she replied. "But do you see what I mean?"

"Yes." He rubbed his face and lifted his head, staring at the door to the courtyard. "Yes, I do see."

Evemer had no idea what they were talking about. He fiddled with the ledgers in front of him and kept his eyes averted, as if that were enough to keep him from being part of the conversation, though he was desperately curious to know what Eozena had said—perhaps she was talking sense into His Highness.

Kadou sighed and looked at Evemer. "You mentioned you'd studied some accounting for the exams?"

"Not much, Your Highness. Like the commander, I can balance my own accounts, but . . ." He cast his eyes across the table and shrugged.

"It's not much more complicated than that," said Kadou, which seemed like a lie, but who was Evemer to disagree? "We just need another set of eyes. Just . . . if you notice anything that seems odd."

"Honestly, I looked over all of this twice last night," Eozena said. "And I do have some other appointments. I'm to meet with Her Majesty before lunch—more nonsense with that dreadful Madam Melachrinos, I believe."

"Oh," His Highness said blankly. "Is that going any better than this?"

Eozena shrugged. "Too soon to tell. Siranos is reminding us at every possible moment that he—and therefore Oissos as a whole, apparently—isn't happy to see one of his countrywomen questioned outside of a fair court trial."

His Highness winced. "Better you than me. I'll—I'll send

word, I suppose, if we find anything useful. I have some things later today as well."

"Right," Eozena said and got up from the table, sketching a very casual bow—Evemer supposed that was one of the privileges of rank. She left, and then they were alone again, Kadou looking more worried now than he had all morning.

Evemer begrudgingly admitted that he could not entirely fault him. Siranos *was* dreadful, and if he were throwing his weight around like that and making a nuisance of himself, then Kadou's concern was understandable.

He could almost see the thoughts circling Kadou's head like buzzards, and it was not at all surprising when Kadou spoke up. "Yesterday was . . . it was strange, wasn't it? The way he acted? I'm not just imagining it, am I?"

"No, Highness," Evemer said.

"No to which part? Sorry."

"Your Highness didn't imagine it. It was strange."

Kadou laughed nervously and shuffled the papers around, flicking through them in random order, picking them up and putting them down again. "I was surprised he went straight for calling my mother an adulteress."

"Highness," Evemer said, for lack of anything else.

"Usually people come at it more . . . sideways. They start with comments about my name, things like that."

He could have just said *Highness* again, but the words that left his tongue were "My apologies, I don't speak Vintish. I have no context for what comments there might be to make." Other than *funny, foreign,* and *why would he be named like a Vint?*

"It's *cadeau,* if you're speaking Vintish." The vowels were different when he said it like that, with the stress on the second syllable instead of the first. "It means gift, and there's zero significance except that my mother didn't speak Vintish well either. I was born at the Araşti embassy in Ancoux, and all the Vintish servants kept coming in to stand around my crib and coo, *Cadeau, un cadeau, un tel cadeau,* and she thought it sounded nice, so she named me that, spelled out phonetically in Araşük." Kadou shrugged one shoulder. "They were all flattered. I'm told it finished the trade deal she was trying to negotiate. Most people bring it up as a lead-in to the 'So did your mother sleep with a Vint?' topic. I was surprised that Siranos didn't."

They'd hardly stayed long enough for Siranos to plumb the depths of the inappropriate comments available to him. "Highness," Evemer said. And then, because his tongue and his better judgment had apparently ended their professional relationship, "Have you mentioned anything to Commander Eozena about yesterday's incident, Your Highness?"

Kadou winced. "No. I don't want to trouble her with . . ." He looked away. "Well. I suppose that sort of thought is what got me into this mess in the first place, isn't it?"

Evemer didn't dare risk saying even *Highness*. "I will send her a report."

"Right," His Highness said faintly. "Of course."

Evemer didn't say another word to him for the rest of the morning. They sat in silence, which Kadou felt was agonizingly uncomfortable, and read through the ream of paper. Evemer fetched a wax tablet and scribbled equations from time to time, double-checking the arithmetic, and had to get up twice to change it for a new one. It was inconvenient to have north-facing rooms at a time like this—if there'd been a sunny windowsill, he could have just left the tablet there to soften until it could be smoothed out again.

Tadek returned at noon with the mended kaftans folded over his arm, a bit of sun-gilded color in his cheeks, and a pair of cadets in mist-colored uniforms behind him carrying trays of lunch. Evemer pointedly cleared up all the papers that Kadou wasn't physically touching, and said, "Highness," in a particular way that Kadou took to mean, *Give me the rest; you're going to eat lunch or else.*

He ate lunch.

Evemer put away the papers and scrawled out a note, presumably the report to Eozena about encountering Siranos the day before, while Tadek sat across the table from Kadou with his hands folded. "I've been thinking," he said.

Kadou was hungry enough at this point that even this sort of ominous comment couldn't ruin his appetite, but it was a close thing. "Oh?"

"You don't have a personal secretary."

"I don't need one. I've never needed one, except around holidays." He didn't receive enough correspondence to warrant foisting it off on someone else to sort through what was relevant or urgent, nor did he have enough appointments that he couldn't keep track of them himself. He usually managed with notes on scraps of paper or, in a pinch, scribbled on his inner wrist, above where the cuffs of his kaftans would hide.

"It would give me something to do. 'The prince's secretary' is more coherent than 'the prince's armsman.' People know what a secretary is for, but armsmen are for country estates. I don't make *sense* in the city—even in a town house, I wouldn't make sense, let alone here in the palace where there's a kahya every twenty feet." Tadek looked away. "And I think it would make both of us look responsible."

Kadou turned these thoughts over several times. It wouldn't step on the kahyalar's toes too outrageously, though around the busy holidays, Midsummer and Midwinter, the person temporarily assigned to manage his schedule always came from their ranks. It would be work that would give Tadek a purpose, because that too was Kadou's responsibility now. If Tadek could be a little happy with it, then it might be enough to assuage some of Kadou's guilt, and it would keep Tadek near him, which would be nice, if Kadou could figure out how to keep himself from making any more mistakes like last night's.

And Tadek was right. It *would* look responsible. It would look like Tadek was settling down into a demure and sober sort of role, and that Kadou was expecting to get more formal correspondence, or that he was intending to make himself busier with official matters. All manner of things. "All right," he said. "That sounds like a good idea." He should say something else too, something about last night, to Tadek, tell him it wasn't going to happen again.

A great deal of tension went out of Tadek's shoulders, and he grinned openly. "Good. Good, then. I'll start keeping a book for you. No more of these paper scraps. Do you know how many times the cadets in the laundry used to shout at me for not going through your pockets before I sent out the washing?"

Kadou made himself smile back. He tried several times to line up in his mouth the other words he should say to Tadek, but none of them sounded right. They were all too harsh and uncaring, and Tadek was smiling and humming again, and . . . gods, Kadou could only imagine how *crushingly* wretched it would be to hear something like "About last night, we can't ever do that again—I mean it this time." He'd have to wait until they were alone, too. Kadou couldn't possibly humiliate him by saying something like that in front of Evemer or the other kahyalar.

After lunch, Kadou ordered in a basin of water and washed up alone in his room like he was ill or on a war campaign. The alternative would have been to go to the bathhouse in the middle of the day with either Evemer or Tadek attending him, or to come up with a plausible reason to take one of the kahyalar at the door instead—he thought it was Yasemin and Sanem today—and *any* of those options was terrible for different reasons. He wouldn't be able to relax with Evemer looming and glowering the entire time. With Tadek, he'd have to either deal with the flirting or completely ruin Tadek's day while both of them then endured the utterly incalculable awkwardness that would follow—he couldn't break things off permanently with Tadek and then make Tadek bathe him; that would be unspeakably cruel. Yasemin and Sanem, too, were little better than Evemer: they were both still angry at him . . .

So. A bucket and a washcloth, in his rooms, alone.

In a small and private fit of anger, he dressed himself as much as he could manage, everything but the black jadeite buttons on the cuffs of his mourning clothes, before he called in Evemer. He got a stony look for his trouble. Evemer pointedly retied his sash for him and made judgmental eyes at his buttons.

He felt sick as he passed out of the Gold Court, trailing kahya-lar and Tadek. Lunch sat in his stomach like rocks, and the velvet was really too warm for the weather. He would have preferred to go straight back to his rooms and lie about on the rugs in his dress-ing gowns, doing anything but what he was expected to do—his duties as the prince and the Duke of Harbors (more of the latter than the former; princes were expected to be largely ornamental), and the arrangements for Balaban's and Gülpaşa's funerals.

Having Tadek with him, standing just behind his shoulder and making notes in a booklet of folded paper, did nothing to help the general air of resentment from the ministers. Just the opposite—people he had always known to be cooperative became stubborn, people who had been stubborn were now actively unhelpful. It wore on Kadou's already frayed nerves, but he breathed through it, and told himself that performing responsibility was the next best thing to actually *being* responsible, and that of course it would take some time to recover his footing. Of course it would.

His tenuous equilibrium lasted right up until the moment, to-ward the late afternoon, when he tried to attend court. He was feeling a little desperate, a little reckless, and there was a voice in his head telling him to just *go* for it, just walk straight into court and see what Zeliha's face did when she looked at him, see if he was allowed to sit in his rightful place, see if he was given leave to speak in front of the ministers and courtiers.

He discovered that he wasn't allowed past the threshold of the building. The kahyalar at the door were polite but firm: He was not allowed to attend court again until he was invited to do so. The knowledge settled over him with a grim feeling of inevitabil-ity. He could not pretend that he was surprised.

He went back to his rooms in a haze. He felt unanchored again, like he wasn't entirely attached to his own body. On one level, it was almost like a meditative state—nothing could touch him when he was drifting like that, but he didn't feel like he could touch anything either. He was detached.

He dismissed Tadek for the evening before his nerves could get the better of him and lead him into another moment of weakness, then stood in the middle of his chambers, his hands feeling very empty and his heart yearning aimlessly for *something*. Direction. Comfort. Solutions. Action. Solid ground.

He could feel, too, the palace wrapped around him: the walls of the three nested courts, the thousands of lives filling them, the crushing weight of responsibility, history, legacy. The knowledge that one wrong word spoken in fear to someone offering comfort could send shockwaves through the whole, like ocean waves after an earthquake. Who had ever thought that this was a good idea? Who had decided to build something so delicate?

He sat with the papers that Eozena had brought. He looked at them. He did not read them. The problem with these reports was that they were boring and therefore couldn't occupy Kadou's attention, leaving his brain free to sing itself right into a tar pit. He found himself tipping from one thought to another, first slowly and then more chaotically as his stomach soured, the whole world feeling like it was made of sharp-edged glass.

There were old sea captains who could read the weather just by the taste of the wind, who could predict a storm when there wasn't a cloud in the sky. He could taste a storm on the wind right now with the way he was worrying, and he could already tell he was set to have a very rough evening of it unless he found some way to avert the oncoming tempest. He could all but hear the growl of that old familiar fear-creature lurking in the back of his mind, feel it like the tremor of exhausted muscles, like the ache of a nearly faded bruise.

Kadou couldn't even pretend that he was focusing on the incomprehensible lines of minuscule script in front of him. His hand was cramped from gripping a pen too tightly, and his palms were sweating, his brain running in circles. He felt restless and breathless, his chest tight. Not just a taste on the wind now, this was the seas getting choppy and a looming tower of clouds on the horizon.

What to do? What to *do*?

Of course he couldn't tell anyone about this. He was too ashamed to tell Eozena, he didn't think that Melek would know what to do, and Evemer would be unsympathetic. Tadek knew already, but—no. He was out of the question now.

Kadou put down the pen, laying his hands flat on the top of the table and pushing down. That was a trick that worked sometimes. When it did, it made him feel more grounded, like he wasn't about to fly out of his own skin.

It did nothing now, just tensed the muscles of his shoulders and arms so he felt instead like he had the *leverage* to fly out of his skin.

He didn't matter anymore. He was a prince in name only, and he mattered to no one, not really, except as an assignment they had to endure. In a way, it was ridiculous. Hilarious. He felt a burst of manic laughter clawing at the inside of his ribs. He didn't matter to anyone, not even Zeliha.

His clothes were too tight. The velvet wasn't just stifling now—it bordered on suffocating.

He went to Evemer, standing as always at the door, and silently held out his wrists. Evemer undid the buttons without hesitation. The moment they were free, Kadou whirled dizzily away to his bedchamber, working the rest of them open with fingers that were almost numbed to sensation. He turned to close the door and started sharply to see that Evemer had followed him. The jangling of his nerves grew more intense.

He couldn't stand this. How was it that he had to steal moments alone so furtively? It was easier to hide a lover than it was to have a second of peace and solitude.

He let Evemer peel him out of the velvet kaftan, watched him fold it neatly and put it away in the wardrobe. "There's a red linen underlayer," he heard himself say. "And a black kaftan. Left-hand side. Bring them."

Plain clothes, possibly the plainest he owned. He'd need those. What else? Something to cover his hair. Evemer would know how the common folk tied a turban. That would do.

And then, all at once, he had a plan. It had come backward, first in the *how*, with the *what* trailing distantly behind it.

He took the clothes from Evemer's hands. "Go have a carriage summoned. A small one. Unmarked." He was being rude. He was running roughshod over Evemer, and he hated himself for it, hated Evemer a little bit too for making it easy to do it. "Leave a note for Melek. Your shift is going to run long."

He had known Melek for too many years. He couldn't be cruel to çem, that was the problem, and what he was going to do would be very cruel to any kahya appointed to him. Melek would talk him out of it, or else go along with it and be hurt or confused the whole time.

Evemer, though.

Evemer, with that stone-wall demeanor masking the perpetual glare hiding just behind his eyes. He could take it. He was an immovable object, or close enough to it. In comparison to Melek or even Tadek, he was invulnerable and untouchable. Kadou could do whatever he damned well pleased, and Evemer would be right there, steady and silent and ferociously disapproving. Already Kadou could count on that like he could count on the moons pulling the sea to a king-tide when they waned to full dark.

Evemer obeyed him, and didn't ask questions. By the time the sun's edge touched the horizon, the carriage was pulling out through the Copper Gate. The rattle of the wheels over the cobblestones began bringing him back to himself, cutting through the fog.

He was alone in the carriage, he noticed with some pleasure, still unmoored and drifting. It gave him a little more time to plan, at least. When the carriage had traversed the seven switchbacks of the road and reached the bottom of the cliff, he knocked on the roof. As soon as they'd pulled to a stop, he climbed out.

He'd been drifting too hard to notice how many kahyalar he'd pulled along in his wake—Evemer sat up with the driver, a kahya of the fringe-guard, and there was a cadet at the back, and no fewer than four kahyalar of the core-guard, fully armed, walking along behind.

"Highness," Evemer said, with just an edge of inquiry.

"I just want to go for a short walk. Stretch my legs." He wouldn't be able to shake all of them, but . . . he could probably get rid of all of them but Evemer. "Come down. Everyone else can wait here. We won't be long."

Evemer's eyes narrowed slightly, but he obeyed. "Highness," he said, more pointedly.

Kadou wasn't going to be able to get away with this sort of thing a second time. Best to make the most of it now, while everyone was all unawares. He forced a smile onto his face. "Don't worry," he said to the others. "Wait right here."

CHAPTER FOUR

$\sim$

Kadou grinned at the man across the table from him and drank straight from the wine bottle, tossing a pair of coins into the center of the table with his other hand. "I'll match your wager." He hadn't the foggiest idea whether he had paid a fair price for the wine. Probably not, considering that it was swill, but that didn't matter. He wasn't drinking for enjoyment.

It had taken walking halfway down the Lifeblood, the main thoroughfare of the city, before Evemer had seemed to realize that Kadou wasn't just looking to stretch his legs. Kadou had been able to feel him growing tenser, and had almost laughed with nervous, manic hysteria when Evemer had finally cracked and said, "Highness."

Kadou had ignored him. It had taken another two blocks before Evemer said, "Highness, we should turn back," and one more after that before Evemer had dared to catch his sleeve.

After that, Kadou mostly had gotten his way through sheer momentum and the element of surprise. He had bets with himself now about how long it would take—and how obnoxious he would have to be—before Evemer threw propriety to the winds, slung Kadou bodily over his shoulder, and hauled him back to the carriage and the Palace Road zigzagging up the side of the cliff face.

He'd tried to mutter something about the safety of the streets, but really, Kadou was safer with one guard than he was even with two. One made him look like a wealthy merchant's son, but two would have been rather suspect. Three would have immediately given him away as a noble of some variety. At the bars where he planned to drink, that could be taken in entirely the wrong way:

The back alleys and shadows had their own princes. They, too, might go out with three or more guards. It would not do to provoke anyone. At least, not unintentionally.

You also couldn't disguise three kahyalar in a group, not like you could disguise one—Kadou had swerved into the first pawnshop they'd passed, bought Evemer another kaftan, and ordered him to put it on over the top of his uniform. It was too narrow for Evemer's ridiculous shoulders, but at least it wasn't terribly stained. That shade of dark pine green was rather good on him, too, though it didn't come close to what the cobalt of the uniform did for him.

Kadou took another drink. The man across the table scowled at him.

He whooped when he won that hand, pulling the man's money into a pile in front of him, feeling the sparkle of the copper kürler in his fingertips: the flickering light of a candle flame, the crack of a log split by an axe, the bitter taste of medicine. There were a few foreign coins mixed in too—unsurprising, this close to the docks. The Oissic asprons were billon, an alloy of silver with copper. The signature of the silver—the crunch of snow under his riding boots high in the mountains of the Northern Marches near the manor house there, the stillness of the temple of Sannesi early in the morning, and the scent of white tea—was muddled up with that of the copper, resulting in a confusing yet quaint impression of cold, still mornings with a crackling fire in the distance that was overlaid with the tang of scalded, oversteeped green tea.

"Again, let's go again," he said. He felt Evemer shift uncomfortably just at his shoulder and ignored it.

He dealt them both another hand of cards and didn't bother to hide his feverish giggle of delight when he fanned his own between his fingers. The man immediately threw down his cards. "Pass."

"Oh, come on," Kadou cried. "Come now, don't be like that. It's just a game, isn't it?"

"Some of us don't like throwing our money away," the man spat. Like his coins, his accent had Oissic mixed in with the

Araşük. "Not everyone can be a wine-sodden *kyrios* with more coin than sense."

Kadou considered this for a moment. "Yes, that's true. Both things. The 'not all of us can be' part, and also me having more coin than sense." He leaned in and said, "I've got only as much sense as any ordinary person, but I've got a *lot* of money." No point in trying to hide it. Although he wasn't wearing any visible jewelry and his long hair, the primary mark of the upper classes, was wrapped up under the turban, the quality of the fabric and tailoring of these, his plainest clothes, singled him out.

"Sir," said Evemer. He'd stopped saying *Highness* when Kadou had dragged them into the less-respectable parts of town and dived into the first filthy tavern he'd set eyes on. "Perhaps you'd like to speak a little more softly."

"I was whispering," Kadou said.

"As you say, sir," said Evemer.

Kadou grumbled at him and drank again from the bottle, or tried to. He held it up to the light—empty. Again. "Get me another of these," he said, and turned back to the man across the table. "And you. Play another round with me. Look, I'll—I'll pay you to play another round." Kadou poked a single billon aspron over to him. The man gave him a filthy look, and Kadou ignored this too.

He dealt a hand.

The game paused when Evemer returned with a fresh bottle of wine for Kadou and very deliberately placed a cup next to it, which Kadou equally deliberately ignored as he wrestled the cork out of the bottle and drank.

Kadou won the hand.

The man was not happy. "I think you'd better leave," he said, as cold as murder.

"Why? I'm doing so well."

The man stood and leaned forward on the table with both fists. Kadou watched him, feeling a strange hunger. Maybe he could get himself punched. Maybe that'd knock the helpless grief out of him, the surging seas of fear that threatened to swamp his boat.

The tempest that he had been running from had only grown.

He'd composed an extravagantly elaborate opera in his own mind of what his kahyalar thought of him, what the ministers and Eozena thought of him, what his sister thought of him. She might not have exiled him *physically*, but she'd still shut him out. Of course she wouldn't say so outright. Clearly the plan had been to let him stew on it until he figured it out himself—she was graceful like that. Sneaky. Joke was on her: He'd figured it out right away. She probably wouldn't even want to have breakfast with him anymore. Probably wouldn't let him hold his niece ever again. Probably wouldn't—wouldn't—

"Too well, some might say," the man was saying. Kadou *had* palmed a few high cards during the fuss with the cork. He'd hoped the man hadn't noticed. "We don't take kindly to cheaters."

"Now, now. There's no call to be rude," Kadou said primly. "I took your comments politely, didn't I? When you said not all of us can be a wine-sodden *kyrios* or whatever it was? And you were right."

"You'd better leave now."

Kadou grinned and kept talking. "You know, not all of us can be ugly goat-fuckers either, but you seem to manage admirably."

He'd seen the punch coming *minutes* ago, before the man had even stood up from the table. The fist slammed into Kadou's face with glorious vibrant pain, and he was thrown half out of his seat. What relief, to feel a physical pain to match that of his own mind clawing itself up from the inside. He scrabbled at the table, pulling himself up, grinning and ready to say whatever it took to get the man to swing at him again—

But Evemer was already there. Ruining it.

He'd laid the man out flat on the floor in the time it took Kadou to find his balance, and Kadou felt the wonderful rush of glee drain out of him. Evemer said nothing to the man, just took stock of the room, the rest of the patrons. Most were still sitting, but a few at the tables nearby had stood or half stood, now frozen. Kadou rose slowly to his feet, rubbing his aching jaw. That was ruined now too. He snatched the bottle off the table, storming to the door.

"Yeah, fuck off!" the man shouted from the floor.

They'd have to find another bar, Kadou mused, striding down the street. He hurled the nearly full bottle down the first alley he found, relishing the shatter and splash, and went on. He didn't look behind to see if Evemer followed; he didn't care whether or not he did.

There were public houses aplenty here in the dockside district—sailors were a thirsty bunch. Kadou turned into the doorway of the very next one he found.

He'd never been so angry in all his life, part of his brain noticed, muffled as if it were someone speaking from a room down a hall. The anger—and, to be fair, it was well blended with his chronic terror—burned in him, like a fire pumped high by the bellows, like a wild animal trapped in a cage that would rip Kadou to pieces if it escaped. Anger was a relief, in a way. It was easier than fear. He was so tired of fear, but he was helpless to resist it or fight it off. It was like heading into a battle at sea against a fleet of ghost ships.

So he might as well turn that desperate energy outward and find someone else to fight with, if he couldn't get a solid hit on what was in his own head. Anything. Anything to make it stop.

Inside the new, equally filthy public house, he grabbed the first person he could reach who looked like they might be drunk enough to want a fight, yanked them around by their shoulder, and said—

He didn't know what he would have said, because then *he* was yanked around, and there was Evemer, not even breathing heavily. Wholly unaffected.

To hell with him and his expressionless face. To hell with him for being so contemptuous of Kadou. To hell with him for all of it—couldn't he see that Kadou was doing worse to himself than Evemer could ever do to him? Could he not see how Kadou tore himself up with guilt and blame, how meticulously he picked over every mistake he'd ever made in his life, how he couldn't even think of Balaban and Gülpaşa's *names* without sending himself into a black despair?

Kadou hated him. "Leave me. Go back to the palace," he said. "No."

Kadou rocked back on his heels. "Excuse me? I've ordered you."

"I will obey all your commands except those that counter-mand one given by a higher authority," said Evemer—the most words Kadou had ever heard from him at once, he thought. "I obey Her"—he caught himself, barely—"*your sister* above you. I am charged with your protection."

Kadou shook Evemer's grip off his sleeve. "Keep your hands to yourself unless I call for you."

"No."

They were getting very close to the breaking point. Kadou was about to be hauled bodily and ignominiously back to the carriage—possibly over Evemer's shoulder, possibly dragged by his hair. "You have not been granted the privilege of disobedience. You could be court-martialed for insubordination."

"I will risk that."

"I know my own business," he said. "I can handle myself."

"No, you can't," Evemer said. "Your choice of establishment and drinking companions has proved that thrice over."

Kadou's nails bit into his palms. He wanted to tear them down Evemer's face—or someone's face, really. It didn't matter who. Just let them stand still long enough for Kadou to gouge into their eyes. How else was he supposed to convince Evemer to stand back and let Kadou get himself hurt? "It's none of your concern."

✺

The world was whirling around Evemer, and the stupid little prince in front of him the center of the hurricane. Where was the man Eozena described, the one she'd known since before he could walk, the one she had sworn had always been quiet and good? Where was the shy and frightened thing from the temple who had shuddered himself to bits over a few cruel words? Where was the prince who had rebuked his armsman and lover and made him apologize to Evemer?

This man was cold and searing by turns, uncontrolled, wild.

His tongue was barbed, his words sharp with venom, but it didn't match the expression in his eyes. There was so much pain there—a quiet, broken kind of pain, and loss, and desperation. Heartbreak. It was, actually, quite close to that of the shy and frightened thing after all, once Evemer was looking for it.

So he wanted to pick a fight, did he? Evemer had seen that impulse in some of the cadets before, ones who were angry or grieving something—he wanted to hurt and be hurt until it broke the shards of glass in his heart into powder that could be scattered with a breath. That, at least, was understandable. But what could have happened to cause it? What was so bad that His Highness would want to wager his life for a brief respite from heartbreak?

"You're being an idiot," Evemer said.

"So what if I am? It's none of your concern," His Highness said again. Evemer wondered if he could hear the waver in his own voice, a waver that was to tears as distant thunder was to the promise of rain. "Leave me be."

Evemer wouldn't have left him in that bar if the sultan herself had ordered him off—a kahya took certain vows. "I cannot."

His Highness whirled around and elbowed his way through the crowd, shoving several people aside, and threw a coin or two on the counter.

Evemer caught up with him just as the barkeep produced another damn bottle of wine and uncorked it. "You've had enough, sir," he said, because if he was telling his liege what an idiot he was, there weren't any boundaries left to trample.

"Why don't you go to hell?" His Highness said. "We don't have to pretend like you actually care, or that you like me. I know you don't. That's fine, because I don't like you either—from the first moment I saw you, I didn't."

"Mm," said Evemer. It wasn't true. That moment at the temple, the night of Princess Eyne's birth, Kadou hadn't thought anything of him. He had barely noticed Evemer. The second time, at the guild—Kadou smiling, *you're a godsend*—still burned, confusing and resentful, in Evemer's chest.

He watched Kadou down a quarter of the bottle and wipe his

mouth on the back of his hand with a sniffle. His nose was red from held-back tears, his lip was split a little from the punch he'd taken, though it'd been a poor punch. The man had been drunk too, and leaning across a table, and standing while Kadou sat . . . Barely more than a clip, and frankly, His Highness probably could stand to take a few more clips like that. No one in his position had the right to feel so sorry for themselves.

"If you are set on fighting someone," he began, feeling a massive effort of will, for this olive branch he was extending to the stupid, careless, flighty idiot seemed to weigh a thousand pounds, "then I can teach you to spar, if you'd like. Sir," he added belatedly. It wasn't safe to call him *Highness* in a place like this.

His Highness gave him a long look. "What?"

"It would let you fight like you want to without putting you in a dangerous situation," Evemer said, warming to the subject. "It would let you turn your emotions to something constructive and work through your anger. And it would teach you a skill that would be useful if anything were to happen to your kahyalar or if for any reason we couldn't come immediately to protect you."

Kadou blinked, as if he couldn't quite believe what he was hearing. Evemer felt a glimmer of pride, even a little excitement—yes, he'd teach the prince to fight, and that would solve so many of the problems with him: His Highness would learn to behave properly and control himself. He'd grow into power—he clearly had the capability already. With enough time, a few months or so, maybe he'd end up being someone that Evemer didn't mind serving.

Kadou nodded. "Right," he said. "Okay. Yes."

Evemer nodded. Small victories, he reminded himself—but it didn't feel small. Kadou turned away from the bar and headed toward the door.

It took a moment, when they were outside, to realize that His Highness was not heading back toward the palace. He ducked into the first alley they encountered, took another swig from the wine bottle, and set it carefully on the ground. "Okay," he said. "Go on, then."

"Sir?"

"You said you were going to teach me. So teach me. Go on."

"Here, sir?"

Kadou nodded and crossed his arms. "Here. Now."

Evemer would have preferred to practice in the quiet gardens just outside Kadou's chambers in the Gold Court, but . . . His Highness did need to be run to exhaustion first, before anything productive could be said or done.

Evemer dusted off his hands. "Yes, sir." He glanced toward the mouth of the alley—there were lanterns lighting the front of the building across the street and another by a doorway farther down the alley. There was a little light. Just enough to see by. "When Your Highness makes a fist, don't tuck your thumb inside," he explained slowly. "Your Highness must do it like this. The thumb over the fingers, do you see? Or Your Highness will break your hand."

Kadou clasped his hands in front of him and nodded, eyes wide. The night did strange things to them, Evemer noticed— they were huge and deep and mysterious, like the darkest depths of the ocean.

Evemer continued, "When you punch, you swivel from the hips. Get the force of your whole body behind it."

"I see," said Kadou.

"Plant your feet about shoulder width apart, so you have some leverage."

"I suppose a person could study for years to learn how to do this," Kadou said.

"Learning to throw a punch properly only takes a week or two, at most. Try it."

Kadou blinked at him two or three times—long eyelashes, Evemer noticed. "Try? You want me to try punching you?"

"The best way to learn is to practice."

"Goodness," Kadou said silkily. "If you insist."

An instant later, a *heartbeat* later, Evemer was flat on his back, staring up at a strip of starry sky framed by the buildings on either side of the alley. Sadık, small and bluish grey and waxing gibbous, still two weeks away from full, had not quite reached its zenith.

Kadou stood over him, shaking out his hand. His expression had changed from attentive to cold. Again.

Evemer wasn't quite sure what had happened. His face hurt.

"Who do you think I am?" His Highness said calmly.

"Sir?" Evemer said. He would get up in a moment. As soon as he finished taking inventory of his body. Gods, his face really hurt.

"Are you stupid? Who am I?"

"My lord," he croaked. He put his hand to his face, but that only hurt more.

"*Who?*"

"Şehzade-Sultan Kadou Mahisti Hazretleri Effendi," said Evemer, as if he were a herald announcing His Highness to the court.

"Right." He heard Kadou pick up the wine bottle. "So are you stupid or what?"

Or what, I think, Evemer mused. He shoved himself up to a seat with one arm and—ah, the stars he'd seen in the sky followed wherever he looked. He blinked them away. "Sir?" he managed.

Kadou leaned down, hands on his knees. "People have been teaching me to kill other people since I was old enough to hold a sword," he hissed. "But thanks for being so condescending."

Evemer deserved that.

It had been genuinely stupid of him. He shouldn't have assumed—His Highness had had tutors for everything else, of course he would have learned a little of this too. Evemer hauled himself to his feet, piece by piece, rubbing and flexing his jaw, trying and failing not to gawk at Kadou.

Kadou picked up his wine. "I'm going back inside," he said in a low voice. "And you're going to follow, and you're not going to say anything."

Evemer swallowed. "Yes, my liege."

He followed His Highness as commanded, his eyes fixed on him like a sailor searching in vain to find the Navigator's Star on a cloudy night while his compass needle swung wildly.

He didn't make sense.

The only comfort was that Kadou didn't try to pick any more fights—he went back in and flung himself into a seat, morosely nursing the bottle of wine, which was better than the gambling, and much better than getting himself punched. At last, and of his own volition, he led Evemer back to the carriage, the palace, safety.

Evemer didn't stop staring at him.

Why was His Highness like this? What was wrong with him? Or perhaps simply: What was wrong? Was it Her Majesty's punishment that was so upsetting him? Why didn't he just make peace with it and do his duty gracefully? He was miserable wallowing like this, so why not just choose something else? The palace had three full temples and a dozen small shrines to Sannesi and Usmim; he could pray for comfort or for guidance with his trials, as he preferred.

What was the *matter* with him?

CHAPTER FIVE

⁓

There was something troubling His Highness, and as Evemer was sworn to his service, he took it upon himself to
figure out how to solve it for him. Sparring seemed unlikely to help, so Evemer tried chess.

Chess was a truly excellent teacher of many essential skills—
patience, attention to both small details and the big picture,
movements of troops, knowing the strengths and weaknesses of
your personnel so that their skills could best be deployed, long-
term planning, holding many possibilities in your head at once,
graciousness toward your opponent . . .

Evemer liked the game more than he liked drilling sword-
forms, though he'd had to work hard to acquire skill at either of
them. If things had been different, if he'd been more than just a
kahya, he might have spent more time on it—lessons with well-
known chess players in the city, perhaps, instead of pouring all his
monthly educational stipend into the study of more practical and
prosaic subjects.

But he was good enough at the game to know that you could
learn things about someone by the way they played, and since
Kadou didn't make sense as a person, this was the best way Evemer
knew to figure out what he was missing.

Kadou played chess in extremely strange ways. He'd sacrifice
a tower to save one of his eight armsmen (Evemer found himself
entirely unsurprised). He hoarded his two kahyalar as if they were
his sultan, but he'd send his archpriests and his general out into
the field as soon as he could. Over the course of a couple weeks,
Evemer found that he could usually get two or three games out

of him a day, and he took to dragging Kadou to the board at odd times to see how it changed things—when he just woke up from a nap, or during a break in the ongoing review of the papers from the Shipbuilder's Guild, or while he was eating lunch, or after he'd had a glass of wine with dinner . . .

At the end of his first fortnight appointed to Kadou's service, Evemer felt he had a general grasp of the shape of His Highness's mind. It came down to what Kadou had called cowardice: On days when he was more fretful, his game was just as much of a wreck—he spent a long time deciding on moves, hesitating over his pieces, visibly second-guessing himself. Evemer won every last one of those games.

But in that fortnight, there were two good days. Kadou had woken early both times. Commander Eozena had arrived for breakfast and, afterward, shepherded him out into the garden for exercise and conversation, joining Evemer, who had been up and training since dawn. It had seemed only natural for the other ka-hyalar to join in too when they ran the more common verses of Beydamur's progression for the sword. On one of these two days, Commander Eozena had sat on one of the benches in the shade and called dozens of forms for them one after another, at random and without a break, until they were all pouring with sweat. Me-lek and Tadek had fallen over from exhaustion, and it was only through sheer force of will that Evemer, shaking, had been able to keep his feet. Kadou, on the other hand, had been winded but laughing. After they'd all gotten bathed and dressed again, Eve-mer had immediately gone for the chessboard and all but pounced on His Highness with it.

And out of *nowhere*, Kadou played a gorgeous game, and Eve-mer had found himself forced to stay on his toes and exert his full force of cunning to stay ahead. He'd still won, but only barely.

He'd gotten four games out of Kadou that day. Kadou had *won* the third, and when he glanced up from the board and smiled at Evemer, he'd looked just like the shining prince on a milk-gold horse again. Evemer had to excuse himself to his room to abso-lutely *boil* with confusion.

Then the next morning there was the funeral at the Grand Temple for Balaban and Gülpaşa. Kadou returned to his rooms immediately after the ceremony, and the one chess game Evemer dragged him into was disaster. Kadou was listless; Evemer, resentful—the funeral had reminded him anew of his anger. Careless-flighty-negligent, he told himself, and he and Kadou didn't exchange a single word for the rest of the day.

And the morning after *that*, Melek reported that Kadou had risen at the crack of dawn and fussed with everything in his chambers, flitting from one thing to another without focus. That day, he refused to play at all, refused to let anyone brush his hair or change his clothes, refused to eat until Evemer was ready to pour broth down the prince's wretched throat himself. Kadou was exhausted and wild-eyed by midafternoon, practically on the verge of tears with worry. In the evening, in a last-ditch fit of desperation, he dragged Evemer out of the palace, back to the bar by the docks where no one would look at him.

Evemer had reported the first incident of this sort to the commander, of course. It didn't do any good. Kadou wasn't forbidden from leaving the palace. He could wander where he pleased, including shadowy alleys and cheap dockside taverns if the whimsy took him, and Evemer could do nothing about it. Eozena, grim-faced, had told him as much, and then she'd solemnly examined the bruise on his face from where Kadou had punched him and told him to be very, very careful. As if he didn't know.

He thought she must have spoken to Kadou about it privately, though, because at least Kadou had stopped cheating at cards and trying to pick fights with the drunkest brawler he could find. Additionally, as much as Evemer loathed admitting it, taking only a single kahya with him was the one thing Kadou was doing right. The one reasonable and insightful thing he'd done with any kind of consistency—two kahyalar would have been too conspicuous. It could have drawn attention, and therefore put Kadou in more danger.

There were two kinds of seedy taverns in the city—ones frequented by the dockworkers, the laborers, the smugglers and

back-alley merchants, and the ones that were the territory of a
more intellectual type, mostly failed poets and students on a rare
visit home from the University of Thorikou in Oissos. The students didn't have much spare cash, but they were willing to pay
with drinks in exchange for academic assistance. Kadou, for his
part, had already spent a lifetime supplied with the very best tutors
anywhere around the Sea of Serpents. He and the students found
mutually satisfactory business arrangements, and Kadou tutored
them in logic, grammar, rhetoric, law, economics, diplomacy, history, and any of his five languages: Araşük, Oissika, Mangarha,
Vintish, and Botchwu, the elegant pidgin of the N'gakan trade
emissaries.

Evemer was not sure *why* Kadou did this when he was the
prince of the richest country in the world and hardly needed
pocket money to afford wine. He did not ask either, because when
the nights wore on so late that Evemer's eyes went gummy and
he ached for sleep and the students began to trickle out of the
bar into the night, then Kadou would turn his attention and his
lectures to Evemer. On a rare occasion, he'd offer a chess game,
but more often than not, he'd continue the topic he'd been in the
middle of explaining or whatever else crossed his mind—usually
money (which meant he was thinking of trade, which meant he
was thinking about the Shipbuilder's Guild), or the ethics of monarchy (which meant he was thinking of Zeliha), or both.

Evemer learned more about economics than he had ever
thought he would care to. But listening to Kadou's lectures, he
had found that he was enraptured. This only added to his confusion. There was something about the prince that relaxed when
he started talking about these things, explaining them from first
principles and in smaller words than were strictly necessary. Even
when he was alarmingly drunk, there was something of the radiant prince smiling down from horseback about him when he
talked like this, and Evemer (to his deep and abiding shame and
chagrin) found it difficult to look away.

"See, because—because it's about *trust*," Kadou said, slapping
his hand on the table. "A coin is a promise, Evemer, it's a bargain.

I say: 'I've made this thing which is going to be worth—' What's it worth, what are you selling me?"

Evemer's body-father had been a horse-tamer, or so his mother had said. She was a weaver. "Horses and cloth," he answered. He'd tried to cajole His Highness into talking about economics during the day, to see if it would cheer him up at all, make his eyes light up like they were now. It hadn't worked; Kadou had been too distracted, all tangled up within himself. But this, now, was . . . strangely compelling.

"Horses and cloth. I say: 'I've made this thing which is worth one horse or six bolts of cloth.' I hand you—" Kadou picked up a coin and pushed it into Evemer's hand. "I hand you a that. It's worth a horse."

Evemer looked down at his open palm. A copper kür. He gave Kadou a long look and waited for him to arrive at the point.

"So I'm—I'm making a promise, I'm saying that I give you that and you give me your horse, and you could use that coin to buy another, similar horse if you wanted."

Evemer *was* familiar with the monetary system. He'd only been a person in the world for, you know, his whole life. He'd only been on the royal payroll for nearly thirteen years. But he carefully did not laugh—if he laughed, then Kadou might stop, and go back to that intolerable wallowing. This was better to watch and to be near. Infinitely better.

"So an interesting thing happens," Kadou said, sipping whatever the students had supplied him with, "when I start breaking promises."

"Oh?"

"What if you find out that the coin I said was worth a horse isn't worth a horse?" Kadou slammed his hand on the table again. "Ruin! Distrust! I come back to you and you don't want my coin as much because you know. You know that I fussed with it. I only gave you a coin worth three-quarters of a horse, and you don't sell quarterhorses." Kadou giggled into his cup. It was a very, very poor joke, and Evemer wasn't going to even smile at it. He wasn't. "Even if I'm embarrassed to be caught out and I fix the coin, you still remember. You're a little more careful, next time. You tell your friends. They're a little more careful too. This is why fineness is so important."

"Is it," said Evemer.

"Fineness means how pure the metal is," Kadou said. His eyes were watery and bloodshot and he swayed a little where he sat. Oddly, his voice didn't slur very much at all. All those rhetoric and elocution lessons, Evemer supposed. "If I give you a coin that is perfectly pure gold, three nines fine—that's nine hundred and ninety-nine parts to a thousand—we'll say it's worth a horse. Not how much a horse costs, but we'll just say it is, because of the arithmetic. And if I give you a coin that has a fineness of seven-five-oh, that's three-quarters of a horse. Again, just because of the arithmetic. Do you see yet?"

"Yes, sir."

"Good, so you see—people like doing business with people they can trust. It's good when everybody trusts you, isn't it?" Kadou sat up very straight. "Like you! Eozena and my sister trust you, clearly. You couldn't do your job without trust either. Coins are the same. You can't cheat people too often, or they stop wanting to take your coins, and if they don't want your coins then they aren't coins anymore, they're just bits of metal. Take Qeteren, for example."

"Yes, sir."

"They were fine, Qeteren were. Then, a long time ago, a few centuries ago—gods, when was that? During our Ahak dynasty, I think—they looked around and decided to join in the very fashionable pastime of building competitive civilizations and, you know, taking part in the world. Then, what, seventy years ago they get into those wars with Yamye and it all comes crashing down on them. Because wars cost money, Evemer, and you can't make money out of thin air. It doesn't grow on trees. Except in Genzhu, where it's paper. That's a whole different thing. Anyway, Qeteren says, 'Oh, damn, we need cash.' So they get a loan from the Pezians, but they're losing the war and they can't get any more loans, so they try some other tricks—war bonds and that, but they're still hard up, so they say, 'All right. We'll *debase the coins.*'" Kadou whispered this last bit with a certain prim disgust. "So they did. You know debasing, Evemer?"

"Yes, sir."

"You take, say, a hundred coins, and you melt them down and put cheap stuff in to bulk it out, then you mint 'em new again, and then you have a hundred and twenty coins. Free money, right? So life is good. Until everybody finds out, and adjusts accordingly, and then you're back where you started. So the Qeter did that over and over, do you see? Until a horse didn't cost one gold coin, it cost ten thousand lead coins with a bit of gold leaf on one side. So they lost the war with Yamye, obviously, and lost a big portion of their northern marches, and now they're all paupers." He paused, looked soulfully into the depths of his cup, the dregs of wine. "It's about trust. That's why Araşt has never, ever debased, not ever. Not once in a hundred and ninety-nine years of the Mahisti dynasty, nor ever during the Shahre dynasty, nor Ahak or Tari or Misba. Because everybody knows trust is really the only thing you have. Trust is *sacred*. We'll assassinate all the heirs of a dynasty every now and then and set up a new one, no problem, but we won't touch the coin fineness regulations. Everybody would find out immediately anyway—how many touch-tasters are there? Roughly one in ten? Maybe one in a thousand who's really gifted? Wouldn't be a point to debasing, we'd just kick ourselves in the teeth. We'd sooner sell the palace or personally starve first. Because what do we have now? Insurance. People build fortunes—empires!—on the foundation of Araşti trustworthiness. That's why the thing with what's-her-name—the Oissika, Madam Azuta Melachrinos— that's why it's such a big deal. Counterfeits."

See, there it was. Kadou would start talking about coins— coins! Commonplace, unromantic things!—and reveal a deep meaning in them, a current of importance and the moral code that went along with it, frame them as symbols of fidelity, and Evemer was just . . . enthralled. He wanted Kadou to keep talking, wanted to listen and look.

"You show someone an altın anywhere in the world—well,

maybe not *anywhere*, but anywhere that matters. Anywhere from the Glass Sea to the Sea of Storms, let's say—you show it anywhere there, and people take it, no questions asked. An Araşti coin is as good as gold because it literally is gold. Nine-eight-six fine. Just a touch of other stuff in there so the gold isn't too soft."

Evemer had never wished that he knew more about economics, of all things, but he did now, if only for the sake of asking intelligent questions that might get Kadou to keep talking.

Kadou yawned. "Getting late. Must finish my wine," he mumbled into his cup. "You know what else, though? You know what else is interesting? When other people start breaking promises. There's things you can do to them besides refusing to take their money. Especially when the money they're offering is yours already."

"Like what?"

"Trade sanctions." Kadou peered at him. "I don't expect you know trade sanctions."

"No more or less than anyone else."

"It's when somebody—and by somebody, I mean usually a government—does something you don't like—and by you, I mean another government—but you don't not like it enough to go to war over it, so you—you know when people snub you at a party and then go off to the other end of the room with all their friends to whisper about you to each other and giggle behind their hands? Like that." Kadou dragged the wine bottle closer and refilled his glass. Tried to refill. He scowled at the mere two fingers of liquid in the cup. "We should go home, I guess."

Evemer felt a trickle of disappointment and squashed it. His Highness was quite right.

Kadou probably had enough material to talk all night long about economics and coin fineness and whatever other damn fool thing that really ought to be as dull and boring as old bread. Evemer would have listened all night too, wondering (and frustrated, and outraged, and confounded) where *that* Kadou went in the light of day.

"Sir," he said. "May I ask you something?"

Kadou peered up at him again, this time startled. "Eh?"

Evemer wrestled with himself for a minute. "It's something personal." Maybe it was fine to ask—if Kadou didn't want to answer, he'd say so. And perhaps he wouldn't even remember this in the morning, if he was offended. But why should he be offended? A kahya might trim his nails for him, or nurse him when he was sick, or die for him. Evemer already knew all His Highness's tailoring measurements by heart, what he liked and didn't like at meals, how sweet and how strong he took his coffee, the softheartedness he showed to his armsmen and kahyalar in chess, and that he couldn't speak to Siranos or even spot him from a distance without fretting himself to bits over it. *Something personal* was, in fact, already fading away in the distance, miles and miles behind them. It had been put behind them the moment Evemer was assigned to His Highness's service. "May I ask?"

"All right," Kadou said slowly, sipping at his wine.

Evemer sat down in the chair beside him and dragged it around so he was fully facing His Highness. "You called yourself a coward."

"Yes?"

"Why?"

"Because I am."

"Why?"

"I don't know. It just comes upon me. Like a tiger leaping on me out of the woods."

"But *why*?"

"Stop saying *why* and ask what you mean to ask," Kadou said peevishly. "Spell it out."

"Why are you afraid? What happened to make you afraid? When did it happen?"

"I don't know," Kadou said. "As long as I can remember? I've always been cowardly. High strung. Once, the tutors took me and Zeliha to the poorest parts of the capital and showed us the orphanages and the charity hospital and the lepers' house, and told us that we'd better be damned careful how we conducted ourselves when we were grown, because those were the people who we'd hurt if we did anything bad. They introduced us to some of them, told us their names, made us ask questions about them and their families and their histories, and then they took us aside and said that if we were bad, then those people would die, and it would be our fault. The first lesson: Misusing our power hurts everyone else before it hurts us. I cried. I wouldn't stop crying. It was very embarrassing for everyone." Kadou drank the last gulp of his wine.

"How old were you?"

"I was five, she was nine. I cried because I thought I already had killed someone, you see," he added. "I remember apologizing and apologizing because I'd thrown a tantrum at breakfast, and I thought that had been bad enough to do it. But instead of comforting me or explaining what they meant, the tutors just nodded and said, 'Yes, imagine if you'd had a very, very big tantrum. Imagine if you were grown-up, and as powerful as your Lady Mother or your Lord Father and you had a tantrum, imagine how bad that would have been. That's why you must be ever so careful.'" Kadou looked pensively down into his empty cup. "I think that's the first time I remember being really afraid. Zeliha handled it well, though. She was serious and solemn the whole time, very queenly. She was old enough to know what they meant. I couldn't even ask for a second cup of tea for weeks after that. Might have killed someone, you know?" He clenched his jaw. "And then it happened just like they said," he whispered. "Gülpaşa, Balaban. One wrong step, and now they're dead, and I might as well have done it with my own hand. I've been trying to write condolence letters to their families for two weeks, and I'm too scared to do that, even. Afraid of making another wrong step, hurting someone else again."

Evemer fit this in to everything else he knew of His Highness and turned it over and over in his mind. There was something there, but it needed to finish brewing, like a pot of coffee set over a dish of coals to keep warm.

※

I can walk, you know, I'm not that drunk," Kadou said, yanking his arm out of Evemer's grasp and deftly avoiding the wall that he nearly swerved into.

"Sir," Evemer said.

Kadou shook himself, smoothed his clothes, balanced himself against the wall with one hand, and set off down the street again. He really wasn't that drunk, no matter what Evemer said—tricksy Evemer, asking him questions like that when his guard was down. No matter, he supposed. What did he have to prove to Evemer, anyway? The man didn't have to like him to be good at his job. He could, come to think of it, tell Evemer anything he wished and be secure in the knowledge that Evemer's opinion of him *couldn't* sink any lower.

But actually taking that step and talking about himself like that? No, unthinkable. Far too terrifying a prospect, even if he was perfectly safe within Evemer's disdain.

That thought, though, gave him an idea.

He'd read over the papers from Armagan's investigation three times in the last two weeks. Evemer had read them too, and Eozena. There hadn't been any conclusions immediately apparent in either direction: either that Armagan had been correct and there wasn't a point to continuing the investigation, or that Armagan had been wrong or (Kadou barely dared to think it—çe was a *kahya*) intentionally dishonest.

Kadou's stupid, anxious fear had kept him from pursuing it further. He kept thinking of the eyes of all the kahyalar watching Tadek run from the dormitories to the Gold Court in his cadet whites, the gossip network through the palace, the way everyone was just holding their breaths for him to make another monumental mistake. If he took a risk and failed, it would be in front of dozens, hundreds, thousands of people.

But now . . . Evemer was the only person around. He, at least, wasn't holding his breath for *anything*.

"Hey," Kadou said. "Let's go to the Shipbuilder's Guild."

"It's night," said Evemer.

"Exactly."

"No one will be there."

"*Exactly*." It wasn't even that far away from where they now stood.

The night air was cool and only faintly salty even when they got closer to the Shipbuilder's Guild and the harborfront—the tall seawalls blocked most of the wind coming off the water—and this, combined with the brisk walk, had Kadou almost one-third sober by the time they reached the guild.

The huge building was well lit. Each door was hung with lanterns, and there had been a double posting of guards since the break-in. Kadou paused, dozens of yards away from the edge of the nearest circle of lamplight, and squinted down the street. "Lots of people here."

"Yes, sir."

"*You* said there wouldn't be anybody here."

"Sir," Evemer said, after a pointed pause.

Kadou decided to let it go. Of course Evemer had meant there wouldn't be anyone who could verify their identities or let them inside the building to poke around. It wouldn't be nice of Kadou to tease him over semantics.

"Take this off," Kadou said, plucking at the sleeve of the pine-green kaftan concealing the uniform beneath. "Might as well show off that you're important."

"Sir," said Evemer.

Kadou was too drunk to bother translating. He peered down the street at the guards. "Any of them kahyalar, you think? Would they recognize *me*?" He didn't even notice his hand was going to his turban, preparing to pull it off and shake out his hair until Evemer caught his wrist.

He snatched his hand back a heartbeat later. "Leave it," Evemer said.

"What if instead I just shout really loudly, 'Here I am, Prince Kadou Mahisti'? How about that?" He really oughtn't tease Evemer. It wasn't fair—Evemer couldn't, or rather *wouldn't*, tease back.

"Sir," Evemer said in a pained voice.

Kadou sighed with his entire heart and led them forward.

It seemed that the guards around the building didn't particularly care if they walked back and forth along the street. They watched, yes, but when the lantern light was bright and near enough to show the colors of Evemer's uniform, they only nodded politely to him and said nothing. Kadou kept his face angled away from the light as much as possible and felt a flare of delight to do so—how strange and novel it was to walk right down the street and at least be dismissed, if not quite entirely unnoticed. How giddy and baffling it was to have someone think *Evemer* was the current ranking authority on this street. It felt scandalous and transgressive, and he wasn't sure that Evemer had even noticed. If he had, he would have gone to throw himself into the harbor.

The delicious vertigo of this uncommon pleasure made Kadou bold. At the end of the street, instead of turning around and pacing back down the length of the building, he turned them toward the guild's shipyard. There were three half-built vessels in dry dock, waiting for decks or masts, and the stale-water and salt scent of the harbor was overlaid here by those of sawdust and pine tar. The tip of Kadou's shoe kicked something small as he walked; it went skittering over the cobbles with a metallic sound. He bent automatically to pick it up—a nail. He knew it was brass, more by common sense than by touch-tasting. He was still drunk enough that the signatures in his fingertips were muffled, muted. All he got was a bit of a juddering sensation and a faint suggestion of autumn leaves. He tossed the nail aside.

"Where do you think they were waiting?"

"Sir?"

"The thieves. The night of the break-in. They must have been nearby, right? Waiting for the fireworks to start." He waved an arm vaguely at the surrounding buildings and the shipyard itself. "Must have had the battering ram and everything ready to go."

"Sir," Evemer said. "Some of us—" He fell silent.

"What?"

"Nothing, sir. Mere speculation."

"I don't have anywhere else to be," Kadou said, which got a faint indignant sound from Evemer. Kadou assumed that meant *Yes, you do! At home, safe in bed, behind three locked gates and four guarded doors!* "Speculate, then. Go on."

"Some of us," Evemer said, "thought they might have taken

something from the wood supply." He gestured toward the end of the shipyard where a massive pile of raw material was covered with oilcloth tarps. "One of the masts, we thought."

Kadou blinked at the pile, then at Evemer. "Why would you think that?"

"The dents in the door." He held up his hands, spanning an invisible circle perhaps ten inches across.

Kadou peered at it. "That'd be a pretty small mast. Maybe for a little sloop, but . . ."

"Sir."

"Nothing about that in Armagan's notes, though."

"Sir."

"Did anyone tell çem about that theory?"

"I believe so, sir."

"Did çe have anyone look around?"

"I couldn't say, sir."

"Hm." Kadou looked back at the wood pile. "It would make sense—why bring your own battering ram when you can borrow one for free right next door?" But it would have been in Armagan's notes.

Unless, of course, there was a reason for it to be missing.

"All right," Kadou said. "Let's go look. Go get a lantern or something from one of those guards at the door." Both moons hung full directly above them, silvery-bright and blue-grey. More than enough light to go wandering, but not enough to look for something specific.

"Sir," Evemer said, a flatness to his tone that Kadou was almost sure meant uncertainty.

"I'm *allowed* to be here," he snapped. "I'm the Duke of Harbors. I'm legally permitted to commandeer any ship they make here." Not that he ever would—the very thought of doing so made him queasy. "They can't stop me from rummaging around in the woodpile if I feel like it. Go on. Need a light."

"Highness," Evemer said pointedly. He'd drawn himself sharply to attention at Kadou's tone, which made Kadou feel just *wretched*, thanks so much. "I cannot in good conscience leave Your Highness alone in a place like this."

Doubly wretched, then. He ought to keep better control of his tongue—being drunk was no excuse for reflexively sniping at Evemer, and it wasn't at all right of him to ask Evemer to disregard his primary duty for—for what? Kadou's convenience? His laziness, because he didn't want to walk all the way back up to the guild for a lantern? Doubly and triply wretched.

"Right. Certainly," he said. "We'll go together."

Kadou indulged, in the most private recesses of his soul, in a tiny moment of annoyance. That was all he could permit himself, like a single bite-sized honeycake devoured privately behind a closed door when he was supposed to be saving his appetite for dinner. Annoying of Evemer to be so inflexible, and moreover to be *right* about it—that was the worst part.

He pushed the thought away firmly, locked it in an iron chest, threw it into the sea.

At the edge of the lamplight, he stopped, crossed his arms, and nodded for Evemer to go ahead. "Evening," Evemer said flatly to the guard. "We're going to borrow a lantern."

She eyed him, her eyes lingering on his cobalt uniform. In polite but suspicious tones, she said, "You're . . . from the palace, then?"

"Yes," said Evemer, already helping himself to one of the lanterns hanging on either side of the door. The guard's eyes flicked to Kadou. "We'll bring this back in a minute."

"Right," she said slowly. "Of course." She drifted after them for several dozen yards as they walked off, far enough back that Kadou wasn't worried about her overhearing them, but nevertheless a watchful presence. She stopped at the edge of the shipyard, where she'd be able to see the door of the guild and keep an eye on what they were up to.

Kadou ignored her and fumbled with the ties on the corners of the oilcloth tarp covering a pile of rough-hewn masts until he could, with a woozy effort, fling the heavy, unwieldy lengths of

fabric back from one end. Evemer stood nearby with the lantern
and did not offer to help. "Right," said Kadou, slightly winded.
"The dents were this big, yes?" He mimicked the circle that Evemer had held up for him before.

"Yes, sir."

Kadou flicked back the skirts of his kaftan and crouched down.
The mast was one of the trickiest parts of the ship to source, since
it had to be in one long piece. They were usually found specially
and earmarked for the exact vessel they'd be fitted to. "Do you," he
said, examining the logs, "know how many shipyards we have?"

"Twelve, sir," Evemer answered immediately.

"That's how many are *in Araşt*. How many do we *have*?"

Silence for a beat. The flame in the lamp flickered. "I couldn't
say."

"Sixty." He stood up. All of these were too big—the wrong
diameter, for one thing. They would have been ridiculously long
to use as battering rams anyway, unless the thieves had come in
a whole squadron. That guard who had apprehended them and
fought them off said there had been only a handful. "Where do
you think they keep the scrap heap?"

Evemer pointed immediately to the other end of the shipyard.
Of course. Most of the fringe-guards on the investigation would
have taken turns patrolling the area and familiarizing themselves
with the terrain. Evemer might know the shipyard better than
he did. Kadou had only been here one or two dozen times, and
then he'd only passed through on Duke of Harbors business. He
was usually escorted by one of the guildmasters when they were
showing him some new advancement in the building technology
for which the Kasaba headquarters of the Shipbuilder's Guild was
most famous.

Halfway down the yard, Evemer said, "Where are they?"

"Where are what?"

"The other forty-eight shipyards that aren't in Araşt."

"Oh. All over. Kafia, Persep, Amariyan. *Six* up north in
Laemuir—lots of good trees in Laemuir, nice dry weather. A
couple in Arjuneh. Ephucca, Quassa sai Bendra. We just signed

a contract to open one in Lapaladi." He squinted into the dark, looking for the scrap heap. Everything outside the lamplight was just dark mounds and shadows, and in the milky moonlight nothing was significantly distinguishable from anything else. "Why do you ask?"

"You asked me how many there were as if you thought I would be interested in the answer. Sir."

"Oh. Are you?"

"Sir," Evemer said. And then, unexpectedly, "Yes."

Kadou hadn't known that Evemer had any interest in ships or shipbuilding, but then Evemer hadn't yet owned to liking or being interested in *anything* beyond sword drills, chess, and the fine art of a perfectly nuanced stony silence. "It was just drunk rambling on my part," he said. "Don't mind me."

"How does it work?"

Kadou resisted the urge to turn and stare at him. The lamplight would go right in his eyes, and then what little night vision he'd adjusted to would be shot. "Uh, shipyards?"

"Foreign ones."

"We sign a contract—usually a twenty- or forty-year one, for a lease on land to build a shipyard on. It's like establishing an embassy—it *is* an embassy in a lot of ways. We send a guildmaster and a handful of overseers and a hundred or so shipbuilders to start with, and we hire locals for felling the trees and a lot of the less-skilled labor. The guildmasters make sure all the ships meet specification before they're launched, and then they're brought to one of the Araşti shipyards and checked again, and if they're properly made, the masters here give them certification of quality." That wasn't very interesting information, and Kadou felt a little bit like he ought to be presenting it better. The shipbuilders and all those shipyards were his, after all—at least, they were his by courtesy as the Duke of Harbors, though they were legally owned by the Araşti government. They were his responsibility, ultimately. It was his job to . . . Well, to make sure that there were people whose job it was to make sure there were *other* people whose jobs involved looking after the foreign shipyards, negotiating contracts, and ensuring that standards of quality were met or exceeded.

He should say something interesting. He should say *anything* that wasn't dreadfully boring. Ugh, and he was leaving the point of drunkenness where he was immune to anxiety. Lovely. "Did you know," he said, thinking quickly, "that the yards in Laemuir each make four ships a week?"

"No."

Damn. Maybe that wasn't interesting enough. "We sell some of them, but the ones that we keep get brought right here to Kasaba to have their hulls painted in all those bright colors and patterns. For good luck." Well, that's what they *told* everyone, anyway. It had to have something to do with the trick of avoiding the sea serpents, but Kadou would never breathe a word of that theory to anyone. "Can't go to sea without luck. Is this the scrap heap?"

It did seem to be—a loose pile of odds and ends, including some yard-long sections of logs, left over from when the masts were sawn to length. Kadou picked around the edges of the pile, nudging boards and beams out of the way until Evemer made an unhappy noise. "Sir," he said, as if he were about to beg Kadou not to drown a bag of unwanted kittens. "*Sir.*"

"What?"

"Your hands."

"It's fine."

"Sir. *Please.*"

Kahyalar! Kadou mentally cursed. Why were they all like this? "It's just bits of wood, calm down."

"Sir."

"Which are you going to start with? 'But it will make your hands rough' or 'But you might crack a nail'?" Kadou unearthed a likely-looking log and hauled it onto its end. Too narrow, distinctly too narrow. More like a piece of a bowsprit than a mast. He tipped it to the side.

"*Sir,*" Evemer said, tortured.

"Funny how none of you kahyalar complain about my archery calluses. Funny how none of you get faint when I prick my fingers doing needlework. If you hate this so much, you can always put the lamp down and help, you know," Kadou said peevishly. "Then my hands would only get half-ruined. Maybe just a chipped nail instead of a broken one."

Evemer . . . did. He set the lantern on the cobbles and stepped in to help.

The clattering of the wood echoed very loudly through the shipyard, and when Kadou glanced up at the guildhall, he saw a few guards standing and watching them at the corner of the building. Too far away to see their faces, but they seemed calm. Sometimes one of them turned a little and said something to another. Kadou put them out of his mind.

He found another large log, primarily by stubbing his toes on it. Even before he was done cursing, Evemer was at his side, helping haul it out from under the rest.

"Hm. That's about the right size, isn't it?"

Evemer frowned, peering at the end of it in the dark, rubbing his fingers over some—smudge? No, it flaked off. Impossible to distinguish color or detail in the scanty moon- and starlight like this. Kadou went for the lantern and held it up so its light fell over the end of the log.

Flakes of red paint. The wood looked a bit worn.

Almost as if it had been used to batter down a red-painted door.

They gazed at it in silence for a long time. "It wasn't that hard to find," Kadou said slowly. "Did Armagan even look?"

"Not as far as I know. And not according to the notes."

"Çe would have recorded it, otherwise. Surely."

"Yes, sir."

Kadou didn't want to say it out loud. Armagan, noted for being a thorough and meticulous investigator, either hadn't found it or had omitted it. Either option was . . . not promising. "Can we carry this back to the palace?"

Evemer gave him a look. "I would prefer to have my hands free, sir."

"Oh, I can probably carry it, then," Kadou said just for the sake of seeing Evemer's barest eye-twitch, which of course meant un-speakable anguish at the very thought of Kadou doing physical labor. It was nice to see him being so expressive. He really oughtn't tease Evemer, though, *especially* when it was easy. "We'll leave it with the guards," he said, nodding up to the guildhall. "I'll send someone to collect it tomorrow."

Evemer seemed to find this acceptable and hauled it out from under Kadou's hands and up onto his shoulder with only the bar-est grunt of effort. Ah, Kadou reflected sagely to himself. That log must have weighed as much as he did. Good to know that one day when Evemer inevitably snapped and hauled him back to the palace over those incredible shoulders, he wouldn't hurt his back or strain a muscle doing so.

Evemer took the lantern too, pointedly.

Kadou let him do the talking when they went up to the guild-hall, once more hanging back as Evemer ordered the guards to keep the discarded battering ram in a secure place.

It must have been past midnight by then—the kahyalar wait-ing with the carriage at the foot of the Palace Road would be quietly having conniptions. Kadou was only half-drunk now, but exhaustion was creeping in, there was a soreness just above his eyes and a gummy feeling when he blinked, and the consensus through all his muscles and sinews was that the thing to do would be to find a cushion somewhere and rest his eyes for a minute. As soon as Evemer turned away from the guards, Kadou said, "Home now, I think."

"Very good, sir," said Evemer, which Kadou translated as *I shall dance and sing in the streets from joy.*

In this part of the city and this late at night, the streets were quiet but for the occasional sweeper picking up trash and debris or sloshing buckets of well water onto the cobblestones to rinse off dust and grime. Kadou watched one of them as he passed, musing absently to himself about the welfare of government employees, the ongoing public works, health and sanitation—perhaps if he came up with some ideas for Zeliha, she might let him back into court—

He was so deep in thought that the hands clamping around his arms and shoulders took him entirely by surprise.

Before he could so much as gasp in shock, he was dragged into an alley and flung against the wall, the breath knocked out of him, then knocked out again with a punch to his stomach. He wheezed, coughing for air, momentarily too dazed to struggle as two assailants fumbled through his clothes, their faces and even their clothes well concealed in the dark. "Quick, quick," one grunted, yanking out Kadou's coin purse as the other cut the fine silver buttons from his kaftan and pulled the knot of his sash loose. "He have rings? Jewels?"

Evemer, where was Evemer? Where in the *gods' names* was—

His vision, hazy from the pain and the drink and not entirely adjusted to the darkness, focused just enough: Evemer, at the mouth of the alley, grappling with two other thieves.

Evemer fought like a wolf. He flung them aside, sending them stumbling to the ground, and then he slammed into the two who held Kadou—they all went down, him and the thieves and nearly Kadou too.

Evemer shot to his feet. "Run. I'll hold them off." Three of the thieves scrambled back up, and Evemer flung himself at them.

But Kadou had heard the slick ring of steel behind him, and then a footstep, and he'd quarter-turned enough to glimpse a lick of starlight glinting off a blade—

He wrenched himself to the side, just as Master Kazar had drilled into his bones for years. The knife missed him by six inches.

Ah.

The knife flashed again and Kadou found himself another six inches away, knees slightly bent, feet apart and weight equally distributed between them as if he were floating between those two points on the ground, his body turned sideways to the person with the knife.

Octem's stance, first position. A flash of the knife—from first position, swivel to *in quartata* (*not* on his toes, knees still bent, still maintaining floating balance), retreat one step, and recover into first position.

He knew this. Like dancing and embroidery and coins and horses and ships and the tides and stars, this was as natural as breathing. It was a gift; a deliberate, intentional gift, a gift from his parents and theirs and generations of House Mahisti before them, who knew with a cold and level certainty what it was to rule and who had seen wisdom in teaching their children to survive unarmed against armed assailants for more than ten frantic heartbeats.

He and his attacker had rotated, and his eyes had adjusted as much as they could to the thick darkness of the alley—the thief had short hair and a rough masculine timbre to his rasping breath. He grunted as he lunged forward again, swinging his knife at Kadou's face—Kadou ducked, stepped to the side, came up in third position. Swivel. Retreat. Recover to first.

He found himself on the outside of the fight's circle. Evemer, deeper in the alley, was an indistinguishable knot of furious movement with the other three assailants—he'd drawn his long dagger, but one of the thieves had pinned his arm, and as Kadou watched, they twisted the blade away from him, sending it clattering to the stones.

Kadou was outside the fight. He could run. Should run.

Evemer caught a bad blow to the side that sent him reeling off balance, and that seemed to be all the thieves needed. They wrenched his arms behind his back, and one of them bent to pick up the dagger.

Kadou's blood ran cold, and things . . . blurred.

The man with the knife lunged at him again, and Kadou abruptly decided that he'd had enough of this. He swiveled, but instead of following through with the retreat-and-recover-to-first, he stepped into fourth with a strange dreamlike clarity, then shifted to *in quartata,* and slammed his foot into the side of the man's knee. He went down with a cry, and Kadou punched him in the neck, planted his foot on the man's chest, and *shoved.*

Somewhere in there, the man had dropped his knife. Kadou left him wheezing on the ground and picked it up.

Now it was a fair fight.

He turned toward the darker part of the alley. His eyes had adjusted now, and Evemer had managed not to get his throat slit yet, thank the gods.

Master Kazar had been a former soldier—a real fighter, not one of the fashionable instructors favored by the upper classes—and he had his own ideas about the kinds of situations in which Kadou would find his training most useful. Formal duels were disgraceful and beneath a prince's dignity; in battle, he would be surrounded by kahyalar—if he went to battle at all, for Araşt had not been at war in generations.

But there was always the possibility of danger, and Mastar Kazar had quite agreed with the philosophy of that deliberate gift that House Mahisti took care to teach its scions. *You're helping your kahyalar,* he had said when Kadou had uncertainly and hesitantly expressed his terror of hurting someone. *You're buying them time to get to you; you're making it easier for them to keep their oaths to protect you.* So Kadou had learned—not formal dueling, not battlefield combat, but brutally efficient knife-fighting that was best suited for . . . this, as it happened. Surprise attacks in narrow, dark spaces.

Kadou took three river-steps forward, ended in Meyhan's second, put the dagger through one of the thieves' throats, swiveled, recovered to Octem's first. He knocked Evemer's dagger out of the other thief's grip and nicked high on their inner arm, roughly in the region of their brachial artery. The third one cursed and released Evemer with one last kick to the back of his knee, felling him before vanishing at speed into the darkness.

As Evemer struggled back to his feet—alive, mostly unharmed, good—Kadou turned his attention back to the last thief, the one he'd only knocked aside.

He'd just killed two people, he realized absently. Or rather, he'd have killed them in about a minute when they both finished bleeding out.

The last man had staggered to his feet again. He had another knife, a quite long, rough thing that looked like it had been beaten out of scrap steel by an overly ambitious apprentice blacksmith who thought they knew anything about making swords. But even if it didn't have an edge on it, it would hurt if it hit him.

Kadou fell into the floating balance of Octem's first, his knife at the ready, and watched the man's elbow. Not his wrist, and certainly not his eyes—not that he could have seen them anyway, stuck in the dark as they were.

"Should have gone for you first," the man rasped. He had a strange accent that Kadou in his blur of adrenaline couldn't place—a foreigner? "You're the dangerous one, eh? Should have known."

The man came at him, swinging wildly and amateurishly. Before he had even completed his first stride, Kadou moved: Shift to second, balestra forward like surging waters, knock aside the knife, slide steel into his throat.

He choked. He fell.

All was still.

Kadou felt and heard his heartbeat roaring in his ears, noticed that the haze of alcohol had faded off. Everything was very clear. Too clear. His hands were shaking. He tasted blood in his mouth, smelled blood. The touch-taste of the steel dagger sang in his fingertips—the thump of a heavy door pushed closed, a lump of incense burning under a clear night sky, the gritty feel of dusty leather.

Kadou dropped the dagger, dropped Octem's second, stumbled back against the wall. He felt like he wasn't quite of himself, like he was an observer in his own flesh, the world pressing in on him from every direction with a terrible, terrible clarity.

※

Evemer felt as though he'd been struck by lightning.

It had all happened so quickly—he'd been grabbed from behind, and he'd seen Kadou grabbed a heartbeat later, and then—that. Heartbeats, that's how long it had taken. Not moments or instants, but heartbeats.

And now there were three corpses at their feet, killed by *His Highness's* hand.

Killed.

By Kadou.

Kadou had killed them.

Lightning. Evemer was full of lightning, his skin prickled with it. It loosened all his joints and raised all the hairs on his arms, sent chills up and down his spine.

Kadou had been . . . resplendent. He'd moved like nothing Evemer had ever seen, like a rip current, like a tidal wave. Kadou. His liege. Evemer realized he was gawking and shook himself. The lightning running through him did not abate.

Kadou was leaning against the opposite wall, very still, hidden in a shadow. Evemer's mouth was dry. He swallowed hard. "Highness, are you all right?" he asked.

He didn't answer.

The lightning in him twisted into fear—had he taken a blow? Was he so still because he was holding a wound closed? Was he even now bleeding out? Evemer lunged forward, his aches and bruises disappearing in this new surge of alarm. "You're hurt. You're hurt? Are you?"

It was only when he was up close that he could see how Kadou was shaking. The shadows had hidden that too. His clothes were disarrayed, he'd lost several buttons—but Evemer couldn't see the wet black of blood in darkness, nor feel it as his hands patted frantically across Kadou's torso—and he saw then that Kadou's hands were hanging limp at his sides, not clasped against any injured part of him.

His Highness's eyes were wide, unfocused, staring into nothing. His mouth, slightly open; he was taking little gasping sips of air, and no more.

"Your Highness?" Evemer whispered. No response. Shit. "You're in shock."

Kadou's eyes focused a little then, drifting to Evemer's face. If there had been enough light to see colors, Evemer was sure his face would have been ash-pale. But even by starlight, he could see the tears standing in Kadou's eyes.

Evemer swallowed hard, picked up his dagger and sheathed it, then steered Kadou out of the alley with one arm around his back. "Home now," he said firmly. "Before anyone finds us and the bodies."

Kadou was crying outright now, still shuddering violently, though he was eerily silent. Evemer shoved aside the lightning and half dragged Kadou down the street.

Kadou had returned to the carriage staggering drunk enough times that the kahyalar did not leap into dismay and panic at the state of him. Evemer bundled him in, hesitated, and climbed in after him rather than going up to sit with the driver.

His Highness shuddered all the way back up the Palace Road, occasionally making soft noises as if the creaks of the carriage and the occasional rough jolt were torture to him, too much to be borne.

Evemer had no idea what to do about it.

He took off the pine-green kaftan that Kadou made him wear over his uniform, folded it neatly, and placed it next to Kadou on the seat, in case he was cold and wanted to use it.

Kadou remained crammed into the corner in a little ball, his hands clutched to his chest, his eyes closed, his breath stuttering. He did not reach for the kaftan. Evemer tried to think of something else to do that might be helpful.

He tried reciting the "Admonishments to the Would-Be Righteous Man" chapter from Beydamur's *Ten Pillars of War*, which was all about prescriptions for correct behavior and which Evemer had found very comforting on those occasions that he found himself troubled or unprepared—though as the third Admonishment was "Be never unprepared for any demand or need or occurrence," that had not happened frequently.

Concerningly, this did not seem to help Kadou either, and any calmness or grounding that Evemer had gained by the recitation was swept away once more by the sight of his lord shuddering so hard that his bones must have been rattling. Could it be an epileptic fit, rather than shock as he'd thought? He held himself tense and poised to leap across the carriage to catch Kadou if he fell.

He had no idea how he managed it, but he got Kadou out of the carriage as near as it could come to his apartments in the Gold Court, across the formal gardens, and, blessedly, to the doors of his own chamber.

Yasemin, the kahya at the door, took one look at them, went wide-eyed and pale, and said as she opened the door for them, "I'll send for the doctor."

"No," said Evemer. "The commander." He half dragged Kadou inside and settled him on the couch next to the fire. Kadou collapsed onto the cushions like a cut flower. Evemer placed the folded green kaftan next to him again.

He second-guessed himself the whole time that he was waiting for Eozena—should he have allowed Yasemin to send for a doctor as well? But Kadou didn't seem to be hurt, and doctors couldn't treat shock. Nor epilepsy, if it was that—but Kadou wasn't frothing at the mouth, and he'd been able to keep his feet on the walk from the carriage . . .

Ah—clutching Evemer's arm hard enough that his nails had dug in through Evemer's uniform. That was how he'd managed getting Kadou across the gardens. His Highness's grip had been astoundingly strong, considering how watery his knees seemed to be.

Evemer hovered around the couch, not sure if he should—or whether he ought to—the commander was coming. She would tell him what to do. In the light of the fire, Evemer saw suddenly that Kadou's hands were splashed with dark blood, and more was spattered and smeared on his face and clothes—Evemer was confounded as to how he could have missed that. Not seeing it in the dark was one thing, but . . . He must be in shock too.

The blood certainly explained Yasemin's reaction.

He should—he should clean His Highness's face and hands.

He went for the ewer and basin and clean cloths. When he

came back and knelt by the divan, Kadou had his eyes scrunched tight, still shivering. Evemer dampened one of the cloths and wiped at the smears on his lord's face.

Kadou flinched away with a sharp sound, the tiniest pleading whimper of "No."

"You're—not clean." He didn't want to say *bloody*. He dipped the cloth in the water again and noticed suddenly that it was icy cold. Ah. That was poor form on his part.

He moved the water close to the fire, swirling it in the polished brass basin to at least take the chill off it. The commander arrived just as the water came above lukewarm. The instant she clapped her eyes on Kadou, she froze. "What happened?" she demanded. She sprang forward, kneeling close to him. "*What happened?*"

"Not Evemer's fault," Kadou stuttered between desperate, juddering breaths.

"Are you hurt?" Eozena took his hands in her own.

"Not that I could tell," Evemer said. Still kneeling, he moved the basin close again and wet a new cloth. Kadou didn't move or reach out for it, so Evemer took Kadou's hands from Eozena, one at a time, wiping the blood from them. The water in the bowl was rust-cloudy by the time he'd finished—new water from the ewer warming on the hearth, then, and a new cloth for cleaning Kadou's face.

The warm touch of the wet cloth against his cheek didn't make him flinch this time, and in fact it seemed to bring Kadou back to himself, at least a little. He blinked hard, took several shuddering breaths. "There you have it," he whispered. "I told you, didn't I?"

"Your Highness?" Eozena spoke quietly.

Kadou's ocean-dark eyes turned to Evemer. "I told you they've been teaching me to kill people since I was little. Didn't I say so?"

"You did, Your Highness," he replied.

"There you have it."

"Yes, Your Highness."

Kadou took another unsteady breath. "I killed them. But they would have killed you. I had to. Didn't I? I had to?"

Eozena moved to sit by him on the couch and pulled him upright so she could put an arm around his shoulders. "You did well, Your Highness. You were victorious. You came home in one piece."

For some reason that just made Kadou start to cry again. The tears left tracks in the smears of blood, and Evemer wiped both away with soft strokes of the cloth, trying to be . . . gentle. It was not a muscle he used often.

Kadou wouldn't stop shaking. Eozena awkwardly patted his hair, and Evemer wiped all the blood off him, but . . . this was like nothing he'd seen, even when Kadou had been so distraught about clashing with Siranos that he'd sent for his armsman.

When Eozena shot a glance up at him, Evemer thought that she must not have seen the prince like this either—and if it were simply battle fatigue or plain cowardice, she would have presumably known what to do about it.

But Kadou hadn't *been* cowardly. Evemer had told him to run, and he hadn't.

"Highness," Eozena said. "Kadou. You're all right. You're not hurt. That's the most important thing—that you're safe." He only shook harder, clutching his hands to his chest, gasping for air like he was being strangled. Eozena backed off, trading another nervous glance with Evemer. "Highness . . . What do you wish? What should we do? Are you ill?"

Kadou tipped sideways again and pressed his face into the fabric of the divan. Every muscle of his body was tense, as taut as a drawn bowstring. "Tadek," he stuttered, over the course of several hitching sips of breath. "Tadek. Now. He knows."

Evemer wasted no time—his heart was beating as fast in his chest now as it had been in the alley, or faster. He slammed down the hall in the direction of the chamber he now shared with Melek. There was another room next to it, barely larger than a broom closet. He slammed the door open, not bothering to be quiet, and hauled Tadek out of bed.

Tadek squawked awake and struggled in his grip. "What the fuck—what—"

"His Highness requires you *immediately*," Evemer snarled. "He's ill."

Tadek, cursing, found his feet and dove out the door without bothering to straighten his clothes or make himself presentable and, with Evemer close at his heels, strode into His Highness's chamber like he owned it.

He brushed Commander Eozena aside and sat himself down on the divan with not even a trace of hesitation. He hauled Kadou up and against him, tucked Kadou's head down to rest against his neck, got his arms tight around the prince, and pulled him half into his lap.

"There, lovely, breathe for me," he said softly. Evemer stood frozen. Eozena had risen to her feet too. "Both of you back away," Tadek said, sharp and warning. "And stop staring at him. You're not helping." Then, returning to his soft tone before: "Breathe, beauty, fill those lungs for me. There, look at you, that's a little better. You're doing so well. Another one, eh?"

Eozena, as commanded, turned away, but Evemer could not— Tadek laid soft, dry kisses against Kadou's forehead and hair, squeezing him around his shoulders and ribs as tight as the bands of a barrel. He kept a continuous low murmur of soft words, calling Kadou lovely and gently coaxing him to breathe, just to breathe.

Tadek must have seen something like this before. He was so calm, Evemer saw, narrowing his eyes. He was the one person in the room who knew what he was doing. Evemer watched him intently.

Kadou's hands were clenched so tight in Tadek's nightshirt that his knuckles were white, and his frantic sips of air had deepened to small gulps and sobs. "I can't—I can't breathe—" Evemer heard him gasp.

"You *are* breathing, lovely," Tadek said immediately, before Evemer could twitch even a muscle toward the door to run for the doctor. "You're breathing, and you're doing so well. You're already halfway through it, mm? Just ride out the rest. You're safe, lovely, you're well."

Eozena quietly left the room; Evemer heard the kahya at the door ask some soft question before it shut. He knew he should leave too. This wasn't for him to see. But he couldn't move, couldn't shake his attention from being wholly bent on what was happening on the divan.

It seemed like it took years for Kadou's breathing to finally ease, the shivers ebbing out of him like the tide, leaving him limp and weak and draped over Tadek. Evemer felt much the same; his muscles ached, and it was only when they released, one by one, that he realized how tightly he had tensed them.

Tadek's iron grip on Kadou eased too, no longer holding him together like he would have otherwise shaken to pieces. His hands moved softly over Kadou's hair, his shoulders, his arms.

Why had Tadek been the only person who knew how to help? Evemer felt a pang of something deeply unpleasant—why hadn't he been told how to help with this . . . affliction? Why hadn't Kadou wanted anyone to know about this? He'd deliberately concealed it from all his kahyalar, but his armsman knew—why? Why? Why?

Kadou shifted, sniffled, and pushed himself up, separating from Tadek. Tadek didn't stop him, only let his hands fall away from Kadou's hair with a few strands pulling through his fingers.

Kadou looked like he'd just begun to recover from an *illness*, and Evemer felt another unpleasant sensation burn through him. Kadou blotted his face dry with the clean inside of his kaftan.

"Do you require anything?" Tadek said, still half lounging.

Kadou shook his head hard. "No. Sorry. I—I shouldn't have had them wake you."

"Yes, you should have," Tadek said. "I'm glad that you did." He looked at Evemer expectantly, as if Evemer was going say something, but by the time he realized he was supposed to chime in and agree, the moment had passed and Tadek had turned his attention back to Kadou. "I'm going to get you something to drink and then I'm putting you to bed."

Kadou twitched at that. "No," he said, his voice clearer now, more determined. "No, I'm all right."

"You had a lot of wine, Highness," Evemer said softly. "You should drink something."

"Fine. I can put myself to bed, though. I don't need . . . nurse-maiding, despite all appearances to the contrary."

"No one thinks you need nursemaiding," Tadek said. He dipped forward to press a kiss to Kadou's temple and got up. "I'll fetch something for you."

"Please go back to sleep after that," Kadou said. "I'm fine now. I won't let them wake you again."

Tadek gave him a surprised look, which Kadou, who was looking at the floor, entirely missed. "Are you sure, Highness?" he said, politely. "As you know, I'm happy to—"

"Yes, I know," Kadou said. "I don't need anything else. Please go. I already feel guilty for disturbing you."

Tadek nodded slowly and left, passing Evemer without a glance.

He and Kadou waited there in the near dark, while the few lamps in the room guttered and wavered now and again. That unpleasant feeling was coiling and writhing in his chest, uniden-tifiable. He ought to say something. He ought to do something.

The force of that last thought finally sparked his limbs into motion again, breaking his paralysis. Evemer put out a few of the lamps, went to the bedroom, turned back the blankets, and loos-ened the ties of the bed's curtains without fully undoing them. He came back into the parlor just as a soft knock came at the door, which he answered. Eozena stood on the threshold with a steaming cup. She handed it to him silently, only glancing over his shoulder and tilting her head toward Kadou inquisitively. *Is he well?*

Evemer nodded in reply.

"I'm taking a watch here," she said, just above a whisper. "Tadek went to bed, and Melek is ready to take over whenever you'd—"

"No," Evemer said. "His Highness may require something else. Tell çir to sleep while çe can."

The commander nodded, and Evemer shut the door, glancing down at the hot earthenware cup in his hand—salep, thick and milky, with a dusting of cinnamon across the top. He crossed the room and pushed it into Kadou's hands, forcing the prince's fin-gers to wrap around the cup's handle.

Kadou shivered a little and cradled it close to his chest, sipping it quietly. He said nothing else.

"Do you require anything else, Highness?" Evemer said.

Kadou shook his head.

"Drink, please," Evemer said, and Kadou sipped slowly, his expression still drawn and wrecked.

When he'd finished the cup, he rose on his own power and dragged himself to his bedroom, shedding the outer layers of his clothing onto the floor while Evemer followed in his wake and picked them up.

Kadou fell face-first into bed. He was asleep before he even got the blankets arranged around himself. Evemer pulled them over him, feeling strangely neutral about the whole affair—as if he were *holding* himself in neutrality by sheer willpower. Two hours ago he would have been frustrated, exasperated, angry. Two hours ago he would have resented Kadou for—for weakness, or cowardice. He would have wondered—demanded, really—why Kadou couldn't be a better prince.

And now?

He stood there in the near dark with only one candle and moonlight, and he looked hard at Kadou's still figure, curled up small and tight in the center of the mattress.

He opened the door and slipped out into the corridor. Eozena, leaning against the wall, raised an eyebrow. "I'm coming back in a minute," Evemer said. She nodded silently.

Evemer went to the primaries' quarters and opened the door.

Melek had a lamp lit, still. Çe was curled up in bed, quiet but awake, and Tadek was sitting on the edge of Evemer's bed on the other side of the room, leaning with his elbows on his knees, his hands clasped between. Evemer shut the door behind him.

"I apologize for dragging you out of bed so abruptly," Evemer said, when Tadek looked up at him.

Tadek shook his head immediately. "If that happens again, you drag me out of bed by my hair if you need to. But you won't need to."

"Is he sick, Tadek?" Melek asked quietly. "We should have been told, if he were sick."

"Not sick in the body, no," Tadek said slowly. "Not sick in a way that a physician could help. Not as far as I've been able to tell. But," and he looked at them both fiercely in turn, "you mustn't tell anyone about it. He doesn't want anyone to know, so keep your traps shut."

"How many times have you seen that happen?" Evemer asked quietly.

Tadek shrugged. "I didn't keep track. Three years ago, I was appointed to his core-guard for five months, and I didn't notice anything out of the ordinary—he was just shy and quiet, and he worried over little things sometimes, and always went out of his way to be polite and careful of all his kahyalar. And then last year, I was appointed to him again for eight months. Still normal, the first two, and then Her Majesty announced her pregnancy. About a week after that, I found him like he was just now. Shaking, scared out of his wits, saying he couldn't breathe and so on, even though I could see and hear him breathing."

"Fuck," Melek whispered.

"If it happens again, come get me," Tadek said firmly. "No matter what I'm doing, no matter what you're doing. If he goes down like that again, you drop everything and you *come get me*."

"Is it likely to happen again tonight?"

"Is he asleep, or did you leave him alone to wring his hands and work himself back into a state?"

"He's asleep," Evemer said tonelessly.

"Then that's probably it for the night. It takes a lot out of him. He'll be useless tomorrow, so everyone just . . ." Tadek opened his hands and made a calming gesture. "Be gentle. *Especially* you, Evemer, you make him nervous. And I know I'm just an armsman now and I don't have any right to be ordering you two around—"

"I don't think either of us cares about that right now, Tadek," Melek said.

Tadek blinked, a little taken aback, and glanced between çem and Evemer.

Evemer shrugged. "We all serve him the same."

"That's the last thing I thought I'd hear from *you*," Tadek said frankly. "I thought you'd be the one to pull rank."

"We all serve him the same," Evemer said again. He felt a little twinge—he probably *would* have pulled rank if given the chance. A personal weakness. Now that he had identified it, he would not give in to it, no matter how he was provoked.

Melek pushed çemself up onto one elbow. "Did you think we'd be awful about it?"

"It seemed like a reasonable assumption," Tadek said crisply. "*I* would have been awful about it."

"We're not witty like you, though," said Melek. "You're clever."

Tadek sighed. "Melek, you wouldn't be a kahya if you were *stupid*."

"No, I wouldn't," çe agreed. "But I have to try hard. Evemer too. You, though, everything comes naturally to you. And you notice things that other people don't."

Tadek looked perplexed, which Evemer could honestly relate to. "Well, darling, by the sounds of it, you've been noticing more things than I have."

Melek cuddled back into the pillows and blankets and gave him a winning smile. "Only because I've been trying hard."

"I have another question," Evemer said.

"Another one? Goodness. Shall we make a game of it? Drag the pillows and blankets onto the floor and build a fort and tell each other all our secrets?" Tadek said dryly, leaning back on his hands.

"What happened on the hunt?"

The amused look melted off Tadek's face until he looked hollow, but to his credit he held Evemer's gaze. He opened his mouth, but it took a long time for him to answer: "I fucked up."

"What happened?"

Melek sat up again, as intent as Evemer was. Tadek's posture didn't change. He didn't even twitch or clench his hands. He was entirely still, and Evemer couldn't help but begrudgingly approve. Tadek asked, his voice low, "Did His Highness say it was his fault? Did someone else blame him?"

"Yes," Evemer said.

"It's my fault. I did it. I fucked up. Not him."

Evemer only waited, looking steadily at him.

"Siranos threatened him," Melek said quietly. "I was with him when it happened. The night the princess was born, Siranos came up and grabbed him, said all sorts of wild things."

"He had an episode that night, after you left, Melek," Tadek said. "I came to his room to congratulate him on his niece, and he was already in the middle of it. He told me everything, and . . . I fucked up. Every other time he'd had an attack, it was always just flinching at shadows. And every other time, I calmed him down and showed him evidence that he was wrong—like you do with a spooked horse, you soothe them and you let them look at the thing that's terrifying until they see that it's not dangerous. He's always worried about taking up too much space, or stepping on people's toes, and every other time I just showed him people who loved him."

People who loved him . . . "Gülpaşa and Balaban?"

"I took them for drinks," Tadek said, finally dropping his eyes. "I asked—too many things. They were on edge by the end of it. Paranoid, worried. I thought it didn't matter because it was just proof of their love that I could show to His Highness. But kahyalar are terrible gossips." He gestured broadly among the three of them in the room. "Nothing like a midnight gossip, is there? Suddenly quite a lot of people were on edge, asking me what had happened or if His Highness needed anything, and I was—I was proud of them. Of us. I was *proud* that we were all so loyal, that we could all be together in loving him. I encouraged them, and when things went wrong, no one was thinking straight. So it was my fault. You may consider yourselves at liberty to lay the blame on me if His Highness starts claiming otherwise. I was careless."

The really frustrating part was how rational it all sounded—Siranos had gotten physical; Kadou had been afraid. Naturally, he'd confided in someone.

What would Evemer have done in that situation? Would he have done anything different from what Tadek had done? If His

Highness had told Evemer that someone had physically threatened him, had dared to *hurt* him, then . . . Well, what *had* Tadek done? Gathered a little group of people he trusted without question? Told them just enough to keep them watchful? That was their job, after all, just as Tadek said. They were supposed to be companions and servants, but before all else, their duty was to protect the lives of the Mahisti scions.

Evemer was not yet sure that his first assessment—either of Kadou or Tadek—had been *wrong,* per se, but evidently he hadn't been entirely right either. "Thank you. I'd better return to His Highness," he said quietly, and left without waiting for another word.

Commander Eozena nodded to him again as he passed by and let himself back into Kadou's bedroom. He gazed for a long time at the too-small lump under the blankets, where Kadou was still curled up tight with the sheets drawn up nearly to his forehead, and the spill of his black hair across the white pillow—he hadn't tied it up, and it was going to be tangled again in the morning.

The prince was, frankly, a disaster. It was like there were two Kadous, or possibly three Kadous, and Evemer hadn't yet found a way to reconcile them—one was cowardly, if that's what you could call it. Like a spooked horse, as Tadek had said, so maybe "persistent nervousness" was a better descriptor, not that one term or another made much of a difference.

And the other . . .

The other had quite literally saved Evemer's life less than an hour before. He could have run away, and he hadn't. He could have left Evemer to do his duty and die in the service of protecting his charge. And he hadn't. *That* Kadou had cut down their enemies—*their* enemies, their *shared* enemies—like they were so many stalks of wheat.

Evemer felt the lightning prickling through his veins again at the very memory. He put a hand off-center of his stomach, where he'd been punched, and the flare of a deep bruise there made it all real.

There'd been an instant, right as Kadou had killed the last one, when Evemer had felt . . .

He'd felt . . .

What had he felt?

It had been as if he'd been standing on a street corner, watching the crowds pass by, and sensed a presence at his shoulder, and turned—and there he was. There he was, familiar and comfortable. That's what it felt like. Like his heart, or whatever part of him it was that yearned for someone worthy to serve, had recognized the person he was meant to follow. The person he was meant to die for. There he was.

Evemer stared harder at Kadou, still shivering a little in sleep. There he was.

Well. All right, then.

CHAPTER SIX

K adou felt like paint scraped thin over a canvas, and it wasn't just the hangover. He'd barely eaten anything, despite coaxing from all the kahyalar as they went on and off of their attendance shifts.

They were all fussing over him, which was only to be expected from the others, but even Evemer was behaving strangely. He'd slept on the divan the night before, waking again as soon as Kadou stirred, sending Melek to bring Kadou tea, fussing quietly with the curtains on the bed so that Kadou was shielded from the light.

All morning, Evemer had been making himself available in a way that he hadn't before, a living *presence* rather than a statue standing at the door and waiting for Kadou's commands.

He'd all but loomed over Kadou during breakfast, watching him nibble halfheartedly at a sesame bun and listening intently when Eozena tactfully asked Kadou to explain his breakdown from the night before and whether it was likely to happen again. Kadou had deflected her questions as best he could, drawing her attention away from his health by telling her in hollow tones about what they'd found at the Shipbuilder's Guild.

Eozena made notes, agreed to send someone to fetch the evidence they'd uncovered, and then deftly brought the conversation around once more to the original topic. It was nothing, Kadou explained to her, just a minor episode, aftereffects of the shock from the attack. Kadou had sent Eozena away after they'd eaten (though "eat" was a generous overstatement for what Kadou had mostly failed to do with the food in front of him), but Evemer would not be dissuaded.

Kadou wished he could say anything to calm what was, for Evemer, a wild rampage of restless fidgeting. It was only making him fretful too.

He tried to read through Armagan's notes one more time, just to make sure he hadn't missed anything, but his head was aching and his nerves felt like they'd been scraped raw with the edge of a shard of broken glass. "Evemer," he said in a small voice, and Evemer's attention, already wholly focused on him, became as intense as a sunbeam through a lens.

"Highness," said Evemer. He had bruises—the imprint of fingers on his neck, a faint black eye, a cut high on his cheekbone and another on the opposite side of his jaw. Probably more under his clothes—the thieves had gotten at least a couple good punches to his stomach. "Is there something troubling you?"

He wouldn't have asked that yesterday. "Only what you'd expect."

"If there is anything you require." Others would have trailed off; Evemer said it as a statement with a definite end.

What had he meant to request, a moment ago? For Evemer to stop fixing so much of his attention on him? "Nothing," Kadou answered. "Never mind." He looked away, out the window, staring out over the garden. He couldn't go out again—not yet. Possibly not ever. Even if he took Eozena and Evemer both—you never knew what might happen. It wasn't safe.

"Highness." Evemer cleared his throat then, and said, "Your Highness seemed shaken last night."

Kadou choked out part of a laugh, more surprised than anything. Shaken—what tactful phrasing. "Yes, I suppose I was."

Evemer was silent for a long time; Kadou couldn't even hear him moving around the room. "I should apologize, Your Highness. I nearly failed in my duty to you."

"There's no such thing as a near failure," Kadou murmured. He didn't have to think about the words, just recited them as they had been taught to him. "Either you succeed or you don't. How close you come to either doesn't matter at all."

"Nevertheless. I was distracted. I didn't protect you as I should have."

Kadou closed his eyes. "There were more of them than there were of us."

He heard Evemer's almost imperceptible huff of frustration, so small that Evemer himself might not have noticed it. "I failed in my duty. I forced you to do what I should have been able to do myself."

"I told you I'd been trained for it." Kadou could feel his throat tightening again. The room seemed stuffy, his sash too tight about his waist.

"Nevertheless. I was charged to protect you. I should have protected you—not just from the thieves, but from having to do that."

"I don't know why you care about it all of a sudden." Kadou swallowed hard and tugged at his collars, loosening them around his neck a little.

"Because you found it . . . distasteful. Your Highness has the kahyalar to take care of all manner of distasteful tasks for you; that one should have been mine. For this, I'm sorry."

"It's forgiveness you want, is it? You have it, you're forgiven." He was sweltering in all these clothes—why had he chosen such a heavy kaftan? Why had he even bothered to change out of bed clothes when he wasn't likely to ever leave this room again?

"Highness, are you well?"

"Fine," Kadou snapped. "I'm fine." He squeezed his eyes shut. His hand drifted to his chest, clenched in the fabric over his heart until his knuckles ached with it. There—the first tremors beginning to course through his bones. Again.

"Respectfully, Highness, you're not."

"Well, what do you expect!" Kadou snarled toward Evemer. "In a situation like this, do you expect me to be fine?"

"Highness," Evemer said.

"You don't understand, do you?" The tremors were coming more strongly now, but Kadou shoved himself to his feet. Evemer rose as well, falling instantly into parade rest. "This isn't normal.

I'm doing everything I can to—to cope, to handle it with grace and dignity! My sister hates me, have you realized that?" Did she? She did, didn't she? Kadou felt as if he were being torn asunder by the teeth of his own uncertainty and those of the fear-creature as it rushed out of the shadows and locked its jaws around him. "She hates me enough that she nearly sent me into *exile*. Just by existing, I'm a threat to her, and it doesn't matter how much I love her. It doesn't matter that she's the only family I have left besides my grandparents—and I'll probably lose them too within the next few years. I made a mistake. I trusted the wrong people, and now she hates me, and she'll never forgive me. She would have *sent me away*! She's banned me from court!" His voice cracked at last. "I don't know who I am anymore. I don't know what to do. I feel like I've been shipwrecked. And now—now I've killed people, and—and you almost *died*—" He was trembling so hard he felt he'd fall apart at the joints, and he couldn't get enough air. His words came in small, frantic bursts as he wheezed for breath. He'd never had attacks two days in a row. He tried to fight it back—why did he have to be so weak? "It wasn't—I thought there were rules—I don't know this game, I don't know how to play this game—I thought the world worked—differently."

Evemer took hold of his arm, trying to guide him to sit on the divan by the open window.

Kadou shook him off. "I don't like hurting people," he managed to snarl. He hated these attacks, hated his body and his brain for crumbling like a cliff into the sea. It took a great effort of will, but he steeled himself against the wracking shivers. He was as power-less to stop them as he would have been to stop the incoming tide, but he set his shoulders, at least, and tightened his jaw, and stared Evemer down. "I'm fine," he said, shuddering and shuddering, his muscles as tight as steel bands. "I'm *fine*. Ignore this."

"Highness, Tadek is right outside the door, let me fetch—"

"*Stop.*"

Evemer froze.

"Don't," Kadou said. "*Don't*. Just ignore it."

Evemer stared him down for a moment and part of Kadou longed for him to refuse the order. "Yes, Your Highness." He clasped his hands behind his back, falling again into parade rest, and let his eyes slide off Kadou. He really was the perfect kahya. Obedient and unwavering. *Damn* him.

"I don't know who I am," Kadou continued.

"You are who you have always been," Evemer replied suddenly, unexpectedly. "You are the prince of Araşt. You're afraid of hurting people by misuse of your power. But you should have more confidence."

"In a position like mine, confidence gets people killed. I don't want any more blood on my hands. I won't do it."

"You could do great things."

"I don't want to be great."

"What *do* you want?"

"To be *good*. To keep my family safe." He wouldn't cry. Not in front of Evemer, of all people; Evemer, who already so obviously disdained him. He fought against it with every sinew. He wouldn't cry as long as he had a point he was trying to make. "The whole kingdom is my family, so it's hard. But if I stop trying, then I might as well be killing them myself." He let himself fall at last onto the divan, his strength gone. The wracking tremors overtook him again and he closed his eyes. Endured, like a ship lashed down tight through a hurricane. There was nothing to do but ride it out. "Even—even self-preservation—it's at the expense of other people. And I *can't*."

"Highness, will you allow me to apologize?" Evemer said. That unidentifiable feeling from the night before was rising again—shame. That's what it was, at least in part.

"What?"

"I'm sorry," he said. "I have served you poorly."

"You apologized already, and I forgave you already."

Evemer stared down at his own feet. He was burning with that shame now; he could feel how hot his face was. "I don't mean for last night, Highness," he said. "I have not behaved as a kahya ought. I have dishonored the oaths I swore."

"What are you talking about?" Kadou's fidgeting had slowed, though he was still trembling fiercely.

"I have been . . . ungracious." He felt as if he should be kneeling, perhaps like he should have his forehead pressed to the carpet or to the back of Kadou's hands in supplication, but he did not deserve even that—he would stand, and confess to his wrongs like a child being scolded. "Last night, after Your Highness went to bed, Tadek and Melek told me the truth of what happened—the hunting party and the circumstances leading to it. I realized that I formed my first conclusions on shaky evidence, and I allowed them to influence my actions. I do not *ask* for forgiveness," he added swiftly. "I would rather prove that I—"

"Do you mean how I can tell that you don't like me?"

Evemer would not stoop to flinching as if he'd been slapped. Kadou's voice hadn't even been particularly sharp, but he was still shivering, worrying at a tassel on the corner of a pillow, though his breathing had steadied. Evemer's treacherous instincts tried to protest it, his mind offering forth more of that nonsense about how a prince should present himself—with poise and confidence and so forth. He shoved the thought back sharply. Perhaps that was true, perhaps it wasn't. It wasn't for him to criticize his liege. "I had . . . hesitations. That was not appropriate to my place."

"Of course it is." Kadou's voice was rough. "A kahya isn't supposed to be an automaton. You're *supposed* to think. You're supposed to be a person."

Evemer wasn't entirely sure how to reconcile this with the rest of what he knew. He was silent for a moment, gazing down at Kadou's slippers—pretty ones of soft fawn-colored suede with pointed toes and beading and piercework decorations, too delicate for outdoor wear. He'd worn tall riding boots the night before, much like the boots the kahyalar wore with their uniforms. They'd been well kept, but showing signs of *use*, though not quite yet *wear*.

The cadets had taken them away last night to try to get the blood polished out.

"I didn't thank you, Highness," he said quietly. "For saving my life."

Kadou went tense again. "You needn't," he said.

"You don't want to hurt anyone, but you did last night. To save me."

"What did you expect me to do? Leave you there to die? You're my kahya, whether or not you like me. You're a person who is sworn to me, and I have obligations. I wouldn't have left you there, or—or Eozena, or the others—"

"Let's not pretend Commander Eozena would have *needed* you to stay," Evemer said, before he could stop himself, and then glanced up at Kadou again for the first time, horrified. He'd *interrupted* his liege.

Kadou didn't seem to have noticed. "No. She wouldn't have. But I don't want to talk about it, and I don't want you to feel like you've failed in anything. It's *nothing.*"

It wasn't nothing, but His Highness didn't necessarily need to know that. If this was something that was just Evemer's, then so be it. He could let it change him, let it change how he thought about his liege without ever letting Kadou know the whys of it, or the way that it had thrown Evemer's world out of balance, the way it had given him a new center of gravity, a sun to orbit, a star to follow.

"As you wish, Your Highness." The hot shame still burned within him, but Kadou had quite rightfully left it between Evemer and his conscience. He was not entitled to forgiveness or even the possibility thereof simply because he had deigned to apologize for his behavior, nor did he require guidance in being better, only his own choice, his own determination and resolve.

His Highness said Evemer was supposed to be a person, not an automaton. If that were true, then by all the laws of fealty, Evemer had to reciprocate and allow the same of his liege: imperfection.

He had to forgive His Highness before he ever deserved the same in return.

It was several minutes before Evemer spoke again. Kadou did not dismiss him or command him to sit, so Evemer still stood there, hands behind his back. "Do you really believe Her Majesty would have sent you away?" he asked quietly.

"Yes. I had to talk her out of it."

"Her Majesty is not unreasonable," Evemer said carefully. "And she would not so easily cast her family aside." He could see what Tadek had meant now, when he'd compared Kadou's nervousness to that of a spooked horse shying from a shadow.

"My sister Zeliha might not, but *Her Majesty* Zeliha might have no choice," Kadou said. "You can't make decisions purely on emotion when you're sultan." He shook his head—he hadn't wanted his hair dressed that morning, evidently, so it was hanging loose and uncombed around his shoulders. "Usmim have mercy on me, will you *please* sit? You're making me nervous."

Evemer obeyed, folding to the carpet right where he stood and crossing his legs tailor-style. "You're not without resources. You have opportunities to change her mind and prove your loyalty, earn her forgiveness."

Kadou laughed sharply. "What, by uncovering whatever Armagan's done and tidying up the mess? By doing the bare minimum I was asked to be responsible for?"

"Highness," Evemer said, and Kadou sighed.

"You're allowed to say you disagree with me. What am I going to do, have you whipped? After I saved your life?"

"If Your Highness doesn't want me to talk about that," Evemer said quietly, "then I'd rather you didn't joke about it either."

Kadou swallowed hard and looked away. "Yes, of course. Sorry." His hands trembled again, and he clenched them tight in his lap around fistfuls of his kaftan. "That was . . . You're right, of course, and I'm sorry."

Evemer bit his tongue—he'd never wanted to talk about anything like this before, not really. He'd never much wanted to talk at all, at least to most people. His mother was the only exception. He wrote ten-page letters to her two or three times a week, and he visited her every time he had a day off and told her everything in

exhaustive detail—at least, everything he was allowed to. These last weeks, he had hesitated to vent to her about all his resentment about Kadou, fearing that it might violate some aspect of the prince's privacy. With everyone else, he rarely saw any need to speak his thoughts. He'd had entire conversations with Eozena by saying nothing but "Yes, Commander. No, Commander. Commander."

So why was he finding himself so *chatty* with Kadou? He had not had more than a glass of small beer for weeks, yet he kept finding his tongue loosened as if he were drunk, stirring to speech before he had a chance to think of what he was going to say and whether it was worth saying it.

Even more bewilderingly, he was *frustrated* with His Highness for forbidding him to speak of what had happened.

Why *couldn't* they talk about it? There were so many things that Evemer was realizing that he didn't understand, and it sounded like there were things His Highness didn't understand either. How ridiculous would they feel if they discovered they each had the other's answer? If they could have just shared what they knew, and how they felt about what had happened, and found . . . common ground? Or at least a way to make sense of their own reactions?

Or even the simplest exchange: "I'm glad neither of us died" and "I'm glad of that too"? That would have been enough.

Evemer had never talked like that to anyone. He'd never shared his thoughts with anyone except, again, his mother. Not even one of the temple aunts, whose *job* it was to listen and help unburden you of your troubles. There'd never been a reason to do so. He didn't know what he would say to Kadou now, if he were permitted. His tongue didn't know the language.

When I was young, he might say, *six or seven, before my body-father died and my mother brought me to the city, I made all my friends play the kahyalar game. We'd all go off into a clearing we knew in the forest, and we'd lay out sticks in a square on the ground and pretend it was a palace—here, the throne room; and here, the barracks; and here, the stables, and the banquet hall, and the royal chambers. And we'd fill*

it with pebbles for treasures and rush around playing at being impor-
tant, the kahyalar of a sultan or a lord . . .

Then, perhaps, Kadou might ask who got to play the lord, and
Evemer would have to tell him: *No one did. I didn't let them. They*
weren't worthy of it.

You, though. You might be, if I can figure out what you are.

You stayed to save me. I'd be dead if it weren't for you.

There's something there, beneath the surface of you. And it might be
the right thing, the thing I missed in all the others.

But he couldn't say any of that.

"I'm sure Her Majesty doesn't intend to shut you out forever,"
he said instead. "And if your goal is to prove your loyalty to her,
then I believe in time there will be some opportune moment. You
can do something that will strengthen Her Majesty's political position somehow. Or rescue someone important, or—or capture a
pirate fleet," he added, and was bewildered with himself about
why he'd say *that*, of all things, until Kadou snorted and he realized with an even stronger wave of bewilderment that he'd been
trying to make His Highness laugh.

And he'd . . . succeeded?

And for some reason that felt good.

He'd never wanted to make anyone laugh, either, any more
than he'd wanted to talk about something troubling. Perhaps that
was just what happened to you when someone saved your life: You
just started to . . . *like* them? Could he go so far as to say he liked
Kadou already? Surely not. He said interesting things about coins
when he was drunk—damned interesting! Interesting enough to
listen to for hours, and a huge relief from watching him mope
about. But . . . Kadou had pointed out, embarrassingly but correctly, that Evemer *didn't* like him. More accurate now to say he
hadn't.

But another opportunity to like him had opened up, a second
chance.

Evemer cleared his throat and sat up straighter. "I should apologize again too," he said, before Kadou could rebuke him, if he
was going to. "I shouldn't make light of subjects like this either."

"It's all right," Kadou whispered, though it was clear it was not, quite.

"But I do think Her Majesty will forgive you, in time. I have faith in her, and in her love for you."

Kadou smiled sadly. "Thank you for saying so." He took a breath. "I suppose I should get dressed and go talk to Armagan," he said.

"Highness," Evemer said, and went to lay out the formal clothes.

❈

As agreed, Commander Eozena met Kadou at the Gold Gate. "Feeling better, Your Highness?"

Not particularly, Kadou thought. His head still ached from the alcohol hangover, and he felt greyish and drained from the emotional one—but it would not do to complain. "A little better, yes," he said.

She came closer and lowered her voice. "This morning you said you'd left that battering ram with the guards at the Shipbuilder's Guild, right? It was supposed to be kept there until we could fetch it?"

Kadou's headache sharpened. "What happened to it?"

"I sent someone. She came back about half an hour ago and said that nobody there had any idea what she was talking about. Nothing to be found, no records of it. There's *something going on,*" she said, her voice now barely louder than a hiss.

Kadou closed his eyes. "Who were the guards at the guild last night? Kahyalar?"

"Two of them were. Fringe-guard, supervising the other eight, employed by the guild. So either *our* people are involved, or theirs are."

"I guess we have an investigation after all," Kadou said. Dammit. He felt rather resigned and unsurprised about the whole thing—perhaps last night and this morning had drained all his reserves of fear. "Let's go talk to Armagan, then."

When they arrived, Armagan was working quietly in çir office in the Copper Court, bent over a writing desk and scribbling what looked like an extremely long letter. "Your Highness," çe said when they came in, surprised but not unwelcoming. Çe rose, came around the desk, and bowed. "And Commander Eozena. I . . . wasn't expecting you. Did you send word?"

"No," Eozena said. She strode forward into the room, looking around briefly—*once a kahya, always a kahya*, Kadou mused to himself. They all checked rooms like that, cataloging doors, windows, dangers.

Evemer and Sanem posted themselves at the door as he followed Eozena in. "We were just passing by," Kadou said. "And we were curious about something. We thought you might have some insights."

Armagan spread çir hands. "Of course. How can I help?"

"The Shipbuilder's Guild," Eozena said. "Funny thing." She helped herself to Armagan's desk chair, tipped it back, and put her heels up on the desk. Her long brown fingers tapped the armrests. "How did the thieves get in?"

Armagan frowned slightly. "They bashed the doors in—you were there, you saw the damage."

"What did they use, though?"

"A . . . battering ram? One presumes?"

"It would have had to be pretty heavy, wouldn't it?"

"I suppose so," çe said. "It would have to be. Sorry, was this what you were wondering about, Commander?" Çir eyes flickered between her and Kadou.

Eozena glanced at Kadou with a question in her eyes—did he want to ask anything? He shook his head. He was busy watching Armagan. She turned back. "Was there any trace of such a thing at the scene?"

"Not that we found, Commander."

"One of the guild guards discovered the thieves in the process of ransacking the offices, isn't that right?"

Armagan was getting tenser now—Eozena wasn't doing a very good job of disguising her tone. She sounded like she was interrogating çem. "Yes," çe said. "I've written as much in my notes."

"She ran them off, did she?"

"That's what she told us."

"So what happened to the ram?"

"I beg your pardon, Commander, I don't quite follow."

Eozena dropped her heels off the desk, the front two legs of the chair slamming back to the ground. She sat forward with her elbows on her knees. "That big heavy battering ram, Lieutenant," she said. "When the thieves got run off, did they stop to collect it and haul it away with them?"

"You're asking me to speculate," Armagan said. Çe was getting frustrated. "But if I have to, then I'd say that seems like a logical conclusion. It couldn't have just walked off on its own."

"Couldn't it? Did you look around for it?"

"Of course."

Kadou's mouth went dry. Evemer had been there for the investigation. Evemer had said that they hadn't looked for it at all. Armagan's notes had never mentioned a search either.

A lie. His heart stuttered and quickened in his chest.

"And you didn't find it?" Eozena asked.

Armagan spread çir hands again. "We don't always get that lucky."

"I did," Kadou said. "Get that lucky, I mean. Though it didn't take much."

Armagan stared at him. "I beg your pardon, Highness?"

"His Highness," Eozena said, "went to the guild last night around midnight. He had one kahya and one lamp. Now, in a shipyard, there's a lot of wood—a whole haystack of wood, one might say. And yet His Highness managed to find the proverbial needle fairly easily. Wooden needle, wooden haystack, and yet—how long did it take you to find it?"

"Less than an hour. Less than half an hour, probably. In the dark," Kadou said. "I was also . . . you know. Drunk."

Eozena slouched back in the chair and laced her fingers together across her stomach. "Thoughts on that, Armagan?"

"I . . . I'm afraid I don't know what to say. Please don't take this the wrong way, Your Highness, but how can you be certain of what you found? Especially if it was dark, especially that late at night when you must have been tired. Especially if you were . . . intoxicated."

"My kahya, Lieutenant Hoşkadem, was with me," Kadou said. "He was posted with the guild investigation just before his promotion, and he says that he's unaware that there were any efforts at all to search the shipyard for evidence."

"He must be mistaken," Armagan said.

"You recorded an exhaustive amount of other details, Lieutenant," Eozena said. "Why not record the search?"

"I—I must have forgotten."

"I wonder what else you forgot to make note of?" Eozena stood slowly. "Highness, may I request a moment alone in the room with Lieutenant Armagan?"

Kadou nodded weakly. "Of course, Commander." She was going to arrest çem. It probably *was* better for him to be out of the room for that, in case Armagan got . . . violent. He retreated just outside, leaving the door open, and leaned against the wall next to Evemer.

"Right," Eozena said from within. "Are you going to make this easy?"

※

Of course Armagan's office and personal quarters had to be gutted and searched.

Kadou left all this to Eozena and her people. It was her jurisdiction, after all, since she was one of Armagan's direct supervisors. She wouldn't appreciate him hanging around behind her, wringing his hands and being useless, and in any case he had a much more daunting task.

He had to go tell Zeliha.

He hadn't seen her in weeks, except at a great distance, surrounded by kahyalar and ministers. He hadn't dared to show up at her rooms for breakfast. To be fair, though, she hadn't invited him either.

She couldn't turn him away again, not today. Not for this. He had an excuse this time. If her kahyalar declined to let him near her, he could say it was important without lying.

"Do either of you know what Her Majesty's schedule is today?" Kadou asked his kahyalar.

"It is the second hour of the afternoon," Evemer replied immediately. "Unless Her Majesty has been detained on some important matter, the official schedule included a gap of an hour and a half. It is presumed she will be at leisure in the gardens near the royal chambers." *It is presumed* was a phrase that meant the kahyalar's gossip network was in good working condition. All the core-guard had access to the sultan's official schedule, though not all of them had reason to keep themselves apprised of it. Through sheer familiarity with Zeliha and her habits, the kahyalar could make reasonable guesses about where she might be and what she might be doing during any unscheduled time in her day.

Evemer's guess was, indeed, correct: They found Zeliha in the pavilion in her garden. White silk curtains hung from the eaves on the sunward side, casting shade over the couches within. Most of her kahyalar were positioned at a bit of a distance—one stood at the corner pillar of the pavilion, but the other three were arrayed fifteen or twenty feet away. Enough space to give her the illusion of privacy, but close enough that a word from her could bring them all to her side.

Zeliha herself was lounging on one of those couches, idly reading a book. Kadou was too close to turn away when he saw that she wasn't alone—Siranos sat cross-legged on the carpeted floor with Eyne swaddled up in the cradle of his lap, brushing her nose with the tip of a soft feather and grinning down at her. Kadou's heart thumped unpleasantly in his chest, and he forced away all his feelings with a frantic shove before they could do anything more than that.

He stopped at the edge of the pavilion and bowed. "Majesty," he said softly. "Good afternoon." Out of the corner of his eye, he saw Siranos look up. Kadou didn't look over, though it took all his will. He kept his eyes fixed on Zeliha.

Looking up from her book, she said blankly, "Oh. Kadou. What are you doing here?"

"There's a matter. That I need to discuss with you. If you have a moment? I'm sorry for interrupting."

"No, no," she said quickly. She sat up, putting a ribbon in the book to mark her place and setting it aside. "Please come in, sit down."

She didn't *seem* like she was still angry with him.

He stepped into the pavilion and sat on the edge of one of the couches, folding his hands in his lap. Gods, he was nervous. He took a breath or two—just one of Usmim's trials, he told himself. Just something that had to be gotten through. And for goodness' sake, this was his *sister*. "If it would be possible for us to speak privately?"

Zeliha grimaced. "How long is this going to take?" she asked. "I've promised Siranos that I wouldn't let business interrupt us this time."

"Only a few minutes," he said hesitantly. "It . . . it can't wait. I'm sorry."

"Only a few minutes," she said brightly to Siranos. "Do you mind?"

Even the mere beat of hesitation before Siranos spoke was agony. "Of course not, Your Majesty," he said. Kadou was almost shocked to hear Siranos speak so calmly and pleasantly. "I'll just take a turn around the garden." He gathered Eyne into his arms and got awkwardly to his feet.

"Oh, wait," Zeliha said. She looked earnestly at Kadou. "Eyne hasn't seen you in a few weeks either. Do you want to hold her?"

Yes. Yes, he did. He missed her suddenly and ferociously. He was about to say as much when Siranos said easily, "Oh. Yes, of course," and that was shocking too. Perhaps Siranos was only being polite because they were in front of Zeliha. Kadou watched him, suspicious, as Siranos stepped forward and handed Eyne over to him.

"Thank you," Kadou said carefully. And he was glad he was already sitting when Siranos . . . *smiled* at him. He hadn't smiled at Kadou in months. Not since before Zeliha had announced her pregnancy, at least.

"Of course," Siranos replied. Then, half to Zeliha, he said, "I'm getting used to everyone wanting a turn with her."

"Can you blame them?" Zeliha said, grinning.

"Not at all. She's as beautiful as her mother." He took her hand, kissed her knuckles, and then dipped to kiss her cheek. Straightening, he nodded once more to Kadou, saying softly, "If you'll excuse me."

He left. Kadou stared after him. Why was he being so polite? What was he up to? Kadou might have spent an hour picking apart every word Siranos had said, but the spite and paranoia vanished like morning mist in the sun the moment he looked down at Eyne. "Mother of all," he said with astonishment. "She's gotten *big*." She was appreciably heavier than the last time he'd held her, two—three?—weeks ago. Her eyes were a purer, darker blue, and her chubby cheeks had gotten so round and fat and *perfect* that he couldn't quite comprehend how she was possible.

He couldn't spare a second thought for Siranos. When Zeliha said something, it wasn't until several moments later that Kadou realized she had been addressing him. He looked up sharply. "Sorry, what did you say?"

"I said, 'What did you want to tell me about?'" she said, with an amused half smile. "But take your time."

"Oh. Um." He tore his attention away from Eyne. "Eozena has just arrested Lieutenant Armagan of the ministry of enquiry."

"Gods above and below. On what charges?"

"Suspicion of çir involvement with the incident at the Shipbuilder's Guild," Kadou said, settling on the reclining couch and shifting Eyne in his arms so she was cuddled against his shoulder. "We've uncovered some new evidence. Eozena is having Armagan's quarters searched."

"But Armagan is a kahya," Zeliha said blankly.

"I know." It wasn't a comfortable thought—the kahyalar were supposed to be unfailingly loyal. "We're not completely sure yet, of course."

"But you had reason to believe it. *Eozena* believed it."

Of course she'd put more stock in Eozena's judgment than his. He couldn't blame her.

"When will she know for certain?"

He shrugged the shoulder that didn't have a baby on it. "Soon, I imagine."

Zeliha nodded. Her expression was drawn, ill at ease.

"I'm sorry," Kadou said suddenly. "For interrupting, I mean."

"Don't be."

"You were having a nice afternoon with Siranos and I've . . . barged in and mucked it up."

"You haven't mucked up anything," she said, half reclining again. She sighed. "I shouldn't have promised Siranos—well. Never mind, that's nothing you need to worry about. Was that the extent of your news for me?"

"Roughly. For now."

She nodded, sighed again. Her gaze flicked up from Kadou to something behind him. She gave another one of those slow, pleased half smiles, though this one was somewhat more tired than before. "Lieutenant Hoşkadem," she said. "I take it you like children?"

"Yes, Your Majesty," Evemer said. Kadou half turned to look at him, and found that Eyne had at some point reached out to him. Evemer had apparently reached back, and now Eyne had one of his fingers gripped in her perfect little hand and was trying to eat it. Evemer apparently had no objection to this. He was nearly *smiling*. Kadou could just see the edges of it around his eyes.

Baffling and unexpected. Kadou turned back.

"Do you have any of your own?" Zeliha asked.

"No, Your Majesty."

"You just like them?"

"Yes, Your Majesty."

"You can hold her if you want," Zeliha said, magnanimous. "If Kadou will let her go."

Kadou felt like he didn't particularly need another person with whom he had to fight for time with his niece, but Evemer was harder to spite than Siranos, and . . . he was sort of curious. He looked at Eyne—she was staring up at Evemer with enormous eyes as if he had just revealed something shocking and life-altering to her, and now she *was* actually slobbering on his hand, and Kadou didn't know what to do with any of this information except wave a white flag and surrender.

"I don't mind," Kadou said slowly. Evemer promptly and decisively plucked Eyne out of his arms.

Siranos didn't return for another ten minutes, and when he did, Kadou was almost grateful to see him. Eyne had gotten all chatty with Evemer, squawking and burbling at him while Evemer got just as chatty in return, carrying on half of a deadly serious conversation with her and calling her *Highness* with the same depth of gravity that he used for Kadou, if not more. Kadou almost wanted to turn around and demand to know whether Evemer had replaced himself with an identical twin, except that *nobody* but Evemer Hoşkadem said "Highness" in that particular way, with that particular incredible nuance of meaning.

Zeliha turned to Siranos with a smile as he entered the pavilion again and held out her hand. He came forward and took it obligingly, sitting on the ground by her couch and watching Evemer. "She's won another heart, has she?" he said.

"She's as charming as her body-father," Zeliha murmured back. Kadou couldn't look at them, and he couldn't look at Evemer (who was murmuring to Eyne, "Yes, Your Highness, did you know that you also have a nose? Thank you for holding on to mine, I was concerned," in the same grave manner he might have said, "Yes, Your Majesty, the harbor tax collected this month totaled one hundred and twenty-six thousand altınlar").

For lack of anywhere else to look that wasn't supremely awkward, Kadou looked out across the garden and was therefore the first to spot Eozena in the distance, walking toward them at a brisk pace, nearly a jog, with her sword strapped to her hip.

"Zeliha, if you've finished," Siranos said, "perhaps His Highness might give us our privacy—"

"Wait, please," Kadou said, rising to his feet. Something was wrong. "Evemer," he said urgently. Evemer stopped in the middle of whatever he was saying to Eyne. "Give her back to Zeliha. Right now." Out of the corner of his eye, he saw Evemer obey instantly.

His heart was pounding. What was it? What had Eozena found?

"Kadou?" Zeliha said.

"Wait, please," he said again. He went to meet the commander. Evemer followed close behind.

Eozena shoved a handful of coins at him as soon as she was close enough. "Highness. Confirm these," she said.

As soon as the metal hit his palms, he knew: counterfeits. The signature of the altınlar clanked hollowly rather than ringing clear; the yiralar tasted bitter in his fingertips, almost medicinal, rather than the delicate notes of white tea and snow.

He didn't even need to say anything. Eozena made a cutting motion at Evemer with one hand, the other gripping the hilt of her sword. *"Distance. Now."*

"Commander," Evemer barked. Immediately, he took ten paces backward from Kadou and jerked to stiff attention, staring straight ahead.

"What?" Kadou said faintly, but Eozena seized his arm, pulling him forward with her.

"Distance!" she snarled at the kahya standing at the corner pillar of the pavilion. The woman's eyes widened and she scrambled away with the same speed as Evemer. Then, to Kadou and Zeliha: *"Stay."*

It was a voice he hadn't heard since he was a child, and he knew Zeliha hadn't either. It was the voice of someone saying, *Your life is in my hands; obey me so that I can save it.* He went to his sister's side and found her coming to his, seizing his hand, clutching her daughter to her chest.

Siranos had risen too and he joined them. "What's happening?"

"Eozena, what is it?" Zeliha said, sounding more like his sister in that moment than she had since the day she had been crowned sultan.

"A moment, Your Majesty," Eozena said. She looked around

at the kahyalar arrayed around the garden. Stabbing her finger at a spot on the ground twenty paces distant from the pavilion, she roared, *"Fall in."*

Every kahya in earshot obeyed. There were eight of them, and they formed two neat cobalt lines of four at perfect attention.

Kadou's hands were trembling. So were Zeliha's, he noticed distantly. He huddled closer to her side and she put an arm around his shoulder, drawing him in still further. Siranos edged in front of them, putting himself between them and the squad of kahyalar.

Eozena barked at the kahyalar, *"Stand.* And with the gods as my witness, if even one of you takes a step forward, the others have leave to *kill them."*

Eight kahyalar stood stock-still. They didn't even twitch or blink. They might have been statues.

Eozena whirled on Kadou and Zeliha, assessed them with a glance. "Majesty," she said. "Highness. I am invoking the privileges of my station."

"Yes," Zeliha said. Her voice was steadier than Kadou's would have been. "Yes, I rather see that you are. What is it?"

"Lieutenant Armagan is guilty," she said bluntly. "I found a *chest* of coins in çir quarters, which His Highness has just confirmed are counterfeits. I also found two other kahyalar in the process of destroying some of Armagan's personal papers."

Kadou felt Zeliha draw a sharp breath. "So it's not an isolated incident."

"No, Your Majesty. It's a fucking conspiracy, right under my nose. Until I can swear on my life about which of your kahyalar are loyal and true, *none of us* are moving from this spot."

Kadou was familiar with fear. It was an old friend. But there was something about being confronted with the idea that the people who stood behind you had blades that they could use *against you* that went beyond fear. It was an open and barren wasteland so cold that it made mere *fear* seem like a cool breeze off the sea.

The core-guard could go anywhere in the palace and barely be questioned. They could walk directly into Zeliha's bedchamber, or Kadou's. The kahyalar dressed them, bathed them, fed them, watched over them while they slept, treated their illnesses. Kadou had never once in his life even idly entertained the idea that they might turn on him. If they wanted to, it would be easy. It would be *appallingly* easy. He and Zeliha wouldn't last five minutes.

"How can we possibly—" Zeliha stopped, took a breath. "That Inachan satyota we consulted about Azuta Melachrinos. Has he left?" Oh, yes, a satyota—a satyota, who could read the lie out of someone's eyes—

"Weeks ago," Eozena said tightly. "And even if he were here . . ."

"There are too many kahyalar," Zeliha said softly. "There's thousands of them. How can we possibly . . . There must be another satyota in the city. There *must* be. We can have them summoned, we can—they could at least test a *few*—"

Except that satyota could lie. Except that perhaps there wasn't one in the city, and even if there were, it would take hours to find them, and it would still be *kahyalar* doing the searching—

Kadou felt rather faint. There were two hundred kahyalar and cadets just to sort through the *flour* in the palace kitchens. In the whole country, counting ministers, there were more than ten thousand.

Kadou found himself looking toward the eight kahyalar standing at attention. Evemer was at one end of the front row. Surely *he* was loyal, wasn't he? He could have let Kadou be killed by those thieves in the alley. He could have reached out and snapped Kadou's neck whenever he wanted to. He could have—

But it was *Evemer*. He wouldn't. Not five minutes ago, he'd held Kadou's niece in his arms, and Kadou had turned his back on them and felt perfectly safe doing so.

Kadou pulled away from Zeliha's side. She clutched at his shoulder, but he pushed her hand away.

"Kadou," Eozena said. "Kadou, *stand*."

"Wait," he said, walking forward. His life was not the most important—Zeliha's and Eyne's were. He was just . . . the spare. So many of his duties were asinine, ceremonial tasks that any decent automaton could have carried out. But this, this was something that only he could do.

He stopped in front of his kahya.

"Evemer," he whispered. "At rest."

Evemer fell into parade rest and looked down at him. "Highness," he said.

Kadou took a breath. "Draw your sword," he said gently. There was only a flicker of hesitation in Evemer's eyes before he obeyed.

"Kadou," Eozena said warningly, and then: "Kahyalar! *Distance.*"

Seven of them retreated. Kadou, trembling all over, held Evemer's eyes. His kahya didn't move.

"My lord," Evemer said. "I am at your service."

"Put your sword to my neck."

"No."

Kadou reached out, took the hand that held the sword, pulled it toward him—

Evemer jerked away and cast the blade aside, falling to his knees, pressing his palms and forehead to the grass even as he said, "*No.*"

"Look at me." Evemer sat back on his heels and looked up at him. Kadou reached out, brushed a piece of grass out of his hair. "Are you true? Do you swear it?"

"My lord, I will not raise a hand against you, even if you order me," Evemer said. "But if you ask it of me, I will cut that hand off for you."

Kadou was no satyota, but Evemer's voice rang like the touch-taste of pure gold in his fingertips. "What if Her Majesty asked you? Would you?"

"Yes, my lord," Evemer said. His gaze didn't waver from Kadou's face. He didn't even blink. His eyes were as black as the night sky, and as resolute and unwavering as the stars. "But first I would beg for mercy."

Kadou held his gaze, yearning to see something that would make him beyond certain. He felt in his heart and his gut that it was enough, that Evemer of all people was the last one who would waver from his oaths. If it had only been Kadou's own life, it would have been enough.

He glanced at the sword lying a few feet away. "Your left hand or your right?" By all Usmim's trials, what was he asking? What *was* this? Did he think this was some kind of epic poem where princes could blithely ask their kahyalar to work miracles?

But . . . Zeliha's life. Eyne's. He *had* to be sure. He had to push. He had to harry Evemer right unto the outermost bounds of his faith.

He looked back at Evemer, who was looking down at his hands where they lay flat on his thighs. "I'm right-handed," he said. "But I obey my lord's command."

"Left, then."

Evemer nodded sharply. "May I tie a tourniquet?"

"Yes."

Evemer unknotted his sash, pulled it free of his scabbard's loops. He tried to push up the sleeve of his kaftan, but it was quickly clear that it would get in the way of his tourniquet's knot. He shook the kaftan off his shoulders and let it pool in the grass around his hips. His smooth bare skin was golden in the sunshine, and his shoulders somehow seemed even broader. His musculature, his form and proportions—he looked like the dream of what a kahya should be. He knotted the sash around his forearm properly now, using his teeth to pull it tight. Not tight enough, Kadou saw. Not as tight as a surgeon's would have been—probably not enough to fully stop the blood flow. But tight enough to reduce it, and better than nothing, the best that Evemer could do on himself without assistance. "Please step back, my lord."

"I'm going to watch."

"I don't want to get blood on your clothes."

Kadou didn't move.

Evemer leaned over to get the sword. He braced his elbow across his leg, took a deep breath, and raised the blade.

"Stop," Kadou said.

Evemer looked up curiously at him. "My lord?"

"Stop."

Evemer lowered the sword. The veins on his strong golden arm were beginning to stand out. "My lord."

"Get up. Get dressed. That's enough."

Evemer gazed at him for a long moment. "Are you sure?"

"Yes."

After a moment, Evemer's shoulders slumped. He didn't look away from Kadou for a moment as he unknotted the tourniquet, flexed his hand to get the blood flowing again, sheathed the sword, pulled his kaftan back on and buttoned it, and tied his sash. He rubbed briefly at the place on his forearm where the tourniquet had been tied—it probably hadn't taken long enough for his skin to bruise or show a mark beyond the imprinted creases of the fabric, but Kadou wondered how long the invisible band of lingering ache would last.

Evemer got to his feet and bowed. "Thank you, my lord."

Kadou led him back to the pavilion. "Here's one, at least."

Eozena was nearly apoplectic. "*What in the gods' names?*"

"Well," said Zeliha. "I suppose that's . . . a method. No good using it on the others, though. They know the ending now."

"Majesty. Commander," said Evemer, and saluted smartly. "I am at your service. What are your orders?"

"First, stop giving me a fucking *heart attack*," Eozena snapped. "That goes for both of you! Gods! What's wrong with you?" She put a hand to her forehead. "Gods, Hoşkadem! Would you really have—"

"Yes," Evemer said.

She seized him by the front of his kaftan and shook him. "You're not supposed to obey orders if they're criminal!" she screamed. "Do you know what a criminal order is?"

"Yes. His Highness asked me to put my sword to his throat."

"He refused, but don't court-martial him," Kadou said. He put his hand on Eozena's arm, tried to pry her off Evemer.

She rounded on him. "And *you*! Do you think I saved you from drowning in ten inches of water to have you pull that kind of nonsense?"

"Someone had to," Kadou said. "Better me than Zeliha." He pulled away and glanced around at the others—Zeliha had gotten distracted by Eyne, who was fussing. Siranos's eyes were darting around as if he felt like bolting and didn't know which way to go.

"Eozena, unless you have some better idea, we're going to go inside," Zeliha said, nodding to the building that housed her quarters. "We will bar the doors. There's still the leftovers of my lunch, which wasn't poisoned, so we'll eat that for dinner."

"I can't secure that building with one other person *and* figure out which of your kahyalar might be disloyal," Eozena hissed.

Zeliha held up one hand. "You're frightened. So am I."

"Three kahyalar! Three! Likely more that stole evidence from the Shipbuilder's Guild last night! And that's just today— Armagan has a dozen kahyalar working under çir command, and there's no way of knowing how many *they* might have turned to their side. Who has Armagan been spying for? What information did çe pass along? Whatever çe told them, it was worth a *chest* of counterfeit coins! Armagan wasn't in charge." Eozena stalked back and forth through the length of the pavilion like a pacing wolf. "Counterfeits! Twice in the space of a month! Do you want to gamble on explaining it as mere coincidence? I don't! Did Armagan know they were counterfeit? Impossible to say, but a payment like that, çe must have been contracted for something more than just spywork. Would you rather wait and see how it plays out?"

"Eozena," Zeliha tried to say.

"Fine, yes, Majesty. Go in the house," Eozena said. "Evemer, escort them and lock all the doors. Don't let anyone near until I come back. I'm going to find some way to—to *deal with this*."

"Send for Tadek," Kadou said.

Zeliha and Eozena both groaned in unison.

"He is loyal," Kadou said firmly. "He fought for me and he would have died for me. He never hesitated—it's hardly any different than what Evemer nearly did just now. And . . ." He gestured helplessly. "He knows *everyone*. He has skills that would be useful to you, Eozena."

"Skills that got him stripped of his uniform a month ago," she growled, but Kadou could see she was relenting—beggars couldn't, after all, be choosers. "Just *go*, please."

❈

Evemer kept his hand on the hilt of his sword and his awareness as sharp as its blade. An hour passed, and then a second—he passed the time by pacing around Her Majesty's chambers, checking each window and balcony, testing the locks on every door, jumping out of his skin at the slightest unexpected noise, and keeping an obsessive inventory of his charges and their personal equilibrium.

Her Majesty was tense, but she was exuding an aura of calm composure that Evemer found both admirable and reassuring. The only tell that gave away her underlying nerves was that she wouldn't let go of Princess Eyne, even when she fell asleep against Her Majesty's shoulder and could have been laid in her cradle.

His lord had found a chair in the shade on the balcony. Part of Evemer wished he wouldn't stray like that, wished he'd just stay together with the others. He felt rather like a sheepdog, herding his flock together into one tight little group, the better to watch over them, but . . . Kadou had put himself in the path of potential danger for the sake of Her Majesty and Her Highness, and if he wanted to sit out on the balcony and be a second pair of eyes on the perimeter, Evemer was going to allow it. *This* time. Only this time.

But equal in weight to the part of Evemer that wanted to herd him like a wandering sheep was a part that wanted to build a wall around his lord to shield him from anything that might set him off into one of his episodes, and at the moment that meant Siranos. Kadou was already quiet and pale enough without being subjected to the man's presence for an indefinite amount of time.

Siranos was deeply unpleasant at the moment. Gone was the agreeable demeanor he had shown in the garden. He paced, he grumbled, he cursed under his breath. He sat down, he got up again. He picked up books, stared at a page, slammed them shut again, asked a thousand questions of Zeliha that were mostly met with "I couldn't say," or "I'm sure the commander will be along to tell us more as soon as there is more to tell." When Siranos finally lost the last threads of his patience and strode toward the door, saying something about how he would go find out more himself, Zeliha said smoothly, "You're still confined to the Gold Court. If you leave this house now, you won't be allowed back in."

Evemer of course said nothing, since there was no one looking to him for an opinion. He only poured a cup of cold tea from the pot on the lunch table and silently took it out to the balcony for his lord.

Around dinnertime, Eozena arrived with six more kahyalar in tow . . . and Tadek, standing out against the little crowd of cobalt in forest green trimmed with bands of black. The colors were those of Şirya Manor, a tiny holding Kadou had inherited from his father, and the uniform was a deliberate attempt to honor Tadek for his service while maintaining a clear separation between him and the kahyalar. Evemer had found it acceptable when Kadou had first hit on the idea a couple of weeks before. It was better than seeing Tadek go around shamefully in cadet whites.

"Right," Eozena said grimly. "I am as sure of these people as I can be. If I have erred and one of them turns out to be a traitor, Majesty, please don't worry about arranging a trial for me. I will handle it honorably by myself. I'm thinking the cliff, so I have plenty of time to think about my errors on the way down."

Zeliha tsked at her. "I'm sure that won't ever be necessary." She looked over the kahyalar, each in turn, and nodded. "All right. Dinner, then. And a bath first, I think." Four of the six kahyalar bowed in unison and dispersed. The other two posted themselves on watch, and Evemer felt a little knot in his chest begin to relax. Her Majesty turned next to Tadek and eyed him. "So you made use of him after all."

"Yes, Majesty," Eozena said, grudgingly. "He does have . . . skills. Little sneak. Turns out he's gotten drunk with nigh on every kahya in the palace. Has a whole mental catalog of everybody's smallest grievance. All I had to do was explain the situation and he had lists ready to go—who he'd trust beyond question, and who we ought to keep an eye on. Little *sneak*."

Tadek bowed and said nothing.

"Lists, is it?" Zeliha said, raising an eyebrow. "And that sort of talent never came up before?"

"That's what I asked," Eozena said, helping herself to the stone-cold tea. "What was it you said, Armsman Hasira?"

"The ministry of intelligence declined my service after my secondary merit exams. I was judged to have a poor aptitude for it."

"Well, yes, we established *that* a month ago," Zeliha said dryly.

"I have no gift for spywork, Your Majesty," Tadek said. He gave her one of his smiles, but at least it was one of the less infuriating ones, in Evemer's opinion. "But I have an excellent memory, sharp eyes, and a great gift for talking to drunk people. They like to tell me secrets."

"And Eozena and my brother both think you're loyal enough to stand in a room with me and the crown princess."

He met her eyes—Evemer thought that really was too bold, but bit his tongue on a rebuke. "Majesty," Tadek said. "You laid my life in his hands. What do I have left besides serving him?"

Zeliha snorted. "He does have a gift for bringing that out in people. Despite his best efforts, I'm sure. Go, then. He's out on the balcony."

Tadek bowed again and headed that way; Evemer followed. Behind him, Eozena began briefing Her Majesty on the handful of other kahyalar she had determined were loyal. She'd put together a squad and sent them down to the city to see if anyone could scrape up a satyota.

Kadou looked up as soon as they stepped out and set aside his teacup, still half full. "Oh, Tadek. Good. Where's—is Melek . . . ?"

"Not to worry about çem, Highness," Tadek said, immediately as bright and merry as he usually was. "Çe will be along shortly, Commander Eozena is just being very careful. Oh, but look at you, lovely, what a day you must have had!" He clucked his tongue and tucked a stray piece of hair behind Kadou's ear. "Have you eaten anything?"

"I'm not hungry."

"You'll waste away to nothing," Tadek said.

"You sound like a grandmother."

"Wise and always right about everything? A great compliment. Thank you, Highness. Why don't you come inside?"

Kadou glanced at Evemer, biting his lip. "Is Siranos still in there?" he whispered. Evemer nodded, and Kadou grimaced.

"Oh, him," Tadek said. "Well, how about a walk? Eozena told us about all the logistical problems, but I think there's enough kahyalar in this house now that you don't have to lock yourself in one room. How long have you been in that chair?"

"Hours," Evemer said.

"High time you got up and stretched your legs a bit, then," Tadek said. "Why don't you give me a tour of the house? I've heard there's a beautiful shrine here."

Evidently getting space from Siranos was a more attractive prospect than lurking out on the balcony. Kadou unfolded himself from the chair and led them out, stopping to have a quiet conversation with Eozena and Zeliha first—they listened to him curiously, and then Eozena handed him something from her pocket and Zeliha got a small pouch out of a locked drawer of her desk.

Evemer couldn't help but notice that Siranos watched them go, arms crossed and resentful. He noticed, too, that Eyne was in Eozena's arms. Good.

Kadou was too busy thinking to give Tadek a very good tour of the royal residence. He'd nearly chewed his lip to shreds out on the balcony, his mind reeling over the Shipbuilder's Guild, Armagan, the counterfeit coins . . .

The coins. In one pocket, the ones Eozena had found in Armagan's chambers. In the other (and he was very careful to remember which was which), several of the counterfeits that had been taken from Madam Melachrinos. He was too cautious to jump immediately to conclusions—first, a test. He needed a pair of scales.

The shrine in the residence occupied a room that butted right up to the edge of the cliff. Like the throne room where he had been taken after the hunt, the long side of the room was left open to a covered balcony spanning its entire width, with the spectacular view of Kasaba City, its famous harbor dotted with tiny islands, the seawall and its two great towers that served as both lighthouses and defensive works, and the ocean beyond.

The altar on the left side of the room had a large niche with a statue of Sannesi, the Mother of All. It was about a foot and a half tall, made of solid gold that had been worn very smooth and shiny on the tops of her feet from years of supplicants touching for luck. Before her was a simple wooden table, holding a basin of water and a long, narrow candelabra with nearly fifty candleholders in two rows. On the right side of the room was Usmim, the Guardian, Challenger, and Judge. His statue was black and marble and silver, likewise worn on the tops of his feet, and there was a set of scales on the altar table before him.

Kadou crossed immediately to Usmim. Distracted, he ran through a few gestures of respect and supplication and offered up a quick prayer. It seemed rude to use the scales without doing so.

"Beautiful view of the city," Tadek said, wandering into the room after him. "How old are these statues?"

"I don't know," Kadou said. "Sorry."

"Tari dynasty," Evemer rumbled.

Tadek grimaced. "I wasn't any good with history. Always mix up the dates—the numbering system is madness, you know."

Kadou was rather inclined to agree. He'd had to memorize everything by rote, or his tutors would have chiseled it into his skull—when a dynasty changed, the new one was numbered from the birth of its founder, but the old one didn't *end* until the last ruler lost the crown, meaning that usually there were at least three or four decades of overlap. Thus, depending on what a historian wanted to emphasize (or their artistic preferences or personal opinions), they might choose to record that the Summer War occurred in the 20th year of the Shahre dynasty, the 236th year of the Ahak dynasty, or (if they were being particularly sycophantic) the negative-26th year of the Mahisti dynasty.

"It isn't that complicated," muttered Evemer, which was really to be expected.

"How do you know they're Tari dynasty, then?" Tadek said, leaning forward to inspect the statue of Usmim.

"I listened. I studied."

"Well, yes, I could have *guessed* that. I meant, did you study art?"

"No."

"So how do you know?"

"There is a book in the kahyalar's library."

"Oh, *reading*," Tadek said airily. "Bad for the eyes, that." He stopped, frowned, and prodded at the scales on Usmim's altar. "Huh. These are out of balance."

"No, they're—" Kadou sighed with frustration, dropping out of the position of prayer. "They're not, they're just old. There's a trick to them." Not that anyone *used* the scales on this altar or needed them to be accurate. They were just symbolic.

"No," Tadek said slowly, standing back and eyeing them from a couple different angles. "They're definitely off."

"They're not."

"Not to contradict my liege lord, but I'm pretty sure they are, gorgeous."

Kadou was at the altar and elbowing Tadek aside before he could stop himself. He flicked back the skirts of his kaftan and knelt, resting his elbows on the altar and fiddling with the scales. "Look, watch."

Tadek crouched next to him. "I swear it, they're off."

"I swear they're *not*. Do either of you have any coins?" With any set of scales, you would want to check the balance first, but with the fiddliness of this particular set, it was essential.

They each had a handful of copper kürler and silver yiralar—Kadou took two yiralar from each of them and placed them in the pans. The scales had been slightly damaged decades before Kadou was born: There was a particular tension screw at the scales' balance point that needed to be fiddled from time to time, especially after damp weather or big changes in the ambient temperature.

Easy enough to do, when you had a few coins that all weighed precisely the same. "There, see." He returned their yiralar and produced the two small coin purses that Zeliha and Eozena had given him. Left, Melachrinos's coins. Right, Armagan's coins. Important to keep them straight.

He kept his mind blank of conclusions. It would be easy enough to say, "Aha, two instances of counterfeits so close together must mean that they come from the same place and were made by the same people." But that sort of thing could lead an investigation astray. No, testing was important. And this test, particularly, might not mean anything.

He counted out five altınlar from each pouch and placed them on the pans: Left, Melachrinos. Right, Armagan.

The scales balanced. Kadou let out a long breath. It wasn't quite definitive confirmation—they'd need a very skilled team of goldsmiths for that, or better yet an incredibly sensitive touch-taster . . .

"Tadek, can you touch-taste?"

"Not a whit. Why?"

"Who is the most sensitive touch-taster you know? And are they trustworthy?"

"Melek," Tadek said immediately. "And I'd wager every last kür in my possession on çir loyalty, yes."

Kadou sat back on his heels and studied the level scales. "Right. We'll go ask Eozena to—"

"What are you doing, Your Highness?" Kadou's muscles locked up—Siranos. He scrambled to his feet.

"I was—we were—"

"Praying," Evemer said smoothly. "Repairing the scales as service to Usmim."

Siranos, standing in the doorway, frowned. "They weren't broken the last time I was here."

"Sir," Evemer said flatly, and Kadou felt terribly grateful to him. His hands were beginning to shake again—damn this affliction! Could it not leave him be for a day? Could it not let him look Siranos in the eye? "We'd just finished," Evemer said.

Siranos laughed—it sounded a little forced. "Is this how many princes and guards it takes to repair a simple set of scales?"

"We're all equal in the eyes of the Lord of Judgment," said Tadek loftily. "Perhaps you ought to spend some time in here contemplating. Oh, or perhaps another shrine would be better, so that you don't get in Her Majesty's way."

Kadou felt another rush of relief and gratitude—Evemer could have stonewalled Siranos all day, but Tadek used words like a rapier.

Siranos blinked. "I didn't mean it as an insult," he said. His eyes flickered to the scales, and he came forward. Evemer angled himself between him and Kadou. From the corner of Kadou's eye, he saw Tadek also drift forward with an air of idleness.

Siranos picked up one of the coins from the pan, looking at the rest in their two piles on either side of the altar. The corner of his mouth quirked in a strange smile. "My," he said. "Araşti princes certainly carry around a small fortune, don't they. You could live for weeks in Thorikou on all this. Months, if you didn't have expensive tastes."

"Sir, His Highness requires solitude," Evemer said.

Siranos picked up the two coin purses and looked in, raising his eyebrows. "Solitude and enough money to buy the best Vintish warhorse?"

"Please put those down," Kadou said.

Siranos shrugged. "As you like." He tossed them on the altar—the coins left in them spilled across the surface, getting hopelessly mixed up. At Kadou's flinch, he held up both hands defensively. "What's that look for?"

Kadou said nothing, only started fumbling the mixed coins into the purses.

Siranos sighed. "Look, Kadou," he said, putting his hands on the altar and leaning forward. "I think we've stepped on each other's toes once too often and—"

"Has he?" Tadek said brightly. "Has he stepped on your toes? Goodness, when was that?"

Siranos half frowned at him. "I am attempting to make amends."

"Are you? Whatever for?"

"I don't wish for there to be any bad blood between us," he said frankly. "He is my daughter's uncle, we are family—"

"We're not," Kadou said. "She's not yours."

Siranos turned to him. After a long moment he said, "Zeliha said she was. I see no reason to disbelieve her."

"You're the *body-father*," Kadou said.

Siranos's finely shaped brows drew together and he pursed his lips with frustration. "I beg your pardon," he said, and now Kadou could hear how carefully he was speaking. "I believe I told you before that I don't understand what the difference is."

Tadek put his hand on Siranos's arm. "Why don't you come out into the hall? Leave His Highness to finish his prayers, and I'll explain it."

Siranos shook him off. "Thank you, no. I'd like to have a conversation with Kadou."

"You're never going to have claim on her," Kadou said, more sharply than he intended.

"But I *have* claimed her," he replied with humiliating patience. "Zeliha admits that Eyne is mine; I believe her, and I want her to be mine. She doesn't have to be a—do you even have a word for it? We'd say *nothos*. Or . . . *bâtarde*, in Vintish?" He drew himself up. "If you are trying to protect your sister's heart, I think that is admirable, but I have been thinking that perhaps I won't return to Oissos after all—I will stay. I want to be in Eyne's life. A child should have two parents."

"What *for*? She has me." But Kadou realized with a sudden clarity that Siranos wasn't just misunderstanding what a body-father was—he misunderstood what an *uncle* was. Even if Zeliha had deigned to share claim on her child, *Kadou's* claim on Eyne would always far outweigh Siranos's, just by dint of the fact that he was Zeliha's brother.

Siranos huffed. "She could have a father and *three* uncles, and an aunt," he said.

"What?" Was Siranos's understanding of the language really that poor? Where had the misunderstanding happened? "I have no other siblings."

"*I* have two brothers and a sister. She should know them too—"

"Whatever for?" Tadek said, sounding just as bewildered as Kadou was.

"Your siblings are not uncles and aunts to Her Highness," Evemer rumbled. "Your family has been granted no claim."

Siranos stood up and rubbed his forehead. He muttered something under his breath—Kadou thought that it was an oath or a curse of some sort, but his near-fluency in Oissika did not include vulgar language. "I am planning to stay," he said, even more carefully patient. "I—" He shook his head, laughed. "I've been loyal to my family for all my life, and they've never been anything but wretched to me. I've only just realized this recently. It's better here. I'm staying."

Kadou didn't have time to deal with this, nor the energy. "That's between you and Her Majesty," he said. "If that was all . . . ?"

If that was all? was a rote phrase his etiquette tutors had drilled into his head, which was supposed to hint that the conversation was over and that someone should imminently excuse themselves. Siranos evidently had not had this lesson from his own tutors. "You think I'm not sincere?"

"Perhaps you could finish this conversation later," Tadek said more firmly, gesturing to the door.

Siranos spared him a single frustrated glance. "Call off your dogs, Kadou. I didn't think you were so arrogant as to—"

"You will address him as *Your Highness*," Evemer said.

"More importantly, you will refrain from calling my kahya and armsman *dogs*," Kadou snapped.

Tadek gave Kadou a polite half bow. "Highness, I'll escort Master Siranos to the door, shall I?"

"*Please.*" Thank the gods for Tadek.

"Sir," Tadek said silkily, turning back to Siranos. "His Highness would like you to leave. Am I going to have to slip my leash?"

"It was a *joke*," Siranos said. "How is anyone supposed to have a conversation with you Araşti when you all close ranks like this the minute someone missteps?"

"Mm, I'm sure that is difficult." Tadek smiled sympathetically. "How is anyone supposed to have a conversation with you, sir, when your tongue would be so much better suited to licking a pig's cock?"

Evemer made a strangled noise, and all Kadou's gratitude disappeared in a wave of horror.

Siranos gaped. "I beg your *pardon*?"

"Granted," Tadek said airily. "You'd better beg His Highness's pardon too, though."

"Tadek," Evemer hissed.

"Tadek, not like that," Kadou said. With fumbling hands, he stuffed the coin purses into his pockets.

"Whyever not? Will he have me beaten?" He leered at Siranos. "Will I have to say *oh, yes, please*?"

"Control your servant's mouth," Siranos snapped.

"Oh," Tadek said, drawing it out long and breathy, as if he'd been offered the most rare and succulent delicacy. "Yes, *please*."

"Tadek!" Evemer snapped again. "Manners!"

"How am I being unmannerly?" Tadek asked, all innocence. "I *said* please! What am I supposed to do, beg? I mean, if you want me to, I certainly can—"

"Excuse us," Kadou said, taking Tadek by the arm and dragging him toward the door.

"Of course, *Your Highness*," Siranos said icily. "A handful, isn't he?"

Tadek turned back and gave him an enormous cheeky wink. "My friend, I can assure you it's much more than one handful."

Kadou was going to die of embarrassment. He dragged a cackling Tadek out of the room and down the hall to the other end of the house, where he shoved him into a spare room. Evemer, close behind them, slammed the door. "Tadek!" Kadou said. "What was *that*?"

Tadek had dropped his fey act. "You're going to tell me I shouldn't talk to him like that. Give me one good reason why not."

Kadou was too aghast to deny it. "Because it's rude."

"And? He's a bully, isn't he? Every time he can corner you, he needles you, even when he claims he's trying to smooth things over. What courtesy do I owe him? We can't do anything else about him, can we, and asking him nicely to leave you the hell alone didn't make any difference. I gave him several chances to leave graciously!"

"It was inappropriate," Evemer intoned.

"Yes, that's the point!" Tadek turned on him. "You tell me, then: You went tense the second Siranos stepped in the room— you've seen him bullying Kadou before, haven't you?" Evemer's expression darkened. "Ah, see, that's what I thought. And I bet you wanted to punch him for it, didn't you?" He put his hands on his hips, meeting Evemer's glare without a flinch—even as tall as Evemer was, they seemed nearly of a height. Tadek had a certain presence, and sometimes appeared taller than he was. "You wanted to punch him and you couldn't, because that would be—oh, my!—inappropriate."

"Illegal," Evemer growled. "Immoral."

"Tadek, leave it alone," Kadou said, pinching the bridge of his nose. "Please leave it."

"He's coming at your prince with weapons," Tadek said, his snapping hazel eyes fixed on Evemer. "Weapons which, unless I'm much mistaken, you don't have proficiency to counter. I do. I know bullies. I know how to put them in their place. If he'd really meant to make up with His Highness, he could have started with *I'm sorry*."

"You won't win against him," Kadou said, catching his arm again and forcing Tadek to look at him.

"I don't *have* to win against him," Tadek said, exquisitely patient, as if explaining a very simple mathematical concept to two people who were deliberately refusing to understand. "I just have to distract him long enough for *you* to make a graceful exit. That's my job, isn't it? Protecting you! You can't go down into the gutter with him, because you're—well, you! Even if you weren't the prince, you wouldn't lower yourself like that. Lovely," he said, holding Kadou by the arms and giving him his most charming smile. "Beauty, I was *born* in the gutter." Kadou wriggled free of his grip; Tadek let go immediately, sighed.

"Please," Kadou said firmly. "Figure out a different way to deal with him. Her Majesty wants a good relationship with him, and with me, and so I—I shouldn't have let that happen. We all took offense much too quickly, and he was *right*—we did close ranks on him. He was trying to repair things between us, and I ought to have listened to him, at the very least." Kadou's voice dropped to a whisper. "Besides that, you baiting him like that isn't going to make Her Majesty any more inclined to forgive you."

Tadek raised his eyes to the heavens. "I don't know how else to explain to you that I don't care about the consequences if it means I can put myself between you and whatever arrows that man shoots at you."

May Usmim show leniency at the hour of judgment, but Evemer found himself agreeing with *Tadek,* of all people. He was right—it wasn't proper or appropriate in the slightest, but it did seem to be the only effective way to stop Siranos in his tracks. The absolute shock on his face when Tadek had opened his mouth for that filth . . .

"We will report this to Commander Eozena," Evemer said. "She will handle it."

Kadou sighed and nodded. "Tadek, go wait at the door."

"At your service, Your Highness," Tadek said, adding a salute that was far too saucy for Evemer to approve of.

Kadou didn't move for a minute. He had that look in his eyes again, like he was working himself up, preparing to shake himself to pieces. Tadek would have to be summoned right back in to cuddle him calm again, Evemer thought resentfully. As if no one else in the room were *competent* enough to be of assistance.

"I need someone to fetch Melek," Kadou said at last. "And—and make sure that çe is loyal."

"The coins," Evemer said.

Kadou rubbed his temples with his fingertips. "Yes."

"What were you testing?"

"Whether they weighed the same."

"And they did." Evemer frowned at the floor.

"It's not too much of a jump to think that they might have been made by the same person, is it?" Kadou said anxiously. "It's not paranoid of me?"

"No."

"I don't want to throw theories at Eozena if I'm just being paranoid."

"Either Armagan and Melachrinos are both involved, or the circulation has become saturated with the counterfeits."

"It's not that. We would have heard from a touch-taster. There wouldn't be a *point* to producing that many for use in this country. People would find out almost immediately. We would have heard."

"And we haven't, except for Madam Melachrinos and Lieutenant Armagan."

"Perhaps they have some plot that hasn't been put into motion yet. Why would you make so many and wait like this?"

"Or they're taking them abroad," Evemer said. "Melachrinos is a merchant. She has ships." Kadou chewed his lip. Evemer watched him intently.

Pretty eyes, he thought. The baby princess was going to have just the same ones, he could tell, that deep Mahisti blue-black. Her Majesty had them too—Her Majesty looked a great deal like Kadou. They had the same long, glossy black hair, the same point to their chins, but Her Majesty was taller and had a broader and more ready smile, and her features were a touch more angular. A great beauty, without question. Both of them were. But . . . Kadou's eyes were prettier.

Kadou shook his head suddenly. "Damn it all. We're going to have to go back to the public houses again."

Evemer's brief reverie shattered. "No," he said. "No. I don't want to go back to the public houses." They'd nearly been *killed* the night before! Where was that cowardice Kadou talked about all the time?

With an air of mild surprise, Kadou said, "Oh. Of course you wouldn't want—I'm sorry, I assumed—I'll take Eozena, then."

That wasn't at all what Evemer had meant. "I don't want *you* to go back to the public houses, my lord," he said. "It's dangerous."

"Yes, it's very dangerous for everyone else if Eozena's there."

"My lord," said Evemer.

"I wish you'd just say what you mean," Kadou mumbled, almost too quiet for Evemer to hear. "I'm tired of guessing whether I've offended you."

Evemer felt that he'd been set off-balance. That seemed to be an ever more common occurrence around His Highness. And then, thinking of that . . . The whole theory of careless-flighty-negligent seemed to have been conclusively disproven. Clearly he did care, clearly he attended to things to the best of his ability . . .

And then there was that moment in the garden earlier, when Kadou had faced him down. When he'd asked for Evemer's blade against his neck. His lord had asked for a great act of loyalty, had granted him mercy, had restored his trust in Evemer—redoubled it, perhaps. That's what it had felt like. Evemer had been trying very, very hard not to think about it. He would allow himself three minutes of thinking about it later, when he was alone with a locked door and his hands firmly clenched on his knees, and then he would definitively never think of it again.

Kadou had seemed so *tall*. He was shorter than Evemer by at least six inches, but even when he'd been looking up at Evemer, it had felt like Evemer was looking up at *him*, shining and serene and assured, like he had never doubted Evemer at all.

Evemer wasn't thinking about it.

If his lord thought Evemer didn't want to go to the public houses again, and if Eozena for some reason wasn't available, then he would very likely take Tadek. For all Tadek's faults, the man could at least lie and keep secrets, and he'd proven that he had a quick tongue, a vicious wit, and a willingness to turn them to His Highness's defense.

But Evemer didn't want Tadek to be the one to accompany His Highness. He didn't want it to be Commander Eozena either. He didn't like either of those thoughts at all—which was nonsensical, at least for the latter one, because if he had wanted Kadou to be safe, then the commander was without a doubt the person who could best accomplish that goal.

He turned his thoughts firmly away from that. His lord had expressed a wish for his behavior. Such a command, even an implicit one, could not be disobeyed.

"I'm not good at being open," Evemer therefore said, with some difficulty. "Or expressing myself."

"You're very expressive," Kadou said, which wasn't a word Evemer had ever heard used to describe himself. Kadou crossed his arms, more as if he were guarding himself than closing off from Evemer in anger. "But sometimes it's too complicated to parse."

"My lord," Evemer said reflexively. Kadou quirked one eyebrow; Evemer cleared his throat. "I mean, my apologies. I shall endeavor to—"

"You don't *have* to change," Kadou said. "If that's how you are, then that's how you are. But . . ." He stopped himself, sighed. "I just wish sometimes that you'd spell it out. But I shouldn't ask. You don't deserve to be burdened with my awkwardness."

"I don't dislike you, my lord," Evemer blurted.

After a very long, horrible moment, Kadou turned to face him, arms still crossed. "I'm glad to hear it," he said. "Is it true?"

"I wouldn't lie to you." *Spell it out,* Evemer told himself. "And I *shall* be offended if you imply that I would, my lord."

"You didn't like me before."

And he'd just backed himself into a corner now, hadn't he? He had just said that he wouldn't lie to his lord—nor could he dissemble, nor evade answering.

"I was wrong. As I said before, I fell to the temptation of gossip and did not do my due diligence to confirm facts for myself. I should have done better by my oaths as a kahya. I should have trusted the people I respect and their good opinions of you, my lord." Another long moment passed in silence. "I was acquainted with Balaban and Gülpaşa. I was angry that they were dead."

Kadou's face fell. "You have the right to your anger," he whispered. "Are you angry still?"

"I mourn that their deaths were wasted on a useless misunderstanding. They deserved better. But they thought they were laying down their lives for the person they were oathsworn to protect, and I honor and respect that sacrifice." Evemer wished he were the type to allow himself to fidget, so that he might have some outward expression of his inner conflict. "I'm sorry, my lord, that I thought their deaths didn't matter to you."

"They did. Of course they did." Kadou looked away. "I hated writing the letters of condolence to their families, you know. *I'm so very sorry* seemed so cheap and thin."

There was silence between them for a time. Evemer wished—he wished . . .

He wished he had anything to say that wouldn't sound cruel or harsh or haughty. He wished he knew how to alleviate this hurt, to offer some small . . . something. Comfort did not seem to be the right word. Shelter, perhaps, as if he could stand over his lord and hold a cloak spread over his arms to protect him from the winds and rains of despair. Shelter, or solace.

"My lord," he said. "If you are set on going back down to the city, I would not rest easy unless I was there with you. But I understand if you prefer Eozena. She is more skilled than I am."

"I would not rest easy if I thought I was putting you into a situation you are uncomfortable with."

Evemer looked him in the eye, stung. "Are you implying I'd let fear get in the way of my service? You don't seem to be afraid to go back, and you're the one who calls himself a coward."

Oh, no. Oh, he hadn't meant to speak so bluntly. All he'd meant to say was *my lord*. What was happening to him, that he had so lost control of his own tongue?

But Kadou only looked surprised, and something in his face seemed to relax, like a door slowly cracked open. All he said was, "I *am* a coward."

"My lord," Evemer said, keeping a tight hold on his treacherous tongue.

"Oh, by all Usmim's trials, speak plainly if you've got something to say!"

"Your Highness nearly got killed last night and you're ready to run right back out tonight," Evemer said, stiff and careful. "I only wonder if that is what a coward would do."

"I have to! Regardless of my feelings, I have to!"

"Why?"

"There's no one else," Kadou said, his voice cracking a little. "Three kahyalar arrested, and more than that involved—people who should have been bound to their oaths with their lives. Eozena is occupied with the garrison so that she can ensure that Her Majesty and Eyne are protected, so who else is there? Who else can I trust with this but myself? Who else can I trust to protect *me*, besides you?"

Evemer felt a hard lump come into his throat. "Do you, my lord?" he asked quietly. "Even after last night? After I—"

"You didn't fail," Kadou said firmly. "You didn't." Softer, gentler, almost tenderly he added, "And yes. Yes, of course I trust you."

You're a godsend. Those words from Kadou that first day at the Shipbuilder's Guild, the shining prince on his golden horse, had swept through Evemer's soul like a breath of unexpected wind and lit a glow in his heart like a single star on a cloudy night. These words now lit him up like a dozen stars.

His lord would be able to see right through him, surely. He would see it, see how much it *mattered* to Evemer . . . But he didn't know yet if he wanted Kadou to see that in him, so Evemer dropped his eyes to the flagstones. "My lord," he said.

Kadou kept speaking, because of course he couldn't hear the tempest of unnameable feeling howling through Evemer. "If those counterfeits make it abroad, then people elsewhere might think we've started debasing. If we've debased that much, and gone to that much trouble to hide it, they'll think something is desperately wrong in Araşt. Ninety percent of our money is imaginary, Evemer. It's just"—he flung one hand out in a broad sweep—"lines of notation in a ledger somewhere. It can vanish like smoke. There's no one else to untangle it all. No one we can trust right now, and there is an *unknown time limit*. I have to do it. It's . . . it's an obligation. Like your oaths of service."

Evemer didn't quite agree that it was anything like the same— Kadou had a duty to be cautious, didn't he? To keep himself safe? To not go running headlong into more dark alleys where who knew what sort of trouble might lurk? "The commander will object."

"She will not."

"She will."

Kadou set his jaw stubbornly. "Want to bet?"

CHAPTER SEVEN

ozena nodded slowly. "Yes, I see. You're right, we do have
to move quickly."

Kadou gave his kahya a dry look; Evemer went to his
blank-stone-wall face. Kadou resisted the impulse to laugh, fighting it down into only a smile, which he directed at Eozena. "I'm
glad we agree. I'll go out and start looking—"

"You? Oh, no, absolutely not. You're going to leave this to me
and your kahyalar."

Evemer gave Kadou an identical dry look. Kadou pointedly
ignored him. "Eozena," he said, entreating. "You're busy—the security of the palace—"

"Yes, that's top priority. But I will handle this as well."

"Are you going to *sleep* at any point? Or eat?"

"Oh, that's rich, coming from you!" she crowed. "Prince Hyp-
ocrite, they'll call you!"

"Eozena."

"Not a *chance*, my love," she said. His heart fell. "You're going
to stay right here, and *you*"—she pointed at Evemer—"are going to
make sure he doesn't leave this house until I say it's safe, and then
you'll make sure he doesn't leave the Gold Court until I say that's
safe, and then you'll make sure he doesn't—"

"Yes, Commander."

She was getting a bit of a manic glint in her eye. "Everyone is
going to be *perfectly fine*."

"*You* came to me to give me this investigation," Kadou said.
"This is important—there's a time limit on it. And I have a duty
to this country! You can't just—"

"Kadou, very best beloved of my heart, you'll find that I certainly can, unless you'd like to ask Her Majesty to have me court-martialed. Let's keep this situation pleasant and familial, shall we? You're not going anywhere. I know it's difficult, I know you want to be useful, and *trust me* that I am aware the investigation is a matter of great concern. But the most useful thing you can do is stay in this house, preferably within eyesight or at least earshot of one kahya at all times. It is also your duty," she said, meeting his eyes steadily, unwaveringly, as firm and immovable as a mountain, "to graciously allow me to do my job and keep you safe."

Kadou could *feel* the waves of smug contentment radiating off Evemer. "Yes, Commander," he said.

"Don't sulk. Find something to keep your hands busy. Read a book. Work on some embroidery." She thought for a moment. "You can go outside and do sword-forms in the courtyard if you take three kahyalar with you."

"It will be dark soon," he said. "I can't do any of those things in the dark."

Eozena shrugged. "I'm sure you'll find something with which to occupy yourself. Chess with Evemer, maybe? You've been playing quite a lot with him lately, no? Nice, safe, indoor sort of game, chess. It'd get your mind off things." She nodded firmly. "As for me, I'll be sending for Melek and having Tadek question çem."

Kadou pressed his lips together hard and nodded. "I understand," he said, trying to keep the bitterness out of his voice. "Thank you for your vigilance, Commander."

She laid a hand on his shoulder, squeezed it. "Don't be angry with me for loving you, my boy," she murmured. He looked up at her—her crooked half smile grew fonder, and her hand left his shoulder to cup his cheek. "Getting an old lady all sentimental, you know."

"You're hardly old, Eozena," he said. His eyes stung a little—from frustration, from the feeling of helplessness, from how warm her hand was on his cheek and how badly he wanted to step forward and bury his face in her shoulder. It wasn't appropriate, now he was grown and had to at least *try* to behave like a prince, rather than having the excuse of being a child who wanted a hug from the closest thing he had to an auntie.

"Ah, give it twenty-five years or so, you'll change that tune. You just watch how quick that niece of yours shoots up, then come back and tell me whether or not you feel a bit like an old man. You'll be nearly fifty then. And I'll be, what, seventy-six or so? Decrepit." Her smile broadened when Kadou gave a soft snort, but when he tried to look away, she turned his face back to hers gently and gave him that steady, immovable-mountain look. "I'm not treating you like a child."

"I know," he said. He swallowed down his upset and whispered, "You're keeping your oaths. You're—using your best judgment. Which you have proven to be sound and—and sensible. And prudent. That's the whole reason you're commander."

"That and the fact that I love you *more than life,*" she said. He had no words to reply to that, could only raise his hand to hers and squeeze her wrist in reply, closing his eyes and trying not to turn his face against her warm hand. "You know that?" she pressed.

"I know," he said, still whispering. "I'm not angry. I just . . ." He exhaled. Shook his head. Couldn't find words.

"Ah, my lad," she said, the fond smile shining in her voice. "Children are a pox, you know. One day they're little enough to drown in ten inches of water; the next, they're all grown-up and *tall* and—ah, no, I can't say anything more, or Lieutenant Hoşkadem will tell the whole garrison that I've arrived irretrievably in my auntie phase and gone soft."

Kadou huffed another small laugh and glanced over at Evemer across the room.

Evemer had his blank-stone-wall face on. He murmured stiffly, "Commander."

"He's offended," Kadou said, giving Eozena a reproachful little pout. "You've cast aspersions on his honor. He wouldn't disrespect you like that."

"Terrible gossips, kahyalar," she snorted. "I should know, I was just as bad about it, back in the days before I started having to be careful of all these state secrets." She cast a cool look at Evemer. "No telling everyone I've gone soft."

"Commander," he said again. And then, to Kadou's pleasure, he added, "His Highness is right, I wouldn't."

Eozena's eyebrows rose in surprise. "My! Evemer Hoşkadem, speaking full sentences! And they say the Mother of All only gave the world one thousand gifts. What a good influence you seem to be, Highness."

Kadou ducked his head, demurring, but Eozena tipped his face back up. She narrowed her eyes at him, mock-stern but smiling. "Don't you go around telling anyone I'm soft either, you hear me?"

He adopted an innocent expression, all wide eyes, and said, "Of course not, Auntie."

"Ooh, *now* you're going to get it, love." She put her other hand to his face, slightly squishing his cheeks like he was a quarter of his age, and said, "What I was going to say about children being a pox is that you turn your back for five minutes and they get all grown-up and tall and *handsome*—"

"Eozena," Kadou said, muffled by her squishing hands as he reflexively pulled a little against her grip.

"—and they go around being terribly good and making you *so proud*—"

Kadou felt his face going hot and began pulling and wriggling harder, trying to escape.

"—all righteous, and brave, and solemn, and serious about duty . . ." Her voice had shifted into a croon. "Doing stupid things now and again to keep you on your toes, yes, making mistakes now and again—but otherwise a *sweet boy* who has grown up into a *good man*—"

"Evemer, help," Kadou whined.

"Don't you move, Hoşkadem, he brought this on himself—a *good man* who tries so very hard and is so very easy to love—I said *don't move*, Lieutenant."

"Commander." Evemer had come forward and set his hand on her forearm.

She harrumphed, smiling, and let Kadou go with a last little rub of her thumbs over his cheekbones. "Good lad, Hoşkadem. Good priorities." To Kadou, she said, "You were asking for that one, though."

"I accept the consequences of my errors," Kadou said—his face was still hot enough that he thought he must be scarlet down to his collarbones. He cleared his throat and glanced up at her. In the smallest whisper, he said, "Thank you."

"For what? Saying things that are true?" That brought another wave of heat to his face. She laughed softly and took the half step necessary to kiss the top of his head. "Everything will be fine. But I really must run now, Highness, there are matters to attend to. I'll be back later, undoubtedly."

Evemer snapped to attention as she turned to the door, which she acknowledged with a nod.

Kadou watched her go, wishing that he could . . . *do something*. It seemed so terribly unfair that he should be so intimately involved in the situation yet be completely barred from affecting any of its outcomes.

He went to the divan by the open window and sat down with a sigh he tried to keep silent. The window looked out over the sprawling gardens of the Gold Court, and the early evening air carried the scents of cypress and cedar and a hundred kinds of flowers.

He didn't know why he'd expected anything different. Of course it was more important for him to . . . just *sit here*. Waiting. Hands empty and useless.

"Highness," Evemer said suddenly.

Kadou half turned. "Yes?"

"Ought I to have stepped in earlier?"

"What, with Eozena? No, she's—she's allowed to do that." She wouldn't have done that in front of just anyone—even in front of Evemer, she'd hesitated before . . . saying those things.

Embarrassing things, and difficult to hear, and so very badly wanted—oh, he wished . . . he wished that . . .

He still didn't have words. He couldn't reject or deny what

she'd said. Eozena did not say things unless she meant them—to disbelieve her would be to disbelieve her honesty, and that was unthinkable.

And yet he couldn't reconcile her view of him—grown-up, brave, serious, a good man, someone she could be proud of, someone she *was* proud of—with what he knew of himself. Small, cowardly, weak. Blood on his hands twice over.

"Can I ask you something?" he heard himself say.

"Yes, my lord," Evemer answered immediately.

Kadou didn't allow himself time to think or second-guess or pick over the thought. "Why do you think she said all that?"

The silence was faintly astonished. "Because she believes it," Evemer answered carefully. It sounded like a guess—was he guessing what Eozena had meant, or what he thought Kadou wanted him to say?

He said nothing more. After a moment, he heard Evemer moving around the room, opening cabinets, adding logs to the fire in the hearth . . . The sound of metal on glass, the sound of water . . .

Evemer moved in his peripheral vision, and a steaming cup of tea appeared on the windowsill by Kadou's elbow. He looked down at it in mild surprise, then up at Evemer, who was setting a neatly folded blanket on the divan next to him, where Kadou had pulled up his feet to be comfortable. "Are these for me?"

"Yes, my lord."

Kadou looked up at him—to gauge his expression, to say thank you if the expression seemed open to it—and found Evemer looking . . . hesitant.

Not uncertain in the way anyone else would—not nearly so obvious as it would be on anyone else's face, and as soon as Kadou had the thought, he wasn't certain that it was correct. What did Evemer have to be hesitant about?

He glanced at the tea, the blanket. For him.

His heart stuttered a little and softened. "Are you trying to make me feel better?" He couldn't help but smile.

"Yes, my lord." Evemer was using his flawlessly neutral voice.

"Ah." Kadou looked at the blanket and the tea again, fighting to keep a smile off his face because he knew—he *knew*—that Evemer would think he was laughing at him. He wasn't. He wasn't, not in the slightest, it was just . . . sweet. Thoughtful.

It was his duty, of course. He would have had training in perception, in *thinking* about the needs of the person he was appointed to attend. But small, unnecessary gestures like these had not been something that Evemer made a habit of—at least that Kadou had seen in these few weeks that Evemer had been in his service. Evemer fulfilled all his duties admirably, even impeccably, when there was a clear and necessary thing that Kadou required. But the less necessary things, the ones that were about simple human pleasures, did not seem to occur to him as comforts that Kadou might desire or appreciate. But then, Kadou wondered suddenly, were they the sort of things that would occur to Evemer as things that *Evemer* might want? Lieutenant Evemer Hoşkadem, who had gotten a near-perfect score on his merit exams, who was known throughout the garrison for being rigid and unyielding and utterly disciplined, the dream of the perfect kahya as Beydamur himself must have imagined when he was writing *The Ten Pillars of War* and establishing the ancient blueprints of what would one day become not just the perfectly loyal army of the sultan, but the ministers and governors of the realm?

No, Evemer Hoşkadem was not the sort to think of simple pleasures unless he meant to deliberately. Unless he had *wanted* to.

Which meant that the tea and blanket were genuine gestures, sincere ones, and not just the dutiful service of a kahya to his lord.

Kadou's heart softened again.

"Thank you," he said, looking up at Evemer.

Evemer was looking rather stiff and formal. He wasn't meeting Kadou's eyes, his gaze lowered respectfully. "If there is something else you require."

Kadou nudged his feet under the edge of the blanket and picked up the tea. "No, this is—good. I like these." He wasn't sure what had made him say it quite like that, just that he wanted Evemer to know.

Evemer nodded sharply.

He stood there in parade rest, tall and imposing and immaculate in every respect, and showing no inclination to step back and give Kadou any more space. Kadou tried not to look at him and sipped his tea, suddenly and unaccountably nervous.

He thought, suddenly, of earlier—in the garden, with Evemer kneeling before him, bared to the sunlight, looking up at him without even a trace of hesitation or uncertainty. He had seemed almost *relaxed* then. Still utterly correct, disciplined, principled, but . . . natural. The Evemer who stood before him now—for all that he was done up perfectly in his uniform, his sword on his hip and his sash neatly knotted—was wooden by comparison. He might have been more imposing like this, but there was something missing—not quite an aura of confidence or an assurance, but a . . . What was it?

In the back of Kadou's head, a voice that sounded rather alarmingly like Tadek's said cheerfully, *Comfort, maybe? Haha, are we trying to reflect on the fact that Lieutenant Hoşkadem looked comfortable on his knees?*

Kadou shut that thought down and pushed it aside so sharply that he had to look out the window and sip his tea to conceal his mortification with himself—and the mortification that came of knowing that the Tadek voice in the back of his head was absolutely laughing at him.

"My lord," Evemer said. "Last night. Armsman Hasira."

Kadou mentally screeched. He cleared his throat. "Yes? What about him?"

Evemer's posture stiffened until he was almost at attention, looking straight ahead out the window. "Armsman Hasira administered aid to you which seemed to be . . . helpful."

"Oh. Yes," Kadou said slowly, suddenly not at all sure where this was going. He hid his face in the teacup, just in case.

Evemer nodded. "Understood, my lord."

What was understood? Kadou looked up over the edge of the teacup, but Evemer's expression was impossible to read. Carefully, he said, "Why do you ask?"

"I wished to refine my knowledge, to better serve you." A pause.

In a different voice, one that did not sound like he was giving a report to a superior officer, Evemer said, "The commander was also helpful, just now. When she . . . touched your face."

"Yes. Sort of. It didn't help the *problem*, but . . ."

"But it helped you feel better about it."

"Well. Yes. A little."

Evemer nodded again. "More than the tea is helping."

Kadou looked at the tea and the blanket again. "I said I liked these."

"My lord."

"Spell it out," Kadou said, a reminder as gentle as he could make it.

Evemer shifted his balance, met Kadou's eyes briefly. "Your Highness finds the most benefit in . . . touch."

A firework of epiphany lit in Kadou's brain. "So you're trying to figure out what I want or what you should do?"

"It is my duty to know Your Highness's preferences in all things."

Oh, what an excellent kahya he was—he *was* trying, wasn't he? And *consciously* so, deliberately looking for ways to improve his service and Kadou's comfort.

As much as it softened his heart to see Evemer trying so hard to make these adjustments and adaptations, ones that clearly didn't come naturally, Kadou felt his heart fall a little, too. He couldn't help but find himself wanting, in comparison to Evemer. No matter how much conscious thought and effort he put into the execution of his duty, the best he could hope for was . . . sufficiency. A man could be good, but a prince? A prince could only be *good enough*. He could, if he tried his utmost, meet expectations. But they were far, far too high for anyone to be able to exceed them.

Wasn't that the whole nature of monarchy? The whole reason his tutors had taught him the way they had? *Get through this without doing harm* had been the explicit lesson. Hold the status quo. Maintain balance. Do not grow ambitious, for ambition too can be a source of harm and suffering, if it leads to failure.

Evemer was permitted to strive to be better. Kadou was not

allowed striving at all—and what else was there for him to strive *for*, in his position? He was the prince of the most financially powerful nation in the world. There was nothing higher than him but the throne itself, and the mere thought of that was enough to turn his stomach.

He sipped his tea. He closed his eyes, feeling the steam on his face, the scent in his nose. Looked for ways to be a good-enough prince for Evemer. "You may always ask me, if you are unsure," he murmured. "Whether it is asking for my opinion of your service, or offering something that you think might help me. I will never punish you for not knowing what I want, or for offering something that I decline. There is no error in that which you would have to be held accountable for."

"Understood, my lord." Evemer was quiet again, but he still stood there, towering over Kadou on the divan.

He must have something else to say, Kadou thought.

When Evemer spoke again, he sounded absolutely neutral—it was only the time it had taken for him to speak that suggested that it was at all effortful for him. "My lord, would you be at all invigorated by visiting the bathhouse?"

Kadou opened his eyes and thought about this. The idea of sitting in the steam-thick air, of sinking into warm water and feeling weightless for a time . . . Yes, that did sound good. He nodded. "Yes. Thank you, Evemer, I would."

The bathhouse of the royal residence was as lavish as the one that served the rest of the Gold Court—and still fully half the size, despite the fact that the only people allowed to use it were the sultan and her immediate family. Evemer didn't know which of these two bathhouses Kadou generally used; the first few days that Evemer had been appointed to him, Kadou had washed with a large basin in his room as if he were on war campaign, and after that, Melek had been attending him, and he bathed in the mornings. Today, since they could not yet leave the royal residence, the matter of preference was moot.

While His Highness finished his tea, Evemer had gotten one of the other kahyalar to run ahead of them and tend the furnaces, ensuring that the water was heated and steam rooms in the baths were fully functional—this was a task delegated most often to a team of cadets, but even they had been temporarily banished from the Gold Court until their loyalties could be verified.

Evemer had never been to the royal baths, though he had heard of them from other kahyalar and had been provided with a floor plan, delivered along with his beautiful new cobalt-blue dress uniform and a number of other items the day after his promotion to the core-guard. The floor plan helpfully pointed out all possible areas of potential danger and what kind of vigilance each room required, from heat exhaustion in the steam room to slipping on the tiles in the washing room to drowning in the therma to "be watchful for intruders; there are many spaces where assailants might conceal themselves" in . . . nearly every room.

After the events of the night before, even remembering that particular warning had set him a little on edge. He had hesitated over the thought of making the suggestion, but Kadou had been so obviously disheartened after the discussion with Commander Eozena, and more than anything, Evemer did *not* want to give his lord the opportunity to work himself into another attack of nerves.

Preventative measures, then.

The frontmost chamber of the baths was a room of low couches and thick, velvety carpets strewn with tasseled silk cushions in vibrant colors. It was much the same as Evemer had found in the nicer public bathhouses down in the city, with the only difference being the splendid quality of the furniture and upholstery. One might invite friends to meet at a bathhouse like this to recline and talk over refreshments—cool sharbat, sliced fruit, sticky pastries—or take in the delicate scent of carefully blended incense, the bright hangings on the walls and the mosaics, the large windows of stained glass that blazed with color when the sunshine hit them and cast dapples of jewellike light below.

Beyond that was another, more private room, where Evemer assisted his lord in taking down his hair and replacing his clothes with a thin white dressing gown of the softest, finest cotton, little more than an underlayer. "Are you taking your weapons in?" Kadou asked.

Evemer was reflexively appalled at the thought of violating the standard of care with which he treated his weapons—the baths were always thick with humidity at the very least, even if they weren't foggy with steam, and regular exposure to such conditions would be bad for both the leather of the sheaths and the steel of the blades.

But . . . *Was* his lord safe here, truly? Was Evemer confident enough to take that gamble? Or would it be better to make an exception, just this once, and violate his standards of how carefully he kept his weapons in favor of maintaining the standards with which he served his lord?

It didn't sit *comfortably* with him, but the answer was inarguable. He lingered over the thought as he changed into bathing robes, although he was fairly certain that Kadou would not require (or even allow) attendance. Still, it was unhygienic to wear outside clothes into the bathing chambers, and even if it weren't, it would be unpleasant to go around for the rest of the evening in a damp, clammy uniform.

He appreciated that Kadou had not pressed him for a quick answer, had given him time to think, so that finally Evemer could say, "Yes, my lord, I am," without any inner conflict as he belted his sword back on over his bathing robes.

The first chamber of the baths proper, the washing room, was cavernous. It was bisected by a waterfall and an artificial brook several feet wide, spanned by a wooden footbridge. The room was elegantly set about with ferns and potted plants; the floor was covered with glistening green tiles in the shape of leaves, and the walls with stunning mosaics of ferocious jungle animals, glittering with gold and copper and brass in the dim, pinkish light of sunset that came through the skylights and the flickering light of the lamps. Like the bathhouse at the kahyalar's dormitories—which was even more cavernous by far—the floor was warm, heated from beneath by steam pipes. (On Evemer's floor plan, the list of potential dangers in the room included but were not limited to: slipping and hitting one's head on the tiles; assailants hiding beneath the footbridge or in the plants or coming in through the skylight; drowning in the artificial brook.)

"Are we in agreement about what will happen if Siranos comes in?" Kadou said, not meeting his eyes.

"I will make him leave immediately, my lord," Evemer said, already vigilant for intruders or assailants—though Siranos would likely come in through the door rather than the skylight.

"Not like Tadek would, though."

"No, my lord." Tadek probably couldn't pick Siranos up bodily and haul him out the door.

Kadou took his first wash, or what passed for it, by simply stepping under the waterfall for the length of a held breath. He proceeded immediately to the steam room, as wet and bedraggled as a half-drowned cat, the fabric of his white bathing robe sticking to his skin.

The steam room was even more beautiful than the washing room, with tall slender pillars supporting a domed ceiling painted Mahisti blue with a fantastic array of stars and constellations in gold and silver leaf. The floor was a mosaic in shades of blue as well: long, swirling, abstract curls that could have been stylized water currents or gusts of wind. Kadou sat in the steam in one of the wall alcoves for a full fifteen minutes. Evemer's floor plan said that the wall alcoves could hide assailants, but that the primary listed dangers of this room were slipping on the tiles (of course), heat exhaustion, or lingering coughs from the excess of moisture in the air.

"Are you annoyed?" Kadou said suddenly.

Evemer jolted. "My lord?" He'd been busy glaring at the door.

"I'm sorry if this is taking a long time."

"My lord," he said. Then, remembering again Kadou's request for him to say what he meant—a difficult habit to form so far—he added, "I would be watching over you regardless of the location, my lord."

Evemer jolted again when the door creaked open and Derya,

the kahya he'd asked to mind the furnaces, stuck çir head in. "Sorry to disturb you, Highness," çe said. "Did you require anything else?"

"No, thank you."

Derya eyed Evemer disapprovingly, as if standing and glaring at the door was insufficient service in some way. "Would you like assistance washing your hair, Highness?" çe asked pointedly.

Evemer flared hot, as much with the implied criticism of his work (criticism that was *correct*, to his shame) as with the image of Derya touching his lord, and the tension of remembering that the other kahyalar might not be as trustworthy as Evemer had thought they were this morning, and the idea *again* that it was much more likely that an assailant would just walk in through the door.

Kadou opened his mouth to reply. "He would not," Evemer snapped. "Leave us."

Derya raised çir eyebrows. "Call me if you need anything, then," çe said, and shut the door.

"Well," Kadou said mildly.

"I don't know Derya," Evemer said.

"Çe got approval from Eozena."

"The commander could be wrong. I *don't know Derya*." He could still feel the bruises in his gut where he'd been punched the night before, and those lists on the floor plan he'd been given flashed again through his mind.

No strangers. Not today, and not here. Not even if they were a kahya.

Kadou conspicuously did not sigh, but gazed steadily at Evemer. Eventually he nodded. "All right. I don't mind washing my hair myself."

Evemer felt another pang of shame—he ought to offer his help. He ought to offer. If he were truly committed to the prevention of another nervous attack, he would offer whatever his lord required. And he knew that Kadou was calmed by touch—*warm* touch, he corrected himself firmly, remembering how Kadou had flinched the night before at the touch of the cold washcloth when Evemer had tried to wipe the blood from his face.

He ought to offer. He knew he ought to. But Evemer was . . . not accustomed to touch.

Kadou moved to another bench where there was a bubbling fountain set into the wall and an elegant little stone table with a tray of cut-glass bottles and wide-mouthed jars. He poked through them, smelling each of them in turn.

Torn, Evemer glanced down at his own hands, then at the archway of the door. If he offered his own services, would he be compromising his ability to protect Kadou in the event of sudden assassination? Or, slightly more likely, Siranos? Was Siranos even allowed in the royal baths? The man had a habit of worming his way into places he wasn't quite welcome . . .

Out of the corner of his eye, he caught Kadou peeling the wet robe off his shoulders so it pooled around his hips, framing the soft curve of his slender waist, the slope of his ribs and the line of his spine as it disappeared up into the black river of his long hair, damp and sticking to his skin in curls and waves . . . the arresting curve from shoulder to elegant neck that was for some reason momentarily the most important thing in the world. Kadou took water from the fountain's reservoir with one of the silver bowls sitting on its lip and poured it over his head to wet his hair again, pulling the slick length of it over his shoulder. He scooped soft soap out of a little glass pot, and Evemer abruptly decided he would not be able to live with himself if he failed to offer. "Please, my lord, would you allow me?"

Kadou blinked at him. "Allow you?"

"I can do that for you, if you wish."

"Oh." Kadou rubbed his hands together, lathering the oily soap. "That's—that's really not necessary." He half laughed. He wasn't meeting Evemer's eyes now. "I always feel strange, asking for things like that—expecting them. Especially from someone I don't know very well. I always worry that they'll think I'm incapable, or that they'll feel that those things are beneath them."

Evemer felt like he'd been dropped into a crucible of molten iron. "In your service, nothing is beneath me," he said softly, just loud enough to be heard over the bubbling of the fountain. "Everything is my job if it makes your life more comfortable."

Kadou looked over at him, that troubled, regretful, *resigned* look in his eyes again. "You're unhappy, aren't you."

"What? No. I—"

"You are, though," Kadou said softly. "You're an infamously dedicated and disciplined kahya of my house. You took the final oaths of service for the core-guard and immediately got assigned to the most disfavored person in the palace. And I . . . I've been making it difficult for you. I drag you out to taverns when you think it's a bad idea, and I get as drunk as I possibly can and you hate that, and I have a hard time asking for help or letting people take care of me. Of course you're unhappy."

Evemer clenched his jaw. "My lord, I'm not. I'm not unhappy." He *wasn't*. He was . . . he was just . . . He was doing his best. He was following all his training and education; he was doing his duty and staying steadfast to his oaths; he was even . . . getting along with His Highness. Sort of—beginning to. The tension of resentment between them hadn't lasted past the night before, when his lord had saved his life. And that moment in the garden, when his lord had made the impossible request and granted him impossible mercy.

"What are you, then?" The soap was dripping off Kadou's fingers. Evemer swallowed. "Because you're not happy either, so what are you?"

Evemer couldn't answer right away. He didn't know how to speak like this. No one had ever asked him to.

"I'll tell you what *I* am," Kadou said, still very quiet. But there was a note of that recklessness underneath, like when he had been trying to pick fights with drunk sailors. "I am a person with no use, Evemer. Her Majesty is the anchor the entire kingdom rests upon. I'm just the spare. The *fail-safe mechanism*." He held Evemer's eyes for a long moment, and then said gently, "What are you?"

It was a very strange sensation, the thing that happened in Evemer's mind. It was like a cloud slipping from in front of the moons and spilling their light over all the things he paid no heed to, the things he ignored or pushed aside or discarded if he held them up against the image of what he wanted most to be and found that they did not fit any more than his childhood clothes would. It was horrifyingly unpleasant.

"What are you, Evemer?" Kadou said again.

"Lost," Evemer said, because he was. Because he didn't have words for this, because he didn't know what was happening to him, because he didn't know how he felt about it or what the rules were or how to hold himself upright and know that he was being correct and righteous. *A ship at sea on a cloudy night,* he wanted to say, but he couldn't get his tongue to move again. *A child who turned the wrong way on a crowded street. A man in a cave, fallen, his torch extinguished.*

Except for that feeling he'd had the night before—that feeling of turning unexpectedly on a crowded street and finding someone familiar beside him. That *ah, there you are* feeling. The same one he'd had in the garden, kneeling at Kadou's feet, prepared to sacrifice anything to that soft voice and its gentlest request.

But had he imagined it? Could that feeling ever be replicated, outside those two extraordinary circumstances? Or was he fated to be wandering the world with this urgent feeling in the back of his mind that could never find an answer? Wandering, and thus . . . lost.

The only sound was the trickle of water into the basins of the fountains, and then Kadou said, in a voice so exquisitely kind that it sent sharp arrows right through Evemer's chest, "Would you please wash my hair?"

Evemer nodded, eyes downcast to the beautiful mosaics on the floor. He removed his sword belt and set it on a neighboring bench, still within reach but well clear of the water, and his lord held out his hands so Evemer could scrape the soap off of them. He moved slowly, and Kadou turned his back. The weight of the water had pulled Kadou's hair otter-sleek over his scalp and down his back, dripping onto the marble seat of the bench. Evemer rubbed the soft oil-soap between his hands and began working it into Kadou's hair, his nose filling with the scent of orange blossom and rare kesarwood.

"I feel like I should apologize too," Kadou said. "I think I understand why you're lost." He was twisting his fingers in his lap in that way he had. "We . . . There aren't . . ." He flexed his hands, made a frustrated noise in his throat. "Fealty works so long as there is a certain amount of trust and loyalty between both parties. It works only when both parties act altruistically to protect each other's interests, otherwise it's just exploitation. I've been so preoccupied with my own troubles that I haven't had a care for yours. If your job is to—to do anything that makes my life more comfortable, then I need to know how I can do the same for you. Because it's only ethical if it's reciprocal and balanced, and I think that you're feeling lost *because* I haven't been reciprocating as I ought to."

Evemer's hands had paused. Kadou's hair was tangled soft and slick around his fingers like rivers of black ink. He heard an echo of Commander Eozena's voice: *A good man . . .* "It's not necessary," he heard himself say, but he knew it wasn't true, his gut twisted and soured with how untrue it was, how much he longed for—

"*Yes, it is,*" Kadou said in a voice as inflexible as the granite bones of the earth, and all the air rushed back into the room. "It is necessary. If I disregard what I owe you, then I am not being a good liege, and you would be well within your rights to withdraw your loyalty. I would not deserve it. I'd be taking from you without giving anything back." He took a breath. "Can you tell me?" His voice was small now—he was lost too, Evemer realized. That's what he meant by being a person with no use. He'd been tugged along by the will of the gods and his own fear for his whole life, and here they were, two ships on a dark cloudy night whose only point of reference was each other. "Can you tell me what you need?"

"I just want to be needed," Evemer whispered. Then, because he thought Kadou would understand what he meant, would understand *him,* he said, "I want to be useful."

"But that's not reciprocity. What do you need from me?"

Evemer forced his fingers to move again, working the soap through Kadou's hair as if he were handling gossamer-thin crystal.

"If we can't be honest with each other, then how are we going to stand each other's company a month from now?" Kadou said.

"We haven't been—it's been better, today. I haven't felt like . . . like there was anger or resentment between us. I don't want to go back to that. I want to make it *right*. I want to know how to care for you. So what do I owe you, as your lord?"

"Fairness. Loyalty. Reciprocal protection," Evemer said, and then, before he could stop himself: "A place in your home. A place at your hearth." Words from the oath of fealty a person took upon becoming a cadet, then again upon promotion to the kahyalar of the fringe-guard, and once more for core-guard, growing longer and more elaborate every time—but that phrase stayed the same. Home and hearth.

Evemer filled one of the fountain's silver bowls with water and poured it slowly over Kadou's hair, shielding his lord's face with his hand. Kadou obligingly tilted his head back—he kept his eyes open, and he looked at Evemer with an expression that he could not quite read. Evemer stared hard at the stream of water.

Very softly, Kadou said, "This morning, you asked to talk about . . . about what happened last night." Evemer inclined his head, just once. "I said no. I told you I didn't want to." Evemer swallowed, his jaw tightening. Kadou took a slow breath. "I'm sorry. I shouldn't have."

"There is no need to apologize, my lord."

"You would have given your life for me last night," Kadou said. "You told me to run. And this afternoon . . ."

"Yes," he said. *I'd do it again. I'd do it a thousand times,* Evemer thought.

"And all you want in return is for your sacrifice to be honored and accepted."

Evemer could only nod, still rinsing oil out of Kadou's hair, letting it stream out of his hands in silky ribbons down the perfect curve of Kadou's spine.

"This was what I meant about my obligations earlier," Kadou added. "How it was my duty to go looking for the counterfeits. I'm bound by fealty too, but my liege is . . . partially abstract."

"The nation."

"The nation," Kadou agreed. "My house. Her Majesty my

sister. Our continued prosperity. The entire populace of Araşt. I'm charged to care for them, as you're charged to care for me."

Evemer felt that warm glow of light in his chest again. This was what he had always felt was right and good—and Kadou understood it. Could verbalize it. "The commander is correct that it isn't your place to run headlong into trouble for their sake. Your death or injury would be a source of chaos—and your duty also includes warding the kingdom against that. Sometimes that is the best way to care for it."

"Would you have stayed out of the fight last night if I'd told you it wasn't your place? If I said your duty was to stand back and protect only yourself?"

His stomach twisted and felt cold and hard at the very thought of it.

"I need to wash your hair again," Evemer muttered, occupying himself with the tray of soap once more. It wasn't at all necessary—it wasn't like Kadou had been caught in a dust storm or walked through a room full of cobwebs. Evemer was just being thorough. Thoroughness was valuable and appropriate.

"Don't dodge the question."

"No, I wouldn't have," Evemer said. "I would have ignored you entirely."

"Obviously," Kadou agreed. "But suppose you had to. Suppose that four or five people—including me, including Commander Eozena—had all held you back from it, or had locked you away so you couldn't be there. Suppose they kept you from my side when I needed you."

Evemer didn't want to suppose any such thing.

"You'd feel lost then too, wouldn't you? You'd feel like you didn't have a direction or a purpose."

"You're trying to convince me to side with you," Evemer said, glaring at the back of Kadou's head as he lathered the soap in his hands and began finger-combing it through Kadou's hair. "You're going to talk to the commander again and you want me to back you up."

Kadou glanced back over his shoulder. "Can you blame me?"

Evemer huffed.

"Just think about it," Kadou said.

He didn't speak again until Evemer was rinsing the next round of thick oil-soap from his hair with bowl after bowl of warm water, leaving it glossy as unspun silk. The water streamed down Kadou's shoulders and back, keeping the white robes around his waist drenched, the water running in rivulets off the marble bench and onto the floor with a sound like rain. Evemer rubbed the impossibly soft locks of hair between his fingers, working the soap out gently, enraptured in a way that felt . . . dangerous. Like standing on a cliff edge and thinking about leaning forward just slightly.

Kadou broke the silence to murmur, "You said earlier that you don't dislike me anymore. Do you . . . think we could be friends, eventually? Or . . . or friendly, at least?"

It took Evemer a moment to find his tongue, and then to put words to it. "I would never wish to presume." The water from Kadou's hair was running clear now, and Evemer found himself acutely disappointed. He couldn't wash it a third time. That would begin to inconvenience His Highness.

"Oh," said Kadou, and his hands twisted in his lap again, fiddling with a hem of the robe. "Would you find it difficult, if we were?"

"I don't know."

"I'd like it if we were," Kadou said softly. "I've never had many."

Evemer stepped away and replaced the jar of soap, occupying his hands with organizing all the little bottles until they were neat. "Of course you have. Everyone loves you."

"At a distance. I haven't had many friends up close. It's . . . hard to get close to someone in my position."

"Tadek," Evemer said, and then his heart stopped in his chest, and for a moment he was too horrified with himself to speak.

Kadou cleared his throat. "Yes. Tadek. I don't know if he'd use the word 'friends' for what we are, but . . . yes, he's a friend of sorts. The closest one I have, anyway. Eozena is more . . . family."

A friend of sorts. Evemer bit his tongue to hold back any further comments and kept his eyes lowered. He supposed it was an *of sorts* kind of friendship for Tadek to feel comfortable taking the kinds of liberties that he did. Evemer clenched his jaw. It was not his place to make judgments about who his liege favored or the choices he made in his personal life. His liege was to be considered above reproach.

Tadek, though. He could judge Tadek all he liked, because regardless of how deft he was at disarming Siranos and how many clever remarks he had prepared and how lightning fast his swordforms were and how many easy talents he possessed, the fact remained that he was a little shit with no regard for propriety and a complete inability to restrain himself around pretty young princes. He was a *flirt*.

"My lord," he murmured, because that was all he had to say.

"May I do yours?" Kadou asked.

"My what?" Evemer said, arranging all of the soap jars in precise regulation-perfect order. He was, frankly, still appalled that Tadek held such little reverence for House Mahisti that he would keep his attentions fixed on Kadou as if His Highness were an *equal*. That Tadek would attempt to *charm* Kadou, as if His Highness could be charmed, calling him lovely and beauty in front of other people as he had earlier—and nearly every other day that Evemer had seen the two of them together. Simply unspeakable behavior.

"Your hair. Can I do it for you?"

Evemer's thoughts wrenched away from Tadek's many sins and improprieties with a jolt. "Why?"

Kadou shrugged one shoulder. "Reciprocity."

Evemer urgently ran through all the rules of duty and honor that he had ever learned or heard allusions to and came up blank but for a confused hunch that he should probably say no, because it was somehow wrong for him to allow Kadou to do such a thing. There were the floor plans—yes, that was it. The floor plans of the bathhouse with all the notes on all the ways one's oathsworn charge could be hurt or killed without the unwavering vigilance of their kahya.

And, on the other hand, there were the ballads—stories of the ancient warlords who brushed and shod their lieutenants' horses with their own hands, or mended their soldiers' armor, or washed their wounds. Evemer flushed with shame and longing to even think of that. Those were gestures of great honor and love, and he had not done anything to be so cherished. He hadn't even been able to protect Kadou the night before. He'd had to be *rescued*.

"You look like you're overthinking it," Kadou said quietly.

Well, he probably was. It came down to Kadou's choice, didn't it? And his liege was above reproach, was he not? "I couldn't impose." But oh, part of him wanted it, wanted to have that proof that he was useful and valued, that his failure could be forgiven . . . Part of him yearned for it so sharply it hurt.

"Reciprocity." And then Kadou added, with a perfectly straight face, "Are you trying to imbalance the whole system of fealty, Evemer? I should have known you'd turn out to be a dangerous revolutionary after all."

Evemer refused to laugh at that, though a sparkle of it gleamed suddenly in his chest, cutting through the ache of all that banked and buried longing. "It's true," he said soberly. "All of this has been a ruse. Soon I will trick you into kidnapping yourself, and I will have you write your own ransom note." The sparkle of mirth was replaced by a wave of horror, and he looked at Kadou properly before he could help himself and—

And Kadou had lit up like the streets of Kasaba's Little Tash district for the Tashaz winter festival of lights. He'd somehow come *alive* in a way that Evemer had never seen on him before—or at least, not since that moment at the Shipbuilder's Guild when he'd looked down and smiled and said, *You're a godsend.*

Evemer felt a wave of strong emotion surging up and promptly slammed a door on it before he could even identify what the feeling was, holding it closed and ignoring whatever spilled through like firelight shining through the gap at the bottom. He looked away from his lord and occupied his attention, as much as he could, with counting tiles at the base of the fountain.

"Evemer!" Kadou said, and that life was in his voice too. "That was a joke!"

"It wasn't a very funny joke."

"But it *was* a joke—that's two now, isn't it? We are pleased, and in place of any honorable titles We could bestow upon thee, We shall wash thy hair."

Kadou sounded like a *person*. Even with the silly, overwrought, archaic language, he sounded like . . . like anyone else. Evemer didn't quite know what had changed, but it was as if a freestanding mirror had been swiveled in place and now reflected a completely novel perspective of the room.

"If you must, my lord," Evemer said, and some part of him, curious to see what would happen, just managed to bite back an assurance that Kadou shouldn't feel obliged to do anything for him.

"You aren't very good at letting people take care of you either, are you," Kadou said, pulling the robe back up over his shoulders, then rising from the bench and nudging Evemer to sit down in his place. Evemer was too gobsmacked at the notion that someone besides his mother might even *want* to take care of him to respond before Kadou tipped Evemer's head back and poured water over him.

He spluttered inelegantly.

"Sorry," said Kadou, unrepentant. The bottles and jars of soaps and fragrant oils clattered on the tray as he rummaged through them, disarraying the perfect order Evemer had constructed them in. Evemer pushed his hair out of his face and wiped his eyes. "You'll have to direct me, I suppose. I've never done someone else's before." His fingers slipped into Evemer's hair a moment later. The scent of the soap—rose, lily of the valley, jasmine, and Arjuni sandalwood—cut a bright note through the humid air.

Through the stunned silence of his own mind, a thought drifted: This soap was, very likely, the most expensive thing he'd ever had on his body, other than his sword and his cobalt-blue uniform. In the kahyalar dormitories they washed with good but simpler scents—mignonette and resin, or zaunwood and citrus.

"It's not difficult," Evemer managed. "This is fine." It was . . . nice. People didn't really touch him. He slammed the door on those feelings too.

A moment later, Kadou said, very quietly, "Did you want to talk any more about last night?"

"This morning, you said it was nothing."

"I did."

"It's not nothing. You know it's not nothing. Why did you say it was?"

"I do know," Kadou said, even softer. "I only thought that I shouldn't let you feel beholden to me. Or like you were obliged to behave as if you were grateful."

"Yes, *obligation* is surely why people feel grateful to someone who's saved their life." Damn, there went his treacherous tongue again. "Apologies, Highness."

"No, don't. I am sorry again for saying it was nothing. It's . . ." He sighed once more, and his hands slipped out of Evemer's hair. "Perhaps this is a foolish way to think of it, but . . . It's a bond. Like the oaths of fealty, but you didn't get a choice. I just did it because I had to, and now there's an extra thread connecting us, and maybe you didn't want that."

A rope, Evemer could have told him. *An iron chain.* "I am honored to have it," he said. "And even if I weren't, I'd prefer that to death." Kadou guided his head back with a soapy hand on his forehead and rinsed his hair, pouring more delicately now. Evemer still squeezed his eyes shut.

"I," said Kadou, "really was pleased, a minute ago. In case that wasn't clear. You made a joke, and it pleased me, and I want you to know that. And I like it when you're sarcastic, too. It . . . helps me worry less."

"Thank you, my lord."

"Just in case *you* were worried."

"Thank you, my lord."

Another sigh. "I'm making you uncomfortable."

"My lord?" Where was Kadou getting an idea like that? Just as Evemer was bringing himself around to it, remembering more of the stories of the lords of ancient times who would wash their servants' feet to show their respect and humility, and how they were remembered in songs as *good men,* just like the commander had said of Kadou . . .

"You're gripping the edge of the bench."

Evemer looked down at his hands, surprised. He hadn't even noticed. He flexed his hands to relax them, placing them flat on his knees. "I wasn't uncomfortable."

Kadou's voice was suddenly very close to his ear. "If you lie to me, I *won't* be pleased," he said. All the hairs on the left side of Evemer's body stood on end. "You said you wouldn't lie to your liege."

"I wasn't. I wouldn't."

"Evemer."

"I swear it." It was nice, in fact—the steady motion of Kadou's hands through his hair and the gentle scrape of his nails over Evemer's scalp. It was going to put him to sleep if it went on any longer, and it was making his shoulders feel *very* odd, sort of loose as if he'd just woken up. "I wouldn't lie to you, my lord."

"Hmm," said Kadou.

Evemer noticed his lungs were burning and took a breath. He unclenched his hands again and laid them very carefully, very flat, on his knees once more. He kept that door in his mind shut tight—he didn't even want to glance at the light shining through the cracks, let alone the immense *something* that burned behind it. He counted tiles on the fountain and, when he had collected himself again, cleared his throat. "Except if I were trying to get you to kidnap yourself," he said, because he had to say something and—and Kadou said he'd been pleased with the joke, hadn't he. "I'd probably lie to you then."

Kadou's hands paused for only a fraction of a second. "Oh? And what lie would you tell me?"

"That I—" A torrent of images tumbled through Evemer's thoughts too quickly to even identify. "That I knew of a beautiful house in the mountains and that I'd take you to it, because there are no rude people named Siranos there." Kadou laughed aloud, and Evemer filled with warmth all the way to his throat.

"Already an improvement over the palace, then. Is there a bathhouse even finer than this one?"

"Fed by a natural hot spring."

"Lovely," said Kadou, and Evemer felt like his very soul was pulling toward the amusement and life in Kadou's voice like a stubborn horse pulling against the reins. He wanted to tell Kadou all about the beautiful house, build it room by room in words like he and his friends had built their imaginary liege's great house as children, the way the wizards in the stories had raised the plateau and built this very palace with their poetry, as exact as any architect. Evemer wanted to tell him about the tall silent pines, and the morning mist veiling the surface of the lake in springtime, the grand main hall and its enormous fireplace, big enough to roast an entire ox, a stable of a thousand white horses whose hooves were shod with silver . . . Rooms and rooms and rooms of every kind for every purpose. There would be a hundred bedrooms alone with huge feather beds and wide fireplaces. It would be a house of endless winding hallways where no one else could ever find Kadou if he wished not to be found.

But it felt so foolish that Evemer could not command his tongue to move, even under the auspices of a jest.

"You grew up in the mountains, didn't you?" Kadou said.

"Yes."

"You don't sound of it, besides your name."

"My body-father died when I was small. My mother moved us to the city after that."

"Were there hot springs near where you lived, before?"

"Yes." He must speak. He *must.* "My mother used to tell me they were a place for the mountain spirits. She said they'd snatch my heart away and replace it with a burning ember if I played too close—but that was just to keep me from drowning."

"Hmm," Kadou said again, but Evemer could hear the smile in it. "There's a therma here, if you're feeling nostalgic. I think I would like to swim today. Shall I rinse out your hair now?"

It felt nice to have someone else washing his hair, Evemer had to admit. It felt . . . warm. Safe. Quiet in his head. The steady gentle motion of Kadou's hands through his hair was so soothing, in fact, that he sank into the sensation rather deeply and didn't come back to himself until Kadou had finished and said he wished to move on to the next stage of the baths. Between the steam room and the therma, they passed by Derya again, who was tidying up and refolding the towels on the shelf in the hall. Evemer realized with a cold shock that his guard had lapsed entirely. Assassins. No weapons anywhere. And he'd let his focus drift—he'd let himself be distracted.

Kadou stepped down into the steaming hot therma, a large bath set into the floor that could have held twenty people easily, and sank chin-deep. His hair flowed around his shoulders, a spreading cloud of black ink, and the thin white fabric of the robe floated over his skin, showing flashes here and there of his wrists, his collarbones, the planes of his chest, the arresting curve of neck and shoulder.

Evemer looked away and counted tiles. In this room, the mosaics were primarily white and silver, bordered with delicate, lacy vinework in shining chips of hematite.

"You're not getting in?" Kadou asked.

"I should be alert and on guard, my lord."

Kadou pulled himself a little ways out of the water, just enough for him to rest his elbows on the edge of the therma near where Evemer stood. "You won't get in trouble. You can say I bullied you into it, if anyone scolds you for it."

"Someone could come in." Traitorous kahyalar, or Siranos, or . . .

Kadou nodded slowly and sank back down into the water until it lapped around his cheekbones, and pushed himself back—the movement of his hair through the water was hypnotic, and it was only by great force of will that Evemer looked away again.

Perhaps there had been something to his mother's warnings after all—the mountain spirits were said to be creatures of surpassing loveliness, all bright eyes and dark hair, who lured men to their deaths in the springs or, as Evemer's mother had warned, snatched their hearts and replaced them with burning embers.

He wondered if this was what that felt like.

※

"Fine," Evemer muttered as they were getting dressed again. Kadou looked up at him, surprised. "What?"

He watched as Evemer found words to put with his thoughts—watched the clench of his jaw and slight pursing of his lips and the frown between his eyebrows that once would have read only as disapproval.

At last, Evemer said, "I would hate to be shut away so I couldn't serve. I would hate to be told there was nothing I could do to help." He let out a long breath. "I will take your side if you speak to the commander, but I have conditions."

"I wouldn't be doing anything differently than I have been, except that I won't get as drunk and I'll be bringing two kahyalar."

"Good. Will one of them be me?"

"Well, I imagine so."

"Every time?"

Kadou wavered. "You'll probably want a night off now and again, won't you?"

"No, I won't. Will it be me every time?" Evemer asked again, more firmly.

"If you want, then—"

"I do. Will it be me *every time?*"

"Yes, it will be you every time," Kadou said, feeling rather bowled-over. "Is *that* a condition?"

"Yes," Evemer said flatly.

"All right." Kadou shook his head and finished knotting his sash—he never could get it as neat as the kahyalar did, but he was feeling . . . shy, a little, of letting Evemer dress him. "You could have been a lawyer, you know."

"I wouldn't be any good at that."

Kadou glanced at him again, curious. "You don't think so? You're not interested in law?"

"I want to serve something bigger than myself."

"A minister, then, or a diplomat. They serve." Evemer gave him a rather puzzled look. "What? You can't be a kahya forever. You won't be allowed. You're too . . ." Kadou waved vaguely. "Competent. Obsessively loyal." He gave Evemer a wry look, unable to hold back a half smile and a breath of amusement. "We're definitely going to try to make use of you if you don't watch out."

Evemer didn't answer, just frowned pensively and opened the door for Kadou.

In the corridor, which felt very cool and breezy after the muggy warmth of the bathhouse, Kadou asked, "Want to practice?"

"Practice?"

"Negotiating. Playing politics."

"How?"

"Talk to Eozena for me?"

"She's my superior. I shouldn't attempt to negotiate with my—" He stopped abruptly and blushed.

"Yes," Kadou said, biting back a laugh. "You already *did* negotiate with me just now."

When they returned to the main room of Zeliha's quarters, they found Melek sitting at the table, bent over the purses of coins. Çe looked up when they entered and grinned. "Evening, Highness! Exciting day, isn't it?"

"I'm glad to see you," Kadou said, smiling back. "When did you get here?"

"Just a couple minutes ago. The commander is talking to Her Majesty in the other room," çe added, nodding to another door.

Kadou glanced at the door, which was shut tight—so no interruptions would be welcome. He moved over to the table with Melek and folded down to sit on one of the beautifully embroidered cushions. Evemer took his station at the door—Kadou had the vague thought that he was awfully far away, standing there, but brushed it aside.

"I'm told you recommended me for this," Melek said, glancing up again with another warm smile, which Kadou returned.

"Tadek did, technically. I wasn't even aware you were a touch-taster at all. Tadek said you had the most sensitive gift of anyone he knows."

"Mm," çe agreed. "Not the *most* sensitive, but I'm pretty sharp." Melek ran çir hands slowly over the coins, spreading them out across the table. "What am I supposed to be looking for, anyway?"

"Composition. Whether there are any patterns of difference. If there are two groups, or just one."

Melek nodded and pressed çir hands down flat, spreading them to cover as many of the coins as possible. Çe picked up a few, one by one, and rubbed them between çir fingers. "Well . . . it's complicated. Where would you like me to start?"

"What do they feel like?"

"The touch-tastes I get from coin gold in general are the flavor of white wine, the smell of cut radishes, and a hazy summer dawn. These aren't coin gold, of course. You already know they're debased." Çe weighed one of the coins in çir hand. "This one was minted in the midafternoon, but all of them were made in the late winter of this year. The gold is from one of the eastern mines, not as far out as Köy, but farther than İsimsiz. The copper is eluding me. I'm not familiar with whatever region or mine it's from."

Kadou blinked at çem. "You're *that* sensitive?"

Melek shrugged. "I guess."

"Why aren't you doing that instead of being core-guard?" he cried. "Do you know how much money you could make, working at the Mint?"

Melek snorted and clapped a hand to çir mouth.

"What?" Kadou demanded. "What did I—oh. It wasn't a joke, Melek."

"How much money I could make," çe said, giggling. "Working *at the Mint*. Where they *make money*."

"Melek."

"Sorry. Sorry. I'm fine. Sorry." Çe composed çemself and cleared çir throat. "Well, it's boring, isn't it! Poking at metal for hours in some dusty room and making notes in a book, doing the same thing every day!"

Kadou shook his head. "What about the others? Is it the same ratio of copper?"

Melek felt another coin. "There's traces of silver in them too, but that's—hmm. If I had to guess, I'd say they didn't mint these from fresh gold. They melted down altınlar, because of course coin gold isn't quite perfectly pure. That's where the silver traces are coming from. The copper, though . . ." Çe frowned, running çir hands across the pile. "I think some of the copper must be from melted kürler—it's not exactly the same ratio, and some of these have enough that I can taste the N'gakan mines, same as I get from the average kür. Some of them, though . . ." Çe shook out çir hand, flexed çir fingers to clear the palate. "Do you think there's any follaro available that I could have for reference?"

"You think the copper might be from the mines in Oissos?"

"I *think* so? I'll need to double-check before I can say for sure—it's been a long time since I touched a follaro. You don't see them much, even in the city. And copper's tricky for me, it always over-whelms everything else."

Kadou picked up one of the silver yiralar. Genuine yiralar had a silver fineness of nine-one-five blended with copper, but eighty-four parts copper per thousand wasn't enough to sense with his touch-tasting. He would have needed a sense as sharp as Melek's for that. "What's the price of copper like in Oissos these days?" he mused aloud. "Is it particularly cheap right now?"

"Er . . ." Melek said, and looked at Evemer. "Do you know that off the top of your head?"

"No. I can find out."

"It's not urgent," Kadou said absently, feeling the bitter, medic-inal signature of the corrupted silver in his fingertips. He looked up as Eozena opened the inner door to Zeliha's chambers and came out.

"Evening, all," she said, striding across the room to the exit—she clearly had no intention of stopping.

Kadou stood up sharply, his chair shrieking against the floor. "Eozena, wait."

She turned back, surprised. "What is it?"

"Where's Zeliha?"

"Feeding the princess," Eozena said, jerking her chin toward the room she'd just come from. "Why?"

"I know you don't think I should have any part of the investiga-tion right now, but I should, and it's urgent. So I'm going to."

She gave him a long look, flicking her gaze briefly to Evemer, who stood by the door in parade rest. "Didn't we discuss this already, Highness? It's not a good idea, and it'd make my job easier if you stayed here where it's safe."

"I'll keep him safe," Evemer said simply. Eozena looked at him again—astonished that he had spoken at all, probably.

"I'll take him everywhere," Kadou added.

"He'll take *two* kahyalar," Evemer said pointedly.

"Cute that you two are scheming together behind my back now, can't say I'm upset about *that*, but, uh . . ." She drew the last syllable out for several increasingly sarcastic seconds. "No."

"I'm going to have to insist," Kadou said.

"By all means," she said warmly. "Be my guest. Insist until you're blue in the face."

"What is he insisting about?" Zeliha exited her room, carrying Eyne in an embroidered linen sling with her kaftan and underlayer pulled off of one shoulder. Evemer immediately dove to arrange the most comfortable cushions on a chair for her, but she waved him off. "Can't sit while I'm feeding her, I get too restless. What's Kadou insisting on?"

"Your Majesty," Eozena said formally. "I'm afraid that it might take a royal decree to get it through this boy's head. He's not going to go out gallivanting around the city to continue with the Shipbuilder's Guild investigation."

Zeliha snorted. "Are you already getting claustrophobic, Kadou? It hasn't even been a day!"

"I have some new ideas," he protested. "This case and the one with Madam Melachrinos have to be related—it pushes the limits of plausibility to think that they're not." At Zeliha's inquisitive eyebrow, he continued: "Melek says the coins were all minted around the same time. The ones we got from her, and the ones we got from Armagan today. They use the same gold—coin gold, probably from altınlar—and Melek thinks the copper they're mixed with might be from Oissos. We've found these two large caches of counterfeits, but we haven't heard any reports from the city. That doesn't mean there aren't any in circulation, it just means that a touch-taster sensitive enough to spot the difference hasn't noticed them yet. There could be some loose in the foreign quarter or the harbor district, so *someone* needs to go down there and ask around."

Zeliha turned back to Eozena. "Commander, do you have the staff to send anyone out?"

"Within the next day, I probably will," Eozena said, eyes narrowed. "Depending on . . . the situation."

Zeliha frowned and paced slowly around the perimeter of the room. "If they came in on an Oissic ship, made with Oissic copper . . . Have we considered that they might be made in Oissos, and that they're being smuggled here?"

"If I may offer an opinion, Your Majesty," Evemer said.

"Of course," she said, turning to him. Eyne, merely a lump hidden in the sling, made a soft noise of protest.

"I believe it is more likely that they would be made here and shipped elsewhere."

"I agree," Kadou said. "It's less risky to distribute them somewhere they might not be immediately noticed."

Zeliha hummed in thought and nodded. "All right."

It took everyone in the room a moment to process what she meant. "Your *Majesty*," Eozena said, aghast.

"I wish *I* could go gallivanting," Zeliha added in a grumble. "Better make the most of it, Kadou."

"Zeliha!" Eozena said. "I need him to stay here until I've gotten the situation under control! It's dangerous!"

"Is it? I think it might be *less* dangerous out there than staying here in the palace, actually."

If Eozena had the complexion for it, Kadou thought she would have gone pale. "How can you possibly—That doesn't make a lick of sense—Zeliha!"

"We're nervous about whether the kahyalar corps has been corrupted, yes? There are many, many fewer kahyalar down in the city. It's much safer for him to be in a crowd of people where a handful of kahyalar might attack him and other people will jump to his defense, rather than for him to be in a *crowd made entirely of kahyalar.*"

Kadou's gaze cut immediately to Evemer. He watched Evemer process this, consider it from every angle, and . . . abruptly relax several degrees. "Ah," Evemer said. "Yes."

❉

Over the next month, Eozena's exhaustive interrogation of the kahyalar corps turned up several smaller crimes. Small compared to treason, anyway—illegal gambling rings, people who had found ways to cheat on the merit exams, drugs, petty thievery. While Eozena grew ever more tense and felt less and less comfortable confirming kahyalar as definitively loyal and true, Kadou continued his own part of the investigation and went down into the city nearly every night.

It was dreadful and tedious, for the most part—and disheartening besides.

After every hand of cards or every lecture with university students, he'd test each coin he'd won or earned against the genuine ones, an altın and a yira he kept in a special pouch so he could be sure that his touch-taste wasn't being changed or skewed—a palate cleanser, of sorts. Every coin of every nationality that came into their hands—his or his kahyalar's—they saved scrupulously until they were able to have it changed into Araşti gold, and then he and Melek tested those too. They changed money at shops and pawnbrokers, a different one every time, and Kadou was not sure whether to be frustrated or relieved when it proved so difficult to find any more counterfeits—perhaps it really was simply a small-time forger working out of a basement or a back room somewhere.

They'd gone out for nine nights in a row, the weather being good. He was once more in his own familiar quarters rather than taking up space in Zeliha's house, grimly preparing for the tenth night in the very, very plain clothes he was becoming more accustomed to than his princely finery—linen for his underlayer, trousers, and knee-length kaftan; battered secondhand boots; a turban to hide his hair; and a short wool cloak on cooler nights.

It made Evemer look like he wanted to die of horror, of course. Sometimes, on good days, he was bold enough to attempt to convince Kadou to wear a finer underlayer or jewelry in his hair under the turban—it wouldn't be seen, but Kadou thought the point was that *Evemer* would know it was there, and find it comforting.

This evening, Tadek was leaning against the wall and watching Kadou tie his turban. "Has Evemer had a day off?" he said, breaking a long silence that had passed beyond awkward and looped back around into neutral.

"Er . . . No, not for a while," Kadou said. "We have a deal. He said he doesn't mind."

"Of course. Who would mind attending their prince on fun evening excursions?"

Kadou closed his eyes and took a breath. He'd been expecting this to come up sooner or later. He'd tried several times to make himself have the much-belated conversation he owed Tadek about where they stood—on two occasions, he'd lost his nerve and changed the subject. On another, he'd worded it so poorly and so vaguely that Tadek had entirely missed his point. "He's not the one having fun, you know. He's just watching me."

"Melek's going with you again tonight?"

Kadou turned, already bracing himself. Tadek had his arms crossed. He was sulking again—not the first time, in these last few weeks. "Is there something wrong?"

"Don't pretend like you don't know. Have I *done* something wrong? Would you even tell me if I had?"

"I've been trying," Kadou said faintly. He was already trembling—this was going to be a fight, then. He braced himself again, breathed through the reflexive clench of terror. It was just another trial from the Lord of Judgment. Just something that had to be gotten through. "Not that you've done wrong, just that I . . . It's difficult, sometimes, with my . . . you know, my affliction."

"I thought I didn't count for that. I thought I was an exception."

"No one's an exception," Kadou said with a weak little laugh.

"I can't control it, you know. It's not about logic. I care about you, and I don't want to hurt you, and so . . ." He gestured broadly, a *what is there to be done?* movement.

"When was the last time we *spoke*? Not just like this, but in the way we used to. You don't look at me as much, and you don't let me touch you anymore." Tadek pushed himself off the wall and came closer, standing in front of Kadou with his hands on his hips. "Do you think I expect anything of you? Do you think I'm—I'm angling for something? I've only wished to serve you, but I thought we were friends, at least."

"We're—"

"Please don't lie to me, Your Highness," Tadek said sharply. "I can take a lot, but I can't take that. I presented myself for your use, and you used me as I'd offered. That was fine. But now you avoid me, and you act like you're embarrassed to be seen with me, and—"

"I am embarrassed," Kadou said—it came out rather sharp, almost a snap. "But I'm embarrassed of myself, not of you. I'm embarrassed that I need help at all, and that I'm so weak that I need to be coddled like a child. I'm embarrassed that I kept saying yes whenever you offered yourself to be *used*, as you so bluntly call it."

"How is that blunt?" Tadek demanded. "That's what it *is*." His jaw clenched, his sharp hazel eyes flashing. "What does Evemer call it?"

Kadou's heart jolted. "He doesn't. He wouldn't—I wouldn't. Not with him. He doesn't want—and I don't either. He's just my kahya."

"Your *favorite* kahya, these days. I was your favorite once." Tadek's expression darkened, grew more wretched.

"I don't have a favorite. Eozena would be my favorite, if I were to have one. Evemer and I aren't friends." Not yet. But it was getting easier, every day, to be around him. Easier to turn to him when Kadou wanted input or a second opinion on something. Easier, too, to trust him, and to feel like he was being trusted in return—in fact, that particular part hadn't been difficult at all since the day in the garden, when Evemer had proved himself so conclusively. Even so, Kadou still felt moments of overwhelming, cringing embarrassment when he misspoke in front of Evemer, and he still had a sneaking suspicion in the back of his mind, whispering in the same voice as his terrors, that Evemer was only being kind, that Evemer secretly didn't like him at all and was only finding graceful, political ways to dance around the fact.

"Right," Tadek said. "So it was never me at all." He shook his head, his mouth a tight line. "After Siranos, that's when it started going wrong?"

"No," Kadou said in a small voice. "It was before that. I just . . ." He sat down heavily on the edge of his bed. "I'm sorry," he said. "I'm really, really sorry."

"If you were sorry, you'd explain. Have I offended you? Have I hurt you somehow?"

"No. It's just—people shouldn't be *used*! They're people! *You're* people! You don't deserve that—you're not a thing." Kadou sighed and pressed the heels of his shaking palms to his eyes. "I pushed you away because I thought I was going to hurt you, but that just made it a self-fulfilling prophecy. I should have been honest with you."

"Why did you think you were going to hurt me?" Tadek demanded. "Do you think I don't know my own mind?"

"I don't think I always know *my* mind," Kadou said.

"Well, *that's* perfectly obvious. You'll dither and wring your hands all night until someone convinces you that you have permission to want something. Melek has to coax you just to let çem file your nails!"

Kadou dropped his hands into his lap with a grimace. Evemer hadn't had to coax about washing his hair in the bathhouse. But that was different too—Evemer needed to do things like that so he'd know he was useful and valued. "I'm not in a position where I feel like I can ask for anything I want just because I want it." He swallowed around the lump that had come into his throat. His eyes stung. "I thought—" What had he thought of it? They weren't lovers—that implied that there had been something more between them. They weren't equals, either. They could never be equals, no matter how much they had pantomimed it in private with each other, no matter how much Tadek was the closest thing he'd ever had to a friend. The gap between them was even wider now that Tadek was his armsman instead of a kahya. "A little while ago," he said quietly, looking down at his hands in his lap. He was wringing them, just like Tadek had said. He made himself stop. "A little while ago, Eozena reminded me of my position. I shouldn't have accepted your offer, even last year. And then you were my armsman, and everything was different, and I thought you—"

"What? What did you think?"

"I thought you'd want more from me. I thought you'd want to be . . . you know. Intimate. Emotionally."

Tadek barked a harsh laugh. "Me? Have *emotions*? Perish the thought. I try to avoid them whenever possible, except when they ambush me without my consent."

"You were being . . . affectionate in front of the others." Kadou glanced up at him. "You were making offers more openly."

"They all knew already," Tadek said, incredulous. "Were we going to bother to pretend we were chaste with each other just for propriety, in front of your *kahyalar*, of all people? The ones who know everything about you? I'd bet a hundred altınlar that even Melek and Evemer could map every freckle on your body, and that's *without* having ever slept with you. It's their—*our*—job to know everything about you, to see you at your worst, and love you anyway." Kadou opened his mouth to reply, but before he could, Tadek made a sharp, cutting gesture with one had. "Don't. Don't you dare say it. You were going to say something about all the reasons we shouldn't love you or that we don't *need* to go out of our way, is that right? Fuck that. Or was it how you shouldn't need anyone to look after you?" Tadek said viciously. "You shouldn't have needs or wants, because then you'd be inconveniencing someone else, is that it? Or was it how you shouldn't even be a person with preferences, let alone with desires? No wonder you get along so well with Evemer. You must find him just *fascinating*."

"I wouldn't say that I do." But he did, didn't he? That was part of it—he didn't want Evemer to think badly of him, and as the days and weeks passed, part of him still wondered with no small amount of yearning how Evemer managed to *be* the way he was, so steady and grounded, seeming so sure of himself even when he said he felt lost.

"No? You, who never wants to admit that you want anything, and him, who might as well be made of stone? You're saying you don't wish you could be like him?"

Kadou bit his lip—he was too obvious with it, then. Another way in which he wasn't at all like Evemer. You couldn't tell what Evemer was feeling unless you were looking straight at him and watching for it.

"Tell you what," Tadek continued, "if I was buried alive in a box with one other person, I'd want it to be him—I think he's found a way not to even *breathe,* just in case you might want to make use of the air."

Kadou stared at him. "Are you *jealous* of him? There's no need. He hasn't replaced you."

"Of course he hasn't." Tadek snorted. "He wouldn't offer to sleep with you, and you obviously wouldn't ever ask him. How can I be replaced, when the two of you would only ever manage to sit quietly on opposite ends of the couch like spinsters?"

The ball of tangled and terrifying emotion in the pit of his stomach kindled suddenly into anger. "Would you stop? Please?"

"Oh, right, of course," Tadek laughed. "You don't like me talking about him like that."

"I don't like you talking about *you* like that!" Kadou said fiercely. "Your duty is to care for me—I accept that. I'm doing the best I can to look after you too, but how can I when you're so convinced that the only thing I value about you is the fact that you're willing to sleep with me?" He glared at Tadek, though he was now shaking like a leaf—hard enough that he wasn't sure he'd be able to keep his feet if he'd been standing. His voice shook too, the words catching and snagging in his throat like silk veils on thorns. "If you think that's all you have to offer me, and if I can't accept that offer anymore, then of course you're going to be hurt!

Of course you're going to think that I've cast you aside! You can be as angry with me as you like, you can be jealous and hurt, but stop talking about yourself like you're nothing!" He covered his face with his hands again, wishing and *wishing* that he could allow himself to cry, just to drain out some of this enormous emotion. "You've been doing that the whole time—talking about yourself like you think you're not important to me. I thought you were just flattering me, or flirting, but that's not it, is it? That's why you kept making those jokes about a kiss being a great gift, right? Like it was something I was *giving* you instead of something we were doing *together*."

Tadek said nothing.

Kadou lowered his hands, but couldn't bring himself to look at him. "I'm sorry," he said. He swallowed hard, eyes closed, clasping his hands so tight in his lap that his knuckles ached and his nails dug into his skin. "I should have . . . noticed. Or something."

"There is no need for Your Highness to apologize," Tadek said. He sounded even more like Evemer now, stiff and emotionless.

Kadou opened his eyes and glared at him. "Stop it."

Tadek huffed a breath. "Thank you, I accept your apology," he said, still without inflection. "Happy?"

"No, of course not."

"Do you wish for me to leave, Your Highness?"

"Do you want to leave right now? Do you want anything from me that I can give?"

Tadek went still and quiet again. "I don't know," he said, and then: "I want you to be angry with me."

"Why?"

"I just do."

Kadou looked up, then. Tadek stood there, his hazel eyes blazing, his hands loose at his sides but his shoulders squared and tense. Kadou got to his feet—his knees were weak with nerves, but he forced them to work so he could step close in front to Tadek and look straight in his eyes. "You still have a place in my home and at my hearth," he said softly. "You will *always* have that. You will always belong. You will always be mine—at least until you tell me you don't want that anymore. Until that day, you are my armsman and you are sworn to me, so I'm going to try to take care of you now, because that's what *I* swore to do. If you don't like it, then you have permission to shove me or hit me. Whatever you like." He waited a beat. Tadek didn't move. Kadou took another half step forward and wrapped his arms around his armsman, the person who was closest to being his friend, hugging him as Tadek himself had so often done for him when he was set upon by terrors.

Tadek was warm and familiar. He smelled like comfort, an easing of worries, affection. It was a scent that called up sense memories of quiet laughter in the dark, of fingers brushing back a stray lock of his hair and tucking it behind his ear before drawing him close into warmth, of kisses pressed to his forehead and cheeks, of unspoken jokes shared with a single twinkling glance, of strong arms holding him so tightly that even the fear-creature in the back of his mind seemed feeble by comparison.

Tadek's head lowered onto his shoulder.

"I chose to save you," Kadou said softly. He tilted his head to rest against the side of Tadek's so that his lips moved against Tadek's hair as he spoke. "And you chose to let Her Majesty lay your life in my hands. You took oaths, and I did too, and those *matter*. I want you to think about them, and if you feel like I have trampled on them, then tell me and I'll do what I can to make it right."

"A place in your home, a place at your hearth," Tadek mumbled.

"Yours for as long as you want them," Kadou said again. "You belong."

Tadek's arms came around his waist, slow and loose. They stood there for several long moments, long enough for Kadou's shaking to fade and ease its grip on him.

At last, Tadek pulled away with an inhale that wasn't quite a sniffle. Kadou let him go, his arms falling slowly until his hands rested on Tadek's arms. "Well," Tadek said, forcing a lightness into his voice that Kadou hated to hear. "This has all been embarrassing, hasn't it? Made a bit of a mess of things, haven't I."

"Don't."

"Don't what?" Tadek smiled.

"Don't start pretending you're fine. Don't pretend it's nothing."

"Please let me pretend it's nothing," Tadek said, still airy. "You've already deconstructed me down to my foundations. The least you can do is let me walk out of here having saved some face."

Kadou subsided. "Right. Sorry."

"It's not in your oaths that you have to act like a priest helping me through an unburdening. That's too much to ask." Kadou wouldn't have known where to start with that anyway—he'd never been offered an unburdening, and he only vaguely knew what it entailed. Long talks in a quiet room with a dedicate of Usmim, laying out your heart and your troubles for her to inspect and interrogate, because supposedly that helped you feel better. "I think," Tadek said, "I think I might go to the temple, while you're out tonight. See if I can—" He stopped, swallowed. "See if there's anyone there to unburden myself to, or else try to do it alone. Lay things out and take a hard look at myself."

"I'm sorry," Kadou said again, squeezing Tadek's arms where his hands still rested on them, for Tadek hadn't yet pulled away entirely. "I'm sorry for hurting you, and for . . . deconstructing you. Did I speak too bluntly?"

Tadek did pull away then with another inhale that wasn't quite a sniff. "No, no, it's nothing. Sometimes you don't see yourself properly until someone says something outrageous, so we'll count it as a learning moment and we won't speak of it again, eh?" His easy smile cracked. "I'd already had a bit of that epiphany anyway. After the incident, after I was made your armsman. I'd already started thinking maybe I'd wasted my . . ." He stopped, shook his head sharply. "No, never mind. You have places to go and counterfeiters to catch. I won't trouble you any more tonight."

"Tadek," Kadou said, when Tadek was at the door, his hand on the knob. Tadek stopped, but didn't turn. "I meant it. I want to make it right if I can." He took a breath. "We're not going to sleep together again. But—I value you, and I'm glad to have you here. Thank you for all your service."

Tadek shot another quick smile over his shoulder, all his walls built right back up—he had as many as Evemer did, Kadou realized. He'd just done a better job of convincing everyone that they weren't there. Perhaps he'd even convinced himself. "As I said, it's an honor. Everything has been worth it."

※

On the walk down the Palace Road, Evemer noticed His Highness was unsettled. His hands weren't shaking, and he wasn't overly pale, but something was off.

"Highness, are you well?"

"Yes."

Well. That settled that.

When they reached the bottom of the cliff, Melek hung back twenty or thirty paces so as not to appear like çe was one of Kadou's guards. Halfway down the Lifeblood, Evemer couldn't help but ask again: "My lord, are you sure you're well?" He should have said *sir*—he always said sir when they were out in the city.

"I'm fine," Kadou said. And then: "Sorry, I'm just thinking."

He clearly didn't wish to be pestered about it. Evemer resolved to let it lie, though it rankled him.

"Evemer," Kadou said suddenly, "what do you think are the most valuable things about you?"

"I work hard," Evemer said slowly. "I'm very disciplined."

"What else? What do you like about yourself?"

Where in the world was His Highness going with this? "I never break promises, even to myself. I like that." It was only the month of practice he'd just had in speaking his true thoughts as he meant them that allowed him to add, "Why?"

"I just wanted to know. I wanted to make sure there was something."

Maybe not careless-flighty-negligent, but still very, very strange.

They had lingered at many different establishments all over the foreign quarter and the harbor district of Kasaba City—public houses of all varieties, gambling dens, a few not-quite-brothels. Two nights ago, they had overheard someone mention a particular incense lounge—the woman was recommending it to a foreign acquaintance as a reliable place to change the rest of her money to good Araşti gold, since they offered a markedly better exchange rate than the average. Not so much better that it was immediately and obviously suspicious, but His Highness had begun to lose his confidence several days ago. An unofficial money changer might be up to some other scheme, and Evemer felt that discovering *anything* at this point, even if it was irrelevant to their investigation, would help greatly in bolstering His Highness's conviction.

Evemer could smell the Jasmine Tree long before he saw it; wafts of delicate perfume filled the street. As required by city ordinance, the incense lounge had a green awning out front, hung with long orange tassels on the corners.

Without needing to be told, Melek stationed çemself inconspicuously on the street corner, and Kadou and Evemer entered the incense lounge alone. Inside, the entire floor was covered with layers of worn carpets, and low wooden tables were scattered throughout the room, each surrounded by several rather flat cushions. Kadou drifted toward a table in one of the front corners, near to the door, where it was more private and shadowed. The rest of the parlor was dimly lit by hanging lamps, many of which were covered with globes of pink glass.

An attendant approached, setting a brass incense burner on the table between them. Evemer eyed it disapprovingly—even in the dim rosy light, he could see that it was flimsily made and gaudy.

"What's the cheapest incense you have?" Kadou asked the attendant before she could say anything.

"Lavender."

His Highness made a face. "All right, what's the second cheapest? Sorry. We don't have much money on us, and I can't stand lavender." This was one of His Highness's little tactics to convince people that he was not rich. Evemer could have told him it didn't precisely work the way he intended it to—his clothes were too clean, the cloth too good, his elocution too refined.

The attendant was clearly bored to tears and didn't care either way. She blinked slowly at them. "There's a spice blend. Or Mistress Sidur's house blend."

Kadou sighed and tipped his head back against the wall, closing his eyes. "Either of those sound fine. Surprise us."

They sat in silence until the attendant returned again. She placed a cake of black incense in the center of the burner and lit one corner of it with a long rushlight, then covered it with a brass dome perforated in botanical patterns (also rather cheaply made, Evemer noted). In a moment, the smoke began trickling through the holes in soft ribbons and twisting up to the ceiling—it would have some intoxicating quality to it, though Evemer doubted that a place like this would provide anything particularly potent. Kadou shifted closer and wafted a breath of smoke into his face, inhaling deeply and sitting back. Evemer watched him with wary eyes—Kadou glanced at him and shook his head, murmuring, "Don't worry, I'm not having much."

"You're better with your head clear," Evemer said. "You need to be sharp."

"I'm going to be sharp. I'll be sharper if I'm not worrying myself into a useless heap."

Evemer eyed him. He hadn't realized that Kadou was that much on edge. He was doing a better job of concealing it today. "Is that why you drink so much?" He was always a little surprised with himself when he managed to ask things outright like that, even after the month of practice. It was much like the first few times he'd managed to perfectly execute one of the verses of Beydamur's progression for the sword—that moment of stumbling surprise that he *hadn't* stumbled, that muscle memory was setting in.

Kadou shrugged, not meeting his eyes. "If there was anything else that helped, I'd take that instead. I don't like the sensation of being drunk, but it's better than . . . you know, the alternative. Embarrassing myself in front of people. Needing to be coddled and petted." He sat back heavily, his hands in his lap. "I really hate it, sometimes. Or all the time."

Evemer hadn't been expecting him to say anything more—His Highness did not like to talk about his condition. Carefully, tactfully, he said, "Surely there are medicines of some sort that would be more effective than drink."

"Sure: Laudanum. Opium. Blueash. More addictive than alcohol, and more dangerous, and they would take me too far out of my own head. Even hashish just knocks me out or leaves me catatonic, which in practice is no better than laudanum—I have to be functional and alert. Tobacco can help calm me, but only for half an hour or so, and then I feel worse when it wears off. Everything else is about as effective as chamomile tea. The incense doesn't do anything for me except take the edge off. It blunts just the sharpest corners." Kadou shook his head. "Don't worry about it."

Evemer shifted, but said nothing for several long minutes. The smoke streamed upward, only getting thicker. He stayed well back from it. He would have had to lean right into the stream and breathe deep several times to feel a significant effect. "Is it that you think we are not making fast enough progress?"

"Partly."

Evemer quietly fumed to himself—not about Kadou, but about the situation in general. If he could have solved it by sheer force of will, surely they would have broken through something by now.

They lingered for an hour or so, until the ribbons of smoke in their burner had long since died out. The incense lounge was, by all appearances, a perfectly normal one, though more than slightly shabby. When contrasted with the generous exchange rate that they were offering for money changing, Evemer couldn't help but find that shabbiness suspicious. Establishments that offered money changing as an afterthought to whatever their main purpose was, as this one did, had a tendency to be geared toward a much higher class of clientele—merchants, business owners, solicitors.

There was *something* off about this place, something that warranted further scrutiny, and Evemer knew without having to ask that his lord thought the same.

✳

When they went out onto the street, Kadou managed to murmur a few words to Melek so that çe would move closer to the door and keep an eye on things both inside and immediately nearby while he and Evemer looked around the back.

The alley was, at first glance, also perfectly normal, cluttered with empty crates and full rubbish bins and water barrels. This part of the city was very old and had not been carefully engineered—the alley was full of strangely shaped nooks and shadowed corners where the buildings butted together unevenly at odd angles.

"Come on," Kadou whispered. The benefit of the low, rosy light of the incense parlor was that his eyes were already fully adjusted to the dark—though it was *very* dark. The night was cloudy and the moons were in the wrong phases to provide much help.

Kadou braced himself for an accustomed moment of terror—every other time this last month that they had come close to an alley like this, he'd felt a small sickening catch in his chest at the memory of that night that he and Evemer had been set upon by those thieves. Just as expected, a few steps into the alley, it hit him.

Perhaps he was primed for it to be worse after the fraught conversation with Tadek and his increasing certainty that he was wasting Evemer and Melek's time. Instead of a catch that he could have brushed off with a little discomfort, this was more of a lurch, like he'd missed a step going down a flight of stairs. His stomach dropped to his feet, his pulse pounded so hard he could feel it in his palms, and he took a shuddering breath. His skin felt wrong.

"Sir?" Evemer murmured, touching his wrist—his nerves screamed as if they'd been flayed with hot wires, but Kadou turned, fumbling for Evemer's arm, grasping it so tight his knuckles hurt.

"Sorry," he gasped. "Just a—it's nothing, it will pass."

Evemer pulled him closer, wrapped an arm around his shoulder.

It was so unexpected that it almost shocked Kadou out of the grips of fear. "I asked earlier if you were well, sir," Evemer hissed.

"I was! I swear I was! It's just—" Kadou leaned against Evemer's side; Evemer carried his weight effortlessly, even as Kadou's knees buckled under him. "Damn, I hate this!" he snarled under his breath. "I hate it, I hate it."

"Come on, let's not do this in the open." Evemer tugged him along deeper into the alley and found a niche, where one building abutted another so closely that it had almost blocked off an arched doorway. The arch was deep, but not deep enough for the door to open all the way; the hinges and straps were rusted and covered in dirt and cobwebs. The nook it made, however, was just the right size for two people to cram into.

Kadou leaned back into the corner, heedless of the cobwebs, and put his hands over his face. "To hell with this," he breathed. "I remembered the—the thieves, and it set me off. Like we were back there, like it was going to happen again." He slapped one shaking hand against the stones. "Gods! I *hate* this."

"Can you breathe?"

Kadou tested his lungs—it felt like iron bands were wrapped around his chest, or like something heavy was sitting on him, but . . . it wasn't the worst it had ever been. "Yes," he said. "I'm sorry. I'm sorry."

"I don't think that—" Evemer began slowly, but a noise in the alley stopped him—someone knocking on a door.

They both went very, very quiet. Kadou's heart pounded louder than ever, and Evemer shifted minutely to shield him from the rest of the alley—but no, Kadou couldn't be having that. He pushed Evemer aside just enough and craned to see over his shoulder, looking past him.

There was a figure standing there, scuffing their shoes against the cobblestones, a lamp set on the ground by their feet. The door they'd knocked on was the one to the incense parlor.

The door opened outward and spilled a pool of reddish light, though not enough to fully see the figure.

"Oh, it's you. I suppose you've heard by now?" one of the voices said, a light soprano. "About our friend's contact?"

"That minister or lieutenant or whatever? Aye. Still moldering in the royal dungeons, last I heard." Kadou stiffened and grabbed Evemer's arm—Evemer seized his in return and gestured for him to be quiet.

"Have you heard from our friend?"

"Not since the big upset in the palace. You?" Kadou craned farther to see, realizing belatedly that they had wedged themselves rather tightly into this space and he'd now pressed himself bodily against Evemer. Evemer did not seem to have noticed. His eyes were as fixed on the scene as Kadou's.

"Same." A sigh. "Last orders I got said to continue as we have been."

The other person, a gravely baritone, said something that Kadou couldn't make out.

"No, I haven't the faintest idea. After Azuta's shipment was confiscated—"

There was a noise farther down the alley—perhaps a footstep, perhaps a cat jumping onto one of the rickety crates. Kadou's heart leapt into his throat. The voices stopped. "Shh! You hear that?"

Evemer pushed him back farther into the shadows.

"Hand it over," the lighter-voiced person said urgently. "Come on."

A rustle of clothing, a jangle of metal—coins?—and the definitive thump of a door closing as the ambient light from inside vanished.

The person left in the alley grumbled to themself. The shadows cast by their lantern swung back and forth. "I don't like this," they mumbled. And then, louder, "Anybody there?" Footsteps came toward them.

Evemer tensed, pushing Kadou into the corner, turning his back on the alley so they faced each other. Kadou squirmed and tried to look out again—if he could just get a glimpse of that person's face—

"Shh!" Evemer said, and the footsteps stopped.

"Who's there?" The shadows on the walls shifted as they raised the lamp, swinging it around. Kadou's already racing heart nearly stopped dead. Was this person alone? Did they have friends nearby? Armed? How many? There was certainly the other person inside the building. If he and Evemer were found, would it be obvious that they'd been spying? Why else would two people be crammed into a dark corner together in an alley in the middle of the night—

Kadou seized the front of Evemer's kaftan and yanked to get his attention. "Kiss me. *Now*," he whispered urgently.

Evemer obeyed without an instant of hesitation.

His mouth was clumsy against Kadou's, his lips heart-wrenchingly soft. When he cupped Kadou's face a split second later, his hands were so gentle and warm that Kadou momentarily forgot where he was. Kadou tilted his head a little to correct the angle and, led by pure force of habit because his mind had gone utterly silent and still, he opened his mouth, kissed back, made it deep and real.

At the barest touch of Kadou's tongue against his bottom lip, Evemer made this *sound*.

Oh, that sound. It was quiet and short, not even a tenth of a groan, yet it was *so fucking genuine* that Kadou's entire body thrilled with sensation, like lightning crackling down his spine as that sound imprinted itself on his bones and arrested the whole of his attention.

His eyes were closed, but he saw the light shift through his lids, the lantern raised. Kadou slipped his hands up around Evemer's shoulders, sank his fingers into Evemer's soft hair—gods, just as he had at the bathhouse—

Evemer made that goddamn *sound* again, that soft sigh into Kadou's mouth that was unmaking his entire world and putting it back together all sideways.

"Do you *mind*?" Kadou turned his face aside just enough to snarl. Evemer's mouth, open and hot, fell against the corner of his jaw.

"Oh." The light swung away. "Sorry to interrupt. Have a good night."

Evemer drew back just enough to part from Kadou's skin, and they both paused, listening intently and breathing each other's air, until the footsteps faded away down the alley. Evemer stepped back, putting as much space as possible between the two of them in the archway.

"I'm so sorry," Kadou said quickly, stamping down the thunder that roared along his every nerve, that urged him to move forward and put his arms around Evemer's shoulders again. He *felt* every excruciating hairsbreadth of the space between them as if each was as vast as a chasm. "It was all I could think of—but even so, I shouldn't have ordered—if there's anything I can—no, shit, what am I saying, I can't just—"

"It's all right," said Evemer. "Quite all right. It was all you could think of."

"Yes."

"They would have found us."

"Right."

"And it was good. Smart, I mean," Evemer added quickly. "Smart of you to think of it."

"I panicked. I thought—the thieves the other night, you know—"

"It was per—it solved the problem perfectly."

"I'm really very sorry," Kadou said. He swallowed, tried not to notice whether he could still taste Evemer on his lips. "I swear I won't ever do that again."

Evemer made some frustrated noise, which sparked echoes of that *other* noise ringing and bouncing around in Kadou's brain like a purse of coins dumped onto stone. "Don't swear that."

"What?"

"If we are in a similar situation and that is a similarly perfect solution, you'll want to have it available. As an option."

"I . . . suppose," Kadou said slowly. His nerves were still singing, his hands could still feel the warmth and . . . and, gods, the delicious *breadth* of Evemer's shoulders under his palms. He couldn't think. "Are you sure?"

"I'm not offended. Even if I were, I'd prefer to endure a small offense if it is the price to keep you out of a greater danger. But I am not offended."

"All right. All right, if you say so." That was good. That was very good. He wouldn't want Evemer to be offended. Kadou tried to shake the fog out of his mind. "I'm glad you're not—I mean, I'm relieved that you—I just don't want to overstep. I'll try to come up with something else and—and next time I'll be prepared, so I won't have to make you . . . endure that."

Evemer was quiet for a long moment. Kadou wished he could see his face. "My lord," he said, eventually, and that seemed to be that.

Evemer swiftly made the executive decision that he wasn't going to think about it.

The lesson here seemed to be that he ought to do everything in his power to keep himself and His Highness out of any more alleys. No good came of lurking about in them.

He wasn't going to think about it any further.

He wasn't going to think about the way he'd felt like his knees had been swept out from under him when His Highness said those three words (*Kiss me, now. Kiss me, now. Kiss me, now*), and he wasn't going to think of His Highness's mouth, or His Highness's mouth, or His Highness's mouth, or His Highness putting his hands in Evemer's hair like he was going to pull him around and show him how to do it better, how he *wanted* it—

No. No, he was really not thinking about any of this anymore. Nor was he thinking about how he wasn't going to think about it.

A moratorium on all thinking generally, in fact. A line in the sand. No more of any of that.

What if, however, his treacherous brain suggested, *we think about His Highness's mouth?*

No. Absolutely not. Hadn't they just had that conversation

about what Evemer valued in himself, and hadn't he bragged (and oh, gods, he cringed in embarrassment now to think of it) about his discipline? Never mind that he hadn't kissed anyone in more than a decade. There was a certain personal standard to uphold.

And really, if you looked at it from one angle, Kadou had been saving their lives again. That person might have been armed. They could have been a much better fighter than even Evemer and Kadou put together. It was entirely possible. They'd had a lamp, and Kadou had been in a vulnerable moment—so many things that person might have used to their advantage! And how cata-strophic would it have been if the counterfeiters knew they were being investigated? They'd pack up their operation and flee, and then His Highness would have to start over.

His Highness really had been terribly smart and quick to assess the situation and come to such an efficient solution. Evemer was being both ungrateful and disrespectful by letting himself become distracted into thinking of anything but the tactical genius of it.

Indeed, His Highness would be ashamed and embarrassed if he knew how Evemer's thoughts were straying. Not even embar-rassed of himself, but embarrassed of Evemer. Embarrassed to have a kahya so . . . so easily swayed into—whatever that line of thinking had been.

He couldn't imagine what sort of brilliant plan Kadou might have come up with if he'd been calm and collected in the moment, instead of seizing upon (seizing him, pulling him in, *ordering* him) whatever first came to hand—oh, gods, no, that was a terrible way of phrasing it. He wasn't thinking about it.

He wasn't thinking about it.

He wasn't.

Who was he, *Tadek*?

There, that seemed to do the trick.

❋

As soon as they returned to the palace, the kahyalar at the gate gave Kadou a message from Eozena, summoning him to Zeliha's chambers. He went immediately, Melek and Evemer following in his wake. He had very nearly calmed down—or so he kept telling himself. He felt more on edge than ever.

Zeliha and Eozena were whispering intensely to one another when they entered, and Siranos was brooding out the window. Zeliha looked Kadou over and clapped a hand to her mouth, muffling a laugh. "Oh, Kadou! You look like a *horsemonger.*"

Was everything in the world out to wear down his patience and wind him to the breaking point? "It's a disguise," he said, more sharply than he'd intended.

"It's *hilarious.* Hey, how much is a pretty pony for my daughter? Do you have any that aren't painted with bootblack?"

Kadou clenched his jaw and tried to keep his temper. "You summoned me?"

"Yes, I also want to buy a mare—but a good one, not just an old nag with some peeled ginger up her ass—"

Kadou tugged at the turban, unraveling it from around his head.

"Oh, no, don't do that!" Zeliha cried, unable to stifle her laughter any longer. "It's not *bad*—you're a very cute horsemonger, Kadou, the very cutest horsemonger in the city—oh, gods—"

Hair loose and tumbling down his back, Kadou bundled the fabric of the turban into a wad and flung it on the divan. "I'm *tired.* Do you have something you want, or should I tell you about what *I* found?" he demanded.

Zeliha got her sniggering under control and cleared her throat. "Right. Yes. Besides the best stallion you have—Sorry! Sorry! I'm fine now. I'm stopping." She wiped away a tear of mirth from each eye and flicked her other hand at the table. "It's nothing in comparison to your *adorable* outfit. I'm just looking over a pile of evidence that suggests you're committing treason, that's all."

All Kadou's irritation and distraction vanished in a flash. "What?" His heart and stomach lurched again and he wobbled, putting out one hand—one of his kahyalar caught him. He wasn't sure if it was Melek or Evemer. Whoever it was lowered him onto a divan near the table.

"Apparently you're trying to raise support to usurp the throne," Zeliha said, perusing the papers and selecting a few of them.

"I'm not! I'd never—I don't even *want* it!" His eyes were stinging—not this, not *again*. What was she going to do now? Maybe she'd really exile him this time.

"Oh, sorry, was I unclear?" she said, glancing over at him with a mild look. "We already know it's a forgery, we got this *days* ago."

He stopped. Stared blankly at her.

May the gods rain curses down on sisters. Except not really, because he very much didn't want the throne, not even the possibility of it. Collecting his wits by hand, one by one, he said, "What?"

"I'm shocked and angered that anyone would try such a thing," Siranos said unexpectedly. "I can't imagine who would care to attempt to blacken Your Highness's good name."

"Right?" Zeliha said cheerfully. "It's actually good news, when you look at it a certain way. It means that either you or Eozena is shaking things up enough that whoever is behind the counterfeits is getting scared. So well done, one or both of you." She tapped the edges of the stack of papers she'd selected on the table to neaten them, then held them out to Kadou. He looked blankly at them.

"This is all the more reason to bring them to justice as quickly as possible," Siranos proclaimed. "I only wish that I could be of any use."

Kadou felt rather faint. He was very glad to already be sitting. Out of the corner of his eye he saw that one of his kahyalar—oh, Melek—had set a cup of tea on the table next to him. He took it and sipped, scalding the tip of his tongue, which didn't help his nerves. Zeliha shook the proffered pages at him insistently, and he finally reached out to take them.

They were written in an unfamiliar, hesitant hand—there were several common misspellings and the letters were rather wobbly, as if shaped by someone who wasn't comfortably literate. Not a kahya, then? They were all given schooling from the moment they joined the cadet corps, beginning with the trivium—arithmetic, grammar, and rhetoric. Some of them, over the course of their careers, received more intense and specialized schooling than even Kadou and Zeliha had.

The papers described scenes that the writer had witnessed, or gossip that they had overheard. *Prince Kadou met with ministers of the government and paid them bribes in the amount of 3500 altınlar . . . Prince Kadou made contact with several prominent merchants and secured funding . . . Prince Kadou wrote letters to the monarchs of Aswijan, Inacha, Kafia, and Persep, and to the governing bodies of Pezia and N'gaka . . . Prince Kadou keeps records of Her Majesty's personal retinue and their schedules, and has plans to replace them with his own people . . .*

He shoved the papers away from him and sipped his tea again. "Right," he said, taking several shaky breaths. "And you don't believe any of this."

"Of course she doesn't," Siranos said. "It's a deplorable affront to the honor of the royal family." Kadou spared him a single glance—why was *he*, of all people, trying to defend him? The last month, he hadn't spoken again of their exchange in the royal shrine, and hadn't acted as if he resented Kadou for it. He'd only been . . . cool but polite. Never quite warm, but impeccably courteous. Kadou hadn't yet figured out what to make of it.

"You're my brother," said Zeliha easily. "I know you. You wouldn't do this."

"You weren't so generous after the hunt," he said, and hated himself for how his voice cracked.

"Well, as far as I can see, nobody has died yet because of these," she said, tapping the papers. "And . . . I was angry, before. And tired. I was perhaps harsher than I meant to be. Having a baby takes a lot out of you," she added, a little defensive.

"It does," Siranos murmured. "It is a demanding situation for everyone."

"I'll say sorry if you want me to," Zeliha added, leaning on the edge of the table and giving Kadou a frank look. "Should I?"

Kadou felt sick all over, and didn't know what to say. "No."

"Let's set this matter aside for now," Eozena said firmly, sweeping the papers up and quite literally pushing them to the other end of the table. "You said you'd found something?"

Kadou paused briefly and glanced at Siranos.

"Ah," Siranos said. "I'll just go check on Eyne."

Very strange. Kadou shoved it all aside as Siranos left the room and shut the heavy oak door that led to Zeliha's more private quarters. "There's an incense lounge," Kadou said tonelessly. He'd had one shock too many today, and he was feeling the edges of that drifting, unmoored sensation that sometimes came on the heels of his panic attacks. He welcomed it, yearned toward it. "The Jasmine Tree. There are people there involved with the counterfeits. They talked about their friend, apparently the person in charge of the scheme. They mentioned a contact in the palace I can only assume was Lieutenant Armagan." He pushed himself up from the chair. "That's all. I'm going to bed."

He didn't wait to be dismissed from Her Majesty's presence. He swept out into the corridor, and then out the front door of the royal house. He crossed the wide span of gardens to the other residence, where his own and several other royal apartments were located—empty ever since the royal family had been reduced so cataclysmically in the same shipwreck that had taken his parents.

At his rooms, Melek posted çemself on watch outside the door, and Evemer followed him in. Kadou flung himself onto the divan by the window, and Evemer went around the room to light the lamps. He'd only done half when there was a knock at the door, and Melek poked çir head in. "It's Eozena," çe said.

"Fine," Kadou said.

Melek let her in. "Evening, Highness," she said, then paused and studied him. "You all right?"

"Long day."

She hummed in response and dragged a chair over to his divan. She sat, crossed her legs, laced her fingers over her knee, and watched him. "Good work tonight," she said. "I'm very proud of you."

"Thanks," he said dully.

"I wanted to have another talk with you now that you've

made progress and found a lead. You seemed quite understandably upset earlier—Zeliha sprang that news on you rather clumsily—so I thought you might prefer it if we talked in private. It's up to you whether you'd like Evemer to stick around for moral support."

Yes came the sudden fierce thought, from . . . somewhere. Kadou fidgeted. "I don't have secrets from him." That was the entirely wrong thing to say, good gods. His face went hot.

Eozena tilted her head and looked for a moment like she was about to say something—and maybe she would have, if they'd been alone. Maybe she would have said, *That seems like a sudden change,* or *I see all that skulking around in the bad parts of town together has really brought you two closer as friends,* and then he might have to explain to her what had happened, and . . . Oh, dear. But all she said was, "Of course, Your Highness, as you wish."

Kadou looked at Evemer and gestured at the other seat; he took it silently.

"Right," said Eozena. "I'm about to speak plainly. Fair warning to both of you, but particularly to Evemer, so that he can brace himself for it. I'm sure we have smelling salts around here if it gets to be too much for you," she added dryly.

"Commander," Evemer said.

"You've accomplished something *very* good today. I hope you have the perspective to know just how much of an accomplishment this is. It's a huge piece of progress, and just what we needed. So, with that in mind, I was wondering if you might now be willing to step aside and let our people handle the rest."

He didn't know. He couldn't make decisions like this.

"I only ask," she continued, "because we've had that one close call already, and I'd rather not keep risking you. Once was enough."

Kadou was so tired and had been pulled in so many different directions in one day that he could only stare at her for a long moment, trying to figure out how she had *already* heard about the—the incident in the alley.

Oh, gods, she already knew what he'd ordered Evemer to do. His nerves, wound to the breaking point, abruptly snapped.

He pulled a pillow over his face as he felt himself go scarlet and groaned, "How do you know *everything*?"

"I beg your pardon? You reported it to me."

Moments too late, it occurred to Kadou's exhausted brain that she was talking about something else entirely. She'd meant the thieves from a month ago. *That* one close call.

He lowered the pillow, hoped his face wasn't too incriminatingly red, and said, "Oh, right. Of course."

There was a beat of silence. He stared up at the ceiling, suppressing a grimace, and felt himself growing, if possible, even redder. There was no way she was going to fall for such a clumsy and glaringly obvious attempt to play it off as nothing.

When he dared to glance at her, Eozena narrowed her eyes. "Why did you say it that way?"

"What way?"

"That way. Did something else happen that I should know about?"

"No," he and Evemer said in unison.

"Right," she said. "And nothing happened, and nothing almost happened."

"Nothing happened," Kadou said.

She held up one finger at Kadou. "Your Highness, will you pardon me a moment?" Without waiting for a reply, she shifted her gaze to Evemer. "Lieutenant, report!" she barked.

He snapped to attention. "Commander. We went to the Jasmine Tree, an incense lounge in the waterfront district, and witnessed an exchange of money happening between someone in the back alley and, presumably, one of the workers in the establishment."

"Were you seen?"

Evemer paused. "Technically," he said.

"What does that mean?"

"We were spotted, but we averted any suspicion."

"How?"

"They would not have found our presence in the alley to be remarkable."

"Anyway," Kadou said loudly, so hot with his blush that he felt like he was roasting. "No need to go into all that! We both got out alive and unharmed, and as Evemer said, they didn't pay any attention to us."

"As His Highness says."

Eozena glanced back and forth between them. "No, I want to know what happened. Report, one of you."

"The person who brought the money came down the alley toward us, and we were hiding in a doorway, and, uh . . ." The words stuck in Kadou's throat as he tried to find a phrasing that was not completely embarrassing.

"His Highness assessed the situation," Evemer supplied smoothly. "And when we were seen, he ensured that we were not found to be suspicious." Kadou had to admire that—Evemer really was doing his damned best, wasn't he?

"Vague, Lieutenant," said Eozena. "And not new information."

Kadou couldn't stand the tension any longer and abruptly threw down the flag of surrender. "I told him to kiss me, and the person who saw us a moment later told us to have a nice evening and walked off," Kadou said. He couldn't meet Eozena's eyes. He was fairly sure his face was burning off.

"It was the only thing he could think of," Evemer added.

"Right," said Eozena.

"It was a very clever ruse," said Evemer. Kadou bit his cheek and still could not bring himself to look at anyone.

"I'm sure it was. Ah, Lieutenant, His Highness looks rather feverish. Would you mind fetching him a damp cloth?"

Evemer paused for . . . longer than he should have. "Yes, Commander," he said.

As soon as the door shut behind Evemer, Eozena turned back. "*Kadou.*"

"I apologized right away," he said. "Abjectly! He was very blasé about it, in that way he has. Utterly unflappable, that man. He simply cannot be flapped by anything or anyone, and—yes, I know! I know! But it really was the only thing I could think of, and I really did apologize, and he really did say it was all right!

I said it several times, and so did he! We just stood there taking turns saying *I'm sorry* and *It's fine.*"

Eozena steepled her fingers together. "Do you see," she said slowly, "how that might not entirely reassure me?"

"Only if you don't trust either of us to be at all competent. Do you think Evemer would say that it wasn't necessary for me to apologize, if it really was? If he'd been unsettled or unwilling, he would have said *Highness* and nothing else. Or he would have accepted my apology. He turned it down! More than once!"

"Hmm," said Eozena forbiddingly. "Be careful. You've already mishandled the situation with your armsman."

"I know," he said miserably, rubbing his hands over his burning face. "I talked to him about that earlier this evening too." Her eyebrow quirked in surprise. "I said sorry, and I made things clear to him, and we yelled at each other a bit and started making up. I'm saying sorry to everyone today. All over the place. Right and left. Eozena, I'm *trying.*"

She sighed. "You do see that's not the end of the work, right? There's a lot more you have to do to have a hope of repairing your relationship with him. He won't be able to continue as your personal secretary if it makes him miserable just to see your face."

"Yes, I know." He put his hands over his face. "I shouldn't have avoided him. I need to—to ask him for help more."

"Tell me your reasoning."

"He needs to feel like I trust him. I need to see him being my armsman, and both of us need to figure out what that means for him, and for me. And—and we need to practice having that sort of relationship again. He needs to feel like he has a . . . nobler purpose."

He peeked out between his fingers at her. She looked at him for a long time, eyes still narrowed, then nodded once. "All right. Good enough to be going on with."

Evemer tapped on the door and let himself back in. "Highness," he said, and handed Kadou a cool, damp cloth.

"Thank you," Kadou said, pressing it against his inner wrists and the sides of his neck. It was actually quite a relief, and it did more to soothe his nerves than he'd expected. "Would you tell Eozena you're not traumatized?"

"I'm not traumatized, Commander," Evemer said.

Eozena put her palm to her face. "Fine. Fine. Kadou . . . I trust you'll not do that again."

"He can't promise that," Evemer said smoothly. "He might have to do it again."

"Like hell he will," she said.

"Commander," said Evemer.

"If it helps, I'm going to try really hard not to do it again," Kadou said, pushing himself to sit up. "It was a very stupid ruse. It was all I could think of."

"I suppose it doesn't matter whether you *try* or not, because— look, you don't need to be doing this anymore. Stay here in the palace, please, where it's safe. You've had your fun, Kadou," she said. "I'm serious. You wanted to help, and you've helped. You found something important, and there are people better equipped to handle it than you are."

"But I'm the one who's *been* handling it." His hands were in his lap, and he was holding the damp cloth so tightly that water was dripping out onto the knees of his kaftan.

Eozena sighed. "You're not supposed to be running around—"

"What? Being useful?" Kadou said sharply. "Better I just stay here and read the reports as they come in?"

"Yes, actually. What happens if you get hurt? Seriously: What happens? I'm not a common kahya anymore, Your Highness, I'm the commander of the guard. I'm entitled to make certain executive decisions about the safety of the royal family. In cases of truly mortal danger—for example, the incident last month—I am allowed to, at my most serious and solemn discretion, *disregard orders* in the pursuit of keeping you from harm. So what happens if you get caught up in something bigger than you? What happens if you're captured, or killed? What happens to me?"

"Zeliha already gave me permission."

"What would happen to me?"

"There would be an inquest to determine whether you're

guilty of negligence in the pursuit of duty," Kadou said stiffly. He felt the fear-creature prowling at the edges of his mind again, as if it were sniffing around in the shadows just past the circle of a campfire's light. "Possibly you would be court-martialed. At worst, you'd be stripped of your titles or—she wouldn't execute you, you know!"

"I think you underestimate how much your sister loves you," Eozena said simply. "Make my job easy, Kadou. Let's handle this through the proper channels. Isn't that why you got in trouble in the first place? Because you tried to handle things yourself? You've done all that you can do at this point. Let's not be reckless."

Kadou hit his absolute limit. It was a singular sensation, one he had only truly experienced a few times before. "Stop. Please, just for tonight, *stop*. I can't."

"Commander," Evemer said immediately, rising from his chair. "His Highness is quite tired. Perhaps there will be time tomorrow to continue. May I get the door for you?"

Eozena sighed and got to her feet. "This isn't the end of the discussion," she said sternly to both of them. Kadou covered his face with his hands and endured just as hard as he could until he heard Evemer bid her goodnight at the door. "Actually," she said. "Could I speak to you outside for a moment, Lieutenant?"

"Highness," Evemer said. "Do you require my assistance?"

"No. No, please go ahead." The idea of a few minutes of solitude was a profound relief.

Evemer followed Eozena as she led him away from His Highness's apartments, down the hall to the courtyard door and outside, and then even farther. She stopped by a bubbling fountain, loud enough to cover their voices from anyone who might try to overhear, and turned to him with her arms crossed. The dim moonlight glinted off the scattered silver bands decorating the ropes of her hair, matching something steely that glinted in her eyes. "Is there anything you want to tell me that you didn't feel that you could say in front of His Highness? Anything at all?"

He stood before her in parade rest, his hands behind his back. "No, Commander."

"Would you tell me if there was?"

"Probably, Commander. If His Highness—" But Kadou would never. He rephrased. "If I were assigned to serve a person who gave me a criminal order, I would report to you and ask for clarification, as per protocol."

"Did you need any clarification tonight?"

"No, Commander."

"Are you frustrated with me for my fixation on this issue?"

"You're doing your duty, Commander, as did I. Mine is to protect His Highness. Yours is to protect all of us."

She sighed. "All right. Is there anything else you need?"

"No, Commander."

Arms still crossed, she tapped her fingers against her elbow. "You remember all your training, don't you?"

"I was only promoted to the core-guard a month and a half ago, as you may recall, Commander."

"Then, as I daresay I have no need to remind you: You know it's not against protocol to begin something with him," she said. "It's just not . . . wise. Not without a great deal of care. Not without feeling that you can confide in him and honestly express what you're thinking." She eyed him. "Would you say you're very good at expressing your thoughts?"

Evemer drew himself up until his spine was as erect as a steel bar. "I assure you, Commander, I have no intention of—"

She moved her hand a mere inch in a gesture to quiet him, and he fell silent immediately. "I'm not asking what your intentions are toward His Highness. That question is wildly outside my jurisdiction both as your senior officer and as an uninvolved third party who is coincidentally in the vicinity. But I am cautioning you. I am advising you. I am giving you something to think about."

"Commander," he said. "His Highness has no intentions toward me either." Such a thing was so unthinkable as to be absurd.

She shrugged. "I was young once, you know. I know how

things just sort of end up happening. But all right. Forgive me for my . . . overenthusiasm."

"Thank you for your diligence, Commander." Though it was quite a lot of diligence—more than was necessary for this particular situation. It had been one kiss, and His Highness would never have done anything remotely like that unless their lives were at stake. That was all. Of course he could not argue with the commander like that, but because the comment about expressing his thoughts had been a little too close to home, he added, "I assure you all is well."

"I appreciate your candor," she said dryly. "Anything else to report?"

"No, Commander."

She nodded. "You're dismissed, then. Return to your post. Goodnight."

"Goodnight, Commander."

She walked away down the garden paths. Evemer returned to Kadou's chambers, nodding to Melek at the door. Inside, Kadou had already extinguished the lights in the sitting room and shut the door to his bedroom. Evemer frowned a little and left again, heading back to his own room.

He would have liked to put out the candles for him.

CHAPTER EIGHT

The lowlands of Araşt were usually very warm and dry in early summer, but Kadou awoke the next morning to a grey, rainy day and a breakfast invitation from his sister, a simple note, signed with her own name. In it, she plaintively wondered what she had to do to bribe him back to her table, and offered a few pieces of knowledge as a temptation: Eozena had recently re-approved the Mistress of the Table for service, and said Mistress had just hired a new chef from Vinte.

Kadou sat in his parlor and sipped at a cup of chamomile tea, a vain attempt to soothe his nerves from the previous night's ordeals. He felt Evemer's absence more keenly now, he noticed. There was an empty space at his shoulder where a silent glowering presence should have stood. It seemed rather cold, like the chill of the room came more strongly on that side.

He stared at Zeliha's note for an embarrassing length of time. Remembering the conversation with Eozena the night before, Kadou sent for Tadek, who arrived pleasant and composed. He was too skilled with his masks for Kadou to see through him.

"As my personal secretary, I thought you should know—I'm going over to Her Majesty's chambers for breakfast."

"Of course, Highness," Tadek said. "Will you be lingering?"

"I don't know."

"There are a few small matters which require your attention, but I shall send word that you will not be available until the afternoon, if you wish."

Kadou hated this. Tadek sounded so distant and formal—surely there was some middle ground between this and the shameless flirting? And then, of course, there was the conversation he'd had with Eozena . . . "Actually, I was wondering if you'd help me dress for it."

Tadek blinked, but recovered smoothly. "Of course, Highness, anything you require."

He followed a few steps behind as Kadou headed back into his bedroom with his tea and settled himself in the chair by the window. "I leave it in your hands. I trust you."

Tadek shot him a thoughtful, almost suspicious look and went to the wardrobes. Kadou had finished his tea by the time Tadek had laid out his choice of clothes—a butter-yellow underlayer, thickly embroidered mahogany trousers, and an ankle-length kaftan of deep burgundy silk brocade woven with gold threads in a pattern of oak leaves and saffron flowers.

He shaved Kadou and dressed his hair simply—he had a much lighter touch than Evemer did, and Kadou hardly felt him working at all—then helped Kadou into his layers. They buttoned up the front together, both starting from the middle and working outward: Tadek up to the high collar, Kadou to the end of the row of jet buttons, halfway down his thighs, after which the long panels of the kaftan hung loose to his ankles, splitting open to show his trousers and slippers beneath. Tadek stepped back and finally looked at Kadou properly, putting his head on one side and his hands on his hips. Kadou rather got the impression that Tadek really was sizing up his clothes for once, rather than leering at him directly. "Are you going to wear jewels?" Tadek asked.

"I can, if you think I ought to."

Tadek opened the jewel box and picked through it while Kadou sat quiet and docile and let him work. "What happened to your padparadscha earrings?"

"They should be in there."

"Ah, here." He held them up to Kadou's ear, studied the effect. "I've always liked how bright they are against your hair."

"I don't like orange." Tadek set them aside, though not back in the jewel box, and tried a pair of honey topaz earrings. "There are garnets in there somewhere."

"I don't want too much matching," Tadek replied absently, digging deeper in the box, and Kadou couldn't help but laugh.

"You're good at this. I didn't know."

Tadek smiled sadly and came to Kadou's side again, his hands full of glittering things. "I haven't . . . I haven't been spending my stipend as wisely as I could have. I've erred too far on the side of cultural enrichment, as they call it, and rather neglected the educational side of it." He clasped a gold bracelet around Kadou's wrist. "Live vibrantly and think nothing of the future, as the poets have warned against."

"And yet have also usually espoused," Kadou said, looking at him curiously.

After a moment, Tadek said quietly, "I was thinking about this last night. I was at one of the shrines. There wasn't anyone around, and I felt silly sitting there all by myself. But I cleaned up the altars, scraped all the old wax out of the candelabras, polished Usmim's scales and Sannesi's bowl. I swept the floors. I shook out the rugs. Hell, I mopped the flagstones. You could *eat* off them now."

"And then?"

"And then I lit candles for the two of us, and I sat there and thought about myself." Tadek shook his head. "I've seen every play and opera and acrobatic troupe that's come through Kasaba City since I became part of the fringe-guard. My ambitions ended with the kahyalar corps—being a minister of something in some dusty little office didn't sound like any fun, certainly not as much as being in the thick of things and getting to watch how everything happened. So I spent my enrichment stipend on silly things that didn't do much except get me out into the city to meet people. By comparison, Melek has a hundred different practical skills, Commander Eozena could *teach* military history, and Evemer's scrounged up books about numismatics and law from somewhere and keeps them in a stack next to his bed. Istani knows how to play every instrument I've ever heard of, Sanem speaks seven languages and can do complex sums in her head, and Firuze can argue legal philosophy until she's blue in the face. And . . . Well, you were right, weren't you? I haven't made myself useful, just entertaining. Melek and Evemer and Sanem and *certainly* Firuze will end up ministers of some sort, and where will I be? Seeing plays and cooling my heels in the garrison, because I never bothered to make anything more of myself. There's not much I can do with skills in dressing people and making snide comments."

"But there *are* people who make a profession of that. Stewards and the masters of protocol and so forth. I've seen discussions of military strategy that were less complicated than some of the banquet seating arrangements that the chief of diplomacy has to manage."

Tadek snorted and held up a teardrop amethyst to Kadou's ear. "They wouldn't give me that sort of responsibility when I've got a record of dishonor. I'll probably die an armsman." He sighed. "No offense."

Kadou's heart ached. "Tadek, I told you I'd still pay your stipend if you want to use it. You still have time—what do you want to do?"

Tadek set the amethyst aside and tried a sparkling thread of diamonds, then set that aside as well. "Too ostentatious," he muttered to himself. "Only breakfast." He shook his head and snorted. "You know, I'm not pious. I don't go to the temple more than once a year, I only participate in the fun holidays, and I don't expect some man who supposedly lives in a cave in the ground to send me fairer trials just because I ask nicely. I don't even care much for philosophy, unless I'm drunk and I get to argue with somebody in person, and then it's more about needling them . . . But when I was trying to unburden myself last night, I got to thinking about sin, and I thought about what I believe."

"Which is?" He had rarely seen Tadek so serious. His expression was rather smooth and serene, other than the slightest tension around his mouth and between his eyebrows. Oh, he really had been trying, hadn't he? He'd been trying as hard as Kadou himself had been.

"Well, I thought about that, and about what you said." Tadek went back to the jewelry box—probably just to have something to occupy his hands with, Kadou thought. "And I decided that if anything is a sin against yourself, it's thinking that you're only good for one use. That there's only one *thing* that makes you valuable."

"I agree," Kadou said.

"I don't want to die an armsman. I don't want to just be forgotten. I want to make a difference to someone. I want to do something that matters." Tadek shot him a sidelong smile. "That's scary. It feels like a risk, because if I care about something, if I *want* something, then when I don't get it I'll be disappointed. But the alternative is living the rest of my life knowing that if I don't even try, then I really am a useless person, and I don't think I'd be able to sleep at night."

"I really, really know what you mean," Kadou said quietly, looking up at him. Tadek gave him another smile—softer, sadder. "I'll wear the padparadschas if you think they're prettiest."

Tadek's smile warmed, and he handed them over. Kadou put them in. "At least there are ways for you to be useful just by existing. You'd hate it and you'd be unhappy, but you could let Her Majesty move you around like a political piece—that would be useful. Do you think she's going to find you someone to marry?"

"Eventually." Kadou shrugged.

"Hmm." Tadek poked through the jewel box again. "Rings, or necklace?"

"As you said, it's just breakfast."

"Humor me," Tadek said mildly. "How often do I get to dress you up pretty? If it's too much, you can take some of it off again." He handed Kadou a few rings—gold bands etched with intricate patterns, and one with an amber cabochon inscribed with a knotted sea serpent on the underside of the jewel. "Do you know who she'll negotiate with?" Tadek paused and asked curiously, "Would she make you marry a woman?"

"Depends, I suppose. She's got her own heir, so that's the dynasty secured, and there's no need for me to worry about having to personally contribute to it. Her Majesty knows my preferences, but if she's negotiating with a foreign state that needs a husband for their crown princess and no one but a Mahisti will do, then . . ." He shrugged again. "Politics might end up outweighing preferences." If he'd been born anyone else in the entire kingdom, he almost certainly would have married for love. At least, the traditional wedding vows were written as if that was the assumed motivation. The acquisition of heirs was of course a separate matter entirely—like Siranos, he would have no claim on children unless it was deliberately granted to him.

Tadek draped a long silver chain and a smooth labradorite pendant around Kadou's neck. "Would you mind it?"

"Being married to a woman? I wouldn't be *happy* with it, but I wouldn't mind, no, as long as I thought we could at least be friends. If it was a choice between her or her brother . . ."

"You'd snap up the brother without a second's hesitation, yes." Tadek studied him again, humming thoughtfully under his breath. "No, you're right, it's too much. Take off the necklace and all but one of the rings. Anyway—the brother, yes. Although . . ." He looked speculatively off into the middle distance. "If it's only the cock that's the issue, you could just buy a—" Kadou burst out laughing, and Tadek turned away, a smaller but much more sincere smile on his face. "I wasn't sure if that sort of joke was going to be overfamiliar," he said when Kadou had handed back all the discarded jewels. "Considering the circumstances."

"No one else makes jokes like that to me."

"Evemer certainly doesn't," Tadek murmured.

"I'd probably faint if he did," he said, half laughing and feeling the sting of heat in his cheeks just at the thought. "Or if anyone else did, really."

Tadek nodded. "I'm sorry, by the way. For *that* part of what I said yesterday. About him. I was upset."

"Forgiven."

"You shouldn't forgive me so easily."

"I'm going to anyway."

Tadek gave him another sad smile. Kadou returned it, and something in the room seemed to ease and settle, like the exhalation of relief after a long-held breath.

※

"You look nice today," Zeliha said, all solicitous, when Kadou met her in her rooms. Siranos was there as well, already waiting at the table with a cup of coffee.

"Not like a horsemonger?" he said, unable to resist the temptation to sarcasm.

She looked a little guilty at that, said, "Here, do you want to hold a baby?" and shoved Eyne into his arms.

This worked fairly well as a distraction—and even better when he looked down at her and was met with the biggest, shiniest grin he had ever seen on an infant. "Oh *gods,* when did she start doing that?"

"Couple days ago," Siranos said.

Zeliha nodded solemnly. "It's brutal, isn't it?"

"She can have anything she wants. What do you want, child?" he said, walking off with her to the breakfast table with no attention at all to spare for Zeliha or Siranos. She was *beautiful,* and she was *his* niece. He was suddenly and marvelously proud of her. Was it foolish to be proud of her just for learning how to smile? He didn't care. He was certain she was better at it than anyone else in the world—that was reason enough to be proud of her. "Name your heart's desire. Anything, as long as you keep smiling like that."

"So I'm going to have to be the stern one, is that it?" Zeliha said wryly. "We can't *both* spoil her, Uncle Kadou."

"I'm not speaking to you," he said loftily. "You called me a horsemonger."

"I said you *looked* like a horsemonger."

"Her Majesty is very rude and hurtful," he crooned to Eyne.

"I'll just have the Mistress of the Table fire the new Vintish chef, then, shall I?"

He spared a glance for the selection of food laid out—a huge amount for three people, but then it usually was. There was thick-crusted bread, butter, eight kinds of jam that Kadou couldn't even begin to identify; poached eggs under blankets of thick, creamy yellow sauce; duck confit; a selection of cured meats sliced paper-thin and rolled into the shape of flowers; two varieties of quiche; a selection of pastry; cream tarts topped with glistening jewels of fruit; a large pancake with edges so puffy and browned that it was bowl shaped, filled with slices of spiced pears; a stack of crepes folded into quarters; coffee, tea, and fresh fruit juices. It wasn't appreciably different from the typical breakfasts they were served in terms of *content*—eggs, meats, breads, jams, and drinks—it was only the quantity and the execution of the dishes that was different, and the fact that so many of them were sweet rather than savory.

"Are you trying to butter me up for something?" Kadou asked suspiciously.

"Not at all. It's the new chef—she's trying to butter *us* up. Well," Zeliha said, thinking again. "I *am* buttering you up, but not with the food. Sit down, I have something to show you."

He sat at the table, arranged a few of the floor cushions next to him into an impromptu cradle for Eyne, and helped himself to the food while Zeliha fetched something from the next room. The silence between him and Siranos was palpable, but Kadou shoved away his nerves.

Zeliha returned with an object, flat and wrapped in cloth, about a cubit long and a foot wide. Kadou set down his bread and jam and took the parcel when she handed it to him—it felt like a picture frame.

"A painting?" he said, unwrapping the cloth.

"Mm," Zeliha said eloquently, and poured them both coffee.

It was a painting of a man—a rather handsome man, with reddish blond hair, light-colored eyes, and pale skin. The man was wearing expensive brocade in the Vintish style with a stupendously complex jewel in the shape of a many-pointed starburst pinned to his left shoulder over his heart. The pearls and diamonds of it were so finely rendered as to look like they might roll right off the surface of the canvas. Only royalty would wear cloth and jewels that fine.

Siranos leaned over to look at the painting. Slowly, he said, "Zeliha, who is this?"

"Phillipe Marcelet du Vigier, Duc de Resti. *La douzième fleur*, I'm told, twelfth in line to the throne. He has a pedigree of other titles, of course, you know how those Vints are. He sent the new chef, along with the painting. What do you think, Kadou?"

Why was she asking him? She surely wasn't thinking of getting married. That would have been entirely ill-advised, *especially* if it bound them with the Vints, who had horrifically complex inheritance laws that didn't at all need to be muddling up the tidy and straightforward Araşti system. "The food looks good, and it's a nice painting," he said cautiously.

"I was thinking of inviting him to visit," she said with the particular glint of cunning mischief that had always meant she'd concocted some scheme that she was particularly looking forward to.

Out of the corner of his eye, Kadou saw Siranos twitch and abruptly turn back to his breakfast.

Oh. Oh! This must be the new Siranos, the potential body-father of another niece for Kadou. He looked at the painting again with fresh eyes. A young man, about his and Zeliha's age, dressed in shining ice-blue overlaying pine-green. He had a short ruddy-blond beard, clipped neatly to his jawline, and the neutral expression that nearly all portraits had—it was, after all, very dull to sit and stare off into the middle distance for hours at a time. The expression was rather like Evemer's stone-wall one. Peeking up from one of the lower corners of the painting was a hunting dog wearing a red, jeweled collar. The dog was extraordinarily badly painted in comparison to the rest of the picture except for the jewels on its collar, which were as finely rendered as the duc's brooch.

He glanced between the painting and Zeliha, imagining her features blended with the duc's—a child with the Mahisti blue-black eyes and a reddish cast to the classic dark Araşti hair might be very handsome. "He looks nice," Kadou said, more warmly. He resisted the urge to glance at Siranos, but couldn't resist saying,

"You should invite him, if you like him." And if that meant that Siranos left sooner rather than later, so much the better.

"You think so?" Zeliha said brightly. "I'll mention it to the ambassador later today, then. If the weather's good, we could expect him here in, say . . ." She tilted her head back and forth. "It's about a month's voyage to Vinte, so . . . Say two and a half or three months, then, to allow him time to pack and get his affairs in order, assuming he wants to come. Right around harvest time!"

"I was thinking of going out to Şirya for the harvest," he said, sipping his coffee. That would be well timed. He'd be out of her hair, and she could have all the space she needed to seduce the duc, or whatever her plan was.

"Perhaps His Grace would like to see some of the country. You could take him with you," she said. Kadou gave her a puzzled look. "What? He's a nice young man, by all accounts. He has land and money and several dogs, reads books, writes poetry, knows how to dance . . ."

"Vints," grumbled Siranos under his breath.

"He sounds very pleasant," Kadou said. More pleasant than Siranos, anyway—*Oh!* he realized with a start. Oh, was Zeliha trying to choose a lover who Kadou might be able to be friends with? Someone who he wouldn't clash so badly with, who might fit in better with the family?

That was . . . rather sweet of her, actually. There really was no need for her to take any notice of *his* feelings in these matters. But then, he *was* the uncle in this family, and as she would never marry, his claim on her children would always outrank that of any of her lovers . . .

Well, it didn't matter whether she was making this gesture out of familial caring or political prudence. The effect was the same either way, and Kadou did feel rather touched that she would give any weight to his opinion.

Eyne made a delightful noise, and his and Zeliha's attentions were immediately arrested. Kadou set the painting aside, and when they had stopped being distracted by the baby, they were

distracted by the excellent food and spoke no more of Phillippe
Marcelet du Vigier, Duc de Resti.

By the end of breakfast, he was stuffed with more food than
he generally cared to eat in the mornings. He couldn't even bring
himself to mind Siranos's presence—after the painting had been
put away, the man had gotten all charming: He'd told an amusing tale that had made Zeliha laugh aloud and had discussed the
political situation in his home country with grace. Araşt owned
over four hundred thousand altınlar of Oissos's debt, and due to a
few extremely unfortunate political events and three years of bad
harvests, their already-debased coinage had been weakened even
further. The exchange rates between their currency and anyone
else's were growing ever more atrocious. Siranos made some off-
hand comment that such things were no longer going to be his
problem and mentioned that he'd written to his sister, who resided
down in the city, and to the rest of his family in Oissos to inform
them of his intentions to stay in Araşt, but Kadou's nerves barely
blinked at the prospect. Siranos had too much pride to stay hanging around for years or decades when there was some nice Vintish
duke around to charm Zeliha.

Kadou nursed a third cup of coffee while Eyne dozed in the
crook of his arm, and during a lull in the conversation, he found
that he was food-stupid enough to sidle up to a hard question and
take it by surprise before his fear-creature could frighten him out
of it. "Am I still banned from court?"

"Yes," Zeliha answered simply. She was lying on the floor next
to the table, a couple cushions shoved under her head.

"Oh," he said.

She rolled her head to the side to look at him. "You don't even
like court. *I* don't like court."

"How much longer?"

"I don't know," she said peevishly. "A couple more months?
Did you expect everyone would have just forgotten by now?"

"No. Of course not."

"Just do something brilliant and heroic so I can forgive you in public. Figure out who wants to frame you for treason and steal from the Shipbuilder's Guild and forge our currency."

Satisfied, Kadou decided not to mention the fact that Eozena had wanted him to step back from that.

Zeliha shoved herself up to a seat with a groan. "Vints," she muttered, eyeing the still-laden table. "We'll be dead of heart disease by the end of the year if we keep eating like this. Blessings of the gods upon their heads. May the Mother smile upon them, and all the Lord of Judgment's trials for them be easy. I shall die happy."

"Those papers from last night," Kadou said carefully. "Can I have them?"

Zeliha squinted at him. "What do you want them for?"

"Evidence?" He shouldn't have eaten so much. Correction: He shouldn't have eaten so much and then opened up difficult and serious conversations. "I'll bring them back if you want them yourself."

She shrugged and got slowly to her feet, moving with great effort. "Blessings on the Vints," she groaned. "A hundred blessings on them." She went to her desk and unlocked one of the drawers, withdrawing the sheaf of papers. "Bring these back when you're done, all right? I might not have believed them, but . . ."

"Someone else might," Kadou said. "Yes."

"I don't see how they could," Siranos said, and added fiercely, "Whoever sent those to Her Majesty ought to be ashamed of themselves. They must think that we're all idiots."

Kadou moved Eyne from his lap back into her little nest of cushions and got to his feet, groaning just as Zeliha had at the uncomfortable sensation of moving when he was so full of food and coffee. Back to his rooms for a nap, then, before he faced the rest of the day—there were letters to be answered, mostly business with his holdings that he had been putting off for several days already and could theoretically put off for several more. But on a dim and dreary one like this, with the rain falling in a soft but persistent hiss and cool breaths of damp air trickling through the windows, even the prospect of opening and answering letters could hold no dread.

He took the papers from Zeliha. She followed him out of the breakfast room into the antechamber, caught his chin and kissed his cheek in a businesslike sort of way. "Don't be angry with me anymore."

"Who's angry?" he said lightly.

"You. You don't come to meals except when I invite you. You avoid me."

"You banned me from court."

"What else was I going to do?"

He sighed and rubbed his forehead. "I don't know," he said. Maybe he was angry, a little bit. Was that a crime, to be upset with his own sister? Who else was it *safe* to be angry at? Not his kahyalar! Not cadets, or ministers, or citizens. There was one person in the whole country who was more powerful than him. One person who he couldn't hurt.

Except that he could hurt her too, judging by her crestfallen expression.

"Sorry," he said. He felt like he was saying sorry a great deal lately—he was abruptly exhausted and utterly disheartened to think of just how many people he'd been apologizing to.

"It's very hard being grown-up like this, isn't it?" she said bitterly. "I wish we could just go have a slap-fight in the garden like we did when we were children, and then I'd dunk you in a fountain and then you'd cry and I'd panic and we'd haggle out a peace treaty. 'Oh, I'll lend you my toys if you promise not to tell—'"

"Eyne needs siblings if she's going to grow up to be a good negotiator," Kadou said, stuffing the papers inside the front of his kaftan so he didn't have to look at her.

"I can't dunk you in any fountains these days," she muttered. "Can't even beat you at horse racing or lawn bowling or—"

"We can spar if you want, sometime," he said. "That should be sufficiently dignified for the sultan of Araşt."

"Gods, no, I'm out of practice."

"Pick champions, then."

"That's not fair either, you'll pick Evemer or Eozena and they'll wipe the floor with mine." Zeliha sighed. "Never mind. I'm only whining because I'm lonely. Siranos is lovely company, but . . ."

He ought to say that he'd do better at being there for her, that he'd start coming to meals again, but he found that there were still tender spots in his heart, and he wasn't yet ready to move on from them. "Well, I would have been lonely too, if you'd exiled me."

She winced. "That the thing you're angry about?"

"I guess." He shook himself. "I'll bring these papers back as soon as I'm done." He opened the door quickly, before she could rope him back into the conversation.

"You all right?" Tadek said when they'd made it downstairs and paused in the entryway for him to drape a cloak over Kadou's shoulders and open a waxed-silk umbrella.

"Yes. It's nothing."

Tadek linked their arms together, the better to keep them both under the umbrella as they stepped out into the rain. The touch felt . . . supportive, rather than companionable, like he was buttressing Kadou up before Kadou even noticed he was wavering. "How was breakfast?"

"The food was good. Siranos was there, but . . . He was fine."

"You know, it's a lot easier to see why Her Majesty likes him when he's not going for your jugular," Tadek said, nodding. "His accent, for example. Mm."

"I suppose," Kadou said. "Talking with Zeliha was good too. Mostly." The rain drummed on the waxed silk above them. "It's no one's fault."

Tadek squeezed their linked arms. "Blame me for it."

Kadou shook his head. "It's not about finding someone to pin the blame on." He put a hand on his chest, safeguarding the papers from falling as they stepped delicately around a puddle on the path. "She said . . . She said I'll be unbanned from court if I can finish the investigation. Find the person responsible."

He felt the first slow gyrations of his mind, vulture-like, as it started to focus in on this idea that he *had* to finish it, he *had to* or all else would be lost, he'd be banned for always, he'd be exiled from the capital or from the country—

He shook himself out of it. The rest of the morning would be for answering letters, not for picking at his scabs.

"You were a little pale when you came out," Tadek mused. "I thought you might be heading into one of your spells."

"No. No, it's not that. Not yet, anyway."

"Let's try to head it off at the pass, then, shall we? A cup of something warm and some sweets, when we get back to your rooms."

Kadou grimaced. "No sweets. I ate my body weight in tarts and eggs and Heyrlandtsche butter sauce already this morning, I don't want to look at or think about food again for a week."

They reached the residence where Kadou's chambers were, on the opposite side of the Gold Court from Her Majesty's villa. They rushed under one of the covered cloisters to shake the rain out of their cloaks and the umbrella, and to laughingly kick off their shoes, which had gotten irretrievably sodden. The stone walkway was slick under their feet, and an unexpected gust blew rain under the eaves of the cloister, sending them scampering for better cover until Tadek stopped and glanced over the garden. "Is he crazy? Look at that—ridiculous."

Kadou looked where Tadek nodded. On the other side of the courtyard, in Kadou's own favorite little corner of the garden, Evemer was still at his morning sword drills, evidently unconcerned with the rain.

He had put off his sash and kaftan and boots. His hair hung in wet curls into his eyes and stuck to his cheeks, and his back and shoulders flexed with every swing of the wooden practice blade, sending a fan of water showering from the edge.

"He's going to catch his death," Tadek said, tsking. "But you have to admit the view is worth it. Look at those *arms*. You know, the scholars say Sannesi blessed the world a thousand times, but I've just found evidence for a thousand and one. Or two, I guess, depending on whether you count 'em separately."

Kadou very carefully did not think about whether he agreed,

nor about how those shoulders had felt under his hands the night before, or the way he'd had to tilt up his face into the kiss because Evemer was just so *tall* . . .

He cleared his throat. "We should go inside."

"Just a moment, I want to see him finish this sequence—what is that, the third verse of Beydamur's progression?"

Kadou hesitated, blushed that he was so easily tempted into lingering. "I think so."

"He's worked a nice variation on it," Tadek said appreciatively. "Fuck, look at the way he uses his height and reach. I can see why the incident in the alley went wrong. Look how much space he needs, look at the *tracks*." Evemer had practiced enough these last weeks that he'd worn paths into the grass—he did indeed tend to cover an incredible amount of ground. "You'd really want him on an open field or—well, anywhere but cramped in an alley fight. I'd kill to see him in a running battle. Do you think he does oil wrestling?"

Kadou forced himself away from the railing, turning toward his chambers. "Come along, let's not gawk."

"Of course, Highness," Tadek said.

The unseasonable rain continued into the next day, though it never got heavier than a steady, drizzling shower that hissed on the windowpanes and the plants in the garden. As he had the day before, Evemer practiced sword-forms in the garden in the morning, pushing himself hard enough that the chill of the rain never sank more than skin-deep, then presented himself at His Highness's chambers once he was dry and dressed.

They had not gone down to the city the night before. Evemer was prepared for another calm day, attending Kadou at home or on some little errand around the Gold Court, followed by another quiet evening that didn't involve dark alleys in any context, for His Highness had received a summons from Her Majesty that morning, which said that his presence was required at dinner that evening with the Oissic ambassador and her delegation.

Evemer had expected Kadou to grumble about the invitation or attempt to wheedle his way out of it, but he said nothing about it until late in the afternoon, when he only heaved a sigh and said, "Tadek, will you dress me for dinner?"

Tadek was at the writing desk, in the middle of scribbling something in the margin of some letter, and replied absently, "Give me two seconds, lov—Kadou. Er. Highness." There was an awkward silence, and Tadek abruptly put down his pen, snapped the inkpot closed, and followed Kadou silently into his room.

Odd. Were they quarreling? A cold knot clenched in Evemer's gut. Had His Highness told Tadek about what had happened in the alley behind the incense lounge?

His instinct was to trail after them, though he knew he wouldn't be much help—it didn't take more than one person to dress the prince. What would he do? Stand in the doorway and watch? He forced himself to stay at his post in the front room.

They left the bedroom door open. Evemer strained to listen, but he heard only an occasional murmur, the sound of the wardrobe's doors opening and closing, rustles of cloth. At length, Tadek called out, "Evemer! The note from Her Majesty is on my desk—bring it in, would you?"

He did so. Kadou was seated in the chair by the window, dressed in a white-on-white embroidered cotton underlayer and an ultramarine blue silk kaftan, several shades richer than the blue of the kahyalar uniforms—the heraldic color of the Mahisti dynasty. Kadou was frowning at the bed, on which were draped three over-robes, all spectacularly beautiful. One was black imperial brocade with glittering silver figuring; the second was a damask precisely the blue-black color of Kadou's eyes; the third was of dove-grey matelassé.

Evemer could spare these only the barest glance—Tadek had smudged kohl onto the corners of Kadou's eyes.

"I've got my hands full here," Tadek said—he did, he was dressing Kadou's hair. "Tell us if there are any hints in there about how formal Her Majesty expects this dinner to be. We would have heard about it before today if it were going to be a full-formal affair."

Evemer forced his eyes down to the paper in his hand. "Nothing, except that it is for the ambassador," he said, after a moment of panic when his tongue seemed to have forgotten all language. "It won't be lower formality than diplomatic standard."

"Told you," Tadek said, and Kadou made a face. "No damask for you. Evemer, could you put that one away?"

Evemer surreptitiously brushed his fingers against the other two robes next to it as he gathered up the damask—the matelassé was cotton. Not a thin fabric like some of Kadou's finest underlayers, either, but as heavy as the damask and brocade, and twice as soft. Evemer's mother was a weaver; she'd faint to hear about this. It was almost completely undecorated, but for the extravagantly intricate patterns of its weave, but the arduous process of producing such fabric would make it just as eye-wateringly expensive as the silk-and-silver brocade.

"An ambassador, but the ambassador of *Oissos*," Evemer found himself saying.

Tadek hummed. "A good point."

"She would have told me if I were supposed to show off for them," Kadou grumbled. "The damask would have been fine."

Tadek rapped him smartly on the shoulder. "None of that. Evemer is right. Diplomatic standard at the very least."

Evemer folded the damask robe and put it away in the wardrobe, then drifted back to the bed. The black-and-silver robe was stunning, and all the candlelight would catch and glitter across it as Kadou moved, but the matelassé . . . It looked as soft as velvet, but infinitely more touchable, and Evemer's fingers itched to brush against it again. The grey color was somehow warm rather than drab, and it would show Kadou's hair better than the black and silver.

He studied the invisible chessboard laid out before him—either of the two options would be fine, diplomatically speaking. Both of them represented political strategy of a different sort: overt power and wealth versus the more subtle kind. But Kadou had little interest in leveraging politics like that, so the scales were so near to being balanced that it made no difference.

The matelassé really was beautiful. Evemer pondered a moment more and moved a pawn one space forward. "His Highness is right, too," he said carefully. "Her Majesty would have sent word if she were planning to send a message."

"You have an opinion?" Tadek asked, sounding mildly surprised.

"I only think understatement is usually preferable."

"You would." Tadek sighed heavily. "Yes, all right, I admit defeat. You both win. I concede the point that the brocade might seem vulgar."

"Told *you*," Kadou murmured, and Evemer found that he very much needed to leave the room and sit in the parlor by himself until they came out. When they did, Tadek was still fussing with the drape and the trailing hems of the dove-grey over-robe, and Kadou was doing the same with the positioning of his coronet, both of them bickering amicably. Evemer drew himself up to parade rest and fixed his eyes on the opposite wall.

"There," Tadek said, hands on his hips and head to one side, studying Kadou. "You look nice. Careful of that over-robe, it's going to show every single spot." He turned to Evemer and pointed a warning finger at him. "Don't let him sit on anything unless it's immaculate, make sure nobody with poor table manners or messy eating is next to him at dinner, and if you let him get within three feet of a blade of grass that might stain his hems green, I swear to the gods I'll fill your bed with itching powder."

"It doesn't matter if I ruin it, I can just buy another," Kadou said reasonably, but Evemer felt faint with horror at the very idea of even a single corner of that beautiful soft fabric getting spoiled.

The rain was heavy enough that the kahyalar had sent for a covered sedan chair to haul Kadou in his finery out to the Silver Court, and Evemer spared a moment to be suspicious when Kadou didn't try to protest in the slightest. He and the other kahyalar made do with umbrellas and only got slightly dampened by the time they made it to the hall.

"You needn't stand attendance on me all evening," Kadou whispered to him as they went in. "There's plenty of kahyalar around.

You can go eat in the antechamber, or play cards with the others, if you like."

"Highness," said Evemer, and might have done so, but Siranos accosted them a moment later.

"Kadou," he exclaimed warmly, coming toward them. Evemer resisted the urge to throw himself between them. "What a pleasure to see you again, twice in two days." He was wearing a fine kaftan that looked new, and embroidered slippers with the extravagantly long, curled-back toe that no one had worn for thirty years. The fashion now was for the point of the toe to tilt up skyward and no further. He still hadn't hired an Araşti valet of his own, then, although Evemer saw that Siranos had, at some point since the last time he'd seen him, gotten his ears pierced. There was still a little scab of blood around each of the gold hoops.

"Hello," Kadou said warily. "Do you want something?"

"Yes, I thought you might like to meet my sister," he said. "She's not with the ambassador's delegation, of course, but everyone in Thorikou knows everyone else, and I convinced Zeliha that it would be nice to make it a sociable sort of evening rather than just business. Will you come?"

Kadou cast a single glance at Evemer. "Ah—"

"His Highness must greet Her Majesty first," Evemer said firmly. "It is proper."

Siranos sighed. "Yes, all right. I'll come with you." He was impossible to shake for the rest of the evening. Despite Evemer's best efforts and Kadou's increasingly panicked glances, Siranos was seated beside His Highness at the dinner table, one seat away from Her Majesty, who had been engaged in intense conversation with the Oissic ambassador all evening.

Beside the ambassador sat a woman who Evemer had glimpsed talking to Siranos just before he accosted His Highness—Siranos's sister, Evemer had to suppose, though they looked almost nothing alike. Their eyes were of a similar color, though hers were several shades lighter, closer to green than hazel, and there was something in their manner and expressions that seemed to echo, but that was all. She was short where he was tall; she, blond and he,

dark-haired. Her features were pretty and delicate; Siranos was
angled and strong-featured like a statue.

She also had an air of great poise about her, as if tempered
steel had learned to be demure, and she listened and watched more
than she spoke. Though her accent was Oissic, she wore an elegant
green dress in the Pezian style, with a bodice and two skirts—the
top one was plainer fabric, and it was looped up here and there to
show flashes of the costly silver silk brocade beneath, as if she had
no need to show it off by wearing it as a top layer. She also wore a
large shiny medal pinned to her shoulder, bearing some elaborate
insignia that Evemer couldn't make out from his position at the
wall behind Kadou.

"Ah, I promised to introduce you to my sister earlier," Siranos said to Kadou. "This is Sylvia. Sylvia, His Highness Prince
Kadou."

"Delighted," Kadou said solemnly. "So pleased you could attend." She and Siranos both smiled expectantly at him, waiting
for him to say anything else, and Evemer could read Kadou's resignation in the set of his shoulders. "How are you enjoying the
city?" he said, as if his tutors had tucked into his pockets a stack of
etiquette practice cards, each bearing a simple, polite question for
making conversation, and Kadou fully intended to read them out
one by one until he could find a way to escape.

"It is bigger than I am used to," Sylvia said. "And busier. And
the prices of everything are just shocking."

"Oh?" said Kadou politely. "Tell me everything about your
home, then."

The dinner continued in this vein for a full two hours. Sylvia
talked charmingly of whatever Kadou asked her—the unfortunate
harvests in Oissos the last few years, the lamentable loss of a harbor full of ships the year previous when the sea serpents' breeding
season had come along weeks early, before the harbor was secured.
She admitted with a sigh that several of her own family's ships,
including most of their half-unloaded cargoes, had been amongst
the wrecks.

However, Sylvia resisted with admirable will Kadou's attempts to make her do most of the talking—she turned questions back on him nearly as often. His Highness had evidently had enough etiquette tutors and enough practice at formal dinners that he navigated the conversation with all appearance of grace and cordiality. Evemer was almost certain that Zeliha was the only other person in the room besides himself who might have noticed that Kadou was doing it by brute-forcing himself into the role he was supposed to be playing, but *she* was occupied entirely with the ambassador.

Evemer did not move from his post, even to shift his weight and relieve the ache in his feet. He had a sharp suspicion that if he left even for a moment, Kadou would require him for something. But when he pictured how upset and disappointed Kadou might be to turn around and find him gone, he knew it was only an exaggeration of his own mind. Kadou had said outright that he wouldn't miss him, if he left. It was a very silly fantasy to imagine otherwise.

After dinner, there was a musical performance in the room adjoining the banquet hall—a very fine quartet from the city who began with one of Evemer's favorite ballads and continued with three more that he did not care for at all. Kadou sat quiet and still, hands folded neatly in his lap and his attention fixed so firmly and obviously on the musicians that no one even tried to talk to him. Evemer stood at his shoulder, but after the first song, his attention drifted.

Zeliha was still in intense conversation with the ambassador on the opposite side of the room, firmly shaking her head about something while the ambassador whispered intensely, gesturing just as firmly with her hands. The small assortment of other guests listened to the musicians with varying degrees of attention. Siranos and Sylvia stood toward the back—her arms were crossed, a dark look thunderous over her face, and she seemed to be firmly ignoring Siranos as he murmured occasionally at her.

In Evemer's boots, one of his socks had shifted and was chafing in an uncomfortable position. He weighed his options: As much as it offended his sensibilities to admit discomfort, a blister would hinder his ability to attend to His Highness, and that would not do. Kadou would be fine for two minutes while Evemer prevented an obstacle to his future service, and then Evemer would return and continue in his current duty without distraction.

He paused only to murmur to Kadou, "I will return," and headed toward the door to the corridor, remembering a low bench he'd seen on the way in.

As he passed by Sylvia, she caught his sleeve. "You're a servant of the palace, aren't you?" she murmured.

"Madam."

"Perhaps you can direct me to wherever a lady might have a moment to rest and reflect?"

By her delicate and pointed tone, Evemer assumed she meant one of the water closets. "Yes, madam. This way."

"Sylvia," Siranos said, his voice almost wheedling. "Just tell me what's the matter."

"Hush," she hissed to him, all delicacy gone, though no less pointed. "Come with me."

Evemer, too, wondered what had upset her so—nothing particular had happened at dinner, at least that he had noticed. He led Sylvia along the hall, Siranos following in her wake. "Just around this corner, madam," Evemer said, gesturing. "The second door."

"So kind," she said with a smile. It didn't have anything on *You're a godsend.* "Siranos, to me. You can wait outside the door and make sure no one comes in."

Evemer left them there, found the bench farther along the hall, adjusted his chafing sock, and took a moment to flex the aches out of his feet. That, perhaps, was a mistake, because the temporary relief meant that it only hurt more when he put his shoes back on and stood up again, but such pains were one of Usmim's simpler trials and could be firmly ignored.

How long had it been? Evemer was seized with the sudden concern that Kadou might have been accosted by one of the guests, might even now be looking around for Evemer or someone to rescue him from an awkward conversation. Evemer strode back down the corridor. Approaching the corner, he heard whispering voices—

Siranos and Sylvia? Some strange instinct made him pause and listen.

"Yes, but why is he *here*?" she hissed—they were speaking Oissika, of which Evemer only had a loose grasp.

"Why wouldn't he be? He's the prince," Siranos replied. "What's gotten into you?"

"Oh, for—me! What's gotten into *me*? Hesthera's saggy tits, Siranos! Perhaps you'd like to answer that yourself?"

"I told you," he said. "I'm staying. I have a *daughter*. Your *niece*."

"Moron, you should have made her marry you first if you wanted that baby to be yours."

There was a sharp *whap*, and Siranos said, "Ow! What was that for?"

"You've been doing it again, haven't you? Getting an idea so firmly in your head that you don't listen to a word that other people say. Doesn't matter how much of a stupid idea it is. You're a moron."

"You can't talk to me like this anymore—"

"Why the hell not? You're nobody, and that baby isn't yours."

"She is."

Sylvia laughed aloud, a sharp and ugly thing. "All right, I'm not going to explain something that you should already know. Moron. You're staying here, to be Zeliha's pampered little pet until she gets tired of you? Fine. Better work hard, though, if you want to keep in favor."

"I am," he said stubbornly. "I misstepped once before, but—"

"*Once?*" she laughed again. "Try seven or eight or nine times, and that's just since the last king-tide. Counting your whole life, though? Oh, goodness, we must have reached ten thousand by now."

"I'm doing what I can." It sounded like he said it through gritted teeth.

As fascinating and tempting as it was to listen to other people's family drama, Evemer couldn't eavesdrop any longer. Kadou would be waiting—he'd have to take the long way around, looping back through the rest of the building to get to the music room.

And then Sylvia said, "Yes, about that. You swore up and down that he was sneaky and conniving and wanted the throne for himself. And yet here he still is, sitting at Her Majesty's right hand at dinner."

Evemer, turning away, paused.

"I jumped to conclusions," Siranos said.

"Are you sure?" she asked, her voice silky.

"What do you mean?"

"Haven't there been any rumors? Hasn't Her Majesty confided anything in you recently? Surely pillow talk has to be good for something."

"It's not that I'm out of favor—"

"I'm sure. Look, you've decided to pin your heart to the sleeve of someone who won't love you back, and I don't really care. You want to be a big man and announce that you're giving up your family for that woman and her daughter? Not my problem. You'll come back to the family in a year or two or three with your tail between your legs. Frankly, if you think you can bear that sort of humiliation in front of our father and your mother and everyone, then go right ahead. But you made me some promises too, and if you fuck me over, then mere humiliation will be the least of your concerns."

"Don't be such a bitch—" There was another, louder crack. "Ow, fuck!"

"Make me hit you a third time. I dare you."

"What do you *want*? Just finish it and leave me in fucking peace!"

"Why is he here?"

"He's the prince. *His* sister doesn't backhand him. I ought to hit you back—"

"You don't have the balls," she said crisply. "You said there was a rift between them. You suspected him of angling for the throne—doesn't she suspect him? Hasn't there been . . . any indication?"

"I don't know why there would be," Siranos said mulishly. "All that rot about Kadou spying—"

"Hush." She huffed. "Fuck, all right. I'll take care of things. Just stay out of my goddamn way."

Evemer couldn't duck away quickly enough, and there wasn't any place to hide. Sylvia came striding around the corner. She froze when she saw him. "How long have you been there?" she demanded. Fortunately, she was still speaking Oissika.

Evemer blinked at her and said in Araşük, "I beg your pardon, ma'am?"

She didn't wholly relax, but subsided somewhat and, with a last suspicious glance, charged past him in the direction of the door out to the Silver Court. Evemer watched her go and went back to the music room, glimpsing only the back hem of Siranos's kaftan as he turned a different corner up ahead and vanished.

Evemer returned to Kadou, who had not been accosted by anyone, and spoke nothing of what he had heard until later that night when he was helping Kadou out of the gorgeous matelassé robe and taking the pins and braids out of his hair. "I overheard a discussion between Siranos and his sister," he began, and was surprised into silence when Kadou flinched hard and yanked away from him.

"You weren't spying on Siranos, were you?" Kadou said, aghast. "Don't do that! Oh, gods. Did I hint to you that you ought to? I shouldn't have. It's my fault. I don't care what you heard. Pretend like you heard nothing. Don't tell anyone."

"My lord," Evemer said. "It was accidental."

Kadou's shock and terror shifted into uncertainty. "Still. You don't need to tell anyone. Certainly not me. I don't need gossip about him."

"It isn't gossip. And I'm going to tell you." And he did, as much of the conversation he could remember and translate, but Kadou shook his head the whole time.

"No, no," he said. "No, we're not going anywhere near Siranos. Or his family."

"My lord." Evemer crushed down his frustration—would Kadou not *listen*? "She, at least, is up to something."

"Of course she is!" Kadou cried. "She's the eldest daughter of a merchant family that's in unfortunate financial straits. Who *wouldn't* be up to something? She probably has fifteen schemes going all at once! But what business is it of ours?"

"She could be linked to the counterfeits, the break-in. Siranos mentioned those papers that accused you—"

Kadou shook his head again and turned away, pulling off his kaftan and underlayer and replacing them with a thin linen nightshirt. He left the buttons at the collar undone.

Clavicles, Evemer's brain pointed out helpfully. He shoved the thought away and tried to remember what his point had been.

"We're not going to bully Siranos," Kadou was saying. "We're not going after his family. We're *not.*"

"My lord," Evemer said.

And for one more day after that, all was quiet.

※

There was a soft sound—a creak, hinges, the door. Kadou stirred and slitted his eyes open. It was still full dark, slivers of moonlight lighting the windowsills, and the rain had abated at long last.

"Evemer?" he mumbled, bleary. If it was past midnight, then Evemer would have had already gone off duty . . . "Melek?"

No answer. Kadou's brain jangled with alarm, that instinctive screech of warning that saved people from tigers and wild boars in the forest—but this was his own room, and if Evemer wasn't asleep or in the sitting room, then he'd be right outside the door, along with several other kahylar. Kadou was quite safe. It was only his tedious brain playing tricks on him again, pouncing on him in the middle of the night and shaking him to pieces like a dog with a rabbit in its teeth. Tiresome, useless thing.

He sighed and turned flat on his back, glaring up at the bed hangings above, willing his heart to calm *down,* for gods' sake, just calm.

Fear! his brain yowled. *Danger! Hello, what if we're about to die!*

Fine, he thought back. *Fine. Suppose you're right. Suppose there is "danger." What are we going to do about it, hmm? Are we going to do anything about it, or are we just going to lie here and let ourselves be torn to pieces by the tiger that's somehow gotten into this room? What's the plan?*

The yowling part of his brain didn't quite know what to do with that. It was almost as if it slunk back, a little embarrassed to be confronted with practical logic. *Fear? Fear?*

Shut up. If there's a tiger in the room, then we grab a weapon and we yell for the kahyalar. Lots of weapons in here, he added sleepily, forcing his muscles to relax. *Tear down the bed hangings to slow it down, then find the dagger in the nightstand and—*

He froze again.

He strained to listen.

Fear, his brain insisted.

Hush, he replied.

Had he imagined that, or was there someone else breathing in this room?

He lay very, very still.

Bed hangings to slow them down. Dagger in the nightstand. Chair at the vanity, could be used to pummel someone. What else?

He shifted, very slowly, breathing as slow and silent as he could, his eyes wide to look into the darkest parts of the room. An instant later, Kadou was certain he saw movement.

More than one.

Fear!

Yes, I know, he snarled at his own mind, and then he drew breath and screamed for the kahyalar.

Everything happened at once: He flung himself out of bed, yanking open the drawer of the nightstand. His fingers wrapped around cold metal. Someone, a strange voice, cursed and a weight crashed into him from the side, shoving him flat on his back and dragging a pillow over his face.

He heard the front door to his chambers burst open, pounding footsteps.

He ripped the blade of the dagger from its sheath; even through the muffling weight of the pillow, he heard the ring of his kahya's blade too. His wrist was pinned.

"Kahyalar!" Evemer bellowed. "Awake, awake!"

Kadou thrashed, clawing with his free hand, kicking at anything he could reach. He twisted his pinned hand free and slashed wildly with the dagger—the person on top of him cried out in pain and released the pressure on the pillow. He flung it free, hot blood on his hand and then dripping on his face, and slashed with the dagger again. The first swipe had caught them across the face. The second thudded into their neck.

There was a thunder of footsteps. He could hear Tadek now too, screaming his name, and Melek shouting for backup, and Evemer across the room, grunting with effort—another cry.

Another person on top of Kadou as the first fell away, this one with something white in their hand that they clapped across Kadou's nose and mouth—cloth? He wrenched his face away, rolling out of bed and out of their reach before they could get a grip on him, and then he was on his feet, stumbling out into the main room.

Fear, his brain said, helpfully.

Actually, yes, he replied. *Useful now. Thank you.*

His head swam—he'd gotten a whiff of whatever sweet-smelling alchemical compound had been on that cloth, but the motions of defense were written into his muscles.

Retreat to Octem's first position.

He needed light. The kahyalar would need light. How many assailants were there? Where were they?

There was an oil lamp on the table in front of the divan. He stabbed at the person rushing him, catching them in the palm— the handle of the dagger, already slick with blood, slipped out of his hand as they wrenched back. *Damn.* He dove backward, scrambling for the oil lamp, and flung it into the fireplace nearby. It shattered on the back wall; the thick oil poured over the banked embers and flames flickered to life.

There were—several? Several people. One already dead on the floor by his bed. One right in front of him, still with his dagger pierced through their hand. They tackled him bodily, bearing him to the floor, getting their injured arm across his neck and pressing down—well, all the better that it was that one. He took his dagger back with a twisting wrench; they howled in pain. He shoved the blade between their ribs and pushed them off.

Abruptly, it was over, or nearly so—all his kahyalar were in the room now, all drenched in blood.

Nasira, one of the secondaries, pulled her sword out of someone's gut and let the body fall to the floor.

Melek was shaken and ashy, clutching çir upper arm, where a thick stream of blood was streaming down çir sleeve—uniform, Kadou noticed vaguely. Çe must have just been switching shifts.

Tadek was there, in nightclothes and likewise bloodied, leaning against the wall and panting, one hand on his hip and his blade held loosely in the other, looking down at a body at his feet.

And Evemer stood silent in the middle of . . . carnage, really, that was the only word for it.

Evemer dropped his sword. Before it had finished clattering on the floor, he had crossed the room and was turning Kadou toward the light, his eyes searing across Kadou's body, looking for injuries. Nasira was there a heartbeat after. "I'm all right," Kadou said—his voice was hoarse; his throat ached. The world swam again in front of him; he staggered. Evemer and Nasira caught him in their arms and lowered him to the divan. "Some kind of drug on a cloth," he rasped. "Didn't breathe much of it. I'm all right."

"Bar the door," Nasira snapped over her shoulder. "Barricade it. Both of them."

Before they could do so, Eozena burst into the room, blade drawn and chest heaving, eyes wild. She took in the room at a glance and sheathed her sword, throwing herself to her knees by Kadou and shoving Evemer aside. "Highness—*Highness*."

"I'm fine, I'm all right," he said, clutching at her hands just as she clutched at his. "Is Zeliha—"

She went very still. "These people, were they trying to kill you?"

"Kidnap, I think," he choked out. "But *Zeliha*—"

"Get him dressed," Eozena snarled at his kahyalar. "Clothes, shoes, cloak. Now."

He'd never been dressed so fast in his life—they didn't even bother replacing his nightclothes with a proper underlayer, just shoved his arms into a warm, quilted kaftan, stuffed his feet into shoes, and flung a cloak over his shoulders.

Perhaps it was the drug still making him hazy, but he only got flashes of the next few minutes: Strong hands on him as he was hauled out the door. The slap of cool air from an open window they passed in the hall. Stumbling on a path in the garden, the scent of night-blooming jasmine. Pricks of lantern light in the distance where the watch stood on the walls and at the gate. Watery moonlight shining off of the kahyalar's blades. Eozena speaking in a low urgent voice. Going indoors, the familiar smell of Zeliha's chambers.

They dumped him into a chair, and they must have gone to wake Zeliha, because with the next flash that he got, the room was lit and Zeliha was being herded out of her bedroom, already dressed, with Eyne carried close to her breast in a sling and Siranos following blearily. "Kadou!" Her voice sounded almost muffled. "Holy hell! What's wrong with him? Is he all right?"

Kadou didn't hear the answer. He tried to say, "I'm fine, stop fussing," but his mouth felt dry and cottony, and his head ached, and he was so very tired . . .

"—get out of the palace—"

"How many were there?"

"—can't take the gates—"

"—tunnels—"

Kadou pinched his arm hard, the sharp pain cutting through the fog. Eozena was facing Zeliha, trying to shout and whisper at the same time, "—need to go to ground! Too many people know about the safe house in the city!"

"Commander," Evemer was saying, standing near her. It sounded like he'd said it several times already.

"—and *none of you* have better ideas," Eozena hissed, turning on the kahyalar. "So—"

"Commander," Evemer said.

"Eozena," Zeliha said, catching her by the arm. "It sounds like *he* has one."

Eozena whirled on Evemer. "Well? Speak, man! Be brief!"

"My mother's house," he said simply.

"Less brief than that, for the gods' sake!"

"It's in the artisans' quarter. It's quiet. Large basement. Beds and food. Easy to defend."

"That sounds perfectly fine," Zeliha said firmly before Eozena could speak. "Let's move."

"Zeliha—" Eozena said.

"Commander. Stay here. Do what you must to secure the palace." Zeliha leaned forward to kiss Eozena's cheek. "We'll be in touch. Don't worry."

Kadou nearly hazed out again at the flurry of motion, but Eozena stepped forward and helped him to his feet, muttering, "You, my boy, are to stay out of any more trouble, do you hear? Evemer, on your life, keep him safe."

"Commander," Evemer rumbled, somewhere behind him.

"I'm fine," Kadou croaked, and Eozena's grip tightened on his arm.

"Of course you are, love," she said. Her voice almost wavered. "Of course you are. Just another close call to keep old Eozena on her toes, eh? Keep him *safe*, Evemer."

"Commander."

Evemer's strong arm came up around Kadou's ribs, taking most of his weight as he dragged Kadou out the door and down the hall with Zeliha and the others. "I'm sorry," Kadou gasped, feeling the world blur again. "I'm sorry, I can walk—"

"Hush, Your Highness," Evemer said. "Mind your feet."

Darkness. A couple lanterns, plucked from their hooks. The shadows they cast wavered on the walls and shuddered with every movement. They made Kadou's head ache horrifically, made the blurring, hazy feeling come in stronger waves.

There were, of course, tunnels from the palace down to the city, held secret by the royal family and only their most trusted kahyalar. Kadou felt Evemer maneuvering them carefully down a narrow spiral staircase, smelled the rising scent of underground damp, heard the echoes change as the group made it to the bottom of the stairs where they opened into the vast underground cistern that supplied the palace with water. Kadou kept trying to shake off the fog, blinking into the dark. They went in single file down the access paths, past columns and arches and huge, deep pools of still water. The vibration of their steps made the surface quiver—the reflections of the lamplight and the columns wobbled violently and Kadou was nearly sick. He squeezed his eyes shut and clutched for a tighter grip on Evemer's clothes. He felt like the world was turning sideways, like the floor would slide out from under him and he'd topple right into the wildly dancing reflections—

Evemer was solid and steady in his grip. Kadou could feel his heartbeat.

He heard splashing in front of them, and Evemer said, "Hmm." Kadou didn't dare open his eyes. If he saw the dancing reflections again, or the wavering shadows, he'd be ill for certain. Evemer didn't ask anything of him, just hauled Kadou right off his feet and waded through the water, setting him down again on the other side. "The stones are wet," Evemer said. "Careful."

Then there were more stairs, and then a downward-sloping path—dirt, by the scuffling feel of it under his shoes, and by the stale, earthy smell of it. He risked another peek through slitted eyes, but it was useless—the walls pressed in on either side, and the ceiling was low enough that Evemer had to walk with his head bowed, and the rest was just the figures of the people in front of them, silhouetted by the vanguard's lamp.

A gust of cool, fresh air washed over them—the smell of the sea and the city, the unmistakable feeling of *space* around them. Someone ahead said Evemer's name.

"Here," said Melek. "Give him to us."

Kadou's grip on Evemer's clothes must have been white-knuckled. It was certainly enough that his hands had begun to cramp, and they hurt more when Melek pried them off and swooped under Kadou's arm, taking it across çir shoulders—someone else did the same on Kadou's other side. Tadek. Kadou recognized the scent of him.

"Where's he—" Kadou choked.

"Hush," Tadek said. "He's got to show us the way now, he's not going far. We have you."

"Zeliha?"

"Up ahead too. Bravest sultan anyone could ask for, eh? The princess too, she's been sleeping the whole way, not a care in the world. Can you manage your feet, Highness?"

Kadou couldn't, quite—Melek and Tadek weren't as tall as Evemer, and even together they weren't taking as much of his weight as Evemer had. He stumbled again and again, gritting his teeth now against the haze and feeling even more woozy and sick.

His arms ached from hanging off Tadek and Melek's shoulders. His ribs ached from where Evemer had held him up. His legs were as steady as thick custard, but somehow Melek and Tadek cajoled him into walking, and they went along through the winding streets of Kasaba, along the foot of the cliff in the direction of the city wall.

"You all right, Tadek?" he heard Melek ask.

"Managing, just about," Tadek said in a tight voice. "But cover for me when we get there, eh? How's your arm?"

"Bad. But thank you for asking."

Kadou tried to force his feet to work. He failed. "Sorry," he said, or thought he said. His kahyalar didn't reply.

And then all at once he was falling—no, being lowered—fabric under him. He opened his eyes. A ceiling above him. A room, around him. People moving in the near dark, lighting candles that stung his eyes, stoking the fire in the hearth. Low voices.

Tadek knelt next to him and got an arm under his shoulders, pulling him up and holding a cup to his lips. "Drink."

When the water touched his tongue, Kadou realized he was thirstier than he could ever remember being and seized the cup, swallowing it down so fast it ached in his throat and chest. "More," he croaked, but Melek was already bringing him another cup. He drank that too, a little slower.

"Give him here," Melek murmured. "Go on."

Kadou caught a glimpse of Melek's arm as he was laid in çir

lap. "Hurt?" he said blearily. He remembered now—çe had been injured in the fight. Had çe had any time to bandage it at all, or clean it out?

"Just a bad scratch, Highness." It didn't look it. Çir sleeve was wet to the cuff. "I'll have a scar to show my friends and a good story."

"Evemer?"

"Not even a chipped fingernail. And Tadek will be fine too," Melek added in a strange voice.

Kadou struggled to sit up. "What?" He looked around. Where had Tadek gone? When had he gone? He'd just been here—

"No, no! Don't worry about him."

"What happened to Tadek?" Another shock of adrenaline was driving the haze back.

"He'll be fine. He's still on his feet, isn't he? He got you here."

"Where is he? Where did he go? Let me up!"

Melek hushed him, tried to tug him back down to lie in the cushions, but Kadou thrashed, suddenly swamped by panic. An instant later, Evemer was there too, holding him down. "My lord," Evemer said in a steady voice that instantly made Kadou go still. "He will be *fine*."

"What happened?"

"Took a knife to the side," Evemer said calmly. "He's cleaning up. He would have already gone down if he were going to. Lie still."

And then he was gone again, and Kadou curled up against Melek's side, shivering. Melek petted his arm and back. "It's all right. Everyone's safe."

Kadou couldn't focus enough to listen to the conversations, and they were all carried out in whispers anyway. It was too dark for him to make out faces clearly from across the room. At length, he was heaved to his feet again. "He'll take your room? And Her—Her Majesty will have mine?" an unfamiliar woman's voice asked.

"Yes, Mama," Evemer said.

"Thank you for your hospitality, ma'am," Kadou wheezed, his

ribs aching again. He wished Evemer would shift his grip, or at least carry him on the other side, to even out the ache. "Honored."

She must have said something in response, but Evemer was dragging him up the stairs with Melek close behind.

Melek helped wrestle Kadou out of his shoes and kaftan, and Evemer rolled him onto a narrow bed. The two of them had a brief, whispered argument, and then Melek left. Evemer covered Kadou with a blanket. It was warm and smelled of clean linen and lavender. The pillows were hard—stuffed with rags rather than down, as Kadou's were. The mattress was a straw tick, but comfortable enough.

"Goodnight, Highness," Evemer said.

Was Evemer about to abandon him? All alone? Was he going to put out the candle? Kadou seized his sleeve. He was beginning to feel the shivering fear come over him. "Don't leave me."

"You won't be alone."

"Stay."

"I'll send Tadek—"

"You. *Stay.*" Tadek was already injured—if they were attacked again, he shouldn't be in harm's way a second time. He might not survive it. And Evemer . . . Evemer *was* safety. He wriggled aside on the narrow bed, all the way against the wall, making as much room as he could. "Please," he said, his voice small. "Please don't go."

Evemer unclipped the sword from his belt and sat beside him, back against the headboard and the sword laid across his knees. "Sleep, Highness. I will keep watch. There are others on watch below, and more patrolling the neighborhood. You are safe."

Kadou squeezed his eyes closed. Tentatively, he pressed his face against Evemer's side. A moment later, one of Evemer's arms draped loosely over his shoulders, gathering him in a little closer.

CHAPTER NINE

⟨⟩

At dawn, Evemer woke still propped up against the headboard and with a horrific crick in his neck, just as the door of his room swung open and Tadek peeked in.

Oh, of all the awkward situations he didn't want to deal with immediately upon waking up. Evemer froze, studying him, but Tadek did not seem to be particularly upset about catching his lover sleeping in a bed next to someone else. Evemer supposed it was obviously innocuous—the sword across his knees, for one thing. He relaxed again. This didn't look like anything but exactly what it was: He was guarding his lord as he slept.

As for His Highness, he was still clinging like a limpet to Evemer's sleeve. Tadek came into the room, shut the door behind him. He had Mama's favorite teapot, gently steaming, and a cup, which he set on the small desk under the window.

Silently, but with eloquent inquisitiveness, he gestured at the tea, then to Evemer.

Evemer stared at him suspiciously for another moment but relented and nodded. Tadek filled the cup for him and handed it over delicately, eyeing the sword across Evemer's knees with a raised eyebrow.

Evemer couldn't do much about it with Kadou occupying one arm and a cup of hot tea in the other. He clenched his jaw and made a dismissive jerk with his head. Tadek nodded, took the sword—carefully, quietly, so it wouldn't jingle and wake His Highness—and set it on the floor by the bed.

Then the presumptuous brat, moving stiffly and wincing, sat down on the floor, put one elbow on the mattress, and propped up his chin with that hand. When Evemer only gazed incredulously at him, Tadek made a *go-ahead* gesture, and Evemer had no choice but to sip his tea and endure.

This was unbearably awkward. Did Tadek expect him to leave? How could he leave without waking Kadou?

Tadek glanced at His Highness again, and mouthed . . . something. Some words.

What? Evemer mouthed back.

Is. He. All. Right? Tadek mouthed again, more exaggerated.

Oh. Evemer peered down at His Highness, shrugged, and nodded. He was breathing easy, and other than a few twitches and soft noises in the night that had woken Evemer with a jolt every time, Kadou slept quietly. No nightmares, no ill effects of that drug. *Are you?* Evemer replied.

Tadek shrugged and shifted onto his knees, pulling up one side of the fresh, unbloodied kaftan. Evemer thought he recognized it as one of his own, discarded when he was twenty or so for being too narrow in the shoulders to fit him anymore. His mother must have given it to Tadek.

Tadek ruched up the side, displaying a bulky pad of bandages, then grimaced and held up two fingers about two or three inches apart, grimacing. "Ugly," he whispered, barely louder than a breath. "Got lucky. Any deeper and I'd be dead." He dropped the fabric and shifted again to sit comfortably.

Evemer sobered. That would have destroyed Kadou. Even the thought of it might. "Don't tell him," he whispered.

"Obviously." Tadek looked at Kadou again with a sad sort of fondness.

Evemer drank his tea. It was licorice root, tasting of the earthy scent of rain after a drought when it first hit his tongue, and blooming into a fabulous, silky sweetness in the back of his mouth. It was his favorite—Mama always kept a jar of it for him.

In a whisper, Tadek asked, "I want your opinion. Will you tell me if I'm mad?"

"For what?"

Tadek dropped his eyes, picked at a loose thread on the quilt by Evemer's knees. "I wouldn't have minded dying for him. Part of me is disappointed that I didn't. I would have felt it an honor."

Evemer stared at him. He took a breath. He set aside his teacup and leaned forward as much as he could without disturbing His Highness. "Don't you dare speak those words again in front of him," he hissed.

"He's asleep."

"I don't care. You don't say that where he can hear."

"So you're saying I *am* mad, then."

"Go to the temple and ask to be unburdened."

"It's only a part of me that's disappointed," Tadek murmured, as if that were a reasonable argument. "I don't *want* to die. I certainly don't want to do it myself. Weren't you a little disappointed when he stopped you from cutting your hand off? It would have been so . . ." He gestured grandly. "Romantic, in the sense of epic poetry. Noble and heroic and—"

Damn Tadek, damn him. "You don't care about things like that."

"Darling," Tadek said, putting one hand to his chest in feigned astonishment. "Why else do you think I spent all my educational stipend on soppy plays?"

Evemer had no answer for that. "Go ask for an unburdening."

"Yes, yes, I know. I just . . ." He tapped his fingers on the blanket. "I wanted to do something that mattered, that's all."

"You think dying could have been it."

"Yes. It could have."

"Have you spared a thought for what it would have done to him?" Tadek didn't answer. "He wouldn't appreciate it the way you intended." Evemer very much would have liked to stalk out of the room then, no matter how haughty it would have made him look. He contented himself with sitting back against the headboard again and primly taking up his tea. When Tadek continued to say nothing, entirely failing to make any kind of smarmy comment that Evemer could have brushed off, he couldn't help but add, "You would have broken his heart."

"I don't have his heart," Tadek said simply. "So I can't break it." A heavy silence filled the room, stretching on and on until

Tadek added, "I never had it, actually—at least, I don't think I did. If I'd asked for it, he probably would have given it to me. But I didn't ask." He didn't sound sad about it, exactly, just . . . thoughtful. After another handful of moments he smiled brightly. "All for the best, really. I'm not the sort to be trusted with a heart anyway. What do you do with one? Buy a pretty box to keep it in, I suppose, and then what?"

Kadou shifted. Evemer and Tadek both froze, watching him.

When nothing else happened, Tadek murmured, "Well, it's all moot. No point in philosophizing about it."

Kadou had a few strands of hair stuck in the corner of his mouth. Evemer set aside his empty teacup again and carefully picked the strands free. Kadou shifted again, sighed. His lower lip looked very soft.

Evemer turned away. He'd already decided not to think about that.

Tadek was watching him with steady eyes that said as clear as text on a page that he'd seen it.

Evemer wanted *badly* to excuse himself. Surely his mother needed him for something—there would be breakfast to prepare for all the people in the house, and tasks to be done for her. He hadn't visited in weeks, surely there would be a list as long as his arm—

"More tea?" Tadek whispered politely, not taking his eyes off Evemer's face.

"Yes. Thank you."

Tadek got to his feet with a grimace and a hand on his side, letting his breath out in a slow, controlled hiss. He filled Evemer's cup again and set it and the teapot on the nightstand. "I won't tell," he said quietly.

"There isn't anything to tell."

Tadek gave him a look.

"His Highness and I aren't—"

"I meant," Tadek said, lowering his voice even further, "that I won't tell *him*."

"Nothing to tell," Evemer said carefully.

"Mm," said Tadek, raising his eyebrows and nodding. "Well, if you decide that there is something."

"There's *nothing* to tell."

"Of course." Tadek offered him a tight smile that didn't quite reach his eyes and left, shutting the door softly behind him.

✻

Kadou woke sore all over, either from the unfamiliar bed, from unknowingly wrenching something in the fight the night before, or most likely, from a combination of the two.

He rolled onto his back and opened his eyes. They felt dry and gritty, and he had to blink several times to get anything to come into focus.

Evemer was still sitting exactly where he'd been the night before, in the same rigid posture. Kadou peered up at him blearily. "Did you sleep?" he croaked.

"Yes, my lord." He pulled his sleeve out of Kadou's grip and immediately got to his feet.

Kadou felt a flush of embarrassment run through him. It was bad form to cling so.

Evemer must have wanted to get away, because he left the room immediately. Kadou heard him stomping down the stairs, voices below . . .

He was in Evemer's room. That's what they'd said last night, wasn't it? There was a shelf of carefully organized papers, a plain wardrobe, a desk and a chair. On the desk, two books in pride of place. One was brand-new, clearly printed with the new presses that had come to the city five or ten years ago and caused something of an explosion of the written word. The other book was older. Kadou rolled out of bed and picked them up.

The new one was Beydamur's *Ten Pillars of War*, a classic and one of the foundational texts for those members of the cadet corps who wished to pursue any of the military-adjacent career tracks. The old book was . . . also Beydamur's *Ten Pillars of War*, but it had been copied out by hand. The early pages were imperfect, the handwriting uneven and a little sloppy. Childish. As the book went on, the work got neater. By the end, the margins were perfectly justified, the lines of text neatly spaced, and the letters regular and clear.

It was too early in the morning for this. Kadou put the books back and went downstairs.

The first floor was one large room, the ceilings generously high to keep the house cool in the summer. The raw wood beams running across were hung with dried herbs, pots and pans, and a leg or two of smoked meat. Tadek sat in a chair at the table near the hearth, shelling beans into a basket and carrying on a lively conversation with a woman bent over a pot on the fire. He smiled when he noticed Kadou. "Highness, good morning."

The woman jerked upright and whirled around. She could only be Evemer's mother—she looked *just* like him, in the color of her eyes and the shape of her jaw, the soft texture of her hair, though hers was generously streaked with grey. Just like him, too, in the stone-wall expression that gave nothing away. "Your Highness," she said stiffly. "Good morning. There will be food shortly."

"We've sent Evemer to the market," Tadek said, with a private smile to himself about something. "He and Madam thought you and Her Majesty would be too good for eggs and porridge. Want to help me with these beans?"

Kadou sat on the bench next to him and began picking loose the papery husks, plucking the beans out one by one. Madam Hoşkadem watched for a moment with a scandalized expression he'd seen a hundred times on Evemer.

"Tea, Highness?" she said, struggling back to composure.

"Is there coffee?"

"There will be when Evemer gets back from the market," Tadek said.

Madam Hoşkadem carefully said, "We didn't tell him to get that."

"Madam," Tadek said. "I'm certain enough of this that I will lay a wager on it, if you fancy it. He will not return to this house without coffee. Trust me."

She clucked her tongue at him. "Such faith in my son! I'm sure he doesn't deserve it."

"Faith in something, anyway," Tadek said mildly.

"Eggs and porridge would have been fine," Kadou said. "You needn't have gone to all the trouble."

She drew herself up and set her chin stubbornly—he recognized that too, and immediately concluded that there wasn't any point arguing with her on this one. At least, not if she dug in her heels the way Evemer did. "I won't have the neighborhood saying Durdona Hoşkadem provided poor hospitality to the sultan and the prince when they turned up on her doorstep."

"I assure you we will only spread rumors of the excellence of your housekeeping," Tadek said with the same air of deliberate charm that he'd so often used to beguile Kadou.

Madam Hoşkadem went a bit pink in the cheeks and turned quickly back to the hearth.

"Where are the rest of the kahyalar?" Kadou asked.

"On patrol around the perimeter, like we arranged last night. A couple of them asleep on pallets in the basement. Siranos is down there too."

Kadou blinked. "Siranos is here? Why?"

Tadek looked at him. "There was a whole argument about it, did you miss that?"

"I must have. It was hard to focus."

"He was with Zeliha when we got to her chambers, and then he just sort of . . . followed along with everyone, didn't make a fuss. No one really paid attention him anyway—you gave everyone a scare," Tadek said easily, though he didn't meet Kadou's eyes. "Falling about half-dead like that. Evemer nearly bit Melek's head off when çe first tried to help move you, and a second time when they put you to bed here and Melek tried to suggest that he go off duty." Kadou didn't remember those either. "How are you feeling?"

"Headache," Kadou said. "Dry mouth. No worse than a bad hangover, really."

"Durdona," Tadek said, getting up from the table. "Do you have willowbark? Ah, thank you, my pearl."

"No respect at all," she muttered at him as he pulled down a jar from a shelf in the pantry. "Keep your flirting to yourself, young fox."

"In the face of such radiance? How could I possibly?" Tadek moved around the kitchen like he owned it, pulling down a cup from the shelf above the worktable and pouring water from a kettle keeping warm on the hearth. "Can I make you a cup of anything, radiant one?"

"I could be your mother," she growled at him, and pointed at the pantry again. "Tea."

Kadou was just finishing his first cup of willowbark tea when Evemer returned with a large woven-wood basket of things on a strap over his shoulder. "What took so long?" Madam Hoşkadem cried, dragging the basket off of his back.

"It's market day, Mama," Evemer said, unruffled. "There were crowds."

"And I suppose you strolled all the way back! His Highness has been waiting here ages for his breakfast!"

Evemer shot Kadou a guilty look. "It's uphill on the way back, Mama," he muttered, helping her to pull things out of the basket and arranging most of them on the table within Kadou's reach. Two big loaves of bread, a dozen simit, olives, several blocks of cheese, butter, a jug of milk, smoked summer sausages, a great variety of fruits, a cake of sugar, and a pound-bag of coffee, which Evemer took immediately to the hearth. Seeing this last item, Tadek made a very strange face as if he were both very angry and holding back hysterical laughter, then stared firmly at the wall. Kadou felt oddly like he'd missed some important bit of context.

Evemer presently brought Kadou a cup of coffee, asked whether he thought Her Majesty would be wanting any, offered some to his mother who was furiously busy at the hearth and the worktable, and finally made the same offer to Tadek.

Priorities, Kadou supposed, and gulped the coffee even though it was nearly scalding. It was perfect—thick and rich and sweet. "Are we safe here?" he asked Evemer.

"Yes," Evemer replied firmly.

One of Zeliha's kahyalar came downstairs—Pinar, Kadou thought her name was. She had skin nearly as dark as Commander Eozena's, and a head of tight curls she kept cropped close to her scalp. Her previous day's makeup remained as smudges around her eyes, and she looked just as tired as the rest of them did. "Her Majesty is awake, and wonders whether there might be breakfast."

"By all means," Madam Hoşkadem said. She shoved a tray into Evemer's arms and assembled pieces of everything she'd been working on, plus more from the pantry, until it was laden.

"And do you have any cloth?" Pinar asked. "The princess needs a change."

"Oh—just linen," Madam Hoşkadem said. "Will that do? Surely even princesses don't have diapers out of silk, do they?"

That got a bark of laughter out of Tadek, who covered his mouth to muffle the rest of his giggles, and a tired but warm smile from Pinar. "Linen will be just fine, thank you."

Madam Hoşkadem finished assembling the breakfast tray, muttering all the while to Evemer that he must mind his manners when he spoke to the sultan, and don't think she hadn't noticed that Evemer hadn't said a word to His Highness when he'd come in the door, not a word, let alone a bow! Had she raised a son to be so disrespectful? All of this was under her breath, and Evemer replied, "Yes, Mama," to everything she said until finally she tsked sharply at him and told him off for sass. "Mama," he replied solemnly, and Kadou had to bite back a smile.

She chivvied Evemer to follow Pinar up the stairs with the food and ducked into her workshop to look for cloths. Tadek turned to Kadou, his expression sober but his eyes dancing with mirth. "I seem to be having a morning of epiphanies."

"You mean, *aha, that's why Evemer is like that*?"

"That's the ongoing theme, yes," Tadek said, and got up to refill Kadou's coffee.

※

A message from the commander arrived before lunch—she'd addressed it to Evemer and his mother, presumably so that whoever was delivering it wouldn't wonder why Kadou and Zeliha Mahisti were hiding in a house in the artisans' quarter.

No one could identify the assailants' bodies. They'd been

wearing kahyalar uniforms, and nobody could say where they'd gotten those from either. There had been another attack elsewhere in the palace—eight people dead, and one prisoner missing: Azuta Melachrinos. Eozena begged Zeliha to stay put.

Evemer took the note into his mother's workshop, where she was at her loom with Zeliha standing behind her and holding Eyne. Mama had been terribly nervous of her and Kadou at first, but Her Majesty was so personable and kind, had inquired so sincerely about her work, and had seemed genuinely delighted when Mama had confessed that she belonged to the partnership of weavers who had been commissioned to make the fabric for Zeliha's own coronation outfit. She herself had woven enough for two panels of one of its layers: Mahisti-blue silk for the warp, a weft of thin ribbons of silver-backed paper, worked in an intricate brocade that had taken her months. Evemer had come home once a week from his duties with the fringe-guard and watched the loom's cloth beam wind steadily thicker with the glimmering, delicate fabric.

Evemer had heard from others that Her Majesty was a diplomatic force to be both admired and feared, and he was not at all surprised when his mother caved to it and shyly offered to show her the workshop.

"Majesty," he said, offering her the letter. "It was addressed to me, so I've already read it. Apologies."

Zeliha shifted Eyne to her shoulder, took the letter, and skimmed it quickly. "Damn," she breathed. "Damn. All right." She handed the letter back to him. "Go tell Kadou. Madam Hoşkadem, it seems like we'll be inflicting ourselves upon you for a little while longer yet."

"It is an honor, Your Majesty," Mama said immediately. "Think nothing of it." She gave Evemer a sharp look. "Why are you still here? Didn't you hear Her Majesty?"

"Yes, Mama," he said. "Majesty, do you require anything? A chair?" She did, as it turned out. He hauled Tadek out of the best chair in the kitchen, ignored his protests, and brought it to her.

Kadou had gone back upstairs earlier in the morning when

Siranos had woken and come up from the basement. He suspected Kadou wasn't as steady as he claimed—if Evemer had been a betting man, he would have wagered that Kadou was even now working himself into a fit of nerves again.

He found Kadou curled up in bed, reading Evemer's book. Kadou looked up, startled, when the door opened. "Sorry," he said, shutting the book carefully. "Sorry. I was bored, I didn't—do you mind that I'm reading it?"

"Letter from Commander Eozena," Evemer said to buy himself time. "Her Majesty has read it." He held out the letter; Kadou took it.

Did Evemer mind? Kadou had the handwritten one, the one Evemer had copied out painstakingly a few years before the printing presses came to Kasaba City and made books like *The Ten Pillars of War* affordable enough to buy. It represented more than a year of dedicated labor, though his work had gotten faster and cleaner toward the end.

He decided he didn't mind. It would have been different if it was Tadek or Melek. They had no call to be poking their noses into Evemer's precious things. Kadou could do as he pleased, of course.

Kadou looked up from the letter. "We're supposed to stay here."

"I know."

"I need to send a letter back to her." Evemer went to his desk, got out paper, ink, pen. "The other night, when you said you thought Sylvia was up to something . . ."

Evemer frowned. He'd been far too busy to think of anything in the world besides the people under his roof. "She did tell Siranos to stay out of her way. She said she'd handle things." He handed the paper and ink to Kadou.

"Do you think . . . didn't Siranos say that everyone in Thorikou knows everyone else? Do you think Sylvia knows Azuta Melachrinos?"

"I am skeptical of coincidences," Evemer said flatly. "I think that involvement in this plot would have significant benefits for Madam Sylvia and her family. They have motive."

"Careful," Kadou whispered. "Careful. Just . . . I don't want a repeat of what happened with Tadek."

"I know."

"We can't make decisions based on paranoia."

"Investigating an option is different from making a decision." He paused. "My lord, if I may be bold?"

"Of course."

"You are overcorrecting for a past error."

Kadou sighed and pressed the heels of his hands to his eyes. "I know." He took a breath. "You're right, of course. We should look at Sylvia. Calmly, quietly, not making any assumptions."

"Should Her Majesty know?"

Kadou opened his mouth to speak, paused, and sighed again. "I don't trust my own judgment on that one. That kind of question keeps getting me in trouble." He added, a moment later, "Probably because I keep *not* telling her things. I could . . . I could try telling her, and see if it makes any difference?"

"You could, Highness."

"And in the meantime . . ." Kadou's brow furrowed in thought. He got out of bed; Evemer stepped back from the desk so he could sit. He straightened the bedclothes while Kadou wrote, blew on the ink to dry it, and looked around the desk. "Do you have sealing wax?"

"In the kitchen." There were too many bits and bobs to keep all to himself in his room, and you needed a flame of some sort to melt the wax anyway.

"I hope Zeliha brought her seal," Kadou mused, and that made Evemer freeze again. Whatever he'd just written wasn't a letter to Eozena, then. It was something official.

"She's with my mother in the workshop," he said.

Kadou took another moment to collect himself—he really was skirting the edge of his terrors today, wasn't he? Evemer wondered if Kadou had even noticed it himself yet, or if he was too accustomed to a low-burn of anxiety to pay it any heed, in the same way that muscles became conditioned to exercise and only noticed a strain when they were being overtaxed.

Kadou went downstairs and into the workshop; Evemer followed.

Zeliha was sitting at the loom, and Mama had gotten over enough of her nerves to scold: "Now *yank* the rope. Sharp, girl, sharper! Look, now your shuttle's died in the middle of the warp, look." Mama stuck her fingers between the threads of the warp to flick the shuttle the rest of the way to the other side. "Then lift your foot from the treadle—yes, then the beater—"

"Zeliha, do you have your seal?" Kadou asked.

"Hold on a moment—how hard, Durdona? Like this?"

"Yes, better, now the next treadle—"

"It's just that I need to shut down the harbors," Kadou said, a little louder to be heard over the clack of the flying shuttle, the clatter of the rising and falling shafts, the thump of the beater.

Zeliha gave him a brief mystified look before her expression cleared. "Oh, because of Melachrinos? We've already impounded her ships. She can't run off by sea."

"She can if she has enough money."

"We've seized all her accounts."

"She might have more counterfeits. Or friends to help her."

"Not if they know what's good for them."

"May I *please* borrow your seal?" Kadou said.

"You're the Duke of Harbors," she said, shrugging. "If you want to close them, then be my guest." She pulled out the seal, hanging on a long chain around her neck. It was not the royal seal, of course. That too would be locked up in the palace, in a safe or a vault somewhere in the sultan's offices.

Kadou hesitated before taking it. "There's someone I want to investigate," he said.

"Is there?" Her gaze shifted to Evemer's mother. "Durdona, if I could have a moment?"

"Yes, Your Majesty," she said immediately, and grabbed Evemer's elbow as she went for the door, pulling him after her.

"He stays, please," Kadou said. "Sorry."

Mama seemed surprised, but she released Evemer with an impressed glance, which filled him with warmth and pride, and swept out, shutting the door after her.

"Who is your suspect?" Zeliha asked, folding her arms on the breastbeam of the loom.

"Not . . . quite a suspect. Just someone to look at. Siranos's sister," Kadou said, very quietly.

Zeliha gazed at him for a long time, expressionless. "Is that so?" Her voice was as soft as silk velvet.

Kadou shot Evemer a panicked glance.

"There was an incident at dinner the other night, Your Majesty. I overheard Madam Sylvia arguing. She was angry. She said she would . . . take care of things. And then, last night's attack."

Zeliha gazed at them both, stony and serious, her jaw tight. "Who was she arguing with?"

"Siranos, Your Majesty," Evemer said.

"And what was his position in the argument?"

"She didn't allow him to speak much, Majesty. She was . . . dismissive of his idea to remain in Araşt."

"He can't be involved," she said in a low, furious voice. "It's a ridiculous idea. Even if his sister is connected to Azuta Melachrinos and her crimes—what motive could *he* possibly have? He's the body-father of the next sultan of Araşt! All he has to do is make himself pleasant enough to stay in my favor and he's set for life! What reason could he have to conspire against that?"

"We're not sure about him. We're not even sure about Sylvia," Kadou mumbled.

"Enough!" she shouted. "Don't speak to me of this again until you find something real!" She subsided immediately, drawing back into herself with a sharp breath and closing her eyes. She held out the seal. "Just take it." Her voice was cool again, controlled. "Shut down the harbors if it pleases you, if you think that freezing trade indefinitely is a reasonable and measured decision to make. I'm sure the fishers don't need to go out to sea. I'm sure that we've imported all the food and goods and raw materials that we need. I'm sure that there aren't travelers coming or going, or news, or diplomatic envoys. I'm sure that a city of twenty thousand people can survive very comfortably with the port closed for days or weeks on end, just to keep one idiot merchant from leaving the city by sea." She glared at him. "To hell with that woman. I was going to be forced to release her within the week anyway."

Kadou didn't take the seal. He turned and left the room, the letter clenched in his fist. Evemer bowed deep and followed him. He'd already rushed back upstairs by the time Evemer was at the foot of the stairs.

"Honeybee," Mama called, stopping him in his tracks. "Will His Highness want lunch?"

"Yes, Mama—"

"You call him *honeybee*?" Tadek said, incredulous and delighted. He was at the kitchen table still, taking care of some of Mama's mending.

"Yes," Evemer said flatly. "What of it?"

"It's adorable."

"Kind of you to say so," Evemer snapped, already turning back to the stairs. "I'm busy."

"Evemer Hoşkadem, we don't speak to guests that way in this house," Mama said darkly.

Evemer closed his eyes and mentally snarled. He was torn in three directions and he did not have time for this. Maintain his pride against Tadek's jibes, obey his mother, or follow his lord? He could pick two, maximum.

"Of course, Mama," he said. "My *apologies*, Armsman Hasira. Now if you'll excuse—"

"You don't sound very sorry, honeybee," Tadek sniffed, and Evemer really would have dragged him out to the garden to strangle him in the rosebushes if there hadn't been more important matters.

"If you will both excuse me," Evemer said, and left.

Kadou had jammed himself into the corner of the bed by the headboard and the wall, all curled up tight, and had Evemer's hand-copied *Ten Pillars* open again on his knees, a few inches from his face. He was reading—or at least staring at the pages—with an intensely focused expression, as if he could block out everything else if he could just fill his eyes with the ink and paper instead.

"Highness," said Evemer.

"Stupid idea, closing the harbors. She was right."

Evemer sat on the end of the bed without waiting for an invitation. Why should he? It was *his* bed, technically. He didn't live here anymore but for one day a week, but it was his. "Mama is bringing you lunch."

"I'm not hungry."

"My lord."

Kadou shut the book with a snap and set it aside, the tight-knotted bundle of his limbs loosening. "I hate this," he said.

"I'm sorry my house is disappointing," Evemer said evenly, hoping Kadou read it as he meant it, as a joke.

"It's not the—it's a lovely house, your mother is very generous—"

"I know. What do you hate?"

"Being trapped here. Not being able to—to *do* anything." He dropped his head back against the wall. Evemer chose not to stare at the inviting column of his throat. "I want to help. I want to do something. And I have to just *sit here*." He sat up sharply and snatched the crumpled letter from the nightstand, tearing it to pieces. "Because if I move at all, I ruin everything," he said furiously. "If I try to use my power at all, it just hurts more people than it helps. I shouldn't have told her anything until I was sure. I knew she'd react like that."

"I imagine it was a shock to her. She is already tired and strained. She is afraid. But she will listen, given time. Her Majesty is fair and just."

"Yes," Kadou said. "But *Zeliha* isn't, always." He flung the shreds of paper to the floor—the violent, ferocious gesture was foiled by the shreds fluttering gently in the air as they fell. "I want to *do* something. But I just sit here and twiddle my thumbs and wait for Eozena to decide that the rest of the kahyalar are trustworthy, so that then I can continue twiddling my thumbs while they handle things themselves. Evemer." Kadou turned a burning gaze on him. "Evemer, what is the point of me?"

He was achingly beautiful like this, his long black hair all tousled from flinging himself about in frustration, the color high in his cheeks, his eyes bright and fierce. "My lord," Evemer managed, barely.

"Answer. What is the point of me? What reason is there for me to be here, instead of retiring to Şirya and being a minor landholder like my father? He used to help bring in the harvest every year, you know. He carried baskets of fruit and helped thresh wheat and take the comb from the beehives, and he lent his horses for the cider-pressing, and—I could do that." He looked down at his hands, flexed them. "I just want problems I can *touch*. I can't touch anything. That's my whole life: Everyone telling me *Kadou, don't touch. Don't touch that, Kadou, you'll ruin it if you're not careful, you'll break it, don't touch it.*"

Evemer wanted to lean forward and take his hands, kiss his palms and the inside of his wrists, just to feel a little of the weight of him in Evemer's hands again. He wanted to press his forehead to the backs of Kadou's hands and swear that he would fix everything—he'd go out and hunt down Sylvia and Azuta Melachrinos himself if he had to—

There was a tap on the door. Tadek let himself in with the lunch tray, and the moment was spoiled.

Kadou surrendered to his kahyalar's coaxing and ate a little, and very much begrudged the fact that it brought him down from his tirade. "I suppose you'll be happy if I'm good and quiet and I stay here like Eozena said," he said, after the lunch things had been cleared away.

"Yes, my lord."

Kadou closed his eyes, nodded. "All right," he said softly. He wasn't going to be able to be gracious about it, not when the walls seemed to press in on him—too many people in the house, not enough space or fresh air. The kahyalar wouldn't even want him to go too near the windows or step outside for a little sunshine. "I'd like to be alone for a little while."

"Of course," Evemer said, standing. "I will be down in the kitchen, should you require anything."

"Thank you."

"My lord." He left. Kadou slumped slowly down onto the bed, his eyes still shut.

When had Evemer started sounding like that when he said *my lord*? Like he meant it as more than just the words themselves? It was gradually growing some deeper, underlying meaning, like a river carving out a canyon from the rock.

It made Kadou feel like he was standing on solid ground. Here, at least, was one certainty. One steady thing to cling to: Evemer, and his loyalty, and the way he said *my lord* every time like it was a promise.

Like Evemer was swearing an oath, each time he said it, that he would be the solid deck of the ship under Kadou's feet when the tempest raged around them. Kadou wished he could be that steady. He wished he knew how.

After some time, he picked up Evemer's copy of *The Ten Pillars of War*. Kadou had read it a dozen times already, as well as many of the other great classics, and like any educated person, he had particular passages of it memorized. But there was something different in looking at the pages written out, tracing the letters that Evemer had shaped, flipping through the book and watching his mastery grow.

Perhaps the making of this book had shaped Evemer just as much as his mother had. Perhaps this was where he had first learned discipline, and exacting measurements, everything fitting neatly into the penciled guidelines. But even by the end, though the spacing and size of the lettering and the layout of the pages became almost mathematical in their precision, they could never quite be described as beautiful. Evemer hadn't bothered with ornamentation, even on the first line of every new chapter. In many older manuscripts, the first line was often lavishly illuminated, a narrow bar of color or intricate art across the width of the text block. This book was plain, with little attention to form but where it contributed significantly to the efficacy of the function.

But when he had been doing sword-forms in the rain, he had worked variations on several verses of the progression, and those had been beautiful.

When Tadek had called him in to settle the debate about Kadou's over-robe, his eyes had lingered on the matelassé one just before he chose it, as if he thought that was beautiful too.

When washing Kadou's hair, his hands had been as gentle as if he'd been handling some rare and fragile treasure.

And he said *my lord* with that deep sense of meaning.

It was strange to think of all those things and hold them up in contrast to the hand-copied book, which gave scant hint of any beauty in the soul of its copyist.

When Kadou looked up from the book again, the light had changed, and there were voices below—the whole afternoon gone. He rose, back and limbs stiff, and descended.

The house was brimming with warm and golden light, though the thin linen curtains over the windows were carefully drawn. The kitchen was full of good smells, and Eozena was sitting there at the table with Zeliha, Tadek, and several kahyalar. Siranos was pacing slowly back and forth across the room with Eyne in his arms, humming softly to her.

"Decided to stop sulking?" Zeliha said with acerbic brightness as Kadou came down the last steps. He stopped in his tracks and just *looked* at her, stung.

Eozena got up from the table and, wordlessly, engulfed Kadou in her arms. "Are you all right?"

"Fine," he said, muffled in her shoulders.

"Scared the wits out of me last night."

"So I've heard."

She pushed him back by his shoulders and held him there so she could study his face. After a moment, she nodded and returned to formality. "Will you come sit, Highness? I have bad news and good."

He sat on one of the long benches between her and Melek and

resisted the urge to curl around her arm and lay his head on her shoulder. "I'll start with the bad news," she said. "The garrison is in chaos. There are several groups of kahyalar who pounced on the first conspiracy theory that presented itself, to wit: His Highness is dead and Her Majesty and the crown princess are either also dead or abducted. I have done my best to disabuse them of this notion, but I suspect that the more passionate ones have begun to suspect that I'm involved." She rolled her eyes. "On the upside, the ones who have come to shout at me about how they're going to un-cover my villainy and avenge House Mahisti have put themselves, to my mind, pretty solidly in the little box I've labeled *trustworthy*. Though perhaps not the one labeled *smart*." She gazed into the middle distance. "Truly, there are benefits to encouraging such passionate loyalties. Makes it easy to sort 'em. Further bad news, though: The chaos has extended to infighting. As of last count, just before I came down from the palace, there were more than thirty kahyalar injured in the infirmary, and two dead since this morning."

"Shit," Zeliha said under her breath. "And how many died in the attacks last night?"

"Six."

Zeliha touched her eyelids, lips, and heart. Kadou did the same. "Usmim, judge them kindly," she murmured. "What else? You said there was good news?"

"Partially good news, partially me asking a favor. How many of your kahyalar—the ones who are here with us—know specifics of the counterfeiting?"

Zeliha thought for a time, glancing around at the handful of kahyalar around the table. "Just Pinar, I think."

Eozena turned to Kadou. "How many of yours do? Or about the Shipbuilder's Guild?"

"Melek and Evemer. My armsman knows as well. The others might have overheard bits and pieces, but . . . I don't actually know which of my kahyalar are here, besides them," he added, trying to keep the peevish tone from his voice. "I've been locked in the house all day, and last night I was too drugged to see who was with us."

"Hmm." She tapped her fingers on the table. "I've been getting a lot of people coming up to me today to prove their loyalty. Selim, the chief of the ministry of intelligence, being one."

"Oh. Yes," Zeliha said. "I trust him."

"Good. As do I. He was worried about that, seems to think that spies might be seen as inherently untrustworthy."

"We don't promote people to the intelligence ministry if we have even a shred of doubt about them," Zeliha said.

"That's what I told him. Nevertheless, he dropped a mountain of half-formed ideas on my desk, vomited everything he knew about anything even remotely sensitive that I was at liberty to hear about. One of those gems was that they may have located where the counterfeits are being produced."

"*May* have?" said Pinar, who was leaning against the far wall with her arms crossed. "I thought the ministry of intelligence dealt in more certainty than that."

"Only because they usually keep their mouths shut if they're uncertain," Eozena said dryly. Kadou stifled a wince. "It's a privately owned warehouse on one of the harbor islands. The one time they managed to get someone inside, it was empty. They found the forge, the workbenches, and a cache of copper ingots. That's it. No dies, no coins."

Eyne made a warning noise of unhappiness, and Zeliha gestured to Siranos. "Bring her," she said. Her voice was just the slightest bit too sharp.

Siranos obliged, pressing a kiss to Zeliha's temple as he laid the baby in her arms. She only twitched slightly at it. "I'll be right back," he murmured to her, and walked out the door.

"You know as well as I do, Majesty," Eozena continued, "that the ministry of intelligence is up to their eyes in work after last night. They don't have the staff to have the warehouse staked out twenty-four hours a day on a hunch, and it's tricky to get to it without being seen by the gods and everybody. They've done a few spot checks over the last couple of weeks—there was one night that there was work going on inside, but the doors were locked— and they know, because god and everybody sees, that there's a boat of workers that goes out to the island most nights. Which brings me to the favor that I'd like to ask."

"Go ahead," Zeliha said.

"Majesty, I'd like to borrow Pinar and see if we can get any more specifics from that warehouse."

"And you want Pinar because she already knows things?" Zeliha only had to consider for a moment. "Yes, all right."

Eozena turned to Kadou. "Highness, I'd also like to ask for two of your three."

"Which two?"

"Your choice, but I would be *very* grateful if Evemer was one of them."

Of course she'd want Evemer. Kadou wanted just as much to guard him jealously, hoarding him away. But that wasn't fair, was it? Evemer was stifled in this house as much as Kadou. And if Kadou himself couldn't leave to put his hands on the problem, then at least he could know that Evemer was doing the very best possible job with it. "All right. Him and . . ." He looked between Melek and Tadek, hoping one of them would volunteer.

Without a word, they turned to each other and played a quick game of taş-makas-kağıt, which Tadek won. "Lucky me," he said, all wreathed in smiles. "I'll go."

CHAPTER TEN

They went out after sunset, their faces and hands rubbed with ash to better hide them in the moonlight. Eozena had a rowboat waiting in a hidden cove at the waterfront. The four of them piled into it, silent but for the black waters that slapped against the hull with a hollow sound.

They rowed across the mile or so of dark water, the wind and waves blowing shocks of chilly sea spray over them. Eozena directed them to the second-biggest of the harbor's islands, rocky and thick with trees. The islands were all owned by various merchant associations, who had built warehouses to store their cargo when the city proper had become too crowded and expensive for new ones.

Evemer jumped out of the boat when they got close to the shore and dragged it up onto the narrow beach, into the shadow of an overhanging tree. Pinar followed and lashed the boat to the tree, leaving the rope taut—easy to cut it free with one slash of a sword if things went poorly and they had to run.

"This way," Eozena said, her voice no louder than the wind. She led them around to the far side of the island, the four of them walking in single file through the wood.

Evemer was so straining his eyes to see, and so straining his ears to hear, that he didn't notice for a moment that the smell came to him before anything else did—bitter smoke on the wind, and the tang of hot metal. Then, the sound: voices, the ringing clang of hammers on metal. Eozena gestured for them to go carefully, and she crept forward, blending seamlessly into the shadows.

Evemer followed her, Pinar beside him and Tadek just behind, as they made their way around the rocky slope.

The wall of the warehouse was stucco-covered brick, built into the side of the island's steep, rocky hill, and the only windows were high above them. They seemed to be covered with thick, black curtains—unusual for a warehouse, which wouldn't require decoration—but in the oppressive darkness they could see just a hint of lamplight limning the edges.

"Is that one open?" Eozena hissed, peering upward.

"No," Pinar whispered back. "But there has to be one some-where, if they've got a forge going in there." Together they crept around the edges of the warehouse, and on the far side, facing away from the city, they found it. A wide window open high above, near to a rocky outcropping that Evemer would have thought too steep to climb without equipment.

Pinar eyed the rock face, speculative. Before any of them could speak, she was scaling it, her fingers finding crevices in the dark and her toes finding every foothold until she was perched high above. She leaned out, trying to get to an angle to see in the window, but the outcropping was too steep to do so without risking a fall that might have broken her neck.

Eozena turned to him and Tadek. "Too old to be spider-crawling up the side of a rock," she said. "One of you will have to."

Evemer and Tadek shared a glance. Tadek's hand drifted to his side, bulky with bandages. "If it's all the same to you . . ."

Evemer nodded.

It was much more difficult for him than it was for Pinar. Though she was nearly of a height with him, very tall and long-limbed, she was perhaps half his weight, all bones and wiry angles. He was winded by the time he reached her, standing on a very narrow natu-ral ledge formed by the boulders. His fingers were sore and scraped from trying to find handholds in the stone, and his boots were surely scuffed beyond salvaging.

"What do you want me to do?" he whispered. Pinar showed him, with whispers and gestures, and he dug his fingers into a crevice in one of the rocks by their heads, gave his other hand to Pinar, and let her lean out over the gap until she was nearly horizontal. She was light, and his muscles hardly strained.

He pulled her back when she'd finished. "Want a turn?" she said.

"You strong enough to hold me?" he asked, only a little uncertain. She was strong enough to haul herself up, after all.

"Yes, of course."

It wasn't as easy as she'd made it look—he had no fear of heights other than that of any rational person, but leaning out over a sheer drop onto hard stone, in the middle of the night, with the only thing between him and gravity being the grip of a strong hand around his wrist . . . There had definitely been places he favored more than this.

The warehouse inside was nearly three times the size of his mother's house. A wave of warmth rushed over his face as he came level with the window. The forge was going, and several stone crucibles amongst the flame-blown coals glowed inside with molten metal. Perhaps a dozen people were working inside, pouring gold or silver and chunks of scrap metal into the crucibles, pouring out the metal into ingots, rolling the cooled ingots into long strips, punching out blanks from the strips, and finally striking each blank between two dies with a powerful single swing of a hammer.

There was a very large chest, already half-full of gold and silver—or at least, what looked like gold and silver—and a knot of people on the far side of the warehouse, arguing. "I don't care!" one of them said, just loud enough to be heard over the noise of the workshop. "Throw this batch in the harbor for all I care, just *pack it up and clear out*!" The man turned, and the light fell on his face: Siranos.

Evemer's foot, braced against the rock, slipped. He fell sharply, his arm yanked in its socket, and he heard Pinar grunt with pain. He scrambled on the rock, trying to find a handhold, and then her grip on his wrist slipped, and he was sliding down the rock, making far, far too much noise, and crashing to the ground with a thud as all the air was knocked out of him.

"Fuck," Tadek muttered, as from inside the warehouse a shout came:

"Intruders!"

Pinar landed on her feet next to Evemer, as light as a cat, and helped Eozena and Tadek haul him up. "Run!"

"Fool!" Eozena hissed at him—yes, he knew. He cursed himself as he ran, feet pounding on the stone and sand as they rounded the warehouse again. They dove into the copse, branches whipping at their faces. There was a great noise behind them, shouting and more running footsteps, and—and just at that moment, the treacherous wind blew a cloud clear of the stars and the moon—one a slipper-sliver, one in its last quarter. Compared to the chthonic darkness from moments before, it was suddenly terrifyingly easy to see Eozena and Pinar before him, darting through the trees.

He heard the hiss of an arrow. It clattered off the side of a tree trunk with a spray of bark and leaves, followed by a second, a third. He urged his legs faster, praying that the ground was level enough that he wouldn't fall and twist his ankle.

Another arrow hiss. A line of fire across the top of his shoulder. At the same moment, Tadek gave a sharp cry and stumbled, falling to the ground. Evemer skidded to a stop and turned back. "Not a chance," he snarled, hauling Tadek up again.

"It's nothing," Tadek gasped. "Just winged me across the calf."

But then their pursuers were upon them. Without even having to think about it, Evemer shoved Tadek behind him and drew his sword, swinging wildly.

He killed two of them and was turning toward the third when another arrow grazed him just below the elbow, deep enough that his hand spasmed and he dropped his sword. He lashed out with his fists instead, seeing out of the corner of his eye Eozena, coming in like a meteor from his left flank, giving him enough cover to retrieve his sword.

Then it was easy—he'd trained for this: the division of the field into two hemispheres, the types of swings and thrusts you could and could not do with a person behind you.

There were more people around them than he had first seen in the warehouse, and they were trained with weapons as the thieves in the alley had not been.

But thinking of that night, comparing it to this, sent an arrow of pain and alarm through Evemer's chest. What would Kadou do if they died here tonight? What would he do without Eozena, without Tadek? "Run!" he shouted, flinging himself anew at their attackers.

Light flooded the area—someone had lit an alchemical flare, and it blazed a blinding greenish white that made spots bloom in Evemer's eyes like dozens of solar eclipses.

But the enemy cursed as well. They had been expecting it as little as he had—all of them, Evemer included, threw their arms up to shield their faces from the scalding-bright light and stumbled, fumbling their weapons and tangling up together. Evemer flailed for Eozena, dragging her away. With his eyes watering and smarting, he stared in the direction of the light. Someone was holding the flare up above their head, the only person still even partially in shadow—Evemer's night vision was ruined too much for him to see, but by the silhouette, he would have guessed it was Siranos.

Siranos, who was looking right at him, who now had seen his face as clear as it would have been in the noonday sun.

"Run, Commander. *Run.*"

"You too, idiot!" she snarled at him.

They caught up with Tadek within seconds—he was staggering, the light hit to his calf clearly not as light as he'd claimed. Evemer ducked under Tadek's arm and took most of his weight, just as he had for Kadou the night before—Tadek was only slightly heavier than the prince, but at least he wasn't drugged.

Siranos—yes, it was him, Evemer recognized his voice— shouted for the others to get themselves pulled together and continue the pursuit. He wasn't a man who knew about fighting in darkness, then. He must have thought he'd been helping his guards by lighting that flare.

Pinar had slashed the rope and was holding the boat ready

to launch. Evemer all but flung Tadek into it, and then he and Eozena were shoving together, wading thigh-deep into the cold water to get the boat out of the shallows.

He heard shouts behind them. He heard a thump, Eozena's sharp cry beside him, the clatter of arrows on the stony beach or hissing into the water around them. He gave the boat a final shove as Eozena leapt up into it. She turned immediately to grab him by the back of his collar and haul him in after her, one-handed, as Pinar and Tadek dug the oars into the water and heaved for all they were worth.

Evemer hit the bottom of the hull with a groan for his sore ribs, bruised by the fall from the window, and pushed himself up, staring desperately back at the island—but the people on the beach had already vanished, either to conserve their supply of arrows or (more likely) to dispose of the evidence and flee, since their quarry had escaped.

"Well, fuck," Eozena said, annoyed.

Evemer glanced over, and his blood went cold. The starlight was just enough illumination to show an arrow lodged in her leg, the wicked point punching all the way through. "Commander!"

"One more thing I did not *motherfucking* need," she snarled, dragging herself to one of the boat's thwarts where she sat heavily, her leg stiff and straight in front of her. Without a wince, she reached down and snapped the arrow's head and fletchings as close to the wound as she could without even a grunt of pain, leaving a length of shaft piercing through her thigh to hold the wound closed. She flung the pieces overboard and only a moment later said, "Oh, fuck me, should have kept those. Might have identified them."

"Gods and fishes, Eozena, don't do any more of that or I'm going to throw up," Tadek said, strangled.

"Oh, calm down," she snapped. "I've had worse."

"Worse than an arrow straight through the thigh?" Pinar asked, breathless with exertion. She hauled harder on the oars.

"Thrice-damned *children*, the lot of you," Eozena snarled. "Shut up and row. Don't know why I thought taking any of you was a good idea. Pinar! Are you hurt?" she demanded.

"Just scrapes and bruises, Commander, ma'am," Pinar said. "Sorry, ma'am."

"At least there's that," she spat. "I'll only have one Mahisti baying for my blood when we get back. Gods!"

"Kadou's not really the baying sort, though," Tadek said. He sounded pained.

Evemer forced himself up, a steadying hand on the gunwale. "Let me," he said.

"I'm fine."

"Tadek, move your sorry ass and let Evemer *fucking row*," Eozena said. "At least he hasn't gotten *punctured* twice in two days like *some people*, by which I mean you, so let him fucking row, and—"

"I'm letting him, I'm letting him!" Tadek said, shuffling off of the rower's thwart and moving to sit in the prow. Evemer took his place and matched the rhythm of his oar to Pinar's.

"—I don't know how you even made it to core-guard with a weak stomach anyway. Threatening to vomit! I can't believe you. What the fuck is wrong with you, boy?"

"Lots of things," Tadek said. "And weak stomachs are one thing, but *watching your commander snap an arrow off when it's going all the way through her leg* is a dramatically different one, I would argue—"

"Are you giving me *backchat*?"

"Yes. And? What are you going to do about it?"

Eozena was agog with rage for a moment. "I can have you whipped for insolence! I can have you demoted!"

"Demoted from His Highness's sworn armsman?" Tadek said, sounding smug now. "You can't. Not actually in your chain of command, am I? You can't touch me. Now speaking of *shut up and row*, that sounds like a good idea, why don't you join us?"

"Tadek," Evemer said. "She can't touch you, but I can."

"Oh? And what are you going to do, *honeybee*? Punch me?"

"*Yes.*"

"I swear to both gods, I will drown the two of you and throw myself on His Highness's mercy!" Eozena hissed. "He'll look me in the eye and do you know what he'll do? *Do you?* He'll cry. And

I'll feel like a fucking monster, and Her Majesty will be furious with me, but at least I'll have one piece of comfort, and do you know what that is? I'll know that it's *all your fault*, because the two of you wouldn't *cut that shit out*."

There was total silence for almost a whole minute.

"*And another thing*," Eozena continued. "Why the *fuck* was Siranos there? Wasn't he just at the house?"

"He said he'd be right back and then . . ." Pinar said breathlessly. "I know I wasn't paying much attention to him. Can't imagine anyone else even spared a second thought."

Evemer took a mental inventory of everyone else who had been in the house. The other kahyalar had gone back out to their watch posts when the meeting had finished, Her Majesty had headed upstairs to rest and feed Eyne, who had been fussing, and Kadou had hovered around the table as Eozena outlined her plan . . . "How much did he hear?" Evemer said. "How much does he know?"

"Fuck," Eozena said again, more fervently. "He knows where your mother's house is, for one thing."

※

Kadou had been pacing for a thousand years, it seemed, and then his worst nightmares walked in through the door and all but collapsed in front of the hearth.

"Someone's already gone to fetch a doctor," Pinar said as Kadou froze in place, unsure whether to rush to Eozena, Tadek, or Evemer first. They were all of them bloodied, and Evemer and Eozena were sodden from the hips down and shivering. The water had washed away some of the bloodstains, but Eozena had half of an arrow sticking out of her leg, and Evemer's clothes were bloody on one side from the shoulder to his waist.

"What happened?" Kadou demanded, when he'd found his voice.

"Went bad," Eozena said. She was sweating profusely, and her skin was clammy when Kadou touched her, helping her onto one of the benches by the kitchen table. Evemer dragged a chair over to the hearth and dropped heavily into it.

Melek was already piling fuel into the fire. "Durdona!" çe called. "Quickly!"

Madam Hoşkadem came clattering up the basement steps, took in the state of the group at a glance, and charged into her workroom, emerging a moment later with handfuls of clean rags to soak up the blood until the doctor could arrive and bandage them properly.

"Get out of your wet things, you two, before you catch your death," Melek said, helping Eozena's fumbling, cold-clumsy fingers with the fastenings of her kaftan. "We're going to leave your trousers on until the doctor gets here, Commander," çe added. "I don't want to pull out that arrow until we have to."

"I'll get some blankets," Pinar said, going for the stairs.

"Do you need help?" Kadou asked Evemer anxiously. "Are you hurt?"

"No," Evemer said. Kadou wasn't sure which of those questions Evemer was answering, or if it was both, but when Evemer peeled off his sodden, filthy kaftan and underlayer, the bleeding gashes in his shoulder and lower arm were answer enough, as were the blooming bruises down his back, the scrapes on his hands.

"What do you mean, *no*? What do you call that?" Kadou shouted. "How did this happen?"

"Is the princess asleep? Don't yell, my lord," Evemer replied.

"And you said he wasn't the baying type," Eozena muttered to Tadek, who had sat beside her on the bench. "Did you forget he's a Mahisti?"

"I said, how did it happen?" Kadou said again, turning on them.

"Collective fuck-up, Highness," Eozena said, straightening her posture as much as she could. "We got caught."

Evemer looked grim, which was all the confirmation Kadou needed. Pinar came back with an armload of blankets, and Kadou snatched one from her, shaking it free and flinging it around Evemer's shoulders. "We're going to have words about this later," he hissed. "All of you! Always scolding me to be careful, and here you are, gallivanting off and getting yourselves cut up and half drowned! I thought this was supposed to be a reconnaissance mission!"

"I'm sorry, my lord," Evemer said.

"And you!" Kadou said, kneeling by Eozena. Fear and alarm twisted in his gut—three of his people, hurt again. All four of them, if you counted Melek's bad arm. Gods. "You can't die, all right?" His voice cracked on the emotion that was welling up in his throat. "You can't. I forbid it."

Eozena laughed weakly. "Haven't died yet, Highness. We all came home safe."

The doctor arrived a few minutes later, a large leather satchel slung from çir shoulder. Kadou, far too distinctively a Mahisti, was obliged to hide in Madam Hoşkadem's workshop for the duration. Çe made quick work of Eozena's injury. Her trousers had to be cut free of her leg, the remaining shaft of the arrow pulled free, releasing a new gush of blood. Çe washed out the wound and applied cleansing poultices, wrapping the leg firmly, and turned to attend to Evemer and Tadek, only to discover that Melek had already done so, placing neat stitches to close their wounds and wrapping them in the same poultice and bandages.

Kadou could only pace uselessly in the workshop and watch from a crack in the door.

He dove back out as soon as the doctor left. "A reconnaissance mission," he spat again. "You could have all *died*."

Madam Hoşkadem silently went into the basement again and came up with a couple bottles of ale. She poured a cup and pulled Kadou toward the fire. "Guests," she said sharply to Evemer, who was occupying the chair, and Evemer obediently moved to the floor by the hearth, his movements stiff and sore. Kadou sat when Durdona prodded him. "Drink, Your Highness," she said, nudging the cup toward his mouth. "Too late for tea and coffee."

Kadou drank, glaring at each of his kahyalar in turn.

"None for you, unfortunately," Madam Hoşkadem said to Eozena, handing around cups of ale to the others. "Not for any hard feelings against what you dragged my only child into," she added primly, and Kadou decided at that moment that he liked her *ferociously*. "It thins the blood, that's all."

"Fair point," Eozena said. "I don't think I'd be in the mood even if I didn't have a hole through my leg."

"Let's not talk about that," Tadek said, a little ashen, and accepted his ale from Durdona with a ghost of his usual smile.

"We're going to talk about what happened, though," Kadou said viciously. "Who wants to start?"

"Well," Tadek began, leisurely sipping his ale as if he weren't the second-most-injured person in the room. "Pinar and Evemer were pulling some stunt on top of a rock so they could look in the windows, and Evemer nearly fell off and broke his neck, and then he *did* fall off, but strategically. Made a hell of a noise, and we got caught. We scampered off into the night, took a couple hits, Evemer saved my life, we all piled into the boat, they shot us a bit more, and there you have it," he finished airily. "Durdona, this ale is very fine, could I have a splash more?"

"Oh," Evemer said, giving Tadek a puzzled look. "I did, didn't I?"

Tadek lifted his refilled cup to him in a little toast and took a huge gulp. "We'll be best friends by the end of the week at this rate."

"Unlikely," Evemer said darkly.

"Wait and see, honeybee," Tadek murmured into his ale. "Now we've been over that, let's talk about the most important question that has ever been asked: Why *do* you call him that, Durdona?"

Durdona seemed only too happy to talk about anything else— she'd grown a little ashen at Tadek's report. "It's because he works so hard," she said, resolutely trying to recover herself. "Even when he was little. Always busy, always flying about looking for important things to do. Too busy even to bring anyone home!" she added, tsking. "In the figurative sense, I mean. Bringing home the sultan and the prince and a pack of kahyalar doesn't count."

"My mother's on me all the time for grandchildren," Pinar said.

"Ah, grandchildren," Durdona sighed. "Never once wished for

a daughter, except for that. But this one's too busy! I've said, *Durdona, let him achieve something for himself, be patient.* And I have been, haven't I?" she said, turning to Evemer.

"Yes, Mama," he said firmly. "Very patient."

"I thought it might get better once he'd gotten that promotion," Durdona added to Eozena. "But it has not."

"Sorry, Mama," Evemer said.

"It's my fault," Kadou said. "I've been giving him too many of those important things to do. I'm afraid he hasn't had a chance to tear himself away."

"Honeybee," she said with dour resignation, as if this were the explanation for everything.

"Wait," Melek said. "Wait. You've never brought someone home to meet your mother?"

"No," Evemer said.

"Never?"

"Not once," Durdona mourned.

"Sorry, Mama," Evemer said, with all evident sincerity.

"Never mind, love. Commander, you're looking tired, can I make you a bed in the workroom?"

"Yes, I think so," Eozena said. She was looking rather frayed around the edges, and it took both Durdona and Pinar to help her up and into the next room.

"Wait, though," Tadek said, squinting at Evemer. "How old are you again?"

"Twenty-seven. Why?"

"And you've *never* brought someone home."

"As I said to Melek."

Tadek exchanged a brief glance with Melek, who shrugged, and turned to peer at Evemer again.

"So it's been more . . . casual friends?" Melek said.

"What do you mean?"

Kadou entertained a brief urgent fantasy of burying his face in his hands. Did Evemer really not know what they were asking?

"Lovers, darling," Tadek said, and Evemer choked a little on his ale. "Except that you're so serious, I can't see you having someone you'd call a lover without introducing them to Durdona immediately, so it must just be . . . casual friends, as Melek puts it."

"Armsman Hasira," Evemer said stiffly. Oh, dear. Kadou was going to have to find some way to change the subject for him.

Before he could think of anything plausible, Tadek said, "Listen. Listen, I've had a glass of ale on an empty stomach and I'm a bit tipsy right now, and we could get you tipsy too if you try harder to catch up, and then we'll have this conversation, and then—like I said! Best friends by the end of the week. What do you say?"

Evemer said, "No."

"Not the sort to kiss and tell?"

"No."

Kadou bit the inside of his cheek. This was going downhill extremely quickly. Was there a way to excuse himself gracefully, at least?

Tadek was looking thoughtful. "You know, I know almost everything about almost everyone, and I don't even know whether you like boys, girls, oryasilar, or none of the above."

"None of your business," Evemer said.

"Come on, this is part of becoming friends," Tadek said brightly. "Here, I'll start: I like everybody. Now Melek."

"None of the above," Melek said gamely.

"Now Evemer."

Evemer glowered. "We're not becoming friends."

"Don't bully him, it's been a long night," Kadou said. "Leave him be."

Melek sat up straight. "Wait, I remember—wasn't there someone when we were cadets?"

"Was there?" Tadek said, surprised. "I don't recall. Honestly, I was busy deflowering everyone who would let me get my hands on them, I wasn't paying much attention to anything else."

Melek scrunched çir nose. "That'd be why I noticed, then, I wasn't preoccupied. But Evemer, wasn't there—Nihani, wasn't it?"

"Nihani Baltakan?" Tadek said. "The one who got an appointment as staff to one of the provincial governors a few years back? Crack shot with a bow and thighs that could crush a melon?"

"That's the one! Weren't you following her around for a bit, Evemer?"

"Everyone was," he mumbled.

"No," Tadek said past rising laughter. "No, honeybee, they weren't. Everyone thought she was *terrifying*."

"Yeah," Melek added. "I think it was just you. Did you like her?"

Evemer took a breath and cast a truly exhausted, beseeching look upward to the gods. "I was sixteen," he said, evidently giving up. "She was sixteen."

"She was angry about everything. All the time. Didn't she throw a chair through a window?"

"Yes."

"So is that it?" Tadek said, amused. "Not boys or girls or oryasilar for you, but angry people who throw chairs through windows and threaten to punch Scholar Arikmas for the appalling crime of daring to teach basic rhetoric?"

"I thought you said you didn't remember," Melek said, wondering.

"My memory's been jogged. Answer the question, Evemer."

"I respected her," Evemer said stiffly. "She was compelling. Powerful."

Tadek snapped his fingers. "There it is. *Power*, he says."

"She *was* terrifying," Melek agreed. "That follows."

"So you and Nihani Baltakan were sixteen together," Tadek said, "and she threw a chair through a window one day and you said, *Now there's a tiger I'd like to offer an opportunity to rip my throat out*?"

"Essentially," Evemer sighed, resigned.

Melek squinted. "Was it you and her that I caught in the broom closet that one time, or someone else?"

"Yes," Evemer said.

"Such unexpected depths!" Tadek said admiringly. "One day he's a walking stone wall, and the next we find out he had sex in a broom closet with Nihani Baltakan of all people."

"I never—" Evemer began, aghast, and snapped his mouth shut with a furious blush.

Tadek and Melek studied him in curious silence. Kadou wondered, again, if this was a good time to leave the room. The conversation kept moving too quickly for him to get traction on it, and he had to fight against his own interest—kahyalar were *awful* gossips. "Never had sex in the broom closet or never had sex with her?" Tadek asked at last, and then turned to Melek. "Should we have made a drinking game out of this?"

"Oh, probably."

"Don't tease him," Kadou said quietly, seizing the first moment he could. "He won't tease you back, so it's not fair."

"You don't have to defend me," Evemer mumbled, but Kadou couldn't have imagined the way Evemer relaxed incrementally and angled himself closer.

"True, he's very capable of defending himself," Tadek said. "He's welcome to retaliate however he likes, and if that means dragging me out into the garden to demand a duel of honor, I'll take those consequences." Tadek refilled his cup one more time. "Now. Evemer, darling, honeybee, new best friend. I want you to look straight into my eyes when I say this next thing. No need to reply, got it? Good. Here we go: You blush like a virgin." Evemer did not reply. He stared stonily into Tadek's face and let himself be scrutinized until Tadek sat back, drank the rest of his ale, and set his cup aside. "Ah, poor pet. That explains why you haven't brought anyone home."

"No, wait, this is great!" Melek said. "Me too! I've never even wanted to! I thought I was the only one, because everybody else seems so obsessed with sex all the time, and I really don't see the appeal—you really haven't?"

"Technically," Evemer growled.

"Technically," Tadek said, suddenly rapt again. "Technically! What does *technically* mean? I mean, I suppose you could say it doesn't count if you're sixteen and shoving your hands down someone's pants in a broom closet."

Evemer muttered something.

"Say again?" Tadek said, leaning forward.

"We didn't get that far," Evemer repeated, crisply.

"You didn't get as far as *handjobs?*"

"I mean, why would you?" Melek murmured sagely. "You don't know where that's been."

Evemer huffed. "I was busy. Classes, training. And . . . people kept walking in on us," he added in a mumble.

"Genuinely shocked that I don't remember this bit," Tadek said, and shook his head. "No matter. Who else?"

"None of your business."

"Fine, fine. But for my own peace of mind—there's been more than just Nihani, hasn't there? Tell me that much at least."

Evemer hesitated.

"Oh, hell," Tadek said. "He has to *think* to remember whether he's kissed anyone else."

"I know I *have,*" Evemer said irritably. "I'm only trying to decide whether the other one counts."

Kadou's heart skipped a beat. That explained why Evemer had been so clumsy about that pretend kiss in the alley—or real kiss. It was a real kiss, wasn't it? They'd gotten the whole lecture from Eozena as if it was. He cleared his throat. "If you have to think about it, it probably counts," he said, and—no, why was he pleased to see Evemer's ears go pink like that? He shoved the thought away and got up. "If we're all done interrogating each other about our personal lives, I'm going to bed."

"Do you require any assistance, my lord?" Evemer asked.

"You know what, I think I do," he said. He'd almost deferred just then, had almost said something like *No, I'm all right* or *Unless you have somewhere else to be.* But Evemer had a look in his eyes like perhaps he did want to be rescued after all, despite earlier claims to the contrary. Kadou wasn't about to leave him here with Tadek in an appalling making-friends mood, asking questions that were outrageous and out of line and—and a whole host of other nascent thoughts that Kadou quashed as soon as he saw the shape of them, before they even fully formed into coherent ideas, let alone rose to the level of verbal arguments.

When they were safe in the upstairs bedroom with the door firmly shut, Kadou whispered, "Sorry."

"What for?" Evemer dropped the blanket from his shoulders, folded it, and got a new underlayer from the wardrobe: loose, pale yellow linen that was somewhat finer than a common artisan's son's would be—the benefits of a weaver mother with commissions from the palace. His bandaged shoulder moved stiffly as he shrugged it on and tied the knots at the waist. Kadou told himself firmly that he was only looking at Evemer's poor bruised back, not stealing glimpses of the way his muscles shifted beneath his skin.

"Sorry that you had to . . . put up with that. The way they talked."

"I don't want to be friends with Tadek," Evemer said grimly.

"Good luck with that, since he's apparently decided he's going to be friends with you regardless of your opinion." Kadou winced. "Sorry for that too."

Evemer grumbled under his breath and fetched another underlayer out of his wardrobe to replace the clothes Kadou had been wearing since the night before. "*You* don't have to apologize for him."

"He's my armsman. His behavior reflects on me."

"For other people, maybe," Evemer muttered, glancing away while Kadou changed out of his clothes. "It's fine. He's said he'll take the consequences. And I didn't . . . mind." He huffed. "I minded, but I didn't mind."

"If you'd minded, you would have . . . ?"

"Smacked him, probably," Evemer said, with a wry quirk of his mouth that had no call to be so terribly distracting. It was just that Kadou hadn't seen him smile much. "He's harmless. He's all mouth. He can say whatever he likes."

Kadou ought to say sorry for the rest—for keeping him too busy to visit his mother or to bring someone home to her, for assuming he wanted to be rescued downstairs and calling him away from an opportunity to have something of a personal life. For being too interested in the conversation to change the subject when he should have, too interested in the idea that Evemer had only kissed two people (and one of them was Kadou, because it counted, it *did*). He couldn't confess any of that, even in the context of apologizing, because then Evemer would know Kadou had opinions about something that was absolutely not Kadou's to have opinions about.

Kadou sat on the edge of the bed and realized that there was another dilemma—Evemer had to sleep, and there wasn't much space in this room, so he would probably leave. *No,* Kadou thought suddenly, fiercely. *No, don't.*

It wasn't strange of him to want his kahya near him after he'd almost been killed, was it? It was merely reciprocal protectiveness. "Where—where are the kahyalar sleeping?"

"Mama made up beds in the basement and the workroom. The day shift is already asleep."

"Sounds . . . crowded."

Evemer shrugged. "No different than the cadet dormitories."

A long silence, while Kadou struggled to find something to say that wouldn't sound whiny or demanding or—or inappropriate. He just wanted Evemer nearby, just within eyesight, that was all. Nothing more than that. "If you like . . . If you don't want to be around the others . . . Up to you, but you're welcome to sleep here if you wanted." He waved vaguely to the corner of the room by the wardrobe. "If you'll be sleeping on floor cushions either way."

"I wouldn't want to impose, my lord." Evemer paused. "Unless Your Highness still feels uncomfortable after last night's events."

Well, that was *part* of it, at least. He didn't feel safe without Evemer next to him, and he wouldn't be able to feel that *Evemer* was safe either, if he went elsewhere. Would it be terrible of him to say just, "Yes, I require you here in case of attack," as if it were that simple?

Kadou, because he was a coward and a fool, shrugged one shoulder as vaguely as he could manage and hoped that Evemer might read whatever he liked out of that.

And he did: He nodded once, left the room, and came back a minute later with a pair of cushions, which he arranged in the corner with the blanket laid over the top. Kadou watched silently, curling up and fussing with his own covers to occupy his hands.

He didn't like Evemer in yellow, he decided. It didn't look right. He'd worn rust-brown to go out on tonight's so-called reconnaissance mission in order to blend in better, and that hadn't looked right either. The blues of the core-guard suited him better. In any other color, he might have been anyone. This was why people gave their kahyalar and armsmen uniforms: so that everyone would know that they belonged somewhere, that there was someone to whom they mattered.

Someone they belonged to, Kadou thought to himself before violently shoving away that thought too. Evemer wasn't his, but he was, but he wasn't, but he *was*.

Coward, Kadou thought to himself. *Pathetic coward. You won't even think it to yourself. You won't even let yourself admit it. Just do it already, get it over with. You're being ridiculous.*

Kadou rolled onto his back, folded his hands on his stomach, stared up at the underside of the roof sloping above his head, and let himself think it.

There was the possibility that he wanted Evemer.

Coward! he screamed at himself. *No possibility about it!* Eozena had stumbled in with an *arrow* through her leg, and still Kadou had been more afraid for Evemer—and yes, admittedly, that was partially because he was unconvinced that *anything* could kill Eozena. He had more iron-bound faith in Eozena's ability to survive an arrow through the leg and a dunking in cold water than he did of anyone else's ability to survive a stubbed toe.

He wanted Evemer. Oh, it must be so painfully obvious to everyone else. Just the way he'd kept touching Evemer—a hand on his arm or his shoulder, sitting near him . . .

He could have continued resisting it consciously, stubbornly holding a dam against putting words to it in the privacy of his mind, but his hands knew. Had known. He wondered when it had started—possibly in the bathhouse, with his hands in Evemer's hair. Possibly in the alley when he'd told Evemer to kiss him (it counted), with his hands on Evemer's back and shoulders. His hands told fewer lies than his mind did.

Evemer was right there, right across the room—less than ten feet away. Kadou was excruciatingly aware of him. A prickling thrill ran up his spine at the thought of . . . of turning over and looking at him. Just *looking*. Letting his eyes linger on those broad shoulders and strong arms and big capable hands, that fine profile, that incongruously plush bottom lip. Those intelligent dark eyes and solemn brow, all those endearingly serious expressions . . .

No possibility about it. He wanted. He'd been wanting.

Tadek would laugh at you so hard if he knew, Kadou thought wretchedly. *He'd say, "I told you so," and crow about it for a week. He'd wiggle his eyebrows at you and make jokes about broom closets and how you should try throwing a chair through a window, and the only way you'd be able to shut him up is to tell him about that kiss, even though it didn't mean anything and he'd only be even more smug that he'd known all along.*

Unless he wasn't smug. Unless he was hurt by it, or felt abandoned. He *had* felt abandoned, before. He'd already thought that Evemer had eclipsed him in Kadou's regard and favor.

Or was that mostly his stupid, treacherous brain coming up with reasons to make himself feel terrible about it so that he could hide from his wanting more easily? Or were both true?

Usmim have mercy on him, was he going to have to talk to Tadek about this? Get into more shouting matches, exchange more hurts? How was he supposed to be friends with his former lover while he was already wanting someone else so soon, and so badly? How could he expect Tadek to be unaffected by that?

"My lord, are you all right?" Evemer asked.

"Fine, why?"

"You keep fidgeting and sighing. Is the bed uncomfortable?"

"No," Kadou said. "I mean, yes, but it's fine. Goodnight."

No more thinking about this. He wanted Evemer, and that was something he'd just have to deal with quietly, secretly, and alone. If he kept it to himself, then that would solve all his problems— Tadek wouldn't be hurt and his friendship would be preserved; Evemer wouldn't be made uncomfortable, and his presence at Kadou's side would be preserved too. That was the crucial point, Kadou decided: Maintaining steady, stable equilibrium. Moving softly through the world and his relationships without capsizing all the boats.

At least this, of all things, was a problem he could touch. He'd wished for one, hadn't he? Usmim, hearing him, had provided. It was a trial, then, a test of Kadou's mettle. That was all. He could solve this, as long as he kept his mouth shut and didn't tell anyone about it.

CHAPTER ELEVEN

❧

The commander was feverish the next morning, and His Highness was in a very strange mood. Understandable, Evemer supposed—he was worried about Eozena. They all were. Melek changed her dressings, smearing the wound liberally with the cleansing poultice the doctor had left and wrapping it again tightly with fresh bandages while Kadou hovered and watched and paced.

Tadek's injured leg was workable, but he was still half hopping through the room when he needed something, and he couldn't sit on the floor or get up from it without a wall to lean on or someone helping him.

"She'll be fine," Kadou said firmly to the room at large, staring at Eozena lying in a sweaty heap by the fire on a cushion of folded blankets.

"Of course she will," Zeliha said, pacing around the room.

"She'll be *fine*," Kadou said again, louder, and Durdona got out some candles from a drawer and a pair of miniature figures of Sannesi and Usmim. She put them on the mantelpiece, and gave the candles to Kadou to light. He stuck them in front of the figures with a few drips of wax, and then sank into several moments of silent prayer. Evemer stood behind him and added his own prayers to Kadou's. "She'll be fine. She will."

He'd said it so many times that it was a prayer in itself by now.

Zeliha paced the length of the room again like a caged tiger with its tail lashing and its teeth bared. "No one is in charge at the palace now," she said. "And some people think that Kadou and I are dead." She turned sharply to Evemer. "Did you get anything useful from that escapade last night? Give me some good news."

"Majesty," he said. "We did get something, but you won't think it good."

"Spit it out." She was splendid in her anger. Her eyes flashed, the rich Mahisti blue-black that was just the same as Kadou's. "I'll take anything at this point."

"Siranos was there," he said simply. "Pinar can confirm it."

Her Majesty went still. "You're sure?" she said quietly.

"As the stars, Majesty."

She turned away, one hand to her forehead. "Fuck."

No one spoke for a long minute, though they all watched Zeliha from the corners of their eyes, waiting for her to react, to show them in which direction *they* should act. She only stood there in the middle of the room, her hand to her face, her shoulders set and her breath steady.

Evemer looked away from her—if this was her moment to be a person rather than a sultan, she was entitled to it, and she deserved whatever grain of privacy he could offer her.

"I'm going back up to the palace," she said, her voice low and calm. "That's the only choice we have."

Kadou looked like he was about to object, but Zeliha only met his eyes, neither of them speaking except, perhaps, for that silent communication that Evemer had heard siblings sometimes had.

Really, what other choice was there? Without Eozena to keep things calm, who else could Zeliha trust to walk into the chaos and bring it to heel?

"Right," Zeliha said. "Right, here's the plan. I go back up to the palace. I make sure that Mahisti stays in power. This is an excellent opportunity for someone to assume the throne is vacant and snatch it for themselves, and I cannot allow that to happen. The first priority is the security of the dynasty and the nation. To that end also, my daughter will stay here, guarded by the current complement of kahyalar and under the care of Madam Hoşkadem. Durdona, I'm sure you can find a wet nurse in the neighborhood? No need to tell her who Eyne is, make something up."

Kadou's face had gone pale. "Zeliha."

"If anything happens to me," Zeliha continued doggedly, "my wishes are that Eyne will be sultan, and that Kadou will rule as her regent until she comes of age. I bind all of you as witnesses. The rest can be found in my will. There are copies with the masters of the Merchant's Guild and Shipbuilder's Guild, and the heads of the ministry of intelligence and the Royal Mint."

"*Zeliha,*" Kadou said desperately.

She spun on her heel to face Kadou at last. "Prince Kadou, I owe you an apology. I should have trusted you. Three times over, I should have trusted you. If there is anything you can do to find and catch Siranos and his sister with only yourself and your three kahyalar—"

"Two kahyalar and an armsman," Tadek muttered from the corner.

"*Three kahyalar,*" Zeliha said firmly, not taking her eyes from Kadou, "then I charge you to do it." She pulled the royal seal on its chain from around her neck and set it on the table in front of him. "Whatever you need to do," she said. "Get him for me, bring him to me."

"He's hired mercenaries, Majesty," Evemer said. "We can't do it with just four."

"You'll have to," she said, and then she turned on him. "And now for you, Evemer Hoşkadem," she said in a dark voice, stalking toward him. She was a handspan shorter than him, just a little taller than Kadou, yet as she came blazing toward him, Evemer felt as small as the footstool in his mother's workshop.

She stopped before him, looking up into his face, her eyes steady on his—not searching. Not at all—firm and sure and *certain.* In ringing tones, she said, "Evemer Hoşkadem, lieutenant of my core-guard, *get on your knees.*"

He fell to the floor before he had told his legs to do anything. "Your Majesty."

She gazed down at him. "You're something special, aren't you?" she said in a soft voice. "Generations upon generations of kahyalar, training and honing their service and teaching it to the next generation, all culminating with you, right here." Her voice was barely above a whisper. He wasn't sure whether anyone else in the room could even hear her. "You've read your *Ten Pillars*, I presume?"

"Yes, Majesty."

She reached out and touched his chin, lifting his face. "Beydamur began your lineage, kahya. Will you serve me as he served his sultan, Asanbughaa?"

"Yes."

"Even unto death?"

"If I'm turned away from Usmim's scales, then I'll serve even beyond that," he said. She was captivating, enrapturing. And yet . . .

There had been a time, Evemer realized, when he wouldn't have been able to look away from her. There had been a time when he would have absolutely tripped over himself for her. She was made of the cold edges of a steel blade and controlled, intense fire. He would have spluttered and blushed and embarrassed himself even worse than he had last night, even worse than he had when he was sixteen and entirely distracted by Cadet Nihani and all her perfect, gorgeous rage.

He would have fumbled, and Zeliha would have looked on impassively and watched him do it. She would have made him earn her approval. She would have commanded him to follow her into battle and carry her banner and her glory. She would have graciously allowed him to die for her, and he would have done so joyfully and felt that his death was not in vain. She would have ruled him by the sheer breadth of her power and fearlessness and by the tight bindings of his oaths, and Evemer would have thought that right and proper. He would have given her everything and never once thought of reciprocity.

Looking at her was like looking into the sun.

But Evemer's north star sat at the kitchen table, the seal in his hands, biting his lip as he watched them. His expression was wary and fearful, and at a single murmured word from him, Evemer would have turned away from Zeliha's blazing fire, would have *crawled*, if he had to, over coals, over broken glass, over mountain ranges and deserts, just to come to Kadou's feet and press his forehead to the backs of Kadou's hands.

Reciprocity was a thing you had to learn. Someone had to tell you, first, that you deserved to be treated well, before you knew it for yourself.

"Lieutenant," Zeliha said, and his attention snapped back to her.

"Your Majesty."

"Besides my daughter, I consider my brother the most precious thing in the world. I've given him a difficult and dangerous task, and now I have one for you." Her voice was very soft now, not even a whisper. "You're going to follow him into whatever trouble he finds, and you're going to do whatever it takes—*whatever* it takes—to make sure he comes back to me."

"Yes," he said.

She leaned down a little and offered him her hand. "Will you swear it, kahya?"

Evemer took her hand and pressed his forehead to her rings.

There was a shriek of wood—Kadou had pushed his chair back from the table. He strode across the room and grabbed Zeliha by the elbow. "What are you doing? You can't," he said. "You can't have him. No." She shook him off. He grabbed her again. "Sister," he said, an edge of desperation coming into his voice before it dropped to a whisper, "This one's *mine*."

"I'm not taking him from you," she replied, shaking him off once more. "He's just making me a promise on his life."

Kadou looked between them, his face all knotted up, and Evemer wanted nothing more than to reach for him. He yearned for it, ached for it.

He took Zeliha's hand again, pressed it again to his forehead. "On my life," he said. "And whatever is left of me beyond that."

"Good." She leaned down close to his ear and murmured one more thing, one single thing that hit him like a physical blow: "I grant you the privilege of disobedience. Use it wisely." She stood straight. "Now get up." Evemer rose, feeling rather wobbly in the knees and hollowed-out with shock. Zeliha put her hands on her hips and looked around. "Logistics next," she said, and went to the table, ordering Melek to bring her paper and ink. Kadou, with another uncertain glance over his shoulder at Evemer, followed her.

Evemer took the opportunity to vanish into the workroom, and indulged in a moment of weakness: He leaned against the wall with one hand, put his other hand to his heart, tried to catch his breath in a room that suddenly seemed to have both too much and not enough air in it.

He nearly jumped out of his skin when, just behind him, Tadek said, "So can I get you a strong drink or a bucket of ice water?"

"Are you part *cat*?" Evemer snapped.

"I got training for the ministry of intelligence, so . . . Yes, nearly. Never mind me, what was *that* about?"

"Nothing. Orders. Oaths."

"Hmm." Tadek put the back of his hand to Evemer's forehead. Evemer batted him away. "I think you're very sick," he said solemnly, "with an illness called 'a Mahisti looked at me,' and as this is sometimes fatal—"

"We're not friends, Tadek."

"Yes, yes," he said patiently, "I know, we're working on it. Anyway, are you dying? You looked like you might have been dying in there."

"I'm not dying."

Tadek waggled an eyebrow at him. "As good as crushing a melon with her thighs? As good as a chair through a window?"

Evemer was heartbeats away from dragging Tadek by his hair out the front door and kicking his ass down the street and halfway across the city to the harbor, where he would dump Tadek bodily into the water if there was anything left of him. The only thing that stopped him was an idea that Kadou wouldn't like it and Eozena's dire warnings from the night before that if Kadou cried it would be their fault. Evemer gathered his patience up in both hands. "I'm not sixteen anymore."

"Well, no, but . . . I mean, come on. Even I felt a bit warm under the collar, and that's not my sort of thing at all. What did she say to you when she leaned down?"

Evemer could have told him it was none of his business, that it would never be his business. He shuffled across the room and sat heavily on the bench in front of his mother's loom and looked down at his hands in his lap.

With half a sentence, she'd made Tadek a kahya again—if he'd understood it right. With another, she'd given Evemer the greatest treasure—and the most serious.

"She gave me a gift," he said quietly.

"What gift?"

"It's none—"

"None of my business, yes, got it."

The door opened again and Kadou looked in, immediately going tense and wary when he saw them. "Tadek. I didn't know you were in here. What are you two talking about?"

"Oh, this and that," Tadek said airily. "Nothing of any great importance, you know me. What can I do for you, Highness?"

"I need to talk to Evemer."

"Certainly. Privately, I expect?"

"It'll just take a moment," Kadou said quickly. "It's nothing of—of any importance, as you said. And then we'll—all four of us, I think—plan something."

Tadek nodded and, favoring his injured leg, half limped and half hopped back through the door. Kadou shut it behind him and leaned on it with his hands behind his back, looking at Evemer. "She's not taking you from me, is she?"

"No, my lord."

Kadou nodded vaguely. "All right. All right."

Evemer drew himself up and spoke before he could stop himself. "My lord, I'd like to request a clarification of my orders."

Last week, Kadou might have flinched. Now . . .

It was like the way Evemer could fight in the dark with Eozena at his back, simply by knowing precisely where she'd be. It must have been a little bit the same for Kadou, because his only reaction was the briefest flicker of his eyes before he said, "Of course, Lieutenant. Please speak freely."

Evemer got off the loom bench and gestured to it. Kadou sat, folding his hands in his lap, and Evemer settled himself cross-legged on the floor in front of him. "Her Majesty granted me something just now. You should know about it before it becomes an issue in an urgent moment."

"Go on."

"The privilege of disobedience, my lord."

Kadou was quiet. "Oh," he said at last. "Oh. Congratulations, that's . . ."

Evemer looked straight in his eyes, beautiful and dark and surprised. "I don't like it."

Kadou blinked. "Oh?"

"I don't want it." He hesitated, coaxing his uncooperative tongue to move. "But I know I need to have it."

"What was the primary objective she gave you?" Kadou was looking at him very strangely.

"To keep you safe at all costs," Evemer said. He thought that should have been obvious.

"Then I suppose you do need it." The privilege of disobedience was an honor reserved for people like Eozena, who held her position precisely *because* her judgment was trusted implicitly. It was given with the mutual understanding that it would never be used except in cases of dire peril. Kadou swallowed. "What—what would you do? If I gave you an order that you had to disobey in order to keep me safe?"

"I don't know. It would depend on the circumstances."

"Give me one example."

Evemer shrugged. "I might tie you to one of the kitchen chairs, put you in the cellar, and sit on top of the trapdoor. I will not allow you to put yourself in unnecessary danger."

"You might have to," Kadou said.

"I have orders."

"So do I. She told me to find Siranos. That will take some risk."

It was good to start negotiations from a place of aspiration, even if you knew you'd be haggled down, so Evemer said, "You don't have to leave this house."

"Yes," Kadou said in steely tones that sent lightning crackling through Evemer's veins, "I do." He sounded a little like Zeliha when he spoke like that, like he could bend Evemer to his will like a bar of iron on an anvil.

"No, my lord," Evemer replied. "You don't."

"We have a duty."

"I agree. My duty is to keep you alive."

Kadou put his elbows on his knees and rubbed his hands over his face. "And if I ordered you to stay here?"

"I will disobey."

"And if I dismissed you from service?" This was Kadou negotiating too, feeling around in the darkness to find out where the walls had been moved to, now that they lived in this new strange world where Evemer had this inexplicable, wondrous new gift. Kadou didn't know what the hell this meant any more than Evemer did.

So he said: "Frankly, my lord, I'd like to see you try."

At these words, Kadou released a slow breath and a great deal of tension.

Kadou snorted, hands still pressed to his face. After a long moment, he said quietly, "I really didn't need to apologize so much for kissing you in the alley, did I."

Another prickle of lightning tingled through him. "I didn't need disobedience then. You've never been able to make me do anything I didn't want to do," Evemer said.

"You have to let me leave the house."

"No, I don't."

"Is that the extent of your argument? Simply digging in your heels and being an immovable object?"

"That's all I need to do. Stay here, where it's safe. Let me and the others be your hands and eyes."

Kadou sat up, and Evemer saw the same expression on Kadou's face that he wore when they were playing chess, right before he started enacting a deliberate strategy. He was going to try to talk

Evemer into it, persuade him with perfect fantasies of honor and heroism and fealty. It was the only thing that would have had a chance of working—Evemer saw Kadou's next four moves as clearly as if the game had been laid out on a chessboard.

Evemer mentally brushed the dust off his hands and moved his general.

Before Kadou could speak, Evemer shifted from sitting before him to kneeling. He took Kadou's hands, pressing his forehead to the backs of them as he had been aching to do. It filled his heart with light to be allowed even just this.

"Şehzade Sultan Kadou Mahisti Hazretleri Effendi, Prince of Araşt, Duke of Harbors and Altınbaşı-ili, Lord of Şirya and Nadırıntepe, and Warden of the Northern Marches, here do I swear myself to service as your kahya. I offer the strength of my arm, the work of my hands, the breadth of my knowledge, the wisdom of my counsel, and above all, the loyalty of my heart. I place my trust in you," he said pointedly, "that you will in return provide me with all that I require for my hands and arms to execute my duties; *that my knowledge and counsel when offered will be heard*; that you will not misuse me for ill purpose which would be a betrayal of my loyalty; and that for as long as I am in service, I will have a place in your home and a place at your hearth." Kadou's hands had clutched his. "Thus swear I, Evemer Hoşkadem, as a kahya of House Mahisti."

He raised his head but did not release Kadou's hands. Kadou looked down at him, stunned.

But he wasn't finished. "Kadou Mahisti," he began anew. This wasn't ritual. "These too, I swear: That I shall not allow harm to come to you, even by your own actions or by your own will, nor shall I allow you to make foolish, ill-advised, or irresponsible decisions. You have a great well of power to draw upon should you wish it, but I have strength enough to match you. Use as much of your power as you like—*you will not move me from your side*."

Kadou didn't look away from him. His eyes were bright, his expression conflicted, but he pulled one hand free and touched Evemer's cheek. "And for that, what do you swear as?"

"Thus swear I, Evemer Hoşkadem," he answered. His cheek tingled. He wanted to turn his face into the warm cradle of Kadou's palm. "As a person who holds your life above all others. As one who cares for you and loves you." And here was the part that felt most presumptive: "As your friend."

Kadou nearly spoke, sighed. "Evemer, I—"

"Would you reject my oaths, my lord?"

A flash of a smile quirked the corner of Kadou's mouth. "You're cheating."

A huffing breath of laughter escaped Evemer, startling both of them. Kadou looked down at him with something like wonder. "I'm not cheating," Evemer said, allowing himself to smile—he so rarely smiled, but it made the wondering look on Kadou's face sharpen, made his eyes widen. "I'm only playing dirty."

Kadou's fingers were still brushing his cheek. "I accept your oaths," he said at last. "As my kahya and as my friend." There should have been more. There should have been a recitation of oaths and acknowledgment of the obligations Evemer had already laid out. Part of him felt it was miserly of Kadou, but . . . It was enough. There were two operative, essential words that Kadou had said: *accept*; *my*.

In other words: *Yes, you're mine.*

Kadou had already said as much to Zeliha—Evemer could have been content with only that, if he'd had to. He could have held those words in his heart like a talisman against despair. What else needed to be said? Wanting to hear anything more was only vanity, wasn't it?

Kadou spoke again: "But you need to listen to me—I can't stay here and wait."

Damn it all, where was Kadou's so-called cowardice when it would have been convenient? "I'll go get the chair. Do you prefer to be tied with ropes, belts, or sashes?"

"Evemer."

"You have duties to me as well," he said. "To Melek and Tadek and Eozena. To Her Majesty."

Kadou's hand left his cheek and gripped him by the chin,

just as Zeliha had. This time, it made his skin prickle. "Lieutenant Hoşkadem, you have given me your counsel and I have listened. Will you do me the same courtesy?" Without waiting for a response—and Evemer could not have moved anyway, would not have moved away from Kadou's grip for all the counterfeit gold in Araşt safely confiscated and minted new and pure again—Kadou continued: "I would have you at my side. I would try to make this as risk-conservative as possible. I can't convince you it will be safe, because it won't be. But there are things that matter more than safety. I've been given a job to do."

This was exactly the gambit that Evemer had tried to head off at the pass. He would have looked away from Kadou's dark, arresting gaze if he'd been able to. Perhaps it would have helped. Perhaps it would keep him from being mesmerized into budging an inch—because Kadou only needed an inch, and then he'd flow around Evemer like water around a stone in the path. But that was haggling for you. He'd known that he wasn't going to win with his first offer. He'd budge. He'd have to, Her Majesty *had* issued an order he did not wish to disobey outright—but perhaps he could manage only half an inch, and direct Kadou on a better course.

Kadou's grip tightened on him.

Evemer wrapped one hand around his wrist, feeling easily the fine slender bones beneath the skin. "If we foresee a physical altercation, either you stay out of it or we all retreat and come at it from a better angle," Evemer said. "If I tell you to run, you run. No heroics. No stopping to save our lives."

"I won't agree to leave you behind."

"You will agree that out of all of us, your life matters most."

Kadou's hand loosened and fell away from his chin. Evemer tried not to be disappointed. "That's an ugly way of looking at it."

"It is necessary." At Kadou's thunderous, frustrated expression, he couldn't help but ask, "Are you angry with me?"

Kadou took his other hand from Evemer's and folded them on his lap. "Do you ever have a moment where you're feeling seven things at once and you can't decide which of them is most important?"

Evemer sat back on his heels and gave this a moment of consideration. "Perhaps two or three at once. I don't think I've made it up to seven."

"I'm angry at the idea that we are sitting here ranking lives in order of importance. I'm angry that we have to play along with pretending that's a real thing—other than Zeliha's and Eyne's." Nice bit of hypocrisy there, but Evemer wasn't going to call him on it. "I'm irritated with Zeliha for giving you the tools to hold me back. I'm scared that we'll be unable to act quickly enough to avert disaster. I'm . . . impressed with you for standing your ground." He lowered his eyes and smiled faintly. "I haven't had many people say no to me before."

"I imagine it's frustrating now."

"Frustrating and . . . comforting." Kadou's voice dropped even lower, so he was barely breathing the words. "I like knowing that you'll be able to stop me when it really matters. It's . . . something of a relief to find that there are limits that you won't let me cross." Kadou tapped his fingers on his knees. "The presence of a stone wall makes the open parts of the field that it surrounds more meaningful."

"My lord," he said, for lack of anything else to say.

Kadou shook his head. "Never mind. Anything else you wanted me to clarify?"

"No. I am at your service."

Before Zeliha left, she kissed Eyne and hugged Kadou and bid him be so, so careful. She shot Evemer a warning look as he helped her mount up on the horse that she'd hired from the best stable in the city, and she rode off with a tiny squad of kahyalar, just enough to get her to the gates. The kahyalar on watch there would announce her, and then it was up to the gods and to fate to determine whether those passionately loyal kahyalar that Eozena had found would flock to her side, and how many, and whether it would be enough, and how many of the others were . . . corrupt.

There had been no news from the palace, and no rumors in

the city. The kahyalar had, to their credit, managed to keep from gossiping for once in their lives.

Kadou spent the afternoon outlining the plan with his own kahyalar at Madam Hoşkadem's kitchen table. They had to assume that the warehouse on the island would be abandoned by now, Siranos having fled somewhere else to regroup, if he hadn't already fled the city.

They only had one lead left, so they went back to the Jasmine Tree.

They came up to the back door of the incense lounge an hour or two after sundown. Kadou and Evemer had lengths of linen fabric like scarves wrapped around their heads and faces—the night was not near chilly enough to really warrant bundling up like that, but with any luck they'd be mistaken for a pair of Tashazi, as long as no one looked closely enough to notice that their hems and scarves lacked the distinctive identifying embroidery that any real Tashazi would have displayed.

But the primary effect of the scarves was that it made it very distracting for Kadou to look at Evemer—it focused all the attention on his eyes. Kadou couldn't afford to be thinking about them now. There was a job to do, a crisis to focus on. No time to get distracted by the memory of Evemer at his feet, the rough stubble-scratch of Evemer's cheek under his palm.

There in the dark, they knocked on the door and waited.

It was opened a few moments later by a tired-looking girl of perhaps sixteen years old, mostly backlit by the rosy light of the incense lounge. "How many more times do I have to tell you people?" she snapped. "You go to the front now."

"We're here to make an exchange," Evemer said.

"Yes," she said. "At the *front*, like I said, stupid."

"The . . . front?" Kadou said.

She rolled her eyes massively. "The front of the *shop*," she said, loud and slow, and slammed the door in their faces.

"I think we're supposed to go to the front," Kadou whispered wryly.

"I don't like it. This isn't the plan."

Evemer had had opinions about the plan—he was the one who had driven most of the discussion, plotting out a dozen different possible gambits, all of which consisted of practical variations on the core mission: *Go to the Jasmine Tree. Get information from the people at the back. Test whether they are still exchanging coins for counterfeits. Retreat and regroup. More tomorrow.*

Clean. Careful. Conservative.

And none of them had involved going to the front. In fact, they had involved the precise opposite of that: *Stay out of sight. Go quietly and sneakily. Shadows, alleys, disguises.*

The disguises wouldn't hold up in the light, other than to make them stick out instead of blending in. No one would identify them as Tashazi in the light, so they would just be two people with their faces suspiciously covered.

They could just ditch the plan. They could wing it. They'd talked enough about strategy, and Kadou had played enough games of chess with Evemer, that he felt like they had a fairly good grasp of each other's instincts and movements.

But Evemer wasn't the sort to improvise anything, and it was foolish and reckless to press onward. Evemer was a better strategist than he was, so Evemer's judgment was the weightier one. "You'll be dragging me back home now, I suppose."

"Would you go quietly if I did?"

"I would go, but not quietly. I wouldn't like it. It'd feel like giving up, and that's even worse than not trying at all. But . . . this wasn't the plan," he said, defeated. He'd exhausted all his rhetorical arguments already—Evemer would insist on taking no unnecessary risks whatsoever.

Evemer said nothing for nearly a full minute, but Kadou could practically hear the whirling calculations. "A wise tactician holds no sentimental attachment to their plans," Evemer said slowly. He was quoting Beydamur, the ancient military strategist who, a thousand years before, had been general to Asanbughaa, the legendary founder of Araşt and the first monarch of the Misba dynasty.

"Bullshit," Kadou said. "Bullshit. You're not about to say you've changed your mind."

"Aren't I," Evemer said.

"Are you? What are you *doing*?"

"Trying to meet you in the middle, sir," Evemer said woodenly. He sighed and rubbed his hand over his eyes. "Let's not get killed. That's my only request."

What a terrifying declaration to make, and what a wonderful one. Kadou pushed away his nerves and the voice in his head that said he was about to make a horrible mistake. They regrouped briefly with Melek, who was watching from a distance in case Evemer was caught in a fight and Kadou needed to flee. Tadek, not in any shape to run or fight with his injured leg, had been left at Durdona's house.

Then, shoving aside his nerves *again*, Kadou led Evemer to the front of the incense lounge.

It was not a very busy night. They hung back, across the street from the entrance. "I don't see anyone standing around out front," Kadou whispered. "She meant we had to go inside, didn't she?"

"Yes," said Evemer. "This is a terrible idea. I'm not changing my mind again," he added quickly. "But it is a terrible idea."

"Yes, I know. Someone should say it." Kadou took a breath, released it slowly. "We'll go in, we'll make the exchange, ask a few questions, and we'll leave."

Evemer seemed to relax slightly. "Be quick."

They went inside, Kadou leading and Evemer close at his heels, and went straight to the counter at the back of the large front room. "We were told at the back that we should come to the front now," he said quietly to the woman there. "We were wondering if a friend from the palace had left any messages here."

She looked at them slowly, calculating. "Go sit down. I'll send someone out."

They sat at the same table that they'd been at before, the first time, in the darkest and most shadowed corner. An attendant came to their table after a few minutes with a burner of keresa and cedar incense—"On the house," she murmured—and repeated the note that someone would be along presently to speak to them.

"Are we taking down our scarves?" Kadou whispered when

she'd left. "It's going to look strange—in this light, they can see we're not Tashazi."

They muttered back and forth between themselves and eventually decided, warily, to unwind the scarves. It was dreadfully warm, the air stagnant and thick with smoke, and they were already sweltering. Evemer grumbled imprecations all the while—Kadou's hair was too obvious a marker of wealth and status, but the scarves weren't long enough to fashion into a turban, so there was nothing to be done about it except to twist it into a loose rope, half tuck it into the back of Kadou's collar, and hope that no one looked too close.

Long minutes passed. Another attendant came with a pot of tea and apologized for the wait.

"Actually, before you go, could we ask you—"

"It will only take a moment, so please relax," she said, and left before Kadou could say anything more.

"Sit closer," Evemer muttered, as soon as she had turned away.

"What?" Kadou said, distracted from his annoyance with the attendant.

"It worked before. And there's someone across the room looking at us."

Kadou shifted closer against Evemer's side, their arms bumping awkwardly. "Put your arm around my shoulders," Kadou said, and Evemer obeyed. He was tense, nervous. Kadou could feel it. "It's all right," Kadou said. He rested his chin in his hand so that his fingers covered at least the bottom of his face and glanced around the room. His heart thudded when he spotted the person Evemer had noticed, and he forced his eyes away. "Do you recognize them? Is it someone from the island?"

"I don't know. I only saw Siranos then."

Kadou leaned forward and blew out the candle that the attendant had used to light the incense. The ribbon of smoke from the wick added an acrid note to the mellow, woodsy smoke from the burner. "There. They don't need any more light. Keep an eye on them."

An age passed without the attendant returning again, and Kadou grew restless and nervous. Evemer's arm tightened around his shoulders, which made him restless and nervous in an entirely different way.

He was torn in two—he kept thinking that maybe they should give up, run back to Durdona's house, and forget trying to get information out of any of the employees here. They could go back to the warehouse and look for clues there. Kadou could order the harbor closed, and as soon as Zeliha had sorted out whatever was happening at the palace, there would be increased security at the city gates to keep Siranos from leaving there either.

He tried to calm himself. They had already waited so long, what was the harm in waiting just a few more minutes? It wouldn't make any sense to run away when they were so close to their goal.

And the other half of him, which apparently had *nothing better to do*, maintained a keen awareness of Evemer next to him, of the warmth of his body and how it was a different quality to that of the room, of the weight of his arm around Kadou's shoulders. Why had his brain caught up to his hands *now*? Why couldn't he have gone on in avoidance for another month?

He despaired of himself. And he despaired of Evemer—it hadn't been fair of him to get on his knees like that and swear his fealty, looking into Kadou's eyes like he was pressing gifts into Kadou's hands. Kadou's hands had entirely betrayed him, clinging to Evemer's, touching his face. And Evemer hadn't jerked away. He'd looked like he wanted Kadou to keep touching him.

And now . . .

Now he had a moment of stillness and the awkward silence between the two of them while they waited for the attendant to return, and all he could think of was the hours and hours they'd spent at Madam Hoşkadem's table, watching Evemer argue with Melek, with Tadek, with *him*. Evemer could have been a brilliant military strategist if he'd set his mind to it—he'd clearly studied enough, and he was methodical and breathtakingly thorough.

He was incandescent when he stopped holding himself back.

Kadou wanted to get right up against him, breathe him in—he smelled still like sea salt and the medicinal poultice, but underneath that was warmth and something unidentifiable and *good*.

He wanted to pull away. He wanted to lean in closer. He wanted to never look at Evemer again, and he wanted to drag him out into the back alley and let his hands tell the truth since he couldn't trust his tongue—his palms starved for Evemer's skin again. He wanted to kiss him senseless and watch him run Beydamur's sword progression without having to look away. He wanted to know what Evemer meant when he said *my lord* in that particular way.

There wasn't anything else to occupy his attention—where *was* that attendant? Was he being paranoid to wonder what was taking them so long?—so he allowed himself to think of what he'd been avoiding all day: *He's only kissed two people and one of them is you.*

He felt Evemer tense against him. "Shit." He pulled Kadou's head around, against his shoulder. "Stay still," he hissed into Kadou's ear. A long, tense moment passed, and Evemer relaxed. "They've left. The person who was watching us. Walked out the front door."

Kadou could have moved away. And on the other hand, Evemer could have let him go.

How pathetic was he? He needed to have his wits together, and yet all Kadou could think about was how close Evemer was, how much of him there was, how solid and warm, and how he wanted to lick Evemer's neck up to his ear, and bite the lobe, and hear that—that *sound*, gods, he'd almost managed to get that sound out of his head. He breathed in deep, and felt Evemer's breath in reply.

There was a plan. They'd wait and watch, two more anonymous faces in the dim gloom of the incense lounge, and as soon as that damn attendant came back . . . It was such a little thing! They only needed her for a minute, less than a minute—just enough time to ask a few questions, find out whether Siranos or Sylvia had been in communication with them.

He drew away slowly, his mouth gone very dry, and poured himself tea from the pot. It was a snowmelt blend, intended to be served cool, but in the oppressive warmth of the room, it had gone lukewarm and the flavor had dulled.

One of the attendants passing by the table glanced over, then looked back, eyes wide with shock. Kadou turned his face away sharply and looked at Evemer—he was on edge, tense all over, his eyes fixed hard on that attendant.

"She recognized you," Evemer said. "Your hair. Too distinctive."

"Even tied back?"

"Sir," Evemer said. "Don't face the room."

Kadou sighed, gulped the rest of the lukewarm tea, and angled himself back toward Evemer, away from the room. He leaned an arm on the back of the divan and propped his cheek on his hand. From a distance, it might look like—well, like a man leaning close to speak to his lover. Kadou's face went hot to think of it.

The minutes dragged past.

"What's taking so long?" Kadou said, trying not to fidget. "Are you watching the room?"

"Yes."

"Hard for me to see anything like this."

Evemer thought for a moment. "Sir," he said. "If you—" He tugged Kadou closer, got his arm around him. A bit of arranging and muttering, and he had his face mostly hidden in Evemer's collar, his hair partially hiding his face—from here he could just watch the room from the corner of his eye.

"Better," he whispered. Evemer shivered, his arm tightening around Kadou's waist and ribs. Kadou wasn't sure what that was about until he realized with a delicious jolt—his eyelashes, it must have been, tickling against Evemer's neck. Just the brush of his eyelashes, and Evemer shuddered for him. Gods.

"No one's watching us now." His voice was so low it rumbled in his chest, vibrating into Kadou's very nerves.

"No one that we can see," he whispered. He tried to tip his mind toward unfettered paranoia and away from distracted lust. The warmth and the sweet smoke in the air were doing their job, relaxing him even though he had not inhaled directly of the incense. That much was probably fine, but he didn't want to blunt the jagged edges of his vigilance further. Such anxiety did have a *function*, after all, at least in some circumstances—it kept him taut, tense, ready. The slight calm from the effects of the ambient smoke in the air was just enough to feel as though the ground under his feet were solid, not enough to keep him off his toes or slow his reaction speed. Frankly, the effect of Evemer's arms around him was a much more intense one than the smoke, but that canceled itself out by both winding up Kadou's tension *and* steadying the ground. "That attendant—do you think she knows? Maybe she was warned. Maybe she was expecting to see us."

"It's possible."

Kadou rested in the curve of Evemer's neck and shoulder. It was only natural, then, for his hand to creep up, laying flat on Evemer's chest, and then slowly moving up over his other shoulder and the back of his neck.

Damn hands. Damn them. Kadou's whole body was committing treason against him now.

Kadou heard the attendant come back and pulled away. "Thank you," he said, but her hands were empty.

She smiled. "Sorry, gentlemen, the person with the message stepped out on an errand for another patron just before you came and she's a little late coming back. It should just be another few minutes. We'd like to offer you another pot of tea for the inconvenience."

Kadou cleared his throat and tried to shake off the haze of incense smoke and warmth and insistent longing. "We never had to wait before," he said. "Is this new? Something wrong?"

"Not at all," she said smoothly. "Merely a busy night. We're short-staffed."

"Is it common for there to be—" But she had already whisked away again.

Evemer tweaked his sleeve and Kadou leaned back into him again, mulishly. "She was probably an expert in getting out of irritating conversations within the first week she started working here," Evemer rumbled—Kadou felt it against his cheek, and through his chest pressed to Evemer's, all the way down to his bones. And then, an instant later, "*Don't move.*" Evemer went very, very still.

"Who is it?" Kadou whispered. He was facing the front wall of the incense lounge here, and most of what he could see was Evemer's neck and a corner of the table.

"*Siranos.*"

Kadou's nerves jangled, and he longed to turn his head enough to peek from under Evemer's chin and see for himself, but he stayed quiet. "What is he doing?"

"He came in. He sat across the room, near the counter."

"Is he looking this way?"

"Not right now. The parlor mistress just came out—she's speaking to him."

"Hide. Hide your face. He knows you too."

Evemer buried his face in Kadou's hair, as if he were kissing Kadou's ear, probably the best he could do in the circumstances without scrambling to throw his scarves around his face again. "We shouldn't have come."

"Be still," Kadou whispered back. "Stay calm. We can get out of this."

"I shouldn't have listened to you. I should have invoked disobedience the minute you wanted to change the plan. I should have hauled you back to my mother's house and barred the door and nailed it shut."

"Yes," Kadou said. "Probably. And tied me to the kitchen chair and put me in the cellar and rolled Eozena on top of the trapdoor to hold it shut. But here we are, so calm *down*."

"There are a few people blocking the door. Talking, getting in the way. We'd have to elbow our way through them if we ran. There's the back door. No windows. An upper floor—the stairs must be in the back."

"Be. Still," Kadou said, and at last, Evemer obediently froze. "You're right. We leave, but slow and steady, like we haven't noticed anything. This is not a moment to panic."

"It is when someone could put your sultan in checkmate in one move."

"I'm not your sultan and you don't have to move me. Your sultan is up at the palace, surrounded by hundreds of kahyalar who I *know* are loyal to her, and you know it too. She will be fine. *We're* not in check. *We* are lesser pieces." It wasn't that he was unafraid—he was terrified—but he had an intimate and daily experience of fear that surely beat out anything Evemer had endured. In this moment, like the night of the attack, he found himself in control of his terror simply by dint of his familiarity with it. "Has he noticed us yet? Has he even glanced over?"

"No."

"Just keep watching him for a moment. The people at the door?"

"Still there. *Fuck*," Evemer said, and Kadou almost twitched in surprise. He'd never heard Evemer curse before. "Siranos looked over. I don't know if he recognized me."

Damn it all. "I will preface this by saying I'm very sorry." A lie, a lie. Not a whole lie, but no better than a half truth. "Be still, please, and—I'm going to kiss your neck. It looks strange for us to just sit here—and if he's watching—"

"Yes," Evemer said without hesitation.

Kadou snarled at himself, at his fear-creature, at his recalcitrant mind, at his traitorous hands to behave themselves, to not give anything away. He would not permit himself to be untoward or ungentlemanly about this situation.

He brushed his mouth against the corner of Evemer's jaw.

Evemer went tense all over—more tense.

Under his palm, he felt the pulse in Evemer's neck stutter and quicken. Evemer let out his breath, slow and controlled, gusting into Kadou's hair and warming his ear and neck. Kadou's own heartbeat leapt in response.

Keep control, Kadou thought to himself. *Think of Siranos looking over and wondering about you.* He should see two people who were paying attention to nothing in the world but each other. He shouldn't have even a moment of opportunity to wonder whether Evemer looked familiar.

But tightening his grip on the back of Evemer's neck was not control; opening his mouth against Evemer's neck was not control. He kept control. He did not do those things. With deliberate intent, he very, very carefully did not do either of those things.

But he couldn't help the way he turned a little more toward Evemer, and his control had nothing at all to do with the way

Evemer's hand on the back of his waist tightened, gripping the fabric of his kaftan and sash.

Control, here in the private space between them. Control, here behind the fall of Kadou's hair, with the humid heat of his breath and Evemer's skin warming his face. To the rest of the room, it had to look like—well, *something*. It had to look like something while *being* nothing.

Kadou brushed his lips, dry and closed, just under Evemer's ear. Another, a little down his neck. Another, nosing just past his collar. It was the worst kind of torment, to be so close, to have his mouth just barely touching Evemer's *skin*, and to have to stay mindful when all he wanted was to taste—just one little taste. Evemer's hand flexed at his waist. His throat bobbed as he swallowed. "Any change? Did he look away?" Kadou whispered.

"Yes," Evemer breathed. "But he's turned toward us. Speaking to the parlor mistress. He'll look up if we leave." His pulse was still racing under Kadou's hand.

"Like an animal that sees movement," Kadou muttered. He felt Evemer shift as slowly as the turning tide, lifting his free arm, laying his hand on Kadou's shoulder blade as if he wanted to hold Kadou close and safe. "We're fine so far. We're not in check." Kadou laid another flat, chaste kiss to his skin, let it have a hint of real pressure rather than the previous, ghost-light imitations.

A very tiny thread of Evemer's control snapped: he tipped his head a mere hairsbreadth away, the slightest baring of his neck.

Kadou couldn't even tell himself that it was unconscious or unintentional. This was *Evemer*. If he didn't mean to move, then he didn't move.

He closed his eyes. Another soft kiss, and Evemer's chest swelled against him with a breath. His hand brushed up, his fingers sliding into Kadou's hair at the back of his head, and Kadou felt his own breath leave him, slow and *controlled*.

He was letting things get out of hand. His heart was pounding, he could feel how high his color was, and a sharp hunger was running through him, overwhelming the terror and paranoia, crashing into all his ideas of propriety and comportment and gentlemanliness—a hunger to see the rest of Evemer's famous discipline fray away to nothing, to find more of the person who lived underneath all those iron bands and stone walls of restraint, to *hear* him again like that night in the alley when Kadou had had only to command him with a word to have Evemer's mouth against his.

No—no, too much. Too much, even for the sake of pretense. Kadou tried to draw away, to turn his head. "Don't," Evemer breathed.

Kadou's heart stuttered. "He's looking?"

"No."

"Don't what, then?"

Evemer said nothing. Did nothing. Except—except the faintest pressure on the back of Kadou's neck. Except another tiny tilt of Evemer's head, which Kadou wouldn't have ever noticed without being pressed up so close to him.

Kadou realized with a jolt—Evemer was *asking*. He was pulling Kadou in, even if it was so light and tentative, and baring his neck like that. His heart thundering in his chest, Kadou set his lips against him again, his mouth softening and falling open just enough to taste the salt of his skin.

Evemer's breath caught, and he made that sound.

Kadou's borrowed control failed him, cracking like a ship in a tempest. He shoved himself closer, pulling Evemer's head aside by his hair and scraping his teeth up the tendons of his neck. Evemer's breath caught silently and he jerked in Kadou's arms, and Kadou's blood was singing, throbbing through him, and he could feel every burning nerve in his body—

Evemer turned sharply, pulling him up, pulling his face up, and Kadou met him in the middle, crashing into him like his mouth was the rocks that Kadou's ship finally wrecked itself upon. He kissed him wildly, ardently, desperately. He clutched at Evemer's coat, at his hair, pushing him back against the seat and licking into his mouth, sinking his teeth into Evemer's impossibly soft lower lip. Evemer made that sound again—not quite a moan, and not quite a whimper, just a soft vocalization of undeniable want in his throat, and Kadou wanted to *drink* it, flood his veins with it, drown himself in it. He wanted to tear Evemer's clothes open and set his palms on Evemer's bare skin and make him make that noise until it was carved as deeply into his memory as the touch-taste of gold was on his fingertips.

But—fuck, one of them should be watching the room, one of them should—

He tried to turn away, and Evemer caught his face in his hands and brought him back, kissed him again, whispering into his mouth, "Wait. He's—he's paying her. He's standing."

Kadou let his breath out slowly. "Leaving?"

"I think. Yes, but—wait—" He pulled Kadou back in, kissing him once more—he wasn't even very good at it, but gods *damn* him, it wasn't making Kadou any less frantic. Evemer kissed like he wasn't used to it (*only two people and one of them is you*, whispered Kadou's brain helpfully), like he'd had better things to do with his life than learn the more elegant points and the artistry of it. And, frankly, like he was distracted—Kadou opened his eyes and saw that Evemer's already were. He was still peering through the curtain of Kadou's hair as someone walked past, coming far too close to their table for comfort.

Then Siranos was gone—Kadou could tell the moment that the danger passed. He could feel it in the muscles of Evemer's shoulders, now no longer tensed to spring into action.

He ought to shift away. He ought to slide out of Evemer's lap, where he had somehow ended up, and give Evemer back his personal space. They ought to run right out of the incense lounge and find better shadows to hide in, or pounce upon Siranos and take him immediately.

But that would not be what Evemer would describe as risk-conservative. Siranos could have his mercenary guards with him. He wouldn't be wandering around the city without protection. Evemer had ruled that they would do this slow and steady, and that there would be no heroics of any kind.

And then there was another consideration: Evemer's arms were still tight around him and his eyes were on Kadou, hot and wild but . . . uncertain. He was waiting for Kadou to make a move, one way or another, so that he could match it. He wouldn't let go until Kadou did, and Kadou couldn't yet.

"It would look suspicious," Kadou ventured, "if we were to stop the very instant he walked out. Wouldn't it?"

"Yes," Evemer breathed. "Yes," and, without waiting a heart-beat longer, kissed him again. He was, to his credit, a quick study when he was paying attention—the clumsy press of his mouth was already refining by leaps and bounds.

Kadou ought to pull away, just as soon as there had been enough of an overlap not to be suspicious. He really ought to pull away—*but now?* his heart whined. Just as Evemer was starting to get a handle on the idea that he had teeth and a tongue and could do interesting things with them?

He stifled a small noise of his own and rubbed his thumbs over Evemer's cheekbones as Evemer bit gently at his bottom lip, send-ing a thrill of starry want sparkling from the top of Kadou's head all the way down his spine.

He forced himself to pull away. He was breathing rather heav-ily, he noticed. They both were, and Evemer looked . . . deliciously mussed. His hair was sticking up every which way, as if Kadou had been running his hands through it—he hadn't noticed. And the color was in his cheeks, and his eyes were bright and a little glassy with—

Kadou licked his lips. "Is anyone watching?" he murmured. His own hair was probably a wreck too, and he could feel that some of his clothes had been yanked out of place, no longer lying comfortably and in alignment.

Evemer stared up at him for a long moment, his mouth open and—and red and soft and wet, kiss-bitten. It made Kadou dizzy to look at him. Evemer seemed to come back to himself suddenly and looked around the room. "No one's watching," he said, and Kadou slid out of his lap.

He was probably imagining the way Evemer's hand lingered on his waist. "We'd better go," he said. He was feeling rather muzzy—between the incense and the kiss, it was no wonder. "Home now. Quickly."

Right before his eyes, he watched Evemer reconstruct his walls of discipline and iron bands of control, watched the wanting anguish disappear brick by brick. "Yes," he said, sounding almost normal. "Yes, we'll go."

Kadou snatched up his scarf and wound it over his hair and face as he walked out the door—

And came face to face with Siranos and five hired blades.

"How convenient," Siranos said. "Take them."

Kadou flung himself back through the door and Evemer slammed it shut. "Out the back," they both said in unison, and then they were scrambling across the room, dodging between the knee-high tables and scattered floor cushions.

Now was the time to run, though his every instinct screamed to look back, to make sure Evemer was behind him. He heard the slam of the door opening, the thunder of footsteps behind them, the crash of wood—Evemer must have upended some furniture to slow them down, to buy Kadou a few seconds.

Kadou shoved aside the parlor mistress, ducking through the cramped back rooms, seeing only glimpses of things as he passed— cabinets with a hundred tiny drawers, bunches of herbs hanging from the ceiling, a quality of light that was no less murky here than it was in the front.

Straight back, an arrowshot to the back of the building. Evemer was still behind him, yanking things to the floor, sowing chaos in their wake.

Kadou yanked open the alley door and leapt down to the cobblestones, straight into the waiting arms of . . . six more hired blades.

If only Evemer had had his sword, he might have had a chance of holding them off, but swords were impractical in the narrow alleys of Kasaba City, and too conspicuous to wear at your belt on the street. Instead, he and Kadou had only brought their daggers.

He didn't have a sword, and some of Siranos's thugs did.

He'd thought for a brief moment that they'd made it. That they'd hit the alley and lose themselves in the warren of the dockside district. Now all he could see was Kadou struggling viciously as three guards tried to hold him, fighting with elbows and knees.

Evemer drew his blade and threw himself into the fray like— like a man whose only reason to live was being captured.

He'd never been so angry before, or so scared.

There was a moment when Kadou broke free. The other thugs were at the threshold now. They were wildly outnumbered, and Evemer wondered if this was what a chess piece felt like when it was captured. "Run. Go," Evemer said. "*Go.*"

He saw the words hit Kadou like a crossbow quarrel to the chest. Evemer didn't need to survive—he only needed to give Kadou time enough to run, to make it to Melek—

Please, please run, Evemer thought, just as one of the thugs knocked his dagger out of his hand and got in a good kick to his knee that sent him to the ground. They dove upon him then, pinning him to the ground by his arms and legs. *Please let him live, let him get away,* he prayed to any god that might be listening.

Kadou didn't run. Stupid, noble little fool.

Kadou drew his own dagger and slashed wildly, fighting his way to the edge of the struggle. One of the women blocked his strikes with her greaves, stepped inside his guard, and punched him in the gut. Another man seized his arm and twisted until Kadou dropped his blade—it rang as it clattered on the cobblestones.

Evemer roared and, with a huge surge of strength, threw off the three thugs that held him down. He dived for his dagger, only to feel a sharp kick to his side, then another to his back, and he was pinned again, *five* people holding him down now, pinning him to the cobblestones as a sixth unlooped a length of stout rope from her belt. "Careful there, friends," she said darkly. She had an Oissika accent. "The Araşti royals have their guards swear blood oaths to die for them, you know. He'll take as many of you with him as he can."

Evemer snarled and thrashed, but the guards' grips were solid, and his shoulders screamed in protest.

They kept him pinned as they tied his arms behind his back with perfect knots that Evemer wouldn't have had a hope of wriggling free from, even without the injuries—a twinge in one shoulder, a flare of hot pain in the other where his stitches from last night's wound had pulled free. A few other, deeper aches were making themselves known too, ones he hadn't noticed in the heat of the fight. But the physical pain of his body was nothing.

He'd failed his lord. His one sworn duty, the thing he had promised Her Majesty with his life and beyond, and he'd failed.

Where was Kadou? Where was he? Evemer thrashed again, looking for him—there, standing now, also being tied up. He was looking back at Evemer with his heart breaking in his eyes.

"I'm sorry," he mouthed. Evemer shook his head. How could Kadou be sorry, when it was Evemer who had been too weak to protect him? Who hadn't lasted even long enough for Kadou to get away safely? If only Kadou had been able to get away, Evemer would have laid down his life at Kadou's feet and done it gladly.

They were probably already dead. How was Evemer supposed to look Usmim in the eye when he came to the divine scales of judgment? How was he supposed to confess to the outcome of this last, great trial? This last, great failure?

The thugs hauled him to his feet, and took them inside.

Evemer hadn't had a chance to see how much of a mess he'd thrown behind them as they'd run—he saw it now. Broken furniture. Overturned cabinets. Powders and herbs covering the floor so thick that their steps crunched as if on dry autumn leaves, sending heady, thick scent into the air.

Siranos was waiting in the front room of the incense lounge, his arms crossed. It had emptied out. There were more overturned tables here too. It looked like a typhoon had gone through.

It hadn't been enough. Perhaps not even his life would have been enough, not even his heart's blood spilled on the cobblestones at Kadou's feet.

"That's them," Siranos said. He snapped his fingers. "Bring them along."

They were dragged out to the street and thrown into the back of a boxy wagon—it looked like an ice-seller's cart. The thugs bound their ankles too, once they weren't required to walk any further, and slammed the doors on them, shutting them in the dark. Evemer heard the *shunk* of a metal bolt, the snap of a lock.

"I'm sorry," he said, his voice cracked. His arms, tied behind him, were already twin columns of agony.

"*I'm* sorry," Kadou replied immediately. Evemer could hear him breathing, slow and deliberate. "Are you hurt?"

"Not in any consequential way. Are you?"

"Barely," Kadou whispered. "I'm sorry," he said again. "I promised to run, and then I . . ." He trailed off. The wagon began moving, and the clatter of the wheels on the cobblestones made it rather too noisy to talk.

Evemer closed his eyes against the sting of tears and tried to think—there must be some gambit, some way out of this. If he could sacrifice himself to let Kadou escape . . .

He had many hurts, but he was used to ignoring them. He had trained specifically so that physical discomfort would not impede him. That, he could push past or set aside.

The shame of failure was more difficult to ignore. It was doubled, and doubled again, by the thought that he had failed with the taste of Kadou still on his lips, the smell of Kadou's hair still in his nose, the burning brands left by Kadou's teeth still on his neck.

If they had run the moment that Siranos had left—if he had invoked his discipline and denied himself that one more moment of bliss—

It still would not have been enough. The thugs were the people who had been blocking the door and talking. Siranos had brought them with him. He probably went everywhere with them.

There must be some way to get out of this.

At least if he sacrificed himself tonight, he'd be dying still feeling the ghost of Kadou's weight in his arms, the memory of how his cheeks flushed and his eyes sparkled when he was kissed, how his breath had caught in his chest. How he'd kissed back. It hadn't been just for the pretense. It had been real.

Evemer closed his eyes against the dark. Is this how it had been for Tadek, when he'd fallen together with Kadou? This slow descent into wanting until, before he knew it, he was wild with it? No, Tadek would have thrown himself into it with his eyes open. He would have known what he was getting himself into, at least well enough to know that it hadn't involved an exchange of hearts. He would have had a map for that wilderness—but Evemer had no map, and both he and his heart were already lost . . . Except for Kadou, burning like the compass star, the center of his sky that all the heavens turned around, steady and constant enough for Evemer to set his course by.

And yet Evemer had given in to base lust, as if he deserved to look upon Kadou in that way and think that he could reach far enough across the vast expanse of space to kiss Kadou's mouth again, to touch him, to hold him.

He could have run. Perhaps Evemer's sacrifice would have been enough, if Kadou had just managed to be a little less goddamn noble. Why couldn't he just accept that Evemer's place was to hang back and hold them off?

But Kadou never left him behind, never turned his back, even before they knew each other well, even when Evemer still disliked him. Every opportunity he'd had to stand with Evemer, he'd seized with both hands. And Evemer (gods strike him down) had thought him careless, flighty, negligent.

Stupid noble little fool. Fools, the both of them. Kadou, for placing too much value on Evemer's life. Evemer, for being so shamefully, wretchedly grateful to not be dead just yet—oh, gods, strike him down. Gods, forgive him.

Kadou had stood and fought, and Evemer's soul sang out toward him.

He didn't know how long they were in the wagon, but eventually it jolted to a stop, and there were voices outside again, and the doors were opened. Their eyes were blinded by the flare of lanterns. While they were wincing, the bonds around their ankles were cut and they were dragged out.

They'd been taken to a very well-to-do quarter of the city, inhabited mostly by merchants, visiting minor dignitaries, business owners, and a few particularly wealthy and exclusive artists and artisans. They were led to a large blocky house of three stories with a grand front door, stained wood with wide beaten-brass straps, framed by a large portico. The building was made all of pale stone, and the entrance hall, when they were dragged inside, was floored with smooth marble.

Lamps were hung everywhere, and fine rugs covered the floors. The thugs dragged the two of them up a flight of stairs, through winding hallways, and into a room where Siranos and Sylvia already waited.

The room was a salon—a wide chamber with tall windows on the long side that overlooked the street. It was floored with polished dark wood and paneled with the same, though the wall panels were extravagantly carved into a series of stylized trees whose lacy branches arced to the ceiling. There was a great fireplace, lying cold now for the warmth of summer.

There was another person in the room besides Siranos and Sylvia: the not-quite-convicted criminal Azuta Melachrinos. He suspected Kadou would have only seen her once, when Her Majesty had hired that Inachan satyota to question her. Evemer had still been on the fringe-guard when she'd been arrested and he'd seen her only a couple times more than that, but there was no mistaking her. She was wearing an Araşti women's kaftan—brocade in shades of umber and burgundy, trimmed with silk braid and closed with gilt buttons—but her iron-and-black hair was pinned up in a distinctly Oissic chignon. She was middle-aged and held her chin high and proud, and the last time Evemer had seen her, she'd carried herself with such icy poise that the iron shackles on her wrists had looked like jewelry.

That poise had vanished now. "Thank the gods," she snarled when she saw them. "What did I tell you, *kyrioi*? Here he is, the nosy little prince who's been causing you so much trouble! I told you he'd come sniffing again!"

"It's certainly a relief," Sylvia said darkly from where she was lounging elegantly across one of the couches by the fireplace. "One prince, a neatly gift-wrapped hostage. But the other one looks familiar . . . ?"

"His guard," Siranos said. "Nobody important." He stalked toward them, furious. "You couldn't have just stayed out of it, could you?" he hissed to Kadou in a low voice. "I tried to be kind to you, and—I was going to undo it. I would have undone it all and come back, and you just . . ." He bared his teeth. "But it's all useless now, isn't it? You've already told Zeliha, and I've lost everything, haven't I? Knew that as soon as I saw *him* last night." His eyes shot to Evemer.

"Yes, yes," Sylvia drawled, rolling her eyes. "If you'd just listened to me the first hundred times I told you that it was all pointless, you wouldn't be in this mess. But here we are, and at least you've come to your senses now. If you're good, I won't even tell Father that you nearly sold us out. First question: What are you planning to do with the prince?"

"You have space enough in this house, don't you?" Siranos said. "You've got entire warrens of cellars, or at least doors that lock. And I have guards enough to watch him. We only need a few days to find a *fucking* ship to get us out of here—"

Sylvia held up one hand, glittering with rings. "Yes, we've heard quite enough of your vulgar language about the ships, brother. Do stop panicking, it's giving me such a headache."

Siranos did look haggard, now that Evemer was looking at him in decent light. He was moving with quick little jerks, his jaw clenched and his hands flexing open and closed, as if he wanted to be pacing or chewing his nails or breaking things. Evemer tried to shift closer to Kadou, but the guards yanked him back.

A few days, they said, and they didn't mean to kill Kadou. That was something, at least. Better a hostage than dead. Evemer looked helplessly at Kadou, wondered if Melek had seen them taken, if çe had followed the carriage . . . But even if çe hadn't, their absence would be noted and the alarm raised—çe would run back to Mama's house and tell the kahyalar there, and they'd take it to Zeliha at once, and then within hours there would be patrols on the street—

Surely there were enough loyal kahyalar for that. Surely.

But if Kadou was locked up in Sylvia's alleged warren of cellars, would they even have a hope of finding him? Zeliha knew of Siranos and Sylvia's involvement, surely had intelligence about the location of their residence . . . Unless this *wasn't* their residence, and they'd already been covering their tracks.

As for Evemer's own fate, it was self-evident what that would be. He let himself keep looking at Kadou, devouring him with his eyes for what felt like centuries . . .

It was true, what Siranos had said—he was nothing. He was not fit to be called a kahya, not even fit to be called a guard. He was bound with ropes, and he had no weapons. There was no more that he could do, besides fight fiercely when they took him away and make their job as hard and tedious as possible.

And then they would kill him.

So he let himself look, he let himself yearn, he let his heart ache for his lord, for that noble little fool—that beautiful, *good* man.

Seconds. Seconds, that was all Evemer had left before someone got around to saying, *The other one, take him away and get rid of him.* Just seconds more to look at Kadou, to think of how many more times he could have kissed him, if Evemer had just been someone besides himself, someone who didn't care at all about the things that were important, and who yet had the strength to destroy Kadou's enemies. Someone like Tadek, who had done the impossible and reached easily across a few feet of space as if it were nothing.

If only Evemer were someone who could take his hand, as if Kadou were merely a person of flesh and blood who had kissed Evemer back.

Seconds more to think of how Evemer had all but carried him out of the palace on the night they'd escaped the attack, his lord mumbling deliriously the whole way. Seconds to think of sitting on the bed beside him in vigil, taking a great and piercing comfort in the steady rise and fall of his lord's chest in sleep—Evemer had done his duty that night, at least.

Kadou's eyes were wide and dark as the sea on a moonless night, filled with panic. It was clear that the same certainty that Evemer held had already dawned on him too. Perhaps he would be generous enough to forgive Evemer his faults and failings before they dragged them apart. Perhaps that would be a weight on the other side of Usmim's scales when Evemer shuffled in shame up to the gates of the afterlife—if he even made it there. More likely, Siranos would have his body dumped in the harbor on the outgoing tide, and Evemer's soul would wander, sinking down to the dark, crushing bottom of the sea.

Kadou tugged at his bindings. "Let me go, please," he said softly. "Please, just untie me."

"Make sure he's unarmed, and then you might as well," said Sylvia, waving one hand airily. "If we want him to write his own hostage notes to Zeliha, we'll need his hands to work. We can't have them dropping off from gangrene."

Evemer didn't look away as the hired thugs came forward to undo his lord's bindings. He would have counted Kadou's eyelashes if he'd been close enough. Seconds left now—he'd already had seconds more than he expected. He'd carry this with him to death—the midnight fall of Kadou's hair, the color of his eyes, the soft bow of his lower lip. Evemer had kissed that mouth less than an hour ago.

What would he have done, if he'd known then how little time he had left? He would have held Kadou a minute longer, savored the shape of him, pulled in the warmth of him to remember as a comfort when his soul was lost in the cold depths. Perhaps it wouldn't be such a terrible fate—those dark fathoms would be just the same color as Kadou's eyes.

"The other one, then, the guard," said Sylvia, and Evemer's heart crashed into his gut. Here it was. "We don't need him, then?"

"I can't see why we would," Azuta said. "Unless Siranos has reason to want to keep him around."

"I don't," Siranos snapped. "Guards, take him away. Get rid of him."

There it was. His death sentence.

Evemer wanted to close his eyes to let it wash over him, but—his lord. Oh, his lord. Evemer would look as long as he could, he'd hold the image of those deep eyes in his heart while they strung him up by his neck, or cut off his head, or tipped poison down his throat, or took him down to the harbor and tied him to a rock and pitched him overboard, or slid steel into his gut. However they thought to do it. Evemer would look and look and look, and he'd close his eyes as soon as they took him out of the room, so that he could tell Usmim that his lord was the last thing he'd seen in life.

"Wait," said Kadou, no louder than a whisper, and then louder, "Wait. Wait, no. Don't—don't hurt him. Listen to me!" His voice grew stronger. "You're keeping me as a hostage, aren't you? You know I'm valuable, and that it would be cataclysmic if Her Majesty finds out you've killed me. If you kill Evemer, you'll be throwing away a second bargaining chip."

Evemer's heart broke—even here at the very end of things, Kadou was trying to stand for him, to be his champion.

Azuta scoffed. "He's a guard."

"He's one of Her Majesty's secret police, and he's here on special assignment from her!" The guards finally finished untying Kadou. He wriggled free of the loosened ropes immediately and took two steps closer to Evemer, seizing his arm. "He's as valuable as I am."

Sylvia quirked an eyebrow. "Lying, is he?"

Siranos frowned, hesitating.

"Think of it," Kadou said quickly, before she could say anything else. "Think of how he never leaves my side. Ever since the night of Eyne's birth, how often have you seen me without him? Her Majesty will pay you money for this man's return—as much as she'll pay for me, I'd wager," Kadou said desperately. "Why keep only one of us alive when you can double your profit? We're talking about hundreds of thousands of altınlar! A million."

"She'd pay that much for one of her officers?" Sylvia asked dubiously. "A mere spy?"

"He's titled as well," Kadou said. "A noble—you know we don't have many of those. There are just a handful of old families left with hereditary titles. Evemer is a count."

Siranos was silent, his frown even deeper. He glanced at Sylvia and Azuta. "Well, don't look at me. I don't know everyone in the court, I've been all but locked up in Her Majesty's jewelry box for the last months."

Sylvia sighed impatiently. "You can do better than that, brother."

Siranos exploded. "How am I to know? Tell me that! How am I to know everything? Especially if he's secret police!" Evemer felt a faint glimmer of hope like a single star twinkling through a cloudy night. "I've done my part, Sylvia! I've done more than my part!" His voice edged toward hysteria. "I got the sultan of Araşt pregnant! I came up with the counterfeiting to pay off our family's debts while *you* were wasting your time on hiring thieves! And at every turn you tell me that it's not enough, that I can do better— what else *exactly* do you want from me?" His voice had risen to a scream by the end. "This is about my mother again, isn't it? It's always about her!"

Sylvia sighed again. "I've asked you once already to calm yourself. If we kill him off and it turns out he's worth half a million altınlar, I'll be rather annoyed with you. So you'd better be quite sure, one way or another. And *please* keep the noise down."

"I don't need to be sure, though, do I?" he said, wild-eyed. "Let's fetch the witch and see if they're lying."

Sylvia rolled her eyes. "Do you know how much she charges me?"

Evemer stiffened, and saw Kadou do the same—a witch—a truthwitch. A satyota.

Any faint hope Evemer had had of surviving the night vanished like a ribbon of incense smoke.

"A wager! I'll wager you for it," Siranos said. His grin was becoming manic. "If it turns out the prince is trying to sell you a vineyard in Pezia, I'll cover the cost of the witch telling us so."

"What, with your little counterfeits? I think not, dear."

"Honest Oissika silver!" he cried, rushing toward her and seizing her hands. "If it's a lie, I'll pay the witch. And if it's true and that man really is a titled noble, then you pay, since you'll likely make your money back anyway."

"Sounds like a fair wager to me," Azuta said.

Sylvia paused for a moment and shrugged one lovely shoulder. "We might as well be sure." Another of those airy waves. "Go fetch the witch for me, would you?"

"She won't be happy to be disturbed at this hour, ma'am," said the guard. "Should I tell her it's urgent?"

"No!" Siranos snapped. "She's got a surcharge for everything, damn her! Just bring her here and don't tell her anything!"

"Untie him, please?" Kadou said loudly. He turned to the guard who was making her way to the door. "Please, before you go. Please untie him. He'll need to be able to write too—"

"Oh, all right," said Sylvia impatiently. "There's enough of us in here, and they don't look stupid enough to try anything."

His lord hovered nearby as the guards loosened the ropes around Evemer's arms. The panic in Kadou's face had settled into a determined terror. Evemer drank it all in—every second now was a gift. Every heartbeat was one more than he had been allotted by the gods.

As soon as the ropes fell away, Kadou was reaching for him again, and Evemer was helpless to do anything but take his lord's outstretched hands. "Follow," Kadou whispered, tugging him across the room.

As if Evemer had to be told. As if his very soul weren't lashed to Kadou like a ship to the compass star.

❊

A satyota. There was a satyota, and she was here in the building, and Kadou had lied. Kadou had lied *so much*. It had all come tumbling out of his mouth as quick as the ideas had risen in his mind.

The ominous growl of the fear-creature in his mind was

drowned out entirely by his heart, snarling ferociously over Evemer like a threatened she-wolf over her cubs—Evemer was *his*. He'd knelt at Kadou's feet just that morning, and pressed his forehead to the backs of Kadou's hands and *sworn* that he was Kadou's. Evemer was not to be touched. He was not to be harmed.

That morning, Kadou hadn't said the answering oaths correctly. He'd seen the disappointment in Evemer's eyes. It had been cowardly of him, to only say, "Yes, I accept," without enumerating his promises in return. Evemer had offered up his whole self and all his devotion, and Kadou should have given him so much more in return. He should have offered something of real significance, of real *meaning* on his own side of the scales to bring it into balance, because *that* was fealty, that was how it worked—Evemer gave his loyalty and his service, and Kadou was obliged to fight with everything he had to protect him in return.

And all he had left was lies.

A *count*. A count! Why had he said that, of all things? He didn't have the authority to raise anyone to nobility! Even if he had, the process took weeks or months, and there was paperwork, and bureaucracy, and if a land grant came with it then there was an even more complicated set of paperwork, not to mention the scholars and clerks who would spend days poring over the old books to assign the new lord their sigils and review all the particulars of the specific title, and all the other tedious minutiae of the process . . .

And then something in Kadou froze in a horrible, wonderful moment of epiphany.

There was one way to do it instantly.

One very, very stupid way.

One way.

Evemer was going to be appalled.

But there was no other way. It didn't matter if Evemer never forgave him. It didn't matter if Evemer chose to go to Eozena or Zeliha afterward and ask for a clarification of his orders so he could be quietly shuffled away from Kadou and *kept* away, out of his reach and rightfully so. It didn't matter, because at least he'd be alive. He'd be alive, he'd be *safe*. Kadou had promised to keep him safe.

He dragged Evemer off into the corner of the room, as far away from the others as possible. He turned to Evemer, and looked into his eyes, as black as the night sky. Evemer was afraid and lost, but he was looking at him like Kadou had some kind of answer, like Kadou *was* the answer. Kadou would never see that look in his eyes again. He was going to destroy it.

He took a breath. "Evemer," he whispered. "I cannot tell you how sorry I am." There was no time. He couldn't waste these few precious seconds on an explanation. "You have to marry me."

CHAPTER TWELVE

You have to marry me," Kadou said, as if he were telling Evemer that someone had died, and Evemer very nearly did.

"My lord?" Evemer managed to choke out. Of all the things—of all the—

Oh. Oh, but then he realized.

Kadou squeezed his eyes shut. "I'm *ordering* you to do it," he said, forcing it out like every word was made of thorns that tore at his tongue. "Right now, immediately."

Kadou was saving his life. Kadou was . . . Oh, clever thing, clever stupid precious thing. Kadou was shielding him under the wing of his protection in the only way he could now. The *titles*. Kadou's titles. He was giving them to Evemer.

And then it wouldn't be a lie when the satyota came.

"Yes. Right now," Evemer echoed. "Immediately." His mouth had gone dry, and he felt rather dizzy. What were the gods-damned oaths? How was he supposed to remember oaths at a time like this, much less oaths that he had never imagined he'd say to anyone? "By the sea—by the—gods, Kadou, I can't—"

Kadou seized his hands. His grip was warm and strong. He wasn't shaking at all.

His own hands were, Evemer noticed distantly.

How could he deserve this? How could he ever possibly hope to repay this kind of loyalty? This was beyond anything that Evemer would have expected from his lord—from any lord, even a perfect one from legend. It was too much.

"I'm not worth this," he whispered.

"You are," Kadou whispered back, simply. His eyes were so bright, so infinitely deep, and so incredibly sad. With no hesitation, with a voice that was as clear and steady and assured as anything Evemer had heard from him, he spoke: "By the sea and in the eyes of the Mother and the Lord of Judgment, I declare myself to you. I come to you without distinctions and without glory, without the trifling and meaningless trappings of mortal honors. I come to you as nothing and no one but myself. Take my hands and see that they are empty—I offer you no wealth but that of my heart, and ask for none but that of yours. Hear my words and know that they are true—I swear myself to you and none other."

"Your hands are empty," Evemer said, feeling rather faint. "Your words, I know, are true. I take you as you are, as nothing and no one but yourself, without distinctions and without glory." Polite lies, those, because Kadou's distinctions and glories were the very reason for doing this. He wanted to sink to his knees and press his forehead to the backs of Kadou's hands once more, wanted to weep and swear his fealty all over again instead. Empty hands? What nonsense. This was as gifts of gold spilling from Kadou's hands like waterfalls.

"By the sea and in the eyes of the Mother," he said, feeling every word of it like a song pulled from his heart, *meaning* it as he had never meant anything before, even more than any oath he'd ever sworn as a kahya, "I declare myself to you. I come to you without distinctions and without glory, without the trifling and meaningless trappings of mortal honors." They *were* meaningless, compared to this. He was daunted by the breadth and depth of this, humbled by the encompassing greatness of it. "I come to you as nothing and no one but myself. Take my hands and see that they are empty—I offer you no wealth but that of my heart, and ask for none but that of yours." Paltry and base, he knew. The wealth of his heart was meager, a deeply inadequate trade when exchanged for Kadou's. "Hear my words and know that they are true—I swear myself to you and none other." This, at least, was true. Beyond true.

"Your hands are empty," Kadou whispered. "Your words, I

know, are true. I take you as you are, as nothing and no one but yourself, without distinctions and without glory." More polite lies, that, because the very fact of being in this room, taking Kadou's hands, hearing him speak these words, was an honor Evemer would never have even begun to imagine.

"I name you my consort," Kadou said then, and Evemer's heart jerked in his chest all over again. "All that I have or will ever have is yours." There was supposed to be more, a long and boring script of much drier language, a recitation of law rather than po-etry, granting each other shared claim on wealth, assets, holdings, heirs. But Kadou stumbled to a halt, his hands gripping Evemer's so hard they hurt.

"I don't have anything," Evemer whispered. He felt like he'd been shattered. He didn't know the rest of the script, and perhaps the rest didn't actually matter. But this, this seemed important. Better to speak truth from the very core of himself, from the basalt foundations of his heart: "But if I did, I'd give all of it to you."

Kadou huffed a nervous, shaky laugh. "Neither of us brought wedding cloaks to exchange."

"I'm sorry," Evemer said, because it was the only thing to say. "I'll try to be more prepared next time."

Kadou was supposed to laugh, but he slipped his hands out of Evemer's. His heart cried out, protesting and forlorn. "I'm sorry too," Kadou said. He glanced at their captors across the room (squabbling energetically with each other and paying little heed), then stepped forward and laid the lightest, briefest kiss on the corner of Evemer's mouth. "There. Done. I'm sorry. I'm so sorry, but I had to. Please don't hate me—I don't mean to hold you to anything. We'll undo it as soon as we can." He stepped back again. "But listen, this is important. These are your titles: Prince of Araşt, Duke-Consort of Altınbaşı-ili, Lord-Consort of Şirya and Nadırıntepe, and Warden-Consort of the Northern Marches. You're rightfully styled Damat Evemer Hoşkadem Mahisti-eş Bey Effendi."

Evemer choked out half a delirious laugh—the full title was something he would have only heard from heralds announcing him to the *court*. A profoundly surreal thought, bordering on absurd.

Kadou continued relentlessly. "Your common-usage address is Prince Evemer. You're of equal rank with me and anyone Zeliha marries, if she were ever to do so."

That was . . . dizzying, in the same way as thin mountain air. "Yes, my lord," he managed.

"Can you remember all that?"

"Yes." The Northern Marches were his home—the mountains where he'd spent his childhood, where part of his heart still lay. That part was Kadou's now too.

The door opened and the satyota entered. She was rather short and plump, with long, dead-straight, glossy black hair tied back in a braid. She had dark, wide-set eyes, rich brown skin, plain clothes—a baggy shirt and drawstring trousers in a matching undyed linen that looked rather bed-rumpled—and a deeply annoyed expression. "What is it now? I was *napping*."

Siranos snapped his fingers at Kadou and Evemer, gesturing them back to the middle of the room. "These two," he said. "We need to know if they're lying."

"Ohh," said the satyota. "Is *that* why you summoned a satyota? I thought we were just going to eat cakes." She heaved a sigh. "Fine, what do you want to know?"

"That one in particular," Siranos said, jabbing his finger at Evemer. "Is he noble?"

The satyota turned sharply on her heel, pivoting to Evemer so sharply her braid swung out behind her. "What's your name?" she demanded.

"Evemer," he replied.

"Full name, with all your titles."

Here it was. He found himself edging closer to Kadou's side, groping for his hand. Kadou's fingers found his and he gripped them tight. His life hung on the words they'd just murmured to each other in the corner, and the ones that he was about to speak. "Damat Evemer Hoşkadem Bey Effendi," he said. Best to drop the *Mahisti-eş* and the *Prince of Araşt* unless he was pressed.

"Duke-Consort of Altınbaşı-ili, Lord-Consort of Şirya and Nadırıntepe, and Warden-Consort of the Northern Marches." Entirely without meaning to, he felt his shoulders straighten, his chin rise.

Kahyalar—the best ones, the smartest and cleverest ones— sometimes ended up titled through positions gained in the civil service. It had been an entirely reasonable possibility to imagine that he might one day be elevated to those heights—a minister or provincial governor, perhaps—but he hadn't thought for a moment that it would come before he was seventy. And *this* altitude was beyond any expectations.

The satyota turned back. "Yeah, anything else?"

"That was *true*?" said Siranos.

She shrugged. "As far as I can tell."

"What!" Azuta cried. "Listen again, use all your powers!"

"Ugh! I keep telling you people it's not sorcery, but do you *ever* fucking listen? No, it's just *Tenzin, Tenzin!*" The satyota's voice took on a mock-whine. "All hours of the day: *Tenzin, Tenzin, come interrogate the prisoner! Tenzin, are you busy? Tenzin, wake up, it's dawn and I can't possibly wait! Tenzin, why are you in the bath? Get out, I need you!* Am I done here? Anything else you want to know about them? Their earliest childhood memories? Their sexual fetishes? Maybe what they ate for breakfast this morning?"

"No, Tenzin," Siranos said through his teeth. "We're terribly sorry for disturbing you."

She scoffed. "Of course you are. Do you want the bill for this separate or added to your total?"

Azuta tilted her head. "You don't have her on retainer?"

"I don't do retainers," Tenzin said sharply at the same moment that Sylvia and Siranos said, "She doesn't do retainers," though more annoyed and exhausted, as if it were an argument that they had lost several times and were now leery of entering into again.

"The amount they nag me as it is?" Tenzin said, crossing her arms. "Absolutely not." She snapped her fingers at Siranos. "Separate bill or running total?"

"Separate bill," he gritted out. "Thank you. Good night."

"Yeah," she said flatly, and left the room.

"Gods, I hate her," snarled Siranos, and then whirled on Evemer. "*Damat?*"

"Yes," he said.

"Who the fuck *are* you? No, better question—who the fuck are you *married to*?"

Evemer stared at him coolly. "Someone very powerful, who would go great lengths to see me in one piece." He squeezed Kadou's hand, and Kadou squeezed back.

"Did you want to bring the satyota back for that?" Kadou asked; Siranos stopped and looked at him. His eyes dropped to their joined hands.

Sylvia sighed. "You Araşti and your labyrinthine titles. I still don't know what all those words meant. You know, we got rid of *our* kings about two thousand years ago; you people really ought to do the same. Makes everything a lot simpler and clearer." She leaned over on the divan and plucked a half-full glass of wine off the side table. She drank deep, looking around with an expectant expression. "Well? Anyone? What's a damat-blah-blah-blah-beywhatever? Siranos? Did you manage to learn *that*, at least, during your little vacation in the palace?"

"Damat bey effendi," said Siranos slowly, "is a title given to the husband of a member of the royal family. All of the titles he gave us are honoraries."

"And you don't know who the . . ." Sylvia waved vaguely. "Who the primary holder is?"

Siranos looked between him and Kadou, calculating. "Seems like it would be this one, wouldn't it?"

"We would have heard if the prince were married, wouldn't we? Someone would have told us."

"Well, *I* don't fucking know," Siranos snapped, turning to her. "But apparently so! Zeliha must have some reason for keeping it under tight wraps, or there would have been announcements and—and stupid parades about it!"

"Secret police," Kadou said mildly. "It's right there in the name."

Sylvia put a hand to her forehead and sighed. "Such a head-ache. Someone take them away and lock them up. And Siranos, by the goddess of mercy, *calm down*."

✳

They were taken away to what seemed to have once been a wine cellar. Beneath the musty smell of the underground, there was an oversweet, rancid tang in the air, as of long-ago smashed bottles whose contents had soaked into the stones and mortar. The cold of the cellar was the sort that crept up and sank into one's bones, rather than biting at one's skin as the wind off the sea did.

The guards did not deign to leave them a lamp. They shut and locked the door behind them, and once more Kadou and Evemer were alone in the dark, the only faint light coming from the crack under the door.

Evemer hadn't let go of his hand, and Kadou also, increasingly, found himself both unwilling and unable to do so.

"All right," Kadou whispered, when they'd stood there in the dark for long minutes, unmoving. Their palms were getting clammy, clasped tight as they were, but it didn't matter. "All right. We're not dead. You're not dead. That's taken care of."

"Yes," Evemer said, and Kadou turned blindly toward him.

"I'm so sorry."

"I won't accept an apology."

"I just—I had to do something, and that was all I could do, and—"

"It was all you could think of," Evemer said. "Kadou. High-ness. My lord." He dropped to his knees and pressed his forehead against the back of Kadou's hand.

"What are you doing?"

"You could have let them kill me," Evemer whispered. "Three times now, you could have left me to die and you didn't. How many of my lives must I owe to you?"

Kadou wrenched his hand away. He regretted it immedi-ately—it made the room so much colder. "Don't say that," he said.

"Don't. I shouldn't—I forced you! I ordered you to do it! You'd be well within your rights to be furious with me."

"Why?"

"I held your life in my hands, you didn't have a choice—"

"You held it in your hands only long enough to wrench it out of theirs, and then you did the one thing you could to give my life back to me," Evemer said, his voice low and . . . angry. Actually angry for once. "Again, you're doing this? Again? My lord, how many more times will you hand me a great gift and then tell me that it's worthless? Stop it."

Kadou backed away a few steps until he bumped into a wall. "I don't know what you're talking about."

"Don't lie to me. You just bid me to hear your words and know they are true. So don't lie."

Kadou flinched. He heard Evemer shifting in the dark, maybe getting to his feet again. "I told you—we talked about it, that time in the bathhouse, I explained—I have so much power over you, I can't be careless, I—"

"Do you?"

"What?"

"Do you have power over me?"

"Yes!" Kadou spluttered. "I'm your lord, I'm the prince, you're—"

"I'm your kahya," Evemer said in a low voice. "And Her Majesty the sultan of Araşt granted me the privilege of disobedience. Whatever power you have over me comes from what I've given to you, and from the oaths I *willingly* swore to you." A footfall in the dark. His voice came a little closer now. "Regardless of the privilege I've been granted, I can take my willingness away. If you broke the oaths between us, I would have nothing binding me to serve and obey you. I could turn my back on you and leave you. A vassal should not give his service to an unworthy lord."

"I am unworthy," Kadou whispered. "I could hurt you before you had time to turn away from me."

Evemer's hands closed on his arms and Kadou squeaked in

surprise—Evemer was so close he could feel the warmth radiating off his skin. "Why don't you trust me?"

Kadou had no answer. He could only stay there, frozen and still in Evemer's hold.

"This morning, I told you *no* in the firmest possible terms. I threatened to tie you up to keep you from going out alone. Upstairs," Evemer said, his voice barely louder than a whisper, "you swore an oath as nothing and no one but *yourself,* without distinctions or glory or the trifling and meaningless trappings of mortal honors. And I *accepted you.*"

"You had to," Kadou whispered.

"I'd do it again."

"There was no other choice but death."

Evemer was quiet. Kadou could hear him breathing. His grip tightened, not quite to the point of pain. "My lord."

Ah. Of course that was all Evemer would say. It was frequently all that he said. What else, really, was there that could be said.

"I," Evemer continued, to Kadou's surprise, "do not . . . go often out of my way to disclose my thoughts." It sounded like he was dragging the words out through sheer doggedness. "My lord bid me once to speak what I meant, and I have been trying to do so. It goes against my . . . my habit, at least, if not my nature. Yet I have tried."

"I know," Kadou whispered. "I know you have, I've seen it. I know. You've been doing it—you've been doing so well. It's so much easier to understand you—"

"And it is all for nothing if you won't *listen* to me," said Evemer sharply. "What is the point of speaking if you don't at least do me that courtesy? You do not need to believe everything I say merely because I say it, but it is an insult to me that you will not accept that *I* believe what I say, and that I am saying it for a reason—namely, that I wish you to *know* the things I believe." There was a beat of astonished silence. "I am *glad to be alive,*" Evemer said relentlessly. "I am glad to have a lord who loves me enough that he would go to such lengths to protect me—not merely honored, mind you, but glad. Ecstatic. Delighted." His voice as he said these was hard, a little sarcastic, but not angry. He added, very firm, a line in the sand that could not be debated or denied: "I am glad that lord is *you*, Kadou Mahisti."

"Oh," Kadou said in a small voice.

After another few moments of silence, during which time the only noise was the too-loud sound of their unsteady breaths, Evemer added with a subtle thread of amused exasperation, "Now you say, *I'm also glad you're not dead, Evemer.*"

That caught him by surprise—he laughed aloud.

The laugh too rather startled him, both the sudden bright sound of his own voice ringing through the empty stone room and the sudden break of tension and fear and guilt. Without allowing himself to think about it, he moved forward and buried his face in Evemer's chest, pulling his arms free from Evemer's gentle hold so he could wrap them around Evemer's waist and hug him tight. "I'm glad you're not dead," he said. The truth of it cut the momentary sweetness of the laughter and brought a lump to his throat. His voice, when he spoke again, was rough and thick. "Gods, I'm *so glad* you're not dead."

Evemer's hands slid around his shoulders and across his back, enveloping him in strength and warmth and security. He felt Evemer tip his head down enough to press the bottom of his face to Kadou's hair—not quite a kiss, but . . . close to it.

Kadou's heart skipped several beats and his mouth went dry. He swallowed. "I'll listen to you," he whispered. "I'll listen now, I promise."

"Prove it. What did I say, a moment ago?"

Kadou again swallowed hard and wished he could do something like pull back from the embrace and recover a scrap of dignity, but—well, there was a wall behind him. That was a good enough excuse not to move. "A lot of things."

"What is the gist of them?"

"That you're . . . not angry with me."

Evemer made an unimpressed noise.

Kadou's breath caught on another half laugh, and he looked up reflexively—it was too dark to see Evemer's face, but he wanted to, wanted to see the expression that went with that noise.

It was only then that he realized how close it brought their faces.

His heart tripped in his chest, and he felt Evemer's breathing stutter, which made it trip several more times in succession as an absolute flock of butterflies erupted in his stomach.

"Try again," Evemer said. His voice was low, husky. Kadou could feel the deep vibration of it rumbling against his chest.

"Try what again?" he whispered, feeling a little faint and mostly wanting Evemer to talk more so he could . . . feel. That.

"Proving that you're listening."

He could feel Evemer's breath—they were close. They were incredibly close. If there had been a scrap of light, he could have seen how close Evemer's face was. How close his mouth was. "You're—" His voice cracked. He trembled, felt Evemer's arms tighten around him. "You're—the—the opposite of angry."

"That'll do," Evemer said, and kissed him.

Kadou exhaled sharply, kissed back as Evemer's arm tightened again around his waist, as his other hand slid into Kadou's hair and cupped the back of his head, as Evemer pressed him against the wall.

Evemer broke off far, far too soon.

Kadou's breath was unsteady—he was almost panting, as if there were no air in the room but what was in Evemer's mouth. His mind was foggy, and he couldn't manage coherent thought, but it was an inarguable fact that Evemer was absolutely, definitely allowed to *stop kissing him* if he felt like it. That was the only certainty Kadou could currently put his hands on, and he clung to it as hard as he could and did not yank Evemer back to him.

Evemer rested his forehead against Kadou's temple, murmuring against Kadou's cheek and ear, "Once more."

Kadou made some noise halfway between a laugh and a wild keen of desperation. His skin was buzzing. His hands were clutching fistfuls of the front of Evemer's kaftan.

"Once more," Evemer said again.

"I," said Kadou. "I, ah . . . Remind me? In small words?"

"I was telling you *I'm fine*."

"You're fine," Kadou echoed, a little delirious.

Evemer had never lied to him. Evemer would never lie to him. By comparison, Kadou's own mind had lied to him on dozens of occasions—hundreds. Why should he listen to those dark, guilty whispers, instead of the one person in the room he could trust?

"I'm fine," Evemer said, crowding him closer against the wall. Oh, the heat of him, the height and breadth of him. He was so strong, so warm, so solid and *real*. Kadou tugged those fistfuls of Evemer's kaftan, wanting him closer, closer, closer. Evemer's mouth hovered a hairsbreadth from Kadou's, as close as he could possibly be without kissing him again. Kadou's pulse was thundering—he could feel the galloping beat of it through every part of his body.

"Could I get away from you if you tried to hold me?" Evemer said. Gods, he was so close, and not nearly close enough.

"Probably. Yes." In an even match of pure physical strength, Evemer would win. He was taller, bigger, better trained.

"If you have power over me here and now, it's because I want you to have it. I'll give that to you, and anything you ask for. I'll give it gladly," Evemer rasped. He was trembling too, Kadou noticed dizzily—he slipped one hand up to cup the back of Evemer's neck. "Command it of me and it's yours."

A few panting breaths between them—both of them unsteady, trembling, tense. Evemer's arm around his waist was as tight and possessive as Kadou's grip on his clothes and the back of his neck.

Kadou's eyes fell closed as he released the last whispering fragments of guilt and hesitation. Easy to do, when every thought in him was eclipsed by pure desire and everything in him yearned toward Evemer like the ocean rising inexorably to the moons when they pulled it to the straining peak of the king-tide, the highest swell of the season.

Evemer . . . waited. Waited for his command.

"Kiss me," Kadou whispered, his heart in his throat.

Evemer made that *sound* and obeyed immediately, kissing him deep and hot and *demanding*. "Again. Ask me again," Evemer murmured into his mouth.

"Kiss me," Kadou said. He couldn't think. "Kiss me. Kiss me."

Evemer groaned outright and kissed him, and kissed him, his hand knotted in Kadou's hair, his arm tight around his waist, his body pressed entirely against Kadou's.

"I wanted you," Kadou confessed in a rush like the breaking of a dam. "I've *been* wanting you."

Evemer made a pleased sound and scraped his teeth against Kadou's lower lip.

Kadou gasped and held him tighter, shuddered as Evemer bit his lip again, as Evemer licked into his mouth. It wasn't enough—he wasn't close enough, he needed—"Closer," he said. "Closer, gods, come here—"

Evemer, as effortless as breathing, shifted his hold and lifted Kadou from his hips, pinning him up against the wall without once breaking the starving, devouring kiss. Kadou wrapped both legs around Evemer's waist, locking his ankles and pulling him impossibly closer.

If there had been any lingering doubt that Evemer wanted him, that first delicious grind together would have torn it to shreds—he was hot even through both their clothes, as hard as Kadou was and probably as aching, and Kadou arched into him, dropping his head back against the wall as he breathed, "Yes, there—like that. Like that."

He was so *fucking close* to throwing every piece of good sense into the sea and bidding good riddance to it. He was shaking with the adrenaline of the kiss, of escaping death, and—gods, he wanted. He wanted to burn out all the adrenaline and the terror and the scrambling, desperate possessiveness with a few scorching minutes up against a wall, just like this—just exactly like this, because against all the odds both of them were, blazingly, still alive.

He pulled Evemer's mouth back to his, cradling his face in both hands, gasping again and again for air that seemed to be in alarmingly short supply as Evemer rocked against him, making that little noise of want almost constantly now, and Kadou would have killed for him again, would have given Evemer anything he wanted, would have happily ordered Evemer to ravish him right here against the wall in this cold, rancid wine cellar if it made Evemer groan aloud like that again, and—

Kadou's eyes flew open. "Stop," he gasped, jerking away from the kiss so sharply he almost cracked his head on the wall behind him.

Evemer froze in place. He was still making those soft wanting noises—oh, god, he'd meant it, hadn't he? He'd do anything Kadou told him to, even right here, and he'd *like* it.

Kadou breathed through a new surge of lust, and forced his legs to unlock from around Evemer's hips. "We have to stop."

"What?"

"Put me down."

Evemer obeyed, still breathing raggedly, letting Kadou slip down the few inches to land, shakily, on his toes. Evemer propped his arm on the wall by Kadou's head, leaning into it hard. "Did I do something?" he panted. "It was too much?"

"No." Kadou closed his eyes once more, not that open or closed mattered at all in the full dark. He laughed miserably. The only other alternative was bursting into tears. "No, not that at all," he said. His voice cracked—his mouth was dry. He swallowed. "We're *married.*" Evemer was still for a moment, and then Kadou *felt* him realize, with his whole body, what Kadou meant. Evemer collapsed against him, his head dropping to Kadou's shoulder, his muscles going lax with defeat. Kadou put his arms around him again, loosely now—it seemed so natural already.

"We're married," Evemer said. He sounded desolate, and Kadou hated himself for it, hated this room, hated anything that made Evemer sound like that.

The lambent want still shimmered through his veins with every wild beat of his heart. If it had only been him, he would have said to hell with it all, and thrown himself back into Evemer's arms, but it wasn't. "Do you—do you understand?" he said. Evemer nodded weakly against his shoulder. "Spell it out. I need to be sure."

"Because of annulment," Evemer said, bleak, "versus divorce."

Kadou hated this so much. Why hadn't he thought of a better plan?

Annulment could be done quietly by a single temple dedicate. A discreet one, for preference.

Divorce, particularly from a prince of the royal family, was a much, much, *much* more complicated affair. And public. So very, extremely public: not one discreet dedicate, but a small army of them, and phalanxes of clerks, and—well, everyone. Everyone in the whole kingdom, and potentially farther. It could even affect places far beyond their borders, kingdoms that might have been making diplomatic advances toward them with the hopes of bargaining to buy that selfsame prince for one of their crown heirs, or to marry off one of their lesser scions and send them away to Araşt. They would be more cautious of bargaining with them if they thought the serenity of the ruling family had been marred.

That's what Kadou very nearly would have thrown into the sea for the sake of another dozen kisses, for the sake of unwinding Evemer's sash, undoing his buttons, letting his clothes fall open to Kadou's touch, for the sake of laying his palms against Evemer's bare skin and unwinding the rest of him too.

But no matter the oaths he'd made upstairs when he was nothing and no one but himself, he *wasn't* just himself.

The thought tore at him as it had never torn at him before in his life—it wasn't fair. It wasn't fair that he should be denied every opportunity for individual decision. It wasn't fair that he could never, even once, consider only his own wants in matters like these. It wasn't fair that the demands of his country should again outweigh his longing for one thing that was, even temporarily, *his.* The thing he wanted so badly he could barely keep his knees from giving out under him.

Even so, he wavered. He hesitated.

But it wasn't just his own life he was weighing on the scales of the country's demands—it was Evemer's too. A quiet and discreet annulment would preserve his career. A public and complicated divorce, even completely amiable, would destroy it. Kadou could weather that storm—whether or not his reputation was dented, he was still a prince—but Evemer would be left with nothing. His career demanded a certain sterling image. A prince's castoff (and that *is* how he would be seen) would not have a place with the kahyalar. There would be no opportunity for advancement, no promotion to government office. No more educational stipend to make something else of himself, if government service did not suit—and Kadou doubted whether Evemer would allow him to simply pay for such things out of his own purse in recompense. He would be worse off than even Tadek had been as an armsman.

"We have to be able to undo it," Kadou whispered.

"Yes," Evemer said. "The kingdom. Your reputation."

"Fuck my reputation. The kingdom, yes. But your *career*."

"Oh," said Evemer, like he hadn't even thought of that. "I suppose."

"Your whole life. I can't save your life and then destroy it myself. And—and if we were divorced, if it was public—"

"And it *would* be public," Evemer said, resigned.

"They'd expect me to get rid of you." He heard Evemer suck in a breath. "If I publicly cast you aside, everyone will expect me to have nothing to do with you afterward. They'll send you away from me, or make me send you away, and I—I don't want to." He hated how petulant he sounded. "I can't do that. I can't abandon you."

"You could. You could turn me away."

Kadou swallowed hard. "I want to keep you," he whispered, but damn, that was a little too close to a shipload of things he wasn't ready to admit even to himself, let alone aloud. But there were layers of oaths he'd made to Evemer, and some more known and quantifiable than others: "I'm your lord, and I owe you a place in my home and at my hearth. I want you there. I don't want you to leave. How would I manage without you?"

"I would stay at your side as long as you'd have me, my lord." He stood up straight again, turning to lean his back against the wall next to Kadou. Their hands found each other in the dark and gripped tight, and the two of them, without speaking, slid down the wall to sit on the hard stone floor. Kadou allowed himself one single moment of weakness and huddled close against Evemer's side, telling himself it was just because of the cold of the room and because Evemer was so warm. "My lord, would you . . ."

"Would I what?" Kadou asked after a moment when Evemer didn't finish.

"Your grandmother, the dowager-sultan, her kahyalar . . . Would it be like that?"

Kadou's grandmother had three kahyalar whom she considered favorites. The oldest of them, Zarghuna, had been at her side for more than fifty years. Grandfather had appointed Zarghuna to her personally on the day Grandmother had arrived in the capital to be married to him. These days, Zarghuna was much too old and frail for most of the duties of a kahya, but she had been an immovable fixture at Grandmother's shoulder for as long as Kadou could remember—she was practically a great-aunt to him. There was no one in whom the dowager-sultan confided more.

"You wouldn't need to stay my kahya. You could take promotions." That would be all right—Evemer would still be near, even if he wasn't right at Kadou's fingertips. "But if you wanted to stay," Kadou said softly, "then you could."

"If it might be like that, I should tell you something." Evemer's thumb ran softly over his knuckles. "I don't expect that I'm going to stop wanting you."

Kadou's breath caught, his hand gripped Evemer's tighter. "Oh."

"That's all. I just wanted you to know."

Kadou couldn't speak for a moment. "Perhaps—perhaps if we get out of this alive, and—and after we get the annulment . . . If that's still true, you could tell me so again."

"When I'm merely your kahya again, and not Damat Evemer Hoşkadem Mahisti-eş Bey Effendi?" There was a strange note of bitterness in Evemer's voice. "Will you let me close to you then? Or will you decide that I'm too vulnerable to your power and that you can't risk hurting me?"

"I might try that, yes," Kadou whispered. "At least at first. Just remind me that I promised to listen to you, and . . . maybe give me a little time to adjust. Let me stew over it for a month or so and I'll lose my conviction." Like the moons, really, turning their faces away from the sun but always, always turning back.

Evemer's thumb rubbed over his knuckles again. "You may take all the time you want. I'll wait. You can take years if you need to. I'll still wait."

"It won't take years. It might not even take months. My convictions have failed me suddenly before," Kadou said with a shaky laugh. "Hold my hand again and do that with your thumb and it'll cut the wait a lot shorter."

"This?" Another rub over his knuckles.

Kadou breathed carefully. "Yes."

"Should I stop?"

"No," he murmured. "Please don't. No one would count holding hands as consummation, and I'll go crazy if we just sit here in the dark."

"We don't have to just sit here. We could drink some of Sylvia's wine."

"No doubt we're sitting amongst a very impressive collection," Kadou said. "But if I get drunk right now, I guarantee you I'm going to try to . . . make poor decisions." He didn't trust himself not to seize Evemer and kiss him again. It was already hard enough not to now, without his reason impaired.

Evemer cleared his throat awkwardly. "Yes, I see."

The chill of the room was beginning to set in. Kadou pressed up even closer against Evemer's side, tucking his face against Evemer's neck to steal more of his heat. *Perhaps we could just kiss,* a calculating part of his brain suggested. *Just kissing would be safe.*

But no, he couldn't have even that right now, though the denial made his entire soul ache wretchedly. That way lay peril—if you walked along the edge of a cliff, you risked falling off it. Better to stay well away from cliffs and not even approach the edge. "I don't suppose there's any hope of a secret passageway out of here?"

"I saw the room before the door closed. There are racks of bottles against that wall," Evemer used their joined hand to gesture, so Kadou could tell which direction he was indicating. "And that one. This is a blank wall. No other exits."

"*Damn,*" Kadou said, squeezing his eyes closed. "The waiting is what's really going to get to me."

"My lord?"

"It's been an emotional evening," Kadou said, trying to sound light. He didn't succeed. "I'm going to be paying for it later."

Evemer squeezed his hand. "Will it help if I look again for another passage?"

"Patting around in the dark? It's useless."

"But would it feel like we were doing something? Would it help take your mind off of it?"

Kiss him again, suggested that stupid voice in Kadou's head again. *That'd take your mind off it nicely.*

No, he said to it firmly. Aloud, he said, "I suppose it's worth a try."

He had a faint idea that Evemer would begin resenting him if Kadou took to a habit of kissing him whenever the whim seized him, but he had a firm enough handle on his thoughts, at least for the moment, to recognize that was merely a whisper from the fear-creature in his head. Easier to deny it now when it was just a whisper, before it spiraled into something far bigger, with far more sharp teeth.

Evemer got to his feet, pulling Kadou up with him. "You're starting to shake."

"Cold, I think, for the moment. Just cold."

※

It was easy enough to stay oriented, at least; the crack of light under the door was not enough to see anything by, but it was a clear flag for the front of the room and, roughly, the midpoint of it. They fumbled with the wine racks, checking that the walls behind them were solid stone, and stamped on the flagstones here and there.

"They'll come looking for us, won't they?" Kadou said, and then immediately: "Silly thing to say. Of course they will. But . . . I mean, will they be able to find us?"

"Yes," Evemer said firmly. "But we'll escape before that." He went to the door, testing it to see that it was locked.

Evemer could sense that Kadou, behind him, was thinking too

hard. He really ought to be kissed more often. It seemed like it had done him a world of good for those few exquisite minutes. Evemer was beginning to see where Tadek had been coming from with all that outrageous flirting—it was a distraction tactic.

There was nothing unusual about the door—it had locked with a key, and . . .

The door had swung inward.

Evemer felt around the edges of the door—aha. Triumph. Kadou was going to be so pleased with him. "My lord, did you want to get out of this room?" he said, modulating his tone to utter neutrality. "Did I understand that right?"

There was a beat of profoundly confused silence from Kadou. "Yes?"

Evemer pounded on the door. "Anyone out there?" he called. "Guards!"

No answer.

"What are you doing?"

"I didn't have a wedding cloak for you," Evemer said simply. Kadou choked, spluttered. "I ought to give you something to make up for it."

"Evemer, *what*?"

Evemer felt again for the hinges of the door. The hinges which were, brilliantly, on the inside. Well oiled, too, they felt.

"Don't be rude to the man who is about to get you out." He was grandstanding, wasn't he? *Showing off.* Well, and who could blame him? Kadou deserved to have someone show off for him.

"How am I being rude?" Kadou asked, his spluttering now colored with laughter.

"I have it on good authority that I'm styled *Prince* Evemer these days," he said crisply. Evemer, with a little effort, pried and twisted the pins out of the hinges. "Hold out your hands." He felt for Kadou's open palms in the dark and dropped the heavy pins into them. "These are the first part of your present."

Then he turned around, found handholds on the door (the knob on one side, a crossbar on the other), and lifted it clear of the frame, angling it so the deadbolt slipped free of its slot. Lamplight streamed into the room. The door was solid wood and enormously heavy, but Evemer only had to shift it a step to the side and lean it against the wall.

He turned around. Kadou was still standing there, framed in the light with the hinge pins in his palms, wide-eyed.

"Happy wedding," Evemer said. "I got you this door."

Kadou's look of astonishment shifted to one of pure hunger. Evemer was certain, for a moment, that Kadou was going to stride forward and seize him by the back of the neck, kiss him until he'd all but forgotten his own name. Again.

"What a thoughtful gift," Kadou said in a low voice. "Thank you, Your Highness. I don't have anything for you."

"You'll think of something."

Setting aside his whirl of outraged bewilderment at the outlandishness of being called *Your Highness*, Evemer grabbed one of the bottles of wine from the rack—it would make a good club for the first guard they ran across and a decent dagger for the rest, so long as it shattered correctly.

They slipped out into the hall, and a surge of pure delight so vivid that it felt alien swamped Evemer as he glimpsed, in the corner of his eye, Kadou pocketing the hinge pins.

Kadou had known the pins were iron before he knew what they were or what Evemer was doing. The unexpected weight of them hit his palms, and as his fingers closed over them, the signature of the metal bloomed into his senses—a memory of carrying something heavy, the creak of leather, the sight of a cloudy night sky, the smell of lightning . . .

Except then, all at once, the signature changed. The heavy weight in his arms became a heavy weight at his back, the pressure of being held against a wall; the creaking leather sound softened into someone sighing into a kiss; the smell of lightning became the taste of salt on skin. Only the glimpse of a sky full of stars remained, but even that changed: the clouds melted away and the stars glinted brighter.

The pins *were* iron, there was no doubt of that. This was not like the wrong, corrupted signatures of the counterfeit coins. He'd *felt* the change happen. This was simply what iron felt like now, a new imprint on his senses. That happened from time to time, he'd heard. Just as someone's palate changed over time, making delicious foods repulsive and vice versa, so too might their sense of a metal change. It was interesting but not, in and of itself, remarkable.

Remarkable, and ominous, was the fact that it had happened *now*. Remarkable was what it had changed to.

He was never again going to be able to touch iron without remembering this: The wine cellar. The door. Kissing Evemer. It was imprinted on him permanently, written into his fingertips. A memory to hold on to for comfort one day when he eventually lost this. Because he *would* lose it, he thought sadly. It couldn't last, except in the way that Grandmother had with her most loyal kahya. But that . . . that wasn't *this*. It wasn't the same.

None of that now. Kadou followed behind Evemer, likewise taking a bottle of wine to arm himself.

There was another locked door at the top of the stairs, and this one had the hinges on the outside. "Do you know how to pick a lock?" Kadou asked.

"No."

"We can't break it down."

"Not unless we want the whole house to come running," Evemer agreed darkly. "We could try picking it anyway. Do you have any hairpins?"

"You were the one who fixed my hair today. You'd know better than I would."

"But in your pockets?"

Kadou checked them—empty, except for the hinge pins. He felt the memory of the kiss again when his fingertips brushed against them and nearly shivered. "We could smash one of the bottles and hope that one of the shards is the right shape."

The doorknob rattled—they both stepped back, almost to the edge of the steps. A moment later, the lock clicked and the door swung open, revealing Tenzin, the satyota, with a half-eaten apple in her hand.

She stared at them for a long moment. "Huh." She finished chewing and swallowed. "I was just coming down here to help myself to the wine," she said conversationally. "How are you gentlemen? How is your day going?" She pointed sharply to Evemer. "I don't need any idiot's idea of sorcery to see you're about to step forward and clobber me over the head with that wine bottle. Consider that I can slam the door and scream before you get anywhere near me."

"My name is Kadou Mahisti, and I'm the prince of Araşt, second in line to the throne," Kadou said quickly. She was a satyota, after all—if he wanted to prove something to her, all he had to do was speak. "My sister, the sultan, would be very, very willing to pay a great deal of money to anyone who helped us out of this mess."

"Hmm," Tenzin said, taking another bite of apple. She pointed at Evemer with the hand holding the apple. "Do me a favor and say what he just said. His sister the sultan would . . ." she prompted. Evemer recited the rest of the words, and she nodded. "Right. Your mind works a little funny, did you know?" she said to Kadou. "What you say is true, but you don't quite believe it, not the way other people do. That's interesting. What if I don't care about money?"

"What do you care about?" Evemer asked. "You don't seem to be on good terms with your employers."

"He's an ass," she said. "She's also an ass."

"Hard to disagree," Kadou murmured. Evemer snorted.

"Do you want a new job?"

Tenzin took another thoughtful bite of the apple. "Make use of satyota very often, do you?"

"I don't, but the sultan of Araşt does, upon occasion." Evemer turned to Kadou. "Would she be likely to quibble over the bill?"

"Quibbling over the bill has been a noble and glorious tradition in my family since before we took over the country," Kadou said solemnly. "But my sister *would* pay fairly, probably more than Siranos and Sylvia do. You could trust her word, if she gave it."

"All true," Tenzin mused. "You believe *that*."

"Also . . . A question, madam," Kadou said. "What have they been paying you with?"

"Coins," she said, as if she thought he was an imbecile. "Money. Good Araşti gold."

"Oh."

"What?"

"Siranos has been making counterfeits," Evemer said.

"You're not Araşti, so you wouldn't have the touch-tasting . . ." Kadou added with a grimace. "So he might have risked paying you with them."

She peered at him for a moment and rummaged in her pockets. He held out his hand at the ready even before she withdrew a few coins and slapped them into his palm.

She watched him carefully. The silver yira bloomed bitter when he rubbed it, and he handed it back with another wince. "Fake."

"Well, shit," she said, looking down at it. Kadou slipped his hand into his pocket to touch the hinge pins again, clearing away the foul taste of the corrupted silver. She sighed, then made a thoughtful noise. "What's in that bottle?" she said, nodding to the one in Evemer's hand.

He looked at the label. "I can't read Vintish."

This whole situation was fast becoming absurd, but Kadou leaned close to see. "It's a port from Bevoie-Lency, bottled in the Vintish year 1562. Converted from their calendar, that's . . . forty years old, roughly."

Tenzin made another thoughtful noise and held out her hand. Evemer gave her the bottle. "Think it's any good? Well, I guess if that asshole has it in her wine cellar, it must be." She shook her head. "No, that's not true. Those two have things because they're expensive, not because they're good." She saluted them with the wine bottle. "Right. You mind waiting a couple minutes?"

"Are you . . . coming along?" Kadou asked cautiously.

"Might as well," she said with a shrug. "Got nothing better to do, and you told the truth about paying me."

"How do we know you're telling the truth about turning coat?" Evemer demanded.

She blinked innocently at him. "A satyota can't lie, didn't you know?"

"Bullshit."

"Worth a shot," she said, taking another bite of the apple. "Do I look like a person who is particularly interested in helping the fuckheads upstairs?"

They had to confess that she did not, and she left to get dressed.

"I don't like her," Evemer said.

"You don't like anybody when you first meet them. But Zeliha wanted to find a satyota in the city, and here one is, so . . ."

"I don't like it."

"Satyota are like kahyalar," Kadou said. "Just act with the assumption that her first loyalty is to Inacha and her second is to money, and we'll be fine."

She returned only few minutes later, dressed in a comfortable linen tunic, trousers, and quilted overcoat, as well as beautifully made turn-toe boots in the style of Map Sut, embroidered around the tops with decorative stitching and silver beads. She also held the now-open wine bottle in one hand and was sipping leisurely from it.

Tenzin took absolutely no agency in the proceedings, ambling after them as they slunk carefully out onto the main floor of the house. She did not offer comments or suggestions on how to get out, even when they found that there was a guard standing at the front door and had to backtrack. She only drank her wine from the bottle and watched them curiously, as if mere observation were her only driving motive.

A very careful, very quiet search through the rest of the house turned up an unlocked study with several windows overlooking the street—only a ten-foot drop or so. They were in the middle of a whispered argument about whether it was safer for Evemer to jump out first or second when there was a sudden distant crash, a cry, and then the sound of shouting and thundering feet. They scrambled out—Kadou later would have no recollection of which of them had actually jumped first.

Tenzin, of course, made them catch her wine bottle before she followed.

CHAPTER THIRTEEN

❧

They didn't stop running until they were dozens of streets away, solidly in the middle of a completely different district of the city. Evemer's legs and lungs were burning, his wounded shoulder throbbing dully and his wrenched one aching—he probably shouldn't have picked up both Kadou *and* a solid oak door.

Even on any other day, it wouldn't have been a late enough hour for the streets to be completely deserted, but tonight there was an extra scattering of people out and about, mostly occupied with hanging decorations in preparation for the following week's Midsummer festival: bright swags of yellow-and-white tassels above the doors, long chains of folded paper flowers spanning the street from window to window, and trailing ribbons of silk or tissue covered in poems and blessings in silver and gold calligraphy that had already been pinned beside a few doors. These last, as the day of the festival drew nearer, would appear nailed or pasted to any and every available surface until the slightest breeze would make the streets appear as though they were covered in gently fluttering swarms of sparkling butterflies.

"Where," Evemer wheezed. He stopped, leaned on his knees, gasped for breath. "Where, my lord? Palace? House?"

The few times Kadou had joined Evemer and the commander for sword drills in the gardens, he'd proven his endurance. Evemer might win in contests of strength, and Tadek in cunning and speed, and Melek in dexterity, but when the game was simply to run drills until they dropped, Kadou was always the last one standing.

Yet even he was flushed and sweating and heaving for breath, his hair sticking to his face and neck.

Tenzin, too, was wheezing and red-faced—and still carrying her half-full wine bottle.

Kadou put his hands on his hips and coughed. "House? Safe there. Kahyalar. Send letters to—gods, to everyone. Tell Zeliha. Shut down the harbor."

"Find Melek," Evemer said.

"Find Melek, yes."

"Who's Melek?" Tenzin asked.

Coughing for breath again, Kadou managed to get out "Important."

The people on the street were hesitating in their work, looking toward them, whispering to each other. Evemer silently groaned. Why had the gods not sent him kinder trials than to go about the city with an appallingly distinctive Mahisti? Even when he was splotchy and pouring with sweat, he was heart-wrenchingly beautiful.

Evemer wearily stood. "People are staring."

"Nothing to be done about it," Kadou said, and gestured them onward.

It was gone midnight by the time they made it back to Mama's house. They startled the kahya standing watch on the far perimeter, but as soon as çe recognized them, çe stood abruptly. "Oh, thank the *gods,* we thought you'd been kidnapped!"

"We *were,*" Evemer said, striding past çem.

There were still lamps on inside the house, and when they entered, they found Tadek and Mama sitting at the kitchen table together, drinking coffee in grim silence.

"Where the fuck have you been?" Tadek howled, standing.

Mama, seeing them, let out a huge sigh of relief and flicked a hand in a gesture of gratitude toward the statues of the gods on the mantelpiece.

As Kadou and Evemer stumbled in and flung themselves into the first chairs they could seize, Tadek shouted, "You scold *us* for fouling up a reconnaissance mission? And then you have the gall to go and *vanish*? And who is *this*?" he added, gesturing at Tenzin, who had already helped herself to the water bucket and was splashing her face.

Mama said, "Tadek, hush, the baby—"

It was too late. Eyne, cuddled in a cozy nest of fabric in a basket, had woken and began to cry.

Evemer took an instinctive step toward her, but Mama was faster—she glared at Tadek, gathered up Eyne, and held her close against her neck and shoulder as she stomped up the stairs.

"Name's Tenzin," Tenzin said, making herself comfortable in another chair. She held out the wine bottle to Tadek. "Do you want the rest of this? I'm done with it."

"Hello, Tadek," Kadou groaned, folding his arms on the table and dropping his head onto them. "Your intelligence network must be very good, if you're mad enough to be shouting at us."

"It damn well is! We got a message from Melek not even an *hour* ago, saying you'd been taken!" Tadek said, barely lowering his voice as he took Tenzin's wine bottle and poured what was left into a cup. "Çe couldn't say when, or by whom, or whether your lives were in danger, or where you'd gone, so here we've been, gnawing our fingernails to the quick and contemplating the various creative ways you might have *died*. But here you are, dancing through the front door, and where the hell is Melek?"

"We don't know," Evemer said. He pushed himself back to his feet, got cups of water for himself and Kadou, and sat again heavily, exhausted down to his core. "Where's Eozena?"

"She was feverish," Tadek said, his jaw tight. "We moved her up to Durdona's room. More comfortable."

Kadou raised his head from his arms and said dully, "I need paper, ink, and Zeliha's seal."

Evemer pushed Kadou's cup of water a little closer to him, encouraging. To Tadek, he said, "In that drawer to your left."

Tadek fetched the writing things from the drawer and the royal seal from around his own neck—*Little heretic,* Evemer thought darkly—and slapped them onto the table in front of Kadou. "Melek's message said çe was going after you. Çe hasn't been back."

"Start the sealing wax, please," Kadou said, setting the cup of water aside and pulling the paper closer.

Tadek grumbled and obeyed, kneeling at the hearth to light a candle for melting the wax. Tenzin, in the chair by the fire, watched him curiously for a moment and then said, turning back to the table, "I'll want to talk about my pay at some point, Highness."

"Pay?" Tadek looked at her as he rose and brought the candle back to Kadou. "What is he paying you for?"

"Services," she answered with an infuriating smile.

"She's a satyota," Evemer said. Gods, why in the world had he thought it was a good idea to bring someone like Tenzin anywhere near Tadek?

"Ruining my fun, Highness," she tsked, looking directly at Evemer.

Evemer's heart stopped, and Kadou fumbled the inkpot, spilling a smear across one edge of the paper.

Unconcerned, Tenzin continued, "Is that a hobby, ruining people's fun? You look the sort."

"Don't—don't call me that," Evemer said, strangled. "There's no need."

"Eh?" said Tadek, narrowing his eyes.

Tenzin gave Evemer a puzzled look. "You *don't* want me to call you Highness? You Araşti always seem so uptight about titles."

"Quiet, please!" Kadou said. "I'm very busy writing these orders and I need complete silence!"

Dutifully, complete silence fell.

Evemer bit his tongue and watched Tadek mentally run through the last few moments of conversation. Giving him time to think had been a mistake.

The only sound was the frantic scratch of Kadou's pen nib against the paper. At last, he signed with a flourish, poured a puddle of the melted wax, and set Zeliha's seal into it to cool.

Immediately, Tadek said, "So I have questions."

"Sit down," Evemer snapped, standing sharply, grabbing Tadek by his sleeve, and dragging him into a chair. Tadek hissed with pain as his bad leg took his weight.

Evemer leaned on the arms of the chair and got down into Tadek's face. Tadek gazed back, unintimidated—even curious.

"You have questions," Evemer growled. "Do not ask them. Do not speak them aloud, do not even think them. There is a situation, and it will be handled without your input."

"Right," Tadek said slowly, putting his head to one side. "Now I have questions *and* theories."

Dammit. Dammit, Evemer should just not talk.

"Theory number one," Tadek said thoughtfully, "is that when Their Majesties' boat was shipwrecked fifteen years ago, with all those nobles and all those heirs, the ugly tangle of inheritance claims somehow ended up dumping a title on you. But no, that doesn't make sense, you wouldn't be ranked high enough to be called—Well. Actually, now that I think about it—"

"I'm not taking part in this conversation," Kadou said with a brightness that was only masking panic. "Looks like you've got this under control, Evemer." He pulled the seal off the cooled wax and went to the door, presumably to hand the letter off to a kahya.

Tadek was looking ever more thoughtful. "I *guess* a case could be made for someone to call you Highness if you were some long-lost Mahisti by-blow. Or a foreigner, of course."

"Tadek. No theories."

"Are you secretly a prince, Evemer?" Tadek asked, his eyes glittering.

"*No questions.*"

"Oh, come on, give me just this one."

"I am not secretly a prince!" Evemer snarled. "No questions!"

Tenzin cleared her throat. "A lie."

Tadek's face lit up. He leaned around Evemer to look at her, gleeful. Evemer glared fiercely. Tadek ignored him and said, "What did you say your name was?"

"Tenzin."

"Hello, Tenzin. My name is Tadek, and I think you're an unmitigated delight. Do you know why he's a secret prince?"

"Said earlier that he's one," she said promptly. "That's all I've got, and I don't really care."

Kadou came back inside. "Oh, dear. Is this still happening? Tadek, please make this not be happening, I have to write a message so Zeliha knows I'm not dead, and then I have to figure out where Melek is so çe knows I'm not dead too. Please have this not happen."

Tadek tried to push Evemer back, out of his space. Evemer made himself an immovable wall. "Did *you* know about this, Highness?" Tadek said, squirming in vain.

Kadou said, slowly, "No?"

"Lie," Tenzin said.

"You're not getting paid for this!" Kadou cried. "You know that, don't you?"

"I'm getting paid as we speak," she said with a grin, slouching down into her chair and crossing her arms. "I'm getting paid in *chaos*."

"An unmitigated delight," Tadek said again, rapturously. "Highness—either Highness—you *must* tell me everything."

Evemer turned his glare on Tenzin. "Another word and you're dismissed."

"Yes," Kadou said. "Yes, we won't take you back to Her Majesty."

She considered this for a moment, shrugged, and nodded. Kadou relaxed and sat down at the table to write again.

"Not a word," Evemer hissed to Tadek. "I will drown you with my own hands."

"But I want to *know*," Tadek whispered back, imploring. "Are you the real Kadou, switched at birth with an impostor in Vinte?"

"*What?*"

"Tadek," Kadou said warningly. "You watch too many plays."

"Are you a forgotten Mahisti scion, the product of a passionate forbidden tryst, returning to make a claim on the throne?"

"Of course not!" Evemer said, appalled.

"Oh, good. Are you—"

"Evemer," Kadou said. "Do whatever you need to do."

"My lord," Evemer said briskly, and he hauled Tadek over his shoulder and out the front door to the street corner—which *hurt*, but that was the price of justice.

The whole way, Tadek chattered at an astonishing pace. "Are

you Zeliha's secret twin? Is Kadou just a decoy to protect you, the real prince, from assassination? Was a witch's curse involved at any point? Did you spend twenty years wandering in the wilderness because the man you thought was your body-father said that—" The rest was lost to gurgles as Evemer pinned him below the spout of the water pump on the corner and hauled on the lever.

"Are you done?" Evemer said, when Tadek had been thoroughly doused.

Tadek spluttered and coughed. "Confidence scheme involving body doubles?"

Evemer gave him another torrent of water.

"I can't think of any more," Tadek said when Evemer next let him breathe. He pushed Evemer's hand off his chest and sat up, wiping his hair out of his eyes. "It's got to be something with the shipwreck and the inheritance claims—" He rolled away as Evemer tried to seize him again. "That's the only plausible one. Hey, is your shoulder bleeding?"

"Tore my stitches," Evemer said, sitting back on his heels. He was damp all down his chest, and the knees of his trousers were soaked. But it seemed to have shut Tadek up, so . . . Worth it, all told.

"What, hauling me around like a sack of grain? Or before?"

"Before. When we were captured."

"Fought like a bull, did you?" Tadek shook the wet hair out of his face again as Evemer stood. "All right. Help me back inside and we'll take care of that." He held out his hand and gave Evemer an expectant look.

"No more questions," Evemer said firmly. "No more theories."

"Yes, Your Highness." Evemer, having taken his hand and pulled him partially up, let him drop again into the slowly draining puddle on the cobblestones and gave the handle of the water pump another half push. "Fine, fine," Tadek yelled, scrambling out of the way. "I get it, you're not ready to reveal your secret identity!"

"Are you not yet drowned?" But he let Tadek go and pulled him back to his feet. He even let Tadek lean on his shoulder as they went back inside.

Kadou was just lifting the seal from his second letter as they came back in. "How'd it go?"

"I am a wet and wretched thing, pity me," Tadek said. He limped to the hearth, peeled off his kaftan, and hung it over the back of a chair in front of the fire.

"He's not going to ask any more questions, Highness," Evemer said.

"Good."

"Kadou, I know we're just friends now," Tadek said, "but you should know that you are *very* pretty when you're being merciless. You should do it more often, suits you."

Evemer squashed the impulse to drag the little twit back outside for another go under the pump.

Kadou ignored Tadek and held out the letter. "Take this out to one of the kahyalar and tell them to *fly* to the palace. We'll follow right away."

As he took the letter, Evemer could see the strain of exhaustion in Kadou's eyes. "We could wait until morning. Or wait for them to send horses down."

"Zeliha needs the satyota to verify the loyalties of the kahyalar. And we need the kahyalar to arrest Siranos and Sylvia, and find Melek." Kadou closed his eyes, clearly worn to the bone. "Half an hour to catch my breath, and then we'll go."

The perimeter guard was a little thin, with one of them already sent to carry the message down to the harbor, so Evemer went down into the cellar, where three more were asleep on pallets. By the time he got one of them out of bed, into clothes and shoes, and out the door, Kadou had fallen asleep at the kitchen table, his head pillowed on his arms. Tadek, half-dressed and still dripping all over the floor, was delicately draping a blanket over him. Tenzin was dozing too, curled up in the opposite corner of the room on some of the floor pillows.

"We're both on the same page about this, right?" Tadek whispered. "We're waiting an hour to wake him, not half an hour?"

That . . . was too good of an idea to pass up. "Yes," Evemer said.

"Coffee?"

"Yes."

Tadek made him coffee—in Evemer's own home, which was strange and uncomfortable, but then Tadek wasn't the one who had brushed up against death that night. As it was brewing, Tadek got him to take down one side of his bloodied kaftan, smeared ointment on the torn wound, and bandaged him up neatly.

"So," Tadek said, when he had poured the coffee. He took a seat across from Evemer, folding his hands on the table. "Will I get dragged back out to the water pump if I ask about tonight's escapades?"

"What do you want?"

"Nothing important. A bedtime story, at most."

"We went to the incense lounge," Evemer said. "We changed our plans. We were captured." And then, because he was tired or because it was the quiet hour of the night when tongues sometimes moved unbidden, he added: "His Highness saved my life."

Tadek's expression softened, cleared, became very fond. "Oh. Yes. He does that."

"Again," Evemer said. "Twice now."

"What happened?"

Evemer mentally shook himself. No details, or else Tadek would start pulling it all out of him one thread at a time. "I don't want to talk about tonight."

"All right," Tadek said easily.

They sat in silence while Evemer drank his coffee. They heard the night watch go past, distantly calling the second hour past midnight.

"You can admit it," Tadek said in a much different voice. Quieter, more serious. "Who am I going to tell?"

"Admit what?"

"You keep looking at him. You're always looking at him. Even when Her Majesty had you at her feet." Tadek was studying the grain of the table's wood, tracing the whorl of a knot with one fingertip as if it occupied his whole attention. "I see things."

Twelve hours ago, Evemer absolutely would have denied it. But he'd already admitted it to Kadou, kissed it into his mouth, pressed it into his hands, whispered it into the dark. *I can't help it,* he might say. *Of all people, you should know that feeling. Look at him. How could anyone help it?* But he wasn't going to be friends with the likes of Tadek.

"Do you have a point to make?"

"No. Just . . . questions and theories. Except I'm not allowed those," Tadek added with a half smile. "And the occasional unexpected, uncomfortable, unwelcome emotion here and there, but no need for either of us to heed those. Do you believe in the gods?"

An odd sort of non sequitur, but perhaps Tadek was going somewhere with it. "Yes," Evemer said slowly.

"You believe there's a woman in the sky who has a galaxy for a navel and who birthed the world and put a thousand blessings into it, and that she has a brother below the ground, who sends us trials, opportunities to test our strength of character? Literal beings?"

Evemer did not particularly care for this flavor of philosophizing. What did it matter? The world was for living in, and the gods were elsewhere, and that was that. "Do you believe that?"

"Oh, goodness, no. I hardly even believe in the abstract forms of them, honeybee. Never been one for temples or prayers to someone whose merciful intercession, if it were ever granted, would still be totally unverifiable and almost totally undetectable." He paused, half smiled again. "But every now and then a trial comes to me, and it's so perfectly crafted to make me stretch to the very limits of myself, and . . . You know, it's just enough make me pause and wonder, from time to time. Maybe there is at least Usmim, and maybe he's genuinely testing me. Or maybe he's just fucking with me. Hard to say. The two can be so close, you know."

"Have you come across one of those trials recently?"

"Oh, yes," Tadek whispered, still tracing the knot in the wood of the table, still half smiling as if there were some amusing secret joke that he had with himself that he certainly wasn't going to share with Evemer. "Very much yes. Like many trials, this one's about who I am, and who I want to be, and acceptance, and kindness, and several other nonsense things about myself that I've been ignoring for far too long."

Totally incomprehensible, of course, because Tadek could only speak in riddles or else be far, far too forthright for comfort. Evemer nodded anyway.

"I think," Tadek continued thoughtfully, "that when we've sorted out everything and I've got a day off, I'll go out and get myself really *spectacularly* laid. I'm thinking at least three other people. At *least*."

Evemer silently put down his coffee cup, put his elbows on the table, and put his face in his hands.

"Cures what ails you, you know," Tadek went on. "You might try it, if—if a trial springs itself upon you. If you suddenly find yourself with . . . unwelcome, uncomfortable feelings and you want to get rid of them."

"I'm in the middle of a trial as we speak, and I am very much uncomfortable," Evemer growled, and Tadek laughed loud enough that Kadou jerked awake.

"How long was I asleep?" he asked blearily.

"Only enough time for Evemer to have a cup of coffee," Tadek said airily. "Would you like one?"

Kadou shook his head and wobbled to his feet. "Got to go to the palace. Bring the satyota to Zeliha. Important." He blinked at them owlishly. "I sent the messages?"

"Yes," Evemer said, getting up too. "One to the harbor, one to the palace."

"Oh. Good." He steadied himself against the table. "Where's the satyota?" The last word was broken on a yawn.

Evemer went to wake Tenzin. She was not pleased about it. "Leave me be," she muttered. "I don't work before the tenth hour of the morning."

Kadou looked even more exhausted at this, and he wavered on his feet again.

"Highness," Tadek said. "Go to bed."

"I can't."

"You're dead on your feet. Evemer would be too, if I hadn't poured coffee into him. If she won't work until morning, then there's nothing else you can do tonight. Go to bed."

"I want to go *home*."

"Tomorrow morning," Tadek said firmly. "You'll be fresh and rested, and you can sweep up to the Copper Gate in high style and present Tenzin to Her Majesty in front of everyone. There's *nothing else to do tonight*."

Kadou's face was setting in a stubborn expression that Evemer recognized from those early days when Kadou had led them through a tour of the capital's seediest public houses. Evemer went to him, touched his sleeve. "My lord. Tadek is offering knowledge and counsel. Time to listen."

"Gods-damned kahyalar," Kadou muttered, but he headed toward the stairs. "Don't remember signing up to be hounded by gods-damned kahyalar at every turn." He stopped at the first step, looked down at it, and heaved a truly heartfelt sigh. "Stairs," he mumbled. "Who thought those were a good idea? Probably another gods-damned kahya, that's who."

Evemer bit back a laugh, lit a candle from one of the lamps, and went to his lord. He nudged Kadou in the center of his back. "Go on."

"*Stairs*, Evemer."

"Go, or I'll pick you up again and injure myself."

Kadou sighed again and took the steps slowly, one by one, as if they were each Usmim's most profound trial.

Upstairs, he toppled face-first into bed without bothering to loosen his clothes. Evemer wedged the candle in a holder and pulled off Kadou's boots for him, and then his own, and switched out his bloodied kaftan for a clean underlayer.

"Sleeping here?" Kadou mumbled, his face half-buried in the blankets.

"Not sleeping. But here, yes."

Kadou frowned and lifted his head. "Lie down. Go to sleep. If I have to, you have to. That's an *order*."

A twisting curl of heat ran through his core. "Yes, my lord," Evemer said.

"And—and don't be all the way across the room. Be right here. Near me. Please."

Evemer dragged the pallet of cushions and blankets right to the edge of the low bed, as near as he could be, and lay flat on his back.

"I'd . . . I'd invite you to share with me," Kadou whispered. "But I worry that it would make you uncomfortable. More than sleeping on the floor would." He peeped over the edge of the bed at Evemer, his eyes amazingly dark in the candlelight and his brow twisted with worry.

"You need your rest." The very *idea* of sleeping next to Kadou intentionally was wildly inappropriate and dangerous. And so, so tempting. What had happened to his discipline? It used to be trivially easy to deny himself desire—now it was all but impossible. "I couldn't . . . impose." He thought of Kadou's hair spread out across the pillow like it had been in the heated pool at the bathhouse, thought of the mountain spirits that his mother had warned him would take his heart and replace it with a burning ember. His mouth was dry.

"It's not an imposition," Kadou said quietly. He was sounding more awake with every passing moment. Kadou's hair was tumbling down his shoulders, and his eyes were so *dark* in the candlelight, unearthly.

Just looking at him like this made Evemer ache all through his chest. It was as if he were being pulled forward by his soul, like a hungry man might be pulled forward by his stomach to a table laden with food.

"I'm trying to take care of you," Kadou said—he must have seen or sensed Evemer wavering. "Like how my ancestors ate from wooden plates and gave their kahyalar ones of silver and gold."

"If we share, it won't count, will it?"

"Count?"

Evemer felt bare and raw and hot under Kadou's eyes. He rasped, "Annulment versus divorce. No one would count that."

"Oh. No, I don't see how it could."

Evemer held his eyes for another long moment and sat up slowly. Kadou's face brightened with pleasure and he shifted over to make room—Evemer moved gingerly onto the edge of the bed.

Maybe Kadou was a mountain spirit after all.

The straw tick crackled softly beneath them as they arranged themselves. The bed was just wide enough that they had a very proper foot or so of space between them, though Kadou was crammed against the wall and Evemer nearly falling off the edge. Evemer blew the candle out and carefully lowered himself into the pillows.

The darkness, the warmth, the closeness—it was all immediately, viscerally, compellingly familiar. Evemer gripped two fistfuls of the pillow to keep himself from reaching out and swallowed down the reflexive clench of desire in his stomach.

He heard Kadou take a breath several moments before he actually began speaking. "I don't want this to be unpleasant for you. You said you—you wouldn't stop wanting me, and I would be terribly upset with myself if that became a burden. I don't want it to become difficult for you to serve me."

"It isn't," Evemer said firmly. "It could never be."

He felt Kadou's fingertips just brush the side of his hand. It made all the hairs on Evemer's arm stand up in goose pimples, made his grip on the pillow instinctively loosen. "I've been wishing I was more like you," Kadou said. "Steady. Calm. You always know what to do."

Evemer did not feel like any of those things were currently true. It felt like he had been set off-balance from the very moment he set eyes on Kadou, and even after weeks it had only become worse instead of better. He was not calm, and he had no idea what to do now.

So he turned his hand up, under Kadou's touch, so that his fingertips fell on Evemer's palm. He curled his fingers, brushing them against Kadou's inner wrist, and he felt Kadou shiver all those miles and miles across the bed—he'd shivered when Evemer kissed him, too.

For several long minutes, their hands were tangled so loosely that Evemer was nearly in physical pain. It was unbearable, agonizing—neither of them gripping, neither of them holding or pulling, just . . . there.

Evemer curled just one finger tighter, just enough to make it a real touch, substantial. He heard Kadou breathe again, felt Kadou's thumb slide over his skin, followed by his fingertips tracing the lines of Evemer's palm. It felt like the first roses of spring, like dawn after a long, starless night.

It was so *much,* and it was not at all what Evemer had ever once pictured for his life.

"Do you want to stop?" Kadou whispered. His gentle strokes stilled on Evemer's inner wrist.

Evemer, dying of barely leashed desire, whispered, "No."

The strokes resumed, brushing blindly over the lines in his palm and wrist, the swell of his thumb, the length of each finger. It sent chills up Evemer's arm and down the length of his spine. All he could do was keep his hand very, very still, and breathe carefully, and feel. His heart was a burning ember, but so too was the rest of him, filled up with glimmering soft heat, a low yet urgent pulse of want. How was it possible for him to feel so unraveled, so *destroyed,* just from a few touches to his hand?

It was too much—he was going to go mad if he had to endure it an instant longer. Evemer caught Kadou's fingers in his own and squeezed them, felt his heart nearly beat out of his chest when Kadou squeezed back.

"I've never wanted anyone so badly before," he said, because the truth of it filled up his mouth and throat until there wasn't anything he could do with it but say it, impulsive.

Kadou gripped his hand tight, and Evemer could feel—he didn't know if it was his own heartbeat or Kadou's or both, but *someone's* heart was racing and he could feel the insistent hummingbird beat between their joined hands.

"We could—if we were careful—" Kadou said. He sounded breathless. Evemer heard him swallow, felt his hand tremble and grip tighter. "If you wanted. You could do something about it."

Evemer couldn't speak for a moment. He wet his lips and whispered, "I could."

Kadou's hand trembled again. "Do you think you might?"

"It's quickly becoming a very real possibility," Evemer said, and he'd meant it seriously but Kadou turned his head and muffled his laugh in the mattress, and . . . There, that.

That.

That laugh tipped Evemer over, blew a gust of wind over the shimmering embers of Evemer's heart, and suddenly the whole of him was engulfed in a conflagration. There was no more resistance left in him—he might as well have stopped the moons in their orbit.

He tugged at Kadou's hand to get his attention. When Kadou lifted his beautiful face, still huffing little breathless hiccups of laughter, Evemer reached out with his other hand and just touched his lord's cheek, stroked the backs of his fingers against his jaw.

Kadou's breath caught, and he went quiet and still. Evemer shifted a little closer, partway across the inches (miles) of bed between them. He hadn't let go of Kadou's hand. He found a lock of Kadou's hair, soft and loose-curling, and twisted it around his finger.

He'd wanted people before. He *had* been a teenager once. But it was always a vague, desultory kind of inclination, and there had always been something more important. That girl he'd kissed when he was sixteen was the only one who had ever noticed that she'd turned his head.

But this. *This.* Kadou only had to laugh and Evemer was hopelessly enraptured, entangled.

Kadou squirmed a little closer, impatient, close enough for Evemer to feel the warmth radiating off him like a tiny sun. His free hand touched Evemer's where it lay against his jaw.

Alight with desire, Evemer succumbed to gravity.

Kissing Kadou was, he noticed with a jolt, beginning to be

familiar—and that was *strange,* alarming, terrifying. Perfect. Kadou's mouth, soft and warm, opened sweetly with a small noise and his grip on Evemer's hand tightened nearly to the point of pain. Icy heat crackled and sparkled down Evemer's spine.

"Come here," Kadou murmured into his mouth. "Oh, come here," and so Evemer wound his arm around Kadou's waist and pulled himself closer, pulled Kadou closer. He felt Kadou's fingers curling around the back of his neck, tracing his hairline until he shivered.

"Careful," Evemer whispered. He pulled Kadou's hand to him, clutching it to his heart.

"Yes. Yes, careful. Just this."

It was nothing like the kiss in the wine cellar—so much warmer, so much sweeter and slower. It was all piercingly beautiful, and most beautiful of all was the fact that Kadou was right here, safe and whole and lying all disarrayed in Evemer's bed, sighing and melting in his arms.

Far, far too soon, Evemer broke the kiss, every nerve in his body singing like the plucked string of a musical instrument. "We should stop," he said, wanting to do anything but that. He wanted to kiss Kadou for another hour or three. He wanted to . . . touch him properly. To push Kadou's clothes off his shoulders and taste the silk-smooth skin of his throat and shoulder, to trace slow fingertips down the tender dip of his spine. Unable to force himself to pull away yet, Evemer rested his forehead against Kadou's and whispered, "I was ordered to lie down and sleep."

"Who told you that?" Kadou demanded, sounding woozy, almost drunk. *Evemer* had done that. Just with kissing, he'd made Kadou sound like that—it felt like mastering a new verse of sword-forms, but a thousand, thousand times better. "Who was the idiot who told you that? I'm going to have words with him. Don't you have the privilege of disobedience so you can ignore things like that?"

Evemer snorted, kissed him once more, and then forced himself to pull away, rolling onto his back. It was, without a doubt, the single most difficult thing he had ever done in his life. "Good-night, my lord." A moment later, he felt Kadou's hand sneak back into his, lacing their fingers together. Evemer didn't sleep for a long time.

CHAPTER FOURTEEN

Kadou woke again at dawn, his head aching from insufficient sleep and his nerves already jangling—he shouldn't have let them talk him into going to bed. He should have insisted, should have dragged Tenzin up to the palace immediately.

He also probably shouldn't have asked Evemer to share the bed, though a quiet whisper in the back of his mind disagreed.

Kadou had to gingerly climb over him to get out of bed and go downstairs.

The morning light was grey, the air cool and soft. Tadek still sat at the kitchen table, rolling a cup between his hands and gazing dully at the front door. "Melek didn't come back," he said, in lieu of any other greeting. "I waited up for çem, but . . ."

Kadou's jangling nerves sharpened into a thousand tiny shards of glass. He'd abandoned one of his kahyalar to fend for çemself just so that he could get a few hours of sleep. He gritted his teeth and tried to push the thought away—they wouldn't have any hope of finding Melek without a search party, and they couldn't make up a search party until they took Tenzin up to the palace . . . His head ached, his nerves already scoured raw. What a lovely day this was going to be. "Anything from Zeliha?"

"About an hour after you went to bed. Instructions were to stay here until dawn. Horses and kahyalar who have been confirmed loyal will be waiting for you at the bottom of the Palace Road," Tadek said. "She couldn't send them here without drawing attention, and we still have to hide the princess until it's over. You'll have to go on foot. How did you know Evemer was secretly a Highness?"

"Magic. Is there coffee?"

※

The enormous arch of the Copper Gate loomed above them as they turned the last switchback of the Palace Road—not at all in high style as Tadek had claimed the night before. Kadou was exhausted, unwashed, in days-old clothes, and dying for at least two more cups of coffee.

They rode through the huge expanse of the Copper Court, past crowds of servants, cadets, and kahyalar. The ones who had been sent to guard and escort them were arranged in a ring around them, weapons drawn, looking at their fellows in the crowds with wary, suspicious eyes.

Kadou could never remember the Copper Court being this silent, or the general air so tense and tightly wound. The Silver Court, when they passed into it, was even more so—dead silent, almost deserted. It set Kadou's teeth on edge. Everything was wrong, and there were no problems that he could touch. All he could do was keep leading Tenzin onward.

Zeliha met them at the Gold Gate, accompanied by a handful of ministers and a double handful of kahyalar. She strode up and flung her arms around Kadou as he slid off his horse.

Surprised, he hugged her back. "I brought you a satyota," he said, muffled into her hair, and pulled back to introduce them.

Tenzin nodded politely, as if Zeliha were a new acquaintance she'd met on the street. "I hear you've got something for me to do. Where would you like me to start, Your Majesty?" Tenzin said.

"Find out how many traitors I have in my kahyalar corps," Zeliha said. "Sift out the corrupt, anyone who has taken bribes, and anyone who can't truthfully say they're loyal to the crown. Minister Selim, I'll leave this to you. The first priority is Siranos and his sister." She looked to Kadou. "Do you have anything?"

"I can confirm they were working together with Azuta Mela-chrinos. I know where we were held captive. I don't know if Sira-nos is still there. And—and Lieutenant Melek Murad went missing sometime last night. Can we—if there are enough people—"

"Could Siranos have captured çem too? Did çe track you?"

"Maybe? It's . . . possible."

Zeliha nodded firmly. "Is that enough to start with?" she asked Selim, who bowed and assented. She turned back to Tenzin. "Sec-ond priority is filling out the staff and guards of the Gold Court so that I can send for my daughter and Commander Eozena. Oh—and as for the issue of payment, rest assured that you will be gener-ously compensated."

Tenzin smiled. "True," she said. "And I appreciate you saying so."

"How long will it take to get one or two dozen together?"

"If each one takes me, oh, five minutes apiece, perhaps an hour and a half. That should be enough for a surface-deep check, though if you want me to really dig into them it'll take longer—an hour or so each."

"Quick will be fine for now, especially for the cadets and the fringe-guard. The core-guard and ministers might require a deeper look."

Tenzin gave her a lazy salute. "Show me who I'm interrogat-ing, then," she said to Selim, who bowed again to Zeliha and led Tenzin away.

Zeliha turned to Kadou. "You've got about an hour and a half. Go clean up and get dressed, you look like—"

"A horsemonger?"

"Like you've been borrowing clothes from a weaver's son who's got several inches and at least sixty pounds on you," she said, plucking at his sleeve—the top of the armscye's seam fell baggy a hand's width below the point of his shoulder, and he'd had to turn back the cuffs. "Go make yourself look like a prince again. You'll have work to do." She paused. "Oh. I had your quarters moved. I hope you don't mind, but I thought you might want a clean slate after what happened the other night. Also there are . . . stains. We're going to have to have that room refloored."

"I don't mind," he said, shuddering. "And you're probably right. Where am I now?"

"Cypress Cliff, but you can move again if you don't like it."

He suppressed a groan. The Cypress Cliff house was all the way at the other end of the Gold Court, the hard end of nowhere. It'd be a trek to get anywhere in the palace from there. "Shoving me in the back corner, are you?" he said, trying to keep his voice light.

"Only so that I can put as much space as possible between you and anyone who's trying to hurt you," she said, and added sarcastically, "Forgive me for being protective. Hurry along."

The Cypress Cliff residence was built into the outer wall of the palace itself, on the edge of an irregular outcropping of the plateau overhanging a sheer vertical drop. The tower's curved outer wall faced toward the city so that each floor's wide windows caught a splendid panoramic view, caught every summer breeze and bit of light . . . and caught every howling winter tempest.

Kadou had the whole thing to himself—three floors, consisting of one enormous room each, with soaring ceilings spanned by huge wooden beams, thick carpets (though these were several decades out of fashion), and sturdy doors that would not have been out of place in a fortress. On the top floor, which had been arranged as his bedroom, a balcony wrapped around the outer wall of the structure.

He'd have to have heavy curtains installed if he wanted to be able to sleep past dawn—it was east-facing, with nothing blocking a view of the horizon, and he could already imagine the way the rising sun would glare into the room every morning. Besides that, it felt very . . . exposed, a sensation that was only increased when a few cadets arrived with buckets of lukewarm water and he was obliged to wash in front of all those expansive windows.

Evemer, who had pointedly left the room for that part, came back in to dress him—he'd spent the time productively, it seemed, and had found where Kadou's clothes had been stashed, though he grumbled about how they had been organized. He himself had changed into his core-guard uniform, and the sight of him in good Mahisti cobalt made Kadou's knees nearly give out, made his palms ache with how much he wanted to run them across the uniform's smoothly tailored shoulders and down Evemer's back, how he wanted to brush his fingertips over the bright buttons down his front, mother-of-pearl in a setting of pale electrum.

But there were other people only a room away, and his nerves, still sharp and raw with that feeling of being exposed to the whole world, wouldn't allow him to risk reaching out.

✳

Evemer had never been more relieved: There were enough proven kahyalar around that at last he could relax his vigilance. Kadou looked tense on the ride down to Sylvia's manor, but he was splendid again in shimmering silk brocade, which Evemer had chosen exclusively because the sun was bright and he wanted to see Kadou catching the light like a jewel as they rode.

He hung back with Kadou as the kahyalar knocked on the door of the manor, then banged on it. In the end, they had to climb up and break a window to get inside—the house was completely deserted.

"There are cellars," Kadou said. His hands were tight on the reins of his horse. "Search them." He turned to Evemer, worry clouding over his face. "If Melek's not here . . ."

"I'll look. Stay here." He dismounted from the horse, a large and solidly built blue-roan gelding the color of polished iron, and went inside.

Sylvia hadn't been exaggerating when she'd said this house had a warren of cellars—three times, Evemer spotted a door out of the corner of his eye that he had almost missed, and each time his heart caught in his chest to think that perhaps Melek was behind it and that he'd come that close to turning his back and walking away.

Even after exhaustive searching, the cellars were empty. "Check the rest," Evemer said to the kahyalar who had come in with him. "Be certain."

The rooms upstairs had been all but sacked—in the bedrooms, drawers and cabinets stood gaping open. Clothes were strewn across the floor, a stray bracelet and a single earring had been dropped on the stairs . . . They'd left in a hurry. Was it when they had discovered that Kadou and Evemer had escaped? It had to have been.

If most of the kahyalar hadn't been working elsewhere in the house, Evemer might have missed it—a faint thumping on the other side of a wall in the corridor. He stopped, listened. Pressed his ear against the wall, thumped hard on the wall with a fist. The thumping stopped, then redoubled, frantic.

Evemer shouted for the other kahyalar and within a minute there were a handful of them banging and kicking the wall, tugging on sconces, wedging their fingernails into cracks in the paneling. All at once, there was a click, and a section of the wall jumped back an inch. It was easy to push it back, then, as easy as opening a door. In a tiny, bare stone room beyond, lit only by a single window, Melek lay on the floor, bound and gagged, bruised and bloodied, but still wriggling.

Evemer cut çir bonds; Melek yanked the spit-sodden gag from çir mouth and groaned. "Thank the gods. How did you get out before I did?" Çir face was bruised and swollen, a few cuts here and there, and three of çir fingers were broken.

"Long story. Let's get you out."

"I'm fine."

"You're not," Evemer said. "Don't be a hero. You followed us here?" He helped Melek to çir feet.

"Yeah," çe said sheepishly, letting Evemer steady the both of them. "Sent a message to Tadek and your mother, and then I tried to scale the wall of the manor and break in, but I picked the wrong window. They caught me. Beat me up for a while."

"Any injuries that need immediate attention?"

"My fingers. Don't think I have a concussion, but I got a clip to the head that made me fuzzy for a minute or two. My shoulder's dislocated, and I can't tell if my ribs are cracked, but my breast-bindings are keeping them in place for now, so that's fine."

Fine was a generous word for it. "When did Siranos escape?"

Melek coughed a bit and winced, pressing çir uninjured hand

to çir side. "No idea. They stopped hitting me when someone came in to say you'd escaped, and they threw me in here while they figured out what to do. It was still dark, that's all I know." Çe nodded to the tiny window. "I managed to get myself standing long enough to watch them load up the carriage."

"Was it distinctive?"

"Gods, no. I've seen two dozen just like it in the city. The horses were, though. Big blocky things. Couldn't see the breed— might have been Galecians from Carrock, or . . . Well, really any of the other Lausanian draft breeds."

"At least we've narrowed it down to a *continent*," Evemer said. Gratifyingly, Melek laughed, apparently able to read in his tone or expression that he'd meant it as a dry joke—Kadou's influence on him again, undoubtedly.

It took him and another kahya to help Melek down the stairs, and then two more for safety after a bad moment when Melek's knee gave out and they all nearly fell and broke their necks.

Kadou's face when they exited the manor was a thing of beauty. He flung himself out of Wing's saddle and ran up to Melek, the gold threads woven through the skirts of his kaftan glittering brilliantly in the sun. "Oh, thank the *gods*." He took stock of Melek's injuries, asked anxiously several times whether çe was well, whether çe was sure . . . "We're taking you to the nearest doctor," Kadou said firmly. "And then we'll send a carriage to come get you. You can't possibly ride in this condition."

"My lord," Evemer said urgently. "They packed in a hurry and left. Melek saw their horses."

"Did they leave the city?" Kadou asked, turning again to Melek. "Do you know which gate?"

"No, nothing."

"Damn." Kadou pinched the bridge of his nose. "All right. All right. Make up two groups of four or five and send them to the North and South gates, give them descriptions of the horses and the carriages, see if we can find out if anyone noticed them leaving." He swung up into Wing's saddle with absolutely enchanting grace and gathered up her reins. "Have them report back to the palace as soon as they hear anything. We'll send people after them when we know which road they took. Melek, are you well enough to ride pillion? Just as far as the doctor's, unless we can find a sedan chair to carry you."

Evemer burned with pride as Kadou gave Melek a hand up into the saddle and called for a couple of the nearby kahyalar to accompany him. How had Evemer ever thought him careless, flighty, negligent? The words seemed starkly foreign now.

Kadou was dazzling in the light, his hair tumbling loose and shining down his back, and quite without permission Evemer's feet stumbled to a stop as he gazed after them, a glow building in his chest until it was as warm as the sun on his back.

※

It was late afternoon by the time they got back to the palace. Tenzin had made great progress—the mood in the Copper Court was already easing, and the Silver Court was beginning to come awake too. As they rode through, Kadou felt all the knots of tension in his soul easing with each familiar face he spotted. Entering the Gold Court, they found almost a festival atmosphere. It was lively with kahyalar, all of them greeting each other joyfully, clapping each other on the back, rushing up to help them with the horses when they dismounted, and talking over each other to tell Kadou the news—Zeliha wanted to see him when he got back, and the commander and the princess and Tadek had been brought back to the palace, and, "Oi, Evemer, we met your mom!"

"I hope you were civil," Evemer said flatly. Kadou stifled a laugh and led him off to Zeliha's chambers.

He didn't have an instant to stop and think for the rest of the afternoon—Zeliha was in a furiously productive mood. She listened intently to everything they told her and immediately sent orders for Sergeant Gülfem—the head of the fringe-guard and Eozena's acting-deputy—to assemble a flying squad to be ready to ride out the very instant that they heard news from the city gates.

That done, she said, "What's next?" and dove on the next issue like a stooping falcon, barely pausing long enough for Kadou to offer any comments. "I've ordered a dinner for tonight—Silver Court, officers, foreign ambassadors—and I expect you to be there. Formal but not high-formal, we just need to show them that House Mahisti is happy and healthy and strong. We also need to be *sure* to rebuild relations with the kahyalar corps in the next few weeks, Kadou. This situation can't have been comfortable for them. You're the one who's best at that sort of thing, so think of something. Next, we also need to be thinking of the Midsummer festival next week. The news of all this is going to be hitting the city, oh, probably tonight, so we'd better have a parade or something—can I leave that with you as well? You know I'm no good at that waving-and-throwing-silver part. You'll need to call for the tailor *right now* if you want to have something new to wear in time for that—oh, do you need to write all this down?"

So off they went to Kadou's new residence, sending for the tailor and for Tadek along the way, only to discover that Tadek was already there, patiently waiting with a pair of crutches leaning against his chair, a lap desk, his handmade notebook, and some very intelligent guesses about the sort of schedule Kadou was being dropped into the middle of.

"Help," Kadou said desperately the moment he clapped eyes on him.

"Dictate," Tadek said, snatching up his pen. "Tell me everything we need to do."

※

What followed might as well have been Vintish for all Evemer understood of it. While Kadou and Tadek shouted at each other about parade routes and budgetary allocations and public relations, Evemer quietly manhandled Kadou so that the tailor and her assistant could take his measurements, and then pulled her aside and narrowed the fabric samples down to a selection of seven. These he threw down like a gauntlet between Kadou and Tadek for them to fight over while he firmly led the tailors out of the residence and informed them that the decision would be made before sunset.

After an hour or two of this, Kadou was looking pale and was showing evidence that he was coming to the limit of his ability to make decisions about inconsequential details. Evemer bundled Tadek out of the room with an earful of instructions, sent for tea, made Kadou drink it, put him in the care of the currently assigned secondary, and ordered them both off to the bathhouse.

Yasemin, the secondary, returned with Kadou scrubbed and shaved and his hair already dressed, and Evemer decided that he approved of her. They poured Kadou, unresisting, into his dinner clothes, draped him with jewels, smudged his eyes with kohl—not that they needed it, with eyelashes like that—and then Evemer sent Yasemin out of the room, shut the door, pushed Kadou against it, and kissed him.

Kadou went liquid and boneless instantly, and Evemer stepped back smartly before Kadou could get himself together enough to grab at him. "Don't wrinkle your clothes."

"What," Kadou said, wide-eyed and flushed.

"You need to go to dinner now."

"I don't want to go to dinner."

"Go to dinner, my lord."

"But I don't *want* to," Kadou said again, plaintive. "Why'd you do that if you were only going to send me off?"

"You looked like you needed it."

"I mean, *yes*. Yes, I did need it. I think I need more of—" Kadou stopped. Breathed. "Right," he said, more quietly. "Dinner."

"Dinner."

"You're not coming?"

"Yasemin is attending you, my lord. I'm going to fix your rooms."

A formal dinner might take three or four hours—it was just barely sunset when Kadou left. Evemer went to fix the atrocious job that someone had done in organizing Kadou's clothes, and presently Tadek returned with a few cadets carrying armfuls of bundled cloth. Evemer eyed the bundles suspiciously. "Did you steal those?"

"Yes," Tadek said. "Obviously. You said go find curtains. I

found curtains. No one will even notice they're gone, and we'll replace them as soon as His Highness commissions new ones. What do you want from me?"

Evemer gave him an incredulous look and flicked his eyes to the cadets, who shuffled nervously. Gods, they looked young. Had he ever been that young? Some of them had *pimples*.

Tadek waved a hand. "They won't tell anybody, it's fine. Do you want the curtains or not?"

They hung them across all the windows of Kadou's bedroom while Tadek sat in a chair in the middle of the room with his crutches across his knees, making annoying comments about the draping and insisting almost everything was crooked, until Evemer was just about ready to throw him off the balcony. He kicked out the cadets as soon as they were done and attempted to kick out Tadek too, but Tadek pled his aching injured leg, and the difficulty of the stairs, and the long, long walk across the Gold Court, and Evemer gritted his teeth again and finished organizing the wardrobes and jewelry cases while Tadek . . . continued to make annoying comments about it.

It was almost exactly four hours from when Evemer had sent Kadou off to dinner that they heard the front door open, followed by weary steps up the stairs. Kadou came in, looking dead on his feet, and saw the curtains immediately. "Oh, *thank you*," he said, and Evemer cleared his throat and pretended to be adjusting things at the very back of the wardrobe so Tadek wouldn't see his blush.

"How was dinner?" Tadek asked.

"Long," Kadou said, going to the windows to run his hands over the fabric. "Whose idea was this?"

"Evemer's," Tadek said, at the same moment Evemer said, "We both did it."

Kadou went all around the room, flicking the curtains closed—they were green silk, backed with heavy linen to keep out the light and trimmed along the hems with a wide band of butter-gold satin. He stood back from them and sighed. "Oh, that's so much better. I felt like I was on stage for the whole city to see." He turned away and removed his earrings, but hesitated at the newly organized jewel boxes. "Where do these go now?" Evemer came forward to take them. "And have we heard any news from the city gates?" He piled the rest of his jewels into Evemer's palms one by one—the rings, the bracelets, the labradorite pendant that looked like a piece of the aurora borealis, the jeweled combs and pearl-ended pins from his hair—and watched as Evemer laid them in their new places, all neat and tidy.

"Not yet," Tadek said. "All I've heard is that the flying squad is waiting around in the Copper Court with their horses saddled and their weapons on." He sighed and stretched his leg, wincing. "There are kahya's quarters here, aren't there?"

"Several," Kadou said. "You want one?"

"If it's not too bold a request. I shouldn't have sat down for so long, it's gone all stiff," he said, tapping his fingers on his knee. "Honeybee, give us a hand out of this chair, eh?"

"Don't call me that if you want help down the stairs."

"Evemer," Tadek said, all wide-eyed and guileless. "Help me down the stairs."

If it would get rid of him, Evemer would have carried him halfway across the Gold Court. By the time he came back up, Kadou had already taken down his own hair and laid his kaftan over the back of the chair, so Evemer had two more reasons to resent Tadek.

"You should go to bed too," Kadou said. "You look like you're ready to fall over."

"So do you."

"It won't get any better, this next week. It'll be like this every day. Go on, get some sleep." Evemer couldn't have even said why he hesitated. Kadou smiled gently. "Everyone's home. Everyone's safe. Eozena's doing well. I went to look in on her after dinner—Zeliha's got the best doctors for her, and they said her fever's broken, and they've given her milk of the poppy for the pain. Melek's in the infirmary tonight, but çe isn't in any danger either. Tadek's here, Eyne's here, you and I are here. You can sleep."

Evemer nodded. The glow in his chest from earlier had turned into an ache. "As my lord commands."

"I'm not commanding," Kadou sighed. "But you haven't gotten a full night's sleep in your own bed in days." He half smiled at Evemer and nodded toward the door to the stairs, the corridor below that led to the kahya's chambers. "A room all to yourself. That doesn't sound appealing?"

The ache sharpened. "No. It doesn't."

"No?"

"Don't send me away from you," Evemer whispered.

Kadou's expression softened. "At least go wash and change. You'll feel better, and you don't want to sleep in your uniform. Go, and come back quickly, and we'll . . . figure something out."

Why was Evemer's heart pounding? Nothing was going to happen when he came back. Nothing *could* happen. He walked slowly downstairs and outside to collect a bucket of water from the font in the little courtyard outside the front door.

With every step further, he felt pulled to go back to Kadou's new chambers—why wait? Why waste even an instant apart from him?

He knew he ought to be sensible. He ought to clean his teeth and at least splash off the dust and sweat and take a moment to collect and recenter himself.

Evemer was scrubbing down in his room with a cloth and the bucket of water and musing about how he really couldn't allow himself to sleep in Kadou's bed again, even if he were invited to do so, when the thought struck him like a bolt of lightning out of the blue, and he nearly sent the bucket toppling.

It was both a terrible shock and something he felt like he had known for a long time. His mind howled in unison both *What!* and *Oh . . . yes, that makes sense.*

He was in love with Kadou.

He dropped the cloth into the bucket and stared into space, turning that thought over and over in his head, examining every detail of it.

It wasn't just the devotion of a kahya for his lord, compounded with common and uncomplicated desire. It wasn't the same thing at all. Being willing to die for someone wasn't the same as being in love with him. Being willing to follow him to the ends of the earth at a snap of his fingers wasn't the same either.

There it was, a raw lightning-crash of truth.

He was in love with his lord.

He was *in love*. With his lord. With Kadou.

Or perhaps *at* Kadou would be a better phrasing. That was the roll of thunder on the heels of the lightning: Kadou could not return his feelings. Kadou would arrange for the annulment, and it seemed a strong possibility they might have some brief physical affair after that, but even that was something that would only be temporary. Zeliha would arrange a *real* marriage for him sooner or later, and then Kadou would owe his loyalty and fidelity to some stranger, someone who didn't know him like Evemer did, someone who had no idea of what they'd endured together.

And Evemer would stand just behind his lord's shoulder for as long as his service was required, and he would say nothing and reveal nothing.

He leaned on the edges of the bucket with both hands and hung his head, looking down into the water. He couldn't tell Kadou about any of this. His Highness would undoubtedly find it a burden—if somehow he returned even a faint ghost of Evemer's feelings now, they would have to pull away from it later when Kadou vowed his heart to someone else. His Highness would find that painful, and he would know that it was painful for Evemer too—he'd see it plain, no matter how Evemer tried to hide it. With all Kadou's kindness and care, he'd fret and worry . . . Perhaps he'd even convince himself that it was his fault and that he was the one who had caused Evemer's pain.

And what if he didn't return Evemer's feelings, but thought that he ought to? What if he got some idea into his beautiful fool head about reciprocity?

Evemer's heart ached, and for the first time in his life, he wondered if he was going to be able to survive this.

Probably not.

Chances were that it wouldn't drive him to a literal death, but it was beyond a shadow of a doubt that the Evemer who endured that heartbreak and came out on the other side was going to be a different person than the one who sat here now, half-naked and dripping wet and miserable.

He'd have to be strong, to watch Kadou marry in truth. He'd have to be careful not to hate them, whoever they were, to not even *begin* hating them.

Evemer plunged his head into the bucket, the water gone cool but not shockingly so, and he held himself down until his lungs burned for air. He rose again, water and hair streaming into his face.

Depending on who Kadou married, there could be children. Evemer would have to be careful of them too, careful not to love them too hard—though he didn't know how he could manage not to, if any of them had Kadou's blue-black eyes. Which they would, because every Mahisti for nine generations had had those eyes, or so it was said.

Evemer dried off, rubbing as much of the water out of his hair as he could. He put on a clean uniform because now it didn't feel right to wear anything else—the uniform marked him as Kadou's. He left the bucket and the washcloth. Left his clothes on the floor too. He stood at the door of his room for what seemed like an eternity, his hand on the knob.

A few stray drips of cold water fell from his hair, ran down the back of his neck.

How had it come to this? After all his training and all his discipline, all he'd ever done to keep himself level and crisply squared-off at his corners. After everything, all these years, how had it come to this?

He leaned his head on the wall beside the door. It didn't help. Made him feel weak.

Discipline, square corners—he straightened up, stiffened his shoulders. There was nothing for it but to endure, and obey, and serve with the same staunch dedication as always. Kadou had said he wouldn't send Evemer away. He'd said Evemer had a place at his hearth and in his home for as long as he wanted.

He could keep a handle on the feelings in his heart. They were his own problem, not Kadou's. He could take joy and honor in serving a lord he knew was honorable and worthy. He could be content with that.

More than content—it was only what he'd always wanted, his whole life.

Wasn't it?

Was it *now*?

He drifted back to Kadou's chambers as if in a dream and let himself in. Kadou had left only two of the lamps lit—the one on the nightstand by his bed, the one on the low table in front of the divan in the middle of the room. He had thrown back a few of the curtains and opened one of the windows. He was leaning on the sill, craning to see something, though he turned when Evemer opened the door.

It was an exceptionally clear night, and the starlight was silvery on his dark hair, and the candlelight made his skin glow warm, and his eyes were bright and unafraid for the first time in days, and then he smiled like the sudden rise of the king-tide, and he was the most beautiful thing Evemer had seen in all his life, and probably the most beautiful thing he'd ever see.

This wasn't going to end well. It couldn't.

It was going to break him. Evemer would not survive this— likely he had already failed to survive it. Likely it had already changed him, and he was only just now beginning to realize. The man who had taken the exams for promotion to the core-guard was not the same one who stood here. That was as true as the knowledge that the man who stood here would not be the one who survived having to watch over Kadou's children without loving them too hard.

And then, in another bloom of raw sorrow, Evemer thought of his own children, which he would now never have, not by any method, and of his mother, who would never see grandchildren. Kadou might one day be required to swear his fidelity to someone else, but Evemer never would. He would have no children, by love, by law, or by body, and he would be granted no claim on an heir. His line would end, some decades hence, if he were very fortunate, ancient and silent and still in service—perhaps still watching over

Kadou's grandchildren or great-grandchildren. Perhaps living long enough to see Kadou die.

The goddess Sannesi had birthed the world and shaped it, filled it with wonderful things and bright opportunities. But the god Usmim, to keep the balance and to test the mettle of his sister's creations, sent trials. Some were small and inconsequential—a chance to be kind to a child instead of terse, a chance to help a neighbor lift a heavy box into a cart. But some were as colossal and mighty as immovable mountains.

What might this trial be? What might Usmim be asking of him? *Well, little kahya, can you hold your tongue for half a century of the dynasty? Can you serve, and serve well? Can you give your heart anew every day and silently let it be broken, and hold your faith and devotion close and unwavering? Can you endure, and if so, for how long? Shall we find out together?*

"Are you all right?" Kadou asked, his smile falling—again like the tide. "Did something happen?"

"No," Evemer forced himself to say. "Just tired. What were you looking at?"

Kadou shook his head, closing the window. "Just a moment of childish whimsy. I was looking for the messengers. I feel like it's good luck, on a voyage or on a mission, if someone's waiting for you at the other end, watching to see you come home."

"Surely it must be," Evemer said. He finally got his feet to work and crossed to the divan, sinking down on it. His heart was quickening and, again for the first time in his life, he felt himself holding words *back*. There were so many things he wanted to say that it felt like they had all gotten jammed in his throat. "Do you need any assistance preparing for bed, my lord?"

"Don't call me that," Kadou said. Evemer glanced at him, surprised. "Please. Not when it's just the two of us, not after . . . all of this."

Evemer ought to resist that. He ought to say that it was his place as His Highness's kahya to show respect and deference. He ought to try to keep Kadou at arm's length, as much for his sake as for Evemer's.

There was no way this could end well.

"Do you need any assistance preparing for bed, Kadou?"

"Would you—you needn't, if you don't wish to, but—would you brush my hair?"

Evemer's heart thudded hard against his ribs. "Yes, of course."

Kadou fetched the brush and got arranged—Evemer perched on the edge of the divan, Kadou sitting on the floor before him with his back to Evemer's knees, the weight of his hair gathered across Evemer's palm like a thick handful of black silk.

"Are you all right?" Kadou asked again, when Evemer was only halfway through brushing. He was making it an exquisitely delicate process, teasing each snarl apart with his fingers before trying to run the brush through. "You're tense."

"I'm always tense," Evemer muttered.

"If this is making you uncomfortable—"

Evemer caught his shoulder. "Let me. Please."

"You're upset about something."

"Nothing that I can do anything about right now."

"Oh. *Oh*," Kadou said, and Evemer could hear the blush in his voice even if the candles didn't show it.

I don't expect that I'm going to stop wanting you, he heard, the echo of his own voice. "Not—that. This is something else."

"You don't want to talk about it?" Did Kadou sound a little breathless?

"I can't talk about it."

Kadou leaned back against Evemer's knees. "I could—if you wanted . . . Take your mind off it?" He sounded *hopeful*. What was Evemer supposed to do with that? How was he supposed to resist or deny it?

He really shouldn't be kissing Kadou. It was only going to make his predicament worse, he already knew that. But what was the alternative? Passing up on his chance, even if it only lasted a few months, and then living the rest of his life not even knowing the taste of Kadou's mouth one more time, or the weight of him in Evemer's arms, the lush heat of his skin where neck curved into his shoulder?

It was not even a choice: Eat now, with the knowledge that you'll starve later.

The next problem, then, was how to say *yes, please*.

His heart was fluttering wildly. He could pass up words altogether and just tip Kadou's head back and meet his mouth. That would almost certainly do the trick.

But Kadou *worried* so, and Evemer longed to undo the knot of this particular worry, even if he couldn't undo any of the others. Kadou should never have reason to doubt him. Not in any realm of their lives. There were so few certainties, but Evemer wanted fiercely to be one of them.

So perhaps the words were important after all. "Yes," he said, his voice rougher than he'd been expecting. "Please."

Kadou turned, already smiling, and slid fluidly up onto the divan beside him. "Just kissing," he said. "It won't count if it's just kissing."

"Yes," Evemer said. His arms had come around Kadou of their own volition, and something in him fell still and calm just to be able to touch him. Kadou met his mouth and draped his arms over Evemer's shoulders.

He felt so clumsy, always, in Kadou's hands. He could run sword-forms with his eyes closed all day and never trip, but whenever Kadou took hold of him, in an instant he felt as blundering and ungainly as a gawkish new cadet, unsure of what to do with his hands or his tongue or his nose. But Kadou was deft and graceful enough for the both of them, correcting for each slight awkward angle as if he didn't have to think about it.

It was better than the kiss in the wine cellar. It was better than the kiss in Evemer's bed, in his mother's house. Evemer wondered with a wild swooping moment of mixed anticipation and dread whether each kiss was always going to be better than all the ones that had come before.

Oh, he was not going to survive this.

He kissed Kadou, ran his hands through all that luxuriously beautiful hair, touched his cheekbones, his neck, his back and waist.

When Kadou broke off to catch his breath, Evemer pulled him close, most of the way into his lap, and nosed beneath Kadou's collar, kissing his clavicles and breathing in the scent of him—warmth and salt and a ghost of fragrant incense and the perfume Yasemin had dabbed at the corners of his jaw. Kadou laid kisses in his damp hair and hugged him close, breathing him in too.

"I should go to bed," Kadou whispered.

"Not yet." He hadn't meant to say that aloud, but it made Kadou laugh and kiss his hair again. "Not yet." He turned his face up, and Kadou kissed that too—his forehead, his cheeks, his chin.

"I know," Kadou breathed against the corner of his jaw. "I know. Me too."

Evemer tightened his arms, burying his face in Kadou's neck, the soft fall of his hair. A little longer, just a little longer. That was probably going to be his unspoken chant right up until Kadou's wedding day. Not yet, just a little longer.

"It's all right," Kadou whispered, kissing the shell of his ear. "It's all right, I'm safe. We made it."

He was being too selfish. Evemer loosened his grip, lifted his head. "I apologize."

"Why?"

"You wanted to go to bed. I shouldn't keep you."

"I said I *should* go to bed." Kadou leaned forward and kissed the corner of his mouth. "I want to stay here and keep kissing you but . . . It wouldn't be a good idea."

Evemer let out his breath slowly. "Of course. You're right."

"You sound so formal suddenly, why?"

Because if he wasn't formal, he might forget himself and say something he shouldn't. "Force of habit." Kadou looked unconvinced—Evemer could see the creeping edges of worry already shifting the set of his shoulders and ducked in to press another kiss to Kadou's neck, letting Kadou catch his mouth again, just briefly, when he pulled away. "You should go to bed."

"You could come to bed too, if you wanted," Kadou whispered. "I liked it, last night, and you'd sleep better than on the divan."

No. No, no, too much, it would be far too much. He couldn't

do that again, now that he knew what was happening to him, and still keep his heart secret—he'd give it all away somehow, by whispering in his sleep those things he shouldn't say or clinging too desperately to Kadou.

It was the thing his heart yearned for with a sharp stabbing pain—just to be allowed to be close to him, to hold him quietly, to rub his face in Kadou's hair and feel the gentle rhythm of his breath in sleep. It was the one thing he could not allow himself to have, not even a second taste, never again. He already knew too much of it from the night before.

But that, he insisted to himself, was *different*. He hadn't known he was in love then.

"Thank you for the offer, but—" No, stop, not like that. Kadou had noticed formality before; doing it again would worry him. He picked up Kadou's hand and laced their fingers together. "I mean to say, thank you, but I . . ." He couldn't lie that it was because of the marriage. It hadn't counted last night; it wouldn't count now. He couldn't even admit that he wanted to sleep next to him, or else Kadou would invite him again sometime in the future, and Evemer would have to come up with some other excuse not to do it.

"You don't have to have a reason, you know," Kadou said, watching him closely. He had a worry line between his brows. "You can just say 'no, thanks.'"

"No, thanks," Evemer said. "I'm sorry."

"Don't be." He squeezed Evemer's hand. "Did that help take your mind off whatever was bothering you?"

"It helped." Not with taking his mind off of things, not in the slightest, but Kadou didn't need to know that. He leaned up to kiss Kadou again, and Kadou held him there a moment longer, kissing him deeper, hotter.

"Don't take this the wrong way, but I'm looking forward to not being married to you," Kadou said with a grin, and Evemer must have blushed because Kadou laughed, too.

"Go to bed," he grumbled.

CHAPTER FIFTEEN

Tadek brought the news in with breakfast and the rest of Kadou's mail. He was still dressed in the green arms-man's uniform, the colors of Şirya. "Message from the gates came in last night around midnight," he said. "The flying squad . . . well, flew."

Kadou set his coffee cup down with a clatter. "Which gate was it?"

"South. I'd wager they're heading down the coast road to grab a ship out of Nadırıntepe."

Kadou exhaled. "Right. No need to keep our own harbor closed, then. Paper and ink, please? I'll draft the order right away."

Tadek smirked and brought them out from under the table, already ready. "Thought you might say that."

Kadou scrawled out the orders, sealed them, and called for a cadet to run the message out to the Copper Court and thence down to the harbor.

"So," Tadek said neutrally. "Couldn't help but notice Evemer slept in your room last night."

Kadou occupied himself with pouring another cup of coffee. "Yes. I didn't feel comfortable, and he was kind enough to sleep on the di-van. New place, you know. New sounds at night. The overwhelming memory of that time I was nearly kidnapped, and then the other overwhelming memory of the time I actually *was* kidnapped . . ."

"Oh, of course," Tadek said. "That's a pretty good line. Solid, plausible, just a sprinkling of passive-aggression to make your audience feel guilty for even asking. Everything you'd want in a cover story, really. Nice."

Kadou, aware that he was stealing a trick from Evemer and that it was probably blindingly obvious, very pointedly said nothing.

"Look," Tadek said, a glass-sharp edge of frustration coming into his voice. "I don't *care*. All right, I do a bit, but I'm working on it and that's my problem. By the way, you need to give me a day off, I've got some business down in the city to take care of. That's not the point. Point is, you can do whatever the hell you want, and you don't owe me shit."

"Home and hearth," Kadou said.

"*Fuck* home and hearth. I'm talking to you as your friend Tadek right now, not your armsman. Don't give me any of that ethical bullshit. I just . . ." He stopped, clearly biting back words. "I don't care about *that*. The thing I do care about is being lied to."

"Sounds like some of that 'ethical bullshit' to me."

"Kadou," Tadek said, leaning forward on the table. "The thing that's driving me crazy right now isn't the fact that it's happening, it's the fact that I don't know for sure whether it is. If you don't want to tell me, fine. Do what Evemer does: tell me it's none of my business and douse me under a water pump. *That's* a fair and reasonable way to handle it."

"Is it?"

"Yes. I like that a lot more than I like you looking demurely down into your coffee and murmuring the same sort of bullshit excuse you're going to give anyone else whenever they get around to asking. You can tell me to fuck off all you want, or you can tell me what's going on. But *don't* lie."

"Fine." Kadou set aside his coffee so that he could not be accused of looking demurely into it. "There's . . . a thing."

Tadek let out a long breath. "Right. All right. Thank you."

"It's not—" Kadou gritted out. "It was never about replacing you, or—"

Tadek held up a hand. "You don't have to tell me anything else. It's none of my business, is it? You can do as you please."

"It's complicated. It's not even really happening. I can't talk about it. It's sort of happening. You don't want to know about this. I don't know if it's happening either, come to think about it. It both is and isn't happening. And yes, it's driving me crazy too." He stopped, suddenly aware that he was babbling. Grabbed his cup again, took a fortifying gulp. "You're in charge of my calendar," he said wildly. "I'll give you as many days off as you want if you can find me a free afternoon."

Tadek said, slow and suspicious, "What for?"

"There's something I need to do at the temple, and I really, *really* can't tell you anything more."

Tadek mulled this over. "Does this have anything to do with Evemer being a secret prince?"

"Since you mention him, where *is* Evemer? There's no water pump around here, will it work if he dunks you in a fountain?"

"I feel like I'm this close," Tadek muttered to himself. "I've almost got it. It's on the tip of my tongue."

"Leave it alone. Do you want your day off or not?"

Tadek huffed. "Fat chance getting a whole afternoon free before, oh, next week, maybe the week after. The dedicates and temple aunts all have their hands as full as we do, what with the festival, and everybody gets so *pious* right after a holiday. The temples will all be booked up for unburdenings and blessings and the like, and you know how they are—they won't give you preference just because you're the prince."

"Damn."

"Just wait a couple weeks. Unless it's urgent." He looked interested again. "Is it urgent?"

"It is not a matter of life and death, no," Kadou said carefully.

On the fourth day, Evemer decided to stop torturing himself alone. He woke just before the sun, as he usually did, but rather than running sword drills until the sun burned off the dew from the leaves, he walked through the cool, damp air, all grey with mist and the first glimmerings of dawn, out through the lush gardens of the Gold Court, through the paved walkways and parks and buildings of the Silver Court, to the Copper Court, dense with the servants' quarters, the cadet halls, the fringe-guards' garrison, the core-guards' dormitories, the butteries and storehouses and stables and training grounds, the workshops and laundries and dungeons, the cadet academy, and—most crucially for Evemer—the Grand Temple.

He walked in. The floor of the first room was a great, open expanse below a bogglingly vast dome, the giant porphyry statue of Sannesi looking out kindly over the whole. There were already a dozen people sitting on the rugs before her, scattered through the room and moving quietly through the positions of prayer. This close to a holiday, the temple would be packed by the time the sun had fully risen.

He continued around the perimeter of the hall and through the door at the back into a second chamber, equally large but much darker. No jewels of light falling through colored glass here, no glimpse of the bright sky through the oculus in the center of Sannesi's dome.

Usmim's hall was somber, the light through the slit windows watery and dim. The floor was bare stone, the walls unadorned. There was no one there but him. He sat on the floor and waited.

He didn't have to wait long—perhaps ten minutes. A hand touched his shoulder and he looked up to see a wizened old woman in simple temple robes. She smiled down at him. "Good morning, and sorry to interrupt," she said, her voice low and soft. "I'm one of the temple aunts. Do you need anything? Or shall I leave you to prayer and contemplation?"

"I was wondering about an unburdening. I've never come for one before," he said.

"Many people find the experience to be quite healing and re-freshing to the spirit, as you probably know," the aunt said. "We will look together at any guilt or fears you feel, examine together the trials Usmim has sent you. Or we can just talk together for a while. Would that help you?"

"I don't know."

She tilted her head toward the back of the chamber. "Perhaps a cup of tea while you think it over?"

He nodded and got to his feet. His legs were already stiff and cold from sitting on the stone floor. She led him out to an area enclosed by high stone walls, overgrown with ivy and climbing roses. The grass was thick and soft, still jeweled with dew, and there was a blanket already laid out, and a teapot on a burner of coals. It was quieter and smaller and more wild than the neatly manicured palace gardens. "I have my own little contemplation here most mornings," she said, gesturing for him to sit at one side of the blanket. "So you arrived just in time for the tea to finish." She poured a cup for each of them and settled back, apparently very happy to sit in companionable silence with him.

"What should I call you, Aunt?"

"My name is Aunt Mihrimah," she said instantly. "And yours?"

"Evemer."

"By your uniform, one of the core-guard, I take it?"

"Yes, Aunt Mihrimah." He could have told her right then and there. He had spent enough time in contemplation already that he had the list of his troubles assembled and ready to declaim.

"As you consider how you'd like to proceed," she said gently after a few moments of silence, "I will remind you that nothing you say here leaves this garden. You won't be punished for any of it, and I doubt that you can even begin to shock me. I am here to take your burdens, not add to them."

He nodded and set aside his cup, placed his hands flat on his thighs. "I have many things that burden me, Aunt Mihrimah." She drank her tea quietly and waited for him to continue. He took a breath, and began at the beginning. "I have been contemptuous of my lord, the prince. I have resented my assignment to his service. I have questioned Her Majesty's wisdom and judgment. I've found flaw with one of my fellow kahyalar when it was not my place to do so, and I have disliked him. I believed gossip more than my own two eyes. I have been stubborn and inflexible. I have lacked the strength to defend myself and I required my lord to do it for me. I have killed people as I defended him. I have required rescue. I have been a burden on my lord in a thousand ways. And I married him," he added, because he felt like at this point he might as well come entirely clean.

That was the only thing that gave the aunt pause. "You . . . married whom? Prince Kadou?"

"Yes. Or he married me. To save my life. It was complicated. We're going to get it annulled, of course."

"I see. Well! Which of these shall we start with?"

"I don't *need* to talk about any of them," Evemer said. He suddenly felt very silly, coming all this way just to blather about himself. "Do you have the ability to annul marriages? Ka—His Highness will be wanting someone discreet."

"I do," she said. "But you mentioned being a burden on the prince. Do you ever find yourself concerned with how much space you take up around other people?"

Evemer sat up straighter. "Of course I do," he said stiffly. "Will there be any paperwork for an annulment?"

"Mm, all right. We can get that topic out of the way first, if you'd like. No, there's no paperwork. It will take several hours, with both of you here, either at this temple or whichever of the shrines in the palace complex you find convenient. Another location is workable, if absolutely necessary, but I prefer solemn occasions to be held in a place of solemnity. Oaths are important, as I'm sure you'll agree, even if it was just an oath of convenience in a moment of desperation. Or so I imagine—you said it was to save your life?"

"Yes, I did. Thank you for the information. I will be sure to tell His Highness."

"Send word whenever you would like, and I will be sure to be ready for you, though timing might be tricky with the upcoming holiday. Do you have any other questions about that topic?"

"No, Aunt."

"Hmm," she said. "I have an instinct . . . You know there is nothing holding you here, don't you? You're free to leave whenever you want, or to linger. My time is yours, within reason." She smiled at him. "Have I taken enough burdens today? Do you want to leave?"

Slowly, he said, "No."

"Ah," she said, and sipped her tea.

"It's difficult for me to speak of things like this."

She nodded again. "Take your time. Find the right words."

He sat in silence for a dozen slow breaths. Finally, feeling that this was going to be what scandalized her enough to kick him out, he said, "There was one more thing. I'm in love with His Highness."

But even that, of all things, didn't confound her. "What's your aim, then?"

"My aim?"

"Yes, your intent for what to do with your feelings for him. Your vision for what your life looks like on the other side of this trial. What happens after the annulment?"

"I will keep serving him until he sends me away."

"You said that you felt contempt for him, is that right?"

"Not anymore. Not for a long time. I thought he was weak—careless, flighty, negligent. I was wrong. I admire him. I trust him. He is a good man, and he tries to be better. He cares fiercely, and I believe he would give a place at his hearth to nearly anyone who asked."

"Are your feelings for him another burden?"

"One that I have chosen to bear." He paused. "But I would not want to inflict them on him. I know this is an ill-fated path I have taken. You can say it. I'm dooming myself to heartbreak."

She sighed and topped up her tea. "I cannot tell you whether a path you take is wise or ill. I cannot tell you what to do with your feelings. I am here to ask you questions that you might not think to ask yourself, and to hear you when no one else might be able to. But several of the things you have said suggest to me that you find certain things difficult. What do you feel when you think of being vulnerable to someone?"

"In what way?"

"Amongst your burdens, you mentioned that His Highness was required to rescue you, as you could not rescue yourself. And you've said just now that you think yours is an ill-fated path."

"He will marry someone else. I will be jealous. I will keep it to myself for his sake, for the sake of serving him. I will be unhappy."

"And yet knowing all this, seeing your future so clearly, you still choose this path," she said. "I wonder why."

"Even a day by his side is worth a lifetime of misery."

"So poets and lovers have said since the dawn of time. You said you wouldn't want to burden him with your feelings. Am I to guess that you have not told him any of this?"

"No. Why would I?"

"What are his feelings toward you?"

"He is kind to me. He is a good and worthy lord. He feels the proper obligations to me." Evemer couldn't stop a slight, wry smile. "He has very strong feelings about reciprocity. Fealty goes both ways, he says."

"Is that all?"

There was no need to squirm, not in front of a temple aunt—she would not be embarrassed or shocked, and she would not scold him for lewd thoughts. "He . . . wants me. As I want him. But we have been very careful, because of the annulment."

There had been moments, the last few days, unbearable, scorching moments that drove Evemer to distraction to think of them. The night before, they'd pulled each other onto the divan, half-tangled together, and Kadou had put his mouth to Evemer's ear and whispered about what might count as sex, and the loopholes of what might *not quite count,* and—and Evemer had made himself pull away through what felt like a superhuman act of will even while he felt like he was going to die of want.

And then there were soft, quiet moments too, which made him ache in an entirely different way—Kadou carding his fingers through Evemer's hair, lacing their hands together. Every time he touched or kissed Kadou, no matter how chaste, it was harder to tear himself away.

"Is he as loyal to you as you are to him?"

"Yes," Evemer said, without hesitation.

Aunt Mihrimah nodded and sipped quietly at her tea. After a moment, she said, "When you say you would not burden him with your feelings, are you protecting yourself or him? Do you fear he would not be kind with your heart? Or do you fear it would hurt him to know this thing about you?"

"The latter," Evemer whispered.

"Ah," she said.

"I only want to be as good as he is, and I'm not. If I were good enough, I wouldn't be weak like this."

"Mm, again you mention weakness, and we are back at vulnerability again. What happens if you are weak?"

"If I am, then what's the point of me? What is the point of my position? How can I serve?"

"You said you were contemptuous of him because you thought he was weak."

Evemer gritted his teeth. She was *very* good at drawing connections between things. "I saw in him the thing I fear in myself."

"And now what do you see?"

"What I aspire to."

"Which is?"

"To be a better man."

She nodded. "Let's put this on the hearth and let it simmer for now. What other of your burdens would you like to discuss?"

✳

Evemer left about an hour later, feeling drained and raw but not as if his burdens had been lightened—if anything they seemed weightier, as a heavy pack did when it was shifted into a new balance that he was not accustomed to.

He thought of going back to the garrison, the training grounds. Kadou wouldn't be expecting him until noon. But he was tired and strangely sore in his heart and brain, the way his body was sore after a hard morning of martial drills.

He wanted Kadou. He wanted him like a small child wanted their favorite soft blanket. He wanted to sit at his feet and rest his head in Kadou's lap and merely exist for a time without having to pick apart everything he thought he knew about himself.

So he trudged all the way back across nearly the full length of the palace, and let himself in just as the cadets who brought breakfast were slipping out.

Kadou used the lower level of the residence, one large trapezoidal room, as his parlor. The windows were all thrown open, letting in the morning breeze and the distant scent of the sea. The cadets had laid out breakfast on the low table, as usual, as well as partially on the carpet next to it, because Tadek was taking up half the available surface with some enormous map and holding forth passionately about parade routes while Kadou nodded placidly and Melek, who had only returned to service the day before, assembled full plates from the breakfast offerings.

Tadek paused his tirade, assessing Evemer with a single glance. "Good gods, is something the matter?"

"No," said Evemer.

"Didn't sleep well?" Melek asked.

"Slept fine." The divan in Kadou's room again. It was getting familiar now—his bed in the kahyalar's quarters remained untested. "I went to the temple."

"Oh?" Kadou said, with a studied casualness that Tadek surely must have been able to see through. "Melek, it seems like it's going to be hot today, and I think this kaftan is a bit warm, can you go get me a lighter one?"

"Of course," Melek said. "Right now?"

"If you wouldn't mind."

As soon as çe had left the room, Kadou turned to Tadek. "Three minutes, please."

"I don't get sent on a trivial little errand to make me leave the room? I just get unceremoniously kicked out?" Tadek said with a mock pout, but he stood up. "I see how it is."

"You didn't have to send him away," he said, as soon as Tadek was in fact safely away with no danger of being called back. "I only went to unburden myself."

"Oh," said Kadou in a rather different tone of voice. "How . . . How was it?"

"She wrung me out like laundry," Evemer said. He all but collapsed onto one of the window seats.

Kadou was giving him guilty, sidelong glances. "My fault?" he asked. "I can—last night—I shouldn't have pushed—"

"You didn't," Evemer said firmly, because if thoughts like that started getting into Kadou's fool head then Evemer was never going to be able to weed them all out again. He forced words onto his tongue. "Disagreement over semantic interpretation doesn't mean I didn't . . . you know." He refused to let himself blush or squirm. He stared hard at the other side of the room.

"Spell it out, please."

Dammit. He braced himself. "I liked it, I just think you are wrong and that it would have counted as sex," he said all at once, before his stubborn tongue could decide to swallow the words. Charging forward stubbornly against all his better judgment, he added, "Anyway, going to be unburdened wasn't about that. I may go to speak to her again. I haven't decided if it was good for me or not."

"Can you say that first part again?" Kadou said. Evemer finally looked over at him. His expression had eased, and there was a faint wry smile around the corners of his mouth.

"I liked it?"

"Oh, that part was good too, but the bit right after."

"I think you're wrong?"

Kadou's smile broadened. "You could have just argued with me in the moment, you know."

"About what *counts*?" Evemer stared incredulously at him. "All of it counts!"

"Kissing doesn't, apparently, or we're already in trouble. In practice it's all shades of grey, but legally and theologically it's worded like there's some kind of definite boundary between black and white, so . . ." He shrugged one shoulder. "I thought there might be something that would go right up to that line and stop just short of it. That's what I meant by loopholes."

The blush that Evemer had been so valiantly keeping back flamed onto his face. Kadou was right—he should have argued in the moment, because then it would have been dark and warm and he could have buried his face in Kadou's hair when the conversation got this mortifying. Instead, he was stuck having it in broad daylight across a breakfast table. "I asked her about an annulment," he said. "A few hours at the temple, no paperwork." His throat tightened. "We can go at your convenience."

Kadou looked away suddenly and occupied himself with the food, smearing jam across a piece of toast far more meticulously than toast usually required. "Yes. Yes, well. Unfortunately, I'm told that my calendar for at least the next week or so is too full to block off that much time. I tried bribing Tadek to find a way, and he said it couldn't be done for love or money." Kadou gave him, or perhaps the toast, an apologetic half smile. "It's terrible timing for a festival week, isn't it? I hope you don't mind."

"No, I understand. Your time is not your own at the moment."

Of course Evemer wasn't going to object. The sweet, insistent gravity of desire had not disappeared or abated, but there were moments now and again when it was eclipsed by a greater, keener want—the yearning to hold on to Kadou for just a day or two longer and to carry the name Mahisti-eş in his pocket like a small and secret treasure, the longing to pretend just for another handful of minutes that Kadou was or could ever be Evemer's, the way that Evemer already was his and suspected he always would be. "Let me know, then, and I'll send word to her."

"I will. Thank you for being patient. Would you like something to eat?"

He joined Kadou at the table, indulging in another piece of poor self-discipline by sitting beside him rather than across the table, and helped himself to coffee. Kadou shifted to bump their knees together under the table. "What are you doing?" Evemer said gruffly.

"Flirting with you," Kadou said. Evemer blushed. "I thought I'd give it another shot."

"No need to flirt," Evemer replied softly. "Except to amuse yourself."

"You don't want me to?"

"I don't mean that."

"What do you mean, then?"

Evemer wished badly, again, that he could be having this conversation in the dark. "That I'm a sure thing."

Kadou leaned a little closer to him. "Oh, are you?"

"I told you before." *I don't expect that I'm going to stop wanting you.*

Kadou's eyes were sparkling. "So I don't need to flirt at all?" He touched Evemer's chest with one finger, hooked it between two buttons. Evemer swayed halfway forward at the slightest pull. "How am I supposed to get you to kiss me if I don't flirt?"

"A snap of your fingers and a word," he said. Another might have said it with a smile. Evemer's voice was low and deadly serious.

"You make it sound so easy."

Evemer's blood sang. "How many more ways would you have me swear myself to you before you understand?"

"I'm starting to get it." He tugged again with the finger hooked on Evemer's buttons. "Come here?" There was a knock on the door. Kadou snatched his hand away at the same moment Evemer jerked back and they both turned to the table as if the food were the most fascinating thing in the room. "Come in!"

Tadek stuck his head in. "It's been three minutes. More than three minutes. The parade route isn't going to fix itself, you know."

"Of course, apologies," Kadou said, waving him in. "You should eat before the food gets cold, too."

Tadek swung himself in on his crutches, the rolled-up map stuck through the side of his sash and the new kaftan slung over his shoulder. "I sent Melek out with the mail," he said, tossing the map onto the table. "Help you change?"

Kadou wiped a smear of jam off the corner of his mouth and sucked it off his thumb, which made Evemer want to die, and rolled up to his feet, already undoing his buttons. Tadek leaned his crutches on the back of a nearby armchair and, standing on one leg, helped Kadou wriggle his top layer off his shoulders and down his arms, replacing it with the new one, a very summery blue-green, the color of the water just outside the city harbor, made of linen nearly as light and sheer as the underlayer. He did up his own buttons and sat back down on his cushion at the table as Tadek shook out the old kaftan and began loosely folding it. "Oh," he said, pausing. "You've left something in your pockets."

Evemer had never seen Kadou's face go so white. He whirled around and dove for Tadek, who wobbled, nearly fell, and hopped back a step. "*Drop it.*"

Tadek froze, dropping both the kaftan, which fell to the floor with a soft noise, and whatever had been in the pockets, which fell with a metallic clink and two soft thumps on the carpet.

"What the hell did I just bumble into?" Tadek said.

Evemer looked back, but he had a feeling already—ah. Yes. The hinge pins. He forced himself to look back at the food like it was nothing and hoped his face wasn't going as red as Kadou's had gone pale.

Kadou snatched them off the floor and stuffed them into the pocket of his new kaftan. "Sorry," he said, his voice forced to light-ness. "Didn't mean to snap. Just startled."

"I'm sure. Hey, why isn't Evemer trying to kill me right now?"

Evemer shrugged. "Why would I be trying to kill you?"

"Because Kadou nearly bit my hands off to get those back, and you're sitting there pretending to be unaffected instead of jumping to draw steel on me at the first sudden movement, or glare me into submission, or haul me off for a little bit of recreational drowning." Tadek came around the table and sat across from them, grinning. "Have I discovered another clue?"

"It's not a clue to anything," Kadou said firmly. "Eat your breakfast."

"Do we need to have another conversation about lying?" Tadek asked mildly. He took a piece of simit from the platter and tore a morsel off it, dipping it in salted olive oil.

"I'm not lying, and they're not a clue. They're—a souvenir. That's all."

"Of what? If you say it's none of my business, then I'll *know* they're important, and I'm going to file them under *Evemer: Se-cretly a Prince?*"

"Strange to assume that it's at all connected," Evemer said.

"Is it? Because recently that seems to be the only issue that you two get so defensive and cagey about when I accidentally meander face-first into it. So if it's not that, then what's to stop you from telling me what those things are a souvenir of?" Tadek smiled like a fox.

"They're from the place we were held captive, if you must know," Kadou said, annoyed. "That time Evemer nearly *died*."

"Excellent use of passive-aggression, I definitely feel guilty for even asking," Tadek said encouragingly. "What are they?"

"Hinge pins," Evemer said. "From a door."

"Right. And that's the sort of thing you want to be reminded of?" he asked Kadou curiously. "You want a souvenir of what must have been a terrifying and traumatic moment?"

Evemer's patience, frayed to its breaking point, finally snapped. "Just tell him," he said. "He'll have it out of us sooner or later."

Tadek beamed at him. "Let's be best friends for always, Evemer."

"I'm not telling him anything!" Kadou hissed back.

Evemer turned fully to face him. "Do you think it might help him coordinate your schedule if he knew slightly more about why you are making certain requests?" Kadou hesitated. "He's already eighty percent of the way to figuring it out. He already guessed my . . . my part of it."

"Which part?" Kadou asked suspiciously.

"The part where I look at you too much."

Tadek lit up. "Oh, yes, that part. I've had that part for ages now. Wait—" He looked back and forth between them, his expression slipping into something a little less giddy. "Does *Kadou* know about that part?"

"I would say Kadou has probably gotten the gist of that part by now," Evemer said flatly.

"He . . ." Kadou cleared his throat, looked away. "He guessed my part too. Couple days ago. Dragged it out of me. Probably should have told you."

"Wait, wait, wait," Tadek said. He'd been industriously applying jam to another morsel of the simit, and this he used to gesture at them. "I was assuming you both were being oblivious and hadn't figured it out yet. You've got his bit. And *you've* got *his* bit. So . . . Wait, give me a moment to think of how to word this." He stopped, ate the bite of bread, chewed thoughtfully. Evemer braced every sinew of his soul, and was still not prepared: "So you've, ah . . . already been getting at each other's bits, eh?"

Evemer spluttered. Kadou covered his face with his hands and, evidently deciding this was not enough, pushed aside his breakfast and his coffee and put his head down on the table. Tadek only chortled under his breath until Evemer got himself together enough to say, "*Inappropriate*, Tadek."

"The pun was *right there*! What was I supposed to do?" Tadek cried, his mouth full of bread and jam. "It's the only comfort I have in these trying times!"

"We haven't," Kadou said, raising his head and enunciating crisply.

"Haven't what?"

"Been . . ." Kadou waved his hand vaguely in irritation. "We haven't."

Tadek stared at him. "You haven't . . . at all. You're telling me you *haven't*. That's what you're saying."

"No water pump, but there's a fountain just outside," Evemer said.

"*Why haven't you?*" Tadek screamed. "Whose fault is this? Not Kadou's, I know he's good for it. Evemer! Evemer, honeybee, look at him!" He gestured furiously at Kadou. "Look at this! Look! Are you a *corpse*? Are you—oh, gods, is it to do with the witch's curse that made you a secret prince? Did she curse your dick also? It can't possibly be nerves, there aren't enough nerves in the world that could stand against *that*," he said, with another wild gesture at Kadou. "Evemer!"

"Either tell him or let me drown him," Evemer said to Kadou, who had laid his head back down on the table.

Kadou sat up on a long inhale. "Tadek," he said. "Shut up."

Tadek reached across the table and seized his hands beseechingly. "Why is Evemer still a virgin, it's been *days*."

"Because when we were captured, they knew he was just a

kahya, so they were going to kill him," Kadou explained tonelessly. He didn't pull his hands out of Tadek's. "So I lied and said he had titles, and then they had Tenzin come in, and I had to act quickly and do something to make him *not* just a kahya so that it could stand up against a satyota questioning us."

Tadek's eyes had gotten very wide. "Holy fuck," he whispered. "Holy fuck, you didn't."

"Quickest thing I could do in the moment was . . . lend him mine. Temporarily."

Tadek took a deep breath, took his hands back from Kadou, and pressed both of them over his mouth, sitting back with his eyes closed.

Kadou sat up too and grimly refilled his own coffee and Evemer's.

Tadek was vibrating slightly, eyes still closed. "You *married* him. You married him, and now you need me to find you a free afternoon to undo it because you *can't fuck until you*—" He collapsed into incoherence and broke into howls and hoots and screeches of laughter until he toppled over onto his side.

"There's a fountain," Evemer said again. "It's right outside."

"*You* told me to tell him," Kadou said peevishly. "Just grit your teeth through the rest and then we can forbid him from ever mentioning it again."

Tadek hauled himself back upright with the edge of the table. "Oh, fuck, I think I just got religion," he said, still wheezing with laughter. He wiped away tears with the cuff of his sleeve. "The gods exist and they *love me*. Every moment of my entire life has been worth it to be here at this moment. Every trial Usmim has sent me has been leading me toward this *priceless gift*. Oh, thank you for this," he said, raising his hands in the third position of prayer. "Thank you for my entire life."

"Are you done?" Evemer demanded.

"Absolutely not. I won't be done for days. And to think I was going around pouting and sulking to myself and feeling stupid about it when right under my nose—*this*. Oh," he said, with a sigh that sounded like he was wrapping up at last. "Oh, thank you both for this. Worth it. Incredibly worth it." He cleared his throat and pulled his notebook from his pocket, still quietly gurgling with laughter. "I'm giving you wedding presents. Evemer, I will buy you a single glass of the worst beer I can find in the city."

"Like hell you will," Evemer said. He could already feel in his gut that he was going to be losing this fight.

"Kadou, I'm clearing tonight's schedule after the seventh hour of the evening, so you can come home early and"—he choked back another laugh—"and have a couple extra hours to do absolutely fucking nothing, may the gods bless you and your *beautiful,* temporary union, at least for the next two weeks until there's time for the temple." Another choked-off laugh. "Don't worry, I'll get you both annulment presents too." He scribbled a couple notes on one of the pages with a pencil and shut the little book with a snap. "Finally, in respectful deference to your non-honeymoon, I will be clearing out of the house at exactly one minute past the seventh hour of the evening so that you can have your privacy, though I don't know why you'd need it. I will be going down into the city, firstly to research which fine establishment sells the worst beer so that I can take Evemer there later, and secondly to hire, oh, perhaps five of the cutest courtesans I can find. I will give Melek a copy of tomorrow morning's schedule just in case I'm late in returning, because someone may have to bring me back to the palace in a wheelbarrow. I might be still drunk, and I will definitely not be able to walk."

"Are you done now?" Kadou said flatly. "Can we get back to figuring out the parade route?"

Tadek heaved one last sigh of delight and wiped his eyes again. "Oh, I suppose we'd better. What have I done with my chalks?" He patted his pockets and looked around the floor. "I put them down in the antechamber, I think. Temporary-Highness, can you go get them for—"

"No."

"Both fair and reasonable, considering," Tadek said, nodding, and managed to get himself to his feet without resting weight on his bad leg. "Be right back."

As soon as he was safely out of earshot of a murmur, Evemer leaned close to Kadou and said, "You mentioned loopholes."

"Spite is a terrible reason to have not-technically-sex," Kadou replied, nudging his knee up against Evemer's again beneath the table.

＊

Just after lunchtime, at long last, the flying squad returned. When the messenger arrived with the news, Kadou fled his meeting with the palace exchequer and went directly across the Silver Court to the hall where the prisoners were already, apparently, being put on trial. The kahyalar at the doors to the courtroom let him in without an objection.

Siranos, Sylvia, and Azuta were grubby with dirt and dust from the road, and chained hand and foot. Zeliha was splendid and terrifying in black-and-gold brocade, the effect not at all diminished by Eyne held in her arms. Tenzin stood at the foot of the dais below Zeliha's glory, having made no concession to fashion or the colors of allegiance except to tie a Mahisti-blue-and-white-striped sash around her waist.

Kadou picked his way through the crowd—they were all too rapt to notice or part for him until the warden of the court banged his staff of office on the floor and demanded that the room be emptied of onlookers. They filed out slowly, but Kadou pressed his back against the wall and waited it out. When they'd all gone, he was startled to see Eozena toward the front of the room—she was seated in a cunningly engineered wheeled chair with her injured leg propped up straight to ease her aches. He drifted over to her and stood at her shoulder; she looked up, smiled, and squeezed his hand.

"Now that we can hear ourselves think," Zeliha said dryly. "Let's have a chat. We know that you, Siranos, were involved in an expansive plot to forge our currency and ship it abroad. We've seized your property in the city, rooted out several more of your agents, found the rest of the kahyalar you bribed or threatened into helping you, and seized the two remaining caches of counterfeits hidden in the city. I'm told you had several chests of coins in your carriage as well, confirmed by two touch-tasters in the squad that captured you. How unfortunate that you were caught with evidence."

"I *told* you it wouldn't work, stupid," Sylvia hissed to her brother. "I said it was a ridiculous plan."

"We are also aware that you hired mercenaries to kidnap or assassinate Prince Kadou, my brother, and in doing so caused the deaths of several kahyalar. We are aware that you later *did* capture him, with the intent of holding him hostage and killing his kahya. Your mercenaries attacked our commander of the guard and several other kahyalar when they discovered your headquarters, and you yourselves personally laid hands on another kahya in violence. Furthermore, we are aware that you hired people to break into the Shipbuilder's Guild with the intent of stealing Araşti secrets." Her smile was like the edge of a sword. "The former lieutenant Armagan was kind enough to tell us everything çe knew in exchange for clemency. So were most of the rest of the people we've found." She tipped her head toward Tenzin. "Of course, the ones who refused to beg for a plea deal ended up telling us anyway. Anything to add, ladies? Gentleman?"

The three of them tried to argue, of course, all talking at once. Zeliha let them talk themselves out—Azuta fell silent first, and then Sylvia, while Siranos still held forth until he was red in the face about unfair trials and international diplomacy. He seemed to think that he and Sylvia were important enough that their imprisonment or death would cause an upset back home in Oissos.

"Do you know how much of Oissos's debt Araşt owns?" Zeliha asked, interrupting him. "Roughly four hundred and fifteen thousand altınlar—or two and a half million Oissic trachy, at current exchange rates. You are nothing. They are not coming for you, and if they do, we won't even need to greet them with diplomats, *only accountants*."

Siranos fell silent.

"Now that we're all on the same page," Zeliha said, "why don't you tell me how many shipments of counterfeits you smuggled out of the country and to which foreign ports you sent them, as well as whether you planned to sell the information you tried to steal from the guild or keep it for yourselves. Cooperation will put me in a good mood."

※

The tides rose higher in the next few days, lapping up to the very edge of the quays, and the last slipper of the crescent of Beyaz, the moon of transformation and impermanence, waned away to nothing. The city was loud with color and noise, and watching from his balcony at night, Kadou could see fireworks going up from six or seven places throughout the city, as well as directly behind him from somewhere in the palace grounds.

For one blazing day, the parade wound around the city. Kadou did not have a pleasant time in the slightest—it was too hot, and the extravagant festival robes were too stifling, and his horse Wing was in a skittish mood and wouldn't stop shying, and he was *starving*, which was made only worse by the redolent scents of festival food filling every single damn street and making him crave everything that was sticky-sweet, or fried, or both.

He didn't have a pleasant time that night at the palace's celebration either, with the gardens of the Gold Court all hung with hundreds of colored lanterns, the residences packed with people for once—all the nobles and provincial governors who had returned from the country for the holiday, and their raucous families. There hadn't been a quiet corner to be found in days, and if by chance there were, it was probably already occupied by a pair of teenagers up to no good.

The food and drink were plentiful, but by that point Kadou was fairly well dying for something fried and sticky, and all that was on offer was roast peacock, roast ox, and a thousand elegant delicacies that he had no stomach for, served on long tables outside while everyone milled around and grew drunker and louder, and worse at dancing, and more and more interested in having shouty drunken conversations with him about policy.

He made Zeliha play five games of noughts-and-crosses to battle for which of them would be allowed to leave and make the

Visit to the kahyalar at the other end of the palace. He only won because she too was already fairly tipsy.

At the kahyalar's party, he managed to nearly enjoy himself—they, at least, had fried-and-sticky things for him to eat, which soothed his frayed edges, and they had wine that was much more drinkable than what was being served at the Gold Court party, and ale besides. Once he was drunk, he flung off the outer three layers of his festival robes, bundling all of them into Evemer's arms and leaving him there to blush while Kadou, in his trousers and unbuttoned underlayer, let Melek drag him into the dancing—and this, too, was better than what had been on offer in the Gold Court.

He should have been happy.

Everyone else was happy.

The walk back home, already interminable on a regular day, was nearly impossible. It took Melek and Evemer both to keep him from veering off the garden paths, more tired than tipsy now. Once they made it home, he refused point blank to attempt the stairs up to his room. Melek and Evemer shrugged at each other, braided his hair, and poured him into bed in the unoccupied fourth room of the kahyalar's quarters.

A soft bed, a safe house, a head full of wine and a belly full of fried things, muscles aching from dancing and from the day's ride . . . He should have fallen asleep instantly.

Yet hours later, there he was, still wide awake, lying on his back in the middle of the bed in the dark, trembling violently and biting his lip so that he wouldn't wake Evemer, who was asleep on a pile of floor cushions on the other side of the room.

The fear-creature tore at him, threw all manner of thoughts at him. It didn't matter that he knew most of them weren't even true. He muffled himself in the pillow, trying and failing to steady his breathing. He wanted to weep, but could not allow it—Evemer would wake up, and the fear-creature was doing an excellent job of convincing him that that would be a very, very bad thing.

He'd lied to Evemer. He'd outright lied to him for no other reason than pure selfishness. Surely his schedule could have permitted a visit to the temple by now—they could have gone at dawn or midnight. There were surely other solutions. Kadou just hadn't wanted to look very hard for them. He suspected Evemer knew all of these things, and he wondered whether Evemer thought him pathetic, as he had in the beginning.

He just wanted another few days. Just a little longer of pretending that Evemer was his before he had to once again deny himself his personal wants in favor of his duty to the kingdom. A few more days of the thrilling catch of his heart every time Evemer walked into a room, rather than the cold rush of knowledge that this wasn't his to keep and never would be.

They'd had a heated debate about what exactly counted as sex for the purposes of annulment. Evemer's sense of where the hard boundary lay was much more conservative than Kadou's—it wouldn't count if there was this condition, and this other condition, and two or three further conditions after that, and Kadou had accepted most of them (fully clothed, hands above the waist, mouths above the collarbones), and protested *vehemently* against the final one on the grounds of, "But *reciprocity*, Evemer, are you trying to imbalance the whole system of fealty?" But Evemer had held the advantageous position in that negotiation, and Kadou had grudgingly acquiesced.

And now he had a white-hot memory of Evemer leaning over him and watching with undisguised reverence as Kadou melted into a satiated puddle of bliss in his arms, of Evemer kissing him worshipfully, of Evemer's eyes, as bright as stars and as lovely.

Of Evemer slipping out of Kadou's bed, unsatisfied because that was the last condition of the technicality, before crossing the room to sleep on the divan again as usual.

Of the way watching that happen had left Kadou cold and how his own satisfaction had not been whole and complete after all, of how he yearned to call Evemer back and undo him like he himself had been undone.

Of the next night, when the same thing had happened. And the next.

And then next, when it *hadn't* because, as it turned out, Kadou couldn't bear to send Evemer off like that every day, and Evemer was getting restless and snappish, traces of strain showing in his eyes that meant there were heaps more beyond that which he was hiding, even though he had claimed on the first night that he wouldn't feel like he was truly suffering. Even a pleasant kind of torture had its limits.

Kadou had put his foot down, and they'd argued about that too, Evemer insisting that he wanted to continue, right up until Kadou said that Evemer's wants could go hang, because *Kadou's* want was "not to live like this" and therefore the whole argument was moot. Restraining themselves to infuriatingly lukewarm chastity was miserable, but at least it was a misery they were enduring together.

That was the last time Kadou was going to be allowed to want something for himself. At some point, there would be a foreign treaty of some kind that stipulated a permanent bond, and off he'd go to the temple to be married to someone he'd have to try to love.

It was, on some level, lucky that he and Evemer were being stymied by their marriage. If he'd had the opportunity, he would have taken Evemer to bed a dozen times before he realized what a terrible idea it was, that he was setting himself up for heartbreak. He was embarrassed by how long it had taken him to think of that, but it was better to do so now, before they'd gone any further down that path. He already wanted too much of Evemer, and if he had been at liberty to do so, he would have wanted the rest.

Selfish, greedy thing—Kadou would have wanted all of him, all for his own and forever.

Perhaps Evemer knew how he felt. Perhaps that's why he was holding back, waiting for Kadou to catch up with the idea that they really *shouldn't* be doing this. Perhaps those few nights had been the bare minimum to help Kadou clear his head. Perhaps, perhaps, perhaps—but no, that was the fear-creature again.

He squeezed his eyes closed and pressed both hands over his mouth to muffle himself.

This was a bad one—nearly as bad as the one he'd had after they were attacked in the alley, the one Tadek had soothed him through. Nearly as bad as the ones he'd had during Zeliha's pregnancy.

Gods, he hated this. Usmim was the god of judgment, and he sent trials to measure a person's mettle, but this? This was stupid. This was *boring*. How would a trial like this prove anything except his own ability to keep himself crushed down to size, like cramming his feet into shoes much too small for him?

That's what he was going to have to do soon. Pack everything in, all his feelings and selfish wants—he'd have to shove it into too-small shoes, because of propriety, because of duty, because simply being *born* a prince meant that you were bound into certain oaths, ones that you never got a chance to choose for yourself as the kahyalar did.

He was going to have to let Evemer go, and then he was really, really going to have to try to put some distance between them, even if it broke his heart, even if it was the very last thing he wanted. He had an obligation, promises to keep, his duty. The country needed him to be a prince more than he himself needed to be Kadou. Those parts of him would get packed away again, folded in paper at the bottom of a trunk somewhere like a forgotten kaftan.

He was not allowed to be himself. He was not allowed to want for himself. Evemer would understand, when he framed it like that. Evemer knew about duty.

CHAPTER SIXTEEN

G ods, I'm happy to have that done with," Zeliha said after
lunch the next day—it was supposed to have been breakfast, but she and Kadou had mutually and simultaneously
sent notes that there was no way they were getting up that early.
"Three whole months until the next one, and that's *sedate* compared to Midsummer."

Kadou nodded drowsily, still dead tired and hungover, both
physically and emotionally. He'd only managed to get an hour or
so of sleep, and now he was lounging in the cushions with Eyne a
heavy weight on his chest. That should have been enough to *finally*
knock him out, except that every few minutes, just as he was about
to drop off, she'd wriggle and he'd come alert again with a start,
terrified that he was about to let her fall.

"And then," Zeliha said, yawning and adjusting her own pile of
cushions. "We'll have His Grace here—"

"Who?"

"The nice Vintish boy. The Duc de Resti. I showed you his
picture and you thought he was handsome."

"Oh, him."

"We'll have His Grace here," she continued, "so we'll have
to have parties, and then it'll be winter and everyone will pile
back into the palace *again*, and you won't be able to hear yourself
think—"

It made Kadou's skin crawl to think of it. "I can use your bathhouse, can't I?"

"Other one too crowded?"

"Packed."

"Mm." After a moment, she said, "Isn't it strange to be so furiously busy and then have a quiet, lazy day? I keep thinking someone's going to come in and drag me off to look at something that urgently requires my personal attention. The only things I'm doing today are eating and napping with Eyne. You?"

Well, sister, he thought to himself. *I happened to get married to one of my kahyalar and now I'm in love with him, so my plan for the day is to keep dragging my feet on the annulment, and also to finish breaking my own heart when I think of letting him go. But don't worry, I know my place and what I have to do. Other than that, naps with Eyne sound lovely.* "Nothing much," he said.

After a time, she said, "Did I apologize yet? I should have been kinder to you about Siranos. I should have listened to you."

"No, you were—you were reasonable and fair."

"Too reasonable. Too fair." She shook her head. "I'm still trying to find an equilibrium between being a sovereign and being your sister. I was trying so hard to be good at one of them that I made a really shameful wreck of the other. I'm sorry."

"Forgiven. Of course, forgiven."

"And I shouldn't have even tried to keep him around. I shouldn't have . . ." He looked over to see her biting her lip, staring at the ceiling. "You can't always control your heart," she concluded at last. "If I'd been better about mine, we wouldn't have gotten into this mess." She nodded firmly. "Next time, no feelings. Feelings are for family, not for people like Siranos. *Men.*" A moment later, she added, "He wrote me love letters. They weren't any good, but I guess they don't have to be, when they're for you. I've decided to keep them, seeing as how I won't be getting any more from anyone else."

"Why not?" He sat up, shifting Eyne's weight. "There will be someone else for you."

"I don't think so. I'd rather not risk the kingdom over it. I don't need love letters to get another child or two."

"So you're just resigning yourself to being alone forever?"

"Not alone, am I? I have you and Eyne, and our grandparents for a little while longer, and more kahyalar than I know what to do with." She considered for a moment. "I could get a dog." She forced a smile, as if he *weren't* her brother, as if he hadn't known her his whole life, as if he couldn't tell when she was hiding her pain. She was better at it than Evemer was, but even so, he could see right through her. She'd been betrayed by someone she'd liked. Of course she was in pain.

Kadou laid Eyne in a nest of cushions and squirmed over to Zeliha, wrapping an arm across her and pushing his head under her chin as he'd done when they sprawled like this as children. She huffed a short, sad laugh and returned the hug for a few moments before she drew back. Her eyes were a little red, but she blinked it away. "Let's not talk about it any more today."

"All right. You never answered about whether I could use your baths."

"Oh. 'Course you can. They're closer to your new quarters, anyway. You can take His Grace along, if you want, if he's still here in the winter when it's crowded again."

"I . . . suppose I could," Kadou said dubiously. He didn't particularly enjoy going to the bathhouse with acquaintances. "Won't you want him to go with you?"

"Why would he go with me?"

They both raised their heads and exchanged bewildered looks.

"Because you're bringing him here to court him, to give me another niece?"

Zeliha sat up in astonishment. "He's not for *me*, he's for you!"

"What?" Kadou's heart stopped in his chest.

"Why did you think I was showing you his picture?"

"I thought you were—I don't know, bragging! Or just excited! Or that you were hoping I'd be friends with him!"

"You told me to invite him here!"

"I was trying to encourage you! I was being supportive!"

"Oh, gods above and below—Asad! Evemer!" she shouted toward the door.

Asad, one of the kahyalar currently standing watch, opened the door and looked in. "Majesty?"

"Come here a minute, both of you." When they had done so,

she said, "Hypothetical question. If you were a reasonable person and your sultan invited you to lunch, and then showed you a picture of someone pretty and asked what you thought of them, could you logically conclude that she had a particular reason? For example, oh, I don't know, *because she was trying to offer them to you as someone you might like to marry?*"

Asad stifled a smile. "To be fair, Your Majesty, you did show that picture of that Vintish duc to about six of us, and none of *us* thought you were trying to arrange a match for us. But if I were a prince . . . I probably would have made that guess."

"See?" she said, turning back to Kadou. "You know, he wrote me a letter to say hello. Did I not tell you about that?"

"No," Kadou said faintly. He was trying very hard not to look at Evemer.

"A very nice letter. And he included a poem that he wrote for you! I am pleased to report that, incredibly, it's not awful. He made a very cute pun on *Kadou* and *un cadeau*, clearly thought he was being clever, though he'd be cleverer if he'd already known the story about your name. I've been wondering—*is* it a pun if it's just the same word?"

Kadou could acutely feel Evemer's presence by the door.

He'd be standing there with his stone-wall face on, as impassive as a mountain. He'd be thinking this was right and good, that Kadou was dutiful and obedient to his monarch, a good prince. There were things that were just right, things that you had to do regardless of your feelings, of your wants, of your heart crying out *no, not yet, I thought I could steal just a little more time.*

"When," Kadou said, voice cracking. He swallowed and tried again, "When were you wanting to arrange this?"

"After he comes to visit and you decide whether you like him. If you do, it'd be several months at least to finalize everything. Perhaps a year," Zeliha said. "Negotiations and contracts and so forth, and then another six months on top of that to plan the wedding."

He wasn't going to look at Evemer. He wasn't. He *wasn't.*

He did.

All he caught was a glimpse. Less than a heartbeat, less than a hundredth of a heartbeat: the most wretched expression he'd ever seen on Evemer, outright wretched, open and honest and unhidden, so that anyone looking at him would have been able to tell that someone had just torn his heart out of his chest.

Their eyes met and then it was gone—well, as gone as Evemer could make it. Gone to the casual observer, but Kadou—Kadou could always see him, couldn't he? It was still there, that despair, that misery.

Kadou ducked his head again sharply and thought, *Oh, he loves me.*

Right on the heels of that, he thought, *I promised twice over to protect him from all harm—as lord and as husband, I swore it.*

And then: *What about duty? What about marrying this man Zeliha's found, and enriching the kingdom and strengthening our alliances, and serving the purpose for which I was born?*

And immediately following: *To hell with that. To hell with duty, with fealty and responsibility. Irrelevant!* To hell with all of them if they meant he had to let Evemer go.

He couldn't do it after all.

He was going to refuse this marriage. Not even because he'd promised to keep Evemer from harm and this would surely, surely harm him, but because he *wanted* Evemer like he'd never wanted anyone or any thing for himself before. This, this was *his.* Who knew how long either of them had? They could have died a dozen times in the last few months. They could die any day here, from illness or misadventure.

What, then, was the point of hesitating as if they thought they had the luxury of time to fritter away on uncertainty? What was the point of doing anything but seizing hold of Evemer and loving him just as hard as he possibly could, with the knowledge that he was pouring all the love he had into every instant just in case there wasn't another instant after it?

Except Evemer wasn't his, not really—Evemer might have sworn his fealty, and he might have said the marriage oaths, yes, and he might have said that he wouldn't stop wanting Kadou, but that didn't mean that he was giving himself away. He hadn't said that at all. Even if he was silently dying by the door, even if Kadou *knew* it, he'd have to wait to hear him say he wanted this. That was reciprocity—reaching out your hand in the dark, offering it, and hoping someone reached back.

Kadou hadn't ever really offered, had he? Not properly, not so Evemer knew he meant it.

He had to make Evemer understand that before anything else could be said or done.

"I . . . I think I need to . . . do something," he said, unsteady.

"Are you all right?" she asked as he scrambled to his feet. "Are you getting cold feet about the visit? No one's going to make you marry him if you don't like him, and I forbid you to take this offer just because you think I want it."

"Understood, thank you, may I be excused?" he said, all in a rush.

"By all means."

He sketched a very perfunctory bow and whirled around, out of the room without looking at the kahyalar.

Evemer, of course, followed. In the corner of his eye, Kadou could just see him moving stiffly, like a puppet or an automaton, as if he had to tell each of his limbs to move individually. Kadou strode down the hall, out the front door into the bright midday sun, and through the twists and turns of the Gold Court garden paths until he was in the very thick of them, as alone as it was possible to get outside of his own bedroom—just a handful of kahyalar he could see in the distance on the watch shift, and his own kahya at his back. His own . . . something, anyway. *His*. Evemer.

Kadou had been meaning to charge all the way back to the Cypress Cliff house before he said anything, but he was trembling too violently to go further, and the words in his throat were going to choke him. He stopped, breathing hard.

Evemer was perfectly silent.

From a nearby folly, an elegant little stone structure where Kadou had *definitely* once been a teenager up to no good, he heard a familiar loud laugh. He flung himself through the archway and around several twists and found Tadek in the center, still wearing his armsman greens and seated on the edge of a fountain with the heir of one of the provincial governors perched on his knee.

They both jumped, the heir pulling away and straightening çir clothes as çe stood to bow to Kadou.

"Highness! Fancy seeing you here," Tadek said. "Have you met Aydin?"

"Yes, hello, wonderful to see you again, your outfit was lovely last night, so sorry to interrupt. *Tadek, I need you.*"

Tadek frowned. "What's wrong? What's happened?"

"Shall I go?" Aydin said, already edging around Kadou.

"Don't go far!" Tadek said. "Give me a moment, my flower!" Çe had already slipped out, Evemer stepping aside to let çem pass. Tadek levered himself off the edge of the fountain. "Highness, what's the matter? Are you having an attack?"

It must look like one, mustn't it? His breath caught. What if he were wrong? What if he'd misread it? What if Evemer didn't take his hand when he offered it?

Tadek came forward, laid his hand on Kadou's arm. "Shit. It's bad, isn't it? What do you need?"

"Watch the door," Kadou choked out. "Just . . . I need . . ."

"All right, all right," Tadek said soothingly, glancing back at Evemer. "Can I fetch you anything? It'll take a while since I can't run right now, but—"

"Just watch the door," Evemer said. How could he sound so steady? "Don't let anyone in."

"Done," Tadek said, and vanished.

"My lord," Evemer said. Kadou hated that title from him now. "You're not having an attack. You're just upset."

"So are you," Kadou bit out. Evemer did not reply.

Kadou put his hands over his face and paced once around the fountain. The sun glittering off the water was almost the same as the touch-taste of gold, and the splashing was noisy enough that it would keep them from being overheard even by Tadek at the door, as long as they whispered.

Kadou leaned heavily against one of the mossy walls, crossing his arms. "I won't do it," he said.

"Highness?"

No, that wouldn't do. That wouldn't do at all. Kadou stormed forward, grabbed him by his sword belt and collar and hauled him close, kissed him once, hard, before breaking off. "I'm not marrying him. I'm not. I won't do it."

"All right," Evemer whispered. He looked rather pale. "She'll find you someone else—"

"No," Kadou said savagely. "I won't have anyone else."

Evemer trembled in his arms. "You have to. You—"

"I want *you*. I only want you. I could have found time to go to the temple," he said. "You *know* I could have, even if it took waiting up half the night to finish it. You live six inches away from me at all times. You know I've only been putting it off."

Evemer pulled away. "Don't. Don't. Kadou, you can't, I'm just—"

"You're not," he snarled, letting go of Evemer's clothes. "You want to know what *just* you are? You're *just* the person who sees right through me, who tells me when I'm wrong, who said no to me, who was with me through every moment of the worst months of my life. You're—" *Say it, just say it,* he thought furiously. *Offer properly. Hold out your hand to him.* "You're *just* the person I'm in love with, and the one I want to be married to. If—if you'll have me."

"Your reputation," Evemer whispered helplessly.

"I'd rather be Kadou and *yours* than a prince and anything else. Zeliha can—can exile me if she's not happy with it, I don't care, as long as she sends you with me." He stopped, reined himself in, pulled away a little. "But . . . Your career? Would you rather—"

"Don't," Evemer said. His voice rasped, cracked. "Don't talk about that like it's something that matters."

Kadou breathed out, slowly. "I need you to tell me what you want. Bold and brazen. Everything. I have to know everything."

Evemer stood there, not even a foot away from him, his hands clenching at his sides. "I want to stand beside you," he said at last. "However—however that looks, whatever I get, even if it's scraps or I have to let someone else—"

"Don't lie. *All* of it, Evemer," he said.

"Of *course* I knew you weren't too busy to go to the temple," Evemer said sharply. "I haven't brought it up again, did you notice? We could have made plans to go today, but I thought—even a few more days, even just—"

"I said *everything*. If you say *just* again—"

He saw the moment Evemer's control snapped, and he only had time for a single heartbeat of ferocious, joyous triumph thudding in his chest before Evemer came surging forward. He reached out to grab the front of Evemer's clothes and yank him close at the same moment that Evemer shoved him back against the wall and kissed him like a man flinging himself off a cliff. "I'm yours," he said roughly into Kadou's mouth. "My hands, my heart, my breath—yours. Every part of me. That's everything, that's all of it. I want you to have it; *take it*."

"If you give it to me, I'm keeping it. Keeping you." In response, Evemer made that god-forsaken wanting sound and yanked Kadou's collar aside, biting his neck as Kadou gasped and clawed at his shoulders. "I'm not letting go," Kadou panted. "I won't be able to."

"Fine," Evemer said, muffled against his skin.

"Fine." Kadou gripped Evemer's hair and pulled him back up into another kiss. This was slower, though no less heated, the world narrowing to just the two of them in this shadowed grassy alcove of the garden with no sound but their breath and the bubble of the fountain. Kadou shivered all over with a thrill of elation.

Evemer broke the kiss and stared at Kadou, rumpled and looking vaguely astonished, as if he were just now realizing what he'd done, what he'd asked for, what he'd gotten. "All right," he breathed. He trembled all over and stepped back. "All right. We'll need a plan."

Kadou blinked. "Um—hold on, now, wait—"

"Give me a moment." Evemer said. "We'll run it like a chess game, and—"

Incredible. Unbelievable. Trying to come up with a scheme at a time like this! "You can run it however you'd like," Kadou said, carefully patient. "But come back here and finish kissing me first."

"This is serious," Evemer said. His stern tone was rather ruined by the wreck of his hair. Kadou did not reach out to fix it. "It's damaging to everyone if this turns into a scandal. We'll have to handle it as delicately as possible. You've studied tactics, haven't you?"

"War tactics?" Kadou said, incredulous. "Who are we going to war against?"

"What's Arikman's first principle?"

"Win the battle before the enemy knows it's occurred," Kadou answered slowly. Evidently he wasn't going to get the rest of his kiss before Evemer had his opening gambits lined up. He crossed his arms and sighed. He'd always heard marriage was about compromise. "All right. Tell me your plan."

Evemer considered, staring blankly at the fountain. "We will keep any connection between us beyond the professional one secret for a little while. Perhaps four to six months."

"You want me all to yourself, don't you? That's what you're saying."

"Can't blame a man for expecting a honeymoon," Evemer said, still dreadfully serious, but there was the touch of a smile at the corner of his mouth. He glanced at Kadou and—there was a bit of that moonstruck look again.

"No, you really can't," Kadou said pointedly, giving him a deliberate and hungry once-over, but it seemed to go over Evemer's head. He should have taken Evemer back to his rooms for this instead of the garden, but they were so much farther away. There was a bed there. There was a door that locked. Kadou could have just taken off all his clothes until Evemer got the point. "You can't start planning six months from now, though. There's matters to attend to in the short term."

Evemer nodded sagely. "Of course. You're quite right. Certainly there may be some rumors about us before then, but Tadek can help with managing them, and he'll make sure no one will believe them—"

"I was thinking even more in the short term. More immediately, you might say."

Evemer frowned. Kadou could almost read the *what have I missed?* thought running across his eyes. "Oh. Yes. Request me to be appointed to your service permanently—probably Melek too, for camouflage. That will help with logistics. No one will think twice about why I'm near you so often."

"As good as done," Kadou said. "But more immediately than that. It's an extremely urgent matter," he said, mimicking Evemer's serious tone.

"What is it?"

He cleared his throat and felt a bit of a blush come to his cheeks. "I was thinking you might like to finish off the last bit of business in regards to marrying me before you start plotting out your entire chess game for the next year."

Evemer paused and, rather choked, said, "Oh. Yes. Of course. Ah, tonight?"

It was barely past lunchtime—tonight was *eons* away. "If you like," Kadou said. "But I'm also thinking, why wait?"

Evemer looked increasingly poleaxed. He swallowed, staring at Kadou, apparently unable to look away. "The house?"

The house might as well have been on one of the moons. There were hundreds of people between them and the locking door, and they'd have to drag Tadek along, and he'd *definitely* catch on and giggle the whole way home, and then there would be excuses to make and kahyalar to dismiss, and they'd have to find a crowbar to get rid of Tadek, and that's if there weren't any urgent messages that interrupted them . . .

And besides, if Kadou gave himself any time to think about this, he could very well work himself into a fit of nerves about it, and that wouldn't at all contribute to the mood of a romantic afternoon alone.

"I'm thinking," he said slowly once again, pitching his voice low and inviting. "Why wait?" And then he reached out again, caught Evemer by the tails of his sash, and dragged him back in.

"Here?" Evemer said, scandalized.

Kadou bit back a laugh and pulled Evemer's face down, close enough to kiss. He brushed his lips over Evemer's cheek, the corner of his mouth. "Against a wall in a garden is nicer than against a wall in a cold wine cellar, isn't it?"

"Kadou—"

"Stop talking," he said. He kissed him slow and deep, and smiled into the kiss when Evemer made that little sound of need. Kadou let his hands run down Evemer's neck, his shoulders, his chest, his ribs and belly, all achingly slow—and then further down, until Evemer gasped, and groaned softly, and pushed into the press of Kadou's hand. "Yes?"

Evemer only made that sound and tugged at the knot of Kadou's sash with shaking hands, fumbling at his buttons, pulling the layers of his fine court robes open, sliding his hands around Kadou's waist.

It was ferociously gratifying to be able to touch Evemer properly, to yank open his clothes in turn and trace the lines of his ribs, the planes of his back and shoulders, the cut of his hip. Kadou had not realized the extent to which his hands were hungry for Evemer's skin until there it was, under his palms and against his chest, so intensely smooth and warm and perfect that it was almost a touch-taste itself. It was almost iron—the pressure of a wall at his back, the taste of salt from Evemer's skin, a sigh into a kiss.

There would be time later, Kadou reminded himself, to do it properly, to push all of Evemer's clothes off his shoulders, to leave him bare and all Kadou's, to take a full inventory of what was his: each of Evemer's scars, each freckle and mole and strangely placed hair, each birthmark, each muscle as magnificently shaped as if it had been individually carved from fine-grained golden wood. All Kadou's. Nothing had been only his before, and likely nothing ever would again—just this. Just Evemer and that soft, barely vocalized breath of sound he made that hit Kadou's veins like sizzling oil.

Gods, that sound. That sound was going to be his doom. It was already unmaking him. One day when he had time and a bed and a locking door between them and the rest of the world, and preferably fifty miles too, he'd take inventory of every place that he could brush his fingertips against to get Evemer to make that sound, and whether he would get the same response with his nails, and at what pressure, and, and, and.

"Kadou," Evemer said, and it was *that sound*, soft and imploring.

It made Kadou dizzy to hear it. "Hush, hush," he murmured, which was the very last thing he wanted at this moment, but they *were* in the garden. Later—later he'd lay Evemer out and see how loud Kadou could make him. Kadou kissed him, licked into his mouth, ran his hands up and down Evemer's gorgeous back, pulled him impossibly closer, discovered a spot just at the base of Evemer's spine that made him jerk convulsively and curse and pant into the kiss at no more than a trace of Kadou's nails across it—made him groan loud enough that Kadou had to abandon the spot, laughing breathlessly, for fear they'd be overheard.

Evemer, so collected a few minutes ago, already seemed to be losing his head, if the frantic, almost bruising way he was grasping at Kadou's hips and back was anything to go by. "Tell me what— *oh*—what to do," he gasped. "Tell me—"

"Stop," he murmured into Evemer's mouth.

Just like in the wine cellar, Evemer froze perfectly in place, his breath coming fast and wild and unsteady. He was shaking with need, every muscle tensed hard, but he waited, and Kadou's entire body sang with delight and pleasure and pride and love.

He wondered how far he could push until Evemer's perfect control broke, how much he could endure with nothing to help him but one single word of command. The thought was heady enough that Kadou's knees went weak—which was a splendid idea in and of itself, oh, yes.

Kadou turned them—Evemer went easily, yielding, until his back hit the wall. Kadou kissed him once more and murmured, "Don't fall over." He flicked the front panels of his kaftan out of the way and sank to his knees, plucking at the ties of Evemer's trousers.

Evemer caught his hands. "Wait—wait, don't—"

Kadou stopped and looked up, sitting back on his heels.

"Please stand up. Please," Evemer said, wide-eyed. He sounded almost panicked.

Kadou got to his feet immediately. "Sorry," he said. "You don't want . . . ?"

"Don't do that, you can't—you'll get grass stains, you can't do that."

Kadou blinked. "I beg your pardon? *Grass stains?*"

"You're wearing nice clothes." He was so openly dismayed at the thought that Kadou couldn't keep a straight face. He laughed aloud, kissed him, and went right back down to his knees again. Amused and terribly fond, he said wryly, "I do have other trousers, and my kaftan hems are longer than my knees. Relax."

Evemer made another outraged, protesting noise and fumbled to stop Kadou as he went for Evemer's waistband again. Kadou tried to slap his hands away, but Evemer was just as quick as he was and, admittedly, significantly stronger.

"Stop," Kadou said again, in that soft voice that had worked so well before. He twisted his wrists out of Evemer's suddenly unresisting grip and placed Evemer's hands firmly at his sides. "Be good."

"*Kadou,*" Evemer said reproachfully.

Kadou looked up from working on the ties of his trousers again and gave him an exceedingly patient look. "Do you understand what I'm currently endeavoring to do here?"

"Yes, but—"

"I'm about to put my mouth on you. Are you familiar with this concept?"

"Yes!" Evemer said, turning scarlet. "I joined the cadets when I was fifteen, I know about—about *that.*"

"Just as soon as you shut up about grass stains," Kadou continued.

Evemer closed his eyes, his mouth twisting in a barely suppressed smile. "Fine."

"Fine?" Kadou laughed. "That's it? It's like you don't even want me to—"

"No, I do," Evemer said quickly. "I do."

"Do you? Say that you don't care about my trousers."

Evemer made a dismayed noise, but managed to say, his voice only a little unsteady, "I don't care about your trousers."

"Shall I proceed?" Kadou kissed the jut of his hip, let his hands stray closer to where Evemer was surely aching for touch.

"Yes, please," Evemer said, his voice cracking.

"Say that last word again," Kadou said, loosening the ties with one hand and slipping his other around Evemer's waist to scrape his nails across that spot at the base of his spine.

Evemer exhaled, slow and shuddering, and whispered, "*Please.*"

"Good." Honestly, stopping everything because of grass stains. *Of all things.*

It was worth it, though, for the absolutely shattered sound Evemer made when Kadou pinned him to the wall by his hips and got his mouth on him. He nearly cracked his head on the wall, and Kadou would have pulled off to tell him, "Careful. And hush," if he hadn't been quite so dangerously close to the edge himself just from *hearing* him.

Evemer couldn't quite stifle all his noises, even when he clapped his own palm to his mouth to muffle them. He kept clenching his free hand in the air by Kadou's head, or touching Kadou's hair lightly before snatching his hand away and pressing his palm flat against the stone wall, over and over again until Kadou huffed and pulled Evemer's hand to his hair. It would have been fine if he'd grabbed it, or pulled a little, or guided Kadou's mouth the way he wanted it, but all he did was touch gently, petting with shaking hands and the kind of stop-and-start repetition that made Kadou suspect, with some smugness, that he wasn't thinking at all, that this was just reflex, raw and unfiltered wants too nebulous to resolve into consciousness.

As long as there *was* another instant that followed this one, there would be time later for showing off, for demonstrating every little trick he'd learned, for drawing it out and making Evemer wait for it. He *liked* waiting for it, after all—those first two or three nights after they'd debated loopholes, he'd been enormously content to leave Kadou's bed unsated.

Time for all of it. All the time in the world, and none of it.

Kadou took the hand that was still gently, helplessly touching his hair and laced their fingers together—that of all things was what seemed to force Evemer over that last shattering edge, his hand clutching Kadou's hard enough to hurt, panting wildly against his own palm as he came, every muscle locked as tight as steel. It only took the pressure of his own hand through the cloth of his trousers for Kadou to follow, every fiber of him singing in such sheer, giddy delight that he wanted to laugh aloud and dance for it.

Perfect.

He sat back on his heels, grinning and nearly as breathless as Evemer, whose knees finally gave out underneath him. He slid slowly to the ground, eyes closed and head tipped back against the wall. He was so handsome, so gorgeous and wrecked that Kadou couldn't help but dart forward and kiss his cheek, loving him so fiercely he thought he might die of it.

Evemer, with some effort, cracked his eyes open.

"Hello," said Kadou, smiling at him.

"Your mouth's all red," Evemer said, raising his hand as if it weighed a thousand pounds and brushing the pad of his thumb against Kadou's lip—he sounded drunk. He sounded like . . . *Kadou's.*

"Yes, that happens," Kadou said, amused. He nipped at Evemer's thumb. "Can I kiss you?"

Evemer's eyes fell closed again and his brows knotted up in great, sleepy confusion. "Why in the world wouldn't you kiss me?"

"Some people don't like to kiss, after. The taste."

Evemer gave a deeply disdainful scoff, apparently the only eloquence he was capable of, and reached for him. Kadou laughed and dipped forward; Evemer's mouth was all soft and slack for him, and Kadou felt another burst of adoring joy. "I can't move any part of my body at the moment," Evemer said blearily. "If you'll give me a moment, I'll—for you—"

"Already taken care of," Kadou said, brushing light kisses across Evemer's flushed cheeks and sweat-damp brow. "And I owed you a few anyway. Take your time collecting yourself. All is well."

"Yes, all right," Evemer said. "Hello."

"You know, I'm honestly shocked you're not having more of a crisis right now," Kadou said, grinning.

"What?" Evemer forced his eyes open and peered at him. He felt entirely disconnected from his body, except for the pins-and-needles tingling throughout his brain. He wanted to nap for a year, preferably next to Kadou (his *husband*), who was perfect. "Why would I have a crisis?"

"Would you look at the state of me?" Evemer did as he was bid, getting his eyes to focus with some difficulty. Kadou had sat back, pulled his legs from under him, was brushing ineffectually at the grass stains on the knees of his trousers.

Evemer could not, at this moment in time, bring himself to feel more than a twinge of concern—Kadou *had* insisted, after all, and his kaftan was long enough to cover it as long as he didn't go striding about so the two front panels billowed open to show anything. "I told you that'd happen," he said. His skin was buzzing, he noticed distantly.

Kadou snorted. "Yes, you did. I suppose my hair's a mess too."

"More easily fixed than grass stains."

Evemer, struggling a little with the concept of balance, leaned forward to finger-comb Kadou's hair for him. They tidied up as best they could with handkerchiefs dampened in the fountain, did up their clothes, and sat back against the wall side by side. By then, Evemer felt much more like himself, besides the fact that he was brimming with the unfamiliar glow of generalized goodwill and delicious languor.

"There," Kadou said. "That's done. You can come up with the rest of your scheme for the year now."

"Yes," Evemer said. He felt a possessive sort of satisfaction. He was married, and Kadou was perfect, and . . . really, the rest of the plan could wait fifteen minutes.

"No going back on it."

"Mm . . . Not without several priests and a lot of bureaucracy.

And public spectacle." Evemer looked at him. "Are *you* having a crisis?"

"No? Probably not?" Kadou took a breath. "Only a small one. Only the *oh, gods, we're really doing this* kind."

Evemer shifted, lacing his fingers with Kadou's again. "We're not telling anyone for a little while."

"About that." Kadou chewed his lip. "I don't want you to feel like I'm keeping you secret."

Evemer gave him a flat look. "Is it a secret if it's nobody's business?"

"It will become their business as soon as Zeliha figures out that I'm refusing all the suitors she's offering me. I have to say it out loud, all right? So I know that you know: It's not that I wouldn't fight for you. I fully expect I will have to, sooner or later."

"I was the one who suggested it," Evemer said, frowning. "It's my own plan."

"Yes, I know." He turned and tucked his face against Evemer's neck. "I want to have you all to myself for a little while too. Put off the fuss, because there *will* be fuss no matter how we play it. I'm just . . . starting to think about logistics." He sighed heavily, hot breath gusting against Evemer's skin.

"Leave logistics to me. I'll handle the scheduling of the watches. I'll be at your side as much as you want."

"You'll take days off now and then, won't you?" Kadou asked warily. "You shouldn't live in my pocket all the time. It's not healthy."

"I'll take one day a week to visit my mother."

"Define *day*."

"Twelve hours, dawn to dusk."

"All the kahyalar get twenty-four," Kadou said firmly. "Dawn to dawn. Don't neglect her. And . . . really, give people a chance to notice that sometimes you sleep somewhere besides my chambers."

"They won't think anything of it. It'll take them at least a month to wrap their heads around the idea that I'd even think of doing something like this."

Kadou laughed under his breath. "Something like me," he mumbled into Evemer's collar.

Evemer snorted, and continued, "We'd have a different approach if the goal was to permanently hide this. As it is, we might as well let them gradually get accustomed to the idea. Tadek noticed fast, but he's right up close and he's sharper than most people anyway. They'll see first that I am excessively devoted to you. Then, they'll wonder about me. Then they'll develop theories. By the time they start looking for concrete evidence, we will be ready to start letting them find some."

"I should tell Zeliha at some point," Kadou said in a small voice. "And Eozena. Not right away, but . . . Well, before they hear it from someone else. And you should tell your—your mother."

"Agreed." He didn't know whether to be elated or apprehensive of that, and he set it aside for later.

"What do you think Zeliha will . . . do?"

"In her role as your sister, I expect she will be bewildered and surprised at the very least, and then she will jump upon the opportunity to tease you. As Her Majesty . . . In the very worst case scenario, she might temporarily kick us out of the capital. You've taken away one of the game pieces in her long-term strategy, and that may be troublesome. But we haven't broken any laws. We've simply . . . not done what we were supposed to. There will be consequences, but they'll all be about reputation. Public opinion."

"Right. Yes." Kadou took a breath. "The court. The ministers." More grimly, "The kahyalar. The populace."

Evemer frowned at the grass. A thought was blooming in his mind, and though it was a necessary shape, it was . . . objectionable. He mentally hauled himself out of the languorous pool of bliss, a full thirteen minutes earlier than he'd intended, and resigned himself to the realities of the situation. He'd wanted a few quiet months, the two of them answering to no one but each other, but . . . "No honeymoon after all," he muttered. "Straight to work."

"Hmm?" Kadou raised his head. "What do you mean?"

Evemer took a deep breath. "I'm Damat Evemer Hoşkadem

Mahisti-eş Bey Effendi, Prince of Araşt, Duke-Consort of Altınbaşı-ili, Lord-Consort of Şirya and Nadırıntepe, and Warden-Consort of the Northern Marches. My husband is second in line to the throne. I'm going to have to learn politics." He tsked. "I thought I'd have another twenty or thirty years of preparation before I got government office."

Kadou stared at him for a long moment and shook his head. "Should have known what you were getting yourself into."

"I intend to be good at it. It's my job now."

"Better you than me. What haven't you prepared for?"

"I know very little about land management or what the industries of your holdings are."

"Mostly agriculture. One or two gold mines. Shipbuilding in Altınbaşı-ili. Forestry in the Northern Marches."

Evemer nodded and filed this away. "And I'll need advice when it comes to courtiers and ministers. I'll need introductions, and I'll have to . . ." He pursed his lips. "I'll have to become *talkative*."

"What? You mean you'll expand your vocabulary beyond flatly saying 'My lord' or 'Commander' when people say something you don't agree with?" Kadou bit his lip on a smile. "You know, Tadek's good at all those things. You could let him be friends with you, pick up his tricks."

"How dare you even suggest such a thing?"

"I know. What is the world coming to?"

Evemer turned and kissed him again rather than dignify that with an answer. "I'll have the rest of the plan worked out in the next day or two."

"Don't tell me all of it, all right? Maybe just the upcoming week of the plan, if there's anything specific I need to do."

"Will it worry you to hear the rest?"

Kadou shrugged. "If something goes wrong, or we have to change course, it very well might."

That made sense—Kadou was best with problems that were right in front of him, things he could see and touch. "There won't be many things for you to do. Just be Prince Kadou. Throw bread and silver. Open an orphanage."

Oh, he thought an instant later. Orphanages. Children. *Heirs.* He went very still, feeling a sudden giddy joy bloom in his heart—he wouldn't have to worry about loving Kadou's children too hard after all.

But that was at least four or five years down the line—there were much higher priority things to give his attention to right now.

He squeezed Kadou's hand and attended, as much as possible, to the near future. "We're heading into some degree of scandal. There's no evading that. It's going to be loud, and irritating, and we'll both get more attention than either of us care for."

"This isn't helping my worry."

"I'm going to get most of the attention, unless I can figure out another way to get us through it."

"Why would you get most of the attention? No one knows who you are."

"That's the problem." Evemer sighed. "The best way to come out of this cleanly is to show people . . . melodrama." He pursed his lips at the very thought—it was going to be like one of Tadek's soppy plays, gods grant him patience. "A common kahya will simply *not do* for the prince of Araşt—I'm going to have to convince the general populace that I'm a hero."

"That's not terribly hard. Zeliha could be convinced to give you a medal or something—you'd deserve one anyway, after the last few weeks."

"There weren't enough witnesses for all that." Evemer mulled over his options. "I might have to get myself stabbed in the line of duty."

Bewilderingly, Kadou seemed to think that was unreasonable.

※

Kadou had not finished fighting with Evemer over whether or not he was going to be allowed to arrange himself a light stabbing in heroic and romantic circumstances by the time they finally heard Tadek calling, "Highness?"

"Are we even going to attempt to hide this from him? He already knows everything else." Evemer's expression grew even more calculating. "I could use a pawn."

"Surely he's an arch-dedicate at the very least, good at diagonal movement." Kadou raised his voice to call, "Here, Tadek."

"Are you well?" Tadek said, coming around the spiral corridor. "It's been ages, I thought I'd check and see whether you needed anything." He stopped in the archway to the center of the folly and took them in at a glance. "Oh, for fuck's sake. Did you even try to put yourselves back together?" He came forward and plucked a leaf out of Kadou's hair, batted the wrinkles out of his clothes and tugged them until they lay straight. "Evemer, you look like you got dragged backward through a bush." He stepped back, eyed them up and down. His eyes caught on the grass stains, which Kadou was not attempting to hide, the edge of a love bite just visible above Evemer's collar. "Well," he said dryly. "Congratulations on your annulment. Did you really just interrupt me seducing a governor's heir to make me stand guard for you? Because if so, I respect that. A valid and fair retaliation for, y'know, me laughing my guts out at you the other day. It has a certain poetic justice to it." He cocked his head. "I thought you'd be at Her Majesty's residence for lunch. When did you go to the temple?"

"We didn't," Kadou said, reaching up to fix Evemer's hair for him.

The wry, amused expression slid off Tadek's face. "Oh. Uh. Skirting a little close to the line of what's plausible as 'we haven't,' aren't you? Or are you just going to lie to the dedicates? Because that's what I would do."

"Evemer's decided to accept your overtures of friendship," Kadou said. "Discuss it on the way back to Zeliha's, I have to go talk to her again."

"Highness," they both said in unison, giving him tactful but pointed once-overs.

Kadou stopped and cleared his throat. Right. He probably should clean up properly before charging into another audience with her. "Goddamn *kahyalar*," he muttered, adjusting the fall of his kaftan so the front panels entirely hid his knees.

❄

In point of fact, there were several other things to do in his chambers before returning to Zeliha—besides brushing his hair and changing into clothes that weren't covered in sex and sweat and grass stains, there was the note to be written to the head of the garrison to inform them that he was requesting Evemer and Melek as his attendants indefinitely and that Evemer should be consulted regarding scheduling for anyone else assigned to him.

Evemer sat near him while he worked, twisting a lock of Kadou's hair around his finger while he scribbled. As soon as he blotted the ink dry and folded the page, Evemer leaned forward and kissed his neck. "Let me carry it to the garrison," he said. "I shouldn't be in the room when you talk to Her Majesty."

"Why not?"

"You're going to tell her that you won't marry that Vint."

"Yes." Kadou sealed the letter—indigo wax, a firm push of the brass seal (a touch-taste of the rattling sensation of a carriage rolling over cobblestones, the sound of a shovel thrust into soft earth, the color of leaves in fall), a streak of silver dust dabbed across it with his fingertip (just a flash of crunching snow and white tea). "And?"

"I'm afraid of giving the game away too soon."

Kadou snorted. "What, by smirking or something? Looking as smug as someone who just got his cock sucked in the palace gardens? You? Famously impassive Evemer Mahisti-eş?"

Evemer ducked his head, hiding a smile in Kadou's shoulder. "I don't want to risk it."

"You'll have to show your face in front of her sometime." He handed over the letter.

"I'll have my composure back by then."

"What about the next time I have to tell her that I'm not marrying some nice boy she's found for me?"

"We'll see." Evemer dropped another kiss on his neck and stood. "Are you nervous about talking to her?"

Kadou thought, looking inward, prodding at the places the fear-creature lurked around the edges of his mind. "Yes and no. I don't know yet. If it comes upon me, it'll be sudden, probably right in front of her door."

"You might think of asking for an unburdening, you know."

Kadou laughed. "What have I to unburden myself about?"

Evemer shrugged. "Just a thought. Aunt Mihrimah would look into your eyes and very kindly force you to talk about why you think you're a coward, and when she's done beating you against a washing board, she'll give you tea and hang you up to dry."

"Is that the sort of thing she did to you, the day you came back and said you felt like laundry?" Kadou said. "What do you mean, why I *think* I'm a coward?"

Evemer gave him a flat look.

"I had an attack last night," Kadou said. "So it's not like it's just gone away. It *doesn't*. It's always there in the back of my mind."

"Yes," Evemer said. "And?"

"So I think there's more evidence than just me *imagining* that I'm a coward."

"And there's a great deal more that says you're not. Like taking down a counterfeiting ring, or every time you stayed to save my life, or the way you're facing the very real possibility of cataclysmic scandal and conflict just to keep me."

Kadou blinked. Frowned at him, puzzled. "You think I'm not scared?"

"I think you'd be a fool if you weren't."

"Are you?"

"Yes and no," Evemer said calmly. "I'd follow you to the ends of the earth. I have nothing to lose, except you. But my fear is different from yours."

"Maybe because you're not a coward."

Evemer sighed. "Whatever it is, it's not cowardice. You just get in your own way sometimes. Think about the unburdening."

"I don't know that it would help."

"All right. I'm going to go back sometime. Since I have to learn to be talkative, I might as well practice." He bent to lay another kiss just on Kadou's temple. "I'll come back here as soon as I've finished at the garrison," Evemer said softly. "Straight back."

Kadou nodded absently, then sat up suddenly. "Actually, can I send you on another errand?"

"Where?"

"The palace jeweler." He reached into his pocket. "I want these made into something—bracelets or rings, or . . . Well, whatever you think is best. Two of them." Evemer held out his hands, and Kadou gave him the hinge pins, his fingertips singing with the touch-taste of iron.

※

Kadou eyed his armsman as they headed back to Zeliha's chambers. Tadek was adept enough with his crutches now that he was nearly as swift as Kadou's regular walking speed, though he'd mentioned that the doctors expected him to be limping for most of a year while the slashed muscles in his calf healed.

"Why haven't you been wearing your blues?" Kadou asked, impulsive. He'd been wondering it for days—the time had never seemed right to bring it up, but perhaps there *wasn't* a right time or a wrong one for such things.

"I think green suits my complexion better," Tadek said.

Kadou gave him a sidelong look. Tadek met it, guilelessly. "Why aren't you wearing your blues, Tadek? You were reinstated. Did they not give you your uniform back?"

"Oh, they did. And then I gave it back to them."

"Why?"

"Well, I was having some feelings about it, and you know how much I hate those, so I . . . went to talk to Commander Eozena."

"Talk?"

"Fine, yes, I went to flirt with Commander Eozena. I thought it might cheer her up. She's so grouchy that she can't just *will* herself back to health. Anyway, I hung around until she started yelling and whacking me with a stick, and—"

"Does that sort of thing happen to you a lot?"

"Oh, constantly. Whacked with sticks, drowned under water

pumps, lovely things helping themselves to a perch on my knee. People are always taking the most shocking liberties with me." He gave Kadou a cheeky wink. "As I was saying, she was shouting, and I thought . . . *She wouldn't be shouting at me if I were in my kahya blues. She'd just order me out of the room.* Mind you, she wasn't *actually* angry with me—she was having a good time. I was just being a twit because I thought it might entertain her. And then I was thinking that if I were a kahya again, I'd eventually be reassigned away from you, given to someone else, and I might not want to be friends with the new person. Or I might be promoted, maybe sent off to the provincial governors. I *like* the capital. And," he said, his voice getting a little more quiet and serious, "you've got a whole garrison of kahyalar. You've only got one armsman." Tadek grimaced. "Let's not make it about feelings. Not my thing, feelings. I'll leave those to you and Evemer. I'm staying your armsman because I look better in green."

Kadou bit back a smile. "You're welcome to wear my green as long as you like. Hearth and home."

"Yeah," Tadek muttered, pleased. "Hearth and home." They stopped just outside Zeliha's residence and Kadou looked up at it—the beautiful architecture, the carved wooden shutters thrown open, the balcony above overlooking all the garden. "Nervous?"

"I'm fine. Just—composing myself." He shut his eyes and breathed. *Peace,* he whispered to his mind. *Peace.*

She'll know the truth as soon as you tell her you don't want that Vintish duke. Or she'll hate you for it. What about your duty?

I've already fouled up my duty, he thought back. *It's too late for that, I can't take it back. That was the whole point.*

Then she'll be angry that you're rejecting her gift, the fear-creature murmured.

Maybe, he whispered back. *But I have to do it.*

It's a MISTAKE!

His eyes snapped open. There—there it was, an outright lie that he could reject entirely. He shoved that thought away from himself with a surge of vicious resentment. If this was a mistake, then it meant *Evemer* was a mistake, and there was simply no way that was possible. How would he deserve something of his very own if he weren't willing to fight for it? How would he earn it if he never faced his greatest fears?

In a way, then, he was a little glad Evemer wasn't with him—the temptation to lean on him would have been too much. This was something he had to do all alone.

Usmim sent trials to measure a person's mettle. This was the trial. This was the moment to find out whether he could best it. How small and trivial it was—telling his sister something that would disappoint her, ruining something she'd worked on, rejecting a gift because it was irreconcilable with what he wanted. Taking the first small step to insist on having something for his own, something that had nothing to do with princes or kingdoms or the rest of the wide world at all, just him.

Just his heart.

And yet, a few months ago he suspected he wouldn't have been able to do it at all.

He went up to Zeliha's private rooms. Asad, at the door, smiled and let him in.

Don't, don't, don't, don't, his fear-creature said.

Zeliha was cuddled up with Eyne in the same pile of cushions that Kadou had left her on, just as she had said she would be. She was drowsing only lightly, and she woke when the door shut. "Oh, you're back," she said, yawning. "You all right? You rushed out of here so quickly."

He kicked off his shoes beside the door, went over to her, dragged a cushion out of the pile, and sat. "I won't be marrying the Duc de Resti."

"What? What, really? You don't even want to meet him?" She pushed herself up, astonished. Her hair, as black as his own but even longer, fell in light disarray around her shoulders, tousled from sleep.

"Really. I'm sure he's nice, but nothing is going to come of it."

"You don't think him handsome?" There was the disappointment—and just a hint of annoyance, he thought. And why not? She'd worked so hard to find someone who was perfect.

"It's not about how handsome he is. I'm just not going to marry him. He's welcome to come and visit if you think he'd enjoy Araşt, and I'm sure we can find someone to marry to him if we need to. But we don't need to—our alliance with Vinte is already strong enough."

"Well, yes," Zeliha admitted. "But oh, Kadou! I thought you'd like him! I went looking specifically for someone you would like. I thought being married might give you something to do." She was cajoling him a little, as if she thought this was up for negotiation. She gave him a reproachful, imploring look. "I already invited him to visit. You don't want to even meet him? Just to see?"

"I have things to do," Kadou said firmly. "I'm going to go to Şirya."

"Şirya?" Zeliha tilted her head, further bewildered. "What's there to do in Şirya? It's barely a village. Has something happened? Does it need overseeing?"

"No, but I need it. I'll be gone for a month or two, and I'll come back just after the harvest is in. I'll be here to meet His Grace and be hospitable. But I'm not marrying him. That's all I came here to say." He paused. "And I've named Evemer and Melek as my favorites; Evemer's informing the garrison as we speak."

"Oh. Well, good," she said, still puzzled. "I'm glad. It's nice to have a friend or two around you. I suppose ordeals like the recent ones really forge strong bonds, don't they?"

Oh, she had no idea. "They do," Kadou agreed. He had to get out of this room; things were going *too well* and the fear, tiresome and dull as it was, could twist even that into poison.

She studied him, her hair tousled from sleep. "You seem different. A good different."

"I'm worrying myself to shreds."

"Well, if you weren't, I'd be concerned that you'd been replaced by an impostor." She smiled again. "All right. Go to Şirya." She gave him a pleading, big-sisterly sort of look. "Are you sure you don't like the Duc de Resti? You don't want to take a little time to think on it? You could take his portrait with you. You might change your mind."

Kadou shook his head. "I'm afraid not. I am quite set on this decision." He took a breath to steady himself and said, "We can talk more when I get back."

"All right, all right." She sighed. "Months of work wasted. When will you leave for the country?"

As soon as the iron cools on the palace jeweler's work bench, Kadou did not say. "Soon."

ACKNOWLEDGMENTS

I started thinking about this book in the early summer of 2016, with no more than the inchoate thought that I wanted to write about a prince and his bodyguard falling in love. I started writing it in January of 2017. And then I scrapped it all and started again.

And again.

And again.

It took six years and six drafts, starting from a blank or nearly blank page every time (and that's not counting all the editorial revisions on the draft that you now hold). Across those six drafts, *almost everything* about the book was replaced, rewritten, or otherwise massively and exhaustively overhauled.

I didn't mind. It sounds improbable—but I really, honestly didn't mind it. From day one, I had consciously set out to write the Book of My Heart, and what I discovered along the way was that if you pursue that goal relentlessly, if you keep your eyes fixed on that one singular aim without blinking or flinching away from it, you find yourself in a place of *unshakable* faith and trust, holding with an iron grip to the conviction that no matter how many drafts it takes, no matter how many years it takes, no matter how much work it takes . . . the story is worth it.

People used to be surprised when they heard how many drafts I had been through with this book—they used to offer their sympathy and commiseration, as if they expected that I would be growing tired of it and were ready to be supportive and understanding. Hell, even *I* half expected to at least have a few moments of being tired of it at some point. It would have been *normal* to feel that every now and then.

But I never did get tired of it. Not *once* that I can now recall. Years before I ever got a contract for this book, I was telling people that I'd already been paid a hundred times over in *joy,* just from how much time I'd gotten to spend with these characters. I still feel that way. It was *easy* to spend time with them—it was even easy to start over, because every time I did, I circled closer to something important to me.

Six years. Six drafts. And so many people who helped me along the way.

Thank you, first, to the small group of beta readers (Alyshondra Meacham, Jenn Lyons, Freya Marske, and Jennifer Mace) who read the draft in which I killed off Tadek and immediately threatened to unionize and go on strike unless I undid that great travesty. You were right! You were right, and I was wrong. Thank you for keeping me from making a really bad decision, and for seeing clearly that that wasn't *at all* the story I actually wanted to tell.

To my agent, Britt Siess, who has been a fierce advocate, an invaluable asset, and *always* a voice of wisdom and prudence: Thank you. You are a jewel, and you've proven it anew every day we've worked together.

A huge, sparkly, heart-eyed thank you to the publishing teams on both sides of the pond: Irene Gallo, Becky Yeager, Caro Perny, Kat Howard, Emily Goldman, Sanaa Ali-Virani, Jocelyn Bright, Samantha Friedlander, Dakota Griffin, Kyle Avery, Bella Pagan, Georgia Summers, Elle Gibbons, and everyone else at Tordotcom Publishing and Tor UK who has loved Kadou and Evemer and contributed to making this into a Real Book—and particularly to my editor, Ruoxi Chen, for believing so wholeheartedly and enthusiastically in it and for knowing *immediately* what it meant to me and what it would mean to so many other people. It has been an honor and a joy to work with all of you, and you deserve to be paid twice as much as you're currently making for your incredible work. Please tell your bosses that I said so.

To Martina Fačková, who illustrated the cover: an ecstatic, incredulous, breathless thank-you! It's stunningly, jaw-droppingly beautiful, and I am *never* going to get over it.

To the gremlins in a certain Discord server that shall remain nameless: You know who you are, and you know what you did. You're all gentlefolk and scholars, and I cannot thank you enough.

To my dearest friend Victoria Goddard, who wrote the *other* book of my heart and who always understands what I mean to say sometimes even before I understand it myself: It's been a hell of a goddamn year, and it would have been so much harder and darker and infinitely less fun without you. Thank you. I'm so glad you were with me on the last leg of this adventure.

A few paragraphs ago, I said that *almost* everything about the book changed between the first draft and the final one. What *never* changed, however, were Kadou and Evemer. From the very first line, they were completely and wholly themselves, and through this whole tempest, they held fast, shining and constant at the center of everything. The vividness with which they have lived in my heart and the conviction that their relationship was what I most wanted to write about was the anchor point that kept me steady and certain and sure along the whole journey to this moment, this last page. All the faith and trust I've had has been built on their love.

And so, finally: Thank you to the book itself for the *wealth* of joy it has paid me over these last six years, and to Kadou and Evemer for *never once wavering.*